M000220877

Class and Gender Politics in Progressive-Era Seattle

The Urban West Series

Class and Gender Politics in Progressive-Era Seattle

JOHN C. PUTMAN

UNIVERSITY OF NEVADA PRESS   RENO & LAS VEGAS

The Urban West Series
Series Editors: Eugene P. Moehring and David M. Wrobel
University of Nevada Press, Reno, Nevada 89557 USA
Copyright © 2008 by University of Nevada Press
All rights reserved
Manufactured in the United States of America

Library of Congress Cataloging-in-Publication Data
Putman, John C., 1963–
Class and gender politics in progressive-era Seattle /
John C. Putman.
p. cm. — (Urban West series)
Includes bibliographical references and index.
ISBN 978-0-87417-736-7 (hardcover : alk. paper)
1. Seattle (Wash.)—Politics and government.
2. Labor unions—Washington (State)—Seattle—
Political activity—History. 3. Women in politics—
Washington (State)—Seattle—History. I. Title.
JS1455.2.A8P88 2008
320.9797'77209041—dc22 2007040970

The paper used in this book is a recycled stock made from 50 percent
post-consumer waste materials and meets the requirements of
American National Standard for Information Sciences—Permanence
of Paper for Printed Library Materials, ANSI/NISO Z39.48-1992 (R2002).
Binding materials were selected for strength and durability.

First Printing
13   12   11   10   09   08
5   4   3   2   1

For Irene, Amanda, and Joncarlo

Contents

Preface

This study evolved out of a paper on political reform in Progressive-Era Denver. Intrigued by the breadth and pace of change—political, economic, social, and cultural—in the United States at the dawn of the twentieth century, I wondered how these forces played out in the American West. Gunther Barth's *Instant Cities* inspired me to look to rapidly growing urban centers to explore how westerners confronted this challenging historical moment. Looking for another locale to compare to Denver, I poured through the census. On discovering Seattle, I dropped Denver.

Seattle seemed to be the perfect city to study, because it offered the chance to test the idea that rapid growth in a short time span would expose in greater relief the conflicts and struggles Americans faced in the industrial age. The city's rich history of labor radicalism and not one but two successful equal suffrage campaigns offers historians a great locale to examine the key regional and national features that mark this transitional period. Both women and organized labor struggled—sometimes together and other times against one another—to construct a new West. Their stories represent, in hindsight, much more than colorful events of early Seattle. Indeed, these episodes reflected often painful but sometimes inspiring struggles of westerners to mold and shape their postfrontier dreams of a new West.

Politics, historian Sean Wilentz has argued, "mattered a great deal." By the early twentieth century, industrialization and corporate capitalism had profoundly transformed the urban landscape of America. This book explores how two prominent political actors—women and labor—asserted through the press, on the streets, and in the halls of government their visions of a new Seattle and a new West. As a major urban center, then, Seattle can also help advance our understanding of western progressivism. Cities witnessed the intersection of class, gender, and political reform as residents struggled to cope with a rapidly changing social order. This study, then, traces the collective and individual efforts, the alliances, forged and broken, and the dreams and unfulfilled promises of Seattle citizens to fashion their sense of community in the far reaches of the Pacific Northwest.

As I conclude this odyssey, I want to take the opportunity to acknowledge the many debts I have incurred during this time. I must begin in Seattle, which provided inspiration and a pleasant environment despite the rainy days. My Sunday jaunts downtown to soak up the city's history, including the famous underground tour and Pioneer Square, rejuvenated my mind and soul after mind-numbing hours in the archives. As an urban historian I had the unique opportunity to walk the same streets where the actors of my study protested, marched, shopped, and rioted. I would also like to thank the staff of the University of Washington's Manuscripts and Archives division for their patience and untiring retrieval of boxes. Likewise, I owe a debt to the staff of the Pacific Northwest Collection for similar aid and the large volume of copying they did for me. The Seattle Public Library greatly helped me at every opportunity.

Research and writing was impossible without the financial assistance of many institutions. The University of California Regents provided me a dissertation fellowship that made the several trips to Seattle possible. Children and a mortgage demanded that I work during these ten years, and I would like to thank the history departments of UC San Diego, Cuyamaca College, and especially San Diego State University for the teaching opportunities. These were more than jobs, as they gave me the chance to hone my teaching and analytic skills. While not providing me financial aid, the Living Room Coffeehouse deserves thanks for the space, the electrical outlet for my laptop, and caffeine stimulants.

My personal debts are many, starting with my dissertation committee: Michael Bernstein, Steve Hahn, Bill Deverell, Steve Erie, and Dan Schiller. I am grateful to Eugene P. Moehring and David Wrobel, editors of the University of Nevada Press's Urban West Series, for their continuing support and advice. Gene read more drafts than he would like to admit, and his sharp eye helped me reconceptualize the study. Charlotte Dihoff and Joanne O'Hare, of the University of Nevada Press, have made this endeavor smooth and painless. My colleagues at San Diego State University also deserve special mention for their constant support and encouragement, especially Harry McDean, Joanne Ferraro, Lisa Cobbs Hoffman, David Christian, Sarah Elkind, Steve Colston, Matt Kuefler, Laurie Baron,

Eve Kornfeld, Andy Wiese, Beth Pollard, Paula De Vos, Kate Edgerton, and Tom Passananti. Michael Bernstein has worn many hats over the last two decades—advisor, mentor, and friend. Without his support, advice, criticism, and unending encouragement, this study would not have been possible. Michael continued to push me forward, while remaining a model of professionalism that I strive to emulate. More importantly, Michael also recognized that other things in life are important and never pressured me to ignore them in order to complete the study sooner. His dear friendship and kind wishes for my family will not be forgotten.

Without family this project would have been meaningless. My parents did not blink twice when I told them four years into college that I no longer wanted to become a physician. They always urged me to do what I wanted and excel at it. I also want to acknowledge the support of my other mom and dad—the term "in-laws" is too cold and impersonal to describe our relationship. Mom and Dad Linayao (and my sisters- and brothers-in-law) have not only fed, housed, and encouraged me along the way, but also have eased my mind by helping raise my children. My precious children Amanda and Joncarlo have grown up alongside this project, and their support, nightly prayers, and sense of humor made this journey possible. That they are in high school now only reminds me how long this effort took. Finally, I cannot put into words my thanks and love for my wife, Irene, who put up with the many days and nights I was away researching and writing. She expended as much blood, sweat, and tears as I have, and her love, patience, and undying encouragement made this all possible.

Class and Gender Politics in Progressive-Era Seattle

Introduction

In 1915, Seattle labor leaders urged working-class women to follow the example of the Industrial Workers of the World (IWW) by dropping out of the craft-oriented women's labor auxiliaries and joining the Women's Card and Label League. Inspired by the King County Legislative Federation—a political organization led by middle-class feminists who sought to bring together women's groups ranging from the Women's Christian Temperance Union to the Label League itself—the league implored its working-class sisters to move "into the vanguard of the advanced Woman Movement" of its day.[1] In the years leading up to the Great War, Label League members focused their energy on the resolution of a variety of political and social problems. As a "training school for women,"[2] the working-class organization sponsored political debates and canvassed Seattle's precincts for support of organized labor's various ballot initiatives. At the same time, Label Leaguers worked with middle-class clubwomen to found a home for single girls, expand women's influence in local and state politics, and gain equal suffrage for their sisters throughout the region and the nation.

As if that was not enough, league officials also formed the Federation of Trade Unionist Women and Auxiliaries to wed the interests and power of unions and working-class women more generally. In all these respects, the league helped redefine the meaning of citizenship and of public life for early-twentieth-century Seattle women as a whole.

Viewed more systematically, the Label League's activities symbolized the general transformation of gender and class politics in the late-nineteenth and early-twentieth-century American West. Indeed, the political and social history of the West, and for that matter the nation, cannot be understood without analyzing the interconnection of class and gender in the political realm. As key figures in arguably the two greatest social movements of their age—feminism and labor unionism—working-class women in Seattle facilitated, if only temporarily, the formation of cross-class and cross-gender political alliances. The Seattle Card and Label League clearly represented the amalgamation of these conditions by combining the feminist mobilization for equal suffrage with the class consciousness of the labor movement overall. In less than a decade, Seattle residents watched the city's women gain the vote and then witnessed them play a central role in one of the greatest labor disputes in American history—the Seattle General Strike of 1919. The transition from "Old West" to the "New West," from the "frontier" to the entry of new states into the Union, had everything to do with this mobilization of political actors in the region along the dimensions of class and gender. How this story unfolded in one of the major urban environments of the "Pacific Slope" is the subject of the study that follows.

The historical legacy of Frederick Jackson Turner's frontier thesis, historian Michael Malone has argued, has "led us to focus too much of our attention upon frontiering and, concomitantly, to neglect the study of the modern West."[3] What is still less understood, however, is the transition from the West of the frontier cowboy and sodbuster to that of Boeing Aerospace and Hollywood. The explanations no doubt are many. To begin, historians must look to the key regional and national features that mark this transitional period. The era from the 1880s to World War I witnessed, first and foremost, the rise and spread of corporate capitalism nationwide. The West was not exempt from this phenomenon; in fact, it was a significant contributor to it. The tremendous expansion of the nation's railroad system, which bound the nation together, was only one example of region's relationship to larger, national forces of change. National corporations, like the Anaconda Copper Mining Company, Northern Securities, and Weyerhaeuser Lumber, invested deeply in the West and maintained a firm grip on the region's political economy. The forces of change engendered by capitalism are an important clue to understanding the rise of the modern West.[4]

While corporate capitalism was the foundation of the rapid transition to the modern West, it was only one part of the equation. Such change is never smooth or pretty. According to William Deverell, "given the timing of industrial expansion and transcontinental conquest, the West stands as the last proving ground of nineteenth-century American capitalism, complete with critical protest and opposition movements."[5] It is here, with the conflict and power struggle among western inhabitants, that we can bring life to the changing nature of the West. These battles took place, as they do in nearly every society, in the household, in the streets, in the factory, and in the halls of government. Two of the most profound power struggles during this transitional period involved women and labor.[6] These were not simply contests over power but involved differing and sometimes conflicting visions of what the West should be.

While the forces of industrial capitalism profoundly reshaped the nation, regional differences produced distinct stories and experiences that were threads woven into the national tapestry. We must avoid, however, the urge to see the West as simply the East or South warmed over. Just as slavery and its legacy have given the South a unique historical experience, scholars have pinpointed several particular themes that make the West worthy of its own regional definition. The general aridity of the trans-Mississippi West has greatly contributed to its distinctive economic and political developments. Similarly, the region's racial and cultural diversity—Native Americans, Latinos, Asians, blacks, and whites—clearly set the western experience apart from the bipolar black/white history of race relations east of the great river. Moreover, the dominating presence of the federal government and the timing of the region's emergence in the midst of a global capitalist economy represent two other defining traits of the West. Despite these regional themes or traits, scholars of the West have to perform a careful balancing act and not marginalize or isolate western experiences from the larger American narrative. In the end, the West "is less than a perfect representation of, and more than only a regional variation on, American history, life, and character."[7]

The West, or subregions like the Pacific Northwest, is more than physical territories created by geographers. Regions, according to William Robbins, are "communities in a broad geographic sense with common cultural features and economic orientation."[8] They are as much creations of people as they are products of climate and natural landscapes. There is no better time, then, to search for the origins of regional identity in the Pacific Northwest than the dawn of the twentieth century. Rapid settlement and economic development compelled residents to make sense of their new environment during a time of profound social, economic, and cultural change. Defining their region was a product of both how they saw themselves and how others perceived them. For scholars, the slipperiness of regionalism reminds us of Supreme Court Justice Potter Stewart's frustration with the concept of obscenity—we may not be able to define it, but we know it when we see it.[9]

While turn-of-the-century westerners, unlike historians, may have spoken little about aridity or the federal government's presence, they did express their sense of region through words and actions. Pacific Northwest inhabitants celebrated their region as a gateway to the Orient and economic prosperity, a land of freedom, and a place of magnificent natural wonders. Competition, jealousy, and pride as much as the area's physical attributes informed their regional identity.[10] Seattle workers, for example, looked both to the dreary factories of eastern industrial centers and San Francisco's Union Labor Party when defining their sense of place in the Pacific Northwest. Likewise, the city's suffragists adroitly employed regional rhetoric in making their case for the vote. At the same time they favorably compared western men's outlook toward women to that of their eastern brothers, exploiting intraregional rivalries to convince, if not shame, Washington men to grant women the ballot. This study, then, is a story of both Seattle and the West and the threads they represented in the national tapestry.[11]

Seattle's storied history reminds us that gender politics and labor radicalism should not be overlooked as key features of the western experience. By the early 1900s the West was not only the site of many of the great labor conflicts, but home to many of the more noteworthy radical labor organizations.[12] The Cripple Creek mining strike, the Ludlow Massacre, the *Los Angeles Times* bombing, and the Industrial Workers of the World (IWW) free-speech fights were just a few of the major conflicts that characterized American labor relations in the early twentieth century. From the anti-Chinese riots of the 1880s to the 1916 Everett Massacre and the infamous 1919 Seattle General Strike, Seattle's working class figured prominently in this era of class conflict and labor radicalism. During the late nineteenth and early twentieth centuries, the Knights of Labor, the IWW, and one of largest Socialist movements in the nation called Seattle home. Moreover, utopian labor colonies that dotted Puget Sound attracted numerous prominent labor radicals, including Bill Haywood, Elizabeth Gurley Flynn, William Z. Foster, and Emma Goldman, while Seattle cultivated the likes of Harvey O'Connor and Anna Louise Strong.

The struggle between labor and capital in Seattle extended beyond the factory to the halls of government. While most scholars have urged the study of how workers understood and used political activity as a form of labor protest, or what I refer to as labor politics, often the definition of politics is so broad as to include any type or form of protest. Union strikes and neighborhood street protests no doubt can, and did, affect the local political landscape. The impact of this activity, however, was usually temporary; more long-lasting change, many working-class leaders understood, could be achieved only through more direct control of the reins of government.[13] From San Francisco to Seattle, labor leaders not only seemed to comprehend this, but also attempted to direct workers toward more independent political power. Driven westward by the onslaught of industrial capitalism, many workers viewed the West in rather idealistic terms. Dashed expectations and the harsh working conditions and remoteness associated with the region's extractive economy combined to infuse workers with a special spirit of militancy, best expressed by the Knights of Labor and the IWW.[14] This militancy, as my study suggests, helps explain the politics of class in Seattle.

Although a seemingly masculine region of loggers, longshoremen, and gold hunters, women also exerted a significant social and political influence in western cities. Already Washington territory's largest city by the early 1880s, Seattle was home to a female population that secured and briefly enjoyed the vote for a majority of that decade. In 1890 the state legislature passed the first equal opportunity employment law in the United States, providing women access to all jobs and professions save public office. By the early twentieth century, a local waitress held an influential office on the Seattle Central Labor Council, and along with her middle-class sisters successfully regained the franchise in 1910, initiating a wave of suffrage victories that by 1914 had secured the ballot for women in ten western states. Seattle women quickly employed the power of the vote to refigure local politics, including the recall of city's mayor in 1911 and the 1926 election of the nation's first big-city female mayor, Bertha Knight Landes.[15]

Thus Seattle's experience reminds us that scholars must look to the west to advance our understanding of the emergence of female political equality. Despite nearly three decades of debate and investigation, historians have been unable to pin down a single and satisfying explanation for the success of suffrage in the West. Seemingly little has changed since one scholar concluded that these victories "depended on complex combinations of factors that varied from state to state."[16] Scholars have learned, however, much about these complex factors. Issues of race and class, along with the particular political and cultural climate of each state, help explain many of the western suffrage victories. Rebecca Mead's recent study of woman suffrage in the West has significantly advanced our understanding of these complexities by placing these struggles within a rapidly changing regional political milieu that marked the turn-of-the-century West.[17] More importantly, historians now understand that female suffragists' actions and words were as important, if not more so, as other external factors. Suffragists' political sagacity, cross-class alliances, use of regional appeals, and the context of Progressivism, as this study argues, help explain the success of the equal suffrage campaign in Seattle and Washington State.[18] Seattle women's early victory also offers us greater insight into what women did with the vote during an era of reform and political engagement. Until we understand these things, we cannot fully understand the politics of gender.

As this study will make clear, women and labor played a crucial role in shaping the contours of the West. While both groups initially existed on the margins of power, the rapid development and transformation of the region offered them the chance to assert their visions of a New West. Sometimes together, but often separate, women and organized labor struggled to redefine the political landscape of their communities. Western politics, scholars have demonstrated, were more fluid and susceptible to short-term forces, which partially explains the ability of labor and women to exert political influence.[19] Politics, in my study, signifies not just elections and campaigns, but also how people and groups attempted to effect change and shape decision making in their community.[20] This allows us to explore, in addition to political parties, voluntary organizations, like the chamber of commerce, anti-immigrant societies, and women's clubs, and demonstrate how they participated in the power struggles that defined the West.

Seattle, Washington, thus provides historians an excellent locale to explore the politics of class and gender in the turn-of-the-century American West. What one scholar has called a "new urban frontier" city, Seattle, like Los Angeles, Portland, and several other western cities, not only grew and developed at a critical moment in American history, it also shared several traits with these communities, including a greater degree of suburban sprawl, a more skilled labor force, and economic dominance over its hinterland.[21] From 1880 to 1920, Seattle evolved from a small frontier community into a large cosmopolitan urban center. Like Denver, Los Angeles, and Portland, Seattle experienced the impact of corporate capitalism during this transformative period in American history. Railroads, timber companies, and other eastern-based corporations imprinted both the visible and invisible hand of the market on Seattle's history. Despite its image of wide-open plains and deserts, interrupted by the imposing peaks of the Rocky Mountains, the West was largely an urban society. As early as the 1890s, a larger proportion of the region's population resided in cities compared to the East and South.[22] Moreover, the years from 1890 to 1920 were decisive for the urbanization, and later suburbanization, of the West. Seattle was no exception, growing from around 40,000 people to more than 315,000 by 1920. The rapid growth helps to bring into sharper relief the political and social struggles associated with America in the age of corporate capitalism.

From direct democracy to worker's compensation, far western states placed themselves at the vanguard of a national progressive movement. Washington State, one scholar has argued "is a forgotten pioneer in the history of insurgent politics and social reform in the United States."[23] As a major urban center, then, Seattle can also help advance our understanding of western progressivism.[24] Cities witnessed the intersection of class, gender, and political reform as residents struggled to redefine their communities and their place in a changing American society. Yet, as Robert Johnston has argued, these social identities are not as neat and clean as we once believed. Definitions of the middle class that scholars have placed on these historical actors were not those that Portland's, or for that matter Seattle's, residents would have recognized or accepted. Moreover, the simple idea that workers were more radical and the middle class more conservative belies the reality of early-twentieth-century urban progressives. Social and political coalitions, in fact, were more complex and constantly evolving in response to the changing political, economic, and social conditions in Seattle and other cities. Struggling to come to grips with the dislocation and negative consequences of corporate capitalism and the market economy, Seattle residents actively looked to the political arena to address their fears and concerns as well as fulfill their dreams and visions. The politics of class and gender, as this study will demonstrate, profoundly refigured the political landscape of progressive America.[25]

This study is organized into five chapters that follow the evolution of Seattle from its founding in the 1850s through World War I, focusing on the first two decades of the twentieth century. Together they explore the nature and impact of gender and class politics during this crucial period in the history of the West and the nation. The first chapter outlines the early history of Seattle from the arrival of the first white settlers in the early 1850s through the tumultuous decade of the 1890s. It examines the community's economic development and how gender emerged as a major social and political issue in Seattle's early years. It explains how vice, especially prostitution and alcohol, drew middle-class women together into a successful equal suffrage movement that momentarily secured the ballot in 1883. The chapter then offers a different view of Seattle's political landscape in the 1880s by examining class issues—in particular, white working-class protests against Chinese labor—and how class conflict helped produce a labor-dominated political movement that successfully seized power in both the city and county government in 1886. Chapter 1 concludes by detailing the changing fortunes of both enfranchised women and organized labor in Seattle following the collapse of this brief working-class political movement in the late 1880s. This intense period of class conflict ended with women's loss of the ballot, the rapid demise of the Knights of Labor, and the ascendancy of more conservative AFL-oriented trade unions in the city.

Chapter 2 explores how and why Seattle's working class increasingly viewed direct political activity as a way both to defend its status and secure a voice in the city's future. It begins with a brief examination of how the numerous utopian colonies that dotted Puget Sound at the turn of the century helped replenish the spirit of disillusioned and dejected local radicals during the hard times of the 1890s. Fortunes quickly changed with the Yukon gold strike and the subsequent revival of organized labor by the early twentieth century. This chapter then details how renewed attacks by employers encouraged workers to ally with, and in some ways direct, local progressive forces to reorient power in the community. Despite limited success, organized labor continued to battle with defiant employers over the fruits of the city's 1909 Alaska-Yukon-Pacific Exposition as well as regarding Japanese immigration. The chapter concludes by examining how these struggles again encouraged labor leaders to engage more actively in local politics, this time as an independent labor party in 1910. When soundly defeated, labor once more had to reevaluate the politics of class.

Chapter 3 turns to gender politics and the history behind the successful 1910 equal suffrage campaign. It emphasizes how the social and economic conditions of the early twentieth century drew middle-class and working-class women together, building the foundation of feminist politics in Seattle. It also outlines the successful strategy and tactics employed by Seattle suffragists, especially cross-class alliances, political maneuvering, and a uniquely western message.

Chapter 4 carries gender politics beyond suffrage by exploring how voting women engaged the political process. It outlines how Seattle women transformed the local political landscape, including engineering the recall of the mayor. This chapter also examines the politicization of women and the continuing impact of moral concerns on city politics. Next it illustrates the maturation of the fruitful but tense cross-class alliance that working-class and middle-class women had forged earlier and how this aided female laborers. The chapter concludes by examining how working-class women inserted their brand of feminism into their class activities.

The final chapter explores the politics of class and gender during the critical half-decade before World War I. It illustrates how middle-class feminists and organized labor joined forces to redefine progressivism in Seattle. It details the changing social and economic conditions of the mid-1910s that severely tested this cross-class alliance. Growing labor militancy, influenced by local Socialists and the IWW, confronted recalcitrant and defiant employers at both the workshop and the ballot box. The chapter concludes by examining a series of key events that escalated class conflict and by World War I destroyed the tenuous progressive alliance between middle-class feminists and organized labor.

When the European conflict came to end in November 1918, the new battle lines drawn by the events of the previous decade created a different war that, like the Great War, would leave in its wake only broken dreams and unfulfilled promises. Indeed, these decades following the turn of the century reflected often painful but sometimes inspiring struggles of westerners to mold and shape their postfrontier dreams of a new West.

CHAPTER 1

Class, Gender, and Politics in Late-Nineteenth-Century Seattle

Early one Sunday morning in February 1886, several hundred white working-class men and women gathered in the Chinese district in Seattle. On the pretense of enforcing local health regulations, they pounded on doors, summarily condemned buildings, and strongly suggested that all Chinese leave the city. The teamsters among the throng of white workers then hauled the outcasts' belongings to a nearby dock where the *Queen of the Pacific* prepared to weigh anchor for its regular run to San Francisco. By the end of the morning approximately 350 Chinese residents—some frightened and others defiant—huddled together at the foot of the *Queen's* gangplank. The workers and others who milled around the docks then passed the hat to raise the seven dollars per head demanded by the ship's captain to transport the Chinese to California. Despite authorities' promises to protect them, nearly all the weary Chinese hostages chose to take advantage of the offer to leave Seattle. However, the *Queen of the Pacific* had room for only 200 passengers; when it set sail for San Francisco, it left roughly 185 Chinese residents behind.[1]

Up to this point, the anti-Chinese crowd had largely avoided direct violence. Had the ship had room for all those forced to the docks, perhaps this event would have quietly come to a close. Yet it was the question of what to do with the remaining Chinese that divided Seattle residents. George Venable Smith, one of the leaders of the anti-Chinese crowd, suggested that the Chinese remain at the wharf until another steamer arrived a few days later. Local militia officers, however, overruled him and decided to escort the Chinese back to their residences in the Lava Bed district. At the corner of Main and Commercial, workers who had not been at the docks—and thus may have been unaware that the *Queen* had no more room—closed ranks and impeded the militia. Exact details of this confrontation vary, but it is clear that an unarmed logger objected to the return of the Chinese, and when one of the guards attempted to arrest him, a scuffle occurred and five men were shot, the logger fatally. By nightfall, a proclamation of martial law by the territorial governor and the dispatch of federal troops a day later concluded the opening chapter of a momentous event in Seattle's early history.[2]

The February riot, in many ways, marked the beginning of modern Seattle history. During the next several decades, labor emerged as a major actor in the social, economic, and political life of the city. With the simultaneous enfranchisement of women during this period, Seattle politics in the late 1880s looked like no other in the entire nation. By the 1890s, however, a fragile political moment had unraveled with the revocation of equal suffrage and the disarray and disillusionment of the city's radical community—two outcomes that were not mutually exclusive. In this time of rapid social and economic change, Seattle witnessed class-based coalitions that supplanted past political factions shaped by cultural issues such as prostitution and temperance. It would be a mistake, however, to confine the importance of these events to Seattle alone. Seattle's experiences in the late nineteenth century speak to several significant issues that dominate the landscape of American history, including the growing significance of class politics, the role of race in shaping class relations, and the increasing presence of the state in the relations between capital and labor. Yet, the presence and actions of enfranchised women in Seattle during the 1880s both distinguished this experience from California's anti-Chinese events as well as foreshadowed the tremendous impact of gender politics in early-twentieth-century America.

Settled by a small band of midwestern migrants who ventured to Puget Sound in 1852 in search of a good harbor and abundant land, Seattle quickly became home to a timber industry that would shape the city's economy for decades to come.[3] The Sound emerged as an early source of lumber for San Francisco merchants, despite the great distance, because it offered safe, deep harbors. The region's promise attracted many entrepreneurs to the Puget Sound, including the father of Seattle's lumber industry, Henry Yesler. Yesler ventured to Puget Sound in the early 1850s to build a steam-driven lumber mill. When he arrived in Seattle he discovered that founding settlers Arthur A. Denny and C. D. Boren had already claimed much of the waterfront. However, Denny and his fellow pioneers saw in Yesler's plans just what Seattle needed—a viable industry. Not willing to let his entrepreneurial spirit slip away, the local leaders rearranged their property holdings so as to give Yesler a narrow strip of land running perpendicular to the coast that expanded to a larger holding in the nearby timber lands. Yesler's mill promised a prosperous and bright future for their new community.[4]

Despite the area having a population of only approximately four thousand, excluding Indians, Congress approved a request for territorial status for what was then the northern portion of the Oregon Territory in May 1853. By 1880, more than twenty-five years after Arthur Denny had paddled his canoe up Puget Sound, Seattle seemingly had changed little. The economy expanded in size as the lumber industry reached further inland to the vast forests of Puget Sound and new mills dotted Seattle and the other small coastal communities. Despite this growth, the city's local economy and businesses overwhelmingly depended, directly or indirectly, on the lumber industry. Likewise, the region's working class also changed little, as most workers harvested trees in nearby forests or labored in the local mills refining and processing the lumber for shipment. The 1880s, however, brought countless and profound changes to the city. Without a doubt the foremost engine of change was the completion of the Northern Pacific Railway (NP) which transformed the local and regional economy, tying it into a truly national market. The railroad carried not only new goods but also new people and ideas to the once isolated Sound. The instability and unpredictability that characterized the national marketplace would also describe Seattle in the late nineteenth century.[5]

In the 1870s the Northern Pacific, under the leadership of eastern financier Jay Cooke, began to construct a transcontinental railroad that would link Lake Superior to the Pacific Northwest. Overspeculation, shady dealings, and Cooke's ego combined to crack the shaky foundation on which he had built the NP. A depression stalled further construction of the railroad until a German immigrant, Henry Villard, reorganized and finally completed the NP, tying the Great Lakes to the Puget Sound in the mid-1880s.[6]

The primary terminus for the NP on the Pacific was not Seattle but nearby Tacoma. The choice of Tacoma over Seattle in 1873 could easily have erased Seattle from the map, yet from this loss the city grew more determined to reclaim its supremacy on Puget Sound. In the early 1870s, the NP's directors encouraged Puget Sound cities to vie for the lucrative terminus of this transcontinental railroad. In terms of infrastructure and financial resources, Tacoma had little to offer. Yet it was precisely the lack of both significant development and an entrenched elite to block Cooke's efforts that enticed him to place the NP's terminus in Tacoma. In short, Tacoma could be Cooke's town. Nevertheless, Seattle's officials continued to up the ante for the terminus by offering the NP $250,000 in cash and bonds, some 7,500 town lots, 3,000 acres of undeveloped land, and approximately one-half of the waterfront.[7]

The decision to build the terminus in Tacoma engendered two important responses from Seattle residents. First, it marked the beginning of anti-eastern sentiment in Seattle. Local citizens were quite upset by this decision and soon recognized that forces back East had great power and control over their lives. Episodes like this one have often encouraged historians of the West to argue that, in terms of its economy, the West was little more than a colony of the East. Second, Seattle's leading businessmen realized that the NP's choice of Tacoma threatened their city's vitality, and they responded by attempting to build their own railroad over the Cascade Range to Walla Walla in the eastern part of the territory. The railroad's proponents floated their own stock locally, and despite community picnics and turns at the pick and shovel, the railroad made it only a few miles out of town. The Seattle and Walla Walla line, however, did reach the excellent coal fields of eastern King County. In the end this little community railroad would help expand Seattle's control over its Puget Sound hinterland by directing economic activity through its port.[8]

Prior to the economic boom of the 1880s, the lumber industry, and to a lesser extent the coal fields east of the city, drove Seattle's economy. Territorial figures for 1870 reveal that $1.3 million of the total $1.9 million invested in Washington's manufacturing was in lumbering. Likewise, two-thirds of total manufacturing wages ended up in the pockets of sawmill workers. Within a few years a fleet of small steam vessels based in Seattle, commonly referred to as the "Mosquito Fleet," carried goods to and from Seattle and the Sound's other ports, making the city the central supply depot for the region. By 1875, the city also established its first regular steamship service to San Francisco. The mid-1870s brought bad economic times to the entire nation, the Pacific coast included. Seattle, however, fared better because the demand for its coal in California remained firm and its aborted railroad in the coal fields increased the profitability of many local mining operators.[9]

The Northern Pacific's laying of its final rail in the mid-1880s stimulated economic growth throughout the Pacific Northwest. Seattle's two key industries—timber and coal—benefited greatly from the line's expansion. Railroad construction strengthened the demand for lumber in the form of railroad ties; the growth of the iron horse in the West whetted the industry's appetite for the region's coal. The NP also opened new markets for Seattle businesses and further expanded the region's economy. Washington's lumber industry in 1879, for example, produced approximately one-half as much as California's, but within a decade its production outstripped the Golden State's by nearly twofold. Seattle likewise witnessed an explosion of new sawmill construction and the updating of many older factories. In particular, more and more mills focused on shingle manufacturing, making the Seattle suburb of Ballard the world's largest producer of shingles by the 1890s. Finally, new industries and businesses arose to feed the railroad market and the growing local demands of the rapidly urbanizing community of Seattle. Iron foundries, machine shops, a street railroad, and even an infant telephone company sprang up during the decade.[10]

While the railroad offered prosperity, eastern consumer goods, and closer ties with the rest of the nation, it also brought vast numbers of people who seemed significantly different—socially, culturally, and racially— from earlier settlers. By the end of the 1880s, Seattle no longer was the sleepy hamlet about which Denny and his pioneer friends so fondly reminisced. The city's population swelled by 1200 percent, growing from about 3,500 residents to more than 42,000 by the end of the decade. Workers, skilled and unskilled, journeyed west both to help build the new railroads and to take advantage of the higher real wages that western cities such as Seattle offered. In particular, the NP brought to the Sound many more single young men whose ancestors harked from Ireland, Italy, and Sweden. As late as 1900, 64 percent of the Seattle residents were male. Seattle, as the Sound's main commercial center, attracted many of these young rootless men during the cold wet winter months to partake of various pleasures found in the city's red-light district. The significance of Seattle's economic development, however, lies not so much in its contours as in its pace. While Seattle's economic development proceeded in much the same manner as in the East, "changes which took a century or more on the Atlantic seaboard were concentrated into a generation or less on Puget Sound."[11] Such rapid growth quickly tested the ability of Seattle's citizens to cope with its consequences.

Excited by the city's potential, yet alarmed by some of the effects, many Seattle citizens stepped up their efforts to exorcise what they perceived as the negative consequences of rapid economic growth. In the fall of 1880, anti-liquor forces united to form the Territorial Temperance Alliance and soon turned to government to curb drinking. Within a year, the Temperance Alliance had successfully lobbied for both a Sunday closing law and a measure that made saloonkeepers liable for injuries attributable to liquor sold in their taverns. In 1883, anti-alcohol forces declared a week in July "Temperance Week," during which ministers expounded upon the evil of alcohol and the necessity for good Christians to work actively to eliminate it. The Temperance Alliance not only condemned alcohol and extolled temperance, but also suggested that woman suffrage could provide temperance forces the political leverage to achieve their goals.[12] Temperance advocates firmly believed that the battle for the life and soul of Seattle was at hand. In early November, the territorial legislature greatly aided their cause by passing a bill granting suffrage to women, which Governor William Newell proudly signed into law.[13]

The governor's signature ended a twelve-year battle that had begun with Susan B. Anthony's western visit in 1871. Anthony told a Seattle audience gathered at a local church that women would use their vote against intemperance and the growing social evil of prostitution. In addition, with the ballot in their hands, women could also protect their property and wages.[14] Much of the credit for securing the vote must be given to Abigail Scott Duniway, who led suffrage forces both in her home state of Oregon and in neighboring Washington Territory. Duniway not only invited Anthony to the Pacific Northwest, but also accompanied her throughout her travels to the far reaches of Washington's frontier. In 1873, the Oregonian suffragist began publishing her own newspaper, the *New Northwest*, which not only helped spread her thoughts on suffrage and women's rights, but also facilitated communication among women throughout the region. By the mid-1870s, woman suffrage and temperance entered public discourse, influencing both local and state politics for much of the next two decades.[15]

Washington's equal suffrage triumph, however, extended well beyond the waters of Puget Sound. Nationally, the woman's suffrage movement had limped along following the movement's split into two competing organizations. While the territories of Utah and Wyoming had granted suffrage to women soon after the Civil War, their importance to the suffrage movement was limited because, in the words of a national suffrage periodical, one had "a very exceptional population and the other a very small one." Washington, however, was a much larger and growing territory that was greater in land size than most eastern states. The national suffrage magazine *Woman's Journal* announced that "while the East lags behind on this great question of equal rights, the young, progressive West leads the way." The magazine also applauded "the brave, true young men of the West" for this progressive move. Suffragists throughout the nation thus looked to Washington Territory as a source of pride, hope, and inspiration for further action in their respective states.[16]

The rapid expansion of gambling, prostitution, and saloons to meet the needs of the city's burgeoning young male population spurred Seattle women to exercise their voting power. Despite the threat to the city's economy, a group of concerned citizens formed a new political organization in early 1884 to confront the vice lords and various illicit activities. Composed of newly enfranchised women and like-minded men, the Law and Order League nominated a slate of candidates for the upcoming municipal elections. Worried businessmen quickly responded with a Businessmen's ticket that advocated "reasonable regulation" of vice that would not undermine the local economy. Support for the Businessmen's ticket came from many of the city's most influential and powerful business leaders, including territorial governor Elisha P. Ferry, Henry Yesler, and other local entrepreneurs who declared that the "corner-stone of the business prosperity of the cities of this coast rests on the saloons, the gambling houses and the houses of prostitution; these are woven and inter-woven with every branch of business. When you strike them, you strike at the business interests of the whole community."[17] The municipal elections ended in a draw, the Businessmen's ticket capturing the mayor's seat but the remaining offices equally divided. Seattle's residents seemed to be sending a message that they wished to find some middle ground between the new Sodom and Gomorrah that an unfettered business elite might create and the economic prosperity that drew them to their western promised land.[18]

Much to the chagrin of their detractors, Seattle women crowded the city's polling places during the 1884 elections. The *Evening Telegram* declared: "Away go two old assertions against Woman Suffrage, that women will not vote if they have the opportunity, and that they will be insulted if they make the attempt."[19] Not only did Seattle women proudly march to the ballot box, but some, like Mrs. Laura E. Hall, hitched up their horses and shuttled women back and forth to the polls all day. Others congregated around the polls, encouraging their sisters and supplying them with the proper ballots. That a large number of women voted was evident by the near threefold increase in voter participation from the previous year when women could not vote. No doubt the political excitement created by the Law and Order League heightened interest in the election and attracted more male voters. Yet, one local paper claimed that of more than 750 women registered, "it is a safe assertion that seven hundred voted." Clearly, the local press concluded, woman coveted the ballot.[20]

Surprised by the Law and Order League's success, Seattle businessmen quickly reorganized the Businessmen's ticket in preparation for the 1885 municipal elections. A stagnant economy that left hundreds jobless and local mines quiet inspired merchants to turn to the Lava Bed's saloons and gambling dens to revive business. Seattle businessmen, including former governor Ferry, announced that removing the shackles from saloons—in particular, the Sunday closing law—would lead to a revival of the real estate, timber, and shipping industries. Seattle, Ferry claimed, "will enter upon an era of prosperity such as she has never seen."[21] The results of the 1885 city elections, however, shocked and "astonished" the editor of the *Post-Intelligencer*. The paper characterized the Businessmen's ticket victory over the Law and Order League as "sweeping and complete" and concluded that the "people have virtually passed a vote of want of confidence in the present city government." Businessmen's candidate Henry Yesler outpaced his opponent by nearly a two-to-one margin, capturing all three wards, including the third ward, which was virtually the home of the Law and Order League.[22]

If the municipal elections of 1884 and 1885 revealed a highly fragile and fractured community, the forced eviction of Seattle's Chinese community in early 1886 completely tore the city apart. Anti-Chinese hostility first erupted in the Pacific Northwest in the fall of 1885 with attacks on Chinese miners in Wyoming and hops harvesters in nearby Squak Valley, Washington. Initially, Seattle's middle-class residents expressed concern about these events and agreed that peace would return to the region if employers let their Chinese laborers go. While residents continued to debate the future of the city's Chinese population, Tacoma's anti-Chinese forces took to the streets to evict the Chinese from their city. In early October, delegates from Seattle, Tacoma, and several western Washington communities formed the Anti-Chinese Congress and set a November 1 deadline for the departure of all Chinese from the Sound. Tacoma's forces succeeded in driving most of the Chinese population out of their city. Seattle's apparent consensus soon evaporated as the city's workers stepped up their demand for the eviction of all Chinese residents. At a mass meeting, more than eight hundred mostly working-class citizens voiced their ill feelings toward the city's Chinese. Daniel Cronin, a Knights of Labor organizer who had arrived in Seattle just a few weeks earlier, stepped to the rostrum and dismissed the rather passive tactics advocated by previous speakers.[23] A gifted and rousing orator, Cronin linked the region's woeful employment conditions to the presence of Chinese workers. By using the Chinese as a rallying point for suffering and disillusioned workers, he tied the Knights of Labor to the anti-Chinese crusade. If the Chinese were not removed from Seattle, he warned, "there will be riot and bloodshed this winter."[24]

The period of détente between anti-Chinese forces and Seattle's elite came to an end by early 1886. After a trial of three working-class leaders charged with conspiracy to deny Chinese residents their civil rights ended in acquittal, Cronin told a crowd gathered to celebrate the verdict that the "Chinese question is only a local affair; useful for [broader] agitation and education."[25] He thereby signaled that the anti-Chinese activity was in fact just the beginning of a greater citywide battle between labor and capital. Class relations soured further when talks broke down in early February between the Knights of Labor and mine operators outside Seattle, flooding the city with angry unemployed miners.[26] On the eve of the anti-Chinese riot, a large crowd of miners and other city laborers met to pass a series of resolutions condemning the presence of Chinese laborers and finished the night endorsing a final statement that vividly expressed the depths of their anger and frustration. This last declaration stated:

> That we, in common with all good citizens, shall treat all such pro-Chinese people with the contempt and scorn which they rightly deserve, and that we shall regard them so far the enemies of good order, of society and free American citizenship as to be unworthy of recognition, or of any social or business intercourse, and shall also treat those who shall countenance or in any manner uphold them as of the same character.[27]

The conflict, as this resolution made clear, no longer simply centered on the presence of Chinese workers in the city: it had become a class war. Anti-Chinese leaders placed the blame for the deteriorating social order squarely on the shoulders of the city's elite. Labor leaders aimed their resolution not only at the vocal defenders of the Chinese but also at those in the community who remained silent and thus tacitly countenanced the presence of Chinese workers. The following day Seattle residents awoke to violence and bloodshed.

Class conflict in Seattle quickly spilled over to the political arena. Believing that political activity went hand in hand with organizing at the point of production, local Knights of Labor leaders called on working-men and workingwomen to elect those who favored labor and who could "handle the reins of government in an American manner."[28] The municipal election in the summer of 1886 pitted the Knights' new political party, the People's Party, against pioneer Arthur Denny and the Loyal League. The league attempted to paint the opposition with the brush of radicalism and disloyalty, never missing the chance to remind voters of the anti-Chinese riots. Behind the law and order rhetoric, however, was a concern for the city's economic future. Simply put, the Loyal League maintained that a People's Party victory would destroy Seattle's pioneer image and scare away badly needed investment capital.[29]

When the polls closed in mid-July, the People's Party candidate for mayor had defeated city father Arthur Denny by fewer than fifty votes. The Loyal League also lost the race for city attorney and police chief and split seats on the city council. The People's Party triumph clearly suggested that Seattle was undergoing rapid social change, as new coalitions, largely organized around class, replaced earlier community factions centered on cultural issues like temperance and morality.[30] By 1887, the promise of the People's Party proved illusory. That summer a new Citizen's ticket reclaimed power in the municipal elections.

The People's Party was not the only victim of this important political moment in Seattle's short history. Many working-class radicals left the city to aid nearby coal miners or to form utopian colonies along the Puget Sound.[31] More importantly, just a few months before the 1887 city elections, Washington women lost the right to vote when the territorial supreme court nullified the original suffrage act. The timing of the party's political demise and the end of woman suffrage in Washington Territory were much more than mere coincidence. Unwilling to address directly the class issues the election exposed, the Loyal League and Seattle's elite searched for an alternative explanation or scapegoat for their loss and found it in the city's changing gender dynamics. One of the interesting outcomes of the political events of 1886 was that two of the leading suffragists, Mary Kenworthy and Laura Hall Peters, found themselves opposing many of the most prominent male supporters of equal suffrage with whom they had campaigned in previous elections. For Seattle's old guard, the devastating loss to the People's Party in both the city and territorial elections of 1886 was only topped by the apparent disloyalty of many female voters, like Kenworthy and Peters. Unable to curb the political independence of many voting women or bend them to their will, Seattle's male elites settled on removing this uncertainty from politics all together. Within three months of the People's Party's sweeping victory in the November elections, the territorial supreme court, using a rather arcane technicality, declared the 1883 equal suffrage act unconstitutional.[32]

When Washington State finally entered the union in 1889, Seattle residents no doubt believed that the worst times were behind them. The social and political convulsions produced by the anti-Chinese episode and the People's Party were soon forgotten after a devastating fire nearly destroyed the city in 1889. While Seattle suffragists struggled to rebuild their movement, the city's working class quickly reorganized their forces by allying in a citywide federation. The Western Central Labor Union (WCLU) sprouted from the ashes of the great fire of 1889 as construction workers flooded the city, swelling the memberships of conservative trade unions. In 1891, a local paper reported that the city was home to nearly fifty labor and trade organizations. That same year some four thousand members of this newly organized labor force paraded in the streets of Seattle in celebration of Labor Day. However, despite this apparent demonstration of solidarity, Seattle workers remained badly divided.[33]

While the building trades fared rather well during the late 1880s and early 1890s, serious problems afflicted organized labor, revealing large rifts that could not be easily closed. Again, the Knights of Labor stood at the center of the simmering controversy. While the Chinese had provided the Knights a powerful issue around which to solidify all types of workers, by 1889–90 Chinese labor was no longer a salient issue. Ironically, the success of the Knights and the People's Party not only had driven nearly the entire Asian population from many Puget Sound communities, but it also removed the topic of Chinese labor from public debate. While the Chinese population would slowly revive in the years that followed, it generated little political interest.[34] Moreover, events in the coal fields east of Seattle and disputes within the WCLU further weakened the Knights' influence and power. The ensuing conflict not only added to the mine operators' contempt for the Knights, but also generated a power play within the WCLU that ended with the purge of the radical labor group from the local federation.

At first glance, the failed miners' strike and a weakened Knights of Labor portended little hope for a renewed working-class political movement in Seattle. The WCLU's victory, however, pushed local Knights further toward politics as the best road to improve the workers' lives. Prior to the outbreak of hostilities in the mines, labor leaders had opened conversations with the Washington Farmers' Alliance about forming a political coalition.[35] Local Knights of Labor assemblies enthusiastically embraced the proposed producers' alliance. At the King County gathering, radical labor leaders commanded the meeting. After delegates debated issues ranging from the needs of labor to prohibition, a separate committee returned with a proposed platform. Reflecting the growing influence of populism, the proposal included planks demanding the coining of silver, the eight-hour day, and the direct election of senators.[36]

The Knights of Labor and the Farmers' Alliance announced the birth of the Washington People's Party in the summer of 1891. At a convention held in Yakima, delegates chose Robert Bridges, leader of Seattle's Knights of Labor, to chair the meeting. Fellow Seattle working-class radicals Con Lynch and Millard Knox also gained key elected positions. The People's Party reaffirmed its support for the eight-hour day, an income tax, and the subtreasury system. Notably absent from this convention, however, were WCLU members, who opposed forming a third party.[37]

The Washington People's (or Populist) Party shared more than a similar name with the 1886 People's Party that seized power in Seattle; they shared the Knights of Labor. Much of the 1886 party platform, for example, reappeared several years later in the Washington Populist Party. Moreover, workers made up a majority of delegates at the 1891 Yakima convention, including representatives from at least fourteen Seattle Knights' assemblies. After 1892, most members of the Knights of Labor in Seattle identified themselves as Populists first and Knights second. Politics, then, increasingly became the primary vehicle for advancing the interests of the working class as well as saving the city and state from corporate political corruption. In the 1892 state and national elections, Populists chipped away at both major parties, claiming 28 percent of the overall vote and eight seats in the state legislature. Analysis of the election revealed that Populism's support from urban labor nearly equaled the rural turnout for the new third party.[38]

The Panic of 1893, however, profoundly changed Washington's social and political landscape, greatly improving the People's Party's chances for success. The deteriorating economy hit farm country quite hard, with farmers clamoring about declining prices for wheat as well as discriminatory railway rates. In the cities, trade unions nearly disappeared under the pressure of the depression. The 1893 Labor Day parade in Seattle saw marchers divided into employed and unemployed groups. Several hundred workers responded to the desperate conditions in 1894 by volunteering as "soldiers" in Washington's regiment of Coxey's Army, a protest march on Washington DC. Eugene Debs's national boycott of Pullman railway cars that year also ignited a great deal of debate in Seattle's working-class neighborhoods. While Seattle's WCLU endorsed the strike by Debs's American Railway Union (ARU), it refused to support the local railway workers' boycott of Pullman.[39]

The class antagonism exposed by both the ARU strike and Coxey's Army accelerated the movement of radicalized farmers and laborers to the Populist Party. In the 1894 fall elections, Washington residents sent twenty-three Populist legislators to the state capital in Olympia. More importantly, the returns revealed the collapse of the Democratic Party, which received only 19 percent of the vote.[40] Between 1894 and the critical 1896 election, Populists struggled to maintain a focused, attractive platform that would finally produce a full and complete victory. Those who desired renewed prosperity and political success chose to merge with William Jennings Bryan and the Democrats. On the other hand, a significant number of Washington Populists envisioned a fundamental restructuring of American society and politics, and thus held firm to the broad platform devised at the famous 1892 Omaha Convention. Other interest and reform groups, ranging from single taxers to prohibitionists, further complicated matters for the third party by demanding that their particular ideas be joined to the Populist's platform. By 1895, John Rogers, an agrarian reformer from Kansas who had moved to a small community outside of Tacoma in late 1880s, emerged as the leading spokesperson for what many referred to as middle-of-the-road Populism. Rogers appealed to Socialists, silverites, single taxers, and other groups to "stay in the middle of the road" and avoid their particular pet issues.[41]

Conditions in Washington in 1896 boded well for a Rogers victory. In Seattle, total construction in the city barely reached $200,000, or one-tenth that of 1890. The price of packing shingles dropped from ten cents per thousand to three cents. In the first three years of depression five private banks and one national bank had failed. Even the seemingly indestructible railway companies suffered, with the Northern Pacific, Union Pacific, and six local street railways going into receivership by 1896.[42] The

severe economic downturn, coupled with the successful fusion of Democrats, silver Republicans, and Populists, produced a resounding victory for
reform forces in the state. Both city and rural residents rewarded Rogers
and William Jennings Bryan, the Democratic-Populist fusion candidate
for president, a majority of their ballots. Fusionists claimed victory in seventeen of the eighteen senate races and sixty-five of seventy-eight state
representative seats. In both houses of the state government, Populist candidates who ran on fusion tickets held a comfortable majority.[43]

With its impressive victory, the future of Populism in Washington
seemed bright. Yet within a few months, serious problems surfaced that
not only tormented party leaders but also virtually destroyed the new
political party. The history of Washington State's Populist Party following
its victory in 1896 was largely dominated by a statewide struggle among
fusionist forces. At what was heralded as a new moment in the state's
young history, Populist politicians set out to address their primary concerns, yet party bickering dominated the press. In 1897, for example, Populists fought publicly over their choice for senator to represent Washington
in the nation's capital. Such an open party conflict not only diminished
the Populist victory in many people's eyes, but also deepened the fissures
within the party.[44] In two short years party bickering had significantly
undermined the consensus that fusion had produced, alienating more
and more of the middle-of-the-roaders. Moreover, although the discovery
of gold in the Yukon Territory may have revived the region's economy, it
undermined the Populists' economic message. After 1898, Governor Rogers moved further into the Democratic Party fold. Rogers again claimed
victory in the 1900 gubernatorial race, yet this time as the candidate for
the Democratic Party. With Rogers's reelection, the Populist Party quietly
disappeared from the state's political scene.[45]

The demise of Washington's Populist Party left Seattle's Knights of
Labor reeling. Losing the struggle with the WCLU in 1891, local Knights
had turned their energy toward politics rather than organizing workers.
For all intents and purposes, the Knights as a labor organization had disappeared into the Populist movement, never to be heard from again in
Seattle. Throughout the 1890s, Bridges, Knox, and other former Knights
played key roles in both city and state politics, however, this time acting
as leaders of the new third party rather than as officials of the Knights

of Labor. The death of the People's Party left Bridges and other Knights without an independent vehicle for social change.[46] The Knights' significance, however, lies beyond the strikes and political battles they waged. This labor organization, according to one historian, "did more to shape the region's culture of radicalism than any other."[47] Through pamphlets, labor and reform journals, debates, picnics, and reading rooms, the Knights of Labor brought together a variety of workers of different nationalities and skill, enhancing their ability to disseminate radical ideas to a great deal of Seattle's working class. As the Populist movement in Washington demonstrated, the Knights, even after the collapse of its assemblies, remained a shaping force in the region, influencing Socialists, anarchists, trade unionists, and utopian communitarians well into the twentieth century. While never able to attract more than a small minority into their organization, the Knights of Labor's legacy was indeed lasting and profound.[48]

By the dawn of the twentieth century, then, class and gender politics had significantly shaped Seattle's early history. Both the city's female activists and its working class exited the 1890s weakened and in disarray. Nevertheless, suffragists and workers looked optimistically to the new century and quickly began organizing and rebuilding their forces with expectations of better times ahead. The Progressive Era would indeed provide them a more conducive environment to try to fashion a Seattle that truly reflected their distinctive visions. To do so, however, middle-class women and organized labor would have to rediscover each other. Their difficult journey would be filled with many challenges, and the trials and tribulations of these westerners would tell the story of the birth of Seattle and the modern West.

CHAPTER 2

Citizens and Workers

In the summer of 1909, the eyes of much of the nation were fixed on Seattle. To celebrate the decade of prosperity that the Klondike and Nome gold strikes had brought to the city, local leaders organized the Alaska-Yukon-Pacific Exposition (AYPE). The exposition showcased the beauty and possibilities of Alaska as well as Seattle's place as the jewel of the Pacific Northwest. Behind the glimmer of the fair's magnificent white buildings and fountains, the festering wounds of organized labor lay exposed. Long gone by the opening of the AYPE was the pride in the city's accomplishments and future potential that workers and the business elite once shared. In the latter part of the first decade of the twentieth century, Seattle's working class butted heads with local businessmen over the employers' mounting recalcitrance to union demands, the rising tide of Japanese immigration, and the distribution of the economic windfall the exposition produced. The politics of class, however, were significantly more complex than labor leaders had realized. While unable to forge a true working-class party, they were willing to form political coalitions with like-minded citizens when these proved advantageous. Whether it be alliances with Populists in the 1890s or middle-class progressives a decade later, Seattle's workers continued to search for respect and security in the new industrial world. The lessons learned in these undertakings would serve them well in the years preceding World War I.

Rather than dismiss opportunistic political efforts as a sign of the weakness of American labor in the age of industrialization, scholars might approach Seattle's experience during the early twentieth century as an opportunity to explore the changing nature of working-class political activity, the causes that compelled labor to choose sometimes paradoxical actions, the methods and political styles they employed, and the larger meaning of both their victories and losses. Perhaps the first step in this process is recognition that workers had myriad strategies available to them and that they often exercised more than one of these options at a time. American labor, in short, spoke not with one but many voices during the Progressive Era. Some labor leaders urged workers to make their stand at the point of production; others used the power of the pocketbook by organizing consumption-oriented protests like boycotts and label leagues. By the early twentieth century, a growing number of union officials set their eyes on the ballot box to confront an ever powerful employing class. The strategies workers opted for, however, reflected particular social, cultural, economic, and political forces. Only when we investigate these forces and the choices made by workers can we better understand this crucial period in the history of American labor.

Seattle's working class likewise chose different strategies to combat the growing power of local employers and to assert its voice in city matters. At the dawn of the century workers focused on rebuilding a labor movement left in shambles following the 1890s depression. The economic boom sparked by a gold rush in the Yukon Territory of Canada accelerated the rebirth of organized labor in Seattle. Organizing at the point of production brought a growing part of the city's working class under the umbrella of the WCLU, save African American and Asian workers who found the union door closed. Emboldened by such growth, union officials tried third-party politics to tip the balance of power away from local employers. Trade unions, however, did not have the stage to themselves. Some Seattle workers looked to more radical solutions proffered by Socialist organizations and the Industrial Workers of the World. Pulled in different directions, the city's working class struggled to find the best strategy to champion its cause in an increasingly competitive economic and political marketplace.

Unlike most eastern labor struggles, class conflict out west was more localized. The lack of large-scale national industrial firms meant that Seattle workers had to battle locally entrenched economic and political elites rather than national corporate leaders.[1] Moreover, the Progressive Era provided a particularly dynamic moment for labor organizing, as the relationship between the state and society changed profoundly during these years. The deterioration of party fealty and the growth of interest-group politics offered organized labor the opportunity to restructure local political power. As Georg Leidenberger argues in his study of Progressive Era Chicago, "given the relative weakness of the national AFL and the importance of local and state-level politics at a time of a relatively weak federal government, an analysis of urban-level politics is most relevant to our understanding of both progressivism and trade unionism."[2]

The unraveling of Populism in Washington in the late 1890s and the collapse of the Knights of Labor left Seattle labor radicals with few vehicles for social change. Organized labor, decimated by the depression of the 1890s, was under the control of more conservative trade unions, while Republican stalwarts and a smattering of Democrats dominated the local political landscape. Puget Sound, however, did offer one refuge—Equality. Equality was a utopian settlement founded in late 1897 by the Brotherhood of the Cooperative Commonwealth (BCC). Christened "Equality" by novelist and socialist Edward Bellamy and sponsored by Eugene Debs's Social Democracy of America (SDA), this cooperative colony provided a place of solace and rejuvenation for radicals disillusioned with American society in the industrial age. More importantly, Equality and other western Washington utopian communities provided a key bridge between the ideas and reforms espoused by the likes of the Knights of Labor and their twentieth-century successors.[3]

The Equality Colony was not the first cooperative community established in western Washington. Following the social and political upheaval generated by the Chinese issue in 1886, George Venable Smith formed the Puget Sound Cooperative Colony the following spring. Smith and the other founders declared that the colony aspired "to establish a system which will fasten and secure ethical culture, correct and progressive life in all grades of society, without class distinctions or special privileges." Along with these idealistic goals, settlers also yearned for the material comfort of good homes and a prosperous economy. Over the next several years, the Puget Sound Cooperative Colony kept close ties with the Knights of Labor in Seattle and the surrounding area. Colonists also came to the aid of numerous reform measures ranging from the eight-hour day to woman suffrage. The settlement, however, seemed to lose direction and soon strayed from its mission. Financial problems beset the colony, and it ended up little more than a real estate venture when it went into receivership in the mid-1890s.[4]

The collapse of the Puget Sound Cooperative Colony did not leave Puget Sound less attractive to other radicals. At the turn of the century, Washington's "hospitable political, social, and economic atmosphere" made the state a major destination for utopians and labor radicals. The experiment with woman suffrage in the 1880s, railroad regulation, and other liberal reforms, along with the strength of the Knights of Labor and Populism, earned the state a fine reputation among utopian proponents, including new converts like Eugene Debs. The 1894 Pullman Palace Car strike organized by Debs generated significant support in Washington for his American Railway Union (ARU). Large and enthusiastic crowds met him a year later as he toured the state drumming up support for the ARU and urging workers to engage in politics. Quite familiar with both the state's favorable social and political environment, as well as the region's rather extensive open and productive lands, Debs chose western Washington as the site for the Equality Colony. Growing distaste with the direction of Washington Populism by 1897 increasingly drove many middle-of-the-road Populists and other radicals in the state to embrace such utopian ventures.[5]

The SDA saw Equality as more than simply a refuge for unemployed railway workers or those dispossessed by the depression. The colony was not the end of the line, but rather the organization's starting point for the socializing of Washington. Colony promoters envisioned it as a place to educate people about socialism who then would spread the message statewide. While idealism motivated many colonists, others moved there for more practical reasons. A poem written by a young girl living at Equality vividly detailed why her family moved to Equality. She wrote, "My pa had tried out politics, / and got a rotten deal— / He said, 'Let's try the colony. / It promises a meal.'" By 1901, the combination of an improving economy and the mismanagement of the colony largely ended SDA's effort to socialize the state. The colony's population plummeted from three hundred to a few dozen. However, those Equality settlers who stayed on remained true to its communal ideal for several more years.[6]

The Equality Colony was one of several utopian settlements that dotted Seattle's rural hinterlands at the turn of the century. While differing in makeup, size, and ideology, the other colonies of Freeland, Burley, and Home shared a similar cooperative spirit and a desire to create a more humane life at the outskirts of industrial America. While the utopian colonies failed to reform American society in any meaningful way, they played a crucial role in sustaining both Seattle and the Washington's "radical heritage" well into the twentieth century.

From Equality to Home, the utopian colonies nurtured numerous radicals of local prominence and attracted many nationally renowned ones also. Harry Ault, editor of the labor paper the *Seattle Union Record* at the time of the 1919 Seattle General Strike, began his journalism career at Equality at the age of seventeen. A fellow colonist of Ault's, Ed Palton, left the colony for more than a year, spending most of this time in Seattle. The Burley Colony contributed a future councilman named Max Wardall to the Sound's leading city. Another radical figure, Jay Fox, wounded in the Chicago Haymarket Riot and a close friend of future American Communist leader William Z. Foster, also spent some time in a nearby utopian colony.[7] Not only did the utopian settlements in Washington supply future left-wing leaders to Seattle, but they also beckoned many nationally renowned radicals to the region. In the early twentieth century, Home Colony, for example, attracted labor radicals Bill Haywood, Elizabeth Gurley Flynn, William Z. Foster, and Emma Goldman to Puget Sound. Goldman especially found the colony quite hospitable in 1898 when speaking engagements at Seattle and Tacoma were canceled. Utopian colonies, in short, shaped turn-of-the-century Seattle by nurturing future labor leaders, attracting nationally prominent left-wing figures, and, just as importantly, by furnishing a kind of "city upon a hill" that could replenish the spirit of disillusioned and dejected local radicals.[8]

The pessimism that pervaded Seattle's neighborhoods and fostered the formation of the several utopian colonies quickly evaporated in July 1897 when the steamship *Portland* docked at the wharf at the foot of downtown Seattle with more than a ton of gold in its hull, a precious cargo that forever changed the city. The discovery of gold in the Yukon Territory generated a decade of unprecedented growth, catapulting Seattle into the elite of western cities. Tales of servant girls and former black slaves scooping up tens of thousands of dollars worth of gold produced expectations beyond the wildest imagination. Even before the steamer had docked, "prospectors" had booked passage for Alaska on the *Portland* and several other ships. Immediately, cities up and down the Pacific Coast vied for control of this fantastic trade. While San Franciscans probably expected to dominate the gold trade as they had all other coastal trade, Seattle held certain advantages over the California city. Not only was Seattle closer to Alaska than San Francisco, Portland, or even Tacoma, but it was large enough to provide a wide array of supplies needed by gold seekers. More importantly, Seattle was the terminal city for the Great Northern Railway and was only a spur line away from the Northern Pacific railroad. Finally, Seattle businessmen had established commercial contacts in Alaska prior to the gold strike. These factors positioned Seattle well to capture and dominate most of the Alaskan trade for years to come.[9]

Natural advantages aside, Seattle businessmen and politicians worked diligently to capture the gold trade and make Seattle synonymous with Alaska. The Seattle Chamber of Commerce quickly formed a committee to make sure its city gained the lion's share of the Klondike and Nome windfall. With much vigor, committee chairmen Erastus Brainerd set out to spread the word of Seattle's advantages. Focusing particularly on the East, he published articles and ads in most of the nation's major newspapers, including six full columns in the widely read *New York Journal*. When the *Seattle Post-Intelligencer* published a special Klondike edition of the paper, Brainerd bought 100,000 copies and sent them to 7,000 postmasters, 600 libraries, and nearly 5,000 public officials. The major railroads serving Seattle distributed thousands of additional copies to communities along their routes. By the time Brainerd's publicity campaign was finished, few American could think about Alaska without also thinking about Seattle.[10]

Seattle's natural advantages combined with Brainerd's aggressive marketing made the gold strike the greatest economic boom period in the city's history. In nearly every conceivable way—banking, real estate, and retail sales—Seattle witnessed tremendous growth. In 1900, the value of trade from the city to Alaska topped $20 million annually, and within three years, that had more than doubled. Banks represented one of the greatest indicators of this windfall. In 1898, total deposits in Seattle banks stood at only $7 million, but by 1906 they had reached $60 million. Bank clearings from the Seattle banks (perhaps a better measure of business activity) doubled in the first two years following the discovery of gold.[11] Retail sales likewise reflected this surging business activity, as grocery and hardware sales more than doubled in the first year following the strike. Seattle's economic growth during the first decade of the twentieth century also produced an exceptionally healthy real estate climate. In 1900, twenty-four new business blocks were developed, and the assessed land value in the city nearly quadrupled from 1900 to 1907. In short, as one contemporary observer summed up the Klondike gold strike: "They [gold seekers] all had that for want of which Seattle suffered long and painfully: money. . . . In one day the destiny of Seattle was changed."[12]

Seattle's economic growth at the turn of the century was quite impressive, yet it did not necessarily translate into significant economic development and diversification. The number of businesses did indeed grow, but by the end of the gold rush in 1910, Seattle still possessed a primarily local-oriented economy dominated by rather small firms. In particular, the city still suffered from a rather anemic manufacturing sector. Despite the doubling of manufacturing firms from 1899 to 1909, the number of wage earners per firm increased little during this period, rising from 12.6 per firm to just over 15. In other words, the average size of Seattle factories increased by just a few employees, thus hardly sufficient to compete against national industrial corporations. In fact, in 1910 the city still lacked a single mass-producing iron or steel firm. After a decade of tremendous growth, the Puget Sound's major city was second to last in manufacturing in the nation for cities of comparable size. The difficulty of competing in a national market economy dominated by eastern and midwestern firms, as well as the limited markets in the rather sparsely populated Pacific Northwest, largely explains Seattle's weaker manufacturing base.

Moreover, Portland's location on the Columbia allowed it to siphon off a significant portion of the hinterland's production. While Seattle possessed a rather vibrant economy in the early years of this century, the city remained a commercial center dependent on a larger regional economy more "devoted to the extractive industries, to extensive agriculture, to mining, and to logging than manufacturing."[13]

In 1910, Seattle leaders still yearned for a stronger manufacturing base, but were hardly disappointed with the city's economic and demographic growth in the previous decade. The city's economy appeared strong, and Seattle had become a true metropolis. During the first ten years of the twentieth century, the city's population nearly tripled to just over 237,000, allowing it to surpass Portland as the largest city in the Pacific Northwest. Yet at the same time this was a rather restless and unsettled population. The Klondike gold strike attracted both immigrants and Americans who thirsted for anything but a permanent settled life. Only slightly more than one of every five men over the age of eighteen living in Puget Sound's major city in 1900 still resided there ten years later. The mercurial nature of mining and timber industries perhaps accounted for some of this transience. Without a doubt, however, the leading cause was gold strikes. As the stepping off point to Alaska, Seattle attracted tens of thousands of rootless men who resided in the city for only a brief period while awaiting transportation to the gold fields, or perhaps, worked odd jobs to raise additional funds needed to make the trek.[14]

Seattle's ethnic composition probably also pleased most city leaders. Native-born whites constituted the vast majority of the population. Japanese immigrants, the largest nonwhite group, represented a mere 3 percent of the total population. The city's African American population remained small, totaling 406, though the first decade of the century would see this jump to nearly 2,300. The foreign-born population, however, was rather significant. From the completion of the Northern Pacific in the 1880s to the collapse of the stock market in 1929, Seattle's foreign-born population hovered around 25 percent, making it one of the highest among American cities.[15] Seattle's rather large foreign-born population, however, differed somewhat from immigration patterns in the industrial Northeast and Midwest. The "new" immigrants—Russians, Poles, Italians—represented a much smaller portion of the city's foreign born. In 1910, Canadians,

Swedes, Norwegians, and Germans constituted most of Seattle's foreign-born population. Italians and Russians together numbered less than each of Seattle's three largest immigrant groups, and overall they made up only 10 percent of the city's total foreign population.[16]

Geographic barriers and occupational patterns help explain the unique character of Seattle's foreign-born population. Proximity to Canada and its similar extractive economy accounted for the large number of Canadian immigrants. The region's large Scandinavian population came to Seattle in a two-step process. Most Swedes and Norwegians had lived in the Upper Midwest for several years. Easy access to rail lines and the new opportunities in the lumber industry, in which many had worked in places like Minnesota, made the move to the Northwest more attractive. By the time most Swedes and Norwegians arrived in Seattle, they were somewhat Americanized. Consequently, there was less need for them to form protective ethnic enclaves, as was the common practice in eastern industrial cities. In contrast, impoverished southern and eastern European immigrants tended to find Seattle less attractive, considering the cost of the trip and the few unskilled jobs the city's meager manufacturing sector had to offer.[17]

Those who ventured to Seattle in the early 1900s discovered a vibrant and rapidly growing city that stretched from the shores of Puget Sound to the magnificent Lake Washington, which rimmed the eastern edge of the city. By 1910, the city was divided up into fourteen political wards populated by numerous ethnic groups and several distinct classes of people.[18] The First Ward began from the original center of the city, Yesler Way, and spread southward to include the lion's share of Seattle's manufacturing firms and its railroad terminals. The First Ward possessed a unique population, including low-income workers, transients, one-half of the city's Chinese residents, and those who lived on the gambling dens and saloons that dotted the area. Extending eastward from the First Ward to Lake Washington was the Second Ward. This diverse district saw small homes and apartments share the streets with some small factories filled with unskilled and semiskilled workers. The Second Ward had the highest percentage of foreign-born whites in the city, including a large number of Russians and Italians.

To the north of these wards were neighborhoods of contrast. Wards three and four housed some of Seattle's wealthier families, who resided on the hills that overlooked Elliott Bay or the shores of Lake Washington, which developers finally opened by 1910. Small homes and apartments dominated the western portion of the Third Ward, while wharves, hotels, shops, and banks dotted the shores and hills along the bay. The Fifth Ward closely resembled the fourth, with its transient workers living in apartments and flophouses while well-to-do businessmen loomed above them on First Hill. Adjoining the Fifth Ward to the north was ward six, which mirrored the First Ward with its numerous manufacturing plants and large percentage of immigrants.

Moving north from the city's business district and occupying opposite shores of Lake Union were wards seven and eight. The Seventh Ward was one of the Seattle's premier residential districts, dominated by Capitol Hill, but like its neighbor across the lake it shared the area with native-born working families and small sawmills and foundries. To the west was the city's Ninth Ward, which changed significantly as the population pressed northward and it was chopped up to make wards ten and eleven. More prosperous workingmen dominated the Ninth Ward; however, they differed a great deal from those in the largely immigrant wards to the south. Here workers owned their homes, and schoolchildren filled the streets. Located northeast of the downtown was ward ten, which was home to the state university and middle-class families. On this ward's northwestern boundary was the Eleventh Ward, home to the popular family outing destinations of Green Lake and Woodland Park. Like the surrounding districts, this ward held a comparable middle-class residential population, yet lacked any industry. Seattle's most northern ward was the thirteenth, which included a large number of mills and shipyards. Unlike its neighboring districts, the Thirteenth Ward was home to a large percentage of the city's Norwegian and Swedish residents, who found steady work in the mills.

The same year that Seattle leaders carved out the Thirteenth Ward in the northern reaches of the city, they annexed two large areas south of Yesler Way. The Twelfth Ward, like wards nine and eleven, was still rather sparsely settled in 1910. The district stretched south of ward two, bounded on the east by Lake Washington. Those who inhabited this area were largely working-class and middle-class homeowners. The last ward city fathers established during the early 1900s was the fourteenth, which ran southward along Puget Sound. The Seattle Steel Company and a few flour and saw mills provided work for residents. Though dominated by mostly home-owning workingmen, this ward also included a good number of immigrants and single men. The southernmost portion of this district remained largely wilderness until World War I.

At the dawn of the twentieth century, Seattle seemed to be a city on the edge of greatness. Economic opportunities abounded as the Klondike gold strike stimulated trade and the tens of thousands of new residents generated jobs and businesses. The prosperity seemed to bode well for the city's working class. In fact, the number of employed workers in Seattle nearly tripled from 1900 to 1910. Almost every trade and occupation witnessed job growth of at least twofold. The number of carpenters, for example, jumped from fewer than two thousand in 1900 to nearly six thousand a decade later, while the number of salesmen increased from one thousand to more than five thousand. Seattle's occupational pattern, however, mirrored its economic development. The city's poor manufacturing base meant that Seattle workers did not generally work in large factories as did their brethren back east. For the most part, workers continued to toil in small or medium-sized firms where skill remained critical to production.[19]

On the surface, laborers in Seattle fared rather well in the first decade of the century. In 1900, 40 percent of skilled workers in the state of Washington owned their own home, and more than 80 percent were married. In most years, if a worker held a steady job he might live comfortably compared to workers elsewhere in the nation. Those without skills, however, found the early 1900s a "period of frustration and unfulfilled hopes." Asian American and African American workers likewise struggled in the face of racial discrimination that barred them from joining white unions. Skilled workers aggressively undertook a concerted effort to secure a better life during this period by reviving a moribund union movement. The dazzling prosperity generated by the Klondike gold strike encouraged workers to rebuild unions that the 1890s depression had virtually destroyed. Seattle barbers, for example, organized a union local in 1900 and within a couple of years reported 176 members. Cooks' and Waiters' Local 239 outpaced the barbers, as it membership topped four hundred in 1904.[20] By 1907, the *Seattle Union Record* reported that the city had over ninety unions with some ten thousand members overall. By the end of the decade, city residents watched more than twelve thousand union workers demonstrate their solidarity and pride in the 1909 Labor Day parade. As one expert later testified, "organized labor ha[d] a stronger hold on the Pacific coast than it ha[d] farther east, and I think the reason for it is there hasn't been in our industries such a great demand for unskilled workers." Compared to steelworkers in Pittsburgh or mill operatives in Massachusetts, Seattle's working class seemed to have had little about which to complain.[21]

Better wages, home ownership, and a rather strong organized labor movement notwithstanding, the early 1900s were not always tranquil years for Seattle's working class. While more conservative trade unions still dominated the Western Central Labor Union (WCLU), the legacy of the Knights of Labor and the various utopian settlements continued to inject a good deal of left-wing radicalism into labor's ranks. For the much of the two decades prior to World War I, a small but persistent socialist movement followed by incessant agitation by the Industrial Workers of the World (IWW) sustained organized labor's radical edge. While socialism and IWW syndicalism could be found elsewhere in the nation, Seattle and Pacific Northwest workers more readily embraced these ideas. Compared to the industrialized East, Carlos Schwantes has argued, the American West added to the national growing conflict between labor and capital the "volatility of frontier ideals of individualism and personal advancement [that clashed] with the dependency inherent in working for wages." This "wageworkers' frontier," as he called it, helps explain the radicalism of western labor as the region rapidly moved from a frontier to an urban industrial society. Up and down Puget Sound, Socialists or Wobbly utopian settlers challenged the disappearing promise the West held out to them, and in doing so sustained the "radical heritage" of Seattle's working class.[22]

The existence of a wageworkers' frontier coupled with Washington's extractive economy did indeed create a peculiar labor market in the state. The abusive nature of timber and coal mining operations in western Washington produced a large and vibrant class-conscious workforce. Living and working in isolated logging camps, "timber beasts" together shared dangerous work, poor pay, and primitive living conditions. Traditional trade unions found it exceedingly difficult to organize this isolated and migratory lot. However, during the winter when the camps closed, timber workers "vacationed" in Seattle, where Socialist and Wobbly stump speakers denounced the exploitation of the workers and called on them to fight for the promise of the West. For most of the first two decades of the twentieth century, then, Seattle witnessed the continual interaction of left-wing radicals and conservative trade unionists. While quite different in philosophy and beliefs, the two sides maintained a peaceful coexistence separated by a semipermeable membrane. This membrane may have precluded the WCLU trade unions from allying with Socialists or Wobblies, but it could not stop the latter's radical ideas from seeping into union ranks.[23]

The startling contradiction of a bustling, advanced urban center in such "proximity to primitive frontier conditions" clearly informed Seattle's early labor history. The cries of labor radicals generally fell on deaf ears for much of the first decade of the century. A vibrant local economy generated jobs and adequate pay for most skilled workers, thus lessening the tension between labor and capital in the city. The radical heritage of the Knights did, however, influence relations between the Western Central Labor Union and the AFL at the turn of the century. Even with the Knights out of the picture, the AFL failed to build close ties with the WCLU. Geographic isolation, the relatively small size of the local federation, and the AFL's unwillingness to organize industrial unions left the WCLU open to outside influence from more radical labor organizations. Not until 1902 did the WCLU finally and officially affiliate with the AFL. What evolved during these important years was a kind of regional unionism that permitted a significant voice to Socialists and Wobblies. Formal affiliation, however, did not quell criticism from the AFL's new western partner. During the next two decades Seattle's citywide federation continually questioned AFL policies and at times publicly defied the demands of President Gompers.[24]

Increasing prosperity and relatively cordial labor relations marked Seattle in the early years of the twentieth century. The few conflicts between capital and labor that resulted in strikes were usually settled quickly. For example, in 1903, Teamsters in Seattle struck for better wages, a ten-hour day, and union recognition. Less than two weeks later they settled the dispute, winning both the wage and hour demands, yet falling short of achieving formal union recognition. That same year, Washington State Labor Commissioner William Blackman spoke before the Seattle Chamber of Commerce about the conditions and outlook of the city's working class. The invitation to Blackman, a former president of Eugene Debs's American Railway Union, illustrates the chamber's rather favorable opinion of labor during these prosperous years.[25] The peaceful coexistence of capital and labor allowed Seattle's labor leaders to expand union membership and prepare themselves for possible future confrontations with employers. Strengthening ties among organized labor groups statewide was one part of organized labor's strategy. To enhance the dialogue among the various local federations and lobby for favorable state legislation, labor leaders from Spokane to Seattle met in 1902 to form the Washington State Federation of Labor (WSFL). Two years later WCLU officials reorganized their local council into the Central Labor Council of Seattle and Vicinity (SCLC). This restructuring not only sought to increase the council's effectiveness, but also reflected the strong current of industrial unionism that pervaded the region. The new SCLC did not sanction industrial unionism, but did create industrially organized trade councils (metal, building, printing, etc.) that appealed to those who favored industrial unions.[26]

Most local employers maintained decent relations with organized labor. The Seattle Electric Company was the one major exception. Seattle Electric was a streetcar system organized in the late 1890s by the Stone and Webster Management Corporation of Boston, Massachusetts. The company consolidated numerous streetcar lines and then acquired favorable long-term franchise rights from the various cities in which it operated. In Seattle, local businessmen Jacob Furth, with financial backing from Stone and Webster, consolidated several rail lines and then received a forty-year franchise from the city council. Strong opposition from local citizens forced the council to adjust the terms of the franchise, but did not stop Furth and his partners from forming the Seattle Electric Company. As both the chief supplier of electricity to the city and the primary operator of Seattle's electric streetcar lines, the company attained a near monopoly of electrical operations.[27]

Seattle Electric soon flexed its economic and political muscle. In 1903, the newly organized Seattle Street Railway Employees Union struck Seattle Electric because the company had sent a number of its employees to break a strike by Tacoma's streetcar operators. The Seattle Chamber of Commerce quickly interceded in the dispute and forged a compromise that established an arbitration panel to settle the matter. Panel member Judge

William H. Moore seized the opportunity to tender his own opinion about the dispute. Moore condemned both Seattle Electric for sending strike-breakers to Tacoma and the twenty-five carmen for heeding the company's orders. He leveled his harshest criticism at the company for acting "arbitrarily and without regard to the rights of the public." A few months later, however, the street carmen again struck Seattle Electric over union recognition and the closed shop. The union did not fare well this time, as Furth quickly recognized a new union of street carmen who sought more amicable relations with the streetcar company. Despite support from organized labor in Seattle, Seattle Electric defeated the striking workers and continued to operate an open shop for years to come.[28]

The stinging defeat at the hands of this powerful corporation forced local labor leaders to consider other options, including electoral politics. By 1905 the peaceful coexistence enjoyed by workers and employers following the 1897 Klondike gold strike had evaporated. Businessmen's pressure on state legislators to pass a bill prohibiting boycotts by organized labor, along with the formation of a local employers' association, clearly signaled a change in this relationship. In response, organized labor initially pinned its hopes on reforms proposed by the Washington State Federation of Labor at its annual convention. "Let us hope they will be radical in some respects," wrote the weekly labor paper the *Seattle Union Record* in January. Seattle labor leaders also hinted that direct political action might be the only way to confront aggressive local employers like the Seattle Electric Company. A March editorial in the *Union Record* concluded that workers would no doubt elect a labor ticket if a vote were held at that moment. The paper at the same time chided the city's laborers for always forgetting their anger and frustration when they went to the polls months or years later.[29]

By the time the winter rains had subsided, the *Union Record* announced that "the unions of the city are being driven into taking independent political action."[30] Organized labor had made similar calls for political action before, yet they produced few concrete results. The latest proposal would likely also have faded away had not a serious rift developed between the city's brewery companies and their employees. In May, local brewery workers struck, reportedly over employers' insistence on the open shop. What made this strike different from other job actions was not the open-shop issue per se, but the apparent effort by a reinvigorated employers' association, the Citizens' Alliance, to launch a full frontal assault on organized labor. Spearheading the new Citizens' Alliance was none other than Seattle Electric's president, Jacob Furth.[31]

Union officials saw the brewery strike as not only a threat to brewery unions, but also "an opening wedge in the strong armor" of organized labor in Seattle. The SCLC immediately pledged its undying moral and financial support to the brewery workers. Moreover, union leaders appealed to local merchants and small businessmen to denounce the efforts by a few large employers to disrupt the relatively peaceful status quo. The *Union Record* intimated that a conspiracy existed among Seattle Electric and other firms to seize control of the city by first destroying the unions. After disposing of organized labor, the conspirators would be free to turn on small businessmen and dictate to them appropriate business behavior and practices. If this plea did not move merchants and small businessmen, the large headline that adorned the front page of June 3 edition of *Union Record* certainly indicated the importance of this struggle: "ARE YOU WITH US OR AGAINST US?" Labor leaders made it clear that Seattle merchants could no longer remain on the sidelines but had to choose sides in this defining conflict between capital and labor.[32]

Hope for a successful end to the brewery strike faded by the fall of 1905, generating renewed calls for a working-class political movement. Despite the *Union Record*'s rosy portrait of labor conditions in its annual Labor Day evaluation, whispers about direct political action soon erupted into cries to "Throttle the Octopus." The eventual victory of the Citizens' Alliance in the brewery conflict convinced labor leaders to take on the employers' association by challenging Seattle Electric's expanding monopoly of the city's streetcar system. That the utility company's president was the primary force behind the Citizens' Alliance was not lost on labor. As the brewery strike came to a disappointing close, labor leaders began a campaign to mobilize citywide animosity toward Seattle Electric into a political movement in which labor would play a more prominent role.[33]

Fashioning a third party and nominating labor candidates in 1905 may have placed the Seattle Central Labor Council (SCLC) outside the general practices of the American Federation of Labor, but such action fell squarely within a pattern of labor partisanship practiced elsewhere in the Far West.

At this time the AFL still opposed such overt political action on the part of organized labor. Labor parties, federation leaders believed, had failed in the past because workers quickly lost control of them to self-seekers and theorists. While many Seattle workers likely agreed with these sentiments, others had only to look several hundred miles south for evidence that the working class could, indeed, build a successful labor party.[34]

In San Francisco, union leaders had organized the Union Labor Party at the turn of the century and successfully assumed control of local government. As the movement to form a municipal ownership party gathered steam during the fall of 1905, the *Seattle Union Record* reminded its readers of San Francisco's accomplishments: "San Francisco has prospered under the administration of a union mayor, and organized labor has had a phenomenal growth. The same thing would happen in Seattle if our unionists would get together politically." The reelection of San Francisco Mayor Eugene Schmitz on a Union Labor ticket in November 1905 only bolstered the confidence of Seattle union officials. The victory in San Francisco, the *Union Record* argued, meant that the "best argument has been taken away from the union opponents of political action by union men." Schmitz's reelection was even sweeter and more telling because he had overcome serious opposition from that city's Citizens' Alliance. Seattle union leaders no doubt viewed events in San Francisco as not only encouraging, but as a good omen for their budding political movement.[35]

Success at the ballot box, local labor officials quickly recognized, depended on their ability to mobilize both the support of workers and the wider community. Seattle Electric's new franchise request was a controversial issue that also touched many middle-class residents. Years before widespread availability of the automobile, the streetcar was the lifeline of the entire city. The city's middle class, seeking refuge from the unsavory character of downtown life or searching for less expensive housing in a rapidly growing city, fled to Seattle's new suburbs. Such a move was only possible if cheap reliable transportation existed to carry them back and forth to the city's commercial district. Seattle Electric's near monopoly of the city's streetcar industry meant, in the eyes of critics, high rates and poor service. Moreover, workers and middle-class residents alike complained that Seattle Electric threatened the democratic character of local government by its reported graft and political corruption. Labor leaders thus found common ground with many middle-class residents regarding Seattle Electric's menace to their community.[36]

Desire for efficient streetcar service and the need to uphold the independence of public office, labor officials correctly understood, largely transcended class distinction in Seattle. For local workers, however, this battle represented much more than cheap transportation and clean government. Seattle Electric not only symbolized monopoly and corruption, but also embodied the Citizens' Alliance and anti-union sentiment. Labor leaders thus connected class-specific concerns with the larger community's welfare. The city's working class, the *Union Record* explained to its readers, had both the opportunity to "show [its] principles" and do "something toward the ultimate punishment of one of organized labor's most pronounced enemies in this city. The Seattle Electric [*sic*]." In short, union politics and city politics went hand in hand.[37]

In the spring of 1906, Seattle's working class seemed, for a brief moment, to express quite forcefully what Richard Oestreicher has called "class sentiment."[38] In a series of mass meetings, workers joined forces with "other progressive citizens" and launched the Municipal Ownership Party (MOP). Unwilling to cede control of the party, or as the *Union Record* put it, "not to be the tail to any political kite," labor leaders formed a committee of workers from each political ward to meet with members of the Business Men's League to propose a slate of possible candidates acceptable to each side. The ticket they chose reflected the diversity of the convention. Nominees for city offices included Democratic and Republican lawyers, a Republican electrical worker, a Democratic printer, and numerous other working-class candidates from both major parties.[39] Immediately, labor leaders called on workers and middle-class citizens to put aside party affiliation and vote a straight MOP ticket. Unions gathered to help finance the election. The linemen's union, for example, assessed members $10 to support the party, while the musicians' union tossed $400 into the campaign.[40]

As the election neared, MOP supporters increasingly attacked Seattle Republicans for backing Seattle Electric. The *Union Record* sarcastically commented that "to make the issue plain the republicans might nominate Jakey Furth for mayor." Tying Republican Party leaders to Furth's streetcar company helped define the election to be as much about defeating

Seattle Electric as securing the municipal ownership of public utilities. Seattle labor officials never passed on the opportunity to remind workers that Furth and his company were enemies of organized labor. The *Union Record,* for example, illuminated the company's harsh treatment of its workers, suggesting that wise streetcar employees should support the Municipal Ownership Party because with "the city in control of the street car system street car operatives would cease to be human chattels [*sic*]." City workers would also benefit from a new administration that would make sure that hardworking laborers received a raise and "the man with the soft job [would] not have special monetary privileges granted to him." With strong working-class support for the MOP, a *Union Record* editorial concluded, "Seattle will be the best union city and the best governed one, in the country." Labor officials, in short, hoped that the 1906 city election would both purify the city and, more importantly, raise the stature of organized labor in Seattle.[41]

The *Union Record* also attempted to tap into the growing belief held by many in the city that the East, or at least eastern corporations, selfishly exploited the West. Alluding to Seattle Electric's parent company, Stone and Webster of Boston, the paper rhetorically asked, "Shall Eastern Monopolists Dictate to Western Americans?" The increasing presence of corporate capitalism in the West touched a raw nerve among working-class residents who saw the promise of the region slipping from their grasp. Middle-class businessmen, however, also viewed corporate capitalism with some ambivalence. While some eagerly welcomed the influx of new capital and business, others felt that eastern capital held a competitive edge and threatened their chance to make it in America's last frontier. Seattle Electric and other eastern-controlled companies thus appeared to many western inhabitants as parasites; they preyed on western communities and gave little in return.[42]

In the March municipal election, workers and middle-class reformers celebrated a partial victory when the MOP nominee, William H. Moore, defeated his Republican opponent by a mere fifteen votes out of more than seventeen thousand cast. Moore captured seven of eleven wards, helped particularly by the middle-class and family-dominated working-class wards eight, nine, ten, and eleven. The Municipal Ownership Party was not as successful in the city council races, where Republicans held onto their majority. Nevertheless, the *Seattle Union Record* perceived the election as a victory for organized labor. Not only had its party captured the city's top office, but Seattle residents had also passed a recall amendment that enhanced the people's voice in local politics. Elated with the gains made in the election, labor leaders did not sit on their victory but eagerly looked to the fall elections to build on it. Whatever the fate of the next contest, what most labor leaders did agree on was that the "'old parties' are not going to run things with a free hand in this city any longer."[43] To this end, the SCLC endorsed the recommendation of the Workingmen's League for Clean Politics—a committee of union leaders who advocated political activity— that organized labor raise funds to support further political action.[44]

The political strategy that organized labor chose to follow soon became clear. "Factory and Farm Will Vote Together" proclaimed the *Union Record* in June. Frustrated by the failure to make any headway at the state capital, William Blackman, president of the Washington State Federation of Labor, announced an alliance with the Washington State Grange to press for favorable state legislation. Farmers and workers would combine as "producers" to expand democracy in the state, and "Fight for the Rights of the People" through the use of the direct primary, the initiative, and the referendum. Like the earlier Populist movement of the 1890s, state labor officials drew upon a rich producers' ideology that dated back to the Jacksonian era. Farmers and workers had little trouble realizing the common ground they shared, as corporate capitalism seemed to turn their lives upside down. Only by exploiting their numbers at the polls, these two groups believed, could they wrest control of the government from corporate-infested political parties and defend their way of life.[45]

Cementing an alliance with the state's farmers was only one first step organized labor took to reshape the political landscape. Reforming state politics demanded not just more friendly votes, but also a refiguring of a political system that favored party officials. To expand the "Rights of the People," the Workingmen's League announced that it would join hands with progressive forces within the Republican Party to secure a direct primary law. The progressive-minded King County Republican Club appeared open to this partnership; however, Republican Party officials, fearing that a direct primary law would threaten their command of the party, quickly snuffed this proposal.[46]

Rebuffed by Republican officials, the Workingmen's League turned to the Democratic Party. Democratic leaders quickly agreed to combine forces and work together to defeat Republicans in the upcoming state elections. While working-class representatives hoped to maintain some independence in the fall elections, Democrats invited fusion by both supporting the WSFL-Grange platform and nominating labor candidates like William Blackman for political office. Democratic leaders no doubt hoped to relive the days when their party had joined with Populist forces to defeat the Grand Old Party. Concerned that events were moving too quickly, some labor leaders now advocated caution. Calling on workers to "dabble in politics but not in partisan politics," the *Union Record* presented labor candidates from both parties that workers should support for state office.[47]

At the same time that the Workingmen's League strove to strengthen labor's voice at the state capital, municipal ownership advocates toiled to sustain interest in the fall local elections. One possible explanation for the apparent lack of interest was the inability of the Municipal Ownership Party to make any headway in constructing a city-owned streetcar system. Both the Republican and Democratic parties, for example, officially distanced themselves from streetcar bonds necessary to finance a city-owned streetcar system, while Seattle Electric officials and a group of local businessmen assiduously tried to convince voters to reject the bonds. The *Union Record,* in turn, reminded workers that the issue was as much about gaining a city-owned streetcar system as it was defeating the anti-union Seattle Electric Company. The paper went as far as to print a story about a desperate visitor who recently migrated to Seattle for work. The worker obtained a job with Seattle Electric and apparently met an old friend who was trying to unionize workers at the company. The article claimed that the two friends did not broach the subject of unions during their brief encounter, but that company spies reported to a Seattle Electric official that the new worker had signed a petition for a union charter. The official fired the worker the following day, leaving the man "insulted, crushed in spirit, bankrupt, [and] alone with his needy family in a strange city." Despite their best efforts, municipal ownership forces lost the bond issue by more than a thousand votes. Less than two months later Seattle residents rebuked all but two of the labor candidates on the Democratic ticket for state office.[48]

The rejection of the streetcar bonds indicated that despite the best efforts of *Union Record* to disparage the Seattle Electric Company, residents' enmity towards the company had faded. State elections likewise confirmed the weakness of labor's new political movement. Without a party organization to mobilize workers and without a clear-cut issue to arouse voters' passions, only two labor candidates triumphed in the November elections. Yet when Seattle voters were asked to take the next logical step in the public ownership of the streetcar, securing funds, passions withered. Raising taxes no doubt led many residents to think twice about how much they despised Seattle Electric. Seattle's experience confirms what historian Shelton Stromquist has argued in his study of Cleveland: "Class conflict and mass protest created conditions that invited reform but did not wholly dictate the outcomes."[49] Such moments of conflict, like those involving streetcars, often produced conditions for new political coalitions that could at times transcend class distinctions. Traditional parties thus often faced insurgencies that stimulated new alliances with interest groups like organized labor, which, if they evolved into third-party challenges, threatened entrenched party officials. Reform sentiment, more often than not, proved insufficient to sustain these coalitions. Party structures, competing social and political issues, and the difficulty of governing worked against intraparty insurgencies and cross-class alliances. Seattle workers quickly discovered that governing and sustaining a political movement proved much harder than winning elections. A year that had begun with so much political promise for organized labor ended with politics as usual.

The issue of municipal ownership did not immediately fade away, but working-class support for the MOP did. Envisioning a much more broadly based political organization, leaders changed the name of the party to the City Party for the 1908 election. While city ownership of public utilities remained a key component of the party's platform, officials added demands for direct legislation, free public markets, and limits on the expansion of saloon districts, among others.[50] The SCLC, however, responded coolly at first to the new group. Hoping to influence the Republican Party's choice of candidates, as well as recognizing the fact that a large number of the city's working class remained in the Republican fold, the *Union Record* instead tossed its support behind John Humphries in the GOP's mayoral primary. Despite the endorsement, Republicans chose Deputy Prosecuting Attorney John Miller, who was less sympathetic to organized labor. Miller's nomination left local labor leaders little choice but to turn once again to the new City Party and Mayor Moore. The day after the election, citizens awoke to a new mayor and a thoroughly defeated City Party.[51]

Analysis of Moore's defeat indicates that both middle-class and working-class voters' concerns had changed in the two years between elections. The lack of a polarizing issue like Seattle Electric and Mayor Moore's poor handling of a growing prostitution problem partly explain the disaffection of the city's middle class. While some residents still chafed at Seattle Electric's poor service, the city's deteriorating moral climate resulting from the apparent proliferation of prostitution in the wake of the Yukon gold strike sparked spirited public debate. Mayor Moore had attempted to reduce prostitution during his term, but evidently acted too slowly for many middle-class residents. His Republican opponent, John Miller, instead promised to eliminate the restricted district, though how he would do so and where the prostitutes would go was not clear. Moore's inability to handle effectively the most pressing issue facing Seattle cost him a good deal of the middle-class support that had catapulted him to victory just two years earlier.[52]

While vice eroded middle-class support for the City Party, the mayor's heavy-handed response to a Socialist free-speech fight in 1906–7 likewise alienated a good deal of working-class support. Perhaps threatened by a competing working-class political movement, Socialists, according to the *Union Record*, undertook free-speech fights that aimed to undermine the MOP because party leaders encouraged Seattle workers to ally politically with middle-class residents. Reflecting on Moore's defeat, the labor daily noted that his jailing of Socialist street speakers cost him votes. Moreover, the mayor appointed a chief of police who many union members felt was a foe of organized labor. Such actions may well have turned off many working-class voters, but the City Party also contributed to its own defeat by failing to politically mobilize and inspire Seattle's workers. In 1906, labor leaders had played an active role in the Municipal Ownership Party's formation and initial success. Two years later, however, labor seemed to take a backseat within the party. Middle-class reformers, like journalist Joe Smith, seized control of the party and reshaped its platform and its choice of candidates. Smith stated that Moore had organized his own personal campaign committee made up of local businessmen. The City Party central campaign committee, on which Smith served as vice chairman, had to pass some policies and plans through the businessmen's committee yet without similar input from labor. Furthermore, in 1906, for example, the MOP's slate of candidates included a good number of working-class office seekers, but in 1908 only a handful ran for office. The disaffection of middle-class voters and the City Party's failure to nourish its once close relationship with labor left it vulnerable to a powerful and entrenched Republican Party.[53]

Whether the Socialists' free-speech fight was largely responsible for Moore's defeat in 1908 is impossible to determine. Nevertheless, Seattle's Socialist Party did influence the political behavior of conservative trade unions for most of the early 1900s. Like the Knights of Labor and utopian settlers in the late nineteenth century, local Socialist organizations helped sustain labor's radical heritage in the early years of the twentieth century. Even at their peak in 1912, local Socialists never spoke for more than a small minority of working-class residents. Statewide, the Socialist Party of Washington (SPW) included, at the most, six thousand dues-paying members. Yet during this period, Socialists would carry the mantle of radicalism that had begun with the Knights before eventually handing it off to the Industrial Workers of the World in the century's second decade.[54]

Socialism as an organized political force in Seattle began in 1900 when Dr. Hermon Titus commenced publishing the *Socialist*. A few years earlier a visit from Daniel DeLeon, a nationally renowned Socialist, inspired a small group of Seattle laborers to form Socialist clubs. The nascent movement languished for most of the 1890s until convening its first convention in 1898. Disillusioned by Populist fusion, left-leaning radicals organized the Socialist Labor Party (SLP) and ran candidates for office in 1898. At about the same time, Eugene Debs formed the Social Democratic Party (SDP), which drew members from a variety of left-wing organizations, including Bellamy Nationalists, single taxers, labor unionists, and disgruntled SLP members. The party's surprising gains in Washington in 1898 and 1899 led Debs to declare the state the "ripest field in the West." In 1900, Dr. Titus called on the WCLU to help him support striking telephone operators, but the local federation turned him down. Upset by organized labor's tepid response, Titus began publishing the *Socialist* in order to "Organize the

Slaves of Capital to Vote their own Emancipation." For the next dozen years Titus remained the most powerful and controversial Socialist figure in both Seattle and Washington State.[55]

Dr. Hermon Titus graduated from the University of Wisconsin and briefly attended a theological seminary before serving as a pastor at a New York Baptist church. Unable to reconcile church activity with Christ's teachings, Titus resigned his position and left to study medicine at Harvard so he could help mankind. After Harvard, he came west to Seattle during the 1890s depressions where he served as a social worker in the city's Skid Row district. After reading Karl Marx's *Das Kapital*, he converted to socialism. Titus preached a rather rigid and doctrinaire socialism that caused constant friction in left-wing circles. In 1901, he helped bring together under one roof various Socialist groups, including the SDP, by merging them with the Socialist Party of America (SPA). The SLP, however, remained outside this new party and for next few years vied with Titus's organization for supremacy among local Socialists. Competition between the two major Socialist groups proved less harmful than the internecine struggle within Titus's Socialist Party of Washington (SPW). This destructive internal struggle left local Socialists weak and divided for much of the early twentieth century.[56]

Ideological differences, in particular how best to apply Marx's teachings to American society, deeply divided Seattle Socialists. On the one hand, Titus represented the revolutionary Socialists (or Reds) who demanded an immediate working-class revolution and the destruction of capitalism. Reform Socialists (or Yellows), however, supported political reforms, like municipal ownership and direct legislation, as part of an evolutionary process to replace capitalism. Such reforms and alliances, they argued, would help the party both spread its message and expand its base. In contrast, Titus believed that reform Socialism blunted working-class radicalism and often allowed middle-class reformers to claim victory. Hulet Wells, a leading Socialist figure in the prewar years, initially favored Titus's revolutionary wing when he joined the SPW in 1905. As he saw it:

> there were two types of socialist philosophy, a sentimental appeal to all mankind to wipe out poverty, waste and war, as against the dynamic class-angled philosophy of Marx. I chose the latter without

hesitation, for I had no faith that preaching the brotherhood of man would have any effect on the politically entrenched interests of a powerful propertied class. The quickest way to change was surely to convince the mass of the people that the prevailing system worked them an economic injury for the benefit of a comparatively small class.

While Wells found working-class revolution the most promising way to change the world, many other Socialists remained open to cross-class alliances like the Municipal Ownership Party, which they envisioned as a giant step in the evolution of socialism.[57]

Dr. Titus had little to say about the MOP's victory in 1905 because he had moved the *Socialist* to Toledo, Ohio, where he could be nearer the industrial heart of America. The following year he moved back west to Idaho where three leaders of the Western Federation of Miners were on trial for the murder of that state's former governor.[58] After the excitement of the trial subsided, Titus returned to Seattle in the fall of 1906 to rebuild his financially troubled paper, but found that reform Socialists had assumed control of the SPW. The battle for Socialist Party control, however, continued for several more years. Since Washington had one of the largest Socialist Party memberships in the United States, national SPA officials finally intervened at the 1909 state convention in nearby Everett to settle the dispute. Expelled by his enemies, Titus and his fellow Reds abandoned the SPW to the reformist wing. In 1912, Titus left Seattle for good.[59]

Destructive factionalism notwithstanding, Seattle Socialists did influence working-class politics for nearly a decade. As long as Titus controlled the SPW and threatened to interfere with working-class political pursuits, relations between Socialists and local union officials remained poor. During the period of Titus's absence from Seattle, however, the SCLC changed its opinion about local Socialists. In 1906, the Seattle *Union Record* stated that "the kind of socialists that are now in the central labor body are a credit to it." The paper suggested that reform Socialists were willing to work with unions rather than "ride rough shod over the interests of organized labor." Labor leaders also admired the local Socialist Party's plan to publish a twelve-page weekly newspaper. Finally, the willingness of reform Socialists to work with like-minded groups in Seattle, in contrast to the Titus wing, greatly impressed the SCLC.[60]

The cordial relations between the trade unions and the SPW quickly soured upon Titus's return to the city. During the internecine struggle within the party, local labor leaders clearly sided with the Yellows. When Titus tried to purge Walter Mills from the SPW in 1907, the *Union Record* defended Mills because he was "a consistent and active advocate of organized labor." Socialists like Titus, the paper concluded, "should be immolated in an African jungle. There they would not be a menace to civilization." His revolutionary Socialism, it claimed, offered no benefit to the working man. Union leaders also feared that Socialist factionalism might harm the image of the city's working class. An editorial in the local labor paper maintained that such infighting placed trade unions in a bad light because Seattle residents assumed that Socialists were part of organized labor, even though many of the labor radicals denounced the SCLC. That local Socialists held their meetings in the SCLC's Labor Temple only added to this perception. Union officials, the *Union Record* concluded, should protect the image of Seattle workers by closing their building to Socialists.[61]

Dr. Titus's firm hold on the reins of the SPW before 1909 not only made for frigid relations between the party and local unions, but it also hampered organized labor's political activity. Seattle's labor leaders refrained from forming an independent labor party because they feared Socialist infiltration. Titus made it clear that he believed that his party should be the only true political party of the working class. Efforts by the SCLC to form a labor party, union officials believed, might only encourage Titus and his followers to infiltrate the movement and seize control of it for their own ends. The decision to engage electoral politics through the Municipal Ownership Party likely reflected this concern. Fashioning a new political movement with the help of sympathetic merchants and professionals was less risky because they made a Socialist takeover nearly impossible. Titus's absence in 1906 further lessened organized labor's fear of Socialist infiltration and interference when it dipped its toes in local political waters.[62]

Despite rather large membership rolls, Seattle's Socialist organizations continually failed to build a potent working-class political movement. Socialist Party electoral victories, in fact, were few and far between throughout the nation during these years. This failure notwithstanding, local Socialists did, indeed, affect the city's working class. While few laborers embraced the party, they could not escape its ideas. Seattle Socialists no doubt wasted much energy on internal party matters, but they did not ignore the city's workers. In the end, "left wing unionism, far more than political power," Carlos Schwantes has suggested, "was the real legacy of revolutionary socialists. . . ." For evidence of Socialism's radical inspiration, one only has to look at coal miners east of Seattle, who, in 1909, "declared for public ownership and democratic management of the means of production" in the mines in which they worked. Seattle Socialists may not have notched any political victories on their guns, but they did succeed in sustaining the region's radical heritage well into the twentieth century.[63]

For nearly a decade following the Klondike gold strike, relative prosperity helped Seattle workers weather the difficult struggles with the city's elites at both the workshop and the ballot box. As the first decade of the twentieth century came to a close, a stubborn depression punctured the city's buoyant and confident outlook. The national economic panic of 1907 slowed Seattle's economy, giving rise to the city's first serious bout of joblessness since the 1890s. Class sentiment in the city, as the events of 1905–6 amply illustrated, antedated the Panic of 1907. By the end of 1907, lumber camps in western Washington had discharged large numbers of timber workers, who then poured into Seattle. Exploiting a favorable labor market, many employers tried to force down wages or break unions by waging a new wave of open-shop campaigns. As the *Seattle Union Record* saw it, employers had declared war on organized labor and thus threatened not only the pocketbooks of the working class but also the city's future.[64]

A building trades' open-shop campaign clearly rubbed Seattle workers the wrong way. Not only did it threaten to weaken the power of organized labor, but employers' tactics further aggravated unemployment during the economic downturn. Even though hundreds, if not thousands, of construction workers were jobless, employers advertised in eastern papers for more workers. The Builders' Exchange, an association of building trades employers, placed ads encouraging bricklayers to come to Seattle to work in nonunion settings. In response, the SCLC sent notices to eastern labor organizations detailing the city's poor economy. Such efforts, however, earned organized labor the contempt of the local chamber of commerce. Chamber officials, despite the economic downturn, had recently undertaken their own publicity campaign to entice people and businesses to migrate to Seattle. They chastised the SCLC for undermining the chamber's effort to help revive the economy. Labor leaders, in turn, argued that such publicity campaigns also attracted more workers, thus aiding the Builders' Exchange open-shop movement. In the SCLC's eyes, the chamber's venture made them collaborators with building trades employers and thus also an enemy of labor.[65]

The escalating tension between organized labor and the Seattle Chamber of Commerce marked an important moment in the city's history. Like the city's working class, business did not always speak with one voice. For years the chamber had largely tried to steer clear of class conflict. In the early 1900s, for example, the chamber refused to support Jacob Furth's revival of the Citizens' Alliance and its open-shop campaign. No doubt the large number of merchants and small businessmen in the chamber, who catered to Seattle's working-class communities, blunted the open-shop arguments emanating from the city's larger firms. In the first decade of the twentieth century, progressive sentiment also percolated throughout this largely middle-class organization. As Seattle entered the second decade of the new century, both the chamber's favorable relationship with labor and its progressive outlook rapidly deteriorated.[66]

Further fueling tensions following the Panic of 1907 was labor's belief that Seattle employers robbed workers of the benefits the Alaska-Yukon-Pacific Exposition (AYPE) promised. Conceived by local businessmen in 1906 to draw attention to Alaska and the Pacific region, the exposition soon emerged as a ray of hope as depression enveloped the city. Newspaper reports announced that the AYPE "[would] do much towards giving the East a proper appreciation of the West." In many ways, local officials envisioned the exposition as a coming-out party for Seattle and the American West. At groundbreaking ceremonies held the next year, Henry Alberts McLean, president of the Washington State Commission for the exposition, declared that the AYPE would bring to an end "one epoch of this Commonwealth's history and open another. The pioneer days, the days of adventure, the days of uncertainty, the days during which we have been practically unknown to the great body of the people of the nation, will, when the exposition is over, be ended forever." The promise of the exposition seemed undeniable.[67] In June 1909, the Alaska-Yukon-Pacific Exposition opened for a 138-day run, drawing slightly less than four million visitors. Upon its close in October, city officials appeared quite pleased with their effort.[68]

Seattle workers likewise initially expressed much enthusiasm for the AYPE. The *Seattle Union Record,* for example, printed favorable articles in late 1907, while the SCLC began discussions with AFL officials to bring its 1909 annual convention to Seattle during the fair. The timing of the fair seemed propitious to many workers, who believed that jobs created by fair construction would offset the impact of the economic downturn. The SCLC even offered to purchase $25,000 in AYPE stock in return for a guarantee that exposition managers would employ only union labor. Exposition officials, however, turned down the offer, stating that they had raised much more money than needed. By 1908, organized labor's positive outlook gave way to public criticism of the exposition's use of cheap, nonunion labor in erecting the fairgrounds.[69]

From late 1907 to the opening of the AYPE in the spring of 1909, organized labor battled local businessmen and exposition officials over the decision to employ nonunion labor. Initially, labor leaders announced their regret that Seattle's fair was not the exception when it came to management's relations with local unions. They also hinted that these events might quickly escalate into a "labor war." As economic conditions further deteriorated in 1908, organized labor intensified its criticism of the fair's position. Both the SCLC and the state federation of labor officially declared the AYPE unfair to organized labor. J. E. Chilberg, president of the AYPE, responded that the "opposition of the unions will be unpleasant, that is all." The exposition's refusal to utilize only union labor coincided with the Builders' Exchange open-shop movement and the chamber of commerce's effort to encourage more eastern workers to come to Seattle. Labor leaders claimed that this was no mere coincidence, but part of a master plan conceived by local employers to destroy organized labor. The AYPE, they concluded, was simply "a union-busting project."[70]

Conflict between fair officials and organized labor continued up to the last days of the event when the exposition management and local newspapers urged workers to spend Labor Day at the fair with other city residents. Indignant that antilabor fair officials would suggest that Seattle workers celebrate labor's holiday at the exposition, union leaders began plans for a traditional Labor Day celebration that did not include the AYPE. "We know the management of the fair," the *Union Record* wrote, "would like to secure the fifty-cent pieces of union men to help pay for the buildings erected by scab labor." On Labor Day, some 12,000 workers paraded in the streets of downtown Seattle and then proceeded to a nearby park where thousands more joined them for a picnic and games. A few miles away, fair officials proudly declared that more than 117,000 people crammed into the AYPE, making it the exposition's most successful day. While officials boasted of the exposition's success, the conflict over the AYPE angered organized labor for many years to come.[71]

As the struggle over the Alaska-Yukon-Pacific Exposition illustrates, the growing complexity of Seattle's economy and the increasing commercialization of leisure in the early twentieth century further complicated labor and capital relations. The fair was not a typical business, nor were its managers typical employers. In most labor conflicts, union officials could easily personalize the enemy by focusing their attack on the company's owners, or in the case of Seattle Electric, a prominent manager. Just as labor waged war against the likes of Carnegie and Pullman in the late nineteenth century, Seattle workers had similarly targeted Jacob Furth of Seattle Electric in 1905. The exposition, however, was another beast altogether. Under the control of a board of directors made up of small and large businessmen and other leading citizens, the exposition's management lacked, like the emerging corporate capitalist enterprises of the new age, an obvious single figure on which the community's anger could be focused. Furthermore, the increasing commercialized nature of leisure in American society in the early twentieth century made demonizing the fair difficult. The working class, as Kathy Peiss expertly described, were drawn into the new commercial forms of leisure, like professional sports, amusement parks, and the motion pictures. Bombarded by ads and newspaper columns promoting the exposition's exhilarating sights and sounds as well as its more educational exhibits, workers no doubt found it difficult to avoid the temptation of spending a Sunday at the fair. The exceptional attendance on the AYPE's "Seattle Day," held Labor Day, strongly suggests that a good number of the city's laborers did not find the SCLC's parade and picnic at the park as captivating as the fair's pleasure zone. The changing face of capital, then, increasingly forced organized labor in Seattle to find other strategies and tactics to improve their lives.[72]

The escalating conflict between Seattle's working class and local employers was not limited to the open-shop movement or labor's exclusion from the financial rewards generated by the AYPE. The economic downturn produced by the Panic of 1907, along with the increasing tension between capital and labor during these years, reignited the flame of anti-Asian sentiment in Seattle's working-class neighborhoods. While the anti-Chinese activity of the 1880s had significantly reduced Seattle's Asian population, growing Japanese immigration and that nation's emergence as a major world power in the wake of Meiji Restoration rekindled anti-Asian sentiment in labor circles.

Even though Japanese residents composed only 3 percent of the city's total population in 1910, labor leaders maintained that the number of Japanese entering the port after 1905 posed a menace to both their jobs and the character of the community. In June 1905, the *Union Record* published a notice that San Francisco had organized the Japanese and Korean Exclusion League to combat "the wholesale immigration to this country of cheap Asiatic labor." The paper urged Seattle unions to join this movement, suggesting that "Oriental labor" was a greater threat to organized labor than even the much-despised Citizens' Alliance.[73]

Segments of organized labor attempted to direct Seattle workers' frustrations toward local employers by laying blame for the rising tide of Asian immigration at their feet. When the SCLC passed one of its first resolutions opposing Japanese immigration in 1905, it attacked local capitalists as much as the new immigrants. The labor federation, for example, held transportation companies, Hawaiian agricultural growers, and certain local employers responsible for proposals that would have both loosened restrictions on Chinese immigration and continued to let Japanese immigrants enter the country freely. Others attempted to expand their message beyond working-class neighborhoods. The Japanese and Korean Exclusion League, a few labor officials argued, was not a "union-labor movement" but rather a gathering of "Americans" seeking to protect "American homes." Through such jingoism labor leaders hoped to link working and middle-class anxieties. In this case, labor leaders argued that Japanese immigration not only undermined Seattle workers' economic well-being, but also proved detrimental to local merchants and landlords because labor competition decreased wages. Lower wages, in short, meant fewer purchases at local stores and more unpaid rents.[74]

As workers' frustration grew, the nature of the debate changed slightly as labor leaders also attempted to exploit widespread racist attitudes. When President Theodore Roosevelt proposed legislation to naturalize Japanese residents, a *Union Record* editorial clearly articulated labor's belief that the Japanese threatened American values, morality, racial purity, and politics. Echoing the sentiments of many working people in Seattle, the editors declared:

> The Japs are non-assimilative with the white race, their instincts and principles are diametrically opposed to those of white people; they are content with moral and physical standards under which white men are dissatisfied; their moral standards are oriental, not occidental; what they esteem as virtuous womanhood [sic] the caucasian looks upon as sexual license. . . . Japanese family ideals are on a plane inferior to that of white men; Japanese laborers consider their wives chattels, white laborers' wives are treated as helpmates on a basis of mental equality . . . to admit them [Japanese] to equal political rights would be to constitute a perpetual menace to American standards—would tend to create less respect for family obligations, would degrade rather than elevate labor, would make the ballot box the whip of the capitalist with which to scourge the people.[75]

Roosevelt's initiative spurred organized labor to launch a sweeping indictment of Japanese immigration. Labor competition was no longer its primary complaint. White labor leaders advanced racial thoughts that proclaimed Japanese immigrants as morally and culturally dangerous to American society, not just the city's labor market. The American political system, family ideals, and female virtue were all at risk unless Seattle residents opposed Japanese immigration and naturalization. In short, to defend the "American home," only a cross-class alliance could save the city from the menace Japanese residents posed. SCLC officials likely saw much promise in such a partnership considering that organized labor had successfully partnered with progressive middle-class citizens when it formed the Municipal Ownership Party earlier that year. Before labor leaders could realize any benefit from this cross-class appeal, President Roosevelt finalized the "Gentlemen's Agreement" with Japan. The trans-Pacific immigration severely curtailed, labor's declaration that Japanese immigrants posed a cultural and political threat to both Seattle's working-class and middle-class residents was sapped of much of its force.

While President Roosevelt seemed to have yielded to organized labor's nationwide pleas, Seattle businessmen did not give up their fight to keep the city open to Japanese laborers. Hoping to maintain friendly business relations with Japan, the Seattle Chamber of Commerce, for example, threw its support behind open immigration and condemned the exclusion league. Chamber officials argued that a majority of local residents approved of unrestricted immigration from Asia. The *Union Record*, in response, disputed this claim, instead maintaining that "true commercialism" motivated the chamber. When the local commercial organization widened its publicity campaign to attract new settlers to Seattle during the Panic of 1907, labor leaders blasted chamber officials for both continuing this campaign and for perpetrating a crime "against the Caucasian race in order that Christless few may have the fleeting benefit of cheap yellow labor."[76] The chamber of commerce's defense of immigration and its apparent support for the open shop did little to lessen labor's anger.

Stiffening resistance from the chamber and the prevailing attitude that the Gentlemen's Agreement made Japanese immigration a moot point only transformed the direction of the debate. Further refining their claims that Japanese immigration posed a threat to the community, Seattle labor officials inserted gender into their oppositional message. The *Union Record*, in an editorial titled "Mongolian Invasion of the United States," claimed that the Japanese immigrants' practice of proxy marriages (better known as picture brides) was nothing more than a ruse to cover up the importation of Japanese prostitutes. In a city that was increasingly sensitive about vice and prostitution, calling attention to the exploitation of "Japanese slave girls" helped organized labor broaden its message beyond the city's working-class neighborhoods. Reviving arguments raised during the 1880s anti-Chinese affair in Seattle, labor leaders asserted that Japanese immigration would induce employers to fire white women, driving them into "less desirable employment," as California's white workingwomen reportedly experienced. Desperate white workingwomen might end up in "ill-smelling factories" or, as was the common belief of the time, might be forced into prostitution or other unsavory activities. Labor's new appeal thus connected its own economic concerns with increasingly powerful middle-class sensibilities and anxieties.[77]

By publicly placing gender rather than class at the forefront of the debate, Seattle's labor leaders possessed a more powerful and potentially persuasive argument in their efforts to lure middle-class residents to oppose Japanese immigration. In other words, Seattle's middle class was more willing to side with the SCLC if they understood the issue as one of protecting American womanhood, rather than simply aiding the city's workers in their struggle with capital. Whether Seattle labor leaders ever truly persuaded middle-class Seattlites to support Japanese exclusion is unclear. The Seattle Chamber of Commerce's support of Japanese immigration strongly suggests that labor's arguments failed to sway many middle-class residents. By 1909, the city's economy rebounded from the Panic of 1907, and labor's cries for relief from Japanese competition subsided. Despite the best efforts of organized labor, the Japanese exclusion movement, unlike the anti-Chinese movement in the 1880s, largely fell on deaf ears outside working-class neighborhoods.

When Seattle labor leaders surveyed the terrain in 1910, then, they likely saw a rather bleak landscape. Since the 1906 Municipal Ownership Party victory, organized labor had met defeat on nearly every political front. Reeling from the economic impact of the Panic of 1907, Seattle workers encountered hostile employers who now had a firm ally in the chamber of commerce. Moreover, they also failed to persuade the city's middle class regarding Japanese exclusion or the AYPE's unfair labor practices. Rather then retreat into a hole, labor leaders decided to make one more stab at political mobilization. The recent defeats, they hoped, might in fact act as corner posts on which to build a powerful political movement.

Organized labor, however, did not have to rely simply on negative events to arouse workers. By 1910, positive factors also encouraged a segment of the city's working class to believe it could finally transform Seattle into a labor-friendly city. Again, local labor leaders looked south to California for inspiration. For nearly a decade, San Francisco's working class had held a firm grip on the reins of city government. There, the *Union*

Record observed, it was "hardly probable that the policeman's club [would] be used on the heads of striking workingmen." Just as encouraging as San Francisco's success was the disarray of Seattle's Socialist forces. Dr. Titus's expulsion from Washington's Socialist Party in 1909 lessened the fear that revolutionary Socialists might infiltrate a local labor party. With the radical organization in the hands of reform-minded leaders, union officials felt confident that they could maintain control of a new labor party.[78]

Since the arrival of the Knights of Labor in the 1880s, a portion of Seattle's working class had continually maintained that labor should battle capital in the political arena as well as at the point of production. Whether this took the form of favoring one major party over the other, supporting prolabor candidates regardless of party affiliation, or allying with other social and economic groups and forming third parties, many labor leaders believed that political activity could greatly improve workers' lives. However, sharing power with middle-class progressives, as workers had attempted with the Municipal Ownership Party, only diluted labor's influence and often forced it to compromise its objectives to keep the fragile alliance afloat. By 1910 recent events had made abundantly clear the limits of middle-class sympathy, leading a number of union officials to believe that only a true labor party could produce tangible results and refigure the local power structure.

The pessimism that permeated the ranks of organized labor following the demise of the City Party in 1908 was cast off when the *Union Record* announced the formation of the United Labor Party (ULP) in February 1910.[79] William Moore's failed bid for reelection two years earlier left many questioning the political heart of Seattle's working class. In particular, union officials wondered why organized labor could not translate solidarity at the factory to the ballot box. One observer suggested that workers were fatalistic and resigned to their political impotence. In a rather perceptive analysis, another bystander intimated that labor leaders were not in tune with the rank and file. He proposed a straw ballot "to find out whether or not there is a desire on the part of a majority of our membership to get together and vote together." Despite such lingering doubt, union officials confidently declared in early 1910 that it was time to organize an independent political party that promised to promote the interests of labor first. In February, the United Labor Party was born.[80]

Hastily organized, the new labor party failed, however, to generate much enthusiasm in Seattle's working-class neighborhoods. With less than one month to prepare for the municipal elections, officials could not organize ward and precinct units to rally support for their party. As if that was not enough, the United Labor Party platform also lacked specific goals to ignite sufficient interest among Seattle's working class. The platform, for example, did admit labor's miserable past political failures, in particular the trail of "broken promises and blasted hopes" produced by labor-supported candidates in recent city elections. Ever optimistic, party officials urged workers to dissolve "old party entanglements" and unite under one banner—the United Labor Party. Yet the platform failed to explain to workers why they should support the new political faction. Party officials offered little more than some vague reference to the "bettering of conditions for the working class." To draw attention to their flagging political organization, ULP officers publicly announced that corrupt interests continued to block the implementation of a new direct primary law, which left organized labor little choice but to enter the political fray independently.[81]

The new party encountered a rather lukewarm response both inside and outside labor circles. Whether reluctant to risk organized labor's reputation in another political campaign, or unable to canvass their members' opinion in such a short time, the Central Labor Council refused to endorse the United Labor Party in the 1910 municipal election. Even without the official blessing of the city's main labor organization, the *Union Record* spilt much ink to marshal support for labor's latest political endeavor. Old allies outside labor circles, however, also responded unfavorably to the new party. W. H. Kaufman, Washington State Grange delegate to the WSFL, favored labor's political activity but not an independent political party. He urged workers instead to form a political league that would rally working-class support behind sympathetic major party candidates. In particular, Kaufman suggested that labor should inject itself into the Republican Party and pass a constitutional amendment providing for only nonpartisan elections throughout the state. Eliminating political parties, he concluded, was better than forming another one.[82]

Middle-class residents reacted, as one might expect, rather coolly to the United Labor Party. To maintain the party's independence, labor leaders excluded middle-class progressives from ULP membership, though they no doubt hoped that many might agree with the party's larger aims and support its candidates. The *Argus,* a Republican newspaper, reminded its readers of labor's rather dismal political record, suggesting that any labor party offered little real threat because "unions seem unable to get together much better than usual." Further indicating that the ULP stirred little political interest, an *Argus* editorial sarcastically noted that there "is a Socialist labor party or something of the kind in the field, too. This statement is made to prevent the readers of The Argus from exhibiting surprise when they reach the polls." Whether the labor party actually surprised Seattle voters on Election Day is unclear; however, election results indicated that few were moved by labor's first independent political party. ULP mayoral candidate Charles Miller, for example, came in a distant third. The United Labor Party was only able to muster a little more than 4 percent of the vote, failing to garner even a hundred votes in half the city's fourteen wards and no more than 177 in any single ward.[83]

Seattle residents likely turned a deaf ear to the United Labor Party because it ignored the most salient issue in the campaign. As in the municipal election two years before, vice surfaced as the central topic of debate in the 1910 election. Both the Democratic and Republican mayoral candidates tirelessly proclaimed how each proposed to handle the burgeoning prostitution industry that seemingly plagued the city. The dispute centered largely on whether Seattle should create a small restricted district to segregate vice. In the preceding couple of years, the city had attempted to strictly enforce antivice laws, which, rather than eliminating prostitution, had dispersed it into nearby residential neighborhoods. The United Labor Party, however, completely ignored the question of vice, focusing instead on its promise to improve the position of Seattle's working class. Gender, not class, aroused the passions of city in 1910.[84]

The resounding rejection of the United Labor Party apparently did little to discourage some Seattle labor officials. Less than three months after the spring election, the *Union Record* announced the revival of the ULP. Responding to a canvass of workers by the bricklayers' union, the SCLC now officially endorsed a call for renewed efforts to build a strong, successful political party. Learning from the mistakes the party had committed in the municipal campaign, labor leaders not only pledged to work with local unions, but also launched their party several months before the fall county and state elections. Officials readily admitted that a few individuals, rather than an organized effort involving all unions, had largely conducted the disastrous spring campaign. To avoid these past errors, organizers requested that all unions send five delegates to help manage the party for the upcoming fall elections.[85]

Signaling that they had learned important lessons, labor leaders formulated a much more comprehensive party platform for the fall campaign. Going beyond vague references to promoting the best interests of labor, the new platform included a lengthy preamble followed by a dozen concrete demands dealing with working conditions and local politics. The United Labor Party preamble also revealed the influence of radical ideas more in line with Socialists and the Industrial Workers of the World. Party officials, for example, declared that while labor represented the real source of wealth in society, employers had seized control of this wealth and "formerly self-employing producers thus have become the helpless servants of their industrial masters." The platform added that trusts and large capital also exploited farmers as well as threatened the economic independence of small merchants. Rather than separating labor from other social groups as the United Labor Party had in the spring, officials attempted to link those who struggled for economic independence in a fight "against trust and capitalist oppression."[86]

The party's demands clearly reflected a concerted effort to expand its base. The platform, for example, insisted that mines, quarries, forests, and water power be included in the public domain, rather than left in the hands of private corporations. It also called for a ban on child labor and more government inspections of factories. That political demands outnumbered those directly related to the workplace signaled the party's new direction. Labor leaders also appealed for a graduated income tax, restrictions on the power of the state supreme court, a majority vote for constitutional amendments, direct election of all judges, and the exclusion of Asian labor. While these political demands no doubt addressed problems and concerns that faced organized labor, many also appealed to the city's middle-class residents. More importantly, they reflected labor's recognition that organizing solely at the point of production could not solve all the ills that plagued the city's working class. As long as judges remained outside the control of workers and employers continued to occupy the full attention of political leaders, organized labor's future was imperiled.[87]

In the fall campaign United Labor Party officials placed before voters a slate of union candidates for the state legislature. As in the spring election, labor leaders were careful to nominate only candidates who held union cards. While they no doubt would have liked middle-class residents to support the party at the ballot box, party leaders did not attempt to court them directly. Perhaps alluding to the City Party debacle, they reminded workers that past political efforts failed because those outside the ranks of labor directed and controlled the parties for their own political ends. Clearly marking their territory, delegates passed a resolution at the United Labor Party convention directly attacking the Seattle Chamber of Commerce for its sustained effort to hurt workers by encouraging migration of additional laborers to the city. Perhaps the best evidence that the labor party had no intention of courting middle-class support was its repudiation of perennial prolabor candidate George Cotterill. For more than a decade, the *Union Record* and most of organized labor had firmly supported Cotterill in every election, including his successful bid for the state senate in 1907. In 1910, however, the labor party ran local carpenter H. A. Patzold against Cotterill in the race for state senator. Patzold, in an open letter to the *Union Record*, reminded readers that United Labor Party candidates, including himself, "are in your class and Mr. Geo. F. Cotterill is not." Clearly, the events of the previous few years profoundly influenced many labor leaders. In 1910, they believed that organized labor had to make a stand and distance itself from middle-class progressives and former political friends if they wished to fashion a Seattle that truly reflected labor's interests.[88]

Whether the United Labor Party's strategy repelled possible middle-class support in the fall election is difficult to determine. What is clear, however, is that the party failed to attract much support from its own ranks. Just as they had done in the spring campaign, Seattle voters soundly rejected the party and its candidates. "Only if political challengers could establish a meaningful niche in the structure of power," Richard Oestreicher suggests in his study of working-class political behavior, "could they maintain their capacity to mobilize voters in the future."[89] Unable to offer even a likely victory, the United Labor Party could not entice either working-class or middle-class voters to switch their political loyalties to a new and unproven party. Following the election, the *Seattle Union Record* searched for some silver lining in this rather dark cloud. "We were like the tree," the paper observed, "which bore so many blossoms but little fruit." Editors encouraged readers to see the election as a learning experience on which to build. While the labor party failed miserably at the polls, Seattle voters did send reform-minded progressive candidates to Congress, and the state legislature would, in the next few years, aid the cause of labor in many important ways.[90]

Although labor's tree may not have borne much fruit, Seattle's working-class remained attentive to many of the key urban reforms that marked Progressive Era America. SCLC officials and many prominent union leaders urged workers to support reform measures ranging from municipal ownership and prolabor legislation to bills funding playgrounds and direct legislation. The city's laborers continued to champion municipal ownership of key urban services despite the collapse of the MOP. Workers voted for numerous bond measures to expand Seattle City Light and, after nearly two decades of complaints from riders, helped convince the city to purchase the entire streetcar system from the Stone and Webster Corporation. SCLC also favored improving services that benefited residents, including passage of a $400,000 bond providing incinerators for garbage plants, laws making it easier for city officials to pay workers, and extending the civil service system.[91] Public work measures and bonds that funded construction projects, like the Port of Seattle, often received working-class consent because, as the *Union Record* explained, "bond issues as a rule mean more work, more work means better wages and less employment—the two things in which the worker is principally interested." Union leaders often looked to municipal ownership as a way to restrict private interests or to enhance the lives of workers. In 1917, for example, officials urged unions to back a bond issue to fund a city-owned and operated public market.[92]

Improving city services naturally led SCLC officials to promote reforms to make local government more efficient and responsive to Seattle residents. Direct legislation, in particular the recall and initiative, garnered spirited support from organized labor throughout the Progressive Era. When conservatives attempted to make it more difficult for residents to sign petitions in 1910, labor leaders encouraged workers to reject this amendment.

Unions also distributed petitions for numerous initiatives, including one on the single tax, which promised to simplify the city's finances but was defeated in 1912 and again in 1913. Finally, SCLC officials favored removing partisanship from local elections by instituting nonpartisan ballots, which they believed would "destroy the corrupting influence of party politics" and produce "better government."[93]

Nonpartisan elections was not the only reform organized labor targeted as necessary to make Seattle a better place to live and work. Initially caught up in the wave of progressive enthusiasm for better-planned cities, SCLC officials joined numerous civic clubs to support a 1910 charter amendment to create a municipal plans commission. The commission was charged with developing a comprehensive blueprint to design a more efficient and beautiful city. After two years, the commission submitted the Bogue Plan, which offered a breathtaking design that would have significantly reshaped Seattle. Labor officials, however, rejected this plan, arguing that it was too rigid and inflexible. By 1912, the city's working class had also become more suspicious of middle-class reforms, as evident by the noteworthy support the Socialist candidate for mayor received that year. Similar concerns also explained organized labor's rejection of playground and park bond measures that same year. Workers, as historian Mansel Blackford has suggested, also seemed wary of the "overtones of social control implicit in the scheme."[94] Two years after Seattle residents spurned the Bogue Plan, voters approved another commission to revise the city charter to create a commission form of government. Again, labor leaders initially endorsed this endeavor; however, when the commission presented a charter that provided for the ward system of representation rather than at-large elections, which the city had enjoyed for several years, the SCLC vehemently denounced it. Labor's objections reflected the fact that the city's working class, unlike in most large cities, was residentially dispersed and thus ward elections would have diluted its power. In the end, Seattle workers demonstrated their willingness to endorse many progressive reforms, but only if, and when, the community's interest overlapped with labor's vision.

Stung by the dismal failure of the United Labor Party, organized labor consciously shied away from further independent political action and, instead, forged a strong relationship with middle-class progressive forces in Seattle. The formation of the Municipal Ownership Party in 1905 had marked the beginning of progressivism in the city, and labor, despite its brief foray into independent third-party politics, remained a major partner in progressive political circles. The events of the previous half decade had made it abundantly clear to organized labor that cross-class alliances remained the best way to refigure power relations in Seattle. Yet the disappointment over the Alaska-Yukon-Pacific Exposition and Japanese immigration also reminded labor leaders that middle-class support had its limits. If workers were going to achieve success in the political arena, then, they had to find some common ground with middle-class residents on which to build a successful alliance. Labor's future success, it soon discovered, would be closely tied to the reemergence of women as a political force in Seattle. Looking to bear more fruit than blossoms, labor leaders allied with middle-class feminists during the equal suffrage campaign of 1910 to fashion a cross-class alliance that shifted, albeit for a brief period, the balance of power in Seattle. The politics of class and the politics of gender, then, went hand in hand in Progressive Era Seattle.[95]

CHAPTER 3

Civic Life and Woman Suffrage

On election day in 1910, Seattle voters no doubt passed working-class residents stumping on behalf of the United Labor Party. If they paid any attention, these men would have most likely heard about capitalist oppression and demands to exclude Japanese workers from the city. Yet the United Labor Party and its Democratic and Republican opponents did not have the street to themselves. Voters could not have missed the posters on the wall, or the banners on street poles, or the presence of numerous women thrusting into their hands leaflets with "votes for women" spelled out in large letters. While most male voters turned a deaf ear to the anticapitalist rhetoric, they did heed the pleas of Seattle women and that day granted the women of Washington equal suffrage.

The 1910 fall election was a turning point in Seattle's political evolution. Although voters defined the limits of progressivism by overwhelmingly rejecting the highly charged class rhetoric of organized labor, they did not wish to backtrack or close the book on progressive reform that had begun with the victory of the Municipal Ownership Party in 1905. While they had repudiated politics in which organized labor defined the issues, voters seemed willing to accept the creation of a more inclusive political environment by providing women greater access to public life than was the case in all but four states in the union. Nevertheless, organized labor and Seattle suffragists recognized in the first two decades of the twentieth century that their dreams for a better future were linked. Unable to fashion a class-based political movement, labor leaders increasingly turned toward middle-class women as potential allies. Likewise, suffragists recognized that any chance to gain the ballot rested on securing working-class support. Class prejudices, however, were difficult to overcome. A cross-class alliance would have been quite difficult to forge without a strong shared interest; working-class women quickly emerged as this bond. The nexus of class and gender politics at the dawn of the twentieth century momentarily, but profoundly, redefined Seattle's political landscape.

Washington's equal suffrage victory offers scholars not only additional insight into the significant political gains western women made during the Progressive Era, but also how these women contributed to the changing nature of American politics. Occurring fourteen years after the last state granted women the ballot, Washington women's success in 1910 launched a tidal wave of similar victories in other western states. By World War I nearly every state west of the Rocky Mountains had granted women political equality. Previous interpretations suggesting that men supported woman suffrage because they wished to thank women for their significant contributions to the untamed region, or that they saw equal suffrage as a way to induce more women to migrate west, do not hold up in Washington's case.[1] The explanation is in fact much more complicated. Progressivism clearly shaped the debate and, perhaps, lent a sense of urgency to the decision to put the ballot in women's hands. As one scholar's recent review of the extant literature has stated, women were not only "empowered by and through Progressivism, but [also] were chiefly responsible for some of the most important democratic reforms of the age."[2] In California, Gayle Gullett has argued, reform women identified themselves as both suffragists and progressives and saw the two to be inextricably linked; each made the other possible and more credible. By directly engaging the political process to which historically they had been denied access, suffragists helped develop alternative strategies and political forms that transformed the political landscape of Progressive Era America. The movement questioned the essence and nature of the nation's democratic ideals and, in the end, redefined the meaning of authority, sovereignty, and citizenship.[3]

Seattle's tremendous growth in the 1880s greatly expanded the size of the city's working class and, along with that, produced the first significant white female wage-earning population. The range of economic activity that accompanied the city's growth added to the need for female workers. In the previous decade, the *Washington Standard* had implored eastern women to come to Seattle to work in dry goods, telegraph, and printing enterprises. Whether the demand for these nontraditional jobs was real is unclear; it is more likely that domestic service was the hidden agenda of such advertisements. Studies of workingwomen in Portland, Los Angeles, and San Francisco in the late nineteenth century confirmed that more women labored in the domestic service sector compared to eastern cities, largely owing to the lack of factory jobs west of the Mississippi. The *Standard*'s pleas for workingwomen, then, likely represented an effort to find more racially acceptable help than the "squaw women" that many residents employed.[4]

By the 1880s, growing occupational opportunities did exist for some women. Both the Knights of Labor and the Seattle Typographical Union, for example, included a few women in their ranks during the 1880s. Sinophobic rhetoric about the apparent threat Chinese workers posed to workingwomen's jobs likewise suggests the growing presence of female workers in the city. An 1883 editorial in the *Seattle Post-Intelligencer* commented on both the growth in the number of workingwomen in the city and the fact that they had begun to branch out to new jobs once held by men. The paper applauded this change because it believed that compared to young male workers, these women were more ambitious and industrious.[5]

Washington officials clearly recognized the state's changing job structure when the legislature in 1890 passed the first equal opportunity employment law in the United States. The new law declared that "every avenue of employment shall be open to women; any business, vocation, profession, and calling followed and pursued by men may be followed by women," with one exception, "public office."[6] While the door to political office was closed to female residents, some women had already taken advantage of new opportunities that a rapidly growing Seattle offered. In 1883, the

newly formed Merchants' National Bank included as new associates leading men such as Thomas Burke as well as a woman named Mary Miller.
By 1900, Seattle sported five female journalists, two women lawyers, and
seventeen female physicians. Whether or not these new job opportunities
enticed women to migrate to Puget Sound, the 1900 census reveals that
most wage-earning women in Seattle continued to labor in domestic and
personal service or traditional light manufacturing jobs like dressmaking
and other needle trades. In the end, the overall impact of the "open avenues" law is hard to gauge. That women still worked in traditional female
jobs, while excluded from the more "masculine" building trades, suggests
that the law altered the job market little. Moreover, ten years later Seattle
remained an overwhelmingly male society.[7]

The open employment law notwithstanding, Seattle's workingwomen
struggled to keep their heads above water. The Western Central Labor
Union, for example, largely ignored the plight of wage-earning women
as it faced off first against the Knights of Labor and then the devastating
depression of the 1890s. The opening of the Woman's Home Society in 1888
was perhaps a more telling sign that workingwomen did not fare well in
the late nineteenth century. The Home Society, according to contemporary
historian Clarence Bagley, was "for the benefit of respectable women and
girls who were dependent upon their own work for a livelihood." As one
of at least four special homes erected during this time for the "fallen" and
"unfortunates," the Woman's Home Society attempted, when other groups
(including organized labor) could or would not, to provide assistance to
those women who lived on the margin of society.[8]

Utopian settlements that dotted Puget Sound, however, remained one
bright spot for working-class women at the turn of the century. As they did
for more radically minded workers, the utopian villages offered a liberal
environment for working-class women. The first of several settlements, the
Puget Sound Cooperative Colony declared that "the emancipation of women
from the slavery of domestic drudgery and narrow opportunities shall be
our first care." In these small colonies female residents largely labored in
traditional jobs associated with the home, like cleaning, cooking, and other
domestic chores. Women, however, were not solely relegated to domestic
roles. Laura Hall Peters, a major participant in both the anti-Chinese activity and the first woman suffrage movement, was a founding member of the

cooperative and the editor of its newspaper. While they did not completely free women from traditional domestic duties, such colonies promoted a broader conception of the home than most of American society.[9]

Endeavoring to secure for all "comfortable homes and the blessings of home-life," Puget Sound Cooperative leaders also aimed to free women from the things that denied them their "equitable rights and just rewards for services rendered." Women, for example, received equal pay for their work as well as the political rights of suffrage and officeholding in the settlement. At the Equality Colony, female residents earned eight hours pay for only five hours of work. In the cuisine department, eight women labored cooperatively to prepare meals. The liberal environment of the various utopian settlements also attracted female activists. Just as they played host to many prominent male radicals, the colonies attracted some of the greatest working-class feminists, who found the settlements friendly and welcoming. Visits by radicals like Elizabeth Gurley Flynn of the IWW and Socialist Emma Goldman to Home Colony in the early twentieth century brought colony residents in direct contact with women who not only spoke but lived the feminist ideas that they so eloquently espoused.[10]

The 1897 Klondike gold strike brought both a continuation of some old trends and added new wrinkles to Seattle's female labor market. The strong demand for domestic workers, for example, continued well into the early twentieth century. At the peak of the 1890s depression, Seattle's free public employment office advertised more jobs for women than men. A favorable economy and more job opportunities in the early twentieth century only aggravated an inadequate supply of domestic laborers. Requests for female help at the free employment office, for example, increased 7 percent from 1902 to 1903, with seven out of every ten requests being for housework or day work. Changes in the services provided by the Seattle Young Women's Christian Association (YWCA) likewise hinted at the growing lack of interest in domestic skills. Educational classes in millinery, cooking, and dressmaking attracted few students in 1901, leading the YWCA to eliminate such domestic classes the following year. The organization's own employment agency struggled to fill even one-third of the requests for housekeepers in 1903–4.[11]

Demographics alone, however, cannot explain the relative scarcity of domestic workers in the city. In fact, the city's historically skewed sex ratio declined significantly in the first decade of the century, eventually leveling off in the 1920s. In point of fact, most single women ventured to Seattle not to work in some middle-class abode in the Queen Anne district, but to find jobs in the city's growing retail trades. Of the nearly twenty thousand employed women in 1910, slightly more than seven thousand worked as domestics, representing a decline from 44 percent to 37 percent during the previous decade. Sales and clerical jobs, in contrast, increased 12 percent in this same period, accounting for nearly one of every three Seattle female wage earners.[12]

Investigations and surveys undertaken by the Seattle YWCA substantiated this shift in the female labor market. The organization's Extension Department in 1904 found 367 women working in twenty-four different laundries, 21 women in one overalls factory, 160 workingwomen in four candy factories, and approximately 50 women employed in the Seattle Net and Twine Company. While the survey excluded clerical and sales jobs, it illustrates the expanding job opportunities available to women in Seattle. The growing labor market, the YWCA observed, encouraged thousands of single young women to migrate to the city. Overwhelmed by new arrivals, the local agency had to direct more than seven hundred young women to "outside homes." The YWCA quickly expanded its assistance to the growing number of young working girls through its lunch programs, employment services, and educational and cultural clubs set up at local businesses.[13]

Seattle's vibrant economy and the upsurge of wage-earning women also motivated organized labor to unionize female workers in the first decade of the twentieth century. By 1905, workingwomen participated in nearly a dozen different unions, including locals for beer bottlers, telephone operators, cigarmakers, and waitresses. In many of these unions, however, women constituted only a small minority of the membership. For example, one of the first unions in Seattle to include women, the Typographical Union, reported only six female members out of a membership of more than three hundred. Such mixed-sex unions typically demanded and received equal pay for men and women. In 1904, female members of the Cigarmakers Council No. 188 secured wages of nearly three dollars per day, which was commensurate with the daily earnings of male cigarmakers. The Tailors' Union, Local No. 71, however, typified the practices of numerous trade unions by establishing a two-tiered wage system where female members were paid fifty cents less per day than male tailors.[14]

Seattle workingwomen's union participation proceeded rather unevenly in the first decade of the twentieth century. Saleswomen were able to gain a foothold in the Retail Clerks' Union, Local 330, after demonstrating support for an early-closing campaign. Female clerks enthusiastically participated in parades and demonstrations that quickly brought a successful conclusion to the campaign. Saleswomen, however, had their own specific concerns, including equal pay and better working conditions. Seattle's largest department store, the Bon Marché, endured constant public criticism in the early 1900s for the poor wages it paid saleswomen. The store was also the first firm to challenge the constitutionality of the state's new ten-hour-day law for women workers. Despite losing the challenge, the Bon Marché continually faced investigations by the state labor commission for violating the law. In July 1903, State Labor Commissioner William Blackman took a rather unusual step and hauled the firm before a local court. Two witnesses maintained that the company subtly coerced workers to toil beyond ten hours. The company, however, presented ten other saleswomen who stated that because of the store's "splendid treatment" of its workers, they felt a duty to demonstrate their appreciation by working overtime. The jury quickly brought in a not guilty verdict.[15]

What was rather remarkable about the court case against the Bon Marché was not the verdict, but the willingness of two saleswomen to testify against the company. In the first few years following the passage of the 1901 ten-hour-day law, Commissioner Blackman continually complained that enforcing the law was difficult because most female workers refused to testify in official proceedings. In April 1903, a complainant employed by a bakery, for example, refused to take the stand, leaving Blackman no choice but to drop the case. A few months later he noted that one of Seattle's largest laundries escaped prosecution because female laundry workers were "afraid to testify for fear of losing their positions." Without a doubt one of the most exploited groups of female laborers in the city, laundry workers endured two decades of employer resistance to unionizing efforts. The "little white slaves of the mangle," as one female labor activist called them, continued to suffer from dangerous working conditions and poor pay until World War I.[16]

In stark contrast to the city's laundry workers, Seattle waitresses formed the most successful and powerful female labor organization in Progressive Era Seattle. According to one craft paper, the fifty waitresses who sought a charter in 1900 braved "the strong prejudice against working women mixing in unions, and the even stronger prejudice against forming their own unions."[17] By 1906, the union counted more than 200 members and had secured wage increases of 15 percent, while decreasing the daily hours of work by three. By the end of the decade the waitresses expanded union membership to 375, claiming to have organized 95 percent of the local trade. What set the Waitresses' Union apart from nearly all other organized workingwomen was its insistence on an all-female union. The waitresses who joined together in 1900 chose to organize separately from male waiters, who formed their own union at that time. This decision helps explain the success of the union and its exceptional influence and leadership in local union circles well into the 1920s.[18]

The fiercely independent waitresses immediately impressed Seattle labor leaders. The *Union Record* styled them the "red-hottest unionists in Seattle" and wished that other unions emulated their sense of solidarity. In his 1901 report, the state labor commissioner likewise complimented Local 240 as the "best conducted union in the state." Seattle's rank and file demonstrated its admiration by electing the waitresses' business agent, Alice Lord, vice president of the WCLU in 1905. Lord developed a reputation as an excellent speaker, who, on occasion, was not afraid to challenge male union members' attitude about a woman's right to work or men's spotty attendance at labor functions. For nearly two decades she remained a prominent figure in both Seattle and Washington State labor circles.[19]

The waitresses' contributions reached beyond the city's restaurants and diners. In 1905, for example, Local 240 dabbled in local politics by registering its members to participate in the school directors' election. However, the union's most important endeavors in the first decade of the century focused on improving the lives of other workingwomen. A Waitresses' Union report in the *Union Record* declared that the "girls are up in arms" about the failure of the labor commissioner to prosecute a local laundry for violating the ten-hour-day law. Local 240's successes often encouraged some workingwomen to call on the waitresses for advice and assistance. In 1906, the *Union Record* reported that a number of wage-earning women had asked Alice Lord to consider organizing a Federal Labor Union. While this issue never appeared again in the paper and such a union did not surface in the following years, the request illustrates working-class women's admiration and faith in Lord and the waitresses.[20]

Despite the Waitresses' Union's achievements and unswerving efforts, Seattle labor leaders had little success in organizing women workers. In this way Seattle differed little from other American cities. Across the country trade union membership among women at the turn of the century was exceptionally low. In certain industries, for example the liquor and beverage trades, female organizing did have some impact. Yet of the more than 80 percent of gainfully employed women outside these key industries, less than one percent were members of trade unions. Even at the height of union activity during World War I, less than 7 percent of the nation's women were organized compared to more than 20 percent of men. For Seattle women, this situation was even more poignant because the percentage of women in the workforce exceeded the national average.[21]

The relative lack of success in organizing women can, in part, be explained by the changing labor market. Sex segregation channeled most of the emerging female workforce into clerical, sales, trade, and domestic service occupations that had no tradition of union activity. More important, however, was the discrimination by male unionists, who often stymied women's organizing efforts. Samuel Gompers and other labor leaders blamed low female union membership on women workers rather than on male-led unions. These officials maintained that employment was not an important or permanent part of women's existence and thus organizing them made little sense. Even the efforts of the middle-class Women's Trade Union League to encourage workingwomen to enter the union movement were continuously frustrated by AFL philosophy and practices. In short, obstacles like male chauvinism and the labor market discouraged wage-earning women and made organizing them exceedingly difficult and rare.[22]

Notwithstanding the general sentiments of the AFL's upper echelon, labor leaders in Seattle seemed to devote "much energy and commitment to organizing women." WCLU officials, the *Union Record,* and several local unions did make some effort to encourage women to join unions in the early 1900s. In 1907, officials of a local retail clerks' union, for example, appointed a saleswoman to organize female clerks and lowered dues to attract more women into the union. Local post office clerks likewise admitted women workers to their organization. In 1905, the *Union Record* stated that women dressmakers seemed ready for organizing and indicated that it would bring the matter to the regional AFL organizer. Growing concern about working conditions led local organizers to announce that they would "turn their attention to organizing female wage earners into unions—for their and the community's protection." In fact, more requests for new unions came from workingwomen, the labor paper maintained, than from their male counterparts. Stoking the unionizing fire was none other than Alice Lord. Exploiting her position on Seattle's labor council, she penned numerous articles for the *Union Record* labor paper outlining to workingwomen the benefits of unionization. Noting the gains of the waitresses and local garment workers, Lord even chastised female teachers and clerks for complaining about conditions but doing little to alleviate them through unionization.[23]

Despite this initial effort, most male labor leaders expressed doubts about women workers' true desire for unions. In response to the struggle to obtain the eight-hour day for women in 1908, the *Union Record* stated that "if women workers of Seattle would unite it would not be necessary to petition the legislature for an eight-hour day." Labor leaders' commitment to organizing women workers, however, was often undermined by male unionists' contradictory attitudes and statements. The cries for organizing women workers that dotted the pages of the labor paper often competed for space with contradictory statements about whether women should work at all. In a tone of apparent resignation about the changing nature of work in industrial America, the *Union Record* hoped that men would marry young women and "take [them] out of the factory and put [them] in a home." Yet, if the young women preferred to work rather than marry, the paper called on men to "induce [them] to join the union; let [them] earn good wages both for [their] sake and yours."[24]

Seattle labor leaders' rather inconsistent and contradictory attitudes about workingwomen was not always so subtle. While one week the *Union Record* might applaud efforts of women to organize, the next it might pronounce that the "sphere of the woman is in the home." In 1907, the paper claimed that even though a woman might be a good union member, she could do more for organized labor "by demanding union label goods in her household than she could ever do as a poorly paid wage slave by paying her union dues." Time and again female readers of the *Union Record* read that, in principle, male unionists opposed women becoming wage earners. When a St. Louis trade union announced its plan to replace female stenographers with married men, the paper applauded this decision, suggesting that it would result in less immorality and "race suicide." A growing concern among many native-born Americans in the midst of rapid immigration from southern Europe, "race suicide" emerged as a rhetorical weapon to be used against the employment of young native-born women. In 1905, the *Seattle Mail and Herald,* for example, suggested that women who worked might be unfit mothers and produce inferior children.[25]

Female workers in Seattle thus received mixed messages from their union brothers. Encouraged to form unions by the WCLU and the *Union Record,* workingwomen were then instructed that they would "be attended to in due time." In their defense, male unionists confronted an American society undergoing a rapid and profound transformation in both class and gender relations. The disintegration of separate spheres, which for several generations had been the measure of middle-class respectability, changed the cultural landscape in which the working class operated. Male workers still struggled to achieve the "living wage"—which promised them the chance to keep their wives out of the labor market—at the same time that middle-class and working-class women fought to eradicate separate spheres. Further complicating the matter were the contradictory statements proffered by some union women. Defending their right to work, Seattle waitresses often explained that workingwomen would be glad to stay in the home, but that necessity drove them to work for wages. At the same time, however, Alice Lord chastised male unionists for their declarations that women belonged in the home. Like men, working-class women also struggled to reconcile themselves to the changing social and economic environment. Recognizing the new reality of industrial America, the waitresses perhaps hoped to lessen the fears and concerns of working-class men, as well their own uncertainty, by employing such domestic rhetoric in defense of their jobs. In the changing landscape of early-twentieth-century America, male workers were quickly learning that women workers might "rather work than wed."[26]

This ambivalence about workingwomen helps explain why labor leaders increasingly pressed working-class women to employ their power as consumers in the battle with capital. By purchasing union-made goods, women would encourage local employers to see the advantages of union shops. Good union wages for men, labor leaders concluded, would alleviate the necessity of working-class women to work and thus permit them to remain in their proper sphere. The use of the union label dates back to the 1870s, but women did not become part of this labor strategy until the turn of the century. In 1899, the wives and daughters of union men in Muncie, Indiana, formed the Women's Union Label League. The purpose, according to its founders, was to help "weak union men to stand up for their rights and to educate the workmen's wives in the labor movement." AFL officials quickly jumped on board this effort, publishing pamphlets encouraging the formation of label leagues because they offered women the opportunity to aid organized labor from the home. Label leagues thus promised to solve the apparent dilemma of female workers by both maintaining traditional gender relations and strengthening labor's relationship with capital.[27]

In 1905, the *Seattle Union Record* first broached the subject of forming a label league during labor's conflict with the local Citizens' Alliance. The timing of this suggestion was not coincidental. While labor leaders fashioned the Municipal Ownership Party in early 1905, they simultaneously, and with some urgency, invited working-class women to form a label league. In its first issue of that year, the *Union Record* urged working-class residents to organize as consumers just as workers had as producers. By mid-February, the paper noted that the Waitresses' Union was staging an entertainment event to launch a woman's label league in the city. Union men, the notice urged, should bring their wives, mothers, and sweethearts to this affair. Apparently, the event did little to inspire women to take up this strategy because a few weeks later the *Union Record* openly chided women for failing to form a label league as women in San Francisco, Portland, and nearby Everett already had.[28]

Undeterred by the poor response, Seattle labor leaders explored another strategy by encouraging women to form female auxiliaries to individual unions. Noting that there was only one woman's auxiliary (printers) in the city, the *Union Record* declared that at least twenty auxiliaries should have already been formed. Such organizations, the paper argued, could greatly advance labor's cause. Moreover, it suggested that a strong auxiliary movement would "naturally" lead to the formation of a successful label league. In short, union officials envisioned auxiliaries and label leagues not as competing organizations, but rather as mutually reinforcing institutions. While WCLU officials struggled to interest women in this consumer strategy, Emma Lamphere, an international organizer of the Retail Clerks Association, spoke before the clerks' local. In her speech, Lamphere extolled the virtues of label leagues and the importance of workers' wives to the success of organized labor. Urging union men to bring the union to the home, she proclaimed: "Make a closed shop of the home and an open shop is impossible in the factory." Excited about these comments, the Union Record provided extensive coverage of Lamphere's speech and implored her to remain in Seattle for another week so she could speak before the weekly WCLU meeting. "She is a good talker before any assemblage," the paper observed, "but is especially effective before a gathering of nuion [sic] men's wives and daughters."[29]

After a month of discussion and debate, Alice Lord and other labor women officially launched the Seattle Women's Card and Label League in April, and labor leaders pleaded for union men to encourage their wives to join the new organization. With the reorganization of the WCLU into the Seattle Central Labor Council complete by the spring of 1905, Lord urged members to turn their attention to building a strong label league. The public confrontation with the Citizens' Alliance offered a favorable environment to arouse support for this consumer strategy. Lord argued that in the event of a strike, wives and daughters of the city's seven thousand union men could force employers to capitulate by refusing to purchase a company's products. In a missive to the Seattle Union Record, Mrs. Anna R. Coleman, secretary of the Seattle Women's Card and Label League, mirrored Lord's sentiments by declaring that support for the league would "strike one blow against the Citizen's Alliance." The new organization not only would aid the union cause, she stated, but also would provide working-class wives the opportunity to rid their "lonely hours and lonely feelings" by forming a shared interest with their husbands. Together, then, working-class men and women could defeat the Citizens' Alliance and defend labor's place in the community.[30]

Recognizing the potential power of consumer strategies that depended on wives' participation, the label league, if narrowly constructed, could help labor leaders achieve their goals without undermining traditional gender relations. It was this narrow construction, however, that helps explain the initial failure of Seattle's Women's Card and Label League. According to one member, the label league suffered from the perception that it was little more than an excuse for social gatherings. After explaining that the league aimed to help union men, Mrs. M. H. Puttrick wrote that "this is exactly the purpose of these Label Leagues, not pink teas, as some think."[31] Working-class men, she charged, were the underlying source of the league's impotence. Local labor leaders readily agreed. Six months after its formation, both the *Union Record* and regional AFL organizer C. O. Young blamed union men for the league's languishing existence. Noting the changing attitudes toward women in the early twentieth century, Young implored men to recognize their wives' intelligence and escort them to a label or auxiliary meeting. Despite one last media blitz that placed three letters to the editor on the front page of the *Union Record*'s New Year's issue in 1906, the league limped along for the rest of the decade.[32]

Disappointed by the meager membership of the Women's Card and Label League, a group of union men announced in 1907 the formation of their own label league. They proposed to publish a booklet each month outlining which local firms sold union-made goods or employed union workers. Interestingly enough, and notwithstanding their announced intention to work with the Women's Card and Label League, sufficient confusion had surfaced to prompt the *Union Record* to print a clarification of the new league's purpose. The men's organization, the paper claimed, was not to rival but rather complement the women's league. Clearly frustrated by the infirmity of the Women' Card and Label League, yet cognizant of its potential to improve their class position, male unionists seemed intent on enhancing the female organization's legitimacy in the eyes of working-class men. Husbands no longer had to feel threatened by their wives' more public, powerful, and, indeed, more equal role. The men's label league would ensure that Label League women did not operate completely outside their husbands' control or influence. Thus the struggle between capital and labor may have stretched traditional gender roles and ideas, but in this case it would not break them.[33]

While union leaders seemed unable to overcome male ambivalence toward the Seattle Women's Card and Label League, they did successfully rally working-class men behind the effort to secure the eight-hour day for women workers. The eight-hour-day movement offered organized labor several benefits beyond simply lessening workingwomen's daily toil. First, it provided labor leaders another chance to chip away at the power of capital, particularly as the relations between the two soured after 1905. The eight-hour battle also enhanced class solidarity. Labor leaders were not hesitant to defend working-class womanhood in order to persuade male workers to join the labor movement. Just as the SCLC targeted Japanese workers to explain white workers' woes at this time, it also used the eight-hour day to rally working-class men against local capitalists.

While Seattle labor leaders never failed to express unease with the plight of workingwomen, in particular, the unfortunate need for them to work outside the home, they did little to defend women once they entered the workplace. From Samuel Gompers down to the SCLC, labor leaders had exerted little effort to organize women unless it served male workers' needs. In the first few years of the eight-hour-day battle, Seattle union officials passed several resolutions in support of the bill, but did little beyond this. In 1905, the *Union Record* bitterly complained that state legislators let the bill die in committee. Yet, the tone of the editorial suggested more concern with employers' political power than with the exploitation of female workers. In the midst of the struggle with the Citizens' Alliance that year, the paper encouraged workingwomen to keep up the fight because "there may be elected next time a legislature that will represent the people instead of the corporations." In short, male labor leaders initially linked the eight-hour day with their larger contest against growing employer recalcitrance.[34]

By 1907, the eight-hour day commanded a great deal of attention, as both the SCLC and the WSFL put their considerable resources behind the effort. The WSFL, for example, passed a resolution offered by Frank Cotterill, a union plumber from Seattle, that declared any firm that employed women "for less than living wages, commits a moral crime." Not only did the state federation support the eight-hour bill, but it also attacked businesses that based female wages on those women who accepted less pay because they did not have to work. Despite encouragement from the state's major labor organizations, several religious bodies, and middle-class women's clubs, the bill failed to muster sufficient support in the state senate.[35]

Over the next several years, Alice Lord, the WSFL, and Seattle labor leaders annually visited the legislature with an eight-hour bill but met similar defeat until 1911. Each time organized labor attempted to sway public opinion by employing many traditional arguments. They maintained, for example, that the eight-hour bill promised to protect women's health by reducing the physical and mental ruin that long hours of toil produced. "Twenty years ago," the *Union Record* wrote, "the mothers of the following generation were seldom employed in stores or factories, wearing out their strength and losing the vitality which should be given in nourishment to the unborn." In a similar vein, Alice Lord added that the shorter workday would permit workingwomen time to rest, expand their education by attending night school, and provide "time to fit themselves for something above slavery." Protecting American womanhood and motherhood, then, was a cogent argument that Lord and other labor leaders believed would stir the passions of Seattle's working class and thus enhance class consciousness.[36]

According to some labor officials, the yearly defeat of the eight-hour day offered one potential silver lining. Failure to secure legislative protection, they suggested, might in the end actually stimulate union organizing among workingwomen. In hearings before the Washington State Senate in 1907, Seattle laundry employers argued that organized labor demanded the bill because it could not successfully organize female laundry workers. In many ways the laundrymen were right. Labor leaders did perceive some connection between the struggle over the shorter workday and efforts to organize female wage earners. The best way to unionize the laundries, the *Union Record* claimed, was to "defeat the eight-hour bill; that will force the employees of laundries to organize for protection under union [*sic*] if they cannot get it under law." SCLC officials believed that the energy produced by the battle in the state legislature, even if they met defeat, could be channeled into organizing women workers at the point of production. If successful, one female laundry employee put it, workers "would not have to beg of a senate committee for relief by law."[37]

Despite high expectations, the annual defeat of the eight-hour law did little to stimulate female union membership, leaving labor leaders little choice but to look to the legislature to help female laborers. In 1910, women who worked in retail sales and manufacturing plants, on the average, labored about the same number of hours per day that men did. Some 62 percent of men and 59 percent of women worked a ten-hour day; only 5 percent of men and a slightly higher proportion of women toiled no more than eight hours per day. As Nellie Higgins of the University of Washington noted in a 1913 report, the eight-hour day potentially touched the lives of more than 90 percent of female wage earners in Washington. Labor leaders were likewise aware that the passage of this bill could, in one fell swoop, improve the lives of more workingwomen than even doubling or tripling female union membership. Considering the uphill struggle they faced expanding the rolls of female union membership, a concerted effort to pass the eight-hour day likely looked easier than expending additional energy and funds on female organizing. Sadly, 1909 brought more disappointment as the state senate rejected the bill by a 22–19 margin.[38]

The difference between the defeat of the eight-hour bill in 1909 and its subsequent passage in 1911 was woman suffrage. The granting of the ballot to Washington women in 1910 profoundly transformed the political landscape in Seattle and the state. Not only did the struggle for political equality bring middle-class and working-class women together, but it also produced a rather powerful, albeit relatively brief, alliance between organized labor and middle-class female activists. The plight of working-women emerged as a common bond connecting these two groups. Unable to assert its vision through an independent political labor party, organized labor successfully exploited this shared bond to construct a political alliance with middle-class suffragists, and in doing so refigured Seattle politics at the height of the Progressive Era.

Middle-class women's interest in the affairs of Seattle's working class arose soon after the Yukon gold strike. The rapid growth of the city and the increasing number of workingwomen prompted both sympathy and concern from middle-class women's clubs. Most of this initial interest focused on defending the virtue and womanhood of young women who worked in the various factories and shops in Seattle. The YWCA perhaps best reflected the efforts of middle-class women to aid workingwomen. YWCA members addressed what they perceived as the denigrating effect of wage work by providing lunches, Bible classes, and what they deemed to be appropriate cultural activities. Such efforts, however, did little to improve wages and hours. In 1906, women from the Presbyterian church began to meet and talk with union waitresses. The *Union Record* observed that this new relationship, if cultivated, could aid female wage earners by educating those women who did not have to work about the plight of female workers. By 1907, the paper applauded local women's clubs, which lobbied alongside Alice Lord and union women for the passage of the eight-hour day.[39]

Differing class sensibilities and prejudices, however, surfaced early in the political partnership between organized labor and Seattle's middle-class female activists. Labor leaders often chided clubwomen who failed to expand their activity and truly help the city's workers. Careful not to alienate these middle-class women, a *Union Record* editorial gently suggested that they could aid workingwomen by demanding the union label when purchasing goods and services in the city. Alice Lord, who likely had more interaction with Seattle's elite women than any other member of organized labor, likewise noted her frustration with their tendency to muddle the primary goal with extraneous issues like prohibition. Lord argued, for example, that if middle-class women would devote "one-half of their attention and direct their energies toward relieving suffering occasioned by merciless employers," they would do more for humanity than the closing of every saloon or tavern could accomplish. Other working-class leaders questioned middle-class women's support for the eight-hour day, since these women often worked their domestic servants twelve to sixteen hours per day. In other words, these women placed their own personal class concerns, in this case a desire for stable and pliant female servants, ahead of their working-class sisters' demand for a more humane workday. These conflicts and problems notwithstanding, union officials recognized the great potential this alliance offered Seattle's working class. When social and political conditions spawned a vibrant feminist movement seeking equal suffrage, labor leaders seized the opportunity to solidify this relationship and by doing so helped tip the political scales back in a more favorable direction.[40]

For nearly two decades following the contentious 1880s, Seattle women laid the groundwork in preparation for the right moment to reclaim the ballot they had lost in the political debacle of 1886–87. Many male voters, wary of the uncertainty voting women brought to the political landscape, or perhaps wishing to maintain their control over the city's political and economic future, dashed the hopes of suffragists on two different occasions during this interlude. Male citizens, for example, overwhelmingly rejected a referendum on equal suffrage included as part of the ratification of Washington's state constitution in 1889. Nearly a decade later, during the heyday of Populism, they again turned down women's plea for the vote. Following the second defeat, women leaders quickly realized that any future success depended on building a strong grassroots movement, employing a wide range of arguments that would appeal to a diverse audience. By 1910, Seattle suffragists had cultivated important powerful alliances and seized the most opportune social and political moment to launch an all-out bid for the franchise.

Following the 1887 decision by the Washington territorial supreme court to take the ballot away from female voters, suffrage forces soon crumbled and spent the better part of the next decade in disarray. Several political and economic factors lay behind the suffrage movement's demise. Seattle's working class changed dramatically during the late 1880s and early 1890s as a booming economy and the great fire of 1889 attracted throngs of construction workers more in line with the conservative philosophy of the fledging and moderate AFL than the militant Knights of Labor. Moreover, Western Central Labor Council officials wished to build a strong trade union movement and believed its success depended on disassociating the council from the Knights' more radical social and political vision. Finally, several key leaders of the Knights' political wing, the People's Party, fled to utopian colonies in the ensuing years, thus stripping Seattle of some of its more passionate and committed radicals.

Seattle's elite, however, also turned their backs on equal suffrage during this period. Whether they were disillusioned with what many perceived as the failure of woman suffrage to reform Seattle in the mid-1880s, or fearful that it contributed to tipping the political balance in favor of the city's working class via the People's Party, a great deal of elite support for equal suffrage quickly evaporated. Reflecting this sentiment, the *Seattle Post-Intelligencer* in 1888 bluntly declared: "Woman suffrage has proven a practical failure in Washington Territory. It has accomplished nothing in the way of public or private good. There has been no moral, social or political reforms as a consequence of it. On the other hand it has made dissension and trouble everywhere." Washington's territorial status further complicated the matter. Territorial politicians worried that giving women the right to vote might upend the tenuous support for statehood in the nation's capital. Suffragists, with the aid of thousands of petition signatures, nevertheless pressured delegates at the state constitutional convention to include equal suffrage in the proposed constitution. Apparently unwilling to risk statehood, delegates chose instead to put the issue before the voters. Perhaps cognizant of the changing political winds, woman suffrage opponents proved victorious as voters validated the new state constitution but soundly rejected equal suffrage.[41]

Crushed by the 1889 decision and painfully aware that the tide had reversed, female suffragists had little choice but to start over and rebuild their movement from the ground up. The loss of key leaders such as Laura Hall Peters, who left to found the Puget Sound Cooperative Colony, and Mary Kenworthy, who apparently withdrew from political activism following the loss of the ballot, further dampened prospects for success.[42] Changing political fortunes, however, seemed to offer suffragists renewed hope just a few years later. The 1890s depression restructured local and state politics as Populist forces captured numerous key offices, including the governor's office and a good deal of the state legislature. Populism and its visionary platform appeared to many women as the best vehicle to reclaim political equality. The 1894 state Populist convention, for example, demonstrated strong support for suffrage by adding it to its platform by a vote of 104 to 25. Governor John Rogers's victory in 1896 only heightened expectations, as the state's highest office was now in the hands of a prosuffrage party. Moreover, the success of woman suffrage efforts in neighboring Idaho that same year raised hopes for a similar victory in Washington.[43]

By the time suffragists had secured a referendum for voters to consider, the climate along Puget Sound had again greatly changed. Looking south to California, however, may have given Washington women reason to temper such expectations. In California, a Populist-Democratic Party fusion had eviscerated much of the radical platform of the People's Party, like equal suffrage, permitting Republican leaders to distance themselves from the measure, which voters soundly defeated in 1896.[44] When

Washington's electorate went to the polls in 1898 to decide once again whether the state should extend the franchise to women, the once promising Populist movement had likewise imploded. Incessant bickering and internal differences devoured the bond that these insurgents once shared. Moreover, the discovery of gold in the Yukon Territory in 1897 virtually eliminated overnight the state's economic woes, thus further undermining the party's momentum.

Despite these setbacks, female suffragists prepared for the fight. In 1897, the president of the western Washington Women's Christian Temperance Union (WCTU) urged members to drop some departments and activities and amass their forces behind the suffrage campaign. Arguing that the ballot was the group's best weapon to secure prohibition, she later declared that "woman's enfranchisement is a matter of justice, and will reinforce moral legislation and the administration of good government." Moreover, the "election in this sunset land," the temperance leader concluded, "will affect the woman question in all lands." As one of the most influential women's organizations in Washington State, the western Washington WCTU spoke for a large number of women. However, by tying prohibition directly to woman suffrage, the WCTU jeopardized the referendum's chances. Not only had male voters overwhelmingly rejected a prohibition amendment in the 1889 state constitution election, but the Washington Populist Party had even refused to add a prohibition plank to its platform in 1894. Thus, the promise of Populism seemingly withered by the time voters went to the polls in 1898.[45]

With woman suffrage rejected twice in less than a decade, advocates largely disbanded their active effort to acquire the ballot. Many Seattle women apparently turned to more informal ways to improve their city by forming various women's clubs and joining reform organizations that historians have associated with progressivism. While suffrage was placed on the back burner, it was not forgotten. Instead, female activists slowly built the foundation for a new battle that they knew would be waged sometime in the future. In 1910, social, economic, and political conditions coalesced in Seattle, yielding a unique environment ripe for waging a new suffrage campaign.

One key feature of Seattle's changing political climate at the turn of the century was the proliferation of middle-class women's clubs. Largely originating as self-improvement organizations, women's clubs throughout the nation quickly shifted their focus to the pressing social and economic ills produced by industrial capitalism. In what one historian has called "an era of separate female organization and institution building," middle-class women cultivated new friendships, expanded their horizons beyond the home, and more importantly, acquired organizing and leadership skills. By 1890, these clubs had built a rather impressive network that soon produced a national federation. By incorporating large numbers of middle-class women into these separate female institutions, the club movement provided the foundation for the growth of feminism and the success of equal suffrage in the decades that followed.[46]

Women's clubs did more than simply bring women together. The new activities and issues clubwomen addressed at the turn of the century, according to Estelle Freedman, "served to politicize traditional women by forcing them to define themselves as citizens, not simply wives and mothers." The rapid industrialization and urbanization of the late nineteenth and early twentieth century exposed these traditionally minded women to a host of new problems that impinged on their domestic sphere. Clubwomen responded by extending their domestic sphere into the historically male public sphere, leading to what historian Paula Baker has called the "domestication of politics." These separate female institutions, in the end, permitted women to challenge the idea of separate spheres because "the concerns of politics and of the home were inextricable."[47]

Many Seattle female activists found refuge in the club movement. In 1897, a number of women's clubs formed a statewide federation that included Seattle cultural clubs, like the Nineteenth Century Literary Club and the Classic Culture Club, as well as the more socially oriented Woman's Century Club and the Women's Industrial Club. The Woman's Century Club stood out in many ways, both because of its vision and its noteworthy members. Initially organized by Carrie Chapman Catt, future leader of the National American Woman's Suffrage Association (NAWSA) in the 1910s, it took its name because Catt believed that the twentieth century would be the woman's century. Charter members in the Seattle club included the city's first female school superintendent, Mrs. Julie E. Kennedy, and one of the city's first woman physicians, Dr. Sarah Kendall. When clubwomen formed the state federation, Kendall attended the meeting along with fellow Woman's Century Club member Kate Turner Holmes, who, two years later, was elected president of the state federation.[48]

By the first decade of the twentieth century, women's clubs had already begun to shed their image as simple literary and cultural organizations. While a segment of clubwomen still favored such endeavors, increasing numbers involved themselves in the budding reform movement that quickly flowered into progressivism. In a speech published in the *Washington Women* in 1896, Dora Tweed observed that club life marked a significant change in the status and place of women in American society. No longer was the "individuality of women . . . absorbed in her family and her church." Clubs, Tweed argued, could promote free and open discussion without limiting one's expression and they could be expected to inquire into subjects once thought taboo. At the third convention of the Washington State Federation of Women's Clubs in 1899, one delegate observed that most of the papers presented at the meeting "concern the practical efforts for the bettering of social conditions." A decade later a Seattle women's magazine confirmed this sentiment when it declared that the power of women's clubs came "not from outside talent but from the personal study, which women are giving to the larger questions of the day."[49]

Under the direction of Seattle resident Kate Turner Holmes, Washington's women's clubs tackled pressing social and political matters. Not only did clubwomen demonstrate a great deal of interest in children's issues, including child welfare and the sale of cigarettes to children, but they also advocated on behalf of traveling libraries for rural areas, the abolition of capital punishment, the curtailment of vice, and the eight-hour day for workingwomen. The rapid industrialization of American society during the late nineteenth and early twentieth centuries lay behind these compelling issues. Urban inhabitants could no longer escape the human suffering and the social upheaval that marked this period. Seattle women were no exception. Yet, as one historian of the women's club movement has argued, "industrialization also worried them because they feared it would unalterably change their role within the home, giving them greater leisure but less sense of purpose." Middle-class female activists, then, increasingly found a sense of purpose in urban reform.[50]

The wide range of reform activities notwithstanding, Seattle clubwomen's initial efforts overwhelmingly centered on issues affecting women and children and, as they understood it, the home. The protection of young women was one such issue. According to one scholar, clubwomen "expanded the traditional idea of sisterhood and applied it to the growing population of working women sometimes exploited in the cities of the Northwest."[51] The Klondike gold strike did more than revive Seattle's economy, it also lured large numbers of young women to the city. As early as 1901, the Seattle YWCA had appointed a full-time matron to keep an eye on young women who debarked at the train depot. The depot matron attempted to cleanse "the moral atmosphere both in and around the depot" and warn young women about the various dangers of the big city, in particular, prostitution. She also steered new arrivals to jobs and safe housing. The matron published her findings and suggestions in the YWCA's yearly report in order to bring these dangers to the attention of "many women heretofore wholly indifferent to their sisters." While prostitution and vice were old news to most Seattle residents, these reports exposed middle-class women to the threat that the notorious vice rings posed to girls and young women who were not yet "lost" or "fallen."[52]

Protecting the city's moral environment brought clubwomen into greater contact with working-class women. By far the majority of young single women who ventured to Seattle in these years came for jobs. While the depot matron protected women from the temptations of a big city, the YWCA's Extension Department labored on behalf of what its members believed was the "class of women who most need our help"—workingwomen. Recognizing the hardships and struggles these women faced, YWCA members attempted to improve working conditions by providing lunch rooms and employment services for these women. Despite the YWCA's interest in workingwomen, the middle-class nature of the Christian organization tended to infuse it with a great deal of class prejudice. Some YWCA officials, for example, maintained that the young workers were not really interested in the lunch rooms and lectures. Improving or teaching these female laborers, leaders concluded, was useless unless they first improved the young women's souls.[53]

The class prejudice that influenced the YWCA's opinion of their clients mirrored similar relations between working-class and middle-class women throughout industrial America during the early 1900s. While some workingwomen may have appreciated the concern for their struggles, it seems that few felt comfortable with the prospects of leaving the solution solely in their middle-class sisters' hands. Female workers, like Alice Lord, instead looked to unions as the best answer. When YWCA leaders admitted that they did not look into issues of wages and hours when investigating working conditions for women, Lord no doubt realized the limits of middle-class feminism. YWCA's investigators ignored these topics because they "in no way [sought] to nor [wished] to interfere at all in the discussions arising from the relations of capital and labor." Lord, however, also realized it was foolhardy to burn these bridges with her middle-class sisters because she understood that political ties could be strengthened over time and eventually exploited to aid the cause of Seattle workingwomen. The fight for the eight-hour day clearly reflected this strategy. Nurturing the relationship between middle-class and working-class women, then, was also the key to the future success of the equal suffrage movement. In the end, this relationship not only fortified cross-class gender relations but also helped foster an alliance between two major political forces of Progressive Era Seattle—organized labor and middle-class women.[54]

By 1905, clubwomen's efforts to aid and support their working-class sisters, however misguided, began to bear fruit. Neither side ventured into this relationship with its eyes closed. As early as the 1860s, middle-class suffragists, who had joined Susan B. Anthony's failed Working Women's Association, attempted to bridge the gap between the two classes. By the early 1900s the number of women who worked for wages had increased significantly, and Seattle suffragists understood that the movement's success rested on this cross-class alliance. Middle-class suffrage leaders recognized, for example, not only that their working-class sisters were valuable foot soldiers in the battle, but that closer ties with them might go far in securing the crucial votes of workingmen. Women workers likewise understood that this alliance could help them improve their conditions of work. Alice Lord willingly acknowledged the significant help that clubwomen provided in the battle for the eight-hour day. Their class position buttressed the arguments Lord and other labor leaders presented to state legislators; their gender provided them the ideological authority to speak on the morality of such protective labor legislation. In short, both sides increasingly realized their mutual dependence.[55]

This budding cross-class alliance first surfaced in late 1906 when the Seattle Women's Card and Label League sent a delegation of working-class women to a state equal suffrage convention. Months later the *Seattle Union Record* publicly recognized the support women's clubs offered the eight-hour-day crusade. In 1908, middle-class feminists returned the favor when they spoke before the annual convention of the Washington State Federation of Labor. The strength of this fledgling alliance soon surfaced on the pages of the local labor daily when it began publishing articles on the benefits of labor colonies. Authored by Adele M. Fielde, a significant leader in various Seattle progressive reform organizations, the articles outlined how state-administered labor colonies would provide badly needed jobs for the unfortunate and unemployed who suffered as a result of the Panic of 1907. Soon thereafter, the Industrial Committee of the Washington State Federation of Women's Clubs announced that it would arrange a public meeting to discuss the formation of such settlements. Fielde's writings thus illustrate the growing relationship between organized labor and middle-class suffragists.[56]

Working-class women, however, refused to leave the debate on the benefits of equal suffrage solely in the hands of their middle-class sisters or male labor leaders. A letter to the *Union Record* from Elmira Bush attempted to explain, from a workingwoman's perspective, the advantages of the vote. She first challenged the common belief that suffragists were "short-haired women desiring to become soldiers, sailors . . . [and] do everything that is now done by men." Bush then argued that political equity was not the sole reason why workingwomen demanded the vote, claiming that it would also prove a valuable weapon in the battle against capital. "It has become a necessity," she declared, "for women, as well as men, to endeavor by their suffrage to better industrial conditions." Seattle's working class, then, suffering at this time from an ailing local economy and worsening relations with employers, increasingly looked to politics "to better industrial conditions." By early 1910, organized labor publicly endorsed woman suffrage. Shortly thereafter, the SCLC formed a committee to expand union support for the measure.[57]

While Seattle suffragists slowly cultivated a cross-class coalition, a moral crisis suddenly flared up and severely fractured the city's political landscape, encouraging some Seattle residents to reinterpret the meaning of equal suffrage. Public anxiety about Seattle's notorious vice activities had waxed and waned since John Pennell's infamous band of "squaw girls" of the 1860s. By 1909, however, a near hysteria gripped the city as local citizens bemoaned the unsavory operations that threatened to bring down Seattle. Cries radiated from all ranks of society that white slavery, fallen girls, and debauchery endangered the city's future. By 1910, a good number of Seattle citizens had concluded that protecting Seattle womanhood, and the community itself, meant meshing women's unique traits and abilities into the local political fabric.

Prostitution, gambling, and other vice activities in Seattle expanded greatly with the Klondike gold strike in 1897. Heralding itself as the staging point for prospectors and other gold hunters, the city experienced tremendous growth in mining suppliers and outfitters as well as attracting less savory businesses to serve this new clientele. The Lava Bed, as the vice district was commonly called, erupted with activity during the heyday of the gold rush. Saloons, gambling dens, dance halls, and brothels quickly dotted the streets south of Yesler Way. The undisputed king of vice at the turn of the century was John Considine. A teetotaler, the "Boss Sport" as many papers called him, operated the People's Theatre, which presented burlesquelike shows combined with heavy doses of alcohol. The actresses in his shows usually doubled as prostitutes and earned their keep by encouraging male customers to drink, and if required, servicing their sexual desires in the dark private box seats. The unquenchable thirst for such activity following the gold strike helped sustain a prosperous and thriving vice district well into the twentieth century.[58]

The lucrative nature of these business operations significantly shaped Seattle politics for much of the early twentieth century. Politicians aligned themselves with local vice kings and made sure that police winked at illegal activity. In 1900, and again in 1902, citizens elected Mayor Thomas Humes, who oversaw the expansion of vice activity in the tenderloin district. Despite the money the Lava Bed generated, political rivalries produced investigations and exposés by party-connected newspapers that often resulted in brief public outcries against vice. John Considine surfaced at the center of one especially notorious incident when he was accused of murdering the chief of police during a confrontation over Considine's testimony that the chief had accepted bribes from him. For most of the first decade of the century, however, other more pressing political issues, primarily municipal ownership, pushed vice onto the back burner. In 1908, the unsavory activities of the tenderloin once again loomed as a major issue in race for mayor. As discussed earlier, William Moore of the City Party failed in his bid for reelection because he did not, in the eyes of many city residents, do enough to close down the Lava Bed. For the next three years vice dominated politics in Seattle.[59]

Promising to shut down the Lava Bed, newly elected mayor John Miller struggled to please all sides in this matter. Pressed to live up to his promise, Miller set, and then reset, deadlines for closing down what most now called the restricted district. However, Miller's effort to suppress vice backfired, with the "social evil" fanning out beyond the tenderloin. By early 1909, the *Seattle Union Record* noted, under Miller's reign prostitution had spread throughout the city. "The streets of Seattle," the paper declared, "are a good place for decent women to keep off after dark." In a later issue the labor paper argued that these conditions frightened workingwomen who toiled past eight at night. Things had become so bad that the *Union Record* claimed that Seattle had been overrun by "cheap amusements of various kinds, among them being many that are revolting and would not be tolerated in a frontier town." The paper demanded that city officials address this issue and announced organized labor's willingness to join with local clubwomen to confront this problem.[60]

Labor leaders were not the only residents concerned about the closing of the restricted district. City elites feared that failure to control prostitution would tarnish Seattle's image, just at the time that boosters hoped to use the upcoming Alaska-Yukon-Pacific Exposition to polish it. As the opening day of the fair approached, several local political reform clubs demanded that Miller and city officials "make an effort to have our city morally clean" during the exposition. The Rainier Heights Improvement Club, for example, passed a resolution urging an investigation of Miller's failure to close the tenderloin completely. Apparently club members possessed evidence that not only had prostitution spread to residential areas, but that it still operated openly in the restricted district. The Beacon Hill Improvement Club went a step further, demanding the mayor's resignation.[61]

Frustrated by Miller's inability to crack down on vice, residents eagerly prepared for the upcoming 1910 municipal election. The main battle took place within the Republican Party. Hiram Gill, president of the city council and a lawyer with reputed ties to tenderloin interests, challenged board of public works official A. V. Bouillion. Gill favored reviving the restricted district but firmly regulating it. Considering the noteworthy failures of the previous administration, many city residents seemed inclined to let Gill try to solve the crisis. The opposition of the city's clergy and the Seattle Federation of Women's Clubs notwithstanding, Gill outdistanced Bouillion in the Republican primary. Reform forces bolted their party and threw their support behind the Democratic candidate, William Moore. Nevertheless, Gill emerged victorious, and his fellow Republicans swept the entire city council.[62]

Gill quickly fulfilled his promise to establish a special district for prostitution, gambling, and other vice activities. Vice operators apparently read the reopening of the restricted district as a sign that they were now welcomed in Seattle. Located in an area of the city where several streetcar lines passed through to reach the downtown business center, the new tenderloin reportedly expanded both in size and in variety of activity. According to its opponents, visitors to the district found "dance-halls, bagnios, 'crib houses,' opium dens, 'noodle joints' . . . openly advertised in the full glare of electric light." Moreover, they charged that Police Chief C. W. (Wappy) Wappenstein not only condoned this activity, but also profited from it by taking bribes and payoffs from numerous vice lords. Within months of Gill's election, a couple of major vice operators formed the Hillside Improvement Company, which began construction of a large crib house where upward of two hundred prostitutes could sell their services.[63]

The restricted district's rebirth and the initial failure of reform forces prompted a group of city leaders and reformers to organize the Public Welfare League (PWL) in June 1910. Formed to advocate for the "enforcement of all laws and ordinances" and "to secure the suppression of vice," the PWL mobilized residents to work for the closure of the tenderloin. The league first obtained an injunction prohibiting Gill, the city council, and several major vice operators from maintaining and operating businesses for immoral purposes. This legal action had negligible impact. After the city council and Mayor Gill granted a franchise to the Hillside Improvement Company and news leaked that the beneficiary of this agreement was Gideon Tupper, a principal owner of numerous gambling dens and brothels, the PWL began to circulate petitions to recall the mayor. While Seattle residents fought over the future of the city's mayor, voters went to the polls to decide the fate of woman suffrage in Washington.[64]

With the dominant Republican Party cleaved by reforming insurgents and local politics in a state of flux as a result of Gill's vice policies, Seattle suffragists found themselves in an enviable position. Yet for the most part, they directed little specific attention to the problems south of Yesler Way. One likely explanation for this strategy was that woman suffrage proponents had already conditioned city residents to see equal suffrage as a possible solution to the ills that plagued Seattle. The concept of "municipal housekeeping," which by the early twentieth century had emerged as the dominant argument on behalf of woman suffrage, held that women possessed special traits necessary to cleanse urban centers of crime, filth, immorality, and political corruption. Middle-class women exploited the ideology of domesticity to defend their demand for the ballot, arguing that only with the power of the vote could they truly solve society's social and political ailments. Already exposed to these ideas, Seattle residents needed only a powerful stimulus to jolt them to concede to suffragists' pleas. In the decade following the Klondike gold strike, government officials and other national experts on prostitution proclaimed Seattle one of the top white slavery cities in the nation.[65] Residents could not escape posters pasted on walls and windows during this period that highlighted the threat vice posed to their community:

> Danger!! Mothers Beware
> 60,000 Innocent Girls Wanted to
> take the place of 60,000 White Slaves
> who will Die this year in the U.S.
> Will you sacrifice your Daughter?[66]

Already disposed to perceive women as moral saviors and faced with the political and social crisis engendered by the tenderloin, Seattle residents likely needed little persuasion to accept woman suffrage as the best medicine for their ill city.

If prostitution and vice plagued many American cities at this time, why did it so profoundly shape the equal suffrage movement in Seattle? A partial explanation lies with westerners' growing concern for their cities' images. Since the days of the anti-Chinese riots, Seattle leaders diligently protected the city's image for fear of losing out to other Pacific Coast communities in the competition for outside capital. During the early years of the Klondike gold strike, the city marketed its special attributes to capture the lion's share of the Alaska trade. A decade after the gold rush, however, Alaska fever had subsided and city leaders sought both to defend Seattle's good name and redefine its image. They envisioned the 1909 Alaska-Yukon-Pacific Exposition as Seattle's coming-out party that would advertise the city's social, economic, and cultural assets to potential settlers and investors. This well-crafted image, however, was threatened by national pronouncements that the city stood near the top of white slavery sites in the country. Fearful that the latter image might outshine the purpose of the fair and, moreover, that it might only confirm eastern perceptions of the wild and untamed West, Seattle residents were willing to place, albeit temporarily, the city in women's hands.

Although this unique political and ideological environment helps explain the ultimate success of the suffrage amendment in Seattle, it does not fully account for suffrage leaders' reluctance to exploit the explosiveness of vice in their statewide campaign. A more likely explanation was that Seattle's prostitution troubles did not sell as well outside the port city and victory ultimately depended on convincing voters throughout the state. More importantly, state campaign leaders had already honed their strategy and message several years earlier. While suffrage officials included "municipal housekeeping" and other similar arguments in their blueprint for victory, these remained just one part of the overall strategy. Any shift in tactics so late in the campaign threatened to derail the movement's momentum; few state or local suffrage leaders seemed willing to risk their well thought out strategy.

The campaign that eventually secured the ballot for Washington women actually had begun several years earlier. Following the defeat of the 1898 referendum, suffrage leaders spent the next eight years rebuilding their forces and waiting for the right moment to test the waters once again. In November 1906, women throughout the state attended a rather "large and enthusiastic convention" in Seattle. At the meeting, delegates elected Emma Smith DeVoe as president of the Washington Equal Suffrage Association (WESA). An experienced suffrage campaigner, DeVoe worked incessantly to rally suffrage proponents throughout the state. Within a year WESA membership jumped from 262 to 800, topping 1,000 by 1909. In early 1909, DeVoe, with the help of state senator George Cotterill of Seattle, submitted a new suffrage amendment to the legislature, which passed it overwhelmingly.[67]

The success of the 1910 equal suffrage campaign was partly owing to the decision of state leaders not to limit or control the diversity of arguments the numerous suffrage organizations employed. In most cases, the character of these arguments fit historian Aileen Kraditor's analysis of suffrage ideology. Women who favored the extension of the franchise employed two general sets of ideas. Some, like Susan B. Anthony, emphasized women's inherent right to the ballot based on their interpretation of the U.S. Constitution, the Declaration of Independence, and the general rhetoric of the American Revolution. Other women, however, tended to focus on women's perceived differences or unique character traits and how they could utilize these to make society better. Municipal housekeeping arguments carried more weight because they drew upon late nineteenth-century ideas rooted in the private sphere, and thus seemed to fit the sensibilities of both men and women. In the end, both strands of thought—justice and political expediency—often worked side by side in the struggle for the ballot.[68]

In newspapers and magazines, on posters and billboards, and in mass meetings and conventions, Washington suffragists employed both the expediency and inherent right arguments. In a 1901 paper, Dr. Alice M. Smith, for example, defended women's natural right to vote by arguing that since the basic biology of men and women was virtually the same at the prenatal stage, denying political equality based on sex made little sense. The Washington State Grange likewise proclaimed that women were "in all matters of an equality [sic] with men." Mrs. George Smith, president of the Alki Suffrage Club of Seattle, stressed the democratic foundations of American society and ideas of citizenship in her message to voters in 1910. Explaining that women did not seek to destroy government or "usurp men's place in the world," Smith argued that equal suffrage was an "inalienable right." She not only stated that government stemmed from the consent of the governed, but also declared that, as citizens and taxpayers, women deserved the ballot.[69]

Motherhood, children, and the home, however, formed the basis of one of the more powerful arguments Seattle suffragists enlisted in their campaign for the franchise. Industrialization, they argued, had radically transformed American society, and women needed the ballot in order to defend and protect their families. Mary G. O'Meara, associate editor of *Votes for Women*, for example, maintained that granting women the vote would alleviate the public concern regarding race suicide. She suggested that the evils of society produced by industrial capitalism thwarted women's natural instinct to reproduce. Women, she concluded, needed the "power to control the food and clothes, the schools and workshops, the streets and resorts which affect your children." These issues and "all questions concerning the vital interests of the home," the Seattle Suffrage Club boldly declared, "ultimately become political questions." The club, in its list of twenty reasons why voters should support the suffrage amendment, did not fail to remind Seattle residents of the most significant political issue they faced—vice. Women, especially those living in Seattle, required "every means of self-defense, including the ballot. It is not true that men protect women. The 300,000 'white slaves' in this country disprove it."[70]

By emphasizing society's need for women to clean up the industrial city, suffrage proponents often contradicted the inherent rights or justice argument. It was not just different groups or classes of women within the movement that expressed such contradictions; many individual women often did so in the same breath. Elizabeth Baker of nearby Kitsap County, for example, argued that she "wish[ed] to see women vote vecause [*sic*] women are different from men" and that this gave them a special perspective and unique abilities to tackle pressing social and political issues. Yet, at the same time, she contended that men and women were equal both in God's eyes as well as in the eyes of the Founding Fathers. In a public appeal to voters, Mrs. George Smith articulated the whole gamut of arguments on behalf of the ballot. She not only drew directly from the Declaration of Independence and the U.S. Constitution to bolster her claim of equality with men, but then stated that "women are different from men in aspirations, needs and point of view."[71]

Such contradictions no doubt reflected the rapid transformation of gender in the late nineteenth and early twentieth centuries. One cannot underestimate the difficulty of challenging and undermining century-old beliefs. That both men and women had drunk from the cup of domestic ideology made the task of renegotiating gender norms quite daunting. Women's differentness, in fact, had formed the basis of their claim to the private sphere. It had empowered them in many ways, but also further isolated them from the public sphere of politics. Employing the unique abilities of their sex, then, was not a simple rhetorical strategy. While some women may have understood the advantages of the political expediency argument in convincing men to grant women the ballot, others likely found it a less troubling and threatening way to confront the profound changes that equal suffrage implied. In other words, they could hold on to the comfortable past while blazing a new trail in the uncertain world of gender relations.

Not all women, however, may have perceived these apparent contradictions as a problem. For some suffragists, equality in the political arena did not necessarily imply or demand that men and women have the same life experiences. Mrs. George Smith, for example, could have easily looked to the nation's revolutionary leaders to support this belief. Had not the American patriots in their published grievances, like the Stamp Act Resolutions, declared themselves equal to Englishmen born in the mother country, but at the same time announced that their experiences, aspirations, and needs also made them different? Difference, as revolutionary leaders suggested, should not deny people their political rights and equality; in fact, their special or unique conditions of life made it imperative. Mrs. Smith, then, could find comforting refuge in the ideas and rhetoric of America's democratic heritage.

Whatever arguments Smith and other suffragists availed themselves of to defend their right to vote, they simultaneously refashioned the public sphere and redefined the meaning of politics. The process, however, often reflected ambivalence with the uncertain implications their actions might have for the nation's political culture. Women often couched their public engagement as civic service or nonpolitical work because politics was a term pregnant with significant gendered meaning. Politics to many women meant assuming power for one's self-interest. Nevertheless, the nineteenth-century conception of politics—running and serving for office—was slowly giving way to broader ideas of civic improvement and state regulation of public behavior for the common good. By the turn of the century, the City Beautiful efforts to build playgrounds provided women a public role and helped make them "accepted, valued participants in civic affairs." Civic participation, then, gave them a political role and a sense of citizenship in which the vote became the logical conclusion of this process.[72]

Ideological inconsistency actually turned out to be one of the strengths of the movement. When they chose "Unity in Diversity" as the campaign's theme, both Seattle suffragists and state leaders acknowledged that victory depended on convincing a diverse population. Not only did they have to incorporate women of all classes and ethnic groups into the movement, but they also had to tailor their arguments to appeal to a similarly diverse electorate. No single argument or idea could sway all voters to break with tradition and grant women the right to vote. Thus the Seattle Suffrage Club offered not one but a score of reasons to extend the franchise to women. Opponents might successfully combat one particular assertion, but could not deflect such a multifront assault by suffrage forces. Ideological purity, then, held much less importance than tasting the spoils of victory.[73]

Seattle women had to not only articulate the reasons why they deserved the vote, but also deflect or neutralize their opponents' attacks. Few of their adversaries concentrated on the natural rights argument or what women might accomplish with the vote. Instead, they took aim at the negative consequences that accompanied the destruction of separate spheres and traditional Victorian notions of gender. The threat to marriage was a key concern raised by opponents. Critics maintained that extending the franchise to women would destroy marriages and produce more divorces, as women spent less time with their husbands and children and more time in the world of politics. Perhaps the most persistent advocate of this line of thought in Seattle was Edward Clayson, publisher and editor of a small newspaper called the *Patriarch*. For more than a decade, Clayson expounded on what he perceived as the increasing effeminacy of Seattle society in the early twentieth century. He incessantly referred to suffragists as "political amazons," while calling their male supporters "bearded effeminates." "Sex equality" and "divorce," he often declared, went hand in hand and threatened to destroy Seattle society. The pitch of Clayson's attacks escalated in the months prior to the suffrage amendment decision. Women who possessed the vote, he argued, "cannot have a husband; they may have a man with fair physical proportions, but with mental and moral femininity."[74]

Few Seattle suffragists took Clayson's attacks seriously; nevertheless they felt compelled to respond to the charge that equal suffrage threatened marriage. Suffragists, for example, maintained that divorce rates were, in fact, lower in the four states with equal suffrage because women had a say in laws affecting the home and children. Going one step further, a *Votes for Women* editorial blamed men for growing divorce rates. Men, it argued, controlled legislation regarding the marriage contract, including the legal reasons to break it. The paper concluded that when women had a say in determining the nature of the contract, more stable and happy marriages would result.[75]

Though many of the ideas and arguments Seattle and state suffragists championed differed little from similar debates throughout the nation, they did have a particular regional flavor. In the inaugural issue of *Votes for Women,* the editor proudly proclaimed the "Spirit of the West." Freedom, she argued, "has always come out of the West—the West which has always been peopled by those free souls who gladly gave up the luxuries of the East in order to escape its slavery." The editor hoped that the West would grant equal opportunity to all and that this would be "washed back over the East with the returning tides of humanity." This idea that the American West was special or exceptional was pervasive among suffrage leaders.[76] Whether it was true that, according to *Votes for Women,* in the West "things material and spiritual seem to grow faster than they do in the East," many settlers firmly believed they did. Washington suffragists understood the power of this line of thought and made sure to include women in this image of the West. They often paid homage to female pioneers who "helped win the West" and maintained that the present generation was "winning not only the West, but helping to win all the land to freedom, to right and justice." Emma Smith DeVoe declared that the response to women's call for political equality "came from the broad-shouldered, big-brained men of our great Northwest who made good their popular Western phrase 'A square deal for men must be accompanied by a square deal for women.'" Soon after Washington men passed the 1910 suffrage law, one female observer concluded that men had accepted the presence of women in politics partly because western men did not want "to be considered out of date, in this part of the world."[77]

Such regional appeals point to one other way suffrage forces employed the West in the debate over the ballot. Proponents of the equal franchise not only played on the sense of competition between the West and the East but also encouraged an intraregional rivalry. Suffragists outlined the benefits the ballot had produced in the four western states in which women already could vote. *Votes for Women,* for example, claimed that property values in these four states jumped anywhere from 37 percent to 160 percent, while California, lacking woman suffrage, had witnessed less than a 3 percent increase. Moreover, the journal insisted that female migration to these suffrage states increased substantially after women gained the ballot, producing a more balance sex ratio than in nonsuffrage states like Washington.[78] Not so subtly, suffragists also suggested that Washington would remain inferior to these four smaller states. An advertisement in *Votes for Women* declared: "WOMEN VOTE FOR PRESIDENT AND ALL OTHER OFFICERS IN WYOMING, UTAH, IDAHO, AND COLORADO. WHY NOT IN WASHINGTON? ARE THE WOMEN OF THOSE STATES MORE WORTHY OR ARE THE MEN OF THOSE STATES MORE JUST?"[79] Whether appealing to men's pride or to their competitive spirit, suffrage leaders exploited the special feelings that westerners had for their home.

Good ideas alone, Washington suffragists perceptively recognized, would not secure victory. Suffragists had to walk a fine line because some tactics might in fact alienate voters and undermine their efforts. Just like national leaders, suffrage workers in Seattle and the state searched for the best methods that fit the sensibilities of local residents. Suffrage officers' keen insight into the inner workings of local and state politics helps explain their ultimate success in convincing first the legislature and then the voters to support equal suffrage. Rather than draw the attention of their political enemies by picketing the capitol, suffrage leaders undertook a more personal one-on-one campaign to cajole legislators to support the proposed amendment without forcing them to declare their position publicly. Likewise, another strategy encouraged suffragists to send equal franchise petitions to individual legislators rather than delivering them en masse to the state body. The twist, however, was that suffrage leaders personalized the issue by dividing the petitions by district and sending those signatures from each district to their respective representatives. Suffrage officials even called on working-class ethnic women to pressure state legislators. WESA leaders, for example, urged ethnic women to write letters to their local Norwegian or Finnish societies to encourage them to join the movement. In the end, such active and behind-the-scenes campaigning paid off handsomely as both the state house and senate passed the bill.[80]

Seattle's effort to showcase the city by hosting an international exposition offered a public stage from which suffragists could build the necessary momentum for the long crusade. Women had already pressured AYPE officials to fund construction of a woman's building that could help suffragists reach women from all corners of the state.[81] Moreover, DeVoe and other officials invited several national women's organizations to hold their annual conventions at the exposition. Both the National American Woman's Suffrage Association and the National Council of Women journeyed to Seattle in the summer of 1909. The conventions not only sparked a great deal of enthusiasm among women attending the exposition, but also attracted substantial local press coverage, thus further aiding the campaign.[82]

Throughout the summer and fall of 1909, Seattle suffrage leaders continued their outreach to women. While articles in newspapers or traditional campaign literature attracted some female support, suffragists tried more innovative ways to get their message out to women. Mrs. George Smith, for example, hosted a "suffrage tea" in her home; others held card parties or put on plays and balls in order to attract younger women into the movement. The WESA published a special cookbook, entitled *Votes for Women: Good Things to Eat,* which helped bridge the public and private spheres with political messages sprinkled among recipes.[83] Suffrage forces opened up the 1910 campaign with a special "Woman's Day" at the Puyallup Valley Fair located just south of Seattle. Following speeches by DeVoe and Marion Hay, the state's governor, women paraded throughout the fairgrounds on a special suffrage float. Reflecting the intraregional rivalry theme, the suffrage float carried six women, four representing the "free" western states where women already voted, another the state of

Washington, and the last depicting the "Goddess of Liberty" who stood ready to remove the shackles from Washington women.[84]

The innovative and symbolic imagery suffragists displayed at the fair was not the only way they captured the attention of Washington citizens. Residents of Seattle and other areas of the state could not escape the presence of this crusade. Leaders printed appeals on theater programs, adorned the curtains of movie theaters with suffrage messages, hung yellow banners across busy streets, planted a pennant advocating the franchise on the peak of Mount Rainier, and placed streamers bearing the words "Votes for Women" on race horses. Suffrage leaders also borrowed strategies from male-dominated political campaigns. Following the example of Seattle businessmen who used billboards in their successful campaigns, Washington women papered the entire state with large posters and billboards. Despite the variety and rather public nature of these campaign tactics, the editor of *Votes for Women* insisted that it was the "cleanest and most womanly campaign ever waged in the history of freedom for women."[85] Female propriety, then, remained a concern throughout this crusade.

While innovative tactics helped attract women to the movement, suffrage leaders also employed more traditional political methods to swell both WESA's ranks and, perhaps more importantly, garner male support for the amendment. Suffrage leaders, for example, adroitly exploited the power of the press. Virtually every newspaper in the state carried news of the campaign, and WESA's publicity bureau ran suffrage columns and suffrage supplements in many of the state's largest papers. One observer estimated that suffrage activists put out more than one million pieces of literature over the two-year effort. Without a doubt, the most important paper to champion equal suffrage was *Votes for Women*. Published by Mrs. M. T. B. Hanna of Seattle, the monthly periodical—the only suffrage journal on the Pacific coast—filled its pages with articles, speeches, cartoons, and even advertisements that extolled the benefits of the ballot. The paper proved a valuable asset. It not only permitted suffrage officials to shape and disseminate arguments in favor of the ballot, but it also acted as a direct, unobstructed conduit between WESA leaders and the rank and file.[86]

Newspaper articles, special days at local festivals, and billboards might help publicize the merits of equal suffrage, but WESA leaders recognized the victory hinged on political alliances with certain key organizations, in particular, organized labor. DeVoe and other officials spoke at union meetings, taking care to underscore the virtues of the equal franchise to the working class of the state's largest city. They argued that labor should support woman suffrage because millions of workingwomen needed political power to defend their interests. DeVoe also suggested that just as employers could not make suitable laws for workers, neither could men do the same for women. National suffrage leaders likewise courted support from Seattle unions. At the 1909 exposition, Florence Kelly of the National Council of Women spoke to local labor officials about the plight of the working class, while NAWSA president Anna Shaw emphasized the importance of suffrage to both male and female workers.[87]

Receptive to these arguments, the Washington State Federation of Labor officially endorsed the suffrage referendum, and Seattle's Central Labor Council extended its support through numerous articles and editorials published in the weekly labor paper, the *Seattle Union Record*. The paper maintained, for example, that the working class had learned the value of freedom through its struggles and that freedom was what suffragists also desired. Mirroring the "municipal housekeeping" argument, a letter to the editor added that women possessed the necessary qualities to purify politics. The labor daily also published several WESA appeals that claimed that the ballot not only aided working-class women, but also would greatly "strengthen the political power of the common people more than any other class." Labor leaders were also quick to challenge opponents of equal suffrage. Just weeks before the election, the *Union Record* published both a resolution and a poem chastising a New England anti-suffrage organization for sticking its nose where it did not belong after the eastern group published the names of prominent women and men who opposed the upcoming Washington amendment.[88]

This support notwithstanding, suffrage leaders believed face-to-face campaigning was the key to victory. Months before the election, DeVoe ordered followers throughout the state to canvass each precinct to determine support for the referendum. This information allowed leaders to shift precious resources to areas where they faced stiffer resistance. The success of this approach, however, rested entirely on women. Female activists did the precinct-by-precinct canvassing, and the wives, daughters, and sisters of male voters provided the responses. The network of women's clubs significantly aided this effort. In 1907, for example, Seattle women's clubs formed a correspondence network by dividing the various clubs scattered throughout the city into precincts and districts to facilitate a city beautification plan for the upcoming 1909 AYPE. This earlier effort paid off handsomely in the battle for the ballot. Not only did women canvass their neighborhoods in the weeks before the 1910 election, but on the day voters went to the polls, Cora Eaton coordinated a precinct-level picketing campaign. As captain of the Seattle's Third Ward, she sent letters to fellow picketers explaining how best to approach male voters. From precinct canvassing to the use of billboards, suffrage leaders thus demonstrated their clear understanding of the inner workings of state and local politics.[89]

The well-oiled campaign, however, was not without its problems. The suffrage movement's diversity, combined with the fear that women could not let this opportunity slip away, greatly amplified the possibility of conflict. The most important crisis erupted at the 1909 Seattle exposition. At the center of this conflict was May Arkwright Hutton of Spokane. Hutton, a flamboyant and rather wealthy woman, possessed an engaging, though unpolished, personal style that rubbed many women the wrong way. Friendly with DeVoe until 1909, Hutton's behavior during the lobbying of the legislature earlier that year severely strained her relationship with many WESA officials. A few weeks before the national suffrage convention in Seattle, Cora Smith Eaton received a letter from a state senator who stated that Hutton had interfered in the proceedings and perilously risked the suffrage bill's passage.[90]

Hutton's apparent interference during the suffrage bill debate and her "habitual use of profane and abusive language" moved Eaton to challenge Hutton's participation at the state and national suffrage conventions. The WESA treasurer returned Hutton's payment for Spokane's delegation because she believed that Hutton had paid the dues for many new members in order to increase Spokane's power at the convention. Eaton concluded that Hutton's past immorality and the questionable nature of Spokane's membership figures made her ineligible for WESA membership. Days before the state convention a Spokane newspaper reported that Hutton and her insurgents, in response to this action, planned to replace DeVoe as the state president.[91]

The timing of this dispute deeply troubled Washington's suffrage officials. Not only did Hutton's challenge take place at the Seattle exposition, which they had hoped would catapult the campaign forward, but it also forced national suffrage leaders to intervene. At the state convention, Eaton and others challenged the credentials of the Spokane delegation, refusing to give them a vote in the proceedings. Hutton and her followers appealed this decision to the NAWSA executive board. The board let the state's decision stand, but as a punishment it deprived both sides of their voting rights at the national meeting held later that week. When the dust had settled, Hutton's insurgents potentially weakened the movement by breaking from the state suffrage association and forming their own political equality league.[92]

Intervention by NAWSA officials in this dispute between Hutton and the WESA leadership may have aided Washington's suffrage campaign in an unintended way. In addition to denying all Washington suffragists a vote in their convention, NAWSA officials fired DeVoe as a paid organizer for the national organization. In 1906, national leaders began to pay DeVoe as an official organizer because they were impressed by WESA's increased membership. Freed from national interference, DeVoe was able to follow the strategic advice she received from Abigail Duniway. Duniway, the mother of Oregon's suffrage movement, blamed national officials for the failure of an earlier failed suffrage campaign in her home state. National suffrage leaders, she later wrote in her autobiography, disrupted Oregon's crusade because they stepped in and controlled the campaign's resources and message. After the Washington State legislature passed the suffrage bill in 1909, Duniway congratulated DeVoe on her victory and cautioned her to "do your own work and keep out the officers of the Inner Circle of NAWSA who used us as their wet nurse in Oregon." In a letter to Carrie Chapman Catt a few months after the Seattle convention, DeVoe stated that she believed that NAWSA's unstated policy was to not fund or help Washington. She then added that she did not want national speakers because their interference in state matters was "an expensive and egregious blunder." DeVoe stuck to her guns and invited no national lecturers, except Catt, who was unable to come.[93]

Election day in late 1910 was a rainy day in Seattle, but hundreds, if not thousands, of women refused to vacate the wet cold city streets. Young women and "whitehaired grandmothers" stood outside polling booths dripping from rain and enthusiastically passed out handbills reminding voters to support the suffrage amendment. While the weather suggests that this was a typical fall day in Seattle, the tally of votes at day's end would make this day anything but typical for the city's women. When they awoke the next day, Washington residents found that they now lived in the largest state in the union in which women were the political equals of men.[94]

The turnout for the fall election was rather light, for few other pressing or controversial issues appeared on the ballot. A persistent rain and the absence of controversial ballot measures notwithstanding, 64 percent of Washington voters cast their ballot to grant the franchise to the state's 175,000 women. Moreover, every county in Washington, led by King County's 12,052 votes, passed the suffrage amendment. Seattle residents alone cast nearly 20 percent of all ballots in favor of equal suffrage. The city's First Ward, home to the restricted district, was the only ward to oppose the measure. Over night, Seattle became the largest city in the country in which women possessed the ballot.[95]

Several factors help explain this remarkable victory. Washington suffrage leaders soft-pedaled what women would do with the vote and avoided directly mixing the ballot "with politics or with other reforms." Prohibition remained the most dangerous threat to a suffrage victory. DeVoe and other officials walked a narrow tightrope by retaining the support of the WCTU and other prohibition groups, yet without turning the election into a referendum on alcohol. Looking south to Oregon, they saw how anti-alcohol forces linked the ballot with prohibition, resulting in residents' rejection of woman suffrage in 1906 and 1908. One Aberdeen, Washington, suffrage leader confirmed the value of this strategy in a letter to DeVoe, explaining that her local WCTU was a powerful force behind the suffrage campaign, but that the best chance for victory was to "stand for that one idea alone." Even May Awkright Hutton seemed to accept this strategy as she urged temperance advocates to "throw in a word for suffrage" when speaking on behalf of the local option plan. She, and other leaders, however, rarely, if at all, called on suffragists to speak in favor of prohibition.[96]

Nevertheless, the emerging sociopolitical movement we call progressivism no doubt aided their success. Many voters in Seattle connected the franchise for women with political and social reform. In the months leading up to the election, local politics were in turmoil. The election of Hiram Gill in the previous spring, for example, triggered a reform-minded insurgency within the Republican Party. Suffrage leaders seemed to benefit from this political crisis and recognized that if they could avoid stirring up the hornet's nest of prohibition, they could indeed achieve victory. While suffrage clubs may have emphasized cleaning up the city, they rarely addressed specific concerns like prohibition or prostitution. WESA officials, for example, steered clear of making concrete "predictions as to what the women would do with the vote when once secured." In Seattle, suffrage leaders offered only vague proclamations about how they could improve the city, but avoided specifically or directly singling out either Mayor Gill or the growing vice crisis on the shores of Puget Sound.[97]

The strategy of DeVoe and suffrage forces notwithstanding, woman suffrage was inextricably linked to the growing tide of progressivism in the American West. *Votes for Women,* for example, asserted that by extending the franchise to one-half of Washington's population, the "wealth and progressiveness" of the state would increase. Citizens of Seattle and other western equal suffrage states thus envisioned "votes for women" as not simply an aspect of the region's political culture, but as an effective political instrument, like the recall, initiative, or direct primary, in achieving other goals.[98]

By the end of 1910, Seattle voters had provided reformers important tools of reform—woman suffrage and the recall. Over the next few years these tools would significantly reshape the landscape of Progressive Era Seattle. Labor was one particular group that both contributed to and benefited from this growing reform spirit. In the first issue following the November election, *Votes for Women* specifically cited women's indebtedness to labor unions, the state federation of labor, and even local Socialists. Labor leaders, in turn, expressed their hope that woman suffrage would aid their struggles, since voters repudiated the Union Labor Party in that same election. The *Union Record* anticipated that "by giving the ballot to the other sex that they will prove better 'strikers at the ballot box' than we were." Voting women, labor officials confessed, might actually hold the future of Seattle's working class in their hands. "Cut the political deck," the *Union Record* concluded, "the kings and knaves have had their try, its [*sic*] the queens' turn now, and the new shuffle should result in either reforming or disfranchising the knaves." The prospects for a better future, the paper observed, rested on the willingness of the city's working class to work with the "queens" and "center [their] efforts on the rights of the people to make their own laws, through the initiative." The "queens," as the next chapter will illustrate, did indeed exploit their newfound political party and significantly transformed the social and political landscape of Seattle.[99]

CHAPTER 4

Chiffon Politics in Progressive-Era Seattle

In 1911, Seattle captured a great deal of national attention for its rather unique political scene. Readers from New York to Los Angeles not only read about Washington's successful suffrage campaign in local papers and national magazines, but also learned how Seattle women exploited this newfound power to remove the city's mayor from office. This triumph soon sparked a tidal wave of suffrage victories in the West that eventually ended with the passage of the Nineteenth Amendment in 1920. For Seattle residents, including many of the more passionate suffragists, the exact meaning of this victory was not so clear. Questions quickly arose. After the excitement of their victory would women seize this opportunity? What would they do with this new power the vote offered them? With the political glue of suffrage eliminated, could Seattle women sustain the energy of that movement and avoid fracturing into numerous competing interest groups? In short, would voting women truly make a difference? The answers to these questions would define progressivism and Seattle politics for years to come.

Scholars have written extensively on the suffrage movement's ideas and methods, but the period after suffrage has been subjected to much less historical scrutiny. The few studies that have been undertaken largely focus at the national level following the passage of the Nineteenth Amendment in 1920. In general, most scholars have concluded that equal suffrage had little, if any, lasting impact on the course of American politics. One problem with this conclusion is that it is based on the assumption that women would vote as a bloc. Students of American politics in the 1920s failed to discover any clear evidence of a distinct woman's vote, and thus determined that women simply voted according to their own class, race, ethnic, and cultural sensibilities. Many scholars who have explored female voting practices seemed to have held women to a different standard than male voters, whose voting behavior for more than a century reflected class, race, and other social factors. No doubt a partial explanation for this is that scholars, as well as contemporary observers, accepted one of the primary arguments suffragists employed in the struggle for the ballot. Most suffrage leaders argued that women would significantly transform politics if granted the vote, and it seems that when this change was not immediately evident, observers concluded that equal suffrage was a failure.[1]

Behind this flawed interpretation of woman suffrage was the rather narrow definition of politics adopted by many earlier scholars. Equating politics with electoral results masked the significant political activity undertaken by women following suffrage victories. Women had engaged in a great deal of civic and public business prior to gaining the ballot. By raising issues, debating them, and lobbying for solutions, women had clearly shaped local and state politics.[2] After suffrage, most women continued the same behavior; voting was simply another means but not the sole indicator of political activity. On the surface, then, it may have appeared to many observers that women's political behavior had not changed.[3] Yet, as this chapter will illustrate, Seattle women engaged in a range of political activity, from organizing campaign committees and lobbying to forging cross-class alliances, that profoundly shaped the look and feel of progressivism along the Puget Sound. Several important factors informed female political behavior in the 1910s, producing a very different experience for Seattle women than for those who gained the ballot in 1920. The timing of Washington's suffrage victory at the height of the Progressive Era was an important factor. However, the existence of a lightning rod issue like prostitution, the belief that suffrage victories elsewhere hinged on Seattle women's behavior, the early effort to educate and politicize women, and important cross-class alliances also contributed to an active and engaged female citizenry.

On Seattle streets in late 1910, suffragists celebrated their great victory and looked forward with much anticipation to the tasks before them. The revitalization and cleanup of the city's tenderloin district was at the top of the list. Prior to the fall election, suffrage leaders stood on the sidelines in the escalating debate over Mayor Gill's handling of the tenderloin so as not to put at risk the campaign for the franchise. Within days of winning the vote, Seattle women immediately found themselves at the center of the Public Welfare League (PWL) crusade to recall the city's mayor. Free to speak and act on the question of the city's moral climate—without fear that it might provoke a backlash and threaten the passage of the suffrage amendment—Seattle women took their first step as full citizens by signing recall petitions and registering to vote in the 1911 city election. In early December the PWL dropped off a bundle of petitions that officially placed Gill's recall on the spring ballot.[4]

The PWL charged Gill with supporting a wide-open vice policy in the restricted district. To this, Gill, unapologetically, pleaded guilty. This was not the first time the tenderloin had generated such political attention. Just six months before the PWL petition drive, Gill captured the mayor's office running on a platform that countenanced vice, but promised to keep it corralled in the area below Yesler Way. With the addition of tens of thousands of newly enfranchised voters, reformers believed that they could now clean up Seattle and transform it into the city they envisioned. The *Western Woman Voter,* a new magazine created to educate and inform women voters, claimed that a restricted district actually attracted more "undesirables" because they were guaranteed protection in that part of town. Furthermore, the editor wondered whether protecting vice because of its financial benefit to the city's economy was worth the exploitation of young girls and ruin of young men. The eyes of the nation, the magazine reminded readers, were fixed on Seattle, and the decision about Gill and his policy would greatly shape the city's reputation for years to come.[5]

Rather than resting on their laurels, Seattle's enfranchised women immediately formed a women's campaign committee for Gill's opponent, George Dilling. Dilling was a member of the Public Welfare League and, according to *Votes for Women*, represented the "typical embodiment of our awakening public conscience now characteristic of American municipal politics." In addition to being "young, clean, vigorous, [and] energetic," he possessed a strong record against gambling and other vice activities. Dilling's Woman's Campaign Committee, however, operated separately from his general campaign organization. Committee leaders claimed that their political meeting was the "first of its kind ever held on the Pacific Coast" and the largest gathering of women ever held in Seattle. In an open letter to Seattle women inviting them to attend a mass meeting at the Opera House, Mrs. Thomas F. Murphine, chair of the executive committee, urged local women to exhort their friends to show up and "rally for the protection of their homes under the banner of civic decency." Heeding this call, throngs of women gathered at the Opera House and hundreds of others spilled into the street as the hall burst at the seams.[6]

The enthusiasm evident at the Opera House meeting was apparently quite infectious, for thousands of Seattle women registered to vote for the upcoming recall election. The *Western Woman Voter* predicted that women would constitute more than 30 percent of those voters who went to the polls in February. Observers also noted that workingwomen and salesgirls appeared eager to register because "they knew from their own personal ordeals, where were the largest recruiting-fields for the restricted district." The opposition, however, also recognized the importance of female voters in this election. Reportedly, Gill's supporters attempted to register prostitutes by the carloads and even resorted to bringing "dissolute women" from Tacoma and Portland to counter the waves of pro-Dilling women. After perusing the registration books, the *Western Woman Voter* confidently dismissed this attempt, stating that its investigations indicated few women of the underworld had registered to vote.[7]

While the opportunity to reshape and clean up local politics drew many women to the polls, female activists clearly understood that this election represented more than simply deciding Seattle's future. The election was a key political test for women, and their actions would go far in shaping attitudes about equal suffrage within Washington as well as throughout the nation. A popular local newspaper, for example, more than once argued that "the burden of proof rests upon the women." The *Town Crier* bluntly declared that Seattle women had to prove that equal suffrage was deserved to discredit critics who maintained that women really did not desire political equality. Recognizing the long-term implications of this first test, women leaders urged female voters to avoid the political traps and pitfalls that had plagued men. *Votes for Women* editors implored them not to be hoodwinked by unsavory political tactics, and instead, "exert all the power and influence they can command by their personal work and by their votes." Independence, the *Western Woman Voter* proclaimed, was the source of real power. Follow this advice, its editors concluded, and Seattle women will hold "the balance of political power."[8]

The importance of female voters was evident in the numerous appeals to women made during the campaign. Dilling's supporters, for example, advised local women to act as both good mothers and good citizens by recalling the mayor. Gill, however, refused to concede the female vote, and, on the eve of the election, the *Seattle Times* printed a half-page picture of Gill and his family. Below the picture the caption stated that a vote against Gill would disgrace his wife and stigmatize his two young boys for life. Despite such pleas, Seattle citizens recalled their mayor and elected George Dilling to replace him. While Dilling outpaced Gill by over six thousand votes, Gill did capture the support of five wards, mostly located in the older downtown district. Dilling swept the outlying wards inhabited by the city's middle class and more skilled workers. Helped by more than twenty thousand Seattle women, representing nearly one-third of the total vote, the *New Citizen* declared the election a "Women's Victory."[9]

Gill's recall was a woman's victory in more ways than one. Not only did Seattle women move the city a step closer to the community they envisioned, but they also passed their first political test with flying colors. Newspapers from Salem, Oregon, to New York City attributed Gill's recall to the turnout by Seattle women. *McClure's Magazine* declared that the recall election "must be regarded as a triumph for woman's suffrage." Even Gill admitted a few years later that women were largely responsible for his defeat. For many Seattle residents, the recall election also signaled a change in their city's reputation; observers later claimed that more than a thousand prostitutes and other unsavory women had left the city within a year. No longer the white slavery capital of the United States, Seattle had been transformed from "one of the most immoral cities on the continent" to one of the cleanest.[10]

Despite boasts that Gill's defeat meant the end of vice, the unsavory activities below Yesler Way continued to haunt Seattle for the next few years. Nevertheless, Seattle women had clearly demonstrated that they could be a potent force in local politics. Coming on the heels of the suffrage victory, Gill's recall aroused women voters and helped continue the momentum of the suffrage campaign. Female activists argued that because of Seattle's fortunate political circumstances, women could immediately "feel their power and will henceforth be ardent suffragists." Local progressive activist Minnie Frazier, for example, declared that the "suffragette likes her 'new broom' so well she is anxious to help keep the city clean." The *New Citizen* cautioned politicians that the political winds had shifted. Club meetings, the women's magazine averred, were no longer the "gossipy affairs they used to be." Instead, clubwomen discussed and debated public issues and, in doing so, refigured local politics. While some politicians might have ignored such bold assertions, Hiram Gill admitted a few years later that a "great many officials can't do some things that they could do before women had the vote—morally, and in a great many other respects." Seattle women not only attended to the city's moral climate, they also brought a gendered vision to what Gilled called the "other respects."[11]

The recall of Mayor Hiram Gill, however, did not eliminate corruption or prostitution from public discourse. Less than one week after the recall, the city's prosecuting attorney, John Murphy, convened a grand jury to investigate Gill's connection to the flourishing vice activity. After a week of questioning owners of gambling halls and local brothels, the grand jury returned an indictment against former police chief C. W. Wappenstein. Wappy, as he was more commonly known, had been hired by Mayor Gill to oversee the restricted district. Walking the streets in his pinstriped suits and derby, Wappy learned the name of every prostitute and gambling den owner. Apparently, his regulation of the district went as far as the imposition of a ten-dollar-a-month "fee" on local harlots, which he deposited in his own pocket. Following the grand jury's investigation, Wappy was arrested and several months later convicted. Gill, however, escaped prosecution, as the grand jury found insufficient evidence that he had committed any crimes.[12]

The release of the grand jury report sparked a public uproar, prompting Mayor Dilling to form a "purity squad." The purity squad roamed the streets of the tenderloin arresting prostitutes, inspecting cafes and hotels for illegal activity, and forcing saloons to close on time. By the end of the year, the squad had reportedly arrested more than 1,200 women, including 119 teenage girls. The Seattle Municipal League confirmed that vice activity had decreased by the fall of 1911, though it admitted that "clandestine" prostitution still existed and was nearly impossible to eliminate. A report to Chief of Police Claude Bannick, for example, indicated that the Washington Annex Hotel, the Log Cabin Saloon, and the Quong Wah Company represented just a few of the establishments where vice still thrived.[13]

The moral crusade that began with Gill's election in 1910 might have withered away had it not been for the former mayor's decision to reclaim his office in 1912. "Gillism" became the cry of those who opposed his campaign. Mayor Dilling apparently had tired of office and refused to run for reelection. The nonpartisan primary election thus pitted Gill against state senator George Cotterill, a Socialist by the name of Hulet Wells, and the businessmen's candidate, County Assessor Thomas Parrish. Gill came away from the primary with a plurality of the vote, as Cotterill and Parrish split the reform vote. As the 1912 municipal election neared, Cotterill, who had outdistanced Parrish, publicly attacked Gill's record and reputation. Supporters, for example, published a multipage exposé of the restricted district during Gill's reign. The pamphlet included numerous excerpts from the 1911 grand jury report as well as interviews with saloon owners and crib house operators. The report also reminded readers of the infamous 500-room crib house that had been under construction when Gill was recalled.[14]

Seattle's women's organizations again mobilized against Gill's reelection, and voter registration surged in the outer residential wards where female voters were heavily concentrated. The Seattle General Federation of Women's Clubs and the Mothers' Congress, for example, printed a short circular with pictures of the notorious huge crib house, which claimed that if Gill won he would reopen the establishment. The *Western Woman Voter* likewise questioned the reported effectiveness of the former mayor's restricted district policy. The magazine stated that most prostitutes not only did business in that district, but lived in uptown hotels or in residential neighborhoods, including two parlor houses located less than a hundred feet from the downtown Seattle Theatre. As they had done just a year before, Seattle female activists called on citizens, especially women, to again defeat Gill and protect their daughters from white slavers and their sons from immorality.[15]

Seattle women, however, added a new twist to their attack on the city's moral climate. While in no way excusing Gill's policy, some women also challenged the double standard of morality that failed to place sufficient blame on men for their role in these activities. A *Western Woman's Outlook* editorial, for example, claimed that society tended to tolerate sexual wrongdoings by men, but inflicted women with "inhuman punishments for doing the same offense." Society, it argued, looked on the fallen woman "as a wasted soul and seeks to forget." An anti-Gill pamphlet likewise questioned the discriminatory health laws that segregated prostitutes for sanitary reasons, but did not do the same to their male clients. "Sex," the pamphlet stated, "may qualify morality but it does not qualify the laws of contagious diseases." Never losing sight of their goal to defeat Gill, female activists nevertheless exploited the public debate on morality. Standards of gender must be changed, the *Western Woman's Outlook* declared, but men "should elevate their moral ideas and practices to the plane of women" rather than women drop to the level of men.[16]

The city's economy further complicated the 1912 public debate about Gillism. Early on, the battle over the restricted district was intertwined with concern about the city's economic vitality, as Gill and his supporters claimed that Seattle benefited from vice. Even the *Western Woman's Outlook* admitted that the economic downturn that punished the Pacific Coast in late 1911 helped explain Gill's impressive performance in the primary. His opponents, however, rejected this argument. Even if the city profited from immoral conditions, another women's magazine argued, Seattle should not "sell itself out to vice for "prosperity." A wide-open city, it maintained, actually discouraged investors and new businesses from settling in Seattle. As one pamphlet succinctly put it: "WHICH SHALL IT BE: Cotterill, Decency and Prosperity or Gillism and Disgrace." Recognizing that city politics was complex, female activists did not simply dwell on the morality issue but attacked head-on Gill's economic argument. In short, they did not see decency and prosperity as mutually exclusive. By convincing others of this fact, Seattle women could help destroy the common belief that they should restrict their political interests to issues of the family and home. In other words, female activists could open the door of public debate widely and thus force a renegotiation of gender politics.[17]

Gill's 1912 campaign once again thrust Seattle women into the limelight. Local women's magazines urged their sisters to register to vote, declaring that they had a "moral duty" to go to the polls. Political activity, one magazine explained, was like keeping house in that it was an ongoing task that one could not ignore. The *Western Woman's Outlook* suggested that turning out at the polls was imperative because women held the balance of political power. An impressive showing in Gill's recall notwithstanding, many observers viewed the 1912 election as another referendum on equal suffrage. An anti-Gill pamphlet, for example, declared that the "eyes of the world will be upon the Women of Seattle next Tuesday." "The Ballot in the hand of women," it continued, "is on trial." Once again women had to prove themselves worthy of suffrage. The *Outlook* further cautioned that more was at risk than the political reputation of Seattle's female population. With California's 1911 equal suffrage victory coming on the heels of Washington's, Susan Marshall has argued, antisuffrage organizations quickly mobilized to thwart any extension of the ballot. Suffrage crusades in other states, the magazine warned, hinged on this "test of 'chiffon politics.'"[18]

In an extremely close election won by Cotterill, Gill kept his hold on the downtown lower-class immigrant neighborhoods, while Cotterill captured the middle-class and skilled-worker wards. The significance of the mayor's race did not escape outside observers. According to the *Literary Digest,* the election's outcome confirmed women's benefit to American politics. Papers throughout the country commented positively on their performance and how women's actions discredited suffrage opponents' claims. Once might have been a fluke, but now twice in less than a year female voters had proven themselves. According to the *New York Evening Post,* this "ought to put an end to the worn-out contention of the antisuffragists that to inject women into the electorate is to add a hysterical element, or one controlled by sentiment." Seattle women's actions, then, shaped attitudes nationwide regarding whether women should possess the ballot. Suffragists from Oregon to New York now had more than theory and wishful predictions as weapons in their struggle to convince the American public that women were worthy of the vote. Gill's defeat confirmed women's political capabilities.[19]

Seattle's highly charged elections, on the heels of the 1910 suffrage victory, no doubt hastened the politicization of the city's female population. Voting and democratic participation in public affairs were not inbred characteristics. In her study of women's political activity following the passage of the Susan B. Anthony amendment in 1920, Kristi Anderson has argued that partisanship and political participation was a learned response. Studies of immigrant political conduct, she notes, indicated that newly enfranchised voters acquired the ideas and tools of politics over a period of time. Women's experience, however, differed from the male immigrant or unpropertied nineteenth-century male who gained the vote. Women, Anderson contends, "were not merely *un*practiced at voting or *un*socialized," but rather "had grown up learning that women were *by nature unsuited* to politics, that by definition politics was a male concern" (author's emphasis). Women thus had to not only renegotiate gender boundaries, but also learn new habits.[20]

Seattle women confronted such circumstances nearly a full decade prior to the new voters Anderson studied. Recognizing this situation, within months of their victory suffragists formed several political organizations to educate women and assist them in this transition to their new citizenship. In January 1911, for example, women from Seattle and the rest of Washington met in Tacoma with delegates from the four other western suffrage states to found the National Council of Women Voters. Delegates chose Washington suffrage leader Emma Smith DeVoe as their first president and then declared that the purpose of the National Council was to "educate women voters in the exercise of their citizenship" as well as to work toward securing legislation that reflected the interests of all citizens. Locally, *Votes for Women* officers organized the Women's Information Bureau to educate women, providing space in the magazine's office for Seattle women to visit and learn about the recall, candidates for election, and major political issues facing the city and the state. In less than two months, then, suffragists fashioned several groups to facilitate Seattle women in their transition to full citizenship.[21]

Over the next several years Seattle activists not only educated female voters, but also formed numerous political organizations to expand their influence from Seattle's city hall to the state capitol. Adele Fielde, a recent migrant to Puget Sound, embodied the untiring efforts of many politically active women to expand Seattle women's participation in politics. Immediately following the 1910 election, she organized the Civic Forum that brought together women and men to discuss pressing issues. Ensuring that men did not dominate the new organization, Fielde declared that the board of trustees of the Civic Forum would be composed of both sexes. While the Civic Forum remained largely an educational club, Fielde also formed another group to engage more directly in legislative matters. The Washington Women's Legislative Committee (WWLC), however, was limited to women. The WWLC not only gathered information on important legislative concerns, but also organized women throughout the state to lobby for and against certain measures. Fielde, like most other female leaders, however, couched her rhetoric in rather familiar terms. The WWLC, on the surface, seemed to limits its objective to "legislation that affects home, children, food," or, in other words, traditional female concerns. Fielde, however, refused to circumscribe women's political role so narrowly, and thus also set within its aims any issue affecting the "general interest of the people of this State" or the people's "domestic or political welfare." Such broad construction permitted the WWLC to support passage of more traditional women's legislation, such as prohibition and antiprostitution statutes, and at the same time press for less gender-specific issues, such as state initiative and referendum bills.[22]

New civic organizations met the needs of the more politically minded women in Seattle, but their success was greatly enhanced by several women's magazines that publicized and disseminated their ideas and pursuits to the city's female citizenry. *Votes for Women* may have been the first magazine published by, and for, women, but during the next few years new magazines appeared to compete with it. While it is often said that imitation is the sincerest form of flattery, Mrs. M. T. B. Hanna, publisher of the *Votes for Women* did not believe this so. One month after winning the vote, Adella Parker and a few other women began publishing *Western Woman Voter*, which they intended "to be a journal of information for women voters of the West." The new magazine not only planned to discuss issues related to the home and national suffrage efforts, but it also intended to address politics, legislation, and legal rights of women. Hanna might have agreed with the *Western Woman Voter*'s objectives, but she chafed at the competition and what she viewed as backstabbing. Parker, editor of the new magazine, formerly edited Hanna's *Votes for Women* before having a falling out with her boss over Hanna's unwillingness to follow the direction of Emma Smith DeVoe and the Washington Equal Suffrage Association. Reflecting a similar shift from suffrage to educating the new voters, Hanna's *Votes for Women* soon changed its name to the *New Citizen*.[23]

Despite the name change, the *New Citizen* quietly disappeared within a year. The *Western Woman Voter*, however, almost immediately faced new competition from the *Western Woman's Outlook*. "Owned, edited, managed, and controlled by women," this latest magazine began publishing in December 1911, and within a year the Washington State Federation of Women's Clubs adopted it as its official mouthpiece. Affiliation with the club movement meant that this new magazine had both a broader readership and range of interests. Besides publicizing club activities, the *Outlook* took aim at political and social concerns affecting Seattle and the Pacific Northwest. Heralded by one reader as "the greatest move toward human progress," the weekly *Outlook* quickly became the dominant women's magazine in Seattle and was published until 1914.[24]

The disappearance of the *Western Woman's Outlook* left Seattle women without the powerful and influential voice that the magazines had provided them. In 1916, the *Legislative Federationist* attempted to fill this void; its scope, however, was much narrower than the *Outlook*. The new periodical attempted to coordinate the various women's organizations in Seattle and the rest of the state in order to lobby for "enactment and enforcement of law for the benefit of the home and child." As the official organ of the King County Legislative Federation, the paper also reflected the seemingly contradictory attitudes of female activists after suffrage. The *Legislative Federationist*, as well as most of the other women's magazines and groups, often couched its views in rather traditional terms that appeared to limit women's political activity to traditional female issues, like the home and children. Yet, at the same time it championed clear feminist ideas, ranging from encouraging women to keep their own names in marriage to reclaiming their rightful role in governing society, which they believed men had wrongly usurped. This contradiction is not difficult to understand if one considers the tremendously rapid pace of social and political change in the early twentieth century. Politics and the public sphere had been transformed to such a great extent that an increasing number of women had come to believe that nothing in society was not related to the home and family. As Sophie Clark, president of the Woman's Legislative Council of Washington, succinctly put it, "the state is simply the larger family." For Seattle women, however, this change was even more dizzying. Standing at the vanguard of this new era, references to traditional notions of gender likely helped eased them through this transitional period. While the actions of female activists accelerated the pace and extent of social change, their rhetoric provided a sense of reassurance that they and the world around them were not spiraling out of control.[25]

While Seattle's assault on white slavery and gambling might have generated most of the headlines, the breadth of political activity undertaken by female voters in the first few years after suffrage was quite impressive. Just months after Mayor Gill's recall, the *Seattle Union Record* observed that women's organizations were "taking a deep interest in the affairs of the city."[26] These affairs included many of the more traditional concerns that captivated women, such as playgrounds, juvenile courts, and reform schools, as well as economic and political issues once left to men. Seattle women had always encouraged city leaders to not forget schools and urban amenities, but with the ballot they intensified their efforts and urged women to use their power to accomplish good. The Seattle Federation of Women's Clubs, for example, reminded its members that improving the community meant more playgrounds and parks and better schools. Clubwomen endorsed free textbooks, free kindergartens, and the expansion of domestic science and manual training in the schools. Bettering the schools, according to the *Western Woman's Outlook*, also meant ending the segregation of the sexes, which it believed was "reactionary," and ending persistent underfunding of educational resources for women at the state university.[27]

Expanding women's role in society led many Seattle women to demand changes to the legal system and the local government as well. The *Outlook*, for example, requested the appointment of a woman to the State Board of Control, which oversaw the outfitting and supply of prisons. Likewise, the paper suggested that the city needed a woman justice and endorsed former deputy prosecuting attorney Miss Reah M. Whitehead for this position.

The debilitating discrimination inherent in the legal system did not escape the attention of Seattle women either. Female activists called on state officials to clarify a law that if a person was killed by wrongful act of another that "his heirs" could sue for damages; some judges had construed "his" not to include women and had denied heirs of widows standing in court. When reformers promoted changing Seattle's charter to embody the commission form of government, some clubwomen joined organized labor in opposition. The *Outlook* argued that the proposed reform was "retrogressive. It is the antithesis of democracy." In particular, the paper maintained that it concentrated authority in too few hands. Finally, the direct democracy movement received much support because women believed that the initiative and referendum continued the expansion of democracy that equal suffrage had began.[28]

The exact role local government should occupy was one of the most debated issues in Progressive Era Seattle. Clubwomen weighed in on numerous discussions about municipal ownership, direct legislation, and the single tax. Like their union friends, middle-class women strongly supported public ownership of key urban services, including water, electric, and streetcars. One woman's newspaper proclaimed that the "people of Seattle have advanced sufficiently in civic development to realize that it is much greater economy to own and conduct their own public-service facilities than to depend on private corporations."[29] Both the *New Citizen* and the *Western Woman Voter* urged their readers to support an $800,000 bond proposition for a municipal streetcar line in 1911. When the Seattle City Council apparently refused to appropriate $2 million for a municipally owned telephone system that voters approved, the *Outlook* scolded city leaders for failing to fulfill their duties.[30]

Clubwomen also challenged many business leaders who publicly questioned the Seattle Port Commission's effectiveness. The Washington Women's Legislative Committee, for instance, commended port commissioners for improving Seattle's shipping facilities in comparison to other Pacific coast ports. The *Western Woman Voter* not only supported public ownership of the city's port, but also indirectly linked its future success to a 1912 single tax proposal. Magazine editors strongly endorsed the Erickson single tax amendment because it promised to promote growth by lowering the cost of land and businesses by exempting improvements on property from taxation. The upcoming opening of the Panama Canal, editors suggested, promised significant business for the port, and Seattle would greatly benefit if it made the city attractive to new settlers. Not all club-women, however, apparently shared the *Western Woman's Voter*'s enthusiasm for the single tax, with the *Outlook*, for example, questioning whether it was fair and just to landowners.[31]

Disagreements about the efficacy of the single tax aside, female activists all agreed that they should keep a careful eye on the city's finances, including urging local officials to undertake a general financial audit and warning voters about "exhausting our bonding power."[32] Such concerns prompted the *Western Woman's Outlook* to join the SCLC in opposition to the 1912 Bogue Plan, a multimillion dollar proposal to redesign the entire city. Unlike organized labor, which objected to the inflexibility of the Bogue Plan, the *Outlook* believed that Seattle could not afford the massive project because it was perilously close to its legal credit limit. Editors of the *Western Woman Voter* agreed and counseled voters to consider this when voting on bonds for parks and a tuberculosis hospital. Whatever the issue or reform women encountered in the years following the suffrage victory, Seattle's new voters actively engaged the political process and their civic responsibilities.[33]

Impressive political activity notwithstanding, Seattle women still confronted the question of their proper place in politics. Few issues of the *Western Woman's Outlook* failed to respond to questions or comments about how women should use the vote or to what level or extent they should involve themselves in politics. These debates reflected the diversity of Seattle women as well as the trepidation many felt about their new power. For example, in an article in the *Outlook*, Mrs. S. B. Hassell maintained that a woman's interest extended beyond the four walls of her domicile to the greater community. She and many other female activists still held to the belief that women had to vote for "a morally clean man" and city. Even when urging women to consider larger economic and political issues, Mrs. John Trumbull of the Washington Women's Legislative Committee suggested that by doing so they would fulfill their role as "the universal mother."[34]

Renegotiating gendered political boundaries was not a one-way process. Women not only had to reconcile their own personal beliefs and anxieties, but also brave criticism from both men and women. During the 1912 presidential campaign, for example, some men still expressed discomfort with women who publicly "address their fellow citizens on their public privileges and responsibilities." When a Seattle women's club passed a resolution supporting Mayor George Cotterill and his purity squad, the *Seattle Times* condemned it for "puttering in politics" and suggested that women steer clear of affairs that were "foreign to the objects of the Woman's Club." Challenging the *Times*'s basic assumption, the *Outlook* chose to define for itself what was political and what was civic. The magazine announced that the resolution was well within the club's purview because it was "a civic matter and not all political."[35]

Equal suffrage opponents also employed old stereotypes to ridicule politically active women. The *Outlook,* for instance, printed a column on a California decision to eliminate a law that made it mandatory that people registering to vote give their age. The male columnist sarcastically suggested that this law had kept many women from voting because they feared announcing their age. Voting women even discovered that some of their male friends harbored reservations about their political behavior. William X. Young wrote to one Seattle women's periodical that he believed that equal suffrage would not "unsex women" or retract from their womanliness. Yet, he then concluded that women would have little impact on grand politics but might accomplish a great deal in preserving the city's moral climate.[36]

Politically active women faced resistance not only from their male counterparts but also from other women. While Seattle's female voters organized political groups and cast ballots, the National Association Opposed to Woman's Suffrage urged them and those who still fought for equal citizenship to remain in their proper sphere. Editors of the *Outlook* dismissed Mrs. Arthur M. Dodge and other leaders of this movement for lacking the vision of those who lived "in the atmosphere of the great broad West." Seattle's women's magazines largely ignored antisuffragists' appeals and instead complained about those women who still failed to vote or held onto antiquated views of politics. Elsie Cox Wilcox, for example, chastised those women who spent more time on unnecessary housework and social functions than studying the issues. The president of the State Federation of Women's Clubs likewise observed that after a year of equal suffrage women had increased their work in civic betterment, but "were not very strong on 'Woman's Rights.'" Other female leaders urged their followers to reject old ideas about politics. "Please do not call legislation politics," wrote one clubwoman, "and in the old reserve of the eternal woman, say that you are not interested." As president of the Woman's Legislative Council of Washington, Sophie Clark maintained that her organization helped women move beyond these outdated ideas. The Legislative Council, Clark declared, was "one body in which politics shall no longer be taboo." Renegotiating gendered political boundaries, then, was much more complex than simply casting a ballot.[37]

When it came to casting ballots, Seattle's female leaders implored women to make a difference and avoid partisan politics. Suffragists had argued that women would revolutionize politics because they stood outside its partisan traditions. Following the 1910 suffrage victory, women activists hailed the advantages of independence and nonpartisanship in the electoral process. In a letter to the *Outlook,* for example, Margaret B. Platt urged women to vote independently and not let some party control their vote. Doing so, she concluded, would be women's best weapon. The *New Citizen* went a step further, stating that women were only "half enfranchised" if they voted as their minister instructed them. Local women's magazines also seemed to relish the frustration of party leaders who could not predict or apparently influence female voting habits. Yet when it came to certain issues, especially equal suffrage, editors encouraged their women to punish political parties for their deeds. In response to the failure of both the Republican and Democratic parties to support a national suffrage amendment in 1912, the *Outlook,* in an angry editorial, urged western women to "play politics, to register your rebuke, to cast your protest, against political parties that demean and ignore your sex, and yet seek your votes to further their success." Considering the two major parties' public stance on suffrage, consorting with them might have been difficult for many women to stomach.[38]

Some women's organizations, however, tried to avoid partisan politics by refusing to endorse any party or candidate. For more than a decade the Washington State Federation of Women's Clubs included in its constitution a policy that prohibited its member organizations from taking part in anything political. The policy even precluded the state federation from officially endorsing the 1910 suffrage amendment, though its president personally favored its passage. By 1914, however, the federation had softened its attitude and permitted "the consideration of public issues and to secure such concerted action thereon as its members may desire."[39] Women leaders, recognizing the power that the clubs and organizations now held after passage of equal suffrage, openly encouraged clubwomen to employ the ballot. The *Western Woman's Outlook,* for example, implored the Washington Women's Legislative Committee to renounce its policy prohibiting the endorsement of candidates and issues. The magazine argued that such a change would enhance women's power to affect elections and hold candidates' feet to the fire.[40]

The 1912 national election, which pitted the Democratic and Republican parties against Theodore Roosevelt's Progressive Party, so enthralled female activists that even the leading women's periodical, the *Outlook,* officially deviated from its nonpartisanship stance. Yet if asked, most of these leaders would have denied such charges because they beheld the Progressive Party as so unique that it could not be branded with the "domain of political interest." In fact, the *Outlook* contended that the progressive movement—which it equated with the new political party—was not a political movement but "a social and moral renaissance." In fairness, the magazine did provide space for the three parties to present their views. The Progressive Party, however, received the *Outlook's* hearty endorsement because of its enlightened views on equal suffrage, its emphasis on cooperation rather than conflict, and because it was "patriotic," not partisan like the Republican Party. Jane Addams's enthusiastic support for the Bull Moose Party only made it easier for many women in Seattle to forsake their nonpartisan philosophy in 1912.[41]

Partisanship and party politics aside, one of the most controversial issues that arose after suffrage was whether women should hold office. For the most part, suffragists had remained silent on this level of political participation. According to most scholars, few women envisioned themselves or other women campaigning for political office.[42] Nevertheless, equal suffrage now afforded women this opportunity, forcing them to reevaluate their earlier attitudes. In the first issue of *Votes for Women* following the 1910 suffrage victory, for example, the magazine's editor noted that the law prohibiting women from serving as representatives in the state legislature would have to be changed to "admit women to such positions as they are able to fill." In nearby Vancouver, Washington, the city's mayor claimed that many women had actively sought appointments to official offices or committees. While accepting the right to hold office, most women initially concentrated on political offices that seemed less threatening.[43] In 1912, a dozen supporters of Mrs. Josephine Preston urged enfranchised women to back her bid for state superintendent of public instruction, arguing that they (and likely many men) regarded schools as "woman's natural sphere in political life." Enthusiasm for Preston's campaign grew because she "elucidate[d] her ideas as clearly and independently as she did and yet with womanly modesty." As with earlier debates regarding women's role in politics, electing female candidates also meant that the gendered political boundaries had to be redrawn. Few women, and even fewer men, could conceive of obliterating these boundaries overnight. Thus newly enfranchised women often began with less controversial positions like superintendent of public instruction or seats on local school boards. Nevertheless, the Preston campaign represented a step forward, not backward or sideways, if for no other reason than by taking this step women publicly laid claim to full and equal citizenship.[44]

The sensitive nature of the debate over a woman's right to hold office was evident when Preston and other women took the fateful step. Preston's supporters, for example, remarked that the success of women in office or at the polls "depends largely upon the care and caution with which we enter the field." Urging caution, Mrs. Francis G. Miller of the Washington Women's Legislative Committee, for example, suggested that women avoid seeking elected offices for a few years. Women, she believed, could "best serve the state by contenting themselves with an honest and intelligent use of the ballot." The *Western Woman's Outlook* supported the right of women to hold office, but admitted that winning was exceedingly difficult. Female candidates, it argued, could not just be competent, but must "excel the male candidate in every instance" in order to prove their worthiness to both male and female voters. Despite these sentiments, the continual resistance of many men to female candidates did, at times, irk activists. When the Seattle Municipal League endorsed only male candidates in the 1913 city election, the *Outlook* chastised the organization, maintaining that since the city was analogous to a family, it needed both mothers and fathers to govern it. In a sarcastic conclusion the magazine commended "the League for its 'man-like' stand in the matter of the 'mere men' it saw fit to endorse."[45]

The lukewarm support from even the rather progressive Municipal League meant that Seattle women witnessed few successful female candidacies. One important exception was the election of Mrs. Frances Axtell of Whatcom County to the state House of Representatives in 1912. The *Outlook* relished her ability to outwit fellow representatives through her expert use of parliamentary procedure when the House attempted to repeal a law protecting women. By mid-decade, Miss Reah Whitehead, former prosecuting attorney for Seattle, was elected justice of the peace of King County. Nevertheless, many female leaders could only look forward to the day that women claimed an equitable share of political offices. In 1917, following the elevation of Jeannette Rankin of Montana to the U.S. Congress, the *Legislative Federationist* hoped that this was a turning point and that a woman could escape her bondage and "take her place BESIDE the man."[46]

Despite the attention spent on educating new voters and debating the role enfranchised women should play in Seattle, middle-class activists did not ignore their working-class sisters. Working with, and sometimes under, labor leaders like Alice Lord, clubwomen had forged close ties with working-class women. For several years middle-class clubwomen had joined the annual excursion to the state capitol to lobby for the eight-hour day, finally securing it less than a year after winning the ballot. Though few of the arguments for or against the measure had changed since Lord and others introduced the bill several years earlier, the balance of power in Washington clearly had. The *Seattle Union Record,* for example, praised clubwomen who "came to the rescue of the eight-hour bill this year and did yeoman service." The timing of the bill's passage so soon after the suffrage victory, the labor paper observed, was no coincidence. Mrs. E. P. Fick, a special representative of the State Federation of Women's Clubs, likewise credited the large number of women who wrote to state legislators on behalf of the measure.[47]

The eight-hour bill marked the beginning of a wave of protective labor legislation on behalf of women. Clubwomen also urged employer compliance with the law, by both pressuring local and state officials and investigating local businesses themselves. Nellie Higgins of the University of

Washington, for example, submitted reports to the *Western Woman's Out-look* on the impact of the bill, and concluded that the "attitude of the club women of Seattle has been a potent factor in forcing the strict observance of the law." In 1913, this cross-class alliance helped produce one of the most far-reaching pieces of legislation when the state legislature enacted the Industrial Welfare Commission, which crafted minimum wage regulations for workingwomen.[48]

Overcoming years of class suspicion, middle-class and working-class women saw a bright future for themselves and their city. Side by side they had fought and gained both the right to vote and the eight-hour day. The suffrage movement's intense focus on women and their place in American society helps explain the strength of this cross-class gender alliance. In February 1911, the *New Citizen,* for example, urged its readers to use their new political power to make the city a better place. "Women must help each other," the magazine cried out in large bold print; "the under-paid, over-worked women need help." The *New Citizen,* the *Western Woman's Outlook,* and other magazines maintained that most women work "out of necessity not choice" and urged all women to support their working-class sisters. The Washington State Federation of Women's Clubs and Seattle YWCA were just two of several women's groups that formed industrial or labor committees to study and report on the relations between capital and labor, especially as they affected women. The King County Legislative Federation as well as the Woman's Legislative Council of Washington, which even incorporated equal pay for equal work in its "Declaration of Principles," embraced working-class women in their meetings and committees.[49]

Outreach and statements of support did not fully exempt middle-class women from criticism. Laura House, chairperson of the Washington State Federation of Women's Clubs' Industrial Committee, for example, chastised clubwomen who failed to confront industrial conditions for reasons of indifference or class prejudice. She noted that many women had taken the next step in their political development, but some clubs still spent too much time on "dainty refreshments . . . [that] often consume time, means and energy that might be employed to fit us to do things worth while [*sic*]." House also complained that some middle-class women still believed that working girls were "ignorant, frivolous . . . unreliable" and that they labored for the fun and excitement that work in a department store or laundry provided. Domestic service, as it had for several decades, remained a sore spot between the two classes of women. Some clubwomen opposed welfare-like legislation for female wage earners because it contributed to the growing dissatisfaction of domestic servants who fled their jobs for better working conditions. The Seattle YWCA, for example, responded by undertaking an educational campaign to promote raising the status and training of domestic workers. If successful, the program would have helped female employers overcome the perception that servants were little more than "cattle whose aspirations, opinions and comforts are of no importance," attitudes that continually strained the cross-class alliance that Seattle women had fashioned.[50]

Working-class women, however, were quick to point out the shortcomings of their more leisured sisters. Alice Lord and other labor leaders had little patience with many clubwomen's condescending behavior. Although grateful to middle-class reformers for their assistance in lobbying for labor laws, working-class women often saw their better-off sisters as interfering busybodies. For example, when Mayor Cotterill formed his purity squad to enforce vice laws—a move heartily supported by nearly all middle-class clubwomen in Seattle—some workingwomen objected to what they perceived as class harassment. In the fall of 1912, Lord and her Waitresses' Union lodged an official complaint against the purity squad, stating that it interfered with women going to and from work. Police reportedly had stopped one waitress on the way to work at 4 AM because the officer believed only women of disrepute walked the streets at that hour. Most middle-class women, however, responded that saving one girl "was sufficient to justify all the effort [even] if all the others had been mistakes." Here again, middle-class women's overwhelming interest with vice and morality impeded their ability or willingness to fully understand the more complex world working-class women inhabited.[51]

Prostitution and morality, however, could at times also aid working-class efforts to improve working conditions. Middle-class women's support for the purity squad also impelled them to help their working-class sisters gain higher wages. Laura House, for example, explained to her fellow clubwomen that poor working conditions and poor pay drove some workingwomen to prostitution in order to make ends meet. The *Western*

Woman's Outlook likewise cited an Illinois study that documented the link between low wages and prostitution. The magazine warned its readers that Seattle was no better than Chicago; its local department stores were filled with young women who spent nights selling themselves on the streets and in the saloons or lived secret lives as mistresses. Another observer wrote that women could not "develop much as an animal, as a human being, as a soul bound by the seven dollar wage." Better pay would not only promote the general welfare of female wage earners, local feminist Adele Fielde argued, but also improve labor relations and help employers mitigate their parasitic nature. By early 1913, a movement was afoot to study the plight of workingwomen and improve their conditions of work.[52]

At the 1913 convention of the Washington State Federation of Labor, delegate Alice Lord introduced a resolution calling for a state minimum wage for women. Clubwomen agreed with Lord that sacrificing the honor of workingwomen was not worth the material benefits new manufacturing operations might bring to Seattle and the state. A few months later, state officials formed the Industrial Welfare Commission (IWC) to study, recommend, and enforce a minimum wage for women. Without a doubt the most controversial commissioner appointed by Governor Ernest Lister was University of Washington professor Theresa McMahon.[53]

A graduate of the University of Wisconsin, where she studied under renowned labor historian John Commons, McMahon joined Professor J. Allen Smith's political science department as an instructor in economics and labor history. Prior to taking up residence in Seattle, however, she spent a few years working for the Associated Charities of Chicago where she met progressive reformer Jane Addams. According to her memoirs, McMahon believed that it was this time working with the poor that radicalized her and "taught me to hate the exploiting employer." Her tenure at the University of Washington was stormy and controversial. Her enemies accused McMahon of being a Socialist, and she constantly struggled with local politicians and university officials to maintain her position at the school. She claimed, however, that her radical character was only partly responsible for these conflicts. Several years after university officials passed her over for an appointment to the economics department, McMahon wrote that they rejected her for both her political views and her gender. Despite McMahon's critical views of employers, Governor Lister, pressured by the SCLC and other members of organized labor, appointed her to the IWC.[54]

For nearly two years the IWC held numerous hearings and meetings to investigate each major industry that employed women in order to set an appropriate minimum wage. Both employers and employees of mercantile, manufacturing, and laundry firms presented their opinions and thoughts to their respective IWC conference. The minimum wage conferences consisted of three representatives from labor, business, and the public. These debates and hearings offer historians a fascinating view into the various attitudes about the place and status of workingwomen in Seattle. Employee representatives, for example, stressed the dire need of better pay for women workers, while employers emphasized the negative impact higher wages would have on their businesses. Mirroring the fears of middle-class women's groups, Mrs. Elizabeth Muir, an employee representative to the Mercantile Conference, urged the commission to pay a living wage and "keep our girls who are Christians as Christians." Likewise, Mrs. Florence Locke of Seattle bluntly stated that underpaid workingwomen were "selling their souls."[55]

The industrial conferences, however, dealt much more with the spending habits of working-class women than the morality of a minimum wage. The nine representatives of the Manufacturing Conference, for example, investigated everything from the price women paid for undergarments to the costs of amusements. Each then submitted what he or she believed were the annual costs of a workingwoman's basic needs. The average of the three employee estimates was $589; those speaking for the general public believed $510 was the correct amount. Employer representatives submitted the lowest average of $484, or nearly 20 percent below the figure labor provided.[56] The Mercantile Conference especially generated a great deal of interest in Seattle. Retail Clerks Local No. 6 charged that the Bon Marché, the largest department store in the city and single largest employer of women in the state, supported the IWC to improve its image with those sympathetic to labor. The clerks stated that they had spent months attempting to negotiate with the Bon Marché before finally deciding to declare it unfair to labor. The department store's sudden support for raising the wages of its female employees, union leaders contended, was simply a stalling tactic. The company realized that it would be months before a decision could be made; it could thus profit from lower wages during this period as well as benefit from the store's public support for the minimum wage.[57]

While the Bon Marché's conflict was rather unique, most employers simply complained about the economic damage the IWC decisions posed to their businesses. State Labor Commissioner Edward Olson actually confirmed their concerns. He agreed that Washington manufacturers could not compete against eastern industrial firms if forced to pay higher wages because the cost of manufacturing in the state was already 15 percent higher than in eastern industrial states. The Employers' Association of Washington likewise claimed that since neighboring Oregon firms could work women nine hours a day, Washington employers needed a lower minimum wage in order to compete. One employer representative to the Mercantile Conference, O. C. Fenelson, actually favored a $10–$12 weekly wage in principle; he made clear, however, that he could not afford much beyond $8 a week. Few employers mirrored Fenelson's attitude that women deserved higher wages, yet most shared his thoughts on the economic impact of a minimum wage.[58]

Housing was another contentious issue between employers and employees. Businessmen alleged that their investigations indicated that most workingwomen lived at home and thus needed less money. Fred Krause, an employer representative at the Manufacturing Conference, added that Spokane and other cities offered subsidized housing by way of local charities such as the YWCA. Workers, however, responded that most private families did not want to board young women. Moreover, most female wage earners could not afford the higher costs and had to resort to renting rooms in commercial establishments. Financial considerations aside, one employee representative at the Manufacturing Conference noted her preference for living on her own because private families often prohibited boarders from washing, ironing, or using the kitchen. The debate over housing costs illustrates the lack of understanding among many employers and middle-class residents about the daily lives of working-class women. While a YWCA room might offer some advantages and savings, for many women workers, it also meant a loss of independence and pride. As one employee perceptively observed, the YWCA and similar organizations were supported by private donations, and thus "girls who stay there are therefore accepting charity."[59]

Charity was what some employers believed the minimum wage for women actually represented. Underlying the employers' economic argument was the belief that female laborers were less valuable than comparable male workers. While some bosses tried to argue that the measure would hurt women because they might have to let them go in favor of young boys or men who had no such protection, many others simply believed that their female workers were not worth $10 a week. Frank McDermott of the Bon Marché claimed that he would fire many female workers whom he paid $5 a week because they were not worth the $9 suggested in the hearings. At the Manufacturing Conference, Fred Krause plainly stated that a "girl that is the minimum is no asset to the producer, consequently, [she] would be an expense to the company." The minimum wage, he concluded, was a "charitable proposition." Even the progressive Seattle Municipal League wondered how workingwomen who "already scarcely earn their five dollars . . . are going to command the nine-dollar wage?" McDermott and Krause's thoughts, in short, simply reflected the strongly held belief in the industrial era that women's work was worth less, thus justifying to themselves and American society the low wages paid to women.[60]

After months of hearings, the various minimum wage conferences published their findings. The Manufacturing Conference determined, after several contentious ballots, that the minimum wage for women in this line of work would be $8.90 per week. Employers at the Laundry Conference refused to grant workers more than $8.50 a week. Women who worked in department stores, however, received the highest minimum wage. Citing the higher costs of fashionable clothes many store workers were required to wear, the Mercantile Conference decided on a weekly wage of $10. Less than three years after securing the ballot, workingwomen in Seattle had achieved some of the best working conditions in the nation, earning the admiration of national reformers like Florence Kelley. The passage of the IWC and the minimum wage law in 1913–14 thus marked the pinnacle of the alliance that organized labor and middle-class women had forged a few years earlier.[61]

Not all Seattle women, however, believed that the eight-hour day and minimum wage law sufficiently protected workingwomen from their employers. During the IWC hearings, Theresa McMahon sparked a great deal of controversy when she questioned the action of certain employers who fired working girls because of their questionable morality. She apparently learned of this practice from Frank McDermott of the Bon Marché when he told her that special markings on certain women's job applications meant that their morals were suspect. In a hearing held in nearby Everett, McMahon interrogated employers about whether they hired investigators to follow some of their female workers to check on their activities. She then suggested that a worker's morality would not be an issue if employers paid their female employees better wages. What touched off the controversy, however, was her statement that she believed it was not the employers' "business as far as the girl's morals are concerned, as long as you are indifferent to the men's morals." Local newspapers apparently left off the second half of her statement and in their headlines printed that McMahon believed that workingwomen's morals were none of the employers' business. Church groups and women's clubs publicly attacked her for these remarks. Realizing Seattle's anxiety over prostitution and public morality, IWC opponents purposely misrepresented her actual statement in order to weaken the commission's findings. McMahon's unpopularity with employers, combined with the public uproar over her statement, led Governor Lister, over protests from organized labor, to refuse to reappoint her to the IWC the following year.[62]

The surprising advances made by voting women so soon after the 1910 election, culminating with the IWC conferences, also helped rekindle the floundering Seattle Women's Card and Label League. The mutually beneficial alliance between clubwomen and organized labor helped awaken the male-dominated SCLC to the potential power of a vigorous working-class women's movement. The crucial turning point was the 1910 suffrage campaign. Prior to that decision, the *Union Record* generally portrayed working-class women as "gentle label-buying helpmeets or endangered maidens pleading for a shorter day." The possession of the ballot immediately transformed the image of working-class women from helpmates to empowered citizens who could advance the cause of labor both as consumers and voters.[63]

The rejuvenated Seattle Women's Card and Label League soon demonstrated a willingness to move beyond its typical concerns. The group quickly severed its ties with the International Label League and Trades Union Auxiliary so that it could focus its energy on Seattle issues. Apparently, the SCLC leadership was not pleased that the league did not consult the body before making this decision, but nevertheless praised its dynamism. By 1913, officials boasted that the group's membership topped five hundred. During the minimum wage conferences, Label Leaguers appointed two members to seek cooperation from middle-class clubwomen to help explain the law to female workers. Claiming that it represented the "right hand of the labor movement," the league also sent a letter of protest to the state legislature regarding a "loophole" in the eight-hour-day law. Despite a flurry of activity, the Seattle Women's Card and Label League again began to slowly wither. Critics argued that only union label activity, not the barrage of political speakers that spoke at meetings, could effectively motivate women to participate.[64]

Rather than let another label league disappear, league officials decided to turn the organization into a "training school for women." The inspiration for this transformation was the King County Legislative Federation, which brought together a variety of women's groups, ranging from the Women's Christian Temperance Union and Parent-Teacher Associations to the Label League. Legislative Federation meetings exposed working-class women to a larger feminist agenda that they shared with their middle-class sisters, leading Label League officers to urge their members to propel the league "into the vanguard of the advanced Woman Movement." To accomplish this, officials permitted male union delegates to attend only evening meetings each month, reserving afternoon gatherings for women.[65]

With its new vision and purpose, the Seattle Women's Card and Label League flourished during the next several years. Members, for example, set aside a special day each month to read and discuss labor literature. They debated topics ranging from what they called "sex hygiene" in the schools to dangerous working conditions to the meaning of the Russian Revolution. The *Union Record*'s decision to add a fashion column to its "Page Especially for Women" prompted some league members to charge that the column demeaned female activists. Reflecting the growing influence of industrial unionism that the SCLC endorsed during this decade, league leaders advised working-class women in Seattle to drop their craft-oriented women's auxiliaries. Instead, working-class women were encouraged to emulate the Industrial Workers of the World's "One Big Union" idea by joining the Card and Label League, which, league officials maintained, was devoid of "craft-consciousness." Union auxiliaries, they declared, dissipated the potential power of working-class women. Rather than build solidarity and strength, the auxiliaries, like male craft unions, divided the working class. Until women overcame this division, Label Leaguers believed, Seattle's working class, male and female, would remain weak and ineffective.[66]

During its renaissance, the Seattle Card and Label League toiled on behalf of both the women's movement and organized labor. Several members, for instance, served as both delegates to, and officials of, the King County Legislative Federation. In 1917, three activists held positions on the federation's executive committee. The league also worked with club-women to establish a home for girls. Yet in doing so it remained sensitive to its class position when it complained that Seattle needed the home because the YWCA seemed to serve middle-class and elite women more than working girls. Class concerns remained an important pursuit of the Label League. In 1916, the league, in concert with union women, formed the Federation of Trade Unionist Women and Auxiliaries (FTUW&A). The new organization was to do for female workers what the SCLC did for male workers—it would organize them into unions and support their causes. Wedding the interests and power of union women with working-class wives, however, was not an easy task. Efforts to stretch the family dollar sometimes conflicted with concerns of union women. Alice Lord, for example, complained that attempts to force cafeterias and diners to decrease prices might help working-class housewives, but often meant lost jobs to workingwomen. Here again, women's roles as producers and consumers made for complex relations between female workers and working-class wives.[67]

The complexity of the issues and problems Label Leaguers confronted, in the decade following the suffrage victory, aptly illustrates the difficulty of fleshing out the meaning and impact of the ballot for women. The politics of gender no doubt further muddled an already complex political environment. Cross-class and cross-gender alliances significantly transformed city politics. Yet the tenuous nature of these alliances, as evidenced by the Label League's debate over the need for a home for young girls or Alice Lord's reprimand of the overzealous purity squad, made it difficult to pin down the exact impact of equal suffrage. The 1910 victory no doubt advanced the national suffrage movement and encouraged women everywhere to demand equal citizenship. Clearly, enfranchised women, however, did not think or vote as a bloc as many contemporaries might have expected, though certain issues, like prostitution, did continue to draw their attention. Seattle women, then, refused to recede to the home and did not shy away from public life.

While middle-class and working-class women may have had, at times, differing agendas, both refused to let men decide what issues they confronted. As mothers they may have been compelled to clean up Seattle, but as equal citizens they also felt obligated to discuss city charter amendments and municipal ownership. What is clear, however, is that working-class women represented the nexus between class and gender politics during the Progressive Era. As key figures in the two greatest social movements of this age—the woman's movement and labor movement—working-class women permitted, albeit temporarily, the formation of a cross-class and cross-gender political alliance. The overlap of these two movements would, in many ways, define progressivism. Yet, as subsequent events would make clear, when circumstances forced them to decide, working-class and middle-class women would place class ahead of gender interests. The ultimate political consequences of that choice were both unintended and unfortunate.

CHAPTER 5

The Demise of Seattle's Progressive Spirit

On a rather warm evening in July 1913, Mrs. Annie Miller climbed on top of her rented speaking platform to deliver a speech to workers and others milling around Seattle's Skid Row district. After heckling Miller, a sailor took to the soapbox to offer his thoughts on the issues of the day. Matters soon turned ugly when the sailor refused to give up the platform to Miller and then reportedly raised his hand to her. A rather well-dressed gentleman, according to several eyewitnesses, proceeded to assault the sailor for threatening a woman. Soon a melee broke out as civilians and servicemen exchanged blows until police arrived. By night's end, several of the servicemen had to be treated at a nearby hospital.[1]

This episode might have been quickly forgotten as a simple street skirmish had not a reporter for the *Seattle Times* sensationalized the conflict in the next day's paper. City residents awoke to news that a radical foul-mouthed woman had insulted the American flag and instigated a riot against a few patriotic servicemen who only protested her attack on the nation's most cherished symbol. Leaders of the National Guard and veterans of the Spanish-American War intimated that their members would not countenance such behavior by radical and un-American people. Later that night a group of sailors proceeded to destroy the meeting halls of two radical labor organizations, including the local Socialist Party. The mob, which local papers numbered from a thousand to as many as twenty thousand, celebrated their handiwork with throngs of bystanders who had gathered to watch the annual Potlatch parade.

In response to civic unrest, Seattle Mayor George Cotterill ordered the saloons closed for the rest of the weekend and employed off-duty firemen to help police the city. The mayor also ordered local officers to make sure no more issues of the *Seattle Times* graced the city until the Potlatch celebration concluded a few days later. The paper's publisher, Colonel Alden J. Blethen, a hyperpatriotic and hot-tempered man, immediately called on a local judge to overturn the mayor's order. Cotterill argued that Blethen's paper not only misrepresented the actual events, but also inflamed and encouraged the sailors to retaliate. Unmoved, the judge gave the mayor a tongue-lashing and then ordered him to reverse his edict. By nightfall, the *Times* had flooded the city with its special riot issue in which it referred to the mayor as "the leader of a red-flag gang." Despite such caustic rhetoric, the paper's tone was much more muted than earlier that week and the 1913 Potlatch celebration quietly came to an end.[2]

The Potlatch Riots of 1913 represented much more than simply another colorful event in Seattle's storied history. In between the 1910 equal suffrage victory and the infamous General Strike of 1919, Seattle rode a roller-coaster of high expectations and dashed hopes. The alliance between organized labor and middle-class suffragists seemed to reinforce the optimism of progressive-minded residents. Seattle, they envisioned, would stand in the vanguard of cities where citizens could walk the streets without confronting prostitutes, gamblers, and drunks, and where employers and employees worked together to build a better community. By 1913, however, such heady sentiments had quickly soured. The Potlatch episode seemed to mark the turning point in the city's progressive spirit. Economic forces and recalcitrant employers soon combined to weaken and virtually destroy labor's alliance with middle-class clubwomen. While the Potlatch Riots did not seem to weaken progressive women's support for labor, largely because of Blethen's reputation for sensational journalism, they did signify a changing mood among Seattle's working-class residents.

By World War I, Seattle was socially and politically polarized as extremists in the camps of both labor and capital pushed their respective moderate forces into the background. After 1913, workers veered leftward as Socialists and the Industrial Workers of the World (IWW) expanded both their membership and influence in labor circles. The cordial and successful alliance that mainstream labor leaders cultivated with local middle-class women's groups was soon tested by deteriorating relations between capital and labor. Battles over prohibition, a stagnating economy, a waterfront strike, and a shoot-out between Seattle Wobblies (as IWW members were commonly called) and officials in nearby Everett, opened a breach in the labor-feminist alliance that, as this chapter will demonstrate, proved impossible to close with the nation's entry into World War I. By the end of the decade, the enlightened city that many had once envisioned had spiraled downward into discord and conflict. Like other western cities, and for that matter, cities elsewhere in the nation, Seattle could not escape the turmoil unleashed by corporate capitalism and world war.

In 1910, however, few workers could have imagined such an amazing turn of events. After the troubled years of the Panic of 1907 and the bad feelings engendered by the Alaska-Yukon-Pacific Exposition, Seattle workers had begun to enjoy the city's prosperity and better relations with employers. The *Seattle Union Record*, for example, noted that the summer of 1910 saw little industrial strife. Both labor and capital, the paper observed, seemed willing to find a middle ground on which to share the fruits of a thriving economy. The only problem that tainted these friendly relations was a dispute between the Metal Trades Association and the Machinists Union. The strike or lockout, depending on whose story one accepts, apparently surfaced over Seattle machinists' demand for a contract that resembled the favorable conditions San Francisco machinists had received from their employers. The lengthy strike notwithstanding, organized labor felt rather good about its relations with capital. Furthermore, by the end of 1910, the new alliance with enfranchised women had tempered the disappointment labor leaders felt over the recent failure of its Labor Party.[3]

Organized labor's upbeat mood continued into 1911. In April, the *Union Record* crowed about labor's growing influence in civic affairs when it noted that various community and reform organizations had requested its assistance. The paper, for example, stated that the city's commercial bodies invited labor leaders to speak to businessmen on various civic topics. A "general feeling of friendliness," the paper concluded, "has been manifest between organized labor and the business interests." It was not only the chamber of commerce's new attitude that encouraged working-class leaders. Several women's groups demonstrated their new alliance with organized labor by publicly announcing their support for many of labor's goals. The Washington Women's Legislative Committee, for example, requested that the federal government help establish an effective savings plan for workers, while the Seattle YWCA sent leaders to the state capitol to lobby against a measure aimed at weakening the women's eight-hour-day law. As late as 1917, the King County Legislative Federation publicly supported female laundry workers' efforts to create a union-operated laundry business.[4]

The fruits of the new progressive alliance extended beyond prolabor declarations. In the 1911 municipal election, the *Western Woman Voter* enthusiastically endorsed working-class candidate Robert Hesketh in his race for a council seat. It backed his candidacy both because he ardently supported the eight-hour-day law and because the magazine believed that labor had a right to a seat on the council. The following year the *Western Woman's Outlook* championed a local bill to provide a municipal lodging house for the growing number of unemployed men in Seattle. Clubwomen also demonstrated their support for the city's working class by toiling beside them in various political endeavors. The Woman's Legislative Council of Washington, for instance, formed a "Division of Organized Labor" headed by two working-class women, Ida Walker and Minnie Ault. Perhaps no middle-class woman aided labor more, publicly or privately, than Professor Theresa McMahon. When the U.S. Commission on Industrial Relations came to Seattle in 1914, McMahon testified on behalf of labor before the committee. She not only endorsed greater state intervention on behalf of workers in their struggle with capital, but she also encouraged the formation of independent labor political parties. In return, Seattle labor leaders clearly showed their appreciation for her efforts by intimating to the president of the University of Washington that if he attempted to fire her, that neither he nor the state governor would remain in office much longer. McMahon later stated that the SCLC's bold stance saved her job.[5]

While support for the eight-hour day may have placed middle-class women squarely within the general reform spirit of the day, public pronouncements on Socialism clearly pushed them to the outermost fringe of progressivism. Close interaction with working-class leaders following the suffrage victory seemed to have softened many middle-class women's opinion of Socialism. Famed middle-class feminist Charlotte Perkins Gilman likewise looked to Socialism in addressing "the twin struggle that convulses the world to-day—in sex and economics—the woman's movement and the labor movement."[6] In the 1912 mayoral election, Socialist Hulet Wells performed quite well in the primary election, capturing more than 15 percent of the vote in a four-man race. While George Cotterill went on to claim the office in the general election, several feminist leaders argued that Socialists and progressives shared common ground on many issues. The *Western Woman's Outlook,* for example, maintained that Cotterill received a great deal of Socialist support in the final election, which clearly contradicted the adage that Socialists voted only for Socialists. "Every progressive, intelligent person," the magazine declared, "believes in socialism."[7] The journal continued its positive portrayal of Socialism after the election, suggesting that Socialism did not signify anarchy but was "the dream of the future." The rapidly evolving opinions about Socialism not only reflected the political reality of Seattle's mayoral race, but also the increasing leftward tilt of progressives throughout the nation. The sudden rise of Theodore Roosevelt's Progressive Party in 1912 no doubt helped further diminish the distance between Socialism and the mainstream political ideas of the day. As progressives lurched leftward, they increasingly recognized that social-welfare ideas associated with socialist theory were not as radically different as they had once thought.[8]

Middle-class feminists' support for labor's radical fringe went beyond simply acknowledging their shared values with American Socialists. When violence broke out during an IWW strike at mills located in Lawrence, Massachusetts, local women's magazines publicly sided with the oppressed workers. One editorial, for example, castigated mill owners for both mistreating their workforce and the decision to employ troops to break the strike. Painting the conflict as the workers' struggle for survival against the employers' desire for profit, the *Western Woman's Outlook* further suggested that labor's natural rights outweighed the legal rights of the mill owners. Later, when a congressman attempted to block an investigation into bloody

1914 Ludlow Massacre because his committee lacked a quorum, the *Outlook* argued that if some "captain of industry" had his property threatened, "no quorum" would not have been the congressman's response.[9]

Defense of Socialist and Wobbly activities, however, was not unqualified. When some eight hundred Socialists took to the streets of Seattle to protest poor treatment of striking timber workers by lumbermen in nearby Gray's Harbor, one women's magazine questioned the Socialists' tactics. While it believed that the protesters stood for "civic betterment and human welfare," the *Outlook* was dismayed that local Socialists did not carry the American flag alongside the party's red flag. The red flag, it proclaimed, represented the past, and that by contrast the nation's symbol celebrated liberty and a more positive future. Even trade unions did not always escape the criticism of middle-class feminists. In response to a call for an employers' association to combat the growing power of Seattle's trade unions, the *Outlook* admitted that it concurred with most businessmen and the nation's courts that labor strikes and boycotts illegally restrained trade. Even the more progressively minded middle-class women, as these episodes suggest, continually struggled to reconcile their class sensibilities with sympathy for the city's working class.[10]

The political and ideological limits of middle-class feminists notwithstanding, their favorable alliance with organized labor paid off rather handsomely in the early 1910s. This progressive partnership not only secured a statewide minimum wage and eight-hour day for workingwomen, but it also helped improve Seattle's social and political climate. Both sides, for example, shared a common antipathy toward prostitution, and together they elected mayors and councilmen who favored a clean city. Favoring public ownership programs, Seattle workers and local clubwomen pressured the city to create the Seattle Port Commission in 1911 to oversee and manage the city's public port facilities in expectation of increased shipping traffic from the soon-to-be-completed Panama Canal. At the height of the Progressive Era, then, Seattle middle-class feminists, more often than not, coordinated reform with the leaders of organized labor out of a shared distrust of elite business interests.[11]

The 1913 Potlatch Riots punctured the optimism of many of Seattle's progressive citizens. Reports of angry, insulting, radical laborers pitted against American servicemen no doubt caused many residents to pause. However, as news surfaced in the following days that *Seattle Times* publisher Colonel Blethen not only sensationalized the actual events, but also had encouraged attacks on local Socialists and Wobblies, most citizens soon forgot the incident. The spilling of blood and the destruction of property on Seattle's streets, however, was not the end, but the first of several events that would further strain and eventually rupture the fragile coalition between labor and middle-class progressive women. Such alliances or coalitions are key, as Daniel Rodgers has argued, to understanding the nature of progressivism. With the decline of political partisanship, interest groups increasingly influenced politics and power relations in American society. Shared political and social interests were the glue that held these coalitions together. In Seattle, protecting workingwomen, eliminating prostitution, and improving the city's port facilities were some of the issues that bound organized labor with middle-class women. Maintaining these alliances, however, was difficult. While the Potlatch Riots temporarily raised the eyebrows of some middle-class women, the troubled relations between capital and labor and the specter of class conflict that followed forced many feminists to reevaluate their partnership with the city's working class. The demise of progressivism in Seattle, then, can be found in the changing relationship between the politics of class and the politics of gender.[12]

Central to the crumbling relations between Seattle workers and employers was an economic slump that struck the Pacific Coast in the prewar years. Longer and deeper than the Panic of 1907, this depression threw thousands out of work and provided fertile soil in which more radical solutions could take root. By 1913, numerous agencies and newspapers commented on the growing unemployment in Seattle. The *Women's Western Outlook,* for example, observed that large numbers of homeless and poor men roamed the streets; the magazine, however, suggested that part of the blame lay with the workers. Arguing that the nation's economy was simply readjusting to the Wilson administration's economic policies, the *Outlook* declared that workers wasted summer earnings on high living and unsavory activities, leaving themselves insufficient funds to weather the seasonal joblessness that winter brought to the region. No doubt exacerbating the situation was Seattle's traditional attractiveness to timber workers, who spent winters in the city enjoying the hospitality of gambling dens and brothels that dotted the Skid Row district.[13]

That the joblessness the city experienced during the winter of 1913–14 was different than usual was evidenced by the city council's appropriation of $7,500 to put men to work. Not since the Panic of 1907 had the council taken such action. Working-class responses further testify to this downturn's severity. In 1912, the Agitator Club held a "hard times ball" that required attendees to wear rags or overalls. More astounding, however, was the effort of a few working-class leaders both to organize the city's unemployed into Hobo Union, Local No. 22, and to operate a shelter in an abandoned hotel. Henry Pauly, chairman of the union and manager of the Hotel de Gink, declared that the purpose of the new labor organization was to "keep the itinerant workers from going and taking strikers' places, to get the men to organize, to better their conditions." When a Tacoma businessman reportedly visited the hotel to find strikebreakers, he was "hooted out of the building" and shown the door. Workers spent their nights in the hotel and during the days took on odd jobs clearing land and vacant lots or repairing local streets. Appeals in 1914 from various working-class organizations for a permanent municipal housing lodge made it evident that employment conditions had improved little.[14]

The punishing economic slump, combined with a major teamsters' strike and a union boycott of the Bon Marché department store, only aided the efforts of local labor radicals. By 1912, local Socialists had begun to rebuild their movement after years of destructive internecine conflict. While still divided on whether to travel the revolutionary or evolutionary road to Socialism, most Seattle Socialists appeared willing to put aside temporarily these theoretical disputes. According to one student of Washington labor history, the more revolutionary-minded Reds, after three years of Yellow rule, had regained control over the Socialist Party of Washington in 1912. Largely as a result of the growing immigrant population from Russia, Germany, and Finland, which SCLC organizers failed to recognize or organize, the Reds expanded their membership and quickly seized control of the SPW. In 1911, former Populist Judge Richard Winsor was the first Socialist elected as the director of the city's public schools. The following year Socialist Hulet Wells attracted more than ten thousand votes in the race for mayor, while Eugene Debs polled more than 12 percent of the state's electorate. Though the state's population was still relatively small, Washington's Socialist Party was purportedly the strongest in the nation.

Socialists also penetrated the ranks of Seattle's trade union leadership during this period. In 1915, union workers, for example, elected Wells as president of the SCLC. Harry Ault, who came to Seattle after a short stint as the editor of the *Young Socialist* at the nearby Equality utopian colony, served as secretary of the SCLC in 1911 before taking over the helm of the *Seattle Union Record* a few years later.[15]

Seattle Times publisher Colonel Alden Blethen was none too pleased about the growing Socialist presence in Seattle. The colonel chafed at both the sizable number of Socialists and Wobblies that filled his city as well as the middle-class progressives who thwarted his vision of Seattle. Attempts by municipal ownership forces to place more of the city's utilities into local government's hands, at the expense of private investors, especially angered the newspaper publisher. Moreover, Blethen vociferously opposed middle-class reformers' efforts to shut down the prosperous but immoral vice activity south of Yesler Way. At times, the colonel's hyperpatriotism got the best of him as he viciously struck out against those who, in his mind, impugned the flag and the nation. By 1913, the *Times* publisher exploited his bully pulpit to spawn public protest against Socialists and Wobblies.[16]

The Potlatch Riots were not the only incident in which Blethen abused his power as editor of the *Times*. A few months after Hulet Wells's impressive showing in the 1912 municipal election, local Socialists received a permit from city officials to stage a parade on May Day. While the details of the event are sketchy, Blethen apparently staged a raid on the paraders in order to frame Wells. The *Times* claimed that Wells had desecrated the American flag and denounced it as a "dirty rag." Splashed across the front page of the paper was a picture of a torn flag, beside a headline announcing that Wells's citizenship might be revoked. In his autobiography, Wells claims that he did not attend the parade and was still at work at his city job. Blethen, however, also used the skirmish to attack Mayor Cotterill, who had given Socialists permission to parade through Seattle's streets, by attempting to smear the mayor with the "red" brush of Socialism. Weeks later a small group of disgruntled residents, with the full support of the *Times*, formed the Seattle Patriotic Recall Association to remove Cotterill from office. The *Western Woman's Outlook*, in response, concluded that this recall was little more than a ruse by liquor and vice interests to punish, if not purge, the mayor from office because of his purity squads' success in cleaning up the city.[17]

Though Blethen failed to oust Mayor Cotterill, his hatred of radicals grew over the next several months. Streets swollen with more unemployed workers, growing support for Socialism, and Hulet Wells's libel lawsuit against the newspaper editor did little to improve his disposition. While Wells awaited his day in court, the *Times* continued to blister him and other prominent Socialists. The paper, for example, accused Wells of whitewashing an internal investigation by local Socialists into the domestic relations of Sam and Kate Sadler. The Sadlers were active Socialists who apparently were not legally married, and some party leaders felt it necessary to purge them from the party for sinful behavior. Wells, however, defended their relationship, and Blethen used this to attack him. Unable to counter the colonel's control of the press, Wells composed a short play loosely based on his recent experiences in Seattle. Entitled "The Colonel and His Friends," the play wryly ridiculed Blethen and the legal system. Originally scheduled to open at the Moore Theatre in late July 1913, the Potlatch Riots caused the theater's owner to cancel the show, fearing damage to his venue.[18]

The Potlatch Riots did not in themselves significantly undermine middle-class support for organized labor; nor did they destroy the political partnership between labor and local feminists. They did, however, highlight the growing radicalism within working-class circles and helped contribute, if not burn into the public's collective mind, a negative image of the IWW. Mirroring similar Socialist advances, Wobbly membership and influence in Seattle expanded tremendously in the years prior to World War I. Together, though largely working separately, the two radical labor organizations steered Seattle's working class to the left.

Seattle's IWW chapter was born out of the growing class consciousness of western workers in the early years of the twentieth century. Founded in 1905 by delegates representing various socialist organizations, the Western Federation of Miners, and a few other left-wing unions, the "Continental Congress of the working class," as one delegate called the delegates of this first IWW national convention, sought to build a harmonious working-class movement. The Wobblies, according to one historian, "epitomized the kind of idealistic radicalism that flourished in Washington" since the days of the Knights of Labor. Harmony, however, was difficult to achieve, and ideological battles raged within the IWW over the efficacy of political action that Socialists advocated. Rejecting direct political action, Wobblies instead focused on organizing those left outside the traditional trade unions, such as unskilled factory operatives, timber workers, and migratory agricultural workers.[19]

The IWW took particular aim at what it perceived to be the failure of the American Federation of Labor to aid the working masses. The exclusive craft-oriented organization seemed increasingly ineffective in a largely unskilled world, leading many workers to call it the "American Separation of Labor." The IWW, in contrast, emphasized industrial unionism, labor solidarity, political nonpartisanship, direct economic action, and an American form of syndicalism. More specifically, the Wobblies wished to ameliorate the conditions of the working class and eventually, after the collapse of the capitalist system, seize industries and run them for the benefit of workers.[20] IWW ideology generally accepted Marx's labor theory of value and the inevitability of class struggle, as well as drew on an American producer tradition dating back to Jefferson and Jackson. Unlike the Socialists, the IWW avoided the political arena for reasons of both principle and pragmatism. The state, Wobblies believed, was a repressive organ of the entrenched powers. At the same time, however, the IWW's constituency saw the state as a "distant and fearful enemy" and did not, or could not, see political power as a "means to alter the rules of the game."[21] Since most Wobblies were migratory workers, residency requirements and other restrictive voting qualifications made it exceedingly difficult to exercise political power.

The IWW's membership, however, also distinguished it from other trade unions. Wobbly rosters were filled with "timber beasts," "hobo harvesters," and other dispossessed Americans who recently had journeyed from a preindustrial to an industrial society and who were often ignored by mainstream unions. Despite charges that the IWW was a foreign-led union, most Wobblies were, in fact, native-born Americans or Americanized immigrants. Carlton Parker, in his 1920 classic study of casual laborers, described the American Wobbly as "a neglected and lonely hobo worker, usually malnourished and in need of medical care." The IWW, he concluded, "can be profitably viewed only as a psychological by-product of the neglected childhood of industrial America." The IWW's attractiveness to lower-class workers varied, yet clearly it spoke to the fears and hardships many Wobbly migrants experienced. As one IWW official put it, a worker should look to the IWW if your job had never kept you long enough in a place to qualify you to vote; if you slept in a lousy, sour bunkhouse, and ate food just as rotten as they could give you and get by with it; if deputy sheriffs shot your cooking cans full of holes and spilled your grub on the ground; if your wages were lowered on you when the bosses thought they had you down . . . if every person who represented law and order and the nation beat you up, railroaded you to jail, and the good Christian people cheered and told them to go to it.[22]

In short, the IWW offered a "social break" for workers in search of jobs, and its local headquarters provided both pleasant conversation and a friendly saloon in generally hostile towns.

Because it often appealed to a community's more transient population, the IWW often utilized street speaking to organize workers. One Wobbly theorist stated that "without the street meetings . . . the jobless, homeless, migratory workers could not be organized."[23] Similarly, another IWW official argued: "the street corner was [the IWW's] only hall, and if denied the right to agitate there then they must be silent."[24] Wobbly organizers often centered their activities in the area of the city where employment agencies were located, and hence where unemployed workers usually congregated. Rather than defending some abstract idea of protecting civil liberties, most IWW free-speech fights erupted over the threat street speaking ordinances posed to the group's ability to organize workers.

The rapidly expanding Pacific Northwest lumber industry, which lured young single men to the mountains and hills that divided Washington State, was particularly susceptible to the IWW's organizing tactics. Inexpensive membership fees and cards, which workers could easily exchange wherever they worked, were quite attractive to migratory laborers. Timber workers found the Seattle's Skid Row district especially hospitable during the winter months when lumber camps closed, and because the IWW was willing to organize the "timber beasts," the city quickly felt the union's presence. Moreover, Puget Sound's deteriorating economy meant that after 1912 many of these laborers chose to extend their "vacations" in the port city.[25]

While clearly not to blame for the street violence that plagued Seattle in the summer of 1913, the IWW's growing presence and influence in working-class neighborhoods cannot be denied. Contemporary observers noted that not only lumber camps but also wheat farms and railroad construction drew itinerant workers to the region. Miserable working conditions and the failure of traditional craft unions to reach out to them ushered them into the IWW. Sawmill towns were not much better, as these were often company towns that controlled the lives of the "sawdust savages," as the sawmill workers were called. Anna Louise Strong, daughter of Reverend Sidney Strong and one of the few middle-class residents radical workers took into their confidence, quoted a government official on the conditions of the lumber camps. "There are conditions so bad," the official stated, "that it would be most discouraging if human beings had not revolted." Further aggravating this situation, Strong argued, was the migratory nature of western labor, which turned workers into "wanderers upon the face of the earth, with no home, no settled abode, no property." For many, then, Seattle became a temporary home.[26]

Street speaking thus became a crucial organizing tool for the IWW. The few weeks or months that timber workers spent in Seattle provided a rather captive audience for Wobbly organizers. Henry Pauly, manager of the Hotel de Gink, told the U.S. Commission on Industrial Relations in 1914 that local employers took advantage of IWW workers because they lacked the power to protect themselves. He related one case in nearby Bellevue where workers hired to clear the land had to change their clothes in the rain because the employer provided no shelter. Other bosses simply refused to pay laborers, forcing them to take legal action. According to Anna Louise Strong, Wobbly leaders wished to set up offices with paid secretaries to keep in contact with its members, so they searched for an uptown location for a hall. Most Seattle landlords, however, refused to rent to them, even when officials offered to pay more than other prospective renters did. It was these offices that felt the hatchet blows of Potlatch rioters.[27]

The wanton destruction of both the Socialist and IWW headquarters and Colonel Blethen's caustic tirades against the radical working-class organizations generated a great deal of discussion in the city's labor paper. The *Seattle Union Record*, for example, spotlighted Blethen's role in the riot and the response of various representatives of capital. The paper, for example, deplored Blethen's use of the flag and patriotism to rile up local residents against labor radicals. It also criticized the police department's poor response to the skirmish and published bystanders' accounts, which claimed that several policemen stood by smiling during the destruction of the buildings. The *Union Record*'s lead editorial, entitled "WHO ARE THE ANARCHISTS," claimed that Blethen and other business leaders were the real anarchists and their actions only confirmed Wobbly and Socialist complaints about the city's elite.[28]

The SCLC and the *Union Record* initially attempted to rise above the conflict by representing themselves as the sane and objective voice of the community. The paper not only reprinted some of the most vitriolic columns from the *Seattle Times,* but also published Mayor Cotterill's comments on the event. The mayor intimated that Blethen wished to discredit him in order to undermine his tight rein on vice. The *Union Record* applauded Cotterill's "manly stand in the face of the hydrophobic [*sic*] attacks of his bitter enemies." Some labor leaders, however, did not let the Wobblies escape partial blame for the incident. E. P. Marsh, president of the Washington State Federation of Labor, stated that "the primal cause must be put down as the reckless, inexcusable street talking of the I.w.w. themselves." He railed against Wobbly speeches that, in his eyes, bordered on indecent, and their songs, which he believed were unfit for anyone's ears. While in the final analysis Marsh held Colonel Blethen and his paper ultimately culpable for the incident, he declared that IWW tactics and strategy "won't work in this country" and urged laborers to look to mainstream trade unions as the solution to their problems.[29]

As the head of the state labor organization and a leading representative of the American Federation of Labor, Marsh no doubt saw the Potlatch Riots as a unique opportunity to discredit both belligerent employers and the IWW. By 1913, the IWW had emerged as the traditional union movement's foremost rival in the Puget Sound region. Considering the growing number of Socialists among organized labor's ranks, including the editor of the *Union Record,* Marsh and SCLC leaders were careful to distance local Socialists from the event. As passions cooled, Seattle labor leaders soon softened their criticism of the IWW. Arrests of several Wobblies, the failure of the city council to provide victims financial redress, the issuance of injunctions designed to prohibit street speaking, and local theaters' refusal to open their doors to Hulet Wells's play convinced labor leaders that Seattle employers were using the riot to destroy organized labor. "From an insidious attack on the right of free speech," the *Union Record* alleged, "the master class have advanced to an open and violent attempt to suppress the expression of any ideas that do not agree with their preconceived notion that they are divinely ordained custodians of the brains, morals, laws, religions and wealth of the community." The real issue, the paper declared, was not where Wobblies spoke or how they acted, but what they said.[30]

Less than a month after the Potlatch Riots, the SCLC not only defended the IWW, but also had increasingly recognized that their shared interests outweighed their differences. Editorials spoke of "workers," not just Wobblies. The *Union Record,* for example, argued that employers objected to street speakers not because they interfered with traffic, but because "they are inculcating in their hearers economic theories having as their basis the contention that the wealth of world is produced by the working class [and] the capitalist class robs the workers of this wealth." Rather than dividing Seattle's working class, Blethen and the Potlatch Riots actually propelled many middle-of-the-road trade unionists toward the IWW. In short, a class attack would be met with a class response. "The workers have a heavy hand," an editorial warned, "and when they are aroused they make it felt. 'Ware the tiger.' "[31]

The leftward shift by organized labor significantly contributed to the demise of Seattle's progressive alliance. The economic downturn that plagued the Pacific Coast permitted radical labor organizations to awaken the city's working class to alternative solutions, especially following Blethen's public attacks. Just as laborers in Los Angeles looked to Job Harriman and that city's Socialist Party following the infamous *Los Angeles Times* explosion, Seattle's working-class found the Wobblies' highly charged class rhetoric as attractive as it found the business elite's class-based attacks infuriating. As labor moved left, then, it stretched the fragile bonds that bound it to middle-class feminists. What remained to be seen was whether these women could, or would, move left with organized labor; the future of Seattle's progressive alliance no doubt depended on it.

In 1914, the "tiger" struck first at the ballot box. Disappointed by the paucity of labor legislation produced by the city's progressive forces, save the minimum wage for women, labor officials shifted their strategy to direct legislation. Labor leaders, for example, circulated petitions for a variety of measures, including adding medical coverage to the state workmen's compensation program, an eight-hour-day law, and a bill to regulate employment agencies. After a brief court battle, the state federation qualified five labor measures for the fall ballot. Unions faced significant opposition, however, from the Stop-Look-Listen League, the brainchild of several leading Republican legislators. The league's campaign and the solid opposition of the state's leading newspapers buried all of the WSFL's initiatives, except for the employment agency bill.[32]

Seattle's unions had more success than the state federation when the SCLC called on the city's working class to support its own kind for city council. Such entreaties usually fell on deaf ears; however, politics had taken a significant turn in 1914. According to one student of Seattle history, the 1914 mayoral race revealed that higher-income workers had ended their alliance with middle-class reformers. Growing class consciousness spawned by the slumping economy, the Potlatch Riots, and progressives' lackluster results propelled conservative workers further leftward. While the candidates who threw their hats into the ring in 1914 differed little from those in previous elections, the outcome marked a clear change in local politics. Seeking redemption, former mayor Hiram Gill led the field of four candidates in the primary, which included an avowed Socialist, a well-known progressive reformer, and a traditional businessman's candidate. Gill easily outpaced his three opponents and confronted the businessmen's candidate, J. D. Trenholme, in the general election. That Socialist Judge Richard Winsor outpolled the middle-class progressive standard-bearer Austin Griffiths by more than two thousand votes in the primary was a sign that the city's progressive alliance had begun to disintegrate.[33]

Pitted against a formerly disgraced mayor, Trenholme tried to evoke the outrage of 1910 "Gillism." He also snared the hearty endorsement of several progressive leaders, including Griffiths, Reverend Mark Matthews, and former mayor George Dilling. Gill, on the other hand, begged voters for the opportunity to redeem himself. He also exploited growing class tensions in the city by promising to expand public ownership of the streetcars and defend labor's right to street speaking. Gill emerged victorious, sweeping all but one of the city's wards. Trenholme did quite well in the upper-class wards, while the new mayor once again captured the downtown region. Higher-income workers who had previously supported Dilling and Cotterill instead cast their ballots for Gill. Perhaps recognizing the crystallizing class sentiment in these working-class neighborhoods, the *Union Record* interpreted the defeat of Trenholme and two businessmen candidates for council as a repudiation of the Employers' Association. The election of union leader Robert Hesketh to the city council, the paper concluded, further proved that Seattle citizens wished to travel labor's, not the Employers' Association's, road to a prosperous and harmonious Seattle.[34]

The 1914 municipal election also offered Seattle's working class a unique opportunity to refashion local politics when voters elected delegates to design a new city charter. The *Union Record* maintained that the charter commission was more important than both the mayoral or council races: "they wear away into insignificance when brought face to face with the great problem of building a charter for the community that will in some measure eliminate the kinks complained of at present and what is more important to labor—preserve the advantages we have at present."[35] Labor leaders were particularly concerned that businessmen would exploit the charter commission to strengthen their position against labor. When the businessmen-dominated charter commission released its proposal to create a city manager style of government and return to district-only elections, organized labor immediately mustered its forces against the measure. In simple terms, the *Union Record* declared that the proposal was "A RICH MAN'S CHARTER." The paper complained that businessmen wished to run the city like a corporation, which no doubt meant that Seattle's working class would suffer. In addition, efforts to economize the city's affairs and decrease taxes implied a move away from public ownership of municipal utilities. The repeal of citywide elections, labor officials declared, spelled the end of democracy for Seattle workers.[36]

The battle lines clearly drawn, Seattle voters went to the polls in late June and soundly defeated the proposed charter revisions by a rather wide margin. Labor leaders, however, spent little time celebrating this political victory because the second front of the employers' battle plan was well under way. In late 1913, the Employers' Association of Washington (EAW) targeted the closed shop in order to assert greater control over the workplace. In response to the depressed economy and growing labor radicalism, employers concluded that the time was ripe to wage another open-shop campaign. The EAW chose the Seattle teamsters' strike of 1913–14 to deal its first blow against organized labor. Local teamsters had apparently made some headway with several local companies, but the Team Owners Association, representing the key teamster companies, held the line against union recognition. In June 1914, Teamsters Local 174 called a strike against the Globe Transfer Company after weeks of fruitless negotiations. At this point, the Seattle branch of the EAW entered the picture, applying pressure on all teamster companies to support the open shop.[37]

By December, local teamsters had seemed to gain the upper hand in the struggle as company strikebreakers proved ineffective. However, on December 19, a strikebreaker for the Seattle Drayage and Storage Company shot and wounded three strikers who surrounded his wagon. The gun blasts helped rally Seattle's working class to the teamsters' side, and labor leaders quickly blamed the EAW for hiring "thugs and gunmen" and introducing violence into what had been a relatively quiet strike. On the floor of the weekly SCLC meeting, delegates urged other unions to aid the teamsters in this crucial and defining struggle. Unnerved by the violence, several teamster companies apparently had agreed to sign contracts with their union members until the Employers' Association threatened these firms if they inked these agreements. What had begun as a dispute between a few teamsters and their employers had evolved quickly into a citywide battle between labor and capital.[38]

Confronted with growing class conflict, Seattle residents ventured to the polls and elected Hiram Gill as the city's new mayor. While union leaders implored fellow workers to cripple the Employers' Association by voting for labor candidates, open-shop advocates quickly secured the support of the city's leading minister, Reverend Mark Matthews, who called for arbitration of the dispute in order to avoid the divisive experiences of Los Angeles and San Francisco. Mayor Gill brought both sides to the bargaining table, and in April, after significant hand-wringing by union leaders, the teamsters ended the strike and settled for a small pay hike. The EAW, however, won the battle, as the open shop survived intact. Even before striking teamsters returned to work, the Seattle Chamber of Commerce proudly reaffirmed its support for the open shop. The campaign soon spread to the Bon Marché, with management announcing that the department store stood for the open shop and would settle a budding strike on these terms only.[39]

By the summer of 1914, Seattle's working class could not help but see their daily lives in class terms. The city's elite had solidified their forces

and waged war against organized labor in both the factory and the political arena. In August, labor leaders had the unique opportunity to vent
their anger and frustration before the federal government. The U.S. Commission on Industrial Relations, formed to study the growing class conflict that afflicted American society in the 1910s, came to Seattle to hold
hearings and gather information for its report. For five days, commissioners listened to complaints from workers and union leaders, including the
Wobblies, as well as the opinions and thoughts of leading employers along
Puget Sound. Professor John Commons, the nation's foremost expert on
labor relations, attended the hearings and commented that in Seattle he
found "more bitter feeling between employers and employees than . . . in
any other city in the United States." While the hearings accomplished little
other than publicly airing the grievances of both labor and capital, they did
seem to leave a lasting impression on many Wobblies. James Thompson,
an IWW organizer, reportedly carried the commission's final report with
him and quoted from it at length during his numerous orations. Com-
paring a behind-closed-door meeting among state government officials
to the Industrial Relations Commission public hearings, another Wobbly
observed that the latter "was a real investigation, not a star chamber."[40]

After nine months of turmoil and conflict, many Seattle residents likely
hoped that the year would close quietly. This, however, was not the case.
As the city prepared for another lean winter, residents experienced "the
most anguished conflict between the evangelical churches and the business community in the city's history." The issue was not a labor strike or
prostitution, but rather prohibition. Despite several earlier prohibition
attempts, including the failed 1889 referendum, prohibition forces once
again turned to the government to impose their moral vision on the state's
populace. This time, however, the Anti-Saloon League (ASL) chose to use
the newly approved initiative process to circumvent the hostile state legislature. While numerous rural counties already employed local option laws
to reduce or eliminate alcohol, ASL leaders knew that the cities would ultimately determine success in Washington. Seattle, then, became the center
of this latest prohibition battle.[41]

Initiative Measure Number 3, as the prohibition bill was officially
called, incited significant opposition from numerous businessmen and
every major Seattle newspaper. Some opponents argued that the measure

threatened property rights and the city's fragile economy, while others complained that it was overly moralistic and unenforceable. Despite the imposing presence of Reverend Mark Matthews, the Seattle Chamber of Commerce voted 632–45 to oppose the initiative. The city's working class, however, was not so unanimous about the dubious value of prohibition. Unlike with any other major political or social issue they encountered, labor leaders struggled to achieve even a consensus on the ASL's proposal. Regardless of the class struggle that plagued the city for more than a year, prohibition produced rather strange political bedfellows.[42]

The Seattle Central Labor Council first addressed prohibition in April 1914 when it went on record against the measure following a stormy debate in which several members questioned whether the council should discuss or even consider such an explosive subject. Nevertheless, the council declared its opposition to Initiative Measure Number 3 because of its adverse economic impact on several local unions. A week later, however, the council reconsidered its decision, and after another contentious debate, delegates chose to table the issue and simply take no official stance. Several leading union representatives once again took up the anti-alcohol measure at a meeting held in September 1914 to consider a WSFL resolution opposed to prohibition. Seattle labor leaders debated heatedly for three hours before endorsing the state federation's action by a vote of 55 to 32. The resolution's supporters argued that the measure, if passed, would dump more than eight thousand workers onto the streets. James Duncan, a longtime teetotaler and member of the national council of the American Federation of Labor, demanded that the SCLC reverse its antiprohibition stance because it threatened support for the several labor initiatives on the ballot. Frank Cotterill added that the measure was a trap, aimed at dividing unions from state Grangers who generally supported prohibition. On the eve of the election, the Engineers and Janitors' Association of the Public Schools broke ranks and passed a resolution in support of Initiative Measure Number 3. The prohibition debate illustrates how complex class politics had become. While the SCLC leadership argued that prohibition could harm a significant number of workers, Duncan feared that publicly opposing Initiative Measure Number 3 would undermine community support for labor at the ballot box. In short, class status alone could not help Seattle workers determine the worthiness of every political issue.[43]

When the polls closed on the evening of November 3, 1914, more Washington residents had cast their ballots on the prohibition amendment than any other initiative or political race in the state's history. In the end, nearly 53 percent of the state voters sided with Initiative Measure Number 3, effectively eliminating the brewing and saloon industries in Washington. Despite the fierce war waged by drys in their city, Seattle residents rejected the measure 61 percent to 39 percent. Tacoma and Spokane joined Seattle in opposing the proposal, yet the strong support for prohibition in the state's rural areas largely explains its success. Not surprisingly, labor leaders were dismayed by the electorate's decision. Not only did the amendment cost thousands of jobs, but voters also rejected the eight-hour-day initiative and, according to the *Union Record,* elected the "the most reactionary legislature ever sent to Olympia."[44]

Lost jobs and a tarnished image were not the only costs to labor. The prohibition battle also pitted the SCLC against many middle-class clubwomen, severely damaging their once mutually beneficial alliance. Numerous women's organizations, for example, actively supported the initiative, including the Washington Women's Legislative Committee. Adele Fielde, a strong supporter of organized labor and frequent contributor of articles to the *Union Record,* poured her heart and money into its passage. Likewise, the *Western Woman's Outlook* printed numerous columns and editorials in support of prohibition. Invoking the memory of Mayor Gill's recall, the magazine declared that Seattle women had to again rise to the occasion and defend the city's morality. Following on the heels of the Potlatch Riots and the growing radicalism of organized labor, the SCLC's public opposition to prohibition further strained the city's progressive coalition.[45]

Female activists' success in the prohibition war did not come without a significant price. Not only did the conflict undermine their credibility with organized labor, it also cost local women the *Western Woman's Outlook.* The leading champion of prohibition in the city, the *Outlook,* drew the enmity of the liquor industry. Two months before the fall election, the Liquor Dealers Political Association, using some rather shady methods, reportedly acquired control of the magazine. Once the pride of female activists—because the magazine was owned and operated by women—the *Western Woman's Outlook* passed into the hands of its enemies. In one of its final issues, an *Outlook* editorial noted that the Washington State Federation of

Women's Clubs had severed its ties with its former official organ. Within a few months, the magazine had ceased operations.[46]

Seattle feminists sacrificed more than a magazine in the prohibition campaign. That nearly two-thirds of city voters rejected the initiative indicates that anti-saloon women's groups expended a great deal of political capital with little return. The anti-alcohol struggle also fractured the unity that had marked female political activity following the suffrage crusade. The Seattle Federation of Women's Clubs' election of a new president, for example, signaled a significant shift in the club movement. President Beatrice Lung vowed to keep the clubs out of politics because it had brought much "discredit" on clubwomen. Instead, she pledged that the federation would return to its roots by emphasizing culture, not reform. "The Federation," she declared, "will do much toward raising the general cultural level in the community." Helen Ross, one of the leading female journalists in Seattle who consistently denounced unions, strikes, municipal ownership, and even the women's minimum wage bill, praised this policy shift.[47]

The Seattle Federation of Women's Clubs' election seemed to reflect a changing mood in local progressive politics. Safer gendered issues, like prostitution and the home, still engaged some women's groups, demonstrated by the passage of a law changing the evidence needed to convict persons of crimes against morality and decency. Yet, Seattle's major reform organization, the Seattle Municipal League, continued to bar women from its ranks. Formed by middle-class businessmen and professionals in 1910 who desired civic progress, the league wished to bridge the gap between the radical masses and business elite by studying urban problems and proposing practical solutions. League concerns ranged from prostitution and civic improvement to the election of clean efficient mayors and councilmen. To avoid any hints of impropriety, the league both prohibited members from campaigning for public office and maintained an official policy of nonpartisanship. At the height of the Progressive Era, the Municipal League embraced nearly every major social, economic, and political issue that the city confronted. Together with women activists and organized labor, the organization helped fuel the engine of progressive reform in the prewar years.[48]

Despite the growing political power of Seattle women and the numerous concerns the Municipal League shared with them, the reform organization refused to grant women official membership. In a 1912 debate about whether to admit women, L. D. Lewis argued that permitting women to join would expand the influence of the Municipal League because of club-women's vast network of organizations. Signaling the growing political influence of Seattle women, an editorial in the *Seattle Municipal News,* the official organ of the league, warned that women might form a competing organization and the resulting rivalry would weaken each. Nevertheless, R. C. Erksine spoke for many members when he claimed that extending membership to women would undermine the group's efficiency since most business was often accomplished at lunch. By late November, the league had still failed to vote on the matter owing to the lack of a quorum. However, the Municipal League's discriminatory policy did not escape the crosshairs of the North End Progressive Club. Composed mostly of female activists, the club castigated the reform group for failing to endorse two women candidates for city council in 1913. Club officials strongly rejected the *Municipal News*'s claim that sex was not a consideration in its determi-nation of political fitness. While it is not clear whether the league decided to grant official membership to women, it did open the doors to its general meetings to both sexes by the summer of 1913.[49]

By 1915, many of Seattle's progressive clubwomen had seemingly turned their backs on political engagement. The King County Legislative Federa-tion still offered an active and stimulating environment for women activ-ists, yet its focus on lobbying local and state governments narrowed its appeal. For large numbers of middle-class women who lacked the passion, skill, and interest of Adele Fielde or Helen Norton Stevens, the Legislative Federation, however active, failed to fit their new political sensibilities. The high hopes and expectations that the suffrage victory had produced seemed to have withered away by mid-decade, and with it Seattle's pro-gressive spirit.

Since 1910, the cross-class alliance between organized labor and middle-class feminists had largely defined and shaped progressivism in Seattle. The two groups had shared an anxiety about the city's moral climate as well as a belief that together they could create a harmonious and prosperous future for all Seattle residents. The economic downturn, labor radicalism, class conflict, and the prohibition campaign, however, drove a wedge between most middle-class feminists and organized labor. The growing chasm was particularly difficult for working-class women, who increasingly had to choose what mattered most to them, class or gender equality. As class tensions rose in the mid-1910s, maintaining membership in, or working with, clubs often dominated by middle-class women proved difficult for working-class women. When local politics became the center of discussion in these organizations, laboring women no doubt felt uncomfortable or angry with their middle-class sisters who criticized striking workers or Wobbly radicals. The events of 1914, then, significantly strained the cordial cross-class relationship that Seattle women had cultivated since the early days of the suffrage campaign. Working-class women demonstrated their willingness to maintain this relationship as long as it did not harm their class interests. After 1914, however, this proved more and more difficult.

The Seattle Women's Card and Label League remained the leading voice of working-class women in the prewar years. In 1913, for example, league members visited the largest laundries in the city to speak to workingwomen about the benefits of organization. Stepping beyond the union label, league officers hoped both to increase membership and "make its influence for organization felt by every local union in the city." In response to the slumping economy, members lobbied the city government for permanent municipal lodging houses for unemployed women and men. They also organized a kitchen to feed jobless women, an employment bureau to aid them in finding work, and an Unemployed Women's League to foster an empowering camaraderie among these unfortunate workers. Their support for workingwomen included pressuring the SCLC to back female barbers who had been denied membership in the Journeymen Barbers' International Union. Label Leaguers also did not ignore the growing hostility between Seattle employers and their workers. The league, for example, offered its fund-raising skills to local unions, including raising money to support local teamsters in their lengthy fight against the open shop.[50]

The workplace was not the only area of interest for the Card and Label League. After the WSFL proposed several initiatives for the November ballot, league members tirelessly worked to secure signatures for the petitions and distributed reams of campaign literature to educate voters. They poured over the voter registration books and urged working-class women to exercise their political power, just as the wives of Seattle's elites did.

The requirement that any political candidate who wished to speak before the group had to be a member of organized labor testified to the league's class consciousness. Moreover, several officials visited a Seattle Federation of Women's Clubs meeting to educate its members about the Teachers' Retirement Fund initiative that appeared on the ballot.[51]

On the crucial issue of prohibition, however, Label Leaguers appeared ambivalent. Considering the rancorous debates male leaders participated in on the floor of the labor council, few working-class women seemed willing to take a public stand on the initiative. Label League columns printed in the *Union Record* failed to address the issue directly. Instead, these columns emphasized the league's strong support for the WSFL initiatives without mentioning the SCLC's opposition to prohibition. The group's relative silence was broken when the *Union Record* printed a terse, three-line notice that an antiprohibition lecturer was scheduled to speak at a Label League meeting a week before the election. The response to this topic, a league member observed, was polite but apparently not enthusiastic. Like many of their middle-class sisters, working-class women largely supported prohibition. After listening to an antiprohibition lecturer, one female spectator concluded that her "talk was a novelty inasmuch as woman as a rule lean toward prohibition rather than against it." Here, again, was evidence that the choice of class or gender-based political strategies was not always so clear cut for working-class women.[52]

The passion and industriousness of working-class women increasingly attracted the appreciation and respect of male union leaders. Witnessing the Label League's wide-ranging efforts on behalf of labor, SCLC officials slowly reciprocated by expanding their support for workingwomen. Before 1915, they opted to work with middle-class feminists to fashion laws to protect women workers. While some union leaders remained comfortable with this strategy because it fit well with traditional gender sensibilities, others wished to incorporate workingwomen more fully into the masculine domain of organized labor. In 1913, the SCLC president, for example, criticized national AFL officials for rejecting a proposal to establish a training school for women union organizers. He added that it is "extremely hard to get a new idea through the heads of the Executive Council of the A. F. of L." When Alice Lord declared that the day male waiters received the eight-hour day she would demand equal pay for equal work for her waitresses, council delegates responded with a hardy applause and instructed the secretary to insert her statement into the official minutes.[53]

Symbolic gestures like the 1916 Lathers' Local No. 104 decision to hold a different kind of smoker, replacing the typical beer and sandwiches with a "bountiful supper" and the presence of their wives, represented only one way male unionists demonstrated their thanks and respect. At least twice during the late 1910s, labor leaders publicly denounced national trade unions that barred women from membership. Seattle machinists, for example, defied national leaders by inducting sixteen women workers into their local and inserting an equal pay for equal work clause into their contracts. SCLC officials went one step further when they granted female barbers their own charter, presented them union cards to place in shop windows, and directed the council's new female organizer to assist them in their efforts.[54]

On some occasions, however, male union representatives struggled to break free of more traditional views of workingwomen. On the same day that the SCLC endorsed a call for a national suffrage amendment, the council clashed with female delegates who urged the hiring of women as streetcar conductors. Male union leaders not only declared that the "employment of women in such laborious work would be little short of criminal," but also condemned married women who wished to work when their husbands had jobs. Episodes like this, however, were the exception. More often than not the SCLC heaped praise on its working-class sisters. The Card and Label League, for example, continued to expand its class-oriented political activities in the prewar years much to the delight and appreciation of male labor leaders. In 1915, Frank Cotterill visited a Label League meeting to thank the women for their outstanding work in securing petition signatures. He warmly applauded their efforts, noting that the league turned in more petitions than any other working-class organization. In a front-page article titled "'HATS OFF' TO THE LABEL LEAGUE," the *Union Record* commended Label Leaguers for their toil on the petition campaign despite facing abuse and rude behavior from numerous "gentlemen."[55]

While the Seattle Women's Card and Label League never completely severed its ties with middle-class feminist groups, its increasing focus on working-class politics and union organizing slowly pushed it along a different path. Label Leaguers' public expressions of class consciousness made it difficult for middle-class women to find and maintain shared interests with them. Obvious feminist issues and more class-neutral concerns could still produce friendly cross-class coalitions. League members, for example, often attended the general meetings of the King County Legislative Federation and joined with it to support various political measures. Likewise, clubwomen continued to find a sympathetic ear among their working-class sisters when they publicly complained that free suitable meeting halls in Seattle were scarce, or when they sought allies to launch another good government measure. The drive for a national suffrage amendment to enfranchise all women remained a powerful unifying issue that cut across the class divide. Nevertheless, by 1916 such shared interests seemed to take a back seat to the Label League's more pressing working-class concerns.[56]

Since its birth, the Label League had actively supported working-women's unionizing effort, but in 1916 its leaders announced that it was no longer content to remain on the sidelines. Edith Levi, a tireless Label League officer, penned an article in the *Union Record* highlighting the natural ties between equal suffrage and trade unionism. Recognizing that politics was inextricably tied to the future of the union movement, she urged working-class women to employ their ballot often and wisely. The next logical step in this growing working-class women's movement was to bridge the gap between wage-earning women and the wives of working men. In the spring of 1916, mirroring what one historian has called the "sisterly solidarity" of the King County Legislative Federation, the Label League formed the Federation of Trade Unionist Women and Auxiliaries (FTUW&A). Simply put, the proposed federation endeavored to empower all working-class women, much like the SCLC did for its largely male membership. Beyond advancing female unions, its founders also envisioned the federation as a new and potent weapon to strengthen organized labor and, in the words of Alice Lord, "perhaps be the means of getting labor recognized more fully before the eyes of our enemies."[57]

The FTUW&A reflected both working-class women's growing awareness of their power, as well as the failure of the male-dominated union movement to organize female laborers successfully. The federation's emphasis on union activity suggests that many working-class women remained frustrated with the SCLC's unwillingness or inability to bring women into its ranks. Rather than lay blame at the feet of male leaders, FTUW&A

officials argued that "the spread of unionism among women must come from themselves, and that only in unity is there strength." In short, male leaders might share certain class experiences with female wage earners, but only working-class women could truly understand the daily life of their sisters. The primary goal of aiding workingwomen notwithstanding, FTUW&A officials firmly believed that success would not be found solely at the point of production. Edith Levi understood quite well the power of the ballot in advancing both the status of women and organized labor; thus the federation's first order of business was securing signatures for organized labor's proposed ballot initiatives. By forging closer ties with local female laborers, the working-class wives of the Card and Label League further expanded women's political voice in Seattle while simultaneously extending the power of organized labor.[58]

These complex relations and political coalitions are what define progressivism in the United States. The seemingly odd political coalitions that arose in American politics during the Progressive period cannot be simply explained by class, ethnicity, or gender. A more fruitful way to understand it, however, is to recognize the multiple identities people possessed. At times, one or more of these identities (and there may be many more) dominated or shaped an individual's political sensibilities. Again, as Daniel Rodgers has so ably explained, one must look to the issue, not the person, to understand progressive coalitions. Certain issues or certain environments touched or evoked these various identities, and thus created strange political bedfellows. During the 1910s, then, growing class conflicts in Seattle increasingly provoked different political responses as gender and class identities were recalibrated to fit the changing social and economic environment.[59]

By the time American soldiers headed to the trenches of Europe, SCLC leaders had not only recognized working-class women's contributions to the labor movement, but had reciprocated by increasingly incorporating them into labor's ranks. The symbolic gestures of resolutions and women-friendly smokers had been replaced by concrete aid and assistance. Male leaders furthered the efforts of workingwomen by granting a charter to lady barbers, appointing an official SCLC female organizer, and by pressuring national unions to admit women into their ranks. Yet it would be a mistake to view these advances as magnanimous gifts bestowed on the "weaker sex." As the actions of the Label League suggest, Seattle's working-class women fought for and earned their rightful place in organized labor. By using gender as an organizing tool, these women not only improved the lives of female workers but also advanced the political power of Seattle's working class.[60]

By 1916, destructive political battles and poor economic conditions had profoundly polarized Seattle society. Progressive alliances, which had earlier expanded citizenship rights and ameliorated labor conditions, withered under the social and economic turmoil. While some middle-class feminists continued to maintain tenuous ties with organized labor, the majority associated with the club movement shied away from the growing militancy of Seattle's working class. Cross-class alliances may have deteriorated after 1914, but laboring men and women discovered both each other and the value of class consciousness. If 1914 marked the crystallization of class sentiment in Seattle, 1916 cemented it.

The growing radical character of Seattle's working class was evident not only in the political battles labor waged with capital, but also in the ranks of organized labor's leadership. Socialists and Wobblies increasingly filled the seats in SCLC meetings, and in 1915 Socialist leader and one-time mayoral candidate Hulet Wells assumed the presidency of the labor council. Wells had built himself a strong following in the working-class neighborhoods of Seattle. Following an impressive showing in the 1912 mayoral campaign, he temporarily put aside his Socialist predilections and "turned to the union movement as a more fruitful field for social activity." Wells did not believe that unionism alone would cure the ills that plagued his class, but did admit that it offered some protection for workers. He hoped that unions might eventually form a powerful and successful labor party, though in the end he believed that the SCLC was established as "an economic organization, not organized for political purposes." Partly frustrated by these institutional restraints and partly bored by the mundane activities of the presidency, Wells turned down a nomination for a second term. Other pressing political matters, in particular, the rising drumbeat for war, captured his energy and attention.[61]

Wells's fellow socialist Harry Ault also rose to power within the SCLC in the years preceding American entry into World War I. A resident of the

Equality utopian colony in the late 1890s, Ault threw himself into Socialist activities by his early twenties. He was a delegate to the national Socialist Party convention in 1904, helped manage presidential campaign tours for Eugene Debs, and worked with various leaders of the Washington Socialist Party, including Dr. Hermon Titus. After the internecine struggles within state Socialist ranks nearly destroyed the party, he moved toward trade union activity and was elected secretary of the SCLC in 1912. By 1915, the erstwhile journalist had become editor of the *Seattle Union Record*. His Socialist credentials notwithstanding, Ault, like Wells, understood that trade unions were not political parties but organizations focused on ameliorating working conditions. Trade unions, he declared to the U.S. Commission on Industrial Relations in 1914, should not affiliate with political parties. Yet, as his newspaper amply illustrated, Ault did not mean that workers should avoid political activity; rather they should not tie themselves to one of the major political parties.[62]

Under Ault's command the *Union Record* left no political stone unturned. Every edition confronted some political issue that affected the lives of American workers. The weekly paper championed working-class political candidates and those sympathetic to organized labor in local and state races. Nevertheless, the failure of prolabor ballot initiatives and the unwillingness of government officials to enforce laws or close loopholes that employers exploited increasingly left workers frustrated with politics. In 1914, Ault told the Industrial Relations commissioners that laborers had little faith in labor legislation, and instead they increasingly looked to unions to put pressure on government officials to enforce the laws. The *Union Record*, in his eyes, aided labor leaders by educating workers and rallying them behind prolabor legislation and candidates. Under his superintendency, the paper nearly doubled its circulation. By 1916, the weekly journal reportedly had 12,000 subscribers and more than 60,000 readers, giving it the largest circulation of any local labor paper in the nation. In a time of growing class consciousness, the *Union Record*, with its Socialist editor and large readership, quickly surfaced as a potent force in Seattle's labor movement.[63]

Socialist influence within the ranks of organized labor was both aided and blunted by the growing IWW presence in Seattle. The 1913 Potlatch Riots not only failed to drive Socialists and Wobblies out of the city, but at times drew them closer together. Both groups generally agreed that workers should someday supplant capitalists and seize control of the tools of production, though they differed on how to achieve this goal. James Thompson, an IWW organizer in Seattle, clearly articulated this difference in his criticism of Ault and the *Union Record:* "Now, our idea of a labor paper is that it should teach the foolishness of going to these politicians to get these laws and that they should pass the law in the union and enforce it on the job." In other words, he declared that he did not believe in a "capitalistic ballot" but rather in "the ballot of the union."[64]

Favoring direct action over political action distinguished Wobblies from both Socialists and traditional trade unions. Yet, the IWW's passionate and untiring effort to organize at the point of production did command the respect of many workers. AFL craft-oriented laborers appreciated the IWW's willingness to fight for the rights of workers. As class consciousness rose in the prewar years, growing numbers of unionists heeded Wobbly calls for more concerted action at the workplace. Their colorful antics—boisterous public demonstrations, satirical plays, and song parodies—only drew more attention to Wobbly organizers and helped them instill greater class sentiment in Seattle workers. While some state labor leaders attacked the radical organization for undermining AFL labor practices, including ignoring union contracts and collective bargaining, Seattle workers could not escape the powerful influence of Wobbly ideas in the prewar years.[65]

Growing class consciousness in Seattle's working-class neighborhoods during these years no doubt aided the IWW's expanding presence in the city. Despite philosophical differences, the SCLC came to the defense of Wobblies in the months following the Potlatch Riots. In 1915, the labor federation agreed to join Socialists and Wobblies in a mass protest meeting to condemn the government's harassment of Joe Hillstrom, an IWW leader in Utah. The SCLC also opened its doors to Wobbly speakers, including Red Doran, who spoke to delegates about the benefits of industrial unionism. On more than one occasion he and other Wobbly leaders urged laborers to recognize that craft unions had grown obsolete in a modern industrial society. In light of Seattle's poor economy, the radical labor organization's One Big Union philosophy increasingly attracted the attention of disgruntled trade unionists who struggled to feed their families during these years. James Thompson, the area organizer for the IWW, even pleaded his case before the U.S. Commission of Industrial Relations in 1914. He maintained that businessmen had formed what he called "one big union of employers," which permitted them to shift production to other shops or members of employer associations. This industry-wide organization thus allowed employers to weather union strikes and boycotts.[66]

The radical heritage of Puget Sound workers provided fertile ground for such class appeals. The IWW followed in the footsteps of earlier labor organizations from the Knights of Labor and the Western Federation of Miners to more recent socialist and labor parties. In addition, the SCLC's organizational structure, which divided unions into several semiautonomous trade councils, only encouraged such sentiment. As early as 1913, the citywide labor federation passed a resolution in favor of industrial unionism, tacitly admitting that traditional craft unions were ineffective in defending workers against strongly allied employers. Moreover, it suggested that employers pitted individual unions against each other because those unions not involved in a dispute continued to work for the company. In 1916, the Building Trades Council urged the SCLC to support a resolution to be sent to the AFL demanding that it abolish all labor agreements so that unions could aid striking brothers. The local federation agreed to encourage its national delegate to the AFL to work toward this end.[67]

The Seattle Central Labor Council gave more than lip service to the Building Trades Council request. From the mid-1910s to the mid-1920s, Seattle continually questioned and challenged AFL national leaders, including Samuel Gompers. Even WSFL president Ernest Marsh, who greatly admired Eugene Debs but refused to support the Socialist movement because it rejected traditional craft unionism, advocated industrial unionism during these years. By 1915, both Hulet Wells and James Duncan, secretary of the SCLC, favored the more progressive union strategy. Duncan's dissatisfaction with the conservative, and what he felt, outdated policies of the AFL led him to twice cast the only dissenting votes against Gompers's reelection as AFL president. Furthermore, Seattle's delegates to the AFL annual conventions continually reintroduced resolutions calling for the AFL to embrace industrial unionism, despite the ire of Gompers and other national leaders. By the time American soldiers landed on European shores in 1917, the IWW and its One Big Union philosophy had cemented a place within Seattle labor.[68]

Recalcitrant employers only aggravated the relations between labor and capital during the 1910s. Throughout the nation businessmen intensified their criticism of the union movement; Seattle was no exception. By the midpoint of the decade, Seattle bosses dismissed any pretense of cordial relations with labor and publicly attacked workers' behavior and union philosophy. When the U.S. Commission on Industrial Relations visited the Puget Sound, several businessmen blamed unions and labor radicals for deteriorating labor relations. For example, J. V. Patterson, the president of Seattle Construction and Dock Company, bluntly stated that unions "are an absolute abomination." He added that they typically attracted men of little character and thus he avoided union workers. Earl Constantine, manager of the Employers' Association of Washington, likewise blamed labor leaders for much of the unrest that plagued Seattle and the state, arguing that union leadership exacerbated the city's unemployment problem with its radical ideas and attitudes. Another EAW official specifically charged that the AFL and its trade unions used coercion and arm twisting of politicians to seek nothing less than full control of industry.[69]

The EAW's position no doubt reflected employers' growing concern about organized labor's political successes following the granting of women's suffrage. By 1915, bosses returned the favor and went on the attack, both in the halls of the state legislature and at the ballot box. Beginning with the Stop-Look-Listen League, business interests lobbied hard to turn back or weaken recently passed prolabor legislation. Moreover, they pressured state politicians to enact an antipicketing law to hamstring labor strikes as well as undertook efforts to undermine the public ownership movement, which organized labor strongly favored. J. V. Patterson, for example, stated that he and his fellow businessmen did not hesitate to demand that politicians "carry out their oaths of office" and "maintain the law." By 1916, lobbying efforts had paid off, as businessmen successfully thwarted or neutralized most of the labor legislation passed during the previous few years. With American entry into World War I, employers felt confident enough to urge the state legislature to enact a law "making it a criminal offense for any man to remain willfully idle."[70]

For many employers, hatred of trade unions was surpassed only by their antipathy toward radical labor organizations. Lumberman Edwin Ames, for example, believed that the IWW attracted "a lot of socialists and anarchists and they only take in the lowest class of laborers." The owner of the Page Lumber Company, Paul Page, declared that workers who listened to agitators and read about the "downtrodden laboring man" and that the worker "is abused because he has to work . . . gets just what is coming to him." Such sentiments no doubt helped employers justify their use of spies within labor's ranks. Ames, for example, admitted that most mill owners had "a detective in or around the plant . . . trying to find out who the I.W.W.'s are, and quietly let them go and get them out of the way." Professor Theresa McMahon confirmed such practices when she related a story about a colleague who sat next to two apparent Wobblies at a SCLC·meeting, only to later discover that the two men were employer-paid detectives who reported her friend's sympathy toward the IWW to the college president. Other employers, like J. V. Patterson, kept records on employee activities and character and passed them on to other members of the Metal Trades Association.[71]

Businessmen's assault on organized labor also included a renewed open-shop campaign under the direction of the Employers' Association of Washington. Formed in 1911, the employers' alliance boasted a membership of six hundred by 1914 and had ties with the Federation of Employers' Associations of the Pacific Coast. Seattle stood out, according to EAW officials, as the best-organized district in the state. Earl Constantine boldly admitted before the U.S. Commission on Industrial Relations that employers combined their forces in order to defend their interests against the growing political power labor exhibited in the state legislature. As with earlier open-shop movements, the EAW portrayed the closed shop as the epitome of "slavery, industrial war, [and] political corruption." The open shop, instead, drew upon America's revolutionary heritage and celebrated "the pursuit of life, liberty, and happiness." In particular, employers stressed that the closed shop interfered with the freedom of the individual contract between a worker and his boss. The EAW also took its message to the public, urging local churches to encourage nonunion workers "to unite into a union based on the principles of brotherly love, efficiency, the square deal." Critical of Seattle clergymen like Sidney Strong, who had often sided with labor in past disputes, the EAW noted that the *Free Methodist,* the official organ of the Methodist church, publicly opposed AFL president Samuel Gompers's request that the church endorse the closed shop. While the EAW walked the halls of the state capitol, Seattle water-front bosses seized the moment to expand the open-shop movement on the docks. By the end of 1916, a waterfront strike and a bloody attack on the IWW further inflamed class friction, helping to accelerate the demise of Seattle's progressive spirit.[72]

The EAW renewed its open-shop campaign by throwing its support and resources behind Seattle waterfront employers who faced a coastwide strike by longshoremen. For more than a year the docks witnessed growing tension between employers and waterfront unions. At the 1916 International Longshoremen's Association (ILA) convention held in Seattle, dockwork-ers complained about Pacific Coast waterfront employers' refusal to grant wage increases and to accept a coastwide closed shop. Before adjourning the meeting, delegates voted to strike all Pacific Coast ports on June 1. Seattle waterfront employers responded by recruiting Asians, blacks, and even college students as strikebreakers, and then pressured Mayor Hiram Gill to beef up police patrols along the docks. Advocating on behalf of the open shop, the EAW warmly acknowledged the support for waterfront employers recently announced by the Seattle Chamber of Commerce, Seattle Commercial Club, and the Seattle Municipal League. The *Business Chronicle,* a new Seattle business journal, likewise urged local citizens to rally to waterfront employers' side and protect the city's economy from the unions' irresponsible actions. The journal maintained that the conflict was controlled by "autocratic" labor leaders, mostly centered in San Francisco, who ruled over a union composed of "mostly foreigners." In this charged atmosphere it was no surprise that violence soon struck the waterfront.[73]

In the summer of 1916 Seattle's waterfront was racked by violence, including the stabbing of one striking laborer and the firebombing of a port pier. Meanwhile, the EAW and the *Business Chronicle* continued to press their case for the open shop. In between reports of daily mob violence by strikers, the business journal prominently publicized the prosperity the open shop brought to cities such as Indianapolis and Detroit, as well as the optimistic feelings Seattle waterfront employers expressed about the state of the labor conflict. In August, the Seattle Waterfront Employers' Asso-ciation (SWEA), for example, published an open letter indicating that local companies had no trouble unloading all ships in port and that they had an ample supply of dockworkers. The employers' association reminded readers that bosses were willing to hire union and nonunion workers, including ILA members. Blaming the dispute on labor leaders who were deeply influenced by the IWW, the SWEA reaffirmed its position that it would not compromise on the open-shop issue.[74]

While waterfront employers maintained a solid front in their battle with longshoremen, only the Seattle Port Commission stood in the way of total victory. Reflecting the strong public ownership sentiment in Seattle, the Port Commission was created in 1911 to oversee and improve the city's port facilities. In its first few years, the three-man port commission successfully lobbied for several bond measures to build new piers and improve the city's harbor. By 1915, Robert Bridges had assumed the presidency of the commission. A former state land commissioner and one-time Populist and member of the Knights of Labor, Bridges was a fervent supporter of public ownership and well respected in Seattle's working-class neighborhoods. He once explained in a letter to Reverend Sidney Strong, for example, that public ownership of the port was part of the solution to social ills plaguing the city and the nation. Ridding private monopoly through public owner-ship represented, in his eyes, a fundamental remedy rather than the more typical "makeshift and palliative plasters."[75]

Expecting great things from the opening of the Panama Canal in 1914, Bridges and the other port commissioners lobbied and cajoled citizens to expand port facilities, or else risk losing business to other Pacific Coast ports. Such desires placed the Port Commission at odds with many Seattle businessmen, who favored leaving the development of the wharf in pri-vate hands. By 1915, businessmen struck back, pushing a bill through the state legislature that added new seats to the commission in order to dilute that body's public ownership sentiment. At this point Bridges and the Port Commission turned to organized labor to petition state officials to place the bill on the ballot for voters to decide. In 1916, the Port Commission published a pamphlet urging voters to reject the new state law. The com-mission painted supporters of an expanded port commission as a small selfish cadre of private businessmen who wished to seize control of the port and exploit it for personal gain. Public ownership sentiment clearly remained strong, as citizens nullified the act at the polls.[76]

If the Port Commission's efforts to expand publicly owned harbor facilities did not ruffle the feathers of waterfront businessmen, its support for dockworkers surely did. Port commissioners, in particular Robert Bridges, demonstrated their willingness to aid union dockworkers in order to maintain peace on public waterfront properties. In 1914, for example, the Port Commission agreed to organized labor's request that it pay prevailing wages when it contracted work on its property. No doubt labor's cordial attitude helped foster good relations between the SCLC and the commissioners. Former Port Commission president Hamilton Higday told the U.S. Commission on Industrial Relations that if a port commissioner refused to support employers, they were branded as an "agitator" or "socialist." Bridges, however, particularly angered many waterfront employers. Soon after assuming the presidency of the commission, he instructed his staff to call the longshoremen's union offices for workers rather than the employers' hiring hall. When longshoremen struck the docks in 1916, Bridges agreed to their demands and settled with union workers who unloaded ships on the publicly owned wharf. The *Business Chronicle* immediately blasted the Port Commission, suggesting that its settlement was a blow to the Seattle Waterfront Employers' Association. The journal claimed that the commission refused to protect nonunion workers from striking longshoremen, and by doing so it implicitly sanctioned the closed shop. While the Port Commission's efforts could not itself ensure victory for striking dockworkers, Bridges and his fellow commissioners did help advance the cause of labor.[77]

The Port Commission, the Industrial Welfare Commission, and other bureaucratic agencies that appeared during the Progressive Era could, and often, did tip the balance of power toward labor. Whether appointed or elected, these agencies could act as a defensive buffer protecting workers from particularly powerful employers, as well as make decisions that could materially improve working-class lives. Theresa McMahon's vigilance as a member of the IWC clearly helped workingwomen gain more favorable wages. Likewise, Bridges' authority over the critical public port facilities not only guaranteed work for union laborers, but also forced private waterfront employers to make some concessions to their striking workers or else fear losing additional business to the public docks. The SCLC and other Seattle labor leaders thus realized that these government commissions and the initiative process offered labor new avenues of political influence—progressive inventions and ideas that labor willingly used to refigure power relations in Seattle.

The efforts of Bridges and the Port Commission notwithstanding, striking dockworkers struggled to gain control of the wharf. Facing injunctions that limited their protest activities as well as strikebreakers who filled strikers' jobs, union officials looked to city and federal mediators to settle the dispute in the fall of 1916. While both sides bickered over the membership of the reconciliation committee, the SCLC called on local unions to raise funds for the ILA affiliates. Several locals agreed, though the Waitresses' Union went one step further by offering to walk the picket line. Meanwhile, SCLC officials also urged delegates to canvass their membership to gauge support for a possible sympathy or general strike on behalf of the longshoremen. By October, federal mediators helped the ILA reach a tentative agreement with the SWEA. Allowed to keep their jobs without penalty, dock workers returned to the wharf but under open-shop conditions. Before year's end, waterfront employers violated this agreement, but brisk business and exhausted union forces produced only a feeble outcry from longshoremen. When the nation entered the war the following year, union working conditions had all but vanished from Seattle's docks.[78]

The longshoremen's failed strike not only dashed hopes for coastwide unity among dock workers, but also severely undermined any remaining middle-class support for organized labor in Seattle. The violence and bloodshed that accompanied the strike, coupled with the waterfront employers' ability to paint striking workers as un-American for challenging the open shop, greatly harmed labor's public image. Fear that conflict on the wharf might threaten Seattle's recovering economy only added to middle-class concerns. The Seattle Municipal League, for example, perfectly reflected changing class relations in the years prior to World War I. When the AFL held its national convention in Seattle in 1913, league officials showered organized labor with praise and support. "The demands of labor," the Seattle Municipal News declared, "are the demands of social conscience." A year later the league's journal announced that its survey of Seattle's industrial climate found that the city had escaped the problems that plagued other cities and urged its members to continue their "present policy toward labor in standing for equal opportunities to all." The News's findings, though contrary to the conclusions of the U.S. Commission on

Industrial Relations, illustrates the Municipal League's rather positive opinion of organized labor.[79]

The Municipal League's optimism about Seattle's class relations, however, soured by 1916. When class warfare erupted on the city's docks, the organization quickly announced its intention to mediate the dispute. Believing that it stood outside the battle between labor and capital and thus could best reconcile their differences, the league initially chastised both sides for threatening the city's economic future. By August, however, officials placed the majority of blame squarely on the shoulders of the longshoremen unions. While the SCLC attributed the waterfront violence to employers' use of strikebreakers, the league disagreed. When strikers refused to heed an injunction against picketing, the *News* condemned them for promoting violence and anarchy. The Municipal League especially criticized union tactics, including boycotts, strikes, and the closed shop, arguing that such methods relied on coercion and were contrary to democratic principles. The reform body implored labor to reject such forceful collective methods or else risk alienating Seattle's middle class. During the final mediation discussions, the *News* noted that capital had learned not to ignore the Municipal League's power and warned organized labor that it better not oppose or ignore it either. The league's public disapproval of any working-class effort to create a "labor trust" to combat capital's collective power clearly indicated where it now stood in this great social struggle.[80]

Class tensions in Seattle barely had a chance to cool before another bloody battle between labor and capital rocked Puget Sound. Middle-class residents might have soon forgotten the troubling waterfront conflict had it not been for a deadly gun battle between the IWW and law officials in nearby Everett. The Everett Massacre was triggered by the Wobblies' decision to assist striking shingle weavers who confronted well-organized anti-union mill owners in Everett. By the fall of 1916, Everett's sheriff had deputized several hundred members of the city's Commercial Club to assist him in keeping that city free of the IWW. Nevertheless, Everett Wobblies continued to test the sheriff's resolve to enforce a new law prohibiting street speaking in the vicinity of a popular free-speech site. Hoping to impede the IWW's practice of using outsiders, Everett's sheriff ordered a blockade and placed deputies at all entrances to the city, including the docks and railroad station. This provocative strategy only encouraged Puget Sound Wobblies to escalate the struggle.[81]

What had begun as a shingle weavers' strike in a small mill town up the Sound from Seattle quickly expanded into a regional class war. Recognizing the fierce resistance that their brothers faced in Everett, Seattle Wobblies joined the battle. In October, IWW leaders recruited forty-one members from Seattle's Skid Row district to challenge the blockade. Greeting the Wobblies at Everett's dock was the sheriff and some two hundred deputies, who immediately grabbed them, transported them to a remote area, and proceeded to make them run the gauntlet. One-by-one, the mob forced the visiting laborers to run between two lines of men armed with clubs, rifles, boots, and fists. Bloodied and mangled, the Wobblies dragged themselves back to Seattle. As news of the beatings spread through the streets of Seattle, IWW leaders declared that "the entire history of the organization will be decided at Everett." Calls for another visit to the mill town produced more than four hundred volunteers, of which two hundred boarded the ill-fated steamer *Verona* on November 5.[82]

While the boisterous Wobbly contingent sang and laughed in anticipation of this opportunity to defend the region's working class, several hundred deputies again assembled at the docks to protect Everett. No sooner did the sheriff demand to speak to the Wobblies' leader, than a shot rang out. Seconds later bodies lay motionless on both the dock and on the *Verona* as the ship's captain quickly piloted the vessel back toward Seattle. In the end, seven men died, five of them Wobblies, and more than fifty were wounded. Who fired the first round is still unclear; however, George Vanderveer, a Seattle defense attorney for the accused IWW members, perhaps put it best:

> It is not a question of who shot first, not a question of which side shot first, it is a question of who was the aggressor, who made the first aggressive movement, who did the first hostile thing. The man who did a thing to excite fear was the aggressor, and that man was McRae [Everett's sheriff] when he pulled his gun. McRae clearly did that before there was any shooting.[83]

The Everett Massacre sent a charge throughout Seattle. Business leaders praised the tough response of Everett's sheriff. The *Business Chronicle*, for example, supported the Everett Commercial Club's request that other citizens should contribute to the effort to "supress [sic] the unlawful activities of the members of this law-defying organization [iww]." The conflict reportedly stimulated anti-iww and open-shop sentiment in Everett, Seattle, and other cities, as well as increased hostility toward the iww among local businessmen and even "women of the upper social strata." Seattle Mayor Hiram Gill, however, publicly criticized the Everett sheriff. He declared that Wobblies had every right to land at a public dock, and he believed they had acted without violence. His defense of the iww brought a blistering attack by the city's "best people" and leading newspapers, some suggesting that it was grounds for his recall. Here again, the ironies of progressivism are apparent. The recall once epitomized the city's progressive spirit, for advocates saw this political invention as a way to save democracy from entrenched elites. In 1916, it was many of these same elite who now threatened to use the recall to remove a mayor who defended the iww's democratic right of assembly.[84]

Seattle's working class rallied to the iww's defense. "Rebel girl" Elizabeth Gurley Flynn came to Seattle to speak and raise funds for those put on trial. Sympathetic to the plight of Wobblies, Anna Louise Strong publicly defended them despite the damage to her own reputation. As the trial unfolded, she reported on the proceedings for several eastern newspapers and magazines. Basing her comments on her own observations and knowledge of the iww, Strong argued that "free speech was only one element in the fight. The back-ground was the industrial struggle and the effort along the entire Pacific Coast to establish the Open Shop." She noted that iww handbills publicizing the trip to Everett emphasized the need to defend workers' constitutional rights and that this clearly indicated that visiting Wobblies had no intention to "burn and slay" that city. Reflecting on the event a year later, Strong commented on how previous labor-capital conflicts, like Ludlow in Colorado or the Wheatland Riot in California, did not really touch her until this bloodbath, only a few miles away from her hometown, invaded her life.[85]

Despite support for the Everett Wobblies from Seattle's mayor and Anna Louise Strong, the Everett Massacre, coming on the heels of the waterfront strike, only further polarized a deeply fractured community. Middle-class support for organized labor evaporated as labor leaders waged war with local businessmen. Judge Thomas Burke, who helped whip up hostility toward the Knights of Labor some three decades earlier, organized a Law and Order Society to encourage Seattle residents to safeguard their community from radical workers. In this environment Strong could no longer straddle the fence between the classes. Where once she comfortably moved back and forth between her father's middle-class acquaintances and the boilermakers and longshoremen she sat beside at SCLC meetings, her defense of the Everett Wobblies no longer made this possible. Having applauded her child welfare activities just a few years before, Seattle newspapers and politicians now portrayed her as a "conspirator" and a "friend of anarchists." Her public writing on the massacre, she explained to the editor of the *Survey*, was the "blackest mark against me in most quarters."[86] Exhausted by nearly a year of constant class conflict, many Seattle residents looked forward to the conclusion of the Everett trial in early April. What the city needed most was time to heal its gaping wounds, yet President Woodrow Wilson's call to arms ensured that time was not on Seattle's side.

Wilson's war declaration surprised few in the nation, for relations between Germany and the United States had deteriorated with the former's resumption of submarine warfare. As long as the country remained outside the fray, most Seattle residents agreed that war was not in the nation's best interest. Despite the Wilson administration's "preparedness" campaign, Seattle city schools initially resisted the militarization of their curriculum. Women's clubs and labor leaders, for example, opposed the addition of military training classes or the use of army recruiters on the city's high school campuses. Such sentiment also extended to the University of Washington. In 1915, SCLC president Hulet Wells published an editorial in the *Seattle Union Record* urging students, faculty, and concerned citizens to ban military training at the university. Wells not only maintained that young boys did not possess the maturity to understand or judge the soundness of military service, but he also argued that businessmen hailed "preparedness" as a way to deflect concern away from the troubles of labor.[87]

From the outset, Seattle labor leaders strongly opposed the United States entering the European conflict. Within months of the assassination of the Austrian heir to the Hapsburg throne in 1914, the SCLC passed a resolution condemning the war and implored American leaders to steer clear of the European struggle. The labor council later announced its opposition to the implementation of compulsory military drills at the university and voted to oppose conscription of soldiers in the event of American involvement. In May 1916, the SCLC passed a resolution criticizing preparedness parades and other public activities, which threatened to "divert our attention from the greater enemies of the workers inside our borders to our less enemies in foreign lands." Within days of Wilson's war declaration, the SCLC voted 250–0 to oppose the nation's entry into the conflict and followed that with a strongly worded resolution supporting Hulet Wells's condemnation of the draft and demanding that Congress repeal the Conscription Act.[88]

Despite overwhelming opposition to American entry into the Great War, Seattle workers were careful to avoid charges of anti-Americanism. Less than a week after condemning Congress's war declaration, SCLC delegates held a flag demonstration and sang the "Star Spangled Banner." One labor delegate explained that the "demonstration was a very fitting rebuke to any and all who questioned the patriotism of the organized workers of Seattle and those who may have sought the limelight at the expense of the movement." Throughout the war most labor leaders actively supported the war effort, particularly the more conservative native-born members of the labor movement. Samuel Gompers and the AFL, along with the Washington State Federation of Labor, unabashedly endorsed the war. Several Seattle working-class leaders willingly served on the King County Council of Patriotic Service (later called the Council of Defense), including the president of the SCLC, R. L. Proctor. AFL leaders saw the war as an opportunity to expand the power of organized labor. Gompers, for example, used the conflict to solidify his ties with Woodrow Wilson, promising labor's loyalty in return for the federal government's guarantee to protect union jobs and wages. Seattle's left-wing unionists, however, viewed the war as a capitalist-bred conflict among imperialist powers, which in the end would only further entrench corporate capitalism. As Seattle's economy geared up for war production, left-wing laborers mobilized their forces, expanding both their numbers and influence in the city.[89]

American entrance into World War I did wonders for Seattle's economy. The economic slump that had plagued the city quickly disappeared. Demands for ships and wood products stimulated industrial activity in the city, and the port burst at the seams as shipbuilding companies expanded production. In the nearby hills and mountains, lumber companies felled trees at unprecedented levels. Organized labor also fared well, as union membership skyrocketed by 300 percent, especially in the metal trades and in the numerous shipyards that dotted the waterfront. Despite the recent open-shop campaign, the combination of high demand for war goods, favorable government contracts, and the relative scarcity of labor forced many employers to hire union workers. By war's end, the SCLC represented more than 60,000 workers, up from less than 10,000 in 1915.[90]

The changing labor market also transformed the face of organized labor in Seattle. WSFL president William Short observed that while Seattle witnessed exceptional growth in union membership during the war, the draft decimated the SCLC's leadership ranks. The loss of more conservative laborers, he suggested, only enhanced the ability of the IWW to increase its power and influence among Seattle's working class. In addition, thousands of Wobbly and disgruntled timber workers poured into the shipyards and other war industries in search of better working conditions. Wobblies and Socialists, already mobilized by earlier antiwar activity, were well positioned to take advantage of these changes. The threatened hanging of Tom Mooney for his alleged bombing of a preparedness parade in San Francisco further exacerbated class tensions in the city. Less than a month after Wilson's call for war, nearly five thousand Seattle workers met at Dreamland Hall to protest the Mooney case. On May Day, some twenty-five thousand local workers participated in a short general strike to demonstrate their outrage. While the Mooney trial stirred class passions, it was the prosecution of several prominent radical labor leaders that propelled Seattle's working class further left by war's end.[91]

Within a few months of American entrance into World War I, radical labor leaders began to pay the price for their antiwar activities. While the SCLC initially criticized President Wilson's decision, in middle-class neighborhoods the conflict quickly bred a strident patriotism that, as many scholars have noted, significantly curtailed free speech and civil liberties.[92] The "time for debate has ended," the staunchly middle-class *Municipal News* announced; "we are and will be unswervingly behind the President." Like other American cities, Seattle witnessed the formation of patriotic leagues and paramilitary groups like the Seattle Minute

Men. These private organizations wished to rally support for the war and encourage patriotism, which meant, as the Municipal League declared, "stamp[ing] out disloyalty wherever [they] may find it."[93]

The first victim of this internal war in Seattle was Hulet Wells. Like many Socialists, Wells opposed American entrance into the European conflict. To counter the preparedness campaign, which he and others saw as little more than a propaganda vehicle, Wells joined a local branch of the American Union Against Militarism organized by Anna Louise Strong. After the April war declaration, the group disbanded because, as Wells later explained, "none of us had the slightest thought of impeding the government in its prosecution of the war." That outlook quickly evaporated when American officials announced a conscription plan. Strong and her pacifist friends responded by organizing the No Conscription League. While Congress worked to pass the Espionage Act, the new league, with the able assistance of Wells, printed and distributed a pamphlet outlining its opposition to the draft. Even though the federal act had not yet become law, local authorities, egged on by inflammatory headlines in several Seattle newspapers, arrested Wells and three Socialist members of the No Conscription League.[94]

Ironically, directing the attack on Wells was not his archenemy Colonel Blethen of the *Seattle Times*, who had died a few years earlier, nor conservative businessmen's groups like the Employers' Association of Washington, but rather the quintessential progressive organization the Seattle Municipal League. The traditionally conservative antilabor forces in Seattle did remain true to form and publicly railed against Wells and other antiwar radicals. What was remarkable, however, were the shrill demands that emanated from the self-proclaimed neutral middle-class organization, which had just a few years before befriended organized labor. Eager to demonstrate Seattle's undying patriotism, the Municipal League slavishly labored to rally support for the war and squash any local opposition to the conflict. The Washington State Council of Defense, headed by Dr. Henry Suzzallo, president of the University of Washington and chairman of the Municipal League's Committee on Industrial Relations, canceled numerous teaching certificates for teachers who demonstrated pacifist tendencies. Before the year ended, the Municipal League called on Governor Lister to convene a special legislative meeting to discuss how the state should assist the war effort. Officials urged state leaders to protect local industries from enemy agents by invoking martial law and building internment camps. Disappointed by the governor's rejection of its proposal, the league nevertheless pushed forward its own efforts to ensure Seattle's support for the war.[95]

Any pretense that the Municipal League represented a middle ground between capital and labor evaporated with the outbreak of war. The organization announced that "the time has passed for discussion or debate on the merits of our entrance into the war." Furthermore, it argued that opposition to the war, whether in word or action, constituted treason, and thus city officials should deny the streets to "agitators and others seeking to voice their disloyal sentiments towards our country in this time of its peril." While Hulet Wells's Socialist leanings and his participation in the No Conscription League made him an easy target, other more respected members of the community also felt the league's wrath. In the summer of 1917, for example, league members voted overwhelmingly to expel Reverend Sidney Strong from the organization. For nearly a decade, Strong had best represented the spirit of progressivism in Seattle. Yet, unlike many of his middle-class brethren, he refused to heed President Wilson's call for Americans to accept the course the country had chosen. Strong's crimes, according to Municipal League officials, included disseminating antidraft material and publicly speaking on behalf of the IWW, which many believed harbored subversives. The decision of Ole Hanson, another longtime progressive, to run for mayor as the businessmen's candidate further reflected Seattle's shifting political sands. Once a strong advocate of organized labor, Hanson declared that he would not countenance sedition or any antiwar activity. In the 1918 city election, Municipal League president Austin Griffiths and other officials rewarded the candidate with their hearty endorsement. The collapse of the progressive middle ground evidenced by Hanson's victory, Strong's expulsion, and the league's charged rhetoric only aggravated a deeply polarized Seattle community.[96]

Hulet Wells's indictment provoked a groundswell of support from Seattle's working class. The SCLC, for example, raised funds for his legal costs, and several labor officials publicly defended the accused traitor. The *Seattle Union Record* also attacked the Municipal League, calling it "a bunch of stay-at-home capitalist patriots." In September 1917, a jury deadlocked and

Wells was set free. However, the prosecuting attorney chose to retry Wells, and in early 1918, with American troops now fighting in the trenches of Europe, a jury convicted Wells of conspiracy and sentenced him to two years in jail. Labor leaders, however, refused to back down and contributed additional resources to bail Wells out of jail and fund an appeal of his conviction.[97]

Seattle labor radicals quickly felt the repressive hand of both government and private organizations like the Municipal League. Less than a month before Wells's conviction, a mob of twenty sailors and two leading citizens broke into the H. C. Pigott Printing Company and destroyed the presses that printed both the *Union Record* and a local Socialist paper, the *Daily Call*. A subsequent trial later revealed that the Seattle Chamber of Commerce had hired the two civilian instigators. In late 1917 and early 1918, federal officials, working side by side with city leaders, organized a sweep of IWW headquarters. Throughout the war the IWW faced constant harassment and repression at the hands of federal officials, while the AFL and conservative labor leaders looked the other way. Seattle's Minute Men added an extralegal twist to these events as they assaulted Wobblies and broke up meetings throughout the war years. As one historian of civil liberties wryly observed, "it was probably safer to be a German agent in the Northwest than to be a Wobbly."[98]

The antiradical milieu in Seattle tragically claimed the reputations and liberties of Hulet Wells, local Wobblies, and many other residents. Yet without a doubt, the most celebrated and controversial victim was Anna Louise Strong. The expulsion of her father from the Municipal League foreshadowed the changing fortunes of left-wing progressives during World War I. As late as 1916, women's clubs, city leaders, and local newspaper editors continued to heap praise on the reverend's daughter. Her Child Welfare Exhibit drew thousands of admiring visitors, and Seattle demonstrated its warm feelings by electing her to a seat on the local school board in 1916. But though once able to move rather freely between working-class and middle-class organizations and clubs, by 1917 Strong's pacifist activities alienated her middle-class friends.[99]

Urged by local progressives and clubwomen to seek a seat on the Seattle School Board, Strong brought a breath of fresh air to the organization that she claimed "had been for two decades a self-perpetuating committee of bankers and business men." Petitions passed around Seattle on behalf of her campaign demanded "a representative of women on all educational boards." In a letter to a Seattle newspaper, Strong added that a woman's voice seemed logical considering that most of the teachers and half the students were female. Labor leaders also actively supported her campaign. Teachers and mothers, they argued, not capitalists, should run the schools.[100] Strong's victory electrified local clubwomen. The Seattle WCTU and Mothers' Congress Parent-Teachers' Association, for example, proudly applauded her victory. In a congratulatory missive, Eva Richardson proclaimed her success "momentous because it . . . proves to Seattle women what may be accomplished when they stand together even though the strong arm of the press is against them." The newly elected board member quickly pushed through her first initiative by opening school buildings to local clubs and citizens' groups as a place for meetings and other community activities. By early 1917, however, Strong's sympathetic magazine articles on the Everett Massacre provoked anger and resentment in middle-class circles.[101]

On the heels of the Everett trial, Anna Louise Strong turned her attention to Seattle's antiwar movement. Not only was she a prominent figure in both the American Union Against Militarism and the No Conscription League, she also gained a great deal of celebrity for her presence in two noteworthy trials in the fall of 1917. Strong's public support for Hulet Wells, along with sympathetic articles in the Seattle *Daily Call*, helped paint her as a radical and brought into question her patriotism and loyalty. Strong further outraged Seattle's middle-class residents by befriending a self-confessed anarchist named Louise Olivereau. Swept up during the government's IWW raids in November 1917, Olivereau was indicted under the Espionage Act for circulating anticonscription pamphlets. Her rather provocative attitudes about sexuality did little to improve her image. During an earlier stint in Oregon, for example, Olivereau publicly challenged the segregation of high school students by sex, as well as advocated the dissemination of birth control. Unlike Wells, however, she refused to put up a vigorous defense, choosing instead to represent herself. Asked by Olivereau to attend the trial and provide emotional support, Anna Louise Strong agreed and paid the price for her friendship in the local press. In her autobiography, Strong ambivalently wrote: "I was neither prepared nor unprepared for the eight column headlines which greeted the fact that the woman school director, already under attack for recall, had befriended an anarchist."[102]

Strong's well-publicized radical activities and the changing mood of Seattle during World War I contributed to her loss of middle-class support in Seattle. The Municipal League and the local dailies soon attacked her for what they perceived as un-American deeds. More importantly, women's clubs, once her greatest allies, also turned on Strong. Before Wilson's demand for war, many clubwomen shared her opposition to the militarization of Seattle's public schools. In 1915, the Washington State Federation of Women's Clubs (WSFWC) went as far as to pass a resolution urging President Wilson to keep the nation out of the European conflict. After Congress's war declaration in April 1917, however, clubwomen immediately announced that they stood firmly behind the president. Months later, the Peace chairperson of the state federation, Mrs. William Goodyear, proclaimed that clubwomen must remain loyal to the government and not comfort the enemy by criticizing its actions. She declared, in no uncertain terms, that each woman was either for or against the United States, for there was "no middle ground." During the war years the WSFWC, the Western Washington WCTU, and the local branch of the National League for Women's Service actively urged women to support the war effort by conserving food, aiding the Red Cross, helping in war industries, and disseminating "Patriotic Propaganda."[103]

While many clubwomen cautiously questioned the government's tepid concern for the dangerous moral climate surrounding army bases, demanding that politicians curb "the moral and physical contamination, which [clubwomen] fear more than bullets," they could not countenance Anna Louise Strong's antiwar activities. In response, the Seattle Federation of Women's Clubs, the University Women's Club, and the Parent-Teacher Association joined with the Municipal League in demanding Strong's removal from the school board. The Recall Committee charged that her antiwar activities, her support for Wells and Olivereau, and her sympathy toward the IWW clearly demonstrated her disloyalty and warranted her recall. "The people of Seattle," the committee concluded, "do not want anyone in charge of their public schools who is not entirely in accord with America and Americanism." Where just a year earlier many middle-class women celebrated Strong's victory as a giant step forward in the women's movement, the vicious public attack left Strong, in her words, "much disgraced in the eyes of all nice ladies."[104]

Persuaded by organized labor's unyielding support, Anna Louise Strong valiantly fought the recall campaign. When her neighbor noted that she had lost the backing of both middle-class clubwomen and the Seattle Ministerial Federation, she retorted that several of Seattle's largest organizations still stood behind her. The Boilermakers Union and its seven thousand members, for example, campaigned for her, along with longshoremen, the Metal Trades Council, and the more conservative Building Trades Council. The SCLC established a committee to investigate the recall effort and later published a brief pamphlet defending Strong. The committee declared that she came from "American revolutionary stock" and was attacked "UNDER THE CLOAK OF PATRIOTISM by certain interests which have always stood against the rights of the people." The report concluded that the charges against Strong were false and urged readers to vote against the recall.[105]

The SCLC also published Strong's personal statement in which she claimed that there was no better proof of her patriotism than her willingness to fight for her constitutional right to free speech. She also challenged the veracity of the Recall Committee's charges that the No Conscription League had released its document weeks before Congress had passed the Espionage Act. Reverend Sidney Strong likewise reaffirmed his daughter's innocence and loyalty. He argued that she befriended Louise Olivereau, not out of some ideological affinity, but because the accused subversive was alone and without friends. The reverend also championed his daughter's journalistic reports of the Everett Massacre and subsequent trial, believing that after passions had subsided her portrait of the events would be validated. Finally, Reverend Strong specifically attacked the motives of his daughter's detractors, alleging that they represented "certain interests in the city which care neither for God nor the people," in contrast to Anna who "stands for the kind of democracy that Woodrow Wilson voices in his 'New Freedom.'"[106]

Despite these passionate pleas, Anna Louise Strong faced an uphill battle, as the local press continued to rail against her while also refusing to publish her side of the story. One newspaper even turned down a paid advertisement she submitted. One of the few periodicals willing to publish her communiqué was the King County *Legislative Federationist*. As the official mouthpiece of the most politically active women's organization, the magazine declared that the same element that had earlier opposed woman suffrage and prohibition now spearheaded the Strong recall effort. The King County Legislative Federation, which in 1918 evolved into the Woman's Legislative Council of Washington, represented one of the few progressive voices left in Seattle by World War I. No doubt the fact that three Seattle Women's Card and Label League activists sat on the federation's Executive Committee in 1917 helps explain its steadfast support for Strong. Weeks before the recall election, Strong wrote in a letter to a friend that many women's groups still stood behind her, but feared organizing public demonstrations on her behalf lest "they be charged with being unpatriotic."[107]

The public and private support notwithstanding, Seattle voters, by slightly more than two thousand votes, recalled Anna Louise Strong from the local school board in March 1918. As she later noted in her autobiography, the course of the war no doubt influenced this decision, for "American troops were already in French trenches and Seattle's temper had changed." Immediately following the recall, Sophie Clark, president of the Woman's Legislative Council of Washington, sent Strong her condolences, condemning the voters' decision and adding that it would "injure the women voters of Washington for many days to come." Clark referred to Strong as a "valiant warrior" who fell victim to the hyperpatriotism of the hour. Recognizing the damage the recall might do to the cause of feminism, Strong wrote a letter to the president of the Seattle School Board requesting that the directors appoint a woman to replace her. She reminded the board that her initial election reflected local citizens' strong demand for a woman on the school committee. The recall, she declared, had been "stirred up by persons averse to the presence of any woman at all" and that it was her questionable patriotism, not her sex, which explained her loss. Despite the tribulations, Strong refused to run and hide. Less than a week after the election, she dispatched a note to a friend in the state branch of the National Council of Defense offering her services. Within a year her fame would extend well beyond Seattle when she emerged as the journalistic voice of the infamous Seattle General Strike.[108]

The celebrated trials, the IWW raids, and Strong's recall signaled the beginning of the First Red Scare in Seattle. In her study of Seattle's working class during this period, labor historian Dana Frank has maintained that Strong was recalled on "an anti-Red platform." In a few short years, Seattle's political environment had been turned on its head. The events of the previous few years had so deeply polarized the city that the once powerful and vibrant labor-feminist middle ground no longer existed. Most middle-class progressives recoiled as a more militant working class insisted on asserting its vision of Seattle. Moreover, the super-patriotism generated by the war provided middle-class reformers a much less threatening and revolutionary cause than refashioning the city's social and political hierarchy. Those like Sidney and Anna Louise Strong, who resisted or objected, were quickly shunted aside. Organized labor, the other half of the middle ground, had generally viewed earlier reform efforts not as the end but the beginning of a new Seattle. The city's changing economic climate and stiffening employer resistance together dashed its dream to build on these earlier reforms. By 1915, more militant visions and tactics best expressed by Socialists and Wobblies resonated well in Seattle's new social and political environment. As Hulet Wells later noted, by 1918 an "aggressive left wing" began to rise and quickly dominated the SCLC and organized labor in the city. The local labor council's hearty endorsement of the 1917 Bolshevik Revolution confirmed this shifting power balance. The favorable showing by "Reds" in the 1918 municipal elections, according to Strong, "expressed and helped create a new political alignment in Seattle." No longer did local politics reflect battles between the "progressives" and the "interests," she argued; rather new struggles pitted the "good citizens" versus the "reds." The trials, raids, and arrests in Seattle during these years, in Strong's eyes, were "part of a war between classes, not part of a war between nations." When the European conflict came to end in November 1918, the new battle lines drawn by the events of the previous decade shaped a different war that, like the Great War, would leave in its wake only broken dreams and unfulfilled promises.[109]

Epilogue: Patriotism, War, and the Red Scare

The growing class divide in Seattle exemplified by Anna Louise Strong's recall from the Seattle School Board continued to widen during and after World War I. The cross-class and cross-gender political alliance born out of the suffrage campaign a decade earlier virtually collapsed under the weight of the class conflict generated by such momentous events as the Potlatch Riots, the Everett Massacre, the hyperpatriotism of the Great War, and the infamous 1919 General Strike. The future of both organized labor and middle-class clubwomen, however, was more complex than one might imagine. The war years offered unexpected benefits to each, yet neither exited the war unchanged. The experiences of labor and middle-class women continued to diverge as they chose, or were compelled, to take very different paths in the postwar years. These paths thus continued to shape the politics of class and gender in Seattle for decades to come.

Despite the political tension and social unrest that the war produced, women discovered new and unique opportunities to exert their collective voice in Seattle. Yet like members of organized labor, not all Seattle women experienced or reacted to the war and subsequent Red Scare in the same manner. For middle-class women these events shaped how they viewed politics and the larger public sphere, often leading them to redefine and reevaluate their progressive sensibilities. Moreover, the profound class consciousness the war generated deeply polarized Seattle residents, testing the progressive impulses that had connected middle-class and working-class women for more than a decade. In many ways the strength of these connections was largely determined by the level of personal ties and social networks women had forged in the previous few years.

In the wake of the nation's declaration of war, Seattle women patriotically offered their services to the nation and their community. Scores of clubwomen jumped at the chance to participate in the numerous new government agencies the war created, like the State Council of Defense and the National League for Women's Service. Inspired by patriotic appeals, thousands of others served as officers and contributed time and money to the Red Cross, soldier aid societies, and war bond campaigns. For example, Bertha Knight Landes, president of the Woman's Century Club, organized five Red Cross auxiliaries and helped found the Washington Minute Women. The latter group raised money for families of needy soldiers and provided lunches, reading material, and moral support to young draftees. The war years, then, only helped improve women's image as citizens and political equals.[1]

While significantly expanding the level of women's public activity during the war, Landes and other more conservative clubwomen narrowly focused their attention on issues associated with the home and children. The Seattle Federation of Women's Clubs, of which Landes would become president in 1920, two years earlier had decided to drop out of politics and focus on raising the cultural level of the city. The direction the Washington State Federation of Women's Clubs took during the war similarly reflected this shift in its largest local branch. In an article titled "What Can Women Do to Win the War," the WSFWC listed three primary duties for women: maintain the home and children, practice conservation in the home, and provide moral support for soldiers. The federation's president also urged women to keep an eye on labor laws and see that the government did not use the war to justify abandoning laws protecting female workers.[2]

Conservation of foodstuffs and other materials needed for the war effort received much attention from clubwomen. The WSFWC president, for example, urged members to take a pledge that they would control wastes produced by their families and try to "live simply." Others encouraged women to purchase goods from Washington firms rather than eastern suppliers because long-distance trade wasted energy and resources. Most importantly, club leaders reminded women that their role as the primary consumer in the family meant that they could significantly impact the war economy. Working girls also were not forgotten. A brochure for the United War Work Campaign titled "How Much Good Can a Girl Do With $5" detailed how they could aid the war effort by donating some of their wages to the YWCA or the Salvation Army. These organizations, the brochure outlined, not only would provide comfort, books, and lectures for soldiers but also might improve the lives of female munitions workers.[3]

For two decades Seattle clubwomen had labored on behalf of female workers to improve their working conditions, including successfully lobbying for the eight-hour day and minimum wage laws. Despite the economic pressures produced by the war, many club leaders urged members not to forget workingwomen. WSFWC officials, for example, suggested that middle-class women's consumer habits could affect the demand for certain products and thus help prevent female workers from "being inducted into employment detrimental to their moral and physical well being." The federation's mouthpiece warned its readers that where women replaced men, the equal pay for equal work doctrine must be vigorously enforced. Wages aside, middle-class women also believed that large number of young female workers migrating to Seattle could greatly benefit from their own social clubs. The Seattle branch of the National League for Women's Service called on women to create Girls Clubs that would provide working girls a place for companionship. Teachers and secretaries composed a majority of the membership of the first clubs established during the war.[4]

Such concern for the workingwomen also reflected a persistent anxiety about female sexuality that Seattle middle-class women had expressed since arrival of the railroad four decades earlier. The Great War exacerbated this anxiety about morality and vice, since nearby Camp Lewis housed nearly fifty thousand young men. A WSFWC resolution passed in 1917 stated that since women offered their sons to fight the war, mothers call on "their nation to protect [our] sons from moral and physical contamination, which we fear more than bullets." More specifically, the Alki Women's Improvement Club implored Montana's congresswomen, Jeanette Rankin, to demand that the federal government "enforce a rigid regime, making prostitution and illicit indulgence a crime with heavy penalty, and the immoral women followers be interned as traitors." While most clubwomen abhorred the "vampires pouring into Seattle and Tacoma on every train," they did not necessarily see jail as the best solution for these immoral women. The wsfwc announced in late 1917 that of the several bills it endorsed, the most important was a measure requiring the state legislature to build a Woman's Industrial Home where prostitutes and other immoral women could be housed and reformed rather than simply sending them to jail from which most would return to their dissolute ways.[5]

Given the proximity of Camp Lewis, Seattle residents were particularly worried about vice. The Western Washington Women's Christian Temperance Union, for example, implored all women's organizations to demand that city officials enforce vice laws. Other female leaders called on women to supervise young girls and soldiers wherever they gathered. One Industrial Welfare commissioner specifically targeted restaurants operated by Greeks because these employers, she proclaimed, hired only the best-looking girls and required them to live in adjoining rooms next to where mostly young men resided. Concerned about Seattle's moral climate, the Woman's Social Hygiene Department of the Washington State Board of Health undertook an exhaustive survey of the city's workingwomen and commercial leisure establishments. The study not only collected information about numerous firms where women worked, including wages, working conditions, and the firm's recreation opportunities, it also examined dance halls and movie houses. Female investigators scrutinized each dance hall's hours of operation, the class of people it attracted, the nature of supervision, and the type of music and dancing that took place. The reports also left room for any remarks the investigators might wish to add, where most commented on the disturbing and improper social interaction between women and men.[6]

While the extreme patriotism produced by the war polarized Seattle and significantly undermined the city's progressive spirit, some middle-class women continued to promote a wide range of social, economic, and political reforms. No doubt the primary vehicle for middle-class feminists was the Woman's Legislative Council of Washington (WLCW). In contrast to most clubwomen who limited their interests to patriotism, the home, and morality, the WLCW declared in November 1917 that "in a true democracy every sane adult has equal opportunity before the law, in industry, commerce, and government, regardless of race, class or sex." Compared to the WSFWC, the Legislative Council expressed a more strident feminism that demanded that society recognize the equality of women in politics and the law. King County women who had organized the WLCW's predecessor, the King County Legislative Federation similarly desired the "removal of all legal disabilities resting on citizens because of sex." Specifically, they insisted on equal control of community property, laws holding fathers financially responsible for illegitimate children, and the removal of double standards.[7]

Legislative Council officials understood that lobbying was not sufficient to achieve their goals, since men dominated city councils and the state legislature. The WLCW did maintain a nonpartisan policy and endorsed only candidates that espoused its principles. Recognizing the central role government played during the war, the group's magazine proffered a radical blueprint for reorganizing the state legislature. The *Counsellor*'s plan proposed the division of the state into twenty districts each with two delegates, one man and one woman. WLCW officials believed that "to have women in equal numbers would give human welfare at least an equal chance with the almighty dollar." Demand for equal participation also extended to government agencies and other institutions. At a 1918 Social Disease Conference held in Seattle, the question of the exclusion of women from decision-making bodies provoked a fierce debate. The *Counsellor* wondered "when will women cease to be auxiliaries? Have they not proved their fitness to stand on a level with their brothers in all kinds of works?" World War I notwithstanding, WLCW women refused to bend to the social and political pressures the war produced and instead continued to press the progressive feminist agenda that they had developed in the years following the 1910 suffrage triumph.[8]

The WLCW's concern for workingwomen reflected both its progressive outlook and the fact that several working-class women held leadership positions in the group. Mrs. Ida Levi, SCLC woman organizer in 1917, and Mrs. Minnie K. Ault, wife of the *Union Record* editor, headed up the council's Organized Labor division and penned articles for the *Counsellor*. Moreover, the WLCW maintained good communication with the Seattle Card and Label League and even listed its meeting schedule in its publications. When Seattle residents recalled Anna Louise Strong in 1917, the Legislative Council was one of the few middle-class organizations to defend Strong by printing her rebuttal statement in its periodical and publicly blaming those who opposed suffrage and prohibition for the recall campaign. Advocating for equal pay laws and better working conditions for female laborers represented only one course of action. WLCW officials, for example, sent several members to lobby for the defeat of the Candy-Makers Bill in mid-1917. When female laundry workers battled for better wages and union recognition, the Legislative Council encouraged women to patronize the union-operated Mutual Laundry.[9]

Seattle working-class women not only informed WLCW reform efforts, they also helped expand the union movement. The SCLC's growing militancy and the tight labor market during the war produced a favorable environment for organizing female workers. By October 1917, the city labor council finally appointed a woman organizer, who immediately helped domestic workers form a union and assisted telephone operators in securing a raise. As women slowly broke into the traditionally masculine trades, male unions opened their doors to women. The electrical workers, for example, announced in December 1917 that they had admitted sixteen women into their union. Union efforts aside, working-class women never lost sight of larger political issues. In response to the Mooney conviction, the Seattle Card and Label League announced that it would support a proposed general strike scheduled for May 1, 1917, by not performing any housework on that day.[10]

That the Card and Label League and the WLCW were able to sustain a positive working relationship despite the centrifugal force of the war, testifies to the strength of their cross-class network. Whereas middle-class women of the Washington State Federation of Women's Clubs nudged rightward during the war, the progressive Legislative Council better understood the world of their working-class sisters as a result of the personal relationships they had fashioned during the late 1910s. Moreover, as Maurine Greenwald has argued, "working-class feminists in Seattle were influenced by the writings, speeches, and public actions of middle-class feminists, but they were equally influenced by and devoted to the working-class ethic of mutualism. Because of their dual devotion to gender and class rights, they tended to think about women's emancipation in more radical terms than did most middle-class feminists."[11] Constant interaction and discussions with workingwomen enabled middle-class feminists to judge from a different angle the class conflict that tore apart Seattle during this period. When the Seattle Federation of Women's Clubs and the University Women's Club suddenly turned on Anna Louise Strong and demanded her recall from the school board, the WLCW sided with organized labor in opposition. In the end, months and years of close personal relationships helped working-class and middle-class feminists to forge strong bonds that would sustain a fragment of the city's progressive voice into the postwar years.

The Great War's impact on organized labor was more complex. While the hyperpatriotism the war evoked raised class tensions and further tarnished labor's image in middle-class eyes, the economic growth the war engendered provided Seattle workers power and influence that they had not possessed since the heady days of the Knights of Labor and the 1886 People's Party. Beginning in 1917, union organizing expanded tremendously, as labor shortages, production pressures, and liberal government contracts encouraged Seattle employers to placate the demands of organized labor. Tens of thousands of workers, for example, were drawn to the city's burgeoning shipyards. By 1918, more than thirty-five thousand new workers toiled in local shipyards. Moreover, workers recognized the shifting power relations between labor and capital, successfully striking for higher wages and union recognition. At the height of the war, more than sixty thousand Seattle workers enjoyed union representation.[12]

It was not just the number but the character of new members that propelled the Seattle Central Labor Council leftward. Workers once ignored by organized labor felt the power of solidarity for the first time. Moreover, IWW timber workers flooded the city in search of higher-paying industrial jobs. By 1918, upward of ten thousand workers attended public speeches by famous radicals, like William Z. Foster, Elizabeth Gurley Flynn, and John Reed. Despite the apparent leftward tilt of Seattle labor, some labor leaders resisted both the growing radicalism and antiwar proclivities of Seattle workers. The Washington State Federation of Labor, for example, followed the lead of the AFL by endorsing the war, and its officers accepted federal appointments to various war labor boards. Likewise, R. L. Proctor, SCLC president in 1917, and several other union officials served on the King County Council of Defense, which encouraged residents to participate in patriotic activities.[13]

While the war pushed Seattle's working class to the left, it simultaneously moved Seattle employers rightward. Businessmen and city leaders decried the pacifist sentiments emanating from organized labor and the growing power of numerous unions, especially in the burgeoning shipyards where union conditions prevailed. The trials of Hulet Wells and the recall of Anna Louise Strong were just the first steps in the class conflict that erupted in the city following the outbreak of war. Beginning in late 1917, local officials undertook a series of highly publicized raids of IWW offices and meetings under the charge that Wobblies violated wartime espionage and sedition laws. Strong interpreted these events as not an effort to ensure victory in Europe but as class warfare. Furthermore, the Seattle Municipal League illustrated that much of the progressive middle class likewise moved from the center when it called on the governor to call the legislature into special session in order to strengthen the state's role in the war effort, including authorizing him to declare martial law and construct internment camps to house enemies and enemy sympathizers. The Washington Employers' Association added that the legislature should pass a law to help alleviate labor shortages by requiring able-bodied men to work if offered a job. Organized labor saw this as nothing more than a backdoor attempt to subvert strikes and was relieved when the governor refused the request.[14]

Strikes and public opposition to the Great War may have angered Seattle's elite, but workers' public endorsement of the 1917 Bolshevik Revolution allowed businessmen to exploit the community's fear of radicalism to weaken labor's power. Not only did Russia's decision to withdraw from the war increase Seattle residents' anxiety about the conflict just as American troops landed in Europe, but local newspapers like the *Seattle Times* claimed that this revolution was a German plot. It was not too difficult, then, for many middle-class citizens to see labor's support for the Bolshevik Revolution as tantamount to treason. In early 1918, vigilantes, who later admitted at trial that they acted at the behest of the chamber of commerce, broke into a local printing company to destroy the presses that published Socialist and IWW newspapers. Weeks later, Seattle residents elected former progressive Ole Hanson as their mayor after a hard-hitting campaign in which he persuaded voters that union leaders were intimately associated with disloyalty and Bolshevism. Unfortunately, these sentiments were so powerful that neither Seattle's middle-class progressives nor its businessmen would forget or forgive workers even after the war ended.[15]

This leftward tilt helps explain the defining moment of Seattle's working class in the early twentieth century—the Seattle General Strike. In February 1919, nearly sixty-five thousand workers embarked on a sympathy strike to aid the shipyard workers' struggle over wages. Relations on the waterfront had quickly deteriorated following the November armistice as federal officials cancelled ship contracts and the pull of war patriotism subsided. Behind the scenes the Bolshevik Revolution continued to shape the character of class relations as business leaders feared the "rising tide of Bolshevism" and castigated labor for "defiantly putting its own class interests above the interests of the nation."[16] Even WSFL president William Short claimed in a letter to AFL leader Samuel Gompers that the SCLC had "gone Bolsheviki mad since the armistice." In early 1919, waterfront workers walked off the job over wages and called on the SCLC for support. Complicating matters further was the absence of moderate labor leaders, who were in Chicago attending a meeting to consider a general strike on behalf of convicted bomber Tom Mooney. With the SCLC in the hands of the Wobbly-influenced rank and file, Seattle unions voted for a general strike to demonstrate union solidarity.[17]

By the time labor officials returned from Chicago the momentum for the general strike was irreversible. SCLC secretary James Duncan and *Seattle Union Record* editor Harry Ault were less than enthusiastic about the strike but went along out of solidarity after it became clear that the rank and file demanded such action. Negotiations to avert the general strike continued into early February, but came to a cold stop following a February 4 *Union Record* editorial by Anna Louise Strong. In a piece titled "WHO KNOWS WHERE," Strong attempted to justify the proposed strike, but the writing's language left the impression that revolution had come to Seattle. Whether this was Strong's intent, the editorial ended any chance of compromise. Businessmen and city officials, according to one historian, would accept nothing less than labor's surrender.[18]

Beginning February 6, Seattle was virtually shut down for several days before the strike concluded owing to pressure from several national unions associated with the AFL. Despite recriminations by employers and many residents, workers attempted to mitigate any significant harm by maintaining key city services, like power, hospital operations, and even milk delivery. The questionable success of this action aside, the strike nevertheless demonstrated the power of organized labor in Seattle.[19] While labor radicals perceived the strike in revolutionary terms, it is not so clear that the rank and file saw it as anything more than an act of class solidarity. Months after the strike, the History Committee of the SCLC published a pamphlet on the general strike that argued that workers had no revolutionary intent. The committee noted that organizers avoided use of inflammatory expressions like "class war" and instead chose "together we win" as the strike's slogan. While confirming that this event was not revolutionary, University of Washington professor Theresa McMahon did conclude that the general strike was "an emphatic expression of class consciousness."[20]

For Seattle workers the cost of this moment of class consciousness and solidarity was high. Any middle-class support for organized labor following war quickly evaporated. Local newspapers, including the once-sympathetic Seattle Star, castigated unions for threatening the city and demanded that they purge their memberships of radicals. City officials, especially Mayor Hanson, likewise painted the city's working class with the brush of radicalism, thus justifying the closure of printing plants, interference with free speech, and the arrests of dozens of Wobblies. Harassment was the least of labor's problems in the wake of the General Strike, as employers exploited public outrage to wage another open-shop campaign and reassert control on the docks and in the factories.[21]

One month after the General Strike, employers formed the Associated Industries of Seattle (AIS) "to promote harmony between employer and employee." Business leaders had already made clear their intent to bring labor to its knees when the chamber of commerce and local bankers organized a boycott of the Union Record in order to drive it out of business.[22] AIS officials maintained that they only wished to destroy the "insidious and destructive forces of Radicalism" that aimed to establish a "Soviet" in

Seattle. The new employers' association was not opposed to strong-arm tactics, including coercing employers to resist signing union contracts in order to maintain the open shop. When labor conflicts surfaced, AIS officials often sent agents or spies to infiltrate unions and report back with information regarding strike plans and internal union disputes. Associated Industries also began printing its own magazine, the *Square Deal*, which helped disseminate its message to area businessmen, reminding them of the advantages of the open shop and the threat that radical labor posed to business.[23]

From the fall of 1919 to the summer of 1920 at least nineteen strikes erupted in Seattle, including ones involving printers, waterfront workers, and tailors. Meanwhile AIS expanded its membership beyond two thousand, securing the support of the chamber of commerce, Rotary Club, and several other business organizations. Inflammatory editorials in the *Business Chronicle*, which referred to labor leaders as foreign anarchists, no doubt aided this membership campaign. For labor, the timing of these strikes was less than propitious, as the combination of shipyard closures and returning war veterans severely softened a once tight labor market. Hoping to demonstrate that employers only sought harmony with labor, AIS officials formed the American Association of Craftsmen and Workmen to provide nonunion workers an organization from which to voice their concerns. By 1921, the *Square Deal* reported, the new labor group had nearly 2,922 members who disapproved of strikes and favored the open shop.[24]

Competition for workers' loyalty by businessmen, however, was not the only challenge AFL trade unionists encountered. Radicals within the SCLC wished to respond to the AIS campaign aggressively and provoke employers to overreact so that labor might regain the upper hand. The radicals' strategy went beyond antagonizing capitalists to shaking up the AFL by pressing both the SCLC and the WSFL to reorganize the national federation by industry rather than craft. The One Big Union (OBU) effort nearly toppled the AFL-dominated state federation of labor; however, SCLC secretary James Duncan, who had advocated for such a reorganization for more than a decade, broke with the radicals. Duncan argued that the AFL offered Seattle workers the best hope to combat open-shop forces. Failing to construct One Big Union, radicals nevertheless demonstrated that their resolve to refashion social relations in Seattle had not diminished despite the backlash following the General Strike.[25]

Facing a powerful employer alliance and the hysteria of the Red Scare, Seattle labor leaders once again turned to politics to right the ship. While state labor officials attempted to fend off the OBU forces at the 1919 WSFL convention, delegates considered how to respond politically to the conservative forces' offensive. Begrudgingly, radicals agreed to an alliance with railroad brotherhoods and the Washington State Grange. Calling their new coalition the Triple Alliance, farmers and workers intended to use their collective power to endorse candidates and issues favorable to the state's producing classes. Radicals, however, understood that an independent labor party might be formed at a later date. SCLC officials, for example, had a couple of month earlier already contemplated revisiting a labor party following a dismal showing in the March municipal elections held in the wake of the General Strike. The formation of the Triple Alliance, however, superseded the local effort. Alliance officials looked optimistically to the fall elections to test the strength of this political coalition when Seattle voters would go to the polls to choose new school board members and port commissioners.[26]

As the fall elections drew near, organized labor embarked on a vigorous voter registration drive in Seattle's working-class neighborhoods to promote the Triple Alliance. Prospects for success were promising until a shootout between American Legion members and Wobblies in nearby Centralia unnerved Seattle voters. In the midst of the national Red Scare, legionnaires and local patriots in the neighboring lumber town attempted to drive the IWW from their community during the summer of 1919, but with little success. Despite at least two assaults on their headquarters, Wobblies remained defiant. Legionnaires chose Armistice Day, November 11, to finally rid their town of the radical laborers. Unlike in previous confrontations, IWW leaders chose to arm themselves and fight back. When a parade of legionnaires approached the IWW hall, shots rang out, felling two of them. The paraders quickly broke into the hall and captured numerous Wobblies and chased several others, including Wesley Everett, who eventually was captured after killing one of his pursuers. That night a group of men broke into the Centralia jail, seized Everett, and hanged him from a local bridge.[27]

News of the Centralia conflict quickly spread, generating outrage and anger throughout Seattle. Harry Ault published an editorial titled "Don't Shoot in the Dark!" which defended organized labor and suggested that the war veterans were largely responsible for the tragedy. More pointedly, Ault claimed that the confrontation was a response to hostile and illegal activity undertaken by those opposed to labor. At the behest of the *Seattle Times* publisher C. B. Blethen, son of Colonel Blethen, federal officials arrested Ault, Anna Louise Strong, and other officers of the *Union Record* and then closed down the paper for a couple of days. Their primary mouthpiece silenced, organized labor faced blistering attacks from local papers and public condemnation by various organizations. The *Seattle Post-Intelligencer,* for example, boldly claimed that organized labor had long supported the iww and that the "*Union Record* is today an i.w.w. organ, and every union man in this city and state knows it. It stands for soviets, proletarian dictatorships . . . and now it is just as anarchist as it dares to be."[28] *Business Chronicle* editor Edwin Selvin advocated for more vicious vigilantism. When the labor paper resumed publishing, Blethen and local businessmen chose to attack the paper by purchasing its newsprint supply and then lowering newsstand prices from five to two cents. The financial impact was particularly damaging because the paper was poorly capitalized and its meager resources were needed to defend *Union Record* officers from sedition charges.[29]

The Centralia Massacre not only reignited anti-Red sentiment in Seattle and emboldened the Associated Industries open-shop campaign, but it also influenced the fall elections. The sclc's prominent role in the Triple Alliance and its support for school board and port commissioner candidates made the election a referendum on organized labor. Since its inception, businessmen had equated the Triple Alliance with "ultra-Radicalism." The *Business Chronicle,* for example, linked the new political organization to the General Strike: "The real purpose of the men back of the Triple Alliance is to accomplish by stealth and political chicanery what the Closed Shop revolutionists failed to accomplish by force in February."[30] On the eve of the election, the Associated Industries clarified how the party threatened Seattle. Officials claimed that the Triple Alliance wished to dominate the school board so that it could teach its ideas to children and control the Port Commission so that labor could rule the waterfront.

With the Centralia episode fresh in voters' minds, employers argued that the alliance was a "class movement, spring[ing] from the same 'class' from which c[a]me the I.W.W."[31]

The connection between Centralia, the Triple Alliance, and the December elections seemed apparent to labor. WSFL president William Short, for example, wrote to Samuel Gompers during the uproar over the Wobbly-American Legion conflict, claiming that the seizure of the *Union Record* was part of the AIS open-shop campaign. He averred that the "Triple Alliance was growing rapidly and bidding fair to become a force politically on behalf of labor, and opposition was expressing alarm."[32] The letter also explained that one of the paper's staff arrested after Centralia was also a Triple Alliance candidate for the school board. Professor Theresa McMahon likewise suggested in the national magazine the *Survey* that the charged political atmosphere surrounding the Triple Alliance candidates was linked to the tragedy. Perhaps the most damming evidence that local employers exploited the outrage over the Centralia Massacre was a report by one AIS agent sent to spy on union meetings, which admitted that employers wanted to shut down the *Union Record* before the election because of the large number of laborers who had recently registered to vote. On the same day that a Seattle grand jury indicted the *Union Record* officers, residents overwhelmingly rebuffed the Triple Alliance candidates.[33]

As an economic depression enveloped Puget Sound in the winter of 1920 and employers published full-page ads in the Seattle dailies promoting the American Plan or open shop, working-class leaders once more turned to politics. When AIS officials endorsed C. B. Fitzgerald for mayor, labor leaders immediately convened a "council of war" to determine how to respond. After much debate, delegates declared that employer aggression had to met head-on and announced that the secretary of the Central Labor Council James Duncan would oppose Fitzgerald and Municipal League officer Hugh Caldwell. Heralding their candidate as the "people's candidate," SCLC leaders marshaled all their resources to defeat the employers' candidate.[34]

Confronting the AIS at the ballot box was a simple decision, but as one union activist concluded, the employers "had all the advantage. They had the government behind them. That fact demonstrated to the workers that before they can accomplish anything that they must acquire political control."[35] The King County Triple Alliance endorsed Duncan and three labor-friendly councilmen; however, the three council candidates quickly distanced themselves from Duncan and the alliance because the public associated both with radicalism and the IWW. Complicating matters further was the more conservative state Triple Alliance's decision to repudiate the King County group's endorsement because it opposed Duncan's left-wing sensibilities. The local press hounded Duncan with accusations that he sought class rule and "Soviet government" and that a victory by him would return Seattle to days of the General Strike. Nevertheless, SCLC support propelled Duncan into second place in the primary, pitting him against Caldwell in the general election. Conservative forces quickly threw their support behind Caldwell and peppered the labor candidate with claims that he desired the "nationalization of women." When all was said and done, Caldwell defeated Duncan by some seventeen thousand votes, though Duncan did record seven thousand more votes than he did in the primary.[36]

Trounced once again in a municipal election, organized labor demonstrated its remarkable resiliency when less than a month later the SCLC joined the National Labor Party (NLP). Upset that the state Triple Alliance rejected his candidacy, Duncan convinced SCLC leaders to commit Seattle workers to an independent labor party and thus formally rejected the AFL policy of nonpartisanship. The NLP was short lived, as it fused with a left-wing Democratic Party splinter group called the Committee of 48 during a convention chaired by Duncan in Chicago. After rechristening the party as the Farmer-Labor Party (FLP), the SCLC immediately encountered resistance from WSFL president William Short, who struggled to control the left-wing and independent political party unionists who continued to rebuff the AFL's political policy. After a series of wild and complicated meetings held throughout the summer of 1920, Short regretfully admitted to Gompers that the rank and file had won and that the WSFL had little choice but to accept the formation of the FLP in Washington. The new party brought together the WSFL, the Washington State Grange, the Triple Alliance, the Committee of 48, and a few other political groups that quickly convened to select candidates for the upcoming fall elections.[37]

The FLP's platform was broad and reflected the goals of farmers, workers, and those opposed to conservative Republican policies. Delegates added planks on the eight-hour day, workmen's compensation, publicly owned grain elevators, more democratic control of the schools, and government control of the telephone and telegraph industries. The party also nominated Seattle Port Commissioner Robert Bridges for governor and James Duncan for Congress. When the polls closed, Bridges claimed 30 percent of the vote, a distant second to the Republican candidate but nearly double the Democratic Party nominee. FLP candidates seeking statewide office all failed to win their seats, and only a couple of its candidates won seats in the state legislature. While the FLP was able to limp along for a few more years, the punishing economic downturn and rightward shift in state and national politics accelerated the unraveling of the coalition, including WSFL's withdrawal in 1921.[38]

By 1922 the goal of creating a vibrant third party in which labor could carry out its vision of Seattle had largely disappeared. The depressed economy produced significant joblessness, especially in the shipyards and metal trades that had been home to many labor radicals. AFL unionists now reasserted their power and pulled SCLC support for the FLP, bringing the labor federation back in line with the AFL's nonpartisan policy. Moreover, the advertising boycott of the *Union Record* increasingly took its toll on the paper's finances, and declining union membership contributed to plummeting subscriptions. No longer able to dominate the SCLC, labor radicals turned on the *Union Record* and its editor Harry Ault. Ault faced charges that he was a "labor-capitalist" because he had helped organize several labor-controlled businesses, like the Mutual Laundry, the Trades Union Saving and Loan, several theaters, and the *Union Record*. Specifically, opponents complained that these businesses aimed to enrich their promoters and not workers and that Ault and other managers were in fact employers and thus should not assume leadership positions in the labor movement. To fend off this offensive the former Socialist Ault turned to conservative unionists, including WSFL president William Short, who helped silence or isolate radicals. By the mid-1920s the *Seattle Union Record* was a shell of its former self and by 1928 had ceased to exist.[39]

In many ways the rapid demise of the Seattle workers' primary mouthpiece mirrored the downfall of organized labor. Just as the *Union Record* faced attacks from both within and without the city's working-class neighborhoods, the SCLC struggled to overcome the oppressive onslaught of the

Associated Industries and the internecine warfare between left-wing radicals and AFL loyalists. As Dana Frank has ably illustrated, Seattle workers increasingly sought to improve their lives not through traditional electoral politics, but rather through politicized consumption. In the labor-hostile environment that followed the First Red Scare, laborers increasingly looked to consumption as a way to resist their employers' power. Boycotts, union label campaigns, and even labor-owned businesses signified the new path of resistance that Seattle workers chose in the 1920s. By the midpoint of the decade, Wobblies, labor party activists, Socialists, and other radicals no longer commanded SCLC meetings, but increasingly gave way to the more conservative teamster unions that would dominate Seattle labor for the next few decades.[40]

Internally divided and its reputation sullied by the general strike, organized labor in Seattle saw its political voice increasingly silenced. By the mid-1920s, Seattle workers had renounced independent political parties and returned to the nonpartisan ways of the AFL. While the SCLC remained focused on consumption strategies to create a more favorable balance of power in the city, they did not completely ignore local politics. The labor council continued to endorse candidates in local and state elections, though these candidates largely reflected middle-class sensibilities.[41] Class, then, would continue to defined Seattle politics but in new and different ways, with different coalitions, agendas, and strategies. Likewise, gender politics remained an important part of the local scene throughout the Jazz Age. Unlike labor, Seattle's clubwomen had exited the war years largely unscathed. Instead, their service to the nation's cause only raised the public image of women in the community's eyes.

Nevertheless, below the surface much had changed since the thrilling days following the 1910 suffrage campaign. The growing class conflict that plagued Seattle following the Potlatch Riots had not only destroyed clubwomen's important political alliance with organized labor, but it also drove many women away from direct political activity. Whereas in the 1910s Seattle women probed nearly every important political issue from city taxes to municipal ownership, the following decade saw voting women narrow their focus to vice and more traditional women's issues. Moreover, female activists no longer enjoyed the important women's magazines that had politicized female voters and cultivated political awareness. Working-class women likewise engaged electoral politics less and, in the class-conscious postwar years, increasingly severed their ties with middle-class clubwomen in order to protect labor's interests. In short, Seattle women did maintain a political voice in the 1920s, yet it was smaller, less organized, and more narrowly focused.[42]

The profound class strife produced by the 1919 General Strike and the Centralia Massacre not only polarized employers and workers, but also severely tested the cross-class alliance between workingwomen and middle-class feminists. With organized labor withering from the attacks by the press and Associated Industries, female workers struggled alongside their union brothers and were no doubt pulled in different directions by the internal disputes inside the sclc. Minnie Ault, for example, watched her husband Harry side with conservative unions in order to salvage his newspaper. Furthermore, the economic depression of the 1920–21 left many women unemployed and their unions weakened or destroyed. By 1922, even the once vibrant Seattle Card and Label League lay prostrate as its left-wing leadership was replaced by the wives of the new conservative sclc leaders or, as in the case of Minnie Ault, slid rightward with the rest of the league.[43]

Minnie Ault shared her move to the right with most of Seattle's middle-class women in the decade following World War I. Clubwomen, however, maintained their organizations, and many continued to thrive well into the 1920s. Public morality and concern about the home remained central to both the wsfwc and the wlcw, though the latter never failed to demand that women be treated equally. Nearly two years after the war, for example, Sophie Clark, president of the Legislative Council, wrote to Dr. Alice M. Smith about the need to ensure that enforcement of health care laws was impartial even if that meant that women, just like men, "should be forcefully detained" if they continued in the immoral ways. Throughout the postwar years the wlcw actively engaged the political process, lobbying or endorsing a variety of legal and political issues, yet its narrow focus on legislation and its assertive feminism limited its appeal to middle-class women in the changing political culture of 1920's America.[44]

Conservative clubwomen, just like their working-class sisters, could not escape the changes the war brought to Seattle. The city's exploding growth and increasing class conflict during the postwar years greatly informed clubwomen's political and social sensibilities. By 1920, Seattle's foreign-born population topped 25 percent, and the association of these newcomers with the radicalism of labor generated calls for Americanization programs. WSFWC minutes revealed growing anxiety about the threat foreigners posed to Seattle and Washington State, and clubwomen took the lead in advocating Americanization. Moreover, just as working-class women struggled with the economic depression following the war, middle-class clubwomen energetically assumed more responsibility for promoting the region's economy. In 1921, for example, the Seattle Federation of Women's Clubs organized the Women's Educational Exhibit for Washington Manufacturers. Under the leadership of federation president Bertha Knight Landes, the exhibition combined women's role as consumers with Seattle manufacturing to showcase and boost the city's businesses. The chamber of commerce and local newspapers heaped praise on Landes and other clubwomen for their passion and business acumen. In an age when Americans celebrated capitalism and the arrival of the "New Woman," Seattle clubwomen chose to leave their progressive beliefs behind them and settle into the comfortable world of 1920's America.[45]

Ironically, while Seattle women as a whole seemed to recoil somewhat from political activity after World War I, one woman reached the pinnacle of power when voters elected her as the city's mayor. In 1926, Bertha Knight Landes became the first female mayor of a major American city. At first glance, Landes would seem to have been an unlikely first female mayor in Seattle. While she was an active clubwoman during the Progressive Era, she was apparently uncomfortable with the political activism of prominent feminists such as Helen Norton Stevens, Adele Fielde, or even Anna Louise Strong. Yet it was exactly her brand of feminism that made her an acceptable candidate to so many Seattle citizens. Landes first won public office in 1922 when various community groups urged her to run for city council. In the postwar years vice continued to plague Seattle, and she exploited this by running a "municipal housekeeping" campaign. Landes used arguments similar to those that Seattle suffragists had employed two decades earlier—the city was like a home and its residents were a family. However, she also acknowledged that a city had to be run like a business. On the day of the election Landes summed up her campaign: "It has been strictly a women's campaign to elect a woman to the city council without entangling alliances, to represent woman's thought and viewpoint.... Our idea was to serve the best interests of the city; not to further the political ambitions of any one woman." In a surprising victory, Landes won a plurality of the vote and joined fellow candidate Kathryn Miracle as a newly elected member of the Seattle City Council.[46]

By 1926, Seattle's mayor was under attack for his lax enforcement of prohibition and prostitution laws. The active encouragement of community groups, combined with concern for the city's reputation, compelled Landes to run for mayor. She defeated the incumbent by several thousand votes. Despite Landes's probusiness views, the SCLC, having both abandoned any prospects for an independent labor party and largely eliminated radicals from the council, endorsed her and seemingly returned to the coalition politics of the Progressive Era. During her two-year term Landes broadened her concerns beyond law enforcement to social welfare and economic development. Despite her apparent success, Landes lost her reelection bid in 1928. No single reason explains her defeat, though scholars have offered a few plausible explanations. For one, Landes had become an insider after two years in office. Her successful crackdown on vice also had removed a key issue from the campaign. Finally, her opponents tapped into the uncertain feelings Seattle residents—male and female—harbored about Landes's public and powerful role, which still challenged traditional gender norms.[47]

The divergent fortunes of organized labor and middle-class clubwomen evident in 1920's Seattle quickly turned by the time of the depression in the next decade. By 1930, the Seattle Federation of Women's Clubs had changed priorities from city politics to social and personal improvement. Clubwomen focused their attention on art projects and community improvement programs, while membership rapidly declined. The arrival of Franklin Roosevelt and his New Deal, however, helped revive organized labor in Seattle. Union memberships increased, and under the leadership of the Teamsters Union, organized labor reclaimed its political voice in Seattle. As the city entered the depression and war years, the politics of class and gender would, as it had for more than a half-century, continue to shape the social and political landscape of Seattle.[48]

Notes

INTRODUCTION

1. Kathryn Oberdeck, "'Not Pink Teas: The Seattle Working-Class Women's Movement, 1905–1918," *Labor History* 32.2 (Spring 1991): 210.

2. Oberdeck, "Not Pink Teas," 208–9.

3. Michael P. Malone, "Beyond the Last Frontier: Toward a New Approach to Western American History," in *Trails: Toward a New Western History,* ed. Patricia N. Limerick, Clyde A. Milner II, and Charles E. Rankin (Lawrence: University Press of Kansas, 1991), 144. See also Gerald D. Nash and Richard W. Etulain, eds., *The Twentieth-Century West: Historical Interpretations* (Albuquerque: University of New Mexico Press, 1989), xi.

4. William G. Robbins, *Colony and Empire: The Capitalist Transformation of the American West* (Lawrence: University Press of Kansas, 1994), 62.

5. William Deverell, "Fighting Words: The Significance of the American West in the History of the United States," in *A New Significance: Re-envisioning the History of the American West,* ed. Clyde A. Milner II (New York: Oxford University Press, 1996), 40.

6. Donald Worster, "Beyond the Agrarian Myth," in Limerick, Milner, and Rankin, *Trails,* 21.

7. Deverell, "Fighting Words," 33. See also William G. Robbins, ed., *The Great Northwest: The Search for Regional Identity* (Corvallis: Oregon State University Press, 2001), 3–4.

8. William G. Robbins, introduction to *Regionalism and the Pacific Northwest,* ed. William G. Robbins, Robert J. Frank, and Richard E. Ross (Corvallis: Oregon State University Press, 1983), 2.

9. William L. Lang, "Failed Federalism: The Columbia Valley Authority and Regionalism," in Robbins, *The Great Northwest,* 66; Patricia Nelson Limerick, "Region and Reason," in *All Over the Map: Rethinking American Regions,* ed. Edward L. Ayers, Patricia Nelson Limerick, Stephen Nissenbaum, and Peter S. Onuf (Baltimore: Johns Hopkins University Press, 1996), 96.

10. See Robert W. Rydell, *All the World's a Fair: Visions of Empire at American International Expositions, 1876–1916* (Chicago: University of Chicago Press, 1984), chap. 7; Michael C. Steiner and David M. Wrobel, "Many Wests: Discovering a Dynamic Western Regionalism," in *Many Wests: Place, Culture, and Regional Identity,* ed. David M. Wrobel and Michael C. Steiner (Lawrence: University Press of

Kansas, 1997), 16–18; David M. Wrobel, *Promised Lands: Promotion, Memory, and the Creation of the American West* (Lawrence: University Press of Kansas, 2002), chap. 1.

11. John M. Findlay, "A Fishy Proposition: Regional Identity in the Pacific Northwest," in Wrobel and Steiner, *Many Wests*, 44–45, 54–55.

12. The classic labor history by John Commons, Selig Perlman, and Philip Taft provides evidence of the shift of labor radicalism westward in the early twentieth century. In volume four, which covers the history of labor from 1896 to 1932, the authors dedicate nearly one-third of the entire 600-page study of American labor to western events. Moreover, a majority of the discussion on labor relations during the two decades prior to World War I focuses on events and organizations west of the Mississippi River. See their *History of Labor in the United States,* 4 vols. (New York: Macmillan, 1921–35).

13. The recent study by Julie Greene has attempted to reevaluate the political ideas and activities of Samuel Gompers and the AFL. She focuses largely on the national leadership of the labor federation, leaving urban labor politics mostly unexplored. See Greene, *Pure and Simple Politics: The American Federation of Labor and Political Activism, 1881–1917* (New York: Cambridge University Press, 1998). For thoughts on and criticism of Greene's study, see "Symposium on Julie Greene: Pure and Simple Politics," *Labor History* 40.2 (May 1999). A fine study of local political activity on the part of trade unionists is Michael Kazin, *Barons of Labor: The San Francisco Building Trades and Union Power in the Progressive Era* (Urbana: University of Illinois Press, 1987).

14. Carlos Schwantes, "The Concept of the Wageworkers' Frontier: A Framework for Future Research," *Western Historical Quarterly* 18.1 (January 1987): 39–55; and his "Patterns of Radicalism on the Wageworkers' Frontier," *Idaho Yesterdays* 30.3 (Fall 1986): 25–30, and *Radical Heritage: Labor, Socialism, and Reform in Washington and British Columbia, 1885–1917* (Seattle: University of Washington Press, 1979).

15. Virginia Scharff, "Else Surely We Shall All Hang Separately: The Politics of Western Women's History," *Pacific Historical Review* 61.4 (November 1992): 535–55. For an outstanding example of Seattle's value as place to study gender and class, see Dana Frank, *Purchasing Power: Consumer Organizing, Gender, and the Seattle Labor Movement, 1919–1929* (New York: Cambridge University Press, 1994). Frank's study dovetails nicely with my own, for she explores the transformation of gender and class following World War I. She does not, however, examine in much depth middle-class women or urban politics.

16. T. A. Larson, "Dolls, Vassals, and Drudges: Pioneer Women in the West," *Western Historical Quarterly* 3.1 (January 1972): 16.

17. Rebecca J. Mead, *How the Vote Was Won: Woman Suffrage in the Western*

United States, 1868–1914 (New York: New York University Press, 2004), chap. 1; Suzanne M. Marilley, *Woman Suffrage and the Origins of Liberal Feminism in the United States, 1820–1920* (Cambridge: Harvard University Press, 1996). For state-based studies, see Michael Goldberg, *An Army of Women: Gender and Politics in Gilded Age Kansas* (Baltimore: Johns Hopkins Press, 1997); Sherry Katz, "Dual Commitments: Feminism, Socialism, and Women's Political Activism in California, 1890–1920" (PhD diss., University of California, Los Angeles, 1991); Joan M. Jensen, "'Disfranchisement Is a Disgrace': Women and Politics in New Mexico, 1900–1940," in *New Mexico Women: Intercultural Perspectives*, ed. Joan M. Jensen and Darlis Miller, 301–31 (Albuquerque: University of New Mexico Press, 1986); T. A. Larson, "The Woman Suffrage Movement in Washington," *Pacific Northwest Quarterly* 67.2 (April 1976): 49–63, and "Women's Role in the American West," *Montana: The Magazine of Western History* 24.3 (July 1974): 3–11.

18. Since the early 1980s, historians of western women have urged scholars to explore, in more depth and with greater rigor, women of color and female working-class laborers in the American West. While this demand for a multicultural perspective of gender in the region is important and long overdue, this should not exclude continual investigation of white women. Because of the small Asian and black population in turn-of-the-century Seattle, this study focuses largely on white working-class and middle-class women. On the call for new approaches, see Joan Jensen and Darlis Miller, "The Gentle Tamers Revisited: New Approaches to the History of Women in the American West," *Pacific Historical Review* 49.2 (May 1980): 173–213; Glenda Riley, "Western Women's History—A Look at Some of the Issues," *Montana: The Magazine of Western History* 41.2 (Spring 1991): 66–70; Virginia Scharff, "Gender and Western History: Is Anybody Home on the Range?" *Montana: The Magazine of Western History* 41.2 (Spring 1991): 62–65; Antonia Casteñeda, "Women of Color and the Rewriting of Western History: The Discourse, Politics, and Decolonization of History," *Pacific Historical Review* 61.4 (November 1992): 501–33; Peggy Pascoe, "Western Women at the Cultural Crossroads," in Limerick, Milner, and Rankin, *Trails,* 40–58.

19. Paul Kleppner, "Politics Without Parties: The Western States, 1900–1984," in Nash and Etulain, *The Twentieth-Century West,* 295–338.

20. For an excellent study of the rise of interest-group politics in the Progressive Era that includes case studies of Washington and California, see Elisabeth S. Clemens, *The People's Lobby: Organizational Innovation and the Rise of Interest Group Politics in the United States, 1890–1925* (Chicago: University of Chicago Press, 1997). For discussions of the meaning of power and politics, see David Hammack, "Problems in the Historical Study of Power in the Cities and Towns of the United States, 1800–1960," *American Historical Review* 83.2 (April 1978): 323–49; Samuel P. Hays, "Society and Politics: Politics and Society," *Journal of Interdisciplinary*

History 15.3 (Winter 1985): 481–99; and Terrence McDonald, "Putting Politics Back Into the History of the American City," *American Quarterly* 34 (1982): 200–209. Some scholars, however, have perceived an overemphasis on cultural and community studies associated with the new social history. See William E. Leuchtenburg, "The Pertinence of Political History: Reflections on the Significance of the State in America," *Journal of American History* 73.3 (December 1986): 585–600; Spencer Olin, "Toward a Synthesis of the Political and Social History of the American West," *Pacific Historical Review* 55.4 (1986): 599–611.

21. Lionel Frost, *The New Urban Frontier: Urbanisation and City Building in Australia and the American West* (Kensington, Australia: New South Wales University Press, 1991).

22. Walter Nugent, "The People of the West Since 1890," in Nash and Etulain, *The Twentieth-Century West,* 35–70, 40 (quote). Earl Pomeroy was one of the first scholars to note the importance of urban centers in the West. See his *The Pacific Slope: A History of California, Oregon, Washington, Idaho, Utah, and Nevada* (1965; Seattle: University of Washington Press, 1973), chap. 6. On the importance of towns and cities in the American conquest of the West in the late nineteenth century, see Eugene P. Moehring, *Urbanism and Empire in the Far West, 1840–1890* (Reno: University of Nevada Press, 2004).

23. Clemens, *The People's Lobby,* 223, 259.

24. On western progressivism, see William D. Rowley, "The West as a Laboratory and Mirror of Reform," in Nash and Etulain, *The Twentieth-Century West,* 339–57; Pomeroy, *The Pacific Slope,* chap. 8; Michael P. Malone and Richard W. Etulain, *The American West: A Twentieth-Century History* (Lincoln: University of Nebraska Press, 1989), 55–66; William Deverell and Tom Sitton, eds., *California Progressivism Revisited* (Berkeley and Los Angeles: University of California Press, 1994); Philip J. Ethington, *The Public City: The Political Construction of Urban Life in San Francisco, 1850–1900* (New York: Cambridge University Press, 1994); Robert D. Johnston, *The Radical Middle Class: Populist Democracy and the Question of Capitalism in Progressive Era Portland, Oregon* (Princeton, NJ: Princeton University Press, 2003); and William Issel and Robert W. Cherny, *San Francisco, 1865–1932: Politics, Power, and Urban Development* (Berkeley and Los Angeles: University of California Press, 1986), chap. 7.

25. See Johnston, *The Radical Middle Class,* chap. 1; Shelton Stromquist, *Reinventing "The People": The Progressive Movement, the Class Problem, and the Origins of Modern Liberalism* (Urbana: University of Illinois Press, 2006); and Stromquist, "The Crucible of Class: Cleveland Politics and the Origins of Municipal Reform in the Progressive Era," *Journal of Urban History* 23.2 (January 1997): 192–220; Georg Leidenberger, "'The Public Is the Labor Union': Working-Class Progressivism in Turn-of-the-Century Chicago," *Labor History* 36.2 (Spring 1995): 187–210;

Michael McGerr, *A Fierce Discontent: The Rise and Fall of the Progressive Movement in America, 1870–1920* (New York: Free Press, 2003); Steven J. Diner, *A Very Different Age: Americans of the Progressive Era* (New York: Hill and Wang, 1998); Kevin Mattson, *Creating a Democratic Public: The Struggle for Urban Participatory Democracy During the Progressive Era* (University Park: Pennsylvania State University Press, 1998); Kazin, *Barons of Labor*.

1: CLASS, GENDER, AND POLITICS IN LATE-NINETEENTH-CENTURY SEATTLE

1. Details of the anti-Chinese episode in Seattle can be found in Murray Morgan, *Skid Road: An Informal Portrait of Seattle* (New York: Viking Press, 1951), 85–102; Robert C. Nesbit, *"He Built Seattle": A Biography of Judge Thomas Burke* (Seattle: University of Washington Press, 1961), 166–207; Robert E. Wynne, "Reaction to the Chinese in the Pacific Northwest and British Columbia, 1850–1910" (PhD diss., University of Washington, Seattle, 1964), chap. 6; and Jules A. Karlin, "The Anti-Chinese Outbreaks in Seattle," *Pacific Northwest Quarterly* 34 (April 1948): 103–29. For a detailed study of the Tacoma anti-Chinese episode, see Murray Morgan, *Puget's Sound: A Narrative of Early Tacoma and the Southern Sound* (Seattle: University of Washington Press, 1979). For California's experiences, see Alexander Saxton, *The Indispensable Enemy: Labor and the Anti-Chinese Movement in California* (Berkeley and Los Angeles: University of California Press, 1971); Tomás Almaguer, *Racial Fault Lines: The Historical Origins of White Supremacy in California* (Berkeley and Los Angeles: University of California Press, 1994), chaps. 6–7.

2. John Putman, "Racism and Temperance: The Politics of Class and Gender in Late 19th-Century Seattle," *Pacific Northwest Quarterly* 95.2 (Spring 2004): 70–81.

3. The Denny party, as the migrants became known, began their westward journey in the same prairie region that John Mack Faragher made famous in his excellent study of Sugar Creek, Illinois. See his *Sugar Creek: Life on the Illinois Prairie* (New Haven, CT: Yale University Press, 1986).

4. Robert E. Ficken, *Washington Territory* (Pullman: Washington State Press, 2002), 12–13; Moehring, *Urbanism and Empire*, 209.

5. Ficken, *Washington Territory*, 10–19.

6. Richard White, *"It's Your Misfortune and None of My Own": A New History of the American West* (Norman: University of Oklahoma Press, 1991), 246–55; Nesbit, *"He Built Seattle,"* chap. 4.

7. Nesbit, *"He Built Seattle,"* 15–18; Roger Sale, *Seattle: Past to Present* (Seattle: University of Washington Press, 1976), 32–33; Morgan, *Skid Row*, 74.

8. White, *"It's Your Misfortune and None of My Own,"* 252, 267–68; Gerald Nash, *The American West in the Twentieth Century* (Albuquerque: University of

New Mexico Press, 1973), 73; Malone and Etulain, *The American West*, 9, 11; Gerald D. Nash and Richard W. Etulain, prologue to *The Twentieth-Century West*, 12; William G. Robbins, "The 'Plundered Province' Thesis and the Recent Historiography of the American West," *Pacific Historical Review* 55.4 (1986): 577–97, and his *Colony and Empire*.

9. Robert Ficken, *The Forested Land: A History of Lumbering in Western Washington* (Seattle: University of Washington Press, 1987), 34; Nesbit, "*He Built Seattle*," 9–13, 25–26.

10. White, *"It's Your Misfortune and None of My Own,"* 257–59; Robert E. Ficken and Charles P. LeWarne, *Washington: A Centennial History* (Seattle: University of Washington Press, 1988), 36; Nesbit, "*He Built Seattle*," 55; Clarence B. Bagley, *History of King County, Washington*, vol. 1 (Chicago: S. J. Clarke, 1929), 252, and his *The History of Seattle From the Earliest Settlement to the Present*, vol. 2 (Chicago: S. J. Clarke, 1916), 603–5; Moehring, *Urbanism and Empire*, 233–38.

11. *Twelfth Census of the United States: 1900 Population*, vol. 1, pt. 1 (Washington, DC: Government Printing Office), 645; Alexander Norbert MacDonald, "Seattle's Economic Development, 1880–1910" (PhD diss., University of Washington, 1959), 286 (quote), 290; White, *"It's Your Misfortune and None of My Own,"* 277–80; Pomeroy, *The Pacific Slope*, 104. While the entire Pacific coast experienced tremendous growth in the 1880s, the number of newcomers to Washington Territory outpaced California by some 2.5 times. California's population grew larger, but much of this was from natural increase.

12. Norman Clark, *The Dry Years: Prohibition and Social Change in Washington* (Seattle: University of Washington Press, 1965), 34.

13. *New Northwest*, November 18, 1883; Clark, *The Dry Years*, 34–35. Clark argues that the Territorial Temperance Alliance leaned much more toward prohibition by demanding the elimination of the saloon.

14. Bagley, *History of Seattle*, 487–88; Abigail Scott Duniway, *Path Breaking: An Autobiographical History of the Equal Suffrage Movement in the Pacific Coast States* (1914; repr., New York: Schocken Books, 1971); Larson, "The Woman Suffrage Movement in Washington," 51.

15. Ruth Barnes Moynihan, *Rebel for Rights: Abigail Scott Duniway* (New Haven, CT: Yale University Press, 1983), 101, 182–83, chap. 6; Larson, "Woman Suffrage Movement in Washington," 54–55 (quote). The 1881 suffrage bill passed in the House, but lost 7–5 in the Council (Senate). The legislature did, however, bring Washington's laws regarding the rights of women up to the standards of many other states and territories. This included the right to own and dispose of property as well as more equitable community property rights.

16. *Woman's Journal*, November 24, 1883; December 22, 1883; April 10, 1886; *New Northwest*, October 25, 1883; Alan Grimes, *The Puritan Ethic and Woman*

Suffrage (1967; repr., Westport, CT: Greenwood Press, 1980), 60; Mead, *How the Vote Was Won*, 44–47.

17. *New Northwest*, July 31, 1884.

18. *Seattle Post-Intelligencer*, July 15, 1884; Morgan, *Skid Road*, 83–84; Nesbit, "He Built Seattle," 363–64.

19. *Evening Telegram*, quoted in *New Northwest*, July 17, 1884. For a similar view, see *New Northwest*, July 24, 1884, 4.

20. Quoted in the *New Northwest*, July 24, 1884. For the activity of women, see *Seattle Post-Intelligencer*, July 15, 1884; *Woman's Journal*, August 2, 1884, 249. The 1884 election had an overall voter turnout of 2,526 compared to 925 in 1883 and 622 in 1882. While population growth might explain some of the increased turnout, anecdotal evidence indicates that a significant number of women did vote in 1884. Unfortunately, voting logs do not indicate the sex of each voter. Recalling this election a few years later, Mrs. G. A. Wood of Seattle claimed that registration books showed that women constituted nearly one-third of those registered. See *Woman's Journal*, January 22, 1887.

21. *Seattle Post-Intelligencer*, July 16, 1884. On the Seattle economy during the mid-1880s, see Norbert MacDonald, *Distant Neighbors: A Comparative History of Seattle and Vancouver* (Lincoln: University of Nebraska Press, 1987), 23.

22. *Seattle Post-Intelligencer*, July 14, 1885. Yesler defeated Leary 1,337 to 689; a margin of victory of 648 compared to 112 in 1884.

23. *Seattle Post-Intelligencer*, September 9, 1885; Wynne, "Reaction to the Chinese in the Pacific Northwest," 209–10; Morgan, *Skid Row*, 87; Nesbit, "He Built Seattle," 173–74; and Morgan, *Puget's Sound*, 212–52. For more on Knights of Labor views of the Chinese, see Carlos A. Schwantes, "From Anti-Chinese Agitation to Reform Politics: The Legacy of the Knights of Labor in Washington and the Pacific Northwest," *Pacific Northwest Quarterly* 88.4 (Fall 1997): 174–84.

24. *Seattle Post-Intelligencer*, September 22, 1885.

25. Quoted in Wynne, "Reaction to the Chinese in the Pacific Northwest," 244.

26. Wynne, "Reaction to the Chinese in the Pacific Northwest," 245–47. On the troubles in the mines, see *Seattle Daily Post-Intelligencer*, January 21, February 6, 7, 1886.

27. *Seattle Post-Intelligencer*, February 7, 1886.

28. *Seattle Daily Press*, May 6, 1886.

29. *Seattle Post-Intelligencer*, June 30, July 2, 3, 9, 12, 1886; *Seattle Daily Times*, June 30, July 19, 1886. The Loyal League represented many of the same people and interests that the Businessmen's Ticket had in the previous city election.

30. *Seattle Post-Intelligencer*, July 13, 15, 1886; *Seattle Daily Press*, May 10, June 30, 1886.

31. Leon Fink, *Workingmen's Democracy: The Knights of Labor and American Politics* (Urbana: University of Illinois Press, 1983), 30–32, 225–26.

32. The opinion of Judge B. F. Dennison and the *Tacoma Ledger* can be found in the *New Northwest,* February 10, 1887; Putman, "Racism and Temperance," 74–80; Mead, *How the Vote Was Won,* 48–50. Also see Morgan, *Skid Row,* 37, for the suggestion that saloon interests might have been behind the case.

33. Ronald E. Magden, *A History of Seattle Waterfront Workers* (Seattle: International Longshoremen's and Warehousemen's Union 19 of Seattle and the Washington Commission for the Humanities, 1991), 27–28; Thomas Riddle, *The Old Radicalism: John R. Rogers and the Populist Movement in Washington* (New York: Garland, 1991), 78–79.

34. Wynne, "Reaction to the Chinese in the Pacific Northwest," 105, 207. The Chinese population in King County dropped from nearly 1,000 to 142 by 1887, representing a decrease from 7 percent of the population to less than 1 percent. As a note of comparison, Wynne found that Tacoma remained virtually Chinese-free into the 1890s.

35. *Seattle Post-Intelligencer,* March 16, April 16, 23, 1891. For a discussion of the Knights of Labor's key role in Montana's populist party, see Thomas A. Cinch, *Urban Populism and Free Silver in Montana* (Helena: University of Montana Press, 1970), 5–12, 45–49. Besides having a similar role in forming the People's Party, Montana's Knights maintained a significant presence in labor circles because of large mining operations as well as anti-Chinese activity that in some way mirrored Seattle's experience. On the origins of Populism, see John Hicks, *The Populist Revolt: A History of the Farmers' Alliance and the People's Party* (Lincoln: University of Nebraska Press, 1961); Norman Pollack, *The Populist Response to Industrial America: Midwestern Political Thought* (Cambridge: Harvard University Press, 1962).

36. *Seattle Post-Intelligencer,* April 16, 1891.

37. *Seattle Post-Intelligencer,* July 9, 19, 1891.

38. Riddle, *The Old Radicalism,* 129–31.

39. Riddle, *The Old Radicalism,* chap. 5; Schwantes, *Radical Heritage,* 54–60, and his *Coxey's Army: An American Odyssey* (Lincoln: University of Nebraska Press, 1985); Magden, *A History of Seattle Waterfront Workers,* 31. For an excellent study of farmers and politics in Washington, see Marilyn Watkins, *Rural Democracy: Family Farmers and Politics in Western Washington, 1890–1925* (Ithaca, NY: Cornell University Press, 1995).

40. Riddle, *The Old Radicalism,* 168. Riddle's survey of selected working-class precincts indicated that the Democrats lost twenty-four percentage points, while Populists gained sixteen and Republicans added just eight.

41. Riddle, *The Old Radicalism,* 175–83; Schwantes, *Radical Heritage,* 60. For more on Rogers's strain of Populist thought, see David B. Griffiths, "Far-western

Populist Thought: A Comparative Study of John R. Rogers and Davis H. Waite," *Pacific Northwest Quarterly* 60.4 (October 1969): 183–92; Riddle, *The Old Radicalism*, chaps. 1–2.

42. N. MacDonald, *Distant Neighbors*, 45–46; Janice L. Reiff, "Urbanization and the Social Structure: Seattle, Washington, 1852–1910" (PhD diss., University of Washington, 1981), 75.

43. Riddle, *The Old Radicalism*, 227–28. Earl Pomeroy has noted that Washington was one of only ten states outside the south that Bryan carried. Moreover, the Democratic presidential candidate did quite well in urban counties of the Far West, including taking King County and Pierce County in Washington. See Pomeroy, *The Pacific Slope*, 176n.

44. Riddle, *The Old Radicalism*, 232–39.

45. Riddle, *The Old Radicalism*, 242–87. Riddle also argues that middle-of-the-road Populists were critical of the Spanish-American War, which further added to their marginalization in state politics.

46. Schwantes, *Radical Heritage*, 119–22; Riddle, *The Old Radicalism*, 278. The Knights remained influential in eastern Washington until the turn of the century, especially among miners and agrarian radicals associated with the Populist Party. Evidence that Bridges remained influential in the Populist Party was his appointment as chairman of the last Populist convention in 1900.

47. Carlos Schwantes, "The Churches of the Disinherited: The Culture of Radicalism on the North Pacific Industrial Frontier," *Pacific Historian* 25.4 (Winter 1981): 54–64.

48. For discussion of the Knights' legacy in Washington, see Schwantes's various studies: *Radical Heritage*, 34–35; "Washington State's Pioneer Labor-Reform Press: A Bibliographical Essay and Annotated Checklist," *Pacific Northwest Quarterly* 71.3 (July 1980): 112; "Leftward Tilt on the Pacific Slope: Indigenous Unionism and the Struggle Against AFL Hegemony in the State of Washington," *Pacific Northwest Quarterly* 70.1 (January 1979): 24–33; and "Churches of the Disinherited," cited in preceding note.

2: CITIZENS AND WORKERS

1. For the significance of local labor federations in western labor history, see Michael Kazin, "The Great Exception Revisited: Organized Labor and Politics in San Francisco and Los Angeles, 1870–1940," *Pacific Historical Review* 55.3 (August 1986): 371–402.

2. Georg Leidenberger, "'The Public Is the Labor Union': Working-Class Progressivism in Turn-of-the-Century Chicago," *Labor History* 36.2 (Spring 1995): 187–210 (quote, 192). On labor and politics during the Progressive Era, see Greene, *Pure and Simple Politics*, 12–15.

3. Schwantes, *Radical Heritage,* 87–88; Harvey O'Connor, *Revolution in Seattle: A Memoir* (New York: Monthly Review Press, 1964), 3. O'Connor was a leading Socialist in Seattle during the first two decades of the twentieth century.

4. Schwantes, *Radical Heritage,* 87–88; Charles P. LeWarne, *Utopias on Puget Sound, 1885–1915* (Seattle: University of Washington Press, 1975), 18–32 (quote, 34).

5. Carlos Schwantes, "Leftward Tilt on the Pacific Slope," 28–29, and *Radical Heritage,* 85–87; LeWarne, *Utopias on Puget Sound,* 9–11 (quote, 11).

6. LeWarne, *Utopias on Puget Sound,* 56–101 (quote, 75); O'Connor, *Revolution in Seattle,* 1–6; Schwantes, *Radical Heritage,* 88–90.

7. LeWarne, *Utopias on Puget Sound,* 73, 163, and 220; Schwantes, *Radical Heritage,* 88–89; O'Connor, *Revolution in Seattle,* 5. Ault was a major labor leader throughout the 1910s and early 1920s. Fox would later write for Seattle's weekly labor paper in late 1910s. Wardall was elected to the Seattle city council in 1908 after spending a few years at the Burley Colony.

8. LeWarne, *Utopias on Puget Sound,* 138, 175, 198–205, and 225.

9. Morgan, *Skid Road,* 160–62; A. MacDonald, "Seattle's Economic Development," 137; Ficken, *The Forested Land,* 88. An example of Seattle's rapid dominance of the Alaskan trade, Ficken suggests, was the Stimson Mill Company of Seattle, which by December 1897 had shipped nearly four million board feet of lumber to Alaska.

10. Morgan, *Skid Row,* 162–65; Carlos Schwantes, *The Pacific Northwest: An Interpretive History* (Lincoln: University of Nebraska Press, 1989), 197.

11. Bagley, *History of Seattle,* 481–82, 540–41; Calvin Schmid, *Social Trends in Seattle* (Seattle: University of Washington Press, 1944), 31–32; Reiff, "Urbanization and the Social Structure," 81.

12. Bagley, *History of Seattle,* 534 (quote); Reiff, "Urbanization and the Social Structure," 81–82.

13. *Thirteenth Census of the United States: Manufactures,* vol. 9 (Washington DC: Government Printing Office, 1912), 1301–2; A. MacDonald, "Seattle's Economic Development," 102, 163, 186–87, 196, 201; Moehring, *Urbanism and Empire,* 233–38; Pomeroy, *The Pacific,* 119 (quote). According to the census of manufactures, the lumber industry remained the city's single largest employer (behind only the "all other industries" category), employing more than three thousand wage earners. Everett, Aberdeen, and other lumber communities soon eclipsed Seattle as both leading producers and exporters of lumber as Seattle increasingly became the center of the lumber industry's other necessary activities, like company headquarters and employment agencies. Nearby Portland mirrored Seattle's dependence on small manufacturing firms, with approximately 90 percent of Portland firms employing fewer than twenty-five employees. See Johnston, *The Radical Middle Class,* 65.

14. Reiff, "Urbanization and Social Structure," 5, 8, 110, 128, and 231.

15. *Thirteenth Census of the United States: Population 1910,* vol. 3 (Washington DC: Government Printing Office, 1914), 989, 1004; Schmid, *Social Trends,* 99; Quintard Taylor, *The Forging of a Black Community: Seattle's Central District From 1870 Through the Civil Rights Era* (Seattle: University of Washington Press, 1994), 108.

16. *Thirteenth Census of the United States: Population 1910,* vol. 3, 1004. Seattle's foreign-born population included 9,850 Canadians (non-French); 8,676 Swedes; 7,191 Norwegians; 6,172 Germans; 5,797 English; 3,454 Italians, and 2,578 Russians. The city's foreign-born population totaled 60,835 in all.

17. Reiff, "Urbanization and the Social Structure," 55, 118, 117, 170, and 257. She notes that Scandinavians made up 26 percent of Seattle's foreign-born population but only 9 percent of the nation's total.

18. The following description of Seattle's fourteen wards is drawn from Mansel Blackford, "Sources of Support for Reform Candidates and Issues in Seattle Politics, 1902–1916" (master's thesis, University of Washington, 1967), 10–20.

19. *Twelfth Census of the United States: Population 1900,* vol. 2, pt. 2 (Washington DC: Government Printing Office, 1901), 590–93; *Thirteenth Census of the United States: Population 1910,* vol. 4, 194–207; Frank, *Purchasing Power,* 15–18.

20. Schwantes, *Radical Heritage,* 19; quote from A. MacDonald, "Seattle's Economic Development," 286; Taylor, *The Forging of a Black Community,* 49–64; Frank, *Purchasing Power,* 20; Bureau of Labor of the State of Washington, *Fourth Biennial Report of the Bureau of Labor of the State of Washington, 1903–4* (Olympia, WA: Blankenship Satterlee Company, 1904), 135–58 (hereafter, *Bureau of Labor Report, 1903–4*). Older unions like for musicians, machinists, and plumbers revealed similarly healthy organizations.

21. *Seattle Union Record,* February 2, 1907, September 9, 1909; "Testimony of Professor Theresa McMahon before the Commission on Industrial Relations," in U.S. Congress, House, *Industrial Relations: Final Report and Testimony Submitted to Congress by the Commission on Industrial Relations,* vol. 5 (Washington DC: Government Printing Office, 1916), 4182 (hereafter referred to as *Industrial Relations Report*).

22. Schwantes, "The Concept of the Wageworkers' Frontier," 39–42; his *The Pacific Northwest,* 251 (quote); and his "Churches of the Disinherited," 56–57. For an earlier discussion of the radical character of western labor, see Melvyn Dubofsky, "The Origins of Western Working Class Radicalism, 1890–1905," *Labor History* 7.2 (Spring 1966): 131–54.

23. Schwantes, *Radical Heritage,* 18–23, 152–54.

24. Schwantes, *Radical Heritage,* 15 (quote), chap. 9. One constant complaint expressed by many Seattle labor leaders was the AFL's repudiation of industrial

unionism. The legacy of the Knights and the IWW's One Big Union had significant sway in the forests of western Washington. The result was dual unionism in which many workers belonged both to a particular craft union as well as to an industrial union, such as the IWW or United Mine Workers. The AFL faced a similar struggle with industrial unionism in Denver during the early 1900s. See David Brundage, *The Making of Western Labor Radicalism: Denver's Organized Workers, 1878–1905* (Urbana: University of Illinois Press, 1994), 143–46.

25. *Bureau of Labor Report, 1903–4*, 48–49.

26. Schwantes, *Radical Heritage*, 135–40; Richard C. Berner, *Seattle 1900–1920: From Boomtown, Urban Turbulence, to Restoration* (Seattle: Charles Press, 1991), 48–53.

27. Berner, *Seattle 1900–1920*, 48–53; Sale, *Seattle: Past to Present*, 72.

28. *Bureau of Labor Report, 1903–4*, 49–51, 71–76 (quote, 76).

29. *Seattle Union Record*, January 7 (quote); March 11, 1905.

30. *Seattle Union Record*, April 22, 1905; Schwantes, *Radical Heritage*, 156.

31. *Seattle Union Record*, May 6 and 13, 1905; Bureau of Labor of the State of Washington, *Fifth Biennial Report of the Bureau of Labor Statistics and Factory Inspection, 1905–6* (Olympia, WA: C. W. Gorham, 1906); Berner, *Seattle 1900–1920*, 51 (hereafter *Bureau of Labor Report, 1905–6*). On the rise of Citizens' Alliances elsewhere in the West, see Kazin, *Barons of Labor*, 115–17, and Brundage, *The Making of Western Labor Radicalism*, 146–47.

32. *Seattle Union Record*, May 20, June 3, November 4, 1905.

33. *Seattle Union Record*, September 2, 1905.

34. *Seattle Union Record*, June 24, 1905; Schwantes, *Radical Heritage*, 159; Michael Kazin, *Barons of Labor*, 3–4, 29; Clemens, *The People's Lobby*, 113, 137–44. For more on the AFL and politics, see Greene, *Pure and Simple Politics*, and David Montgomery, *Fall of the House of Labor: The Workplace, the State, and American Labor Activism, 1865–1925* (Cambridge: Cambridge University Press, 1987), chap. 4.

35. *Seattle Union Record*, September 23 (quote), October 14, November 11, 1905. Michael Kazin has argued that few California labor leaders "subscribed to the national AFL's vaunted policy of "voluntarism"—the notion that electoral partisanship and labor legislation would only restrict the freedom of unions and embroil them in endless factional disputes." See his "The Great Exception Revisited," 377–79.

36. *Seattle Union Record*, September 9, 16, November 11, 1905; Blackford, "Sources of Support for Reform Candidates and Issues," 27–31, and his "Reform Politics in Seattle During the Progressive Era, 1902–1916," *Pacific Northwest Quarterly* 59.4 (October 1968): 178–79. Georg Leidenberger found similar concerns among working-class and middle-class Chicago residents that aided that city's municipal ownership campaign. See his "'The Public Is the Labor Union,'"

202–6. For a similar example of how political organizations exploited public animus toward powerful corporations, see William Deverell, *Railroad Crossing: Californians and the Railroad, 1850–1910* (Berkeley and Los Angeles: University of California Press, 1994).

37. *Seattle Union Record,* October 7 (quote), 14, 28, 1905.

38. Richard Oestreicher, "Urban Working-Class Political Behavior and Theories of American Electoral Politics, 1870–1940," *Journal of American History* 74.4 (March 1988): 1257–86. Oestreicher defines class sentiment as "a relatively unfocused sense of grievance, for example, a feeling that workers were treated unfairly and unequally, were underpaid and overworked, and a positive response to notions like "we have to stick together" or to phrases like the "rights of labor" (1269).

39. *Seattle Union Record,* December 16, 1905; January 20 (quote), 27, 1906; Blackford, "Sources of Support for Reform Candidates and Issues," 29. The formation of the Municipal Ownership Party exemplifies Oestreicher's contention that for class sentiment "to lead to strategy and action, it must be linked to particular symbols and programs and mobilized by specific individuals and organizations." See Oestreicher, "Urban Working-Class Political Behavior," 1269–70.

40. *Seattle Union Record,* February 10, 17, 1906; Jonathan Dembo, *Unions and Politics in Washington State, 1885–1935* (New York: Garland, 1983), 58; Blackford, "Sources of Support for Reform Candidates and Issues," 29. Labor leaders initially backed Mathew Dow as their candidate for mayor, but compromised with middle-class progressives by nominating Moore. Blackford states that the Democratic Party held a convention but did not nominate any candidates because most of the leading Democrats had deserted to the Municipal Ownership Party.

41. *Seattle Union Record,* January 27 (third quote), February 17, 24 (second quote), and March 3 (first quote), 1906.

42. *Seattle Union Record,* January 27, March 3 (quote), 1906. For discussion of western settlers' perception that eastern corporations exploited the region, see Robbins, "The 'Plundered Province' Thesis," and his *Colony and Empire;* White, *"It's Your Misfortune and None of My Own,"* 354; Nash, *The American West in the Twentieth Century.*

43. For election results, see *Seattle Daily Times,* March 7, 1906; *Seattle Union Record,* March 10, March 17 (quote), 1906; Blackford, "Sources of Support for Reform Candidates and Issues," 11–18; Berner, *Seattle 1900–1920,* 112–13. Chicago's successful municipal ownership campaign resembled Seattle's, as local unionists allied with middle-class reformers to elect the city's mayor. However, in Chicago the mayor ran on the Democratic ticket. See Leidenberger, "The Public Is the Labor Union," 206–7.

44. *Seattle Union Record,* April 14, May 12, 19, and June 2, 16, 1906; Dembo, *Unions and Politics,* 60–61.

45. *Seattle Union Record,* April 14, May 12, 19 (last quote), June 2, 16 (first quote), 1906; Dembo, *Unions and Politics,* 60–61. For more on the revival of farmers' organizations in early 1900s, see Schwantes, *Radical Heritage,* 159–62.

46. *Seattle Union Record,* June 16, 1906; Dembo, *Unions and Politics,* 61–62.

47. *Seattle Union Record,* August 11, 1906; Dembo, *Unions and Politics,* 61–62.

48. *Seattle Union Record,* September 8 (quote), 15, November 10, 1906. Two labor candidates, L. E. Kirkpatrick and George Cotterill, won their races by rather narrow margins. Cotterill's brother Frank was an officer of the SCLC and a major voice in Seattle labor circles in the first two decades of the twentieth century.

49. Stromquist, "The Crucible of Class," 205. Chicago's municipal ownership movement also failed to achieve its goals, as the problem of paying for a municipal takeover and a business backlash proved insurmountable obstacles. For more, see Leidenberger, "The Public Is the Labor Union," 207–8.

50. Municipal Ownership Party committee report, October 26, 1907, box 10, folder 6, Joseph Smith Papers, Manuscripts and Archives, Suzzallo and Allen Library, University of Washington.

51. *Seattle Union Record,* January 25, February 1, 22, 29, 1908; Berner, *Seattle 1900–1920,* 113. Moore lost by more than 5,000 votes out of 31,150 cast.

52. Berner, *Seattle 1900–1920,* 112–13.

53. *Seattle Union Record,* February 22, 29, March 14, 1908; Joseph Smith, "Autobiography," chapter 10C, box 1, folder 18, Joseph Smith Papers; Berner, *Seattle 1900–1920,* 112–13; Schwantes, *Radical Heritage,* 160, 171.

54. Schwantes, *Radical Heritage,* chaps. 6, 12. The actual membership of the Socialist Party of Washington is difficult to nail down. Local Socialist Hulet Wells stated in his memoirs that membership totaled six thousand in 1912. For more on socialism in early Seattle, see Hulet Wells, "I Wanted to Work," box 2, folders 3–5, Hulet Wells Papers, Manuscripts and Archives, Suzzallo and Allen Library, University of Washington. Another contemporary radical, Harvey O'Conner, confirmed this figure, indicating that in 1909 the state party had over one hundred locals and several thousand members. See his *Revolution in Seattle,* 137.

55. O'Connor, *Revolution in Seattle,* 12; Schwantes, *Radical Heritage,* 80–97 (quotes, 93, 96).

56. Schwantes, *Radical Heritage,* 104–6. Titus's background is drawn from O'Connor, *Revolution in Seattle,* 13. In Washington and Seattle, the SLP remained largely insignificant for most of the first decade of the century. Thus, this study will emphasize the impact of Titus's SPW, which was Washington State's SPA affiliate. Further complicating the history of Socialism in Washington is the large number of agrarian Socialists located in the farming counties of eastern Washington. Titus, in particular, had trouble reconciling the farmers' demands with his Marxian working-class Socialism.

57. Wells, "I Wanted to Work," 1–3; Schwantes, *Radical Heritage,* 105–6. Wells noted that early leaders, besides Titus, included William Z. Foster, later head of the American Communist Party; Harry Ault, editor of the *Seattle Union Record* in the 1910s; Floyd Hyde, later a speaker and organizer for the ɪww; John McCorkle, a trade union leader; a journalist; and even a Seattle high school principal.

58. Schwantes, *Radical Heritage,* 170.

59. *Seattle Union Record,* March 14, 1908; O'Connor, *Revolution in Seattle,* 15; Schwantes, *Radical Heritage,* 171–77. Evidence of the success of reform Socialism is a party membership in 1906 that topped 1,500, the third highest in the nation following Pennsylvania and California.

60. *Seattle Union Record,* October 27, December 22, 1906; Schwantes, *Radical Heritage,* 81.

61. *Seattle Union Record,* March 23, April 27 (quotes), 1907; December 19, 1908.

62. Schwantes, *Radical Heritage,* 160.

63. O'Connor, *Revolution in Seattle,* 13 (second quote); Schwantes, *Radical Heritage,* 183 (first quote).

64. For details of the economic impact of the panic on Seattle, see A. MacDonald, "Seattle's Economic Development," 278–79, 315. For the impact on labor, see Bureau of Labor of the State of Washington, *Sixth Biennial Report of the Bureau of Labor Statistics and Factory Inspection, 1907–8* (Olympia, WA: C. W. Gorham, 1908), 5–7, 47–50, 110–37 (hereafter *Bureau of Labor Report, 1907–8*); *Seattle Union Record,* January 4, 11, 18, 1908; Dembo, *Unions and Politics,* 63–68. Dembo notes that sclc membership declined by more than 10 percent from 1907 to 1908, despite an overall tripling of employed workers during this decade.

65. *Seattle Union Record,* February 1, March 28, 1908.

66. Berner, *Seattle 1900–1920,* 49–50, 161. The chamber officially declared itself in favor of the open shop in 1910.

67. Seattle A.Y.P. Exposition Scrapbooks, vol. 1 (June 1906-December 1906), Pacific Northwest Collection, University of Washington (first quote); An Address by Henry Alberts McLean, June 1, 1907, Seattle A.Y.P. Exposition Miscellany, Pacific Northwest Collection, University of Washington; President J. E. Chilberg, "How the Exposition Was Made Possible," *Argus,* February 20, 1909.

68. Seattle Alaska-Yukon-Pacific Exposition Scrapbooks, vol. 1, Northwest Collection, Seattle Public Library; letter from Will Parry, AYP Exposition chairman of Ways and Means committee to F. G. Whitaker, September 22, 1906, box 1, folder 4, F. G. Whitaker Papers, Manuscripts and Archives, Suzzallo and Allen Library, University of Washington; "Alaska-Yukon-Pacific Exposition: Seattle, June 1 to October 16, 1909," issued by Northern Pacific Railway, in Seattle Alaska-Yukon-Pacific Exposition Scrapbooks, vol. 1; Bagley, *History of Seattle,* 524, 527.

69. *Seattle Union Record*, October 13, 1906, November 2, 1907; October 17, 1908. Apparently, labor disputes affected the 1893 World's Columbian Exposition, where fair officials refused to offer a minimum wage or guarantee that they would employ only union labor. Officials seemed unconcerned because they maintained that if the fairgrounds were not completed on time, residents would know whom to blame. See Clinton Keeler, "The White City and the Black City: The Dream of Civilization," *American Quarterly* 2.2 (Summer 1950): 113.

70. *Seattle Union Record*, November 16, 1907; January 11 and 18, 1908; January 16, 1909 (last quote); Seattle Alaska-Yukon-Pacific Exposition Scrapbooks, vol. 3 (first quote). The SCLC's business agent wrote in a letter to Joe Smith dated July 25, 1908, that union members "have been debarred from honorably going to work on these grounds, wages were slaughtered and conditions imposed which union men could not consistantly [*sic*] accept." See box 7, folder 20, Joseph Smith Papers.

71. *Seattle Union Record*, June 6, 1909; July 10, 31, August 7, 14, September 9, 1909; *Seattle Post-Intelligencer*, September 5, 7, 1909. After the close of the exposition, the *Union Record* (October 23, 1909) stated that the local money expended might as well have been burned for the good the general public received for its [AYPE] having been here."

72. On commercial leisure and the working class, see Kathy Peiss, *Cheap Amusements: Working Women and Leisure in New York City, 1820–1920* (Philadelphia: Temple University Press, 1986); Roy Rosenzweig, *Eight Hours for What They Will: Workers and Leisure in an Industrial City, 1870–1920* (New York: Cambridge University Press, 1983).

73. *Seattle Union Record*, June 24, September 2, 1905. *Thirteenth Census of the United States: Population 1910*, vol. 3, 989, 1004; Schmid, *Social Trends*, 99. While the *Union Record* ran columns about the need to organize against Japanese immigration, there is little evidence that workers organized a formal club or organization; rather, they seemed content with discussing it at SCLC meetings.

74. *Seattle Union Record*, November 11, 1905.

75. *Seattle Union Record*, December 8, 1906.

76. *Seattle Union Record*, March 23 (quote), 30, 1907; March 23, 1908. In early 1907, the chamber of commerce passed a resolution declaring its support for Japanese immigration, which it reaffirmed in 1908. See *Seattle Post-Intelligencer*, February 19, 1908.

77. *Seattle Union Record*, June 15, 29, August 17, October 5 (quote), 1907.

78. *Seattle Union Record*, November 13, 1909; September 3 (quote), 1910.

79. *Seattle Union Record*, February 5, 1910.

80. *Seattle Union Record*, August 8 (quote), November 7, 1908. For the announcement of the United Labor Party's formation, see *Seattle Union Record*, February 5, 1910.

81. *Seattle Union Record,* February 5, 19, 1910.

82. *Seattle Union Record,* February 12, 1910.

83. *Argus,* January 28 (first quote) and February 26 (second quote), 1910; *Seattle Daily Times,* March 9, 1910. The United Labor Party was able to muster only a little more than 4 percent of the vote, failing to garner even a hundred votes in half the city's fourteen wards and no more than 177 in any single ward. For a discussion of the 1910 election, see Blackford, "Sources of Support for Reform Candidates and Issues," 38–44.

84. *Seattle Union Record,* February 5, 12, 1910. On the significance of vice in the 1910 election, see Blackford, "Sources of Support for Reform Candidates and Issues," 39–41.

85. *Seattle Union Record,* July 16, 23, 30, 1910.

86. *Seattle Union Record,* July 30, September 3, 1910 (quotes).

87. *Seattle Union Record,* July 30, September 3, 1910.

88. *Seattle Union Record,* September 10, 17, 24, November 5, 1910. Cotterill was a city engineer before his election to the state senate. In the early 1900s he had run for office on a Democratic-Populist fusion ticket, served as chairman of the 1908 City Party, before returning to the Democratic Party in the 1910 election. In 1912, he was elected mayor of Seattle. Cotterill's brother Frank was a longtime labor leader in the SCLC and had encouraged labor's support of the Municipal Ownership Party in 1905. In his study of Los Angeles's 1911 Socialist Campaign, Daniel Johnson noted similar demands within Socialist leadership not to actively court middle-class votes because the middle class shared the capitalist values and beliefs of the enemy in that city's contest. See Daniel Johnson, "'No Make-Believe Class Struggle': The Socialist Municipal Campaign in Los Angeles, 1911," *Labor History* 41.1 (2000): 25–45.

89. Oestreicher, "Urban Working-Class Political Behavior," 1273.

90. *Seattle Union Record,* November 12, 1910. For discussion of the WSFL and state politics, see Dembo, *Union and Politics,* 75–78.

91. *Seattle Union Record,* February 19, 26, 1910; Blackford, "Reform Politics in Seattle," 178; William J. Dickson, "Labor in Municipal Politics: A Study of Labor's Political Policies and Activities in Seattle" (master's thesis, University of Washington, 1928), 111–18. In 1911, the labor weekly urged support for an $800,000 bond to build a streetcar trunk line in order to thwart Seattle Electric Company. See *Seattle Union Record,* February 25, 1911.

92. *Seattle Union Record,* March 1917, quoted in R. B. McKenzie, "Community Forces: A Study of the Non-Partisan Municipal Elections in Seattle II," *Journal of Social Forces* 2.3 (March 1924): 417; *Proceedings of the Central Labor Council of Seattle and Vicinity,* January 10, 24, 31, and February 14, 1917, box 8, Central Labor Council of King County, Manuscripts and Archives, Suzzallo and Allen Library,

University of Washington. For labor's consistent support for the Port of Seattle and the Port Commission, see Blackford, "Sources of Support for Reform Candidates and Issues," 55–77.

93. *Seattle Union Record*, February 26, 1910 (quote); Robert D. Saltvig, "The Progressive Movement in Washington" (PhD diss., University of Washington, 1966), 103–4; Blackford, "Sources of Support for Reform Candidates and Issues," 42.

94. Mansel Blackford, "Civic Groups, Political Action, and City Planning in Seattle, 1892–1915," *Pacific Historical Review* 49.4 (November 1980): 561 (quote), 563–74; William H. Wilson, "How Seattle Lost the Bogue Plan," *Pacific Northwest Quarterly* 75.4 (October 1984): 178; Lee F. Pendergrass, "Urban Reform and Voluntary Association: A Case Study of the Seattle Municipal League, 1910–1929" (PhD diss., University of Washington, 1972), 61–62.

95. For more on the Seattle suffrage movement and the actions of voting women, see John Putman, "A 'Test of Chiffon Politics': Gender Politics in Seattle, 1897–1917," *Pacific Historical Review* 69.4 (November 2000): 595–616.

3: CIVIC LIFE AND WOMAN SUFFRAGE

1. See Mead, *How the Vote Was Won;* Larson, "Dolls, Vassals, and Drudges: Pioneer Women in the West," 5–16; Larson, "The Woman Suffrage Movement in Washington," 49–63; Larson, "Women's Role in the American West," 3–11; Goldberg, *An Army of Women;* Marilley, *Woman Suffrage and the Origins of Liberal Feminism;* White, *"It's Your Misfortune and None of My Own,"* 355–59; Katz, "Dual Commitments,"; Katz, "A Politics of Coalition: Socialist Women and the California Suffrage Movement, 1900–1911," in *One Woman, One Vote: Rediscovering the Woman Suffrage Movement,* ed. Marjorie Spruill Wheeler, 245–62 (Troutsdale, OR: NewSage Press, 1995); Jensen, "Disfranchisement Is a Disgrace."

2. Robert D. Johnston, "Re-Democratizing the Progressive Era: The Politics of Progressive Era Thought," *Journal of the Gilded Age and Progressive Era* 1.1 (January 2002): 11.

3. Gayle Gullett, *Becoming Citizens: The Emergence and Development of the California Women's Movement, 1880–1911* (Urbana: University of Illinois Press, 2000), 152; Ethington, *The Public City,* 326; Kristi Anderson, *After Suffrage: Women in Partisan and Electoral Politics Before the New Deal* (Chicago: University of Chicago Press, 1996), 147; Clemens, *The People's Lobby,* chap. 6.

4. Karen Adair, "Organized Women Workers in Seattle, 1900–1918," (master's thesis, University of Washington, 1990), 1–2; Mary Lou Locke, "Out of the Shadows and Into the Western Sun: Working Women of the Late Nineteenth-Century Urban Far West," *Journal of Urban History* 16.2 (February 1990): 177–82. Locke notes that San Francisco was rather exceptional because it did possess some factory work, being the only significant industrial city in the West

during the late nineteenth century. Domestic labor may have been even greater in Seattle by the 1890s because of its large female Scandinavian population, who, because of both cultural factors and limited occupational opportunities, participated in domestic service at exceptionally high rates compared to native-born women. See Janice Reiff Webster, "Domestication and Americanization: Scandinavian Women in Seattle, 1888–1900," *Journal of Urban History* 4.3 (May 1978): 279–84. While regional differences, according to Locke, limited women to certain occupations, Paula Petrik has argued in her study of Helena, Montana, that that city's service-oriented economy benefited women's employment in the last few decades of the nineteenth century. See her *No Step Backward: Women and Family on the Rocky Mountain Frontier, Helena, Montana, 1865–1900* (Helena: Montana Historical Society Press, 1987), 23. A small number of female Indian wageworkers also continued to supplement the local labor market into the 1880s. See Alexandra Harmon, *Indians in the Making: Ethnic Relations and Indian Identities Around Puget Sound* (Berkeley and Los Angeles: University of California Press, 1998), 58–66.

5. *Seattle Post-Intelligencer* editorial reprinted in the *New Northwest,* December 6, 1883. On workingwomen in 1880s, see Adair, "Organized Women Workers in Seattle," 3, 24–25. She states that while the percentage of Washington's female population that earned wages was 11.6 percent (less than most eastern states), it more than doubled in the next decade.

6. Reprint of law in *Bureau of Labor Report, 1905–6,* 331. Gayle Gullett has argued that in California the campaign to advance women's work was closely related to the effort to fight for citizenship, including the ballot. See Gullett, *Becoming Citizens,* 3–5.

7. Occupational figures from *Twelfth Census of the United States: 1900 Population,* vol. 2, pt. 2, 590–94; Adair, "Organized Women Workers in Seattle," 9–11; Lloyd Spencer and Lancaster Pollard, *A History of the State of Washington,* vol. 1 (New York: American Historical Society, 1937), 364. Domestic and personal service employed 44 percent of Seattle workingwomen; of this more than one-half were servants or waiters. Twenty-one percent of women were employed in manufacturing, 20 percent in trade and transportation (mostly sales and telephone operators), and about 15 percent in professional ranks (largely teachers). Overall, Seattle's population in 1900 was 64 percent male. Native-born residents represented a lower share (61 percent) than foreign-born residents (71 percent). For more detail, see *Twelfth Census of the United States: 1900 Population,* vol. 1, pt. 1, 645.

8. Bagley, *History of Seattle,* 490–91. In addition to the Woman's Home Society, Seattle had the Orphan's Home, the Refuge Home, and the House of Good Shepherd that cared for fallen and other unfortunate women. In 1891, Bagley notes, the House of Good Shepherd was home to fifty "unfortunates."

9. LeWarne, *Utopias on Puget Sound,* 34, 96; Barbara Cloud, "Laura Hall Peters: Pursuing the Myth of Equality," *Pacific Northwest Quarterly* 74.1 (January 1983): 29–33.

10. LeWarne, *Utopias on Puget Sound,* 30 (first quote), 34 (second quote), 80–96, 225.

11. *Seattle YWCA: Annual Report, 1903–4,* accession #3919, box 1, folder 16, Seattle Young Women's Christian Association: King County Records, Manuscripts and Archives, Suzzallo and Allen Library, University of Washingto, 4; Adair, "Organized Women Workers in Seattle," 4, 6, 106–7. Adair states that the free employment office placed notices in eastern newspapers advertising that Seattle's domestic servant wages had increased 25 percent from 1897 to 1898. An additional explanation for the changing course offerings by the YWCA is that working girls joined these organizations in such large numbers that they soon outnumbered genteel women and influenced the activities offered by the organization. See Priscilla Murolo, *The Common Ground of Womanhood: Class, Gender, and Working Girls' Clubs, 1884–1928* (Urbana: University of Illinois Press, 1997), 16.

12. *Thirteenth Census of the United States: Population 1910,* vol. 3, 989; vol. 4, 194–207; Adair, "Organized Women Workers in Seattle," 10–11. The city's sex ratio misrepresented the proportion of female workers when compared to national averages. In 1900, the number of Seattle female workers as a percentage of total labor force was just more than half the national average (10.6 percent to 18 percent); however, the percentage of workingwomen out of the total female population was slightly higher than the national average (20 percent to 19 percent). By 1920, Seattle workingwomen eclipsed national work participation rates in both categories. The changing distribution of Seattle women workers, according to Adair, continued in the next decade as domestic service dropped to 26 percent and sales and clerical work increased to 45 percent. This trend was not exclusive to Seattle, but reflected national changes associated with a maturing industrial society. For more, see Philip Foner, *Women and the American Labor Movement: From Colonial Times to the Eve of World War I* (New York: Free Press, 1979), chaps. 14, 25; Ileen A. DeVault, "'Give the Boys a Trade': Gender and Job Choice in the 1890s," in *Work Engendered: Toward a New History of American Labor,* ed. Ava Baron, 191–201 (Ithaca, NY: Cornell University Press, 1991); Leslie Woodcock Tentler, *Wage-Earning Women: Industrial Work and Family Life in the United States, 1900–1930* (New York: Oxford University Press, 1979).

13. *Seattle YWCA: Annual Report, 1901–2,* 5–6; *Seattle YWCA: Annual Report, 1903–4,* 6; *Seattle YWCA: Annual Report, 1905,* 21; Reiff, "Urbanization and the Social Structure," 114.

14. *Bureau of Labor Report, 1903–4,* 141, 148; Adair, "Organized Women Workers in Seattle," 32–34.

15. Adair, "Organized Women Workers in Seattle," 154–64. The court case is covered in *Bureau of Labor Report, 1903–4,* 14.

16. *Bureau of Labor Report, 1903–4,* 12, 18 (first quote); *Bureau of Labor Report, 1905–6;* Adair, "Organized Women Workers in Seattle," 87–102 (quote, 92).

17. *Mixer and Server,* quoted in Dorothy Sue Cobble, *Dishing It Out: Waitresses and Their Unions in the Twentieth Century* (Urbana: University of Illinois Press, 1991), 63.

18. Membership figures found in *Bureau of Labor Report, 1905–1906,* 105, and *Seventh Biennial Report of the Bureau of Labor Statistics and Factory Inspection, 1909–10* (Olympia, WA: C. W. Gorham 1910), 59; Adair, "Organized Women Workers in Seattle," 177–81. Local 240 was the first permanent waitresses union in the nation and affiliated with the WCLU, the Hotel Employees and Restaurant Employees International Union, and the AFL. According to Mary Lee Spence, the Pacific Coast possessed the most vigorous union effort in the nation at the turn of the century. San Francisco soon followed Seattle's example when that city's waitresses formed their own local in 1906. See Mary Lee Spence, "Commentary," in *Western Women: Their Land, Their Lives,* ed. Lillian Schlissel, Vicki Ruiz, and Janice Monk (Albuquerque: University of New Mexico Press, 1988), 147–48.

19. *Proceedings of the Washington State Federation of Labor, 1907,* Pacific Northwest Collection, University of Washington, 4; *Proceedings of the Washington State Federation of Labor, 1914,* 9; Adair, "Organized Women Workers in Seattle," 189–92. In addition to her several terms as vice president of the local labor council, Alice Lord served on numerous union committees, attended every annual convention of the Washington State Labor Federation into the 1920s, was appointed chairperson of the credentials committee at the 1907 WSFL convention, was the only woman to serve on state committees (other than the Committee on Labels and Unfair Lists) in the 1914 WSFL session, and was an active member and contributor to the Hotel Employees and Restaurant Employees Union.

20. *Seattle Union Record,* December 12, 1905; March 31 (quote), June 23, 1906.

21. Foner, *Women and the American Labor Movement,* 471; Tentler, *Wage-Earning Women,* 14–15; Adair, "Organized Women Workers in Seattle," 9–10.

22. Foner, *Women and the American Labor Movement,* 294, 322, 471–72; Ava Baron, "Gender and Labor History: Learning from the Past, Looking to the Future," in Baron, *Work Engendered,* 9–11; Tentler, *Wage-Earning Women,* 14–15; Cobble, *Dishing It Out,* 61.

23. On Lord's thoughts, see *Seattle Union Record,* January 6, 1906; Adair, "Organized Women Workers in Seattle," 189. On support for organizing female workers, see *Seattle Union Record,* October 28, 1905, December 1, 1906 (quote); March 27, 1909; Adair, "Organized Women Workers in Seattle," 36 (first quote), 162.

24. *Seattle Union Record,* November 14, 1908 (first quote); April 9, 1904 (second quote); Adair, "Organized Women Workers in Seattle," 36.

25. On the race suicide issue, see *Seattle Union Record,* January 13, 1906; Adair, "Organized Women Workers in Seattle," 15–16. For examples of union sentiments concerning women working, see *Seattle Union Record,* April 15, 1905; November 16, 1907.

26. Adair, "Women Workers in Seattle," 14, 36, 45.

27. Kathryn Oberdeck, "'Not Pink Teas': The Seattle Working-Class Women's Movement, 1905–1918," *Labor History* 32.2 (Spring 1991): 194–95; Foner, *Women and the American Labor Movement,* 240–41 (quote); Dana Frank, "At the Point of Consumption: Seattle Labor and the Politics of Consumption, 1919–1927" (PhD diss., Yale University, 1988), 447–48; and Frank, *Purchasing Power.*

28. *Seattle Union Record,* January 7, February 11, March 4, 1905. For a discussion of the Citizens' Alliance and the Municipal Ownership Party, see chapter 2 above.

29. *Seattle Union Record,* March 4, 18 (quote), 1905.

30. *Seattle Union Record,* April 15, May 13, 27 (quote), 1905.

31. Quoted in Oberdeck, "Not Pink Teas," 200.

32. *Seattle Union Record,* October 10, 19, 1905; January 6, 1906.

33. *Seattle Union Record,* January 26, March 2, June 24, 1905. On the limited activity of the Seattle Women's Label League, see *Seattle Union Record,* March 16, 1907; December 5, 1908; Oberdeck, "Not Pink Teas," 200.

34. *Seattle Union Record,* February 4, 1905.

35. *Proceedings of the Washington State Federation of Labor, 1907,* 33, 57, 63 (quote); *Seattle Union Record,* February 9, 23, March 2, 1907; Adair, "Organized Women Workers in Seattle," 91–92, 200.

36. *Seattle Union Record,* February 9, 1907 (second quote); February 27, 1909 (first quote).

37. *Seattle Union Record,* February 9 (first quote), 23 (second quote), 1907.

38. On working hours for men and women, see A. MacDonald, "Seattle's Economic Development," 311. Higgins's report can be found in *Western Women's Outlook* 6.11 (May 29, 1913): 15–17. For reference to the need for state intervention in the working lives of women, see *Seattle Union Record,* January 16, 1909; Adair, "Organized Women Workers in Seattle," 164–65.

39. *Seattle YWCA: Annual Report, 1901–2; Seattle YWCA: Annual Report, 1903–4; Seattle YWCA: Annual Report, 1905; Seattle Union Record,* April 7, 1906; February 9, 1907; February 1, 1908.

40. *Seattle Union Record,* September 28, 1907; July 16, 1910; Adair, "Organized Women Workers in Seattle," 201–4.

41. *Seattle Post-Intelligencer,* August 15, 1888, quoted in Bagley, *History of*

Seattle, 490; Mead, *How the Vote Was Won,* 45; Schwantes, *The Pacific Northwest,* 256–58. The suffrage amendment lost by 35,527 to 16,613, while the proposed state constitution passed by a wide margin, 42,152 to 11,879.

42. Morgan, *Skid Row,* 103–4; Cloud, "Laura Hall Peters," 32–33.

43. Schwantes, *The Pacific Northwest,* 259; Riddle, *The Old Radicalism,* 161, 213.

44. Gullett, *Becoming Citizens,* 89–96.

45. *Report of the 14th Annual Meeting of Women's Christian Temperance Union of West Washington, 1897,* Pacific Northwest Collection, University of Washington, 26–27; *Report of the 15th Annual Meeting of Women's Christian Temperance Union of West Washington, 1898,* Pacific Northwest Collection, University of Washington, 17; Cora Smith Eaton King, "History of Washington Suffrage," manuscript, box F, folder 29, Emma Smith DeVoe Papers, Washington State Library; Riddle, *The Old Radicalism,* 161. Voters rejected the suffrage amendment 30,540 to 20,658. Despite the loss, the gap between victory and defeat had decreased since the 1889 amendment attempt. For a fine study of gender politics and woman suffrage elsewhere in the West, see Goldberg, *An Army of Women.*

46. For an excellent study of the club movement, see Karen J. Blair, *The Clubwoman as Feminist: True Womanhood Redefined, 1868–1914* (New York: Holmes and Meier, 1980). See also Paula Baker, "The Domestication of Politics: Women and American Political Society, 1780–1920," *American Historical Review* 89.3 (June 1984): 620–47; Maureen Flanagan, "Gender and Urban Political Reform: The City Club and the Woman's City Club of Chicago in the Progressive Era," *American Historical Review* 95 (October 1990): 1032–50. On the concept of female institution building, see Estelle Freedman, "Separatism as Strategy: Female Institution Building and American Feminism, 1870–1930," *Feminist Studies* 5.3 (Fall 1979): 517 (quote). Jo Freeman has suggested that even though many literary or civic clubs did not become political clubs, they "provided experience and contacts that were easily transferable to political work." See her *A Room at a Time: How Women Entered Party Politics* (Lanham, MD: Rowman and Littlefield, 2000), 65.

47. Baker, "The Domestication of Politics," 642; Freedman, "Separatism as Strategy," 517; Clemens, *The People's Lobby,* 196–201; Blair, *Clubwoman as Feminist,* chaps. 1–2.

48. Classified List of Delegates to First Convention of Washington State Federation of Women's Clubs, June 22 and 23, 1897, at Olympia, Washington, accession #3463, 3463 (2–5), box 1, folder 13, Suzzallo and Allen Library, Manuscripts and Archives, University of Washington; Serena Mathews, "History of the Washington State Federation of Women's Clubs," 1949, accession #3463, 3463 (2–5), box 1, folder 10, Manuscripts and Archives, Suzzallo and Allen Library, University of Washington, 7, 8, 13–14,; Lillian Long, "The Birth of a Club" [ca. 1980], Federation of Women's Clubs: Seattle Federation District, accession #3463-10, box 1, Manuscripts and

Archives, University of Washington. Dr. Sarah Kendall became state chairman of correspondence with the national General Federation of Women's Clubs. Holmes was elected president for a two-year term in 1899 and, in addition to membership in the Women's Century Club, helped found the Seattle City Federation and served as president of the Seattle Kindergarten Association. Catt expected members of the Woman's Century Club to present original papers to club members on topics dealing with women and society. See Sandra Haarsager, *Organized Womanhood: Cultural Politics in the Pacific Northwest, 1840–1920* (Norman: University of Oklahoma Press, 1997), 210–11.

49. Dora P. Tweed, "Woman in Club Life: Her Duties and Responsibilities," *Washington Women*, n.d., Federation of Women's Clubs: Seattle Federation District, accession #3463-10, box 4, Manuscripts and Archives, University of Washington; *Clover Leaf* 1.1 (June 1899), Federation of Women's Clubs: Seattle Federation District, accession #3463-10, box 4, Manuscripts and Archives, University of Washington (second quote); *Western Woman's Outlook* 1.1 (December 21, 1911) (last quote). Holmes's commitment to social problems was evident early on when she presented her formal paper "The Relation of the Laborer to the Employer" to the Woman's Century Club. See Haarsager, *Organized Womanhood,* 211.

50. Mathews, "History of the Washington State Federation of Women's Clubs"; Bagley, *History of Seattle,* 496; Gayle Ann Gullett, "Feminism, Politics, and Voluntary Groups: Organized Womanhood in California, 1886–1896" (PhD diss., University of California, Riverside, 1983), 2 (quote). For an excellent study of middle-class women who participated in such reform efforts as part of growth coalition aimed at enhancing both their own investment endeavors and improving the city, see Lee M. A. Simpson, *Selling the City: Gender, Class, and the California Growth Machine, 1880–1940* (Stanford, CA: Stanford University Press, 2004).

51. Haarsager, *Organized Womanhood,* 179.

52. *Seattle YWCA: Annual Report, 1901–2,* 7 (first quote); *Seattle YWCA: Annual Report, 1902–3,* 8 (second quote); *Seattle YWCA: Annual Report, 1903–4,* 8.

53. *Seattle YWCA: Annual Report, 1903–4,* 5–6 (quote); *Seattle YWCA: Annual Report, 1905,* 21–22.

54. *Seattle YWCA: Annual Report, 1903–4,* 5–6; Priscilla Murolo has suggested that workingwomen needed help from genteel women to improve their lot by way of protective legislation, vocational education, and other means, especially if organized labor was weak in their community. See Murolo, *The Common Ground of Womanhood,* 117.

55. On Anthony's cross-class association, see Ellen C. DuBois, *Feminism and Suffrage: The Emergence of an Independent Women's Movement in America, 1848–1869* (Ithaca, NY: Cornell University Press, 1978), chap. 5. California middle-class

suffragists also admitted the importance of broadening their coalition to include working-class women when they rejected the "society plan" advocated by national suffrage leaders. See Gullett, *Becoming Citizens,* 149. On Oregon's 1906 failed suffrage campaign, see Mead, *How the Vote Was Won,* 102–7.

56. *Seattle Union Record,* October 13, 1906, January 18, 1908 (quote), October 10, 1908; Mathews, "History of the Washington State Federation of Women's Clubs," 33–34; Helen Norton Stevens, *Memorial Biography of Adele M. Fielde: Humanitarian* (Seattle: Fielde Memorial Committee, 1918), 309–10. Fielde came to Seattle in 1907 and immediately became engaged in numerous progressive reform groups, including the Anti-Tuberculosis League of King County and the Direct Legislation League. She wrote numerous articles that the *Union Record* published, ranging from the obligation of government to provide jobs for the unemployed and establishing a cooperative bank in Seattle, to the benefits of the commission form of government. For example, see *Seattle Union Record,* February 8, 1908; February 5, May 28, 1910.

57. Bush letter published in *Seattle Union Record,* October 3, 1908. On organized labor's public support for the suffrage amendment, see *Seattle Union Record,* November 28, 1908; January 15, March 19, 1910. Spokane's Central Labor Council also publicly and overwhelmingly endorsed equal suffrage as early as 1908.

58. Morgan, *Skid Road,* 124–38; Kathryn Brandenfels, "Down on the Sawdust: Prostitution and Vice Control in Seattle, 1870–1920," unpublished paper, 1981, Pacific Northwest Collection, University of Washington, 33–37.

59. Berner, *Seattle 1900–1920,* 33–37, 113; Brandenfels, "Down on the Sawdust," 35–38; Clark, *The Dry Years,* 59.

60. *Seattle Union Record,* January 9, April 7, July 17, 1909; *Argus,* January 22, February 26, 1910; Berner, *Seattle 1900–1920,* 114–15. In her study of Butte, Paula Petrik has argued that confining prostitution to a specific location opened up the rest of the city or public space to "respectable women." See her *No Step Backward,* 58.

61. *Seattle Post-Intelligencer,* April 7, 8, May 5, 7, 8, 1909. Both the Seattle Woman's Christian Temperance Union and the YWCA also expressed concern about protecting female morality by appointing members to police the fairgrounds throughout the exposition's run in order to watch over unchaperoned young women.

62. Burton Hendrick, "The 'Recall' in Seattle," *McClure's Magazine,* October 1911, 647–49; Berner, *Seattle 1900–1920,* 114–16.

63. Harry E. Moore, "The Moral Cleansing of Seattle," *The Light* [ca. 1911], pp. 13–16, Scrapbook of Seattle Material, 1911–17, Northwest Collection, Seattle Public Library; "Turn on the Light," pamphlet [ca. 1911], Scrapbook of Seattle Material, 1911–17. For an excellent, though perhaps somewhat exaggerated, view of vice activity after Gill's election, see Hendrick, "The 'Recall' in Seattle," 651–57.

64. Hendrick, "The 'Recall' in Seattle," 657–58; Moore, "The Moral Cleansing of Seattle," 16–20; Blackford, "Sources of Support for Reform Candidates and Issues," 46–50.

65. Aileen Kraditor, *The Ideas of the Woman Suffrage Movement, 1890–1920* (1965; repr., New York: W. W. Norton, 1981), chap. 5; Morgan, *Skid Row*, 166. Seattle was listed as one of three main centers of white slavery in the nation in 1900.

66. Poster found in Scrapbook of Seattle Material, 1911–1917, Northwest Collection, Seattle Public Library.

67. King, "History of Washington Suffrage," 1–5 (quote, 1). Membership figures from Cora Smith Eaton, M.D., treasurer of WESA, box 2, folder 2, Emma Smith DeVoe Papers, Washington State Library. According to DeVoe, there were more than 1,700 official members of suffrage clubs in the state in 1909. See E. S. DeVoe, president, WESA, to Fellow Suffragist, January 1909, box 1, folder 18, Emma Smith DeVoe Papers.

68. Kraditor, *Ideas of the Woman Suffrage Movement*, chap. 3; Baker, "The Domestication of Politics," 642; Freedman, "Separatism as Strategy," 521. Kraditor contends that the political expediency argument eclipsed the justice idea as the chief rhetorical claim of suffrage leaders sometime around the turn of the century. One scholar, however, argues that suffragists, from the inception of the movement until victory in 1910s, employed both ideas in the American West. For more, see Larson, "The Woman Suffrage Movement in Washington," 51.

69. Alice M. Smith, "Why I Believe in Political Equality," 1901, accession #4155, box 5, Alice Smith Papers, Manuscripts and Archives, Suzzallo and Allen Library, University of Washington; *Votes for Women* 1.6 (May 1910), 1.10 (October 1910). For an example of the wide range of arguments suffragists enlisted in their campaign, see "The Seattle Suffrage Club Offers a Score of Reasons Why Women Should Be Enfranchised," accession #123, box 2, Nellie M. Fick Papers, Manuscripts and Archives, Suzzallo and Allen Library, University of Washington. On the concept of citizenship and equal suffrage, see Gullett, *Becoming Citizens,* chaps. 2, 4.

70. *Votes for Women* 1.3 (February 1910): 4 (first quote); "The Seattle Suffrage Club Offers a Score of Reasons Why Women Should Be Enfranchised" (quotes). For other examples, see various articles in the special suffrage issue of *Votes for Women* 1.10 (October 1910). For a national perspective of the connection between white slavery and prosuffrage arguments, see Marilley, *Woman Suffrage and the Origins of Liberal Feminism,* 202–4.

71. *Votes for Women* 1.10 (October 1910): 4, 9. On the apparent contradictions within suffrage ideology, see Kraditor, *Ideas of the Woman Suffrage Movement,* chap. 3; Marilley, *Woman Suffrage and the Origins of Liberal Feminism,* 220–26; Victoria Bissell Brown, "Jane Addams, Progressivism, and Woman Suffrage," in Wheeler, *One Woman, One Vote,* 186–95; Katz, "A Politics of Coalition," 251.

72. Gullett, *Becoming Citizens*, 3–5, 108, 143; Freeman, *A Room at a Time*, 73; Maureen Flanagan, *Seeing With Their Hearts: Chicago Women and the Vision of the Good City, 1871–1933* (Princeton, NJ: Princeton University Press, 2002), 87–88.

73. On the campaign strategy, see King, "History of Washington Suffrage," 15. On the similar strategy employed by national suffrage leaders, see Marilley, *Woman Suffrage and the Origins of Liberal Feminism*, 188.

74. *Votes for Women* 1.3 (February 1910); *Patriarch*, June 6, 1903; May 14, November 5, 1904; October 22, 1910 (last quote). The exact circulation of Clayson's paper is difficult to determine. Much of Clayson's advertising originated from the liquor industry, and he published the paper until just before the outbreak of World War I. His ties to the saloons help explain some of his animosity toward woman suffrage, for he believed that the ultimate goal of the movement was prohibition. In 1905, Clayson spelled out what his paper stood for. Its first principle was the "Patriarchal Republic," followed by the "People's Party," "Anti-Woman Suffrage," "Temperance vs. Prohibition," and lastly, "Masculine Virtue and Authority." In the October 1910 edition of *Votes for Women*, the editors made a subtle reference to him and his long opposition to equal suffrage.

75. *Votes for Women* 1.3 (February 1910): 1, 4. In a pamphlet by the Washington Equal Suffrage Association, the editor of the *Puyallup Valley Tribune* also attempted to push aside the perceived threat to marriage and instead emphasized the benefits it produced. See Robert Montgomery, "Female Suffrage: From the Viewpoint of a Male Democrat," 1909, n.p., Pacific Northwest Collection, University of Washington.

76. *Votes for Women* 1.1 (October 1909), 1.11 (December 1910). For more on the West in the American mind, see White, *"It's Your Misfortune and None of My Own,"* 57–58, 612–29; Wrobel, *Promised Lands*. Many westerners believed that one of the special or unique qualities the West possessed was a penchant for reform, or what many at that time referred to as progressivism. In a speech before the King County Political Equality Club in 1909, Professor Edward McMahon of the University of Washington made an urgent appeal to western settlers to grant women the franchise. He stated that they must hasten reforms "before we are swamped by conservative settlers from the East." See *Votes for Women*, January 1910.

77. *Votes for Women*, December 1909, January 1910; Emma Smith DeVoe, "What Next?" November 1910, folder 20, box 1, DeVoe Papers; *Western Woman's Outlook*, January 1912, 5.

78. *Votes for Women*, June 1910, October 1910.

79. *Votes for Women*, October 1909.

80. Letter from Headquarters Secretary, Washington Equal Suffrage Association, to Mrs. M. LaReine Baker, October 10, 1908, box 1, folder 2, Emma Smith

DeVoe Papers; King, "History of Washington Suffrage," 5–6; C. H. Baily, "How Washington Women Regained the Ballot," *Pacific Monthly* 26.1 (July 1911): 9. Rebecca Mead has argued that Washington suffragists represented a transitional phase in the shift to more modern political techniques California women employed in the 1911 campaign. See Mead, *How the Vote Was Won,* 112, 118.

81. Seattle AYP Exposition Scrapbooks, vol. 3, June 28, 1907–April 5, 1908.

82. "41st Annual Convention of the National American Woman Suffrage Association, Seattle, Washington, July 1–6, 1909," Seattle A.Y.P. Exposition Miscellany; Bagley, *History of Seattle,* 495; *Seattle Post-Intelligencer,* June 30, 1909.

83. On the social activities, see *Seattle Post-Intelligencer,* April 23, May 27, 1909; Adella M. Parker note, Notes and Correspondence on history, box 5, folder 29, Emma Smith DeVoe Papers. On the cookbook, see *Washington Women's Cook Book* (Seattle: Washington Equal Suffrage Association, 1909), Seattle Public Library; King, "History of Washington Suffrage," 7.

84. On the various suffrage activities at the fair, see *Votes for Women* 1.2 (January 1910); letter to Women of Washington from Emma Smith DeVoe, n.d., box 1, folder 21, DeVoe Papers.

85. *Votes for Women* 1.2 (January 1910); 1.3 (February 1910); 1.11 (December 1910, quote); letter to Mrs. Baker (no author), October 28, 1908, box 1, folder 2, Emma Smith DeVoe Papers; *Patriarch,* October 22, 1910.

86. King, "History of Washington Suffrage," 7–10; Bagley, *History of Seattle,* 494; *Votes for Women* 1.2 (January 1910); 1.10 (October 1910). *Votes for Women* was the official organ of WESA, and its editors included some of the leaders of the ballot movement, such as Adella M. Parker and Mary G. O'Meara.

87. *Seattle Union Record,* July 9, 1910; form letter from Emma Smith DeVoe, 1910, box 1, folder 20, DeVoe Papers; *Seattle Post-Intelligencer,* April 28, May 16, July 11, 17, 1909. The National Council of Women was established 1889 by Susan B. Anthony, and by 1909 it had a membership of nearly two million women. According to its leaders at that time, the council focused on major social problems facing the nation, including immigration, illiteracy, and the legal status of women and children. On the Washington State Grange and rural support for equal suffrage, see Watkins, *Rural Democracy,* 66–101, 104–7.

88. Washington State Federation of Labor, "Resolution No. 62," box 3, folder 17, Emma Smith DeVoe Papers; *Seattle Union Record,* September 24, October 1, 22, November 5 (quotes), 1910. On the antisuffrage effort, see *Seattle Union Record,* September 24, October 1, 1910; Charles P. Taylor to Emma Smith DeVoe, August 2, 1910, box 3, folder 17, DeVoe Papers.

89. Emma Smith DeVoe to Suffrage Co-Worker, July 22, 1910, box 1, folder 17, DeVoe Papers; Cora Eaton to Fellow Campaigner, October 31, 1910, in Emma Smith DeVoe Scrapbooks, vol. 7, DeVoe Papers; Seattle AYP Exposition Scrapbooks, vol.

2, January 1, 1907–June 27, 1907; King, "History of Washington Suffrage," 6; Duniway, *Path Breaking*, 242. Grassroots, precinct-level organizing proved to be effective in California's 1911 suffrage campaign. See Gullett, *Becoming Citizens*, 166.

90. George V. Piper to Cora S. Eaton, June 1, 1909, box 5, Emma Smith DeVoe Papers; Larson, "The Woman Suffrage Movement in Washington," 57–58.

91. Cora S. Eaton to Mrs. M. A. Hutton, June 17, 1909 (quote); Cora S. Eaton to Mr. J. H. DeVoe, June 4, 1909; Cora S. Eaton to Mrs. [Carrie Chapman] Catt, October 24, 1909, box 2, folder 5—all in Emma Smith DeVoe Papers; Larson, "The Woman Suffrage Movement in Washington," 58–59.

92. For a complete version of this conflict, see Larson, "The Woman Suffrage Movement in Washington," 57–61; Mead, *How the Vote Was Won*, 107–12.

93. Duniway, *Path Breaking*, 224; A. S. Duniway to E. S. DeVoe, February 23, 1909 (first quote), and Rachel Avery Foster to E. S. DeVoe, March 5, 1907, box 1, folder 17, DeVoe Papers; E. S. DeVoe to C. C. Catt, November 23, 1909 (second quote), box 4, folder D, DeVoe Papers; Moynihan, *Rebel for Rights*, 110; Larson, "The Woman Suffrage Movement in Washington, 61. Apparently, California suffragists either followed Washington's example or learned it on their own, because they also attempted to keep national speakers and organizers out of their 1911 campaign. See College Equal Suffrage League of California, *Winning Equal Suffrage in California: Reports of the Committees of the College Equal Suffrage League of Northern California in the Campaign of 1911* (San Francisco: National College Equal Suffrage League, 1913). One interesting difference between national leaders and some local women who demanded the ballot was in the terminology used to describe such women. Miss Adella Parker responded rather positively to the local press's use of "suffragette" to describe her and other prosuffrage women in Washington. Carrie Chapman Catt, however, noted her displeasure with this term, which she believed denoted militancy, and instead declared that she was a suffragist. For more, see *Seattle Post-Intelligencer*, June 28, 1909.

94. *Western Woman Voter* 1.1 (January 1911); King, "History of Washington Suffrage," 13.

95. *Votes for Women* 1.11 (December 1910); *Western Woman Voter* 1.1 (January 1911); 1.3 (March 1911); 2.2 (February 1912); *Seattle Municipal News* 2.22 (September 1912): 1. Because of the rapid growth of Seattle in the previous decade, the political clout of the First Ward had dropped significantly. The region south of Yesler Way, the dividing line of the restricted district, contained only 30 percent of the city's population, while north of this line lay nearly two-thirds of city residents. Of the three Pacific Coast states that granted women the vote in the 1910s, Washington passed it with the largest majority; it squeaked by in California and Oregon. See Susan E. Marshall, *Splintered Sisterhood: Gender and Class in the Campaign Against Woman Suffrage* (Madison: University of Wisconsin Press, 1997), 154.

96. King, "History of Washington Suffrage," 11 (first quote); Ida A. Allen to Emma Smith DeVoe, November 11, 1909 (second quote), box 1, folder 1, DeVoe Papers; Mary Awkright Hutton to Senator George F. Cotterill, November 22, 1909, (third quote), box 8, folder 51, George Cotterill Papers, Manuscripts and Archives, Suzzallo and Allen Library, University of Washington; Larson, "The Woman Suffrage Movement in Washington," 62.

97. On Republican insurgency in Seattle and Washington, see Blackford, "Sources of Support for Reform Candidates and Issues," 38–42. On the significance of the state political environment for the suffrage election, see King, "History of Washington Suffrage," 5, 11.

98. Rebecca Mead likewise sees progressivism as central to the suffrage victories western states achieved beginning with Washington in 1910. See Mead, *How the Vote Was Won*, 2, 171–72.

99. *Votes for Women* 1.11 (December 1910); *Seattle Union Record,* November 12, 1910 (quotes). The Seattle Suffrage Club passed a resolution thanking union men for their aid in passing the amendment. See *Seattle Union Record,* November 26, 1910.

4: CHIFFON POLITICS IN PROGRESSIVE-ERA SEATTLE

1. Baker, "The Domestication of Politics," 643; J. Stanley Lemons, *The Woman Citizen: Social Feminism in the 1920s* (Urbana: University of Illinois Press, 1973); William Chafe, *The American Woman: Her Changing Social, Economic, and Political Roles, 1920–1970* (New York: Oxford University Press, 1972), 299–300. Kristi Anderson has argued that scholars "generally ignored the aftermath of suffrage, implicitly admitting that nothing very interesting happened, with regard to women and electoral politics, until the 1970s." See Anderson, *After Suffrage,* 1.

2. Jo Freeman argues that politics is largely local, and consequently "the study of women and politics is the study of grassroots political activity." See Freeman, *A Room at a Time,* x.

3. Nancy Cott argues that much continuity existed before and after the Nineteenth Amendment. See her "Across the Great Divide: Women in Politics Before and After 1920," in *Women, Politics, and Change,* ed. Louise A. Tilly and Patricia Gurin, 153–76 (New York: Russell Sage Foundation, 1990).

4. Hendrick, "The 'Recall' in Seattle," 659–61. The effort to recall Gill was the first time that this political procedure was used in Seattle. Adella Parker, a high school teacher and graduate of the University of Washington Law School, wrote the charter amendment and led the movement to pass the law in 1907. Journalist and politician-in-waiting Joe Smith joined Parker's effort and helped expand support for the recall amendment. Parker, however, had to work behind the scenes and often used her father's name rather than her own in her more

public activities. For more on the recall and the Direct Legislation League, see Joseph Smith, "Autobiography manuscript," chapter 10B, box 1, folder 17, Joseph Smith Papers, Manuscripts and Archives, Suzzallo and Allen Library, University of Washington.

5. *Western Woman Voter* 1.2 (February 1911).

6. *Votes for Women* 1.12 (January 1911); *New Citizen* 2.13 (February 1911) (last quote); "The Moral Cleansing of Seattle," *The Light*, n.d., Scrapbook of Seattle Material, 1911–17, vol. 1, Northwest Collection, Seattle Public Library; "To the Women of Seattle from Mrs. Thomas F. Murphine," Woman's Dilling Campaign Headquarters, n.d., box 8, folder 1, Joseph Smith Papers; Hendrick, "The 'Recall' in Seattle," 662. For a brief biography of Dilling, see Blackford, "Sources of Support for Reform Candidates and Issues," 51.

7. *Western Woman Voter* 1.2 (February 1911); Hendrick, "The 'Recall' in Seattle," 662 (quote).

8. *Town Crier*, November 12, 1910, January 14, 1911; *Votes for Women* 1.12 (January 1911); *Western Woman Voter* 1.2 (February 1911).

9. *New Citizen* 2.13 (February 1911) (quote); *Western Woman Voter* 1.10 (October–November 1911); "Our Restricted District Under Mayor Gill," pamphlet, 1912, Scrapbook of Seattle Material, 1911–17, vol. 1; Hendrick, "The 'Recall' in Seattle," 663; Blackford, "Sources of Support for Reform Candidates and Issues," 53. In its analysis of voting turnout by sex, the *Western Woman Voter* noted that considering the city's sex ratio, which favored men, the number of women who voted was even more impressive. Cora Smith King also observed that women, though outnumbered by men, voted in the same proportion as the other sex. See Cora Smith King, "Washington," in *History of Woman Suffrage*, ed. Elizabeth Cady Stanton, Susan B. Anthony, and Matilda Joslyn Gage (New York: Fowler and Wells, 1881–1922), vol. 6, chap. 46.

10. *Western Woman Voter* 1.3 (March 1911); *Report of the 28th Annual Annual Convention of the Woman's Christian Temperance Union of Western Washington*, 1911, Pacific Northwest Collection, University of Washington, 3; Hendrick, "The 'Recall' in Seattle," 663 (quote); "The Moral Cleansing of Seattle," 11; King, "History of Washington Suffrage," 16; U.S. Congress, *Industrial Relations Report*, 4110. On the recall and Gill, see Blackford, "Sources of Support for Reform Candidates and Issues," 50–54; Morgan, *Skid Road*, 170–81.

11. *Votes for Women* 1.12 (January 1911) (first quote); Minnie B. Frazier to Joe Smith, March 3, 1911, box 8, folder 3, Joseph Smith Papers; *New Citizen* 2.13 (February 1911). Gill's comments found in *Industrial Relations Report*, 4110.

12. Blackford, "Sources of Support for Reform Candidates and Issues," 56–57; Morgan, *Skid Row*, 171–74. Interestingly, editors of the *Western Woman's Outlook*, a separate periodical formed in late 1911, questioned Wappenstein's conviction,

suggesting that it was based solely on the uncorroborated testimony of underworld figures. For more, see *Western Woman's Outlook* 2.1 (March 28, 1912).

13. "Our Restricted District Under Mayor Gill"; *Municipal League News* 1.8 (August 12, 1911); Report of Robert Boggess to C. G. Bannick, June 27, 1912, box 7, folder 13, George Cotterill Papers; Blackford, "Sources of Support for Reform Candidates and Issues," 57. The Quong Wah Company along with the Nongang Company apparently ran a lottery.

14. "Our Restricted District Under Mayor Gill." In his study of Seattle elections, Blackford states that Gill carried ten of the fourteen wards and had a popular vote of 24,522, while Cotterill captured three wards and 14,420 votes and Parrish received 12,700 votes. One of the more telling results of this primary was that Wells received more than 10,000 votes, foreshadowing the growing class consciousness that would mark Seattle in the years surrounding World War I. See Blackford, "Sources of Support for Reform Candidates and Issues," 60–66. According to Minnie Frazier, the candidates understood the importance of women to the primary election. Parrish asked her to serve on his "board of campaign women," though she refused because of his stance on various city issues. See Minnie Frazier to Joe Smith, January 22, 1912, box 8, folder 12, Smith Papers.

15. "An Appeal to Mothers and Fathers," pamphlet [ca. 1912], Scrapbook of Seattle Material, 1911–17, vol. 1; *Western Woman Voter* 2.2 (February 1912); *Western Woman's Outlook* 1.11 (February 29, 1912).

16. *Western Woman's Outlook* 1.6 (January 25, 1912) (last quote); 1.8 (February 8, 1912); 1.14 (March 21, 1912) (first quote); *New Citizen* 2.15 (April 1911); "Turn on the Light," pamphlet, 1912, Scrapbook of Seattle Material, 1911–17, vol. 1.

17. *Western Woman's Outlook* 1.7 (February 1, 1912); 1.10 (February 22, 1912); 2.2 (February 1912) (quote). Untitled pamphlet found in Scrapbook of Seattle Material, 1911–17, vol. 1. Several women thought that the city's business operations also needed overhauling, and a group of them formed a campaign committee to support Andrew J. Quigley for city comptroller. On the economic conditions and the election, see Blackford, "Sources of Support for Reform Candidates and Issues," 60–69; Saltvig, "The Progressive Movement in Washington," 185–86.

18. *Western Woman's Outlook* 1.1 (December 21, 1911) (last quote); 1.6 (January 25, 1912); untitled pamphlet, Scrapbook of Seattle Material, 1911–17, vol. 1. In a congratulatory letter to Cotterill after his victory, Margaret Haley thanked him for sparing Seattle women "from the nationwide shame of Gillism which the women of the nation would have had to bear." See Margaret Haley to Honorable George F. Cotterill, March 7, 1912, box 9, folder 8, Cotterill Papers; Marshall, *Splintered Sisterhood*, 189.

19. *Literary Digest* 44.12 (March 23, 1912): 577. An attorney from nearby Snohomish also recognized Seattle's women as the key to Cotterill's victory. See John Miller to George Cotterill, March 6, 1912, box 5, folder 17, Cotterill Papers.

20. Anderson, *After Suffrage,* 68–69.

21. On the formation of the National Council of Women Voters, see James H. Brady, governor of Idaho, to Mr. W. H. Foster, January 6, 1911, box 4, folder 4, Emma Smith DeVoe Papers; letterhead of National Council of Women Voters (quote), box 4, folder 7, Emma Smith DeVoe Papers; King, "Washington," in Stanton, Anthony, and Gage, *History of Woman Suffrage,* 6:683; *Western Woman Voter* 1.1 (January 1911); Duniway, *Path Breaking,* 241–50. The National Council later merged with the National League of Women Voters in 1920 and became the Washington State League of Women Voters. Some suffrage clubs, including the Seattle Suffrage Club and the College Suffrage League at the University of Washington, also shifted their focus to educating new voters. Other cities in Washington saw similar educational groups formed in the year following suffrage victory. Tacoma (and Seattle) formed Voter Educational Associations, while in Spokane women formed a new club for the nonpartisan study of local, state, and national politics. See *Western Woman Voter* 1.1 (January 1911); *Western Woman's Outlook* 1.3 (January 4, 1912); *New Citizen* 2.13 (February 1911).

22. *Seattle Union Record,* November 19, 1910; January 21, 1911; *Western Woman's Outlook* 1.3 (January 4, 1912); 8.1 (September 25, 1913); Helen Norton Stevens, *Memorial Biography of Adele M. Fielde,* 323–26. Fielde was an officer in both the Civic Forum and the Washington Women's Legislative Committee, as well as founder of the Seattle Good Government League in 1913.

23. On the controversy over the creation of *Western Woman Voter* and the new magazine's objectives, see *Votes for Women* 1.11 (December 1910); Abigail Scott Duniway to Emma Smith DeVoe, January 23, 27, 1911, box 1, folder 17, DeVoe Papers; *Western Woman Voter* 1.1 (January 1911). For discussion of the change in the name of *Votes for Women,* see *New Citizen* 2.13 (February 1911).

24. The *Western Woman's Outlook* was incorporated in late 1911, with its major stockholders including several leading suffragists (Helen Stevens, Mrs. H. J. Trumbull, Ellen S. Fish, and twelve others). A weekly magazine with a circulation of five thousand, the *Outlook* was largely controlled by Stevens, who was its managing editor during most of its run. For more on the magazine's aim and corporate officers, see *Western Woman's Outlook* 1.1 (December 21, 1911); 1.2 (December 28, 1911) (last quote); 3.4 (July 18, 1912); 4.9 (November 21, 1912). The demise of the *Outlook* will be discussed in chapter 5.

25. *Legislative Federationist* 1.7 (November 1916); 2.4 (May 1917); 2.8 (December 1917) (quote); Baker, "The Domestication of Politics." By 1918, the *Federationist* changed its name to the *Legislative Counsellor* and became the official voice of the Woman's Legislative Council of Washington. See *Legislative Counsellor* 3.4 (April 1918) for review of the first annual convention of the statewide council. Clark's feminist sentiments filled her speech at the convention. Not only did she emphasize

the importance of children, but also questioned the homemaker's absence from the census department's listing of occupations and society's devaluation of housework performed inside the home. An editorial in the *Western Woman's Outlook* held a slightly different view of the state, arguing that it was "to become both more paternal and maternal" (3.4, July 18, 1912).

26. *Seattle Union Record,* May 27, 1911 (quote). For evidence of women's keen interest in local politics, see *Western Woman's Outlook* 1.4 (January 11, 1912); 1.5 (January 18, 1912); 1.6 (January 25, 1912); 2.7 (May 9, 1912); 2.9 (May 23, 1912); 5.8 (February 6, 1913); 5.9 (February 13, 1913); 7.12 (September 11, 1913); 10.10 (May 21, 1914); *New Citizen* 2.14 (March 1911); *Western Woman Voter* 1.3 (March 1911); 2.1 (January 1912).

27. *Western Woman's Outlook* 2.7 (May 9, 1912); 4.8 (November 14, 1912); 11.6 (August 16, 1914).

28. *Western Woman's Outlook* 5.9 (February 13, 1913) (quote); 6.3 (April 3, 1913); 11.9 (August 20, 1914). On the ties between direct democracy and equal suffrage, see Clemens, *The People's Lobby,* 223.

29. *Western Woman's Outlook* 7.12 (September 11, 1913).

30. *New Citizen* 2.14 (March 1911); *Western Woman Voter* 1.3 (March 1911); *Western Woman's Outlook* 5.8 (February 6, 1913).

31. *Western Woman's Outlook* 1.6 (January 25, 1912); 2.9 (May 23, 1912); *Western Woman Voter* 2.1 (January 1912); 2.2 (February 1912). Report to the Port Commissioner of Seattle, Washington [ca. 1915], box 2, folder 19, Seattle Port Commission Papers, Manuscripts and Archives, University of Washington.

32. *Western Woman Voter* 2.2 (February 1912).

33. *Western Woman's Outlook* 1.4 (January 11, 1912); *Western Woman Voter* 2.2 (February 1912).

34. *Western Woman's Outlook* 1.10 (February 22, 1912) (first quote); 3.6 (August 1, 1912); 4.3 (October 10, 1912) (last quote); 6.2 (March 27, 1913); 7.2 (July 13, 1913); *Report of the 32nd Annual Meeting of the Woman's Christian Temperance Union of West Washington,* 1915, Pacific Northwest Collection, University of Washington.

35. *Western Woman's Outlook* 3.12 (September 12, 1912) (first quote); 4.4 (October 17, 1912) (second, third quotes); *Western Woman Voter* 2.1 (January 1912). For more on how suffragists viewed and defined politics, see Gullett, *Becoming Citizens,* 5, 143; Anderson, *After Suffrage,* 25–26.

36. *Western Woman's Outlook* 3.12 (September 12, 1912); 4.4 (October 17, 1912); *Western Woman Voter* 1.1 (January 1911).

37. *Western Woman's Outlook* 1.1 (December 21, 1911) (second quote); 4.8 (November 14, 1912) (third quote); 6.5 (April 17, 1913) (first quote); 10.13 (June 11, 1914); *Welfare: A Journal of Municipal and Social Progress* 2.7 (September 1914); *Washington Women's Legislative Counsellor Yearbook, 1917–1918,* Pacific Northwest

Collection, University of Washington. For more on the antisuffragists, see Kraditor, *The Ideas of the Woman Suffrage Movement,* chapter 2.

38. *Western Woman's Outlook* 1.3 (January 4, 1912); 3.2 (July 4, 1912) (quote); 3.7 (August 8, 1912); 3.9 (August 22, 1912); 3.11 (September 5, 1912); 4.5 (October 24, 1912); *New Citizen* 2.14 (March 1911). Adele Fielde was one female leader who stood firmly behind nonpartisanship. In 1913, she organized the Seattle Woman's Good Government League on a strictly nonpartisan basis. The league attracted several prominent women leaders, including Adella Parker, Helen N. Stevens, Dr. Sarah Kendall, and Mrs. Homer Hill. For more, see *Western Woman's Outlook* 8.1 (September 25, 1913). Kristi Anderson has argued that many women who participated in electoral politics did not believe they were involved in politics if they remained nonpartisan. See Anderson, *After Suffrage,* 25–26; Flanagan, *Seeing with Their Hearts,* 131.

39. Washington State Federation of Women's Clubs, Article of Incorporation, July 1914, accession #3463, box 1, folder 1, Washington State Federation of Women's Clubs Records, Manuscripts and Archives, Suzzallo and Allen Library, University of Washington; Serena Mathews, "History of the Washington State Federation of Women's Clubs," 1949, accession #3463, 3463 (2–5) box 1, folder 10, Manuscripts and Archives, Suzzallo and Allen Library, University of Washington, 38; *Western Woman's Outlook* 1.1 (December 21, 1911). The national General Federation of Women's Clubs finally endorsed woman suffrage in 1914 despite a policy prohibiting such political action (*Western Woman's Outlook* 11.1 [June 18, 1914]).

40. *Western Woman's Outlook* 3.3 (July 11, 1912).

41. *Western Woman's Outlook* 3.9 (August 22, 1912); 3.11 (September 5, 1912); 3.12 (September 12, 1912) (quotes); 4.4 (October 17, 1912); 8.8 (November 13, 1913); Anderson, *After Suffrage,* 40–41. The Progressive Party's stance on direct legislation, government control of monopolies, and social and industrial justice also appealed to the *Outlook.* Thus, the magazine maintained that clubwomen were generally nonpartisan, but felt closer to the Progressive Party.

42. Female candidates faced particular obstacles, including state laws banning women from holding office, gender prejudice, and the fact that parties that nominated women were usually weak and had little chance for victory. See Anderson, *After Suffrage,* 124.

43. *Votes for Women* 1.11 (December 1910) (quote); *Western Woman's Outlook* 1.2 (December 28, 1911). Apparently, Mrs. Homer Hill considered running for city council in 1912. In a letter to Emma Smith DeVoe, Cora Eaton explained that she would support Hill "on principle," though she did not care for her defection from DeVoe's leadership during the last months of the suffrage campaign. See Eaton to DeVoe, November 28, 1911, box 4, folder 10, DeVoe Papers.

44. *Western Woman's Outlook* 3.11 (September 5, 1912); 6.3 (April 3, 1913); 8.9 (November 20, 1913); 8.10 (November 27, 1913); Anderson, *After Suffrage,* 120–21.

The *Outlook* continued to support female candidates for school position in 1913 when it endorsed Miss Mary G. O'Meara and Mrs. Eva H. Schroeder for two school board offices. The magazine stated that women best understood the needs of children. Both women lost in the election. The same gendered arguments also were used to request that the governor appoint a woman to the State Board of Control, which oversaw the outfitting of prisons and state wards. Since children made up nearly one-third of those residing in these institutions, the *Outlook* argued that women were well suited for the Board of Control because it was analogous to outfitting and caring for a household.

45. *Western Woman's Outlook* 3.6 (August 1, 1912) (second quote); 3.9 (August 22, 1912); 3.11 (September 5, 1912) (first quote); 4.8 (November 14, 1912) (third quote); 5.9 (February 13, 1913) (last quote).

46. *Western Woman's Outlook* 5.8 (February 6, 1913); 11.6 (August 16, 1914); King, "Washington," 684; *Legislative Federationist* 2.4 (May 1917); *Bulletin: Washington State Federation of Women's Club* 2.3 (May 1918), Washington State Federation of Women's Clubs Records, Manuscripts and Archives, Suzzallo and Allen Library, University of Washington. The *Outlook* publicly urged Seattle residents to consider Whitehead for office in 1914 (August 20, 1914). As will be discussed in the next chapter, Seattle finally elected a woman to the school board in 1917.

47. *Seattle Union Record*, March 11, 1911; Adair, "Organized Women Workers in Seattle," 202–3.

48. Higgins quote, *Seattle Union Record*, May 29, 1913; Kathryn Oberdeck, "Not Pink Teas," 197–206.

49. *New Citizen* 2.13 (February 1911) (quote); *Western Woman's Outlook* 1.3 (January 4, 1912); 3.2 (July 4, 1912); 7.11 (September 4, 1913) (second quote); 9.3 (January 1, 1914); *Legislative Federationist* 2.7 (November 1917); *Washington Women's Legislative Counsellor Yearbook, 1917–1918,* 16; Oberdeck, "Not Pink Teas," 197.

50. *Western Woman's Outlook* 3.2 (July 4, 1912) (first quote); 8.3 (October 9, 1913) (last quote); 9.3 (January 1, 1914) (second quote); Oberdeck, "Not Pink Teas," 207–8; Adair, "Organized Women Workers in Seattle," 203.

51. *Western Woman's Outlook* 4.5 (October 24, 1912); *Seattle Municipal News* 2.25 (October 5, 1912); "The Truth About the Seattle 'Purity Squad'" [ca. 1912], Scrapbook of Seattle Material, 1911–17, vol. 1 (quote); Oberdeck, "Not Pink Teas," 207.

52. *Western Woman's Outlook* 1.3 (January 4, 1912) (quote); 1.10 (February 22, 1912); 3.12 (September 12, 1912); 5.13 (March 13, 1913).

53. Adair, "Organized Women Workers in Seattle," 205; Saltvig, "The Progressive Movement in Washington," 321–22.

54. Theresa S. McMahon, "My Story," unpublished manuscript, box 1, folder 1, pp. 3–43 (quote, 18), Theresa S. McMahon Papers, Manuscripts and Archives,

Suzzallo and Allen Library, University of Washington. McMahon maintained that she and Alice Lord had more to do with the passing of the minimum wage law than anyone else. While she admired Addams, McMahon disagreed with her strategy of winning exploiters over to her side and instead advocated "swatting the exploiters." Her feminism was quite apparent in her analysis of women and economic evolution in which she argued that women were the mothers of modern industry. Women began agriculture, were the first weavers and spinners, and it was men who displaced them. Thus, she dismissed the idea that working-women were invading the "economic realms of men" and argued rather that they were reclaiming their rightful place (6). For a study of trade union women's attitude toward the value of the minimum wage in California, see Rebecca J. Mead, "'Let the Women Get Their Wages as Men Do': Trade Union Women and the Legislated Minimum Wage in California," *Pacific Historical Review* 67.3 (August 1998): 317–47.

55. Quotations from testimony before the U.S. Commission on Industrial Relations; see *Industrial Relations Report*, 4427 (first quote), 4437 (second quote).

56. *Industrial Relations Report*, 4468–69, 4473.

57. *Seattle Union Record*, March 29, 1913; *Western Woman's Outlook* 6.3 (April 13, 1913). The Retail Clerks leadership sent a letter to the *Outlook* hoping to counter what they perceived as the department store's stalling tactic. The clerks noted in their letter that federal government studies linked low wages and vice. They also charged that the Bon Marché hired very young women because they could live at home, survive on lower wages, and were less likely to unionize. One employer representative suggested that large department stores, like the Bon Marché, should also set up separate time clocks for men and women because he observed that working men and women spent too much time in close contact while waiting to punch the clock. See *Industrial Relations Report*, 4440–41.

58. *Industrial Relations Report*, 4124–25, 4444–45, 4450, 4455.

59. *Industrial Relations Report*, 4452, 4457, 4462–63, 4467–68, 4473, 4486. Mr. Black, the owner of a Seattle overall factory, dissented from the popular view of employers. He believed that the minimum wage was necessary to protect "the girl who might go wrong." Moreover, he argued that the single workingwoman "has no business living down town in a steam-heated hotel." While the Seattle YWCA did provide rooms for some workingwomen, a pamphlet published at the time of the IWC hearings noted that it had room for only a few hundred, while more than ten thousand women worked in the city. The organization urged local citizens to donate funds to help it "provide suitably for its Young Women." For more, see "What Seattle Needs *Most*," YWCA pamphlet, 1913, accession #3919, Seattle Young Women's Christian Association: King County Records.

60. *Industrial Relations Report*, 4459, 4464 (first quote), 4467; McMahon, "My

Story"; *Seattle Municipal News* 4.25 (October 17, 1914); DeVault, "Give the Boys a Trade," 192–200.

61. *Industrial Relations Report,* 4115, 4419, 4428, 4435–39, 4463, 4481–82, 4499; Adair, "Organized Women Workers in Seattle," 205. The $10 figure decided upon by the Mercantile Conference, however, included a one-year apprenticeship paying $6–8/week and limited apprentices to no more than 17 percent of all female employees in a firm. Representatives at the Manufacturing Conference, unlike at the other meetings, wanted a unanimous vote in order to give their decision more force. They voted on several different figures ranging from $8.75 (backed by the three employer representatives only) to a high of $10 before settling on $8.90 per week. A year later Labor Commissioner Edward Olson stated that he felt that the minimum wage standards were insufficient to cover a workingwoman's cost of living.

62. *Industrial Relations Report,* 4165–66; McMahon, "My Story," 30–31; *Western Woman's Outlook* 8.6 (October 30, 1913); Saltvig, "The Progressive Movement in Washington," 323–24. While the *Outlook* attempted to defend McMahon by explaining how her statement had been misrepresented, it did observe that she had "learned something of practical politics."

63. Oberdeck, "Not Pink Teas," 203–5. For an outstanding study of organized labor, gender, and consumption in the post–World War I period, see Frank, *Purchasing Power.*

64. *Seattle Union Record,* October 5, 1912; February 1, 8 (quote), 1913; May 23, 1914; Oberdeck, "Not Pink Teas," 206.

65. Oberdeck, "Not Pink Teas," 208–10.

66. Oberdeck, "Not Pink Teas," 210–16 (quote, 210); *Seattle Union Record,* September 25, 1915.

67. Oberdeck, "Not Pink Teas," 212–219.

5: THE DEMISE OF SEATTLE'S PROGRESSIVE SPIRIT

1. The following description of the Potlatch Riots is taken from Morgan, *Skid Row,* 188–92.

2. Blethen's military title was honorary, for he never served in the military.

3. *Seattle Union Record,* June 18, 1910; U.S. Congress, *Industrial Relations Report,* 4337–40, 4422–27, 4520–32. Confident of its status in 1910, the SCLC sent union leader Frank Cotterill to Medford, Oregon, to help that city's workers form a central labor council. See Frank Cotterill to George Cotterill, December 23, 1910, box 2, folder 65, Cotterill Papers.

4. *Seattle Union Record,* April 1, 1911; *Western Woman's Outlook,* November 24, 1912; Governor Marion Hay to Honorable P. L. Allen, Senator, April 2, 1912, box 4, folder 12, Emma Smith DeVoe Papers; McMahon, "My Story," 25, Theresa

S. McMahon Papers, Manuscripts and Archives, Suzzallo and Allen Library, University of Washington; *Welfare: A Journal of Social Progress* 1.10 (November 1913): 7; *Legislative Federationist* 2.5 (June 1917). The Legislative Federation continued to back labor into the early years of World War I. Lobbyists, including member Alice Lord, helped defeat the Candy-Makers Bill in 1917, which would have permitted female candy workers to work ten-hour days in the months prior to Christmas. The federation also announced that one of its goals in 1917 was to extend the eight-hour day to all workers and establish a living wage in all industries. In a clear sign of its feminist outlook, the group also sought the "removal of all legal disabilities resting on citizens because of sex." See *Legislative Federationist* 2.4 (May 1917).

5. *Western Woman Voter* 1.3 (March 1911); *Western Woman's Outlook* 1.7 (February 1, 1912); *Washington Women's Legislative Counsellor Yearbook, 1917–18*, 16. For McMahon's views of capital and labor, see *Industrial Relations Report*, 4167–83, and McMahon, "My Story," 33.

6. Quoted in Mark W. Van Wienen, "A Rose by Any Other Name: Charlotte Perkins Stetson (Gilman) and the Case for American Reform Socialism," *American Quarterly* 55.4 (December 2003): 621.

7. *Western Woman's Outlook* 1.11 (February 29, 1912). In addition to complimenting Socialist city council candidate David Burgess, the *Western Woman Voter* likewise believed that Wells and Cotterill had similar ideas, but it was only Cotterill's experience that made him a better candidate. See *Western Woman Voter* 2.1 (January 1912); 2.2 (February 1912).

8. *Western Woman's Outlook* 1.8 (February 8, 1912); 4.5 (October 24, 1912) (quote). On the complex nature of relations between Socialists and middle-class feminists, see Katz, "Dual Commitments," and Katz, "A Politics of Coalition," 245–62; Mari Jo Buhle, *Women and American Socialism, 1870–1920* (Urbana: University of Illinois Press, 1986). For more on relations between socialists and progressives, see Nick Salvatore, *Eugene V. Debs: Citizen and Socialist* (Urbana: University of Illinois Press, 1983); Johnson, "No Make-Believe Class Struggle," 25–45; McGerr, *A Fierce Discontent*, 134–38. Robert Johnston's study of Progressive Era Portland, Oregon, adds an additional layer to the complex class relations that marked this period. He argues that Portland possessed a radical middle class or petite bourgeoisie that supported labor and promoted powerful democratic populist values, thus blurring the class divisions most scholars emphasize in studies of progressivism. See his *The Radical Middle Class*, 16–17, 59–73, 75–80.

9. *Western Woman Voter* 2.1 (January 1912); *Western Woman's Outlook* 1.10 (February 22, 1912); 8.9 (November 20, 1913) (quote).

10. *Western Woman's Outlook* 2.3 (April 11, 1912); 9.2 (December 25, 1913). During the 1913 municipal election, the *Outlook* published a letter to the editor criticizing Seattle's Socialist Party for refusing to endorse two female candidates for

council and then encouraging a group of Socialist women to publish a statement announcing that they did not object to the party's stance. The letter's author noted that she was willing to sacrifice the party's cause because she maintained that the national party supported sexual equality. For more, see *Western Woman's Outlook* 5.9 (February 13, 1913).

11. Blackford, "Sources of Support for Reform Candidates and Issues in Seattle Politics," 55–77, and his "Civic Groups, Political Action"; Bagley, *History of King County*, 36; Pendergrass, "Urban Reform and Voluntary Association, 38–39; Padraic Burke, "Struggle for Public Ownership: The Early History of the Port of Seattle," *Pacific Northwest Quarterly* 68.2 (April 1977): 60–71.

12. Rodgers, "In Search of Progressivism," *Reviews in American History* 10 (December 1982): 121–27; McGerr, *A Fierce Discontent*, chap. 2, 134–38; Johnston, *The Radical Middle Class*, chap. 5; Diner, *A Very Different Age*, chap. 8.

13. *Western Woman's Outlook* 8.12 (December 11, 1913); Berner, *Seattle 1900–1920*, 184–86. Local charity officials in Seattle noticed an upsurge in unemployment as early as 1911 and found that most were healthy single men less than thirty-five years of age. See *Annual Report of Charity Organizations of Seattle, 1911*, 19–30, Pacific Northwest Collection, University of Washington. Richard White has argued that the vagaries of extractive capitalist enterprises made such seasonal unemployment common in the American West. Places like Skid Row in Seattle or Larimer Street in Denver attracted jobless men, who waited out these annual lags in the economy. See his *"It's Your Misfortune and None of My Own,"* 278–80.

14. *Seattle Union Record*, December 13, 1913; March 14, December 5, 12, 1914; *Industrial Relations Report*, 4242–47 (second and third quotes); Schwantes, *Radical Heritage*, 59 (first quote).

15. Schwantes, *Radical Heritage*, 207–10; Hulet Wells, "I Wanted to Work," 130–37, box 2, folders 3–5, Hulet Wells Papers, Manuscripts and Archives, Suzzallo and Allen Library, University of Washington; Pomeroy, *The Pacific Slope*, 184. Ault remained editor of the labor daily well into the next decade. For a more thorough history of the battle within the SPW, see Dembo, *Unions and Politics*, 86–94.

16. Wells, "I Wanted to Work," 138–40; Berner, *Seattle 1900–1920*, 153–55.

17. Wells, "I Wanted to Work," 140–43; *Western Woman's Outlook* 3.12 (September 12, 1912); 4.1 (September 26, 1912); 4.8 (November 14, 1912); 4.12 (December 12, 1912); Dembo, *Unions and Politics*, 94; Berner, *Seattle 1900–1920*, 155; Schwantes, *Radical Heritage*, 187; Saltvig, "The Progressive Movement in Washington," 186–87. In his personal history of Seattle, Judge Cornelius Hanford also blamed Mayor Cotterill for tolerating "I.W.W. insolence when they marched in processions flaunting the red flag of anarchy." See C. H. Hanford, ed., *Seattle and Environs, 1852–1924* (Chicago: Pioneer Historical, 1924), 314–15.

18. Wells, "I Wanted to Work," 146–77; Berner, *Seattle 1900–1920*, 155–56. The

circumstances behind the Sadlers' relationship, according to Wells, resulted from Sam's first wife's refusal to grant him a divorce. He also maintained that Kate Sadler not only was a fine Socialist but also a good wife and mother whose reputation was above reproach. Apparently, Well's play likely would have never opened before audiences even if the Moore Theater hadn't closed its doors. Judge John Humphries, who supported Blethen's actions in the 1912 conflict, had appointed a rather biased committee to study the play, expecting to gain support for an injunction against it. Wells finally won his suit against the *Times* four years after the case had begun and a year after Blethen had passed away.

19. Melvyn Dubofsky, *We Shall Be All: A History of the Industrial Workers of the World* (Urbana: University of Illinois Press, 1988); Selig Perlman and Philip Taft, *History of Labor in the United States, 1896–1932* (1935; repr., New York: Augustus M. Kelley, 1966), chap. 21; McGerr, *A Fierce Discontent*, 140–43; Schwantes, *Radical Heritage*, x.

20. Dubofsky, *We Shall Be All*, 73, 152, 155. According to Joseph Conlin, the iww's tenet of industrial organization distinguished it from craft-centered European syndicalism. See Joseph Conlin, *Bread and Roses Too: Studies of the Wobblies* (Westport, CT: Greenwood, 1969).

21. Dubofsky, *We Shall Be All*, 157–69.

22. Conlin, *Bread and Roses Too*, 68–70; Melvyn Dubofsky, "The Origins of Western Working Class Radicalism, 1890–1905," *Labor History* 7.2 (Spring 1966): 153; Carlton Parker, "The i.w.w.," in Parker, *The Casual Laborer and Other Essays* (New York: Russel and Russel, 1920), 100–106. Parker, though trained as an economist, was very interested in the new science of psychology and thus considered himself a "psychological economist."

23. Quoted in Ronald Genini, "Industrial Workers of the World and Their Fresno Free Speech Fight, 1910–1911," *California Historical Quarterly* 53.2 (Summer 1974): 102.

24. Philip Foner, *History of the Labor Movement in the United States*, vol. 4 (New York: International Publishers, 1947), 172.

25. Schwantes, *Radical Heritage*, 184–87.

26. On causes of migration, see *Industrial Relations Report*, 4246–47, 4285; Anna Louise Strong, untitled manuscript on iww [ca. 1918], preface, pp. 2–3 (quote), chap. 2, pp. 1–3, box 9, folder 61, Anna Louise Strong Papers (hereafter referred to as "iww Manuscript"); Schwantes, *Radical Heritage*, 152–53 (quote). The *Western Woman's Outlook* suggested that the increased deskilling of labor as a result of new technology and the failure of traditional craft unions to organize these workers encouraged their drift into socialism and the iww. See *Western Woman's Outlook* 3.6 (August 1, 1912).

27. *Industrial Relations Report*, 4248; Strong, "iww Manuscript," chap. 1,

pp. 8–9. Strong noted that these same landlords and businessmen often criticized the IWW for the location of its offices in the Skid Row district.

28. *Seattle Union Record,* July 26, 1913.

29. *Seattle Union Record,* July 26, 1913.

30. *Seattle Union Record,* August 9, 30, 1913.

31. *Seattle Union Record,* August 9, 30, 1913.

32. On the statewide initiative effort in 1914, see Saltvig, "The Progressive Movement in Washington," 350–51; Dembo, *Unions and Politics,* 105; Schwantes, *Radical Heritage,* 197–99. The "seven sisters" bills—the name given to the original seven proposed initiatives of which only five qualified for the ballot—were conceived by the Joint Legislative Committee, a farmer-labor political organization. The JLC believed these measures would counter the lumber trust and other special interests that it felt had gained control of the state legislature.

33. Dembo, *Unions and Politics,* 104; Saltvig, "The Progressive Movement in Washington," 198–99; Berner, *Seattle 1900–1920,* 190. Winsor, a "Yellow" or evolutionary Socialist, ran on a platform advocating public ownership and labor solidarity. Griffiths tried to appeal to the morality vote that had decided several earlier elections, including Gill's recall. When the votes had been tallied, Gill captured 23,419, Trenholme 11,897, Winsor 11,517, and Griffiths 9,087. See Blackford, "Sources of Support for Reform Candidates and Issues," 83–84.

34. *Seattle Union Record,* February 21, March 7, 1914; Blackford, "Sources of Support for Reform Candidates and Issues," 83–86.

35. *Seattle Union Record,* January 13, 1914.

36. *Seattle Union Record,* January 13, June 13 (quote), June 20, 1914; Dembo, *Unions and Politics,* 104–5; Blackford, "Sources of Support for Reform Candidates and Issues," 89–90; Saltvig, "The Progressive Movement in Washington," 197–98. Seattle was a reversal of the traditional debate over ward versus citywide elections because, unlike with immigrant workers in eastern cities, Seattle's working class was dispersed throughout the city and actually benefited from citywide elections. For contemporary discussions of progressive attitudes regarding ward politics and the city manager and commission form of government, see Clinton Rogers Woodruff, ed., *City Government by Commission* (New York: D. Appleton, 1911); Ernest S. Bradford, "History and Underlying Principles of Commission Government," *Annals of the American Academy of Political and Social Science* 38.3 (November 1911): 3–11. For more recent analysis of this debate, see Robert Wiebe, *Businessmen and Reform: A Study of the Progressive Movement* (Cambridge: Harvard University Press, 1962); James Weinstein, "Organized Business and the City Commission and Manager Movements," *Journal of Southern History* 28 (1962): 166–82; Samuel P. Hays, "The Politics of Reform in Municipal Government in the Progressive Era," *Pacific Northwest Quarterly* 55 (October, 1964): 157–69; Steven Erie, "Bringing the

Bosses Back In: The Irish Political Machines and Urban Policy Making," *Studies in American Political Development* 4 (1990): 269–81; William Issel, "'Citizens Outside the Government': Business and Urban Policy in San Francisco and Los Angeles, 1890–1932," *Pacific Historical Review* 57.2 (May 1988): 117–45.

37. For a breakdown and analysis of the charter referendum, see Blackford, "Sources of Support for Reform Candidates and Issues," 90–91. On the role of the Employers' Association of Washington and the teamsters strike, see Berner, *Seattle 1900–1920*, 166–69, and Saltvig, "The Progressive Movement in Washington," 418–20.

38. *Seattle Union Record*, December 20, 27, 1913; January 3, 17, 1914; Berner, *Seattle 1900–1920*, 167–68. In the January 17 issue, the *Union Record* printed a cartoon on the front page that pictured a hog with the label "capital" beside a man in overalls. The caption stated, "MAN OR HOG, WHICH?" The paper then boldly stated that the most pressing issue before the city was the open-shop campaign and that Seattle's fate was in the hands of local citizens.

39. Saltvig, "The Progressive Movement in Washington," 419–20; Berner, *Seattle 1900–1920*, 168–70; Dembo, *Unions and Politics*, 103. The Seattle Municipal League blamed the economic downturn for Gill's victory. It then concluded that many Seattle residents "expect a relaxed puritanism to produce as much real morality as we do now have and better business." See *Seattle Municipal News*, March 7, 1914.

40. *Welfare: A Journal of Municipal and Social Progress* 2.7 (September 1914): 6; Strong, "IWW Manuscript," chap. 1, p. 13; chap. 3, p. 10 (second quote); Saltvig, "The Progressive Movement in Washington," 420 (first quote).

41. Clark, *The Dry Years*, 108–12.

42. Clark, *The Dry Years*, 108–12.

43. *Seattle Union Record*, April 4, 11, September 19, October 31, 1914; Clark, *The Dry Years*, 112.

44. *Seattle Union Record*, November 7, 1914; Clark, *The Dry Years*, 113–20.

45. On Fielde's role in the movement, see Stevens, *Memorial Biography of Adele M. Fielde*, 333–36. For samples of women's public support for prohibition, see *Western Woman's Outlook* 11.4 (April 11, 1914); 10.10 (May 21, 1914); 11.7 (August 16, 1914); *Welfare: A Journal of Municipal and Social Progress* 2.7 (September 1914). An official history of the Washington State Federation of Women's Clubs likewise noted the strong support both women and the *Outlook* gave the measure. See Serena Mathews, "History of the Washington State Federation of Women's Clubs," 1949, accession #3463, 3463 (2–5) box 1, folder 10, Manuscripts and Archives, Suzzallo and Allen Library, University of Washington, 49.

46. *Western Woman's Outlook*, May 21, September 3, 1914; Stevens, *Memorial Biography of Adele M. Fielde*, 336–37; Mathews, "History of Washington State

Federation of Women's Clubs," 49. According to the *Outlook,* liquor interests had used "pseudo club women" to misrepresent the paper to advertisers as well as encouraged boycotts of the magazine in order to force a change in its editorial policy. Eventually, these liquor interests apparently purchased a debt the magazine had incurred with a local printer as a way to control it. In a diary entry, Adele Fielde confirmed what she believed were the underhanded methods the liquor industry employed to destroy the magazine. Several months earlier, editors commented on recently formed women's groups that had attacked prohibitionists, maintaining that the female leaders of these groups were paid representatives of the liquor and brewery industries.

47. Quoted in Berner, *Seattle 1900–1920,* 189.

48. For a study of the Seattle Municipal League, see Pendergrass, "Urban Reform and Voluntary Association."

49. *Seattle Municipal News* 2.27 (November 2, 1912); 2.28 (November 9, 1912); 2.30 (November 23, 1912); 2.26 (January 4, 1913); 2.42 (February 15, 1913); 3.11 (July 12, 1913). Pendergrass notes the shared concerns and various alliances the Municipal League had with women's clubs, yet his study ignores the struggle over membership.

50. *Seattle Union Record,* May 3, 1913 (quote); February 7, April 25, May 9, December 5, 12, 1914; Oberdeck, "Not Pink Teas," 211–13.

51. *Seattle Union Record,* February 21, September 5, 1914.

52. *Seattle Union Record,* October 24, October 31 (quote), November 7, 1914.

53. *Proceedings of the Central Labor Council of Seattle and Vicinity,* February 21, 1917, Central Labor Council of Seattle and King County Records, Manuscripts and Archives, Suzzallo and Allen Library, University of Washington, quoted in Adair, "Organized Women Workers in Seattle," 38.

54. *Seattle Union Record,* June 24, 1916; Foner, *Women and the American Labor Movement,* 81–82.

55. *Seattle Union Record,* May 15, June 12 (quote), 1915; Foner, *Women and the American Labor Movement,* 63.

56. *Seattle Union Record,* May 30, October 24, 1914; March 11, April 8, 29, 1916; Oberdeck, "Not Pink Teas," 211–12.

57. *Seattle Union Record,* February 27, December 4, 1915; March 11, 18 (Lord quote), April 1, 15, June 17, 1916; Oberdeck, "Not Pink Teas," 216–18.

58. *Seattle Union Record,* June 17, 1916.

59. Rodgers, "In Search of Progressivism," 121–27.

60. Oberdeck, "Not Pink Teas," 219–25.

61. Wells, "I Wanted To Work," 180–81; *Seattle Union Record,* August 7, November 6, 1915; Schwantes, *Radical Heritage,* 207–11.

62. O'Connor, *Revolution in Seattle,* 16; *Industrial Relations Report,* 4188–4202; Schwantes, *Radical Heritage,* 207–8.

63. *Industrial Relations Report*, 4185, 4202; *Seattle Union Record*, June 24, December 23, 1916. Theresa McMahon, appearing before the Commission on Industrial Relations, supported Ault's perception of working-class frustration with government's failure to enforce labor legislation, which, in her opinion, only served to fuel worker unrest in the city. See *Industrial Relations Report*, 4174.

64. *Industrial Relations Report*, 4239–40.

65. On the importance of Wobbly plays, music, and hospitable meeting halls, see Strong, "IWW Manuscript," chap. 1, pp. 3–4, chap. 3, pp. 2, 8; William Short, "History of the Activities of Seattle Labor Movement and Conspiracy of Employers to Destroy It and Attempted Suppression of Labor's Daily Newspaper, the Seattle Union Record," November 28, 1919, Pacific Northwest Collection, University of Washington, 3–4. Short was the president of the Washington State Federation of Labor and a strong supporter of the AFL and its practices.

66. *Proceedings of the Central Labor Council of Seattle and Vicinity*, October 6, 1915; Strong, "IWW Manuscript," chap. 1, pp. 10–11; *Industrial Relations Report*, 4232–35 (quote); Pendergrass, "Urban Reform and Voluntary Association," 65–66. Joe Hillstrom, better known as Joe Hill, was a Wobbly songwriter and organizer in Utah, who had been sentenced to death for robbery and murder. Many unions and labor leaders, however, believed that Hill had been framed, and throughout the United States numerous working-class organizations protested his conviction. He was eventually executed in late 1915.

67. *Seattle Union Record*, August 16, 1913; *Proceedings of the Central Labor Council of Seattle and Vicinity*, November 1, 8, 1916; Schwantes, *Radical Heritage*, 140, 151, 184. In 1915, several printing trade unions formed an industrial union educational league to expand support for industrial unionism among printers. For more, see *Seattle Union Record*, October 9, 1915. In an article for the *Survey* in 1919, Theresa McMahon wrote that the American West provided the right conditions for industrial unionism, not only because of the IWW's strong presence in the fields and woods, but also because Seattle's Metal Trades Council bridged the differences between the IWW and the AFL by organizing all crafts into one industry. The council, she concluded, "is an excellent example of the tendencies in western labor organization." See Theresa McMahon, "The Strike in Seattle," *Survey* 41.23 (March 8, 1919): 821–23.

68. *Seattle Union Record*, July 5, 1913; Wells, "I Wanted to Work," 129, 181; Schwantes, *Radical Heritage*, 188–89; Sale, *Seattle: Past to Present*, 116; Dembo, *Unions and Politics*, 109–10.

69. *Industrial Relations Report*, 4140, 4313–16 (quote, 4314); Leigh Irvine, *Government by Labor Unions*, 1916, Pacific Northwest Collection, University of Washington, 8. J. Bruce Gibson, president of the Sumner Iron Works in nearby Everett and president of the Federation of Employers' Associations of the Pacific

Coast, claimed that the greatest cause of social unrest was "the allowance of yellow journalism, cartoonists that send out these bloody things depicting capital, and all the sort of thing, in the most abhorrent way." In particular, he singled out the *Washington Socialist* for calling on workers to arm themselves in order to resist employer oppression. See *Industrial Relations Report,* 4333.

70. *Industrial Relations Report,* 4314, 4325 (first quote); letter from Governor Ernest Lister to Miss Anna Louise Strong, December 20, 1917, box 1, folder 103 (second quote), Strong Papers. Businessmen challenged recent bills that instituted direct legislation and that added new medical benefits to the state's workmen's compensation law. On the statewide efforts of employers, see Dembo, *Unions and Politics,* 110–12; Berner, *Seattle 1900–1920,* 203–7.

71. Ames quoted in Ficken, *The Forested Land,* 136–37; *Industrial Relations Report,* 4313, 4254 (second quote); McMahon, "My Story," 53–54.

72. *Industrial Relations Report,* 4144–45, 4153–55, 4313–14, 4501, 4516; Leigh Irvine, *Labor Unions and the Law of Love,* 1916, Pacific Northwest Collection, University of Washington, 10 (second quote), 14, and his *A Conspiracy Against Liberty,* pamphlet #1, n.d., Pacific Northwest Collection, University of Washington, 3–15 (first quote, 7).

73. *Business Chronicle* 1.2 (June 10, 1916); 1.4 (June 24, 1916); Seattle Chamber of Commerce, *Annual Report,* 1916, Northwest Collection, Seattle Public Library, 16; Pendergrass, "Urban Reform and Voluntary Association," 67; Magden, *A History of Seattle Waterfront Workers,* 78–91.

74. *Business Chronicle* 1.5 (July 1, 1916); 1.6 (July 8, 1916); 1.7 (July 15, 1916); 1.12 (August 19, 1916); 1.14 (September 2, 1916); Seattle Chamber of Commerce, *Record* 4.8 (August 1, 1916), Northwest Collection, Seattle Public Library; Waterfront Employers' Association, "An Open Letter," dated August 1, 1916, Pacific Northwest Collection, University of Washington; Leigh Irvine, pamphlet #6, 1916, and his *The Story of Detroit,* pamphlet #11, 1916, Pacific Northwest Collection, University of Washington. Despite the efforts of the ILA, the IWW had infiltrated waterfront unions, including ILA Local 38–12. In the spring of 1916, the IWW organized various maritime unions into the Marine Transport Workers. The lead organizer was none other than Red Doran, who, at the same time, was attempting to increase support for industrial unionism within the SCLC. See Magden, *A History of Seattle Waterfront Workers,* 76–77, 83.

75. Robert Bridges to Reverend Sidney Strong, president of the Seattle Central Council of Social Agencies, December 24, 1914, box 4, folder 11, Seattle Port Commission Papers. For a brief history of the Seattle Port Commission, see Berner, *Seattle 1900–1920,* 142–52, 196–200.

76. On the referendum battle, see "A Call for the People's Veto," Port of Seattle Commission, *Bulletin No. 9,* 1916, Municipal Reference, Seattle Public Library. The

pamphlet also reminded Seattle residents of the widespread support for its development plans as evidenced by the numerous successful bond measures the voters had passed. Another bill that affected the port, which voters also rejected in a referendum ballot, attempted to restrict the commission's debt limit and thus undermined its plans to expand public facilities. To rally opposition to this measure, port commissioners played upon civic pride and rivalry by publicizing the efforts of San Francisco, Los Angeles, and other coastal cities to expand their port facilities in order to capture the lion's share of the new business most cities expected the Panama Canal would bring to the Pacific.

77. *Seattle Union Record,* March 21, 1914; June 3, 1916; *Industrial Relations Report,* 4398; Seattle Chamber of Commerce, *Record* 4.8 (August 1, 1916); *Business Chronicle* 1.4 (June 24, 1916), 1.5 (July 1, 1916); Robert Bridges to Sydney Lines et al., April 11, 1919, box 4, folder 26, and James Duncan to Mr. Robert Bridges, May 17, 1917, box 3, folder 1, Seattle Port Commission Papers. In the 1917 fall election, Bridges wrote a public letter to King County voters urging them to support a labor candidate, Frank Cotterill, for a seat on the port commission. See Robert Bridges to voters of King County, Seattle Port District, November 12, 1917, box 4, folder 24, Port Commission Papers.

78. *Proceedings of the Central Labor Council of Seattle and Vicinity,* September 27, 1916, box 8; *Seattle Union Record,* December 30, 1916; Berner, *Seattle 1900–1920,* 216; Magden, *A History of Seattle Waterfront Workers,* 93–100.

79. *Seattle Municipal News* 3.31 (November 29, 1913) (first quote); 4.7 (June 13, 1914) (second quote); 4.25 (October 17, 1914).

80. *Seattle Municipal News* 6.10 (July 15, 1916); 6.19 (September 23, 1916); 6.21 (October 7, 1916); 6.29 (December 2, 1916); Pendergrass, "Urban Reform and Voluntary Association," 67–69; Berner, *Seattle 1900–1920,* 216.

81. *Its Earliest Beginnings on the Shores of Puget Sound to the Tragic and Infamous Event Known as the Everett Massacre* (Seattle: University of Washington Press, 1970), 179–214.

82. Clark, *Mill Town,* 195–201.

83. Clark, *Mill Town,* 201–14 (quote, 211); Berner, *Seattle 1900–1920,* 218–19; Dembo, *Unions and Politics,* 116.

84. *Business Chronicle* 1.24 (November 11, 1916) (first quote); Strong, "IWW Manuscript," chap. 1, pp. 2, 3 (second quote); Berner, *Seattle 1900–1920,* 219.

85. Anna Louis Strong to editor of the *Survey,* March 13, 1917, box 3, folder 96, Strong Papers; Strong, "IWW Manuscript," chap. 1, p. 1.

86. Anna Louise Strong to Mr. Kellogg, March 12, 1918, box 7B, folder 68, Strong Papers; Pendergrass, "Urban Reform and Voluntary Association, 68. Strong blamed her damaged reputation on the intolerance of many Seattle residents, which prevented them from distinguishing between her sympathy for workers

revolting against inhumane conditions and their tactics and methods. See her "IWW Manuscript," preface, p. 3.

87. *Seattle Union Record*, September 18, 1915; Berner, *Seattle 1900–1920*, 229–30.

88. *Seattle Union Record*, April 24, August 8, 1914; May 15, 22, 1915; May 20, 1916 (quote); *Proceedings of the Central Labor Council of Seattle and Vicinity*, June 16, September 15, 1915; April 4, 1917; January 5, May 24, 1916; Dembo, *Unions and Politics*, 128. Portland's labor leaders also opposed growing militarism associated with the outbreak of the Great War. See Johnston, *The Radical Middle Class*, 41–43, 174.

89. *Proceedings of the Central Labor Council of Seattle and Vicinity*, April 11, 1917 (quote); Hanford, *Seattle and Environs, 1852–1924*, 351; Dembo, *Unions and Politics*, 124–27; Schwantes, *Radical Heritage*, 214–15. On Gompers and the AFL's position on World War I, see Montgomery, *The Fall of the House of Labor;* and Lizabeth Cohen, *Making a New Deal: Industrial Workers in Chicago, 1919–1939* (New York: Cambridge University Press, 1990), 370–88. Although the Washington Grange initially joined with organized labor to oppose American entry into the war, labor's radical activity on Puget Sound led farmers to shy away from this stance.

90. Short, "History of the Activities of Seattle Labor Movement," 1–2; Berner, *Seattle 1900–1920*, 234–35; Frank, *Purchasing Power*, 25–30.

91. Short, "History of the Activities of Seattle Labor Movement," 1–2, 7; Berner, *Seattle 1900–1920*, 238; Wells, "I Wanted to Work," 207; Frank, *Purchasing Power*, 25–29; Ficken, *The Forested Land*, 138–42. Philip Foner noted that the trial and conviction spurred working-class women in Seattle's Women's Card and Label League to prepare to join their union brothers after labor leaders called for a general strike to protest the conviction. See Foner, *Women and the American Labor Movement*, 32.

92. McGerr, *A Fierce Discontent*, 288–92; Richard Polenberg, *Fighting Faiths: The Abrams Case, the Supreme Court, and Free Speech* (New York: Viking Press, 1987); Zechariah Chafee Jr., *Free Speech in the United States* (Cambridge: Harvard University Press, 1941); David Kennedy, *Over Here: The First World War and American Society* (New York: Oxford University Press, 1980); Perlman and Taft, *History of Labor in the United States, 1896–1932*, chap. 33.

93. *Seattle Municipal News* 6.46 (April 7, 1917) (first quote); second quote found in Berner, *Seattle 1900–1920*, 237; Pendergrass, "Urban Reform and Voluntary Association," 72–75.

94. Wells, "I Wanted to Work," 186–92; Anna Louise Strong, *I Change Worlds* (Seattle: Seal Press, 1935), 61; Berner, *Seattle 1900–1920*, 255–56.

95. Pendergrass, "Urban Reform and Voluntary Association," 72–74; Dembo, *Unions and Politics*, 131–33.

96   Pendergrass, "Urban Reform and Voluntary Association," 74–84; Pomeroy, *The Pacific Slope,* 224. According to Pendergrass, Port Commissioner Robert Bridges and Warren D. Lane, another well-known middle-class progressive and city councilman, were dropped from the league's ranks for questioning the war. On the war's impact on progressivism nationwide, see Arthur S. Link and Richard L. McCormick, *Progressivism* (Arlington Heights, IL: Harlan Davidson, 1983), 106–12.

97.   Wells, "I Wanted to Work," 200–204; Pendergrass, "Urban Reform and Voluntary Association," 77 (quote).

98.   Memorandum regarding the Pigott Printing Company, 1918, box 9, folder 17, Joseph Smith Papers; Berner, *Seattle 1900–1920,* 250–59 (quote, 255); Dembo, *Unions and Politics,* 133–45. The federal IWW sweeps coincided with similar federal intervention in the lumber camps. Wobbly-led strikes in the summer of 1917 encouraged federal officials to use soldiers to overcome labor shortages in the production of spruce. Simultaneously, the government formed the Loyal Legion of Loggers and Lumbermen to act as a more conservative competitor to Wobbly unions. The organization combined both timber workers and employers and utilized patriotic appeals to increase lumber production and, at the same time, undermine the IWW. For more, see Ficken, *The Forested Land,* chap. 11; Perlman and Taft, *History of Labor,* chap. 32.

99.   Strong, *I Change Worlds,* 51; Berner, *Seattle 1900–1920,* 189.

100.   Strong, *I Change Worlds,* 51 (first quote); petition and newspaper letter found in box 7B, folders 98–99, Strong Papers.

101.   Della Wood Manney to Anna Louise Strong, December 13, 1916, box 7B, folder 84, Strong Papers; Ada C. Caufield to Anna Louise Strong, n.d., box 7B, folder 74, Strong Papers; Mrs. Dis Richardson to Anna Louise Strong, December 4, 1916, and Eva H. Richardson to Anna Louise Strong, December 3, 1916, box 7B, folder 91 (quote), Strong Papers; Anna Louise Strong to Mr. Kellog, n.d., box 3, folder 96, Strong Papers. Strong believed that that "labor vote" was largely responsible for her victory.

102.   Strong, *I Change Worlds,* 61–64 (quote); letter to editor from Louise Olivereau, September 12, 1913, and letter from Louise Olivereau to Reverend C. Bertran Runnels, July 5, 1915, box 1, folder 8, Minnie Parkhurst Papers, Manuscripts and Archives, Suzzallo and Allen Library, University of Washington. According to Joe Smith, the *Seattle Daily Call'*s decision to print a rather controversial speech given by Olivereau provided fodder to those who broke into the Pigott Printing Company a month later. See Memorandum regarding the Pigott Printing Company, 1918, box 9, folder 17, Joseph Smith Papers. For a brief overview of Olivereau's activities during World War I, see Sarah E. Sharbach, "A Woman Acting Alone: Louise Olivereau and the First World War," *Pacific Northwest Quarterly* 78.1–2 (January–April 1987): 32–40.

103. *Bulletin: Washington State Federation of Women's Clubs* 1.4 (August 1917) (first quote); 2.3 (May 1918) (second quote), Washington State Federation of Women's Clubs Records, Manuscripts and Archives, Suzzallo and Allen Library, University of Washington; Mathews, "History of the Washington State Federation of Women's Clubs," 57–59; National League for Woman's Service, *Washington State Report for 1917–1919,* Pacific Northwest Collection, University of Washington; Report of the *34th Annual Meeting of the Women's Christian Temperance Union of West Washington,* 1917, Pacific Northwest Collection, University of Washington; Program, Twenty-Second Annual Convention of the Washington State Federation of Women's Clubs: Program, June 4–8, 1918, Washington State Federation of Women's Clubs Records, Manuscripts and Archives, Suzzallo and Allen Library, University of Washington. For an examination of the war's impact on workingwomen, see Maurine W. Greenwald, *Women, War, and Work: The Impact of World War I on Women Workers in the United States* (Westport, CT: Greenwood Press, 1980).

104. Strong, *I Change Worlds,* 62–64; Anna Louise Strong to Leonard, March 9, 1918, box 3, folder 10 (second quote), Strong Papers; "Why Annal Louis [*sic*] Strong Should Be Recalled" and "Dear Friend" letter from Recall Committee, pamphlets by and about Anna Louise Strong concerning her recall as a member of the Seattle School Board, Northwest Collection, Seattle Public Library; Pendergrass, "Urban Reform and Voluntary Association," 81–82. On clubwomen's concerns about vice, see *Bulletin: Washington State Federation of Women's Clubs* 1.4 (August 1917); 2.1 (November 1917).

105. Strong, *I Change Worlds,* 64; "Statement by Anna Louise Strong, Member of the Seattle School Board, and Report of the Central Labor Council Investigating Committee Regarding the Proposed Recall," n.d., pamphlets by and about Anna Louise Strong concerning her recall as a member of the Seattle School Board.

106. "Statement by Anna Louise Strong, Member of the Seattle School Board and Sidney Strong, Concerning Anna Louise Strong and the Proposed Recall Election," February 28, 1918, pamphlets by and about Anna Louise Strong concerning her recall as a member of the Seattle School Board.

107. Anna Louise Strong to president of School Board, March 7, 1918, box 7B, folder 68, Strong Papers; Anna Louise Strong to Mr. Kellog, February 26, 1918 (quote), and letter to King County Democratic Club, February 1, 1918, box 7B, folder 66, Strong Papers; *Legislative Federationist* 3.2 (February 1918).

108. Strong, *I Change Worlds,* 64 (first quote); Sophie L. W. Clark to Anna Louise Strong, March 8, 1918 (second quote), and Anna Louise Strong to president of School Board, March 7, 1918 (last quote), box 7B, folder 68, Strong Papers; Anna Louise Strong to Leonard, March 9, 1918, box 3, folder 10, Strong Papers. Strong had also earlier turned down an offer from the Socialist *Seattle Daily Call* to become the paper's editor. She believed it was not wise considering her recall

campaign. See Anna Louise Strong to Board of Directors of the *Daily Call,* December 12, 1917, box 8, folder 17, Strong Papers.

109. Frank, *Purchasing Power,* 28–30, 110 (first quote); Wells, "I Wanted to Work," 207; Strong, *I Change Worlds,* 65–66 (second quote); Strong, "IWW Manuscript," chap. 5, p. 9 (third quote).

EPILOGUE: PATRIOTISM, WAR, AND THE RED SCARE

1. Sandra Haarsager, *Bertha Knight Landes of Seattle: Big-City Mayor* (Norman: University of Oklahoma Press, 1994), 34–41.

2. *Bulletin: Washington State Federation of Women's Clubs* 1.4 (August 1917): 1, 23–24; Mathews, "History of Washington State Federation of Women's Clubs," 1949, accession #3463, 3463 (2–5) box 1, folder 10, Manuscripts and Archives, Suzzallo and Allen Library, University of Washington, 57.

3. Mathews, "History of Washington State Federation of Women's Clubs," 57; *Bulletin: Washington State Federation of Women's Clubs* 2.3 (May 1918): 16–17, 22. Brochure, accession #204, box 16, folder 18, Naomi Benson Papers, Manuscripts and Archives, Suzzallo and Allen Library, University of Washington Library.

4. *Bulletin: Washington State Federation of Women's Clubs* 2.3 (May 1918): 22; 1.4 (August 1917): 1; National League for Women's Service, *Washington State Report for 1917–1919,* Pacific Northwest Collection, University of Washington.

5. *Bulletin: Washington State Federation of Women's Clubs* 1.4 (August 1917): 42; 2.1 (November 1917): 18–19, 25.

6. *Report of the 34th Annual Meeting of Women's Christian Temperance Union of West Washington,* 1917, Pacific Northwest Collection, University of Washington, 51; *Bulletin: Washington State Federation of Women's Clubs* 1.4 (August 1917): 29–33; 2.1 (November 1917): 24–25; Woman's Social Hygiene Department of the Washington State Board of Health, *Survey of Seattle and Bremerton District,* April 1, 1919, Pacific Northwest Collection, University of Washington, 30–167.

7. *Legislative Federationist* 2.7 (November 1917): 3; 2.4 (May 1917): 6.

8. *Washington Woman's Legislative Counsellor Yearbook, 1917–1918,* Pacific Northwest Collection, University of Washington, 26; *Legislative Counsellor,* 3.6 (June 1918): 6.

9. *Washington Woman's Legislative Counsellor Yearbook, 1917–1918,* 16; Oberdeck, "Not Pink Teas," 221–23; *Legislative Federationist* 2.4 (May 1917): 4–5; 2.5 (June 1917): 4; 3.2 (February 1918): 2–3; Anna Louise Strong to Mr. Kellog, February 26, 1918, box 7B, folder 66, Strong Papers.

10. Oberdeck, "Not Pink Teas," 221–25; Foner, *Women and the American Labor Movement;* Maureen Weiner Greenwald, "Working-Class Feminism and the Family Wage Ideal: The Seattle Debate on Married Women's Right to Work, 1914–1920," *Journal of American History* 76.1 (June 1989): 125–26.

11. Greenwald, "Working-Class Feminism and the Family Wage Ideal," 148.

12. Frank, *Purchasing Power*, chap. 1; Berner, *Seattle 1900–1920*, chap. 15.

13. Dembo, *Unions and Politics*, 128–29; Hanford, *Seattle and Environs*, 351; Frank, *Purchasing Power*, 25, 29–30.

14. Saltvig, "The Progressive Movement in Washington," 444–45; Berner, *Seattle 1900–1920*, 234.

15. Saltvig, "The Progressive Movement in Washington," 452–53; Dembo, *Unions and Politics*, 160; Berner, *Seattle 1900–1920*, 248; Albert F. Gunns, *Civil Liberties in Crisis: The Pacific Northwest, 1917–1940* (New York: Garland, 1983), chap. 1.

16. Frank, *Purchasing Power*, 30, 34–36; *Business Chronicle* 6.1 (November 30, 1918): 12; 6.4 (December 21, 1918): 38; Robert L. Friedheim, *The Seattle General Strike* (Seattle: University of Washington Press, 1964).

17. Berner, *Seattle 1900–1920*, 276–80; Dembo, *Unions and Politics*, 188–92.

18. Dembo, *Unions and Politics*, 192–95; Friedheim, *The Seattle General Strike*, 111–12.

19. Frank, *Purchasing Power*, chap. 1; Berner, *Seattle 1900–1920*, chap. 20–22.

20. History Committee of the Seattle Central Labor Council, "The Seattle General Strike: An Account of What Happened in Seattle, and Especially in the Seattle Labor Movement During the General Strike, February 6 to 11, 1919," Pacific Northwest Collection, University of Washington, 18; McMahon, "The Strike in Seattle," 822.

21. Berner, *Seattle 1900–1920*, 293–95.

22. Berner, *Seattle 1900–1920*, 301.

23. *Square Deal* 1.4 (October 30, 1919): 2; Berner, *Seattle 1900–1920*, 307.

24. *Business Chronicle* 7.3 (June 14, 1919): 25; "Special Meeting of Board of Trustees of Seattle Chamber of Commerce and Commercial Club, October 27, 1919," Seattle Chamber of Commerce: Minutes, Northwest Collection, Seattle Public Library; Margaret J. Thompson, "Development and Comparison of Industrial Relations" (master's thesis, University of Washington, 1929), 69–71; *Square Deal* 2.28 (February 29, 1921): 4; Berner, *Seattle 1900–1920*, 302.

25. Dembo, *Unions and Politics*, 203–4, 206–20.

26. Letter from Charles Doyle, Secretary of SCLC, to William Short, president of the State Federation of Labor, June 7, 1919, box 15, folders 9–20, Washington State Federation of Labor Papers, Manuscripts and Archives, Suzzallo and Allen Library, University of Washington; Saltvig, "The Progressive Movement in Washington," 474; Dembo, *Unions and Politics*, 209–20; Dickson, "Labor in Municipal Politics," 54–55; Berner, *Seattle 1900–1920*, 305; McKenzie, "Community Forces: A Study of the Non-Partisan Municipal Elections in Seattle II," 416.

27. Tom Copeland, *The Centralia Tragedy of 1919: Elmer Smith and the Wobblies* (Seattle: University of Washington Press, 1993); O'Connor, *Revolution in Seattle*, chap. 8; Dembo, *Unions and Politics*, 222–26.

28. Quoted in O'Connor, *Revolution in Seattle*, 181.

29. Berner, *Seattle 1900–1920*, 307–8; Dembo, *Unions and Politics*, 231; Mary Joan O'Connell, "The Seattle Union Record, 1918–1928: A Pioneer Labor Daily" (master's thesis, University of Washington, 1964), 103–22; Gunns, *Civil Liberties in Crisis*, 44–46.

30. *Business Chronicle* 7.5 (June 28, 1919): 50; 7.8 (July 19, 1919): 85.

31. *Square Deal* 1.4 (October 30, 1919): 3–5; O'Connell, "The Seattle Union Record," 100.

32. W. M. Short to Samuel Gompers, November 14, 1919, box 41, Washington State Federation of Labor Papers.

33. Theresa S. McMahon, "Centralia and the i.w.w.," *Survey* 43.6 (November 29, 1919): 173–74; O'Connell, "The Seattle Union Record," 116; Berner, *Seattle 1900–1920*, 307.

34. Dickson, "Labor in Municipal Politics," 56–58.

35. Quoted in Frank, "At the Point of Consumption," 269; Dickson, "Labor in Municipal Politics," 57.

36. Quoted in Dembo, *Unions and Politics*, 255; *Square Deal* 1.15 (January 15, 1920): 10; O'Connell, "The Seattle Union Record," 156; Berner, *Seattle 1900–1920*, 313.

37. Dembo, *Unions and Politics*, 258–63.

38. Dembo, *Unions and Politics*, 264–69; Berner, *Seattle 1900–1920*, 314–15; Frank, *Purchasing Power*, 182.

39. Frank, *Purchasing Power*, 152–61; O'Connell, "The Seattle Union Record," 181–90; Dembo, *Unions and Politics*, 276–90.

40. Frank, *Purchasing Power*.

41. Frank, *Purchasing Power*, 184; Richard C. Berner, *Seattle 1921–1940: From Boom to Bust* (Seattle: Charles Press, 1992), chap. 1; Berner, *Seattle 1900–1920*, chap. 23.

42. Haarsager, *Bertha Knight Landes*, chaps. 1–2.

43. Frank, *Purchasing Power*, 178–79, 221–23.

44. Sophie L. W. Clark to Dr. Smith, April 16, 1920, box 3, folder 18, Alice Smith Papers.

45. Haarsager, *Bertha Knight Landes*, 37–38, 52–54; Mathews, "History of Washington State Federation of Women's Clubs," 62.

46. Haarsager, *Bertha Knight Landes*, 70–75; Doris H. Pieroth, "Bertha Knight Landes: The Woman Who Was Mayor," in *Women in Pacific Northwest*

History: An Anthology, ed. Karen J. Blair, 89–91 (Seattle: University of Washington Press, 1988).

47. Haarsager, *Bertha Knight Landes,* chaps. 2–6; Berner, *Seattle 1920–1940,* 79, 87–90.

48. Haarsager, *Bertha Knight Landes,* chap. 6; Berner, *Seattle 1920–1940,* chaps. 25–27.

Bibliography

MANUSCRIPTS

Manuscripts and Archives, Suzzallo and Allen Library, University of Washington, Seattle, Washington
Central Labor Council of Seattle and King County Records
George Cotterill Papers
Nellie M. Fick Papers
Theresa S. McMahon Papers
Minnie Parkhurst Papers
Seattle Port Commission Papers
Seattle Young Women's Christian Association: King County Records
Alice Smith Papers
Joseph Smith Papers
Anna Louise Strong Papers
Hulet Wells Papers
F. G. Whitaker Papers
Washington State Federation of Labor Papers
Washington State Federation of Women's Clubs Records
Pacific Northwest Collection, Suzzallo and Allen Library, University of Washington, Seattle, Washington
Seattle A.Y.P. Exposition Scrapbooks
Seattle A.Y.P. Exposition Miscellany
Northwest Collection. Seattle Public Library, Seattle, Washington
Seattle Alaska-Yukon-Pacific Exposition Scrapbooks
Scrapbook of Seattle Material, 1911–17
Washington State Library, Olympia, Washington
Emma Smith DeVoe Papers

NEWSPAPERS AND PERIODICALS

Argus, 1909–10. Seattle.
Bulletin: Washington State Federation of Women's Clubs, 1917. Seattle.
Business Chronicle, 1916–22. Seattle.
Legislative Federationist, 1916–18. Seattle.
Legislative Counsellor, 1918. Seattle.
Literary Digest, 1912. New York.

Municipal League News, 1911–12. Seattle.

New Citizen, 1911. Seattle.

New Northwest, 1875–87. Portland.

Patriarch, 1903–10. Seattle.

Seattle Chamber of Commerce Record, 1916. Seattle.

Seattle Daily Post-Intelligencer, 1883–87. Seattle.

Seattle Daily Press, 1886. Seattle.

Seattle Daily Times, 1886–87. Seattle.

Seattle Municipal News, 1911–17. Seattle

Seattle Post-Intelligencer, 1883–1920, Seattle.

Seattle Star, 1909. Seattle.

Seattle Times, 1909. Seattle.

Seattle Union Record, 1905–22. Seattle.

Square Deal, 1919–21.

Town Crier, 1910. Seattle.

Votes for Women, 1909–10. Seattle.

Welfare: A Journal of Municipal and Social Progress, 1913–14. Seattle.

Western Woman's Outlook, 1911–14. Seattle.

Western Woman Voter, 1911–12. Seattle

Woman's Journal, 1883–87. Boston.

GOVERNMENT DOCUMENTS

Bureau of Labor of the State of Washington. *Fourth Biennial Report of the Bureau of Labor of the State of Washington, 1903–1904.* Olympia, WA: Blankenship Satterlee Company, 1904.

——. *Fifth Biennial Report of the Bureau of Labor Statistics and Factory Inspection, 1905–1906.* Olympia, WA: C. W. Gorham, 1906.

——. *Sixth Biennial Report of the Bureau of Labor Statistics and Factory Inspection, 1907–1908.* Olympia, WA: C. W. Gorham, 1908.

——. *Seventh Biennial Report of the Bureau of Labor Statistics and Factory Inspection, 1909–1910.* Olympia, WA: C. W. Gorham, 1910.

U.S. Bureau of Census. *Report on Population of the United States at the Eleventh Census: 1890,* pt. 1. Washington DC: Government Printing Office, 1895.

——. *Twelfth Census of the United States: Population 1900,* vol. 1–2. Washington DC: Government Printing Office, 1901.

——. *Thirteenth Census of the United States: Manufactures,* vol. 9. Washington DC: Government Printing Office, 1912.

——. *Thirteenth Census of the United States: Population 1910,* vol. 3–4. Washington DC: Government Printing Office, 1914.

U.S. Congress. House. *Industrial Relations: Final Report and Testimony Submitted* to *Congress by the Commission on Industrial Relations,* vol. 5. Washington DC: Government Printing Office, 1916.

Woman's Social Hygiene Department of the Washington State Board of Health. *Survey of Seattle and Bremerton District.* April 1, 1919. Pacific Northwest Collection, University of Washington, Seattle.

PAMPHLETS AND RARE MATERIALS

Annual Report of Charity Organizations of Seattle, 1911. Pacific Northwest Collection, University of Washington, Seattle.

College Equal Suffrage League of Northern California. *Winning Equal Suffrage in California: Reports of the Committees of the College Equal Suffrage League of Northern California in the Campaign of 1911.* San Francisco: National College Equal Suffrage League, 1913. Berkeley, California. Bancroft Library.

"Dear Friend." Pamphlets by and about Anna Louise Strong concerning her recall as a member of the Seattle School Board. 1916. Northwest Collection, Seattle Public Library.

History Committee of the Seattle Central Labor Council. "The Seattle General Strike: An Account of What Happened in Seattle, and Especially in the Seattle Labor Movement During the General Strike, February 6 to 11, 1919." Pacific Northwest Collection, University of Washington, Seattle.

Irvine, Leigh. *A Conspiracy Against Liberty.* n.d. Pacific Northwest Collection, University of Washington, Seattle.

———. *Government by Labor Unions.* 1916. Pacific Northwest Collection, University of Washington, Seattle.

———. *Labor Unions and the Law of Love.* 1916. Pacific Northwest Collection, University of Washington, Seattle.

———. *The Story of Detroit.* 1916. Pacific Northwest Collection, University of Washington, Seattle.

Montgomery, Robert. "Female Suffrage: From the Viewpoint of a Male Democrat." 1909. Pacific Northwest Collection, University of Washington, Seattle.

National League for Women's Service. *Washington State Report for 1917–19.* Pacific Northwest Collection, University of Washington, Seattle.

Proceedings of the Washington State Federation of Labor, 1907–14. Pacific Northwest Collection, University of Washington, Seattle.

Report of the 14th Annual Meeting of Woman's Christian Temperance Union of West Washington, 1897. Pacific Northwest Collection, University of Washington, Seattle.

Report of the 15th Annual Meeting of Woman's Christian Temperance Union of West Washington, 1898. Pacific Northwest Collection, University of Washington, Seattle.

Report of the 32nd Annual Meeting of Woman's Christian Temperance Union of West Washington, 1915. Pacific Northwest Collection, University of Washington, Seattle.

Report of the 34th Annual Meeting of Woman's Christian Temperance Union of West Washington, 1917. Pacific Northwest Collection, University of Washington, Seattle.

Seattle Chamber of Commerce. *Annual Report*, 1916. Northwest Collection, Seattle Public Library.

Seattle Chamber of Commerce. "Record of the Minutes of the Meetings of the Seattle Chamber of Commerce." Northwest Collection, Seattle Public Library.

Seattle Port Commission. "A Call for the People's Veto." *Port Commission of Seattle Bulletin*, No. 9. 1916. Municipal Reference, Seattle Public Library, Seattle.

Short, William. "History of the Activities of Seattle Labor Movement and Conspiracy of Employers to Destroy It and Attempted Suppression of Labor's Daily Newspaper, the Seattle Union Record." Pacific Northwest Collection, University of Washington, Seattle.

"Statement by Anna Louise Strong, Member of the Seattle School Board, and Report of the Central Labor Council Investigating Committee Regarding the Proposed Recall." Pamphlets by and about Anna Louise Strong concerning her recall as a member of the Seattle School Board. n.d. Northwest Collection, Seattle Public Library.

Stevens, Helen Norton. *Memorial Biography of Adele M. Fielde: Humanitarian*. Seattle: Field Memorial Committee, 1918. University of Washington Library, Seattle.

Washington Women's Cook Book. Seattle: Washington Equal Suffrage Association, 1909. Seattle Public Library.

Washington Women's Legislative Counsellor Yearbook, 1917–18. Pacific Northwest Collection, University of Washington, Seattle.

Waterfront Employers' Association. "An Open Letter." 1916. Pacific Northwest Collection, University of Washington, Seattle.

"Why Annal Louis [sic] Strong Should Be Recalled." Pamphlets by and about Anna Louise Strong concerning her recall as a member of the Seattle School Board. 1916. Northwest Collection, Seattle Public Library.

DISSERTATIONS AND UNPUBLISHED STUDIES

Adair, Karen. "Organized Women Workers in Seattle, 1900–1918." Master's thesis, University of Washington, 1990.

Blackford, Mansel. "Sources of Support for Reform Candidates and Issues in Seattle Politics, 1902–1916." Master's thesis, University of Washington, 1967.

Brandenfels, Kathryn. "Down on the Sawdust: Prostitution and Vice Control in

Seattle, 1870–1920." Unpublished paper, 1981, Pacific Northwest Collection, University of Washington.

Dickson, William. "Labor in Municipal Politics: A Study of Labor's Political Policies and Activities in Seattle." Master's thesis, University of Washington, 1928.

Frank, Dana. "At the Point of Consumption: Seattle Labor and the Politics of Consumption, 1919–1927." PhD diss., Yale University, 1988.

Gullett, Gayle Ann. "Feminism, Politics, and Voluntary Groups: Organized Womanhood in California, 1886–1896." PhD diss., University of California, Riverside, 1983.

Katz, Sherry. "Dual Commitments: Feminism, Socialism, and Women's Political Activism in California, 1890–1920." PhD diss., University of California, Los Angeles, 1991.

MacDonald, Alexander N. "Seattle's Economic Development, 1880–1910." PhD diss., University of Washington, 1959.

O'Connell, Mary Joan. "The Seattle Union Record, 1918–1928: A Pioneer Labor Daily." Master's thesis, University of Washington, 1964.

Pendergrass, Lee F. "Urban Reform and Voluntary Association: A Case Study of the Seattle Municipal League, 1910–1929." PhD diss., University of Washington, 1972.

Putman, John. "The Emergence of a New West: The Politics of Class and Gender in Seattle, Washington, 1880–1917." PhD diss., University of California, San Diego, 2000.

Reiff, Janice L. "Urbanization and the Social Structure: Seattle, Washington, 1852–1910." PhD diss., University of Washington, 1981.

Saltvig, Robert D. "The Progressive Movement in Washington." PhD diss., University of Washington, 1966.

Thompson, Margaret J. "Development and Comparison of Industrial Relations." Master's thesis, University of Washington, 1929.

Wynne, Robert E. "Reaction to the Chinese in the Pacific Northwest and British Columbia, 1850–1910." PhD diss., University of Washington, 1964.

PUBLISHED BOOKS AND ARTICLES

Almaguer, Tomás. *Racial Fault Lines: The Historical Origins of White Supremacy in California.* Berkeley and Los Angeles: University of California Press, 1994.

Anderson, Karen. "Work, Gender, and Power in the American West." *Pacific Historical Review* 61.4 (November 1992): 481–99.

Anderson, Kristi. *After Suffrage: Women in Partisan and Electoral Politics Before the New Deal.* Chicago: University of Chicago Press, 1996.

Armitage, Susan. "Women and Men in Western History: Stereoptical Vision." *Western Historical Quarterly* 16.4 (October 1985): 381–95.

August, Jack, Jr. "The Future of Western History: The Third Wave." *Journal of Arizona History* 20.2 (Summer 1986): 229–44.

Ayers, Edward L., Patricia Nelson Limerick, Stephen Nissenbaum, and Peter S. Onuf. *All Over the Map: Rethinking American Regions.* Baltimore: Johns Hopkins University Press, 1996.

Bagley, Clarence. *History of King County, Washington,* vol. 1. Chicago: S. J. Clarke, 1929.

———. *History of Seattle From the Earliest Settlement to the Present,* vol. 2. Chicago: S. J. Clarke, 1916.

Baily, C. H. "How Washington Women Regained the Ballot." *Pacific Monthly* 26.1 (July 1911): 1–11.

Baker, Paula. "The Domestication of Politics: Women and American Political Society, 1780–1920." *American Historical Review* 89.3 (June 1984): 620–47.

———. *The Moral Frameworks of Public Life: Gender, Politics, and the State in Rural New York, 1870–1930.* New York: Oxford University Press, 1991.

Baron, Ava. "Gender and Labor History: Learning From the Past, Looking to the Future." In *Work Engendered: Toward a New History of American Labor,* edited by Ava Baron, 1–46. Ithaca, NY: Cornell University Press, 1991.

———, ed. *Work Engendered: Toward a New History of American Labor.* Ithaca, NY: Cornell University Press, 1991.

Berner, Richard C. *Seattle 1900–1920: From Boomtown, Urban Turbulence, to Restoration.* Seattle: Charles Press, 1991.

———. *Seattle 1921–1940: From Boom to Bust.* Seattle: Charles Press, 1992.

Blackford, Mansel. "Civic Groups, Political Action, and City Planning in Seattle, 1892–1915." *Pacific Historical Review* 49.4 (November 1980): 557–80.

———. "Reform Politics in Seattle During the Progressive Era, 1902–1916." *Pacific Northwest Quarterly* 59.4 (October 1968): 177–85.

Blair, Karen J. *The Clubwoman as Feminist: True Womanhood Redefined, 1868–1914.* New York: Holmes and Meier, 1980.

———. *Women in Pacific Northwest History: An Anthology.* Seattle: University of Washington Press, 1988.

Bordin, Ruth. *Women and Temperance: The Quest for Power and Liberty, 1873–1900.* Philadelphia: Temple University Press, 1981.

Bradford, Ernest S. "History and Underlying Principles of Commission Government." *Annals of the American Academy of Political and Social Science* 38.3 (November 1911): 3–11.

Brown, Victoria Bissell Brown. "Jane Addams, Progressivism, and Woman Suffrage." In *One Woman, One Vote: Rediscovering the Woman Suffrage Movement,* edited by Marjorie Spruill Wheeler, 186–95. Troutsdale, OR: NewSage Press, 1995.

Brundage, David. *The Making of Western Labor Radicalism: Denver's Organized Workers, 1878–1905.* Urbana: University of Illinois Press, 1994.

Buhle, Mari Jo. *Women and American Socialism, 1870–1920.* Urbana: University of Illinois Press, 1986.

Burke, Padraic. "Struggle for Public Ownership: The Early History of the Port of Seattle." *Pacific Northwest Quarterly* 68.2 (April 1977): 60–71.

Cantor, Milton, and Bruce Laurie, eds. *Class, Sex, and the Woman Worker.* Westport, CT: Greenwood Press, 1977.

Casteñeda, Antonia I. "Women of Color and the Rewriting of Western History: The Discourse, Politics, and Decolonization of History." *Pacific Historical Review* 61.4 (November 1992): 501–33.

Chafe, William. *The American Woman: Her Changing Social, Economic, and Political Roles, 1920–1970.* New York: Oxford University Press, 1972.

Chafee, Zechariah, Jr. *Free Speech in the United States.* Cambridge: Harvard University Press, 1941.

Cinch, Thomas A. *Urban Populism and Free Silver in Montana.* Helena: University of Montana Press, 1970.

Clark, Norman. *The Dry Years: Prohibition and Social Change in Washington.* Seattle: University of Washington Press, 1965.

———. *Mill Town: A Social History of Everett, Washington, from Its Earliest Beginnings on the Shores of Puget Sound to the Tragic and Infamous Event Known as the Everett Massacre.* Seattle: University of Washington Press, 1970.

Clemens, Elisabeth. *The People's Lobby: Organizational Innovation and the Rise of Interest Group Politics in the United States, 1890–1925.* Chicago: University of Chicago Press, 1997.

Cloud, Barbara. "Laura Hall Peters: Pursuing the Myth of Equality." *Pacific Northwest Quarterly* 74.1 (January 1983): 28–36.

Cobble, Dorothy Sue. *Dishing It Out: Waitresses and Their Unions in the Twentieth Century.* Urbana: University of Illinois Press, 1991.

Cohen, Lizabeth. *Making a New Deal: Industrial Workers in Chicago, 1919–1939.* New York: Cambridge University Press, 1990.

Commons, John, Selig Perlman, and Philip Taft. *History of Labor in the United States.* 4 vols. New York: Macmillan, 1921–35.

Conlin, Joseph. *Bread and Roses Too: Studies of the Wobblies.* Westport CT: Greenwood, 1969.

Copeland, Tom. *The Centralia Tragedy of 1919: Elmer Smith and the Wobblies.* Seattle: University of Washington Press, 1993.

Cott, Nancy. "Across the Great Divide: Women in Politics Before and After 1920." In *Women, Politics, and Change,* edited by Louise A. Tilly and Patricia Gurin, 153–76. New York: Russell Sage Foundation, 1990.

———. *Bonds of Womanhood: "Woman's Sphere" in New England, 1780–1835.* New Haven, CT: Yale University Press, 1977.

Cronon, William, George Miles, and Jay Gitlin, eds. *Under an Open Sky: Rethinking America's Western Past.* New York: W. W. Norton, 1992.

Daniels, Roger. *Asian Americans: Chinese and Japanese in the United States since 1850.* Seattle: University of Washington, 1988.

Dembo, Jonathan. *Unions and Politics in Washington State, 1885–1935.* New York: Garland, 1983.

Denny, Arthur. *Pioneer Days on Puget Sound.* Seattle: C. B. Bagley Printer, 1888.

DeVault, Ileen A. "'Give the Boys a Trade': Gender and Job Choice in the 1890s." In *Work Engendered: Toward a New History of American Labor,* edited by Ava Baron, 191–201. Ithaca, NY: Cornell University Press, 1991.

Deverell, William. "Fighting Words: The Significance of the American West in the History of the United States." In *A New Significance: Re-envisioning the History of the American West,* edited by Clyde A. Milner II, 29–61. New York: Oxford University Press, 1996.

———. *Railroad Crossing: Californians and the Railroad, 1850–1910.* Berkeley and Los Angeles: University of California Press, 1994.

Deverell, William, and Tom Sitton, eds. *California Progressivism Revisited.* Berkeley and Los Angeles: University of California Press, 1994.

Diner, Steven J. *A Very Different Age: Americans of the Progressive Era.* New York: Hill and Wang, 1998.

Dubofsky, Melvyn. "The Origins of Western Working-Class Radicalism, 1890–1905." *Labor History* 7.2 (Spring 1966): 131–54.

———. *We Shall Be All: A History of the Industrial Workers of the World.* Urbana: University of Illinois Press, 1988.

DuBois, Ellen. *Feminism and Suffrage: The Emergence of an Independent Women's Movement in America, 1848–1869.* Ithaca, NY: Cornell University Press, 1978.

———. *Woman Suffrage and Women's Rights.* New York: New York University Press, 1998.

Duniway, Abigail Scott. *Path Breaking: An Autobiographical History of the Equal Suffrage Movement in the Pacific Coast States.* 2d ed. 1914. Reprint, New York: Schocken Books, 1971.

Epstein, Barbara. *The Politics of Domesticity: Women, Evangelism, and Temperance in Nineteenth Century America.* Middletown, CT: Wesleyan University Press, 1981.

Erie, Steven. "Bringing the Bosses Back In: The Irish Political Machines and Urban Policy Making." *Studies in American Political Development* 4 (1990): 269–81.

Ethington, Philip J. *The Public City: The Political Construction of Urban Life in San Francisco, 1850–1900.* New York: Cambridge University Press, 1994.

Faragher, John Mack. *Sugar Creek: Life on the Illinois Prairie.* New Haven, CT: Yale University Press, 1986.

Faue, Elizabeth. *Community of Struggle: Women, Men, and the Labor Movement in Minneapolis, 1915–1945.* Chapel Hill: University of North Carolina Press, 1991.

Ficken, Robert E. *The Forested Land: A History of Lumbering in Western Washington.* Seattle: University of Washington Press, 1987.

———. *Washington Territory.* Pullman: Washington State Press, 2002.

Ficken, Robert E., and Charles P. LeWarne. *Washington: A Centennial History.* Seattle: University of Washington Press, 1988.

Findlay, John M. "A Fishy Proposition: Regional Identity in the Pacific Northwest." In *Many Wests: Place, Culture, and Regional Identity,* edited by David M. Wrobel and Michael C. Steiner, 37–70. Lawrence: University Press of Kansas, 1997.

Fink, Leon. *Workingmen's Democracy: The Knights of Labor and American Politics.* Urbana: University of Illinois Press, 1983.

Flanagan, Maureen. "Gender and Urban Political Reform: The City Club and the Woman's City Club of Chicago in the Progressive Era." *American Historical Review* 95 (October 1990): 1032–50.

———. *Seeing With Their Hearts: Chicago Women and the Vision of the Good City, 1871–1933.* Princeton, NJ: Princeton University Press, 2002.

Foner, Philip. *History of the Labor Movement in the United States,* vol. 4. New York: International Publishers, 1947.

———. *Women and the American Labor Movement: From Colonial Times to the Eve of World War I.* New York: Free Press, 1979.

———. *Women and the American Labor Movement: From World War I to the Present.* New York: Free Press, 1980.

Frank, Dana. *Purchasing Power: Consumer Organizing, Gender, and the Seattle Labor Movement, 1919–1929.* New York: Cambridge University Press, 1994.

Freedman, Estelle. "Separatism as Strategy: Female Institution Building and American Feminism, 1870–1930." *Feminist Studies* 5.3 (Fall 1979): 512–29.

Freeman, Jo. *A Room at a Time: How Women Entered Party Politics.* Lanham, MD: Rowman and Littlefield, 2000.

Friedheim, Robert L. *The Seattle General Strike.* Seattle: University of Washington Press, 1964.

Frisch, Michael H., and Daniel J. Walkowitz, eds. *Working-Class America: Essays of Labor, Community, and American Society.* Urbana: University of Illinois Press, 1983.

Frost, Lionel. *The New Urban Frontier: Urbanisation and City Building in Australia and the American West.* Kensington, Australia: New South Wales University Press, 1991.

Genini, Ronald. "Industrial Workers of the World and Their Fresno Free Speech Fight, 1910–1911." *California Historical Quarterly* 53.2 (Summer 1974): 100–114.

Goldberg, Michael. *An Army of Women: Gender and Politics in Gilded Age Kansas.* Baltimore: Johns Hopkins Press, 1997.

———. "Non-Partisan and All-Partisan: Rethinking Woman Suffrage and Party Politics in Gilded Age Kansas." *Western Historical Quarterly* 25.1 (Spring 1994): 21–44.

Greene, Julie. *Pure and Simple Politics: The American Federation of Labor and Political Activism, 1881–1917.* New York: Cambridge University Press, 1998.

Greenwald, Maurine W. *Women, War, and Work: The Impact of World War I on Women Workers in the United States.* Westport, CT: Greenwood Press, 1980.

———. "Working-Class Feminism and the Family Wage Ideal: The Seattle Debate on Married Women's Right to Work, 1914–1920." *Journal of American History* 76.1 (June 1989): 118–49.

Griffiths, David B. "Far-western Populist Thought: A Comparative Study of John R. Rogers and Davis H. Waite." *Pacific Northwest Quarterly* 60.4 (October 1969): 183–92.

Grimes, Alan. *The Puritan Ethic and Woman Suffrage.* 1967. Reprint, Westport, CT: Greenwood Press, 1980.

Gullett, Gayle Ann. *Becoming Citizens: The Emergence and Development of the California Women's Movement, 1880–1911.* Urbana: University of Illinois Press, 2000.

Gunns, Albert F. *Civil Liberties in Crisis: The Pacific Northwest, 1917–1940.* New York: Garland, 1983.

Haarsager, Sandra. *Bertha Knight Landes of Seattle: Big-City Mayor.* Norman: University of Oklahoma Press, 1994.

———. *Organized Womanhood: Cultural Politics in the Pacific Northwest, 1840–1920.* Norman: University of Oklahoma Press, 1997.

Hammack, David. "Problems in the Historical Study of Power in the Cities and Towns of the United States, 1800–1960." *American Historical Review* 83.2 (April 1978): 323–49.

Hanford, C. H., ed. *Seattle and Environs, 1852–1924.* Chicago: Pioneer Historical, 1924.

Harmon, Alexandra. *Indians in the Making: Ethnic Relations and Indian Identities Around Puget Sound.* Berkeley and Los Angeles: University of California Press, 1998.

Hays, Samuel P. "The Politics of Reform in Municipal Government in the Progressive Era." *Pacific Northwest Quarterly* 55 (October 1964): 157–69.

———. "Society and Politics: Politics and Society." *Journal of Interdisciplinary History* 15.3 (Winter 1985): 481–99.

Hendrick, Burton. "The 'Recall' in Seattle." *McClure's Magazine* 37 (October 1911): 647–63.

Hicks, John. *The Populist Revolt: A History of the Farmers' Alliance and the People's Party.* Lincoln: University of Nebraska Press, 1961.

Issel, William. "'Citizens Outside the Government': Business and Urban Policy in San Francisco and Los Angeles, 1890–1932." *Pacific Historical Review* 57.2 (May 1988): 117–45.

Issel, William, and Robert W. Cherney. *San Francisco, 1865–1932: Politics, Power, and Urban Development.* Berkeley and Los Angeles: University of California Press, 1986.

Jensen, Joan M. "'Disfranchisement Is a Disgrace': Women and Politics in New Mexico, 1900–1940." In *New Mexico Women: Intercultural Perspectives,* edited by Joan M. Jensen and Darlis Miller, 301–31. Albuquerque: University of New Mexico Press, 1986.

Jensen, Joan M., and Darlis Miller. "The Gentle Tamers Revisited: New Approaches to the History of Women in the American West." *Pacific Historical Review* 49.2 (May 1980): 173–213.

———, eds. *New Mexico Women: Intercultural Perspectives.* Albuquerque: University of New Mexico Press, 1986.

Johnson, Daniel. "'No Make-Believe Class Struggle': The Socialist Municipal Campaign in Los Angeles, 1911." *Labor History* 41.1 (February 2000): 25–45.

Johnston, Robert D. *The Radical Middle Class: Populist Democracy and the Question of Capitalism in Progressive Era Portland, Oregon.* Princeton, NJ: Princeton University Press, 2003.

———. "Re-Democratizing the Progressive Era: The Politics of Progressive Era Thought." *Journal of the Gilded Age and Progressive Era* 1.1 (January 2002): 68–92.

Karlin, Jules A. "The Anti-Chinese Outbreaks in Seattle." *Pacific Northwest Quarterly* 34 (April 1948): 103–29.

Katz, Sherry. "A Politics of Coalition: Socialist Women and the California Suffrage Movement, 1900–1911." In *One Woman, One Vote: Rediscovering the Woman Suffrage Movement,* edited by Marjorie Spruill Wheeler, 245–62. Troutsdale, OR: NewSage Press, 1995.

Kazin, Michael. *Barons of Labor: The San Francisco Building Trades and Union Power in the Progressive Era.* Urbana: University of Illinois Press, 1987.

———. "The Great Exception Revisited: Organized Labor and Politics in San Francisco and Los Angeles, 1870–1940." *Pacific Historical Review* 55.3 (August 1986): 371–402.

Keeler, Clinton. "The White City and the Black City: The Dream of Civilization." *American Quarterly* 2.2 (Summer 1950): 112–17.

Kennedy, David. *Over Here: The First World War and American Society.* New York: Oxford University Press, 1980.

Kleppner, Paul. "Politics Without Parties: The Western States, 1900–1984." In *The Twentieth-Century West: Historical Interpretations,* edited by Gerald D. Nash and Richard W. Etulain, 295–338. Albuquerque: University of New Mexico Press, 1989.

———. "Voters and Parties in the Western States, 1876–1900." *Western Historical Quarterly* 14.1 (January 1983): 49–68.

Kraditor, Aileen S. *The Ideas of the Woman Suffrage Movement, 1890–1920.* 1965. Reprint, New York: W. W. Norton, 1981.

Lang, William L. "Failed Federalism: The Columbia Valley Authority and Regionalism." In *The Great Northwest,* edited by William G. Robbins, 66–79. Corvallis: Oregon State University Press, 1983.

Larson, T. A. "Dolls, Vassals, and Drudges: Pioneer Women in the West." *Western Historical Quarterly* 3.1 (January 1972): 5–16.

———. "The Woman Suffrage Movement in Washington." *Pacific Northwest Quarterly* 67.2 (April 1976): 49–63.

———. "Woman Suffrage in Western America." *Utah Historical Quarterly* 38 (1970): 7–19.

———. "Women's Role in the American West." *Montana: The Magazine of Western History* 24.3 (July 1974): 3–11.

Leidenberger, Georg. "'The Public is the Labor Union': Working-Class Progressivism in Turn-of-the Century Chicago." *Labor History* 36.2 (Spring 1995): 187–210.

Lemons, J. Stanley. *The Woman Citizen: Social Feminism in the 1920s.* Urbana: University of Illinois Press, 1973.

Leuchtenburg, William E. "The Pertinence of Political History: Reflections on the Significance of the State in America." *Journal of American History* 73.3 (December 1986): 585–600.

LeWarne, Charles P. *Utopias on Puget Sound, 1885–1915.* Seattle: University of Washington Press, 1975.

Limerick, Patricia. *The Legacy of Conquest: The Unbroken Past of the American West.* New York: W. W. Norton, 1987.

———. "Region and Reason." In *All Over the Map: Rethinking American Regions,* edited by Edward L. Ayers, Patricia Nelson Limerick, Stephen Nissenbaum, and Peter S. Onuf, 83–104. Baltimore: Johns Hopkins University Press, 1996.

Limerick, Patricia, Clyde A. Milner II, and Charles E. Rankin, eds. *Trails: Toward a New Western History.* Lawrence: University Press of Kansas, 1991.

Link, Arthur, and Richard L. McCormick. *Progressivism.* Arlington Heights, IL: Harlan Davidson, 1983.

Locke, Mary Lou. "Out of the Shadows and Into the Western Sun: Working Women of the Late Nineteenth-Century Urban Far West." *Journal of Urban History* 16.2 (February 1990): 175–204.

MacDonald, Norbert. *Distant Neighbors: A Comparative History of Seattle and Vancouver.* Lincoln: University of Nebraska Press, 1987.

Magden, Ronald E. *A History of Seattle Waterfront Workers.* Seattle: International Longshoremen's and Warehousemen's Union 19 of Seattle and the Washington Commission for the Humanities, 1991.

Malone, Michael P. "Beyond the Last Frontier: Toward a New Approach to Western American History." In *Trails: Toward a New Western History,* edited by Patricia N. Limerick, Clyde A. Milner II, and Charles E. Rankin, 139–60. Lawrence: University Press of Kansas, 1991.

Malone, Michael P., and Richard W. Etulain. *The American West: A Twentieth-Century History.* Lincoln: University of Nebraska Press, 1989.

Marilley, Suzanne M. *Woman Suffrage and the Origins of Liberal Feminism in the United States, 1820–1920.* Cambridge: Harvard University Press, 1996.

Marshall, Susan E. *Splintered Sisterhood: Gender and Class in the Campaign Against Woman Suffrage.* Madison: University of Wisconsin Press, 1997.

Mattson, Kevin. *Creating a Democratic Public: The Struggle for Urban Participatory Democracy During the Progressive Era.* University Park: Pennsylvania State University Press, 1998.

McCormick, Richard L. *The Party Period and Public Policy: American Politics from the Age of Jackson to the Progressive Era.* New York: Oxford University Press, 1986.

McDonald, Terrence. "Putting Politics Back Into the History of the American City." *American Quarterly* 34 (1982): 200–209.

McGerr, Michael. *A Fierce Discontent: The Rise and Fall of the Progressive Movement in America, 1870–1920.* New York: Free Press, 2003.

McKenzie, R. B. "Community Forces: A Study of the Non-Partisan Municipal Elections in Seattle II." *Journal of Social Forces* 2.3 (March 1924): 415–21.

McMahon, Theresa. "Centralia and the i.w.w." *Survey* 43.6 (November 29, 1919): 173–74.

———. "The Strike in Seattle." *Survey* 41.23 (March 8, 1919): 821–23.

Mead, Rebecca J. *How the Vote Was Won: Woman Suffrage in the Western United States, 1868–1914.* New York: New York University Press, 2004.

———. "'Let the Women Get Their Wages as Men Do': Trade Union Women and the Legislated Minimum Wage in California." *Pacific Historical Review* 67.3 (August 1998): 317–47.

Milner, Clyde A., II, ed. *A New Significance: Re-envisioning the History of the American West.* New York: Oxford University Press, 1996.

Milner, Clyde A., II, Carol A. O'Connor, and Martha A. Sandweiss, eds. *The Oxford History of the American West*. New York: Oxford University Press, 1994.

Moehring, Eugene P. *Urbanism and Empire in the Far West, 1840–1890*. Reno: University of Nevada Press, 2004.

Montgomery, David. *The Fall of the House of Labor: The Workplace, the State, and American Labor Activism, 1865–1925*. New York: Cambridge University Press, 1987.

Morgan, Murray. *Puget's Sound: A Narrative of Early Tacoma and the Southern Sound*. Seattle: University of Washington, 1979.

———. *Skid Road: An Informal Portrait of Seattle*. New York: Viking Press, 1951.

Moynihan, Ruth Barnes. *Rebel for Rights: Abigail Scott Duniway*. New Haven, CT: Yale University Press, 1983.

Murolo, Priscilla. *The Common Ground of Womanhood: Class, Gender, and Working Girls' Clubs, 1884–1928*. Urbana: University of Illinois Press, 1997.

Nash, Gerald D. *The American West in the Twentieth Century*. Albuquerque: University of New Mexico Press, 1973.

———. *Creating the West: Historical Interpretations, 1890–1990*. Albuquerque: University of New Mexico Press, 1991.

Nash, Gerald D., and Richard W. Etulain, eds. *The Twentieth-Century West: Historical Interpretations*. Albuquerque: University of New Mexico Press, 1989.

Nesbit, Robert C. *"He Built Seattle": A Biography of Judge Thomas Burke*. Seattle: University of Washington Press, 1961.

Nugent, Walter. "The People of the West Since 1890." In *The Twentieth-Century West: Historical Interpretations,* edited by Gerald D. Nash and Richard W. Etulain, 35–70. Albuquerque: University of New Mexico Press, 1989.

Oberdeck, Kathryn. "'Not Pink Teas': The Seattle Working-Class Women's Movement, 1905–1918." *Labor History* 32.2 (Spring 1991): 193–230.

O'Connor, Harvey. *Revolution in Seattle: A Memoir*. New York: Monthly Review Press, 1964.

Oestreicher, Richard. "Urban Working-Class Political Behavior and Theories of American Electoral Politics, 1870–1940." *Journal of American History* 74.4 (March 1988): 1257–86.

Olin, Spencer. "Toward a Synthesis of the Political and Social History of the American West." *Pacific Historical Review* 55.4 (1986): 599–611.

Parker, Carlton. *The Casual Laborer and Other Essays*. New York: Russel and Russel, 1920.

Pascoe, Peggy. "Western Women at the Cultural Crossroads." In *Trails: Toward a New Western History,* edited by Patricia Limerick, Clyde A. Milner II, and Charles E. Rankin, 40–58. Lawrence: University Press of Kansas, 1991.

Peiss, Kathy. *Cheap Amusements: Working Women and Leisure in New York City, 1820–1920.* Philadelphia: Temple University Press, 1986.

Perlman, Selig. *A Theory of the Labour Movement.* New York: Macmillan, 1928.

Perlman, Selig, and Philip Taft. *History of Labor in the United States, 1896–1932.* 1935. Reprint, New York: Augustus M. Kelley, 1966.

Petrik, Paula. *No Step Backward: Women and Family on the Rocky Mountain Frontier, Helena, Montana, 1865–1900.* Helena: Montana Historical Society Press, 1987.

Pieroth, Doris H. "Bertha Knight Landes: The Woman Who Was Mayor." In *Women in Pacific Northwest History: An Anthology,* edited by Karen J. Blair, 89–91. Seattle: University of Washington Press, 1988.

Polenberg, Richard. *Fighting Faiths: The Abrams Case, the Supreme Court, and Free Speech.* New York: Viking Press, 1987.

Pollack, Norman. *The Populist Response to Industrial America: Midwestern Political Thought.* Cambridge: Harvard University Press, 1962.

Pomeroy, Earl. *The Pacific Slope: A History of California, Oregon, Washington, Idaho, Utah, and Nevada.* 1965. Reprint, Seattle: University of Washington Press, 1973.

Putman, John. "Racism and Temperance: The Politics of Class and Gender in Late 19th-Century Seattle." *Pacific Northwest Quarterly* 95.2 (Spring 2004): 70–81.

———. "A 'Test of Chiffon Politics': Gender Politics in Seattle, 1897–1917." *Pacific Historical Review* 69.4 (November 2000): 595–616.

Riddle, Thomas. *The Old Radicalism: John R. Rogers and the Populist Movement in Washington.* New York: Garland, 1991.

Riley, Glenda. "Western Women's History: A Look at Some of the Issues." *Montana: The Magazine of Western History* 41.2 (Spring 1991): 66–70.

Robbins, William G. *Colony and Empire: The Capitalist Transformation of the American West.* Lawrence: University Press of Kansas, 1994.

———, ed. *The Great Northwest: The Search for Regional Identity.* Corvallis: Oregon State University Press, 2001.

———. "The 'Plundered Province' Thesis and the Recent Historiography of the American West." *Pacific Historical Review* 55.4 (1986): 577–97.

Robbins, William G., Robert J. Frank, and Richard E. Ross, eds. *Regionalism and the Pacific Northwest.* Corvallis: Oregon State University Press, 1983.

Rodgers, Daniel. "In Search of Progressivism." *Reviews in American History* 10 (December 1982): 113–32.

Rosen, Ruth. *The Lost Sisterhood: Prostitution in America, 1900–1918.* Baltimore: Johns Hopkins University Press, 1982.

Rosenzweig, Roy. *Eight Hours for What They Will: Workers and Leisure in an Industrial City, 1870–1920.* New York: Cambridge University Press, 1983.

Ross, Steven J. "The Politicization of the Working Class: Production, Ideology, Culture, and Politics in Late Nineteenth-Century Cincinnati." *Social History* 11.2 (May 1986): 171–95.

Rowley, William D. "The West as a Laboratory and Mirror of Reform." In *The Twentieth-Century West: Historical Interpretations,* edited by Gerald D. Nash and Richard W. Etulain, 339–57. Albuquerque: University of New Mexico Press, 1989.

Ryan, Mary P. *Women in Public: Between Banners and Ballots, 1825–1880.* Baltimore: Johns Hopkins University Press, 1990.

Rydell, Robert W. *All the World's a Fair: Visions of Empire at American International Expositions, 1876–1916.* Chicago: University of Chicago Press, 1984.

Sale, Roger. *Seattle: Past to Present.* Seattle: University of Washington Press, 1976.

Salvatore, Nick. *Eugene V. Debs: Citizen and Socialist.* Urbana: University of Illinois Press, 1983.

Saxton, Alexander. *The Indispensable Enemy: Labor and the Anti-Chinese Movement in California.* Berkeley and Los Angeles: University of California Press, 1971.

Scharff, Virginia. "Else Surely We Shall All Hang Separately: The Politics of Western Women's History." *Pacific Historical Review* 61.4 (November 1992): 535–55.

———. "Gender and Western History: Is Anybody Home on the Range?" *Montana: The Magazine of Western History* 41.2 (Spring 1991): 62–65.

Schlissel, Lillian, Vicki Ruiz, and Janice Monk, eds. *Western Women: Their Land, Their Lives.* Albuquerque: University of New Mexico Press, 1988.

Schmid, Calvin. *Social Trends in Seattle.* Seattle: University of Washington Press, 1944.

Schwantes, Carlos. "The Churches of the Disinherited: The Culture of Radicalism on the North Pacific Industrial Frontier." *Pacific Historian* 25.4 (Winter 1981): 54–64.

———. "The Concept of the Wageworkers' Frontier: A Framework for Future Research." *Western Historical Quarterly* 18.1 (January 1987): 39–55.

———. *Coxey's Army: An American Odyssey.* Lincoln: University of Nebraska Press, 1985.

———. "From Anti-Chinese Agitation to Reform Politics: The Legacy of the Knights of Labor in Washington and the Pacific Northwest." *Pacific Northwest Quarterly* 88.4 (Fall 1997): 174–84.

———. "Leftward Tilt on the Pacific Slope: Indigenous Unionism and the Struggle Against AFL Hegemony in the State of Washington." *Pacific Northwest Quarterly* 70.1 (January 1979): 24–33.

———. *The Pacific Northwest: An Interpretive History.* Lincoln: University of Nebraska Press, 1989.

———. "Patterns of Radicalism on the Wageworkers' Frontier." *Idaho Yesterdays* 30.3 (Fall 1986): 25–30.

———. "Protest in a Promised Land: Unemployment, Disinheritance, and the Origin of Labor Militancy in the Pacific Northwest, 1885–1886." *Western Historical Quarterly* 13.4 (October 1982): 373–90.

———. *Radical Heritage: Labor, Socialism, and Reform in Washington and British Columbia, 1885–1917.* Seattle: University of Washington Press, 1979.

———. "Washington State's Pioneer Labor-Reform Press: A Bibliographical Essay and Annotated Checklist." *Pacific Northwest Quarterly* 71.3 (July 1980): 112–26.

Sharbach, Sarah E. "A Woman Acting Alone: Louise Olivereau and the First World War." *Pacific Northwest Quarterly* 78.1–2 (January–April 1987): 32–40.

Simpson, Lee M. A. *Selling the City: Gender, Class, and the California Growth Machine, 1880–1940.* Stanford, CA: Stanford University Press, 2004.

Spence, Mary Lee. "Commentary." In *Western Women: Their Land, Their Lives,* edited by Lillian Schlissel, Vicki Ruiz, and Janice Monk, 145–50. Albuquerque: University of New Mexico Press, 1988.

Spencer, Lloyd, and Lancaster Pollard. *A History of the State of Washington,* vol. 1. New York: American Historical Society, 1937.

Stanton, Elizabeth Cady, Susan B. Anthony, and Matilda Gage, eds. *History of Woman Suffrage.* New York: Fowler and Wells, 1881–1922.

Steiner, Michael C., and David M. Wrobel. "Many Wests: Discovering a Dynamic Western Regionalism." In *Many Wests: Place, Culture, and Regional Identity,* edited by David M. Wrobel and Michael C. Steiner, 1–30. Lawrence: University Press of Kansas, 1997.

Stromquist, Shelton. "The Crucible of Class: Cleveland Politics and the Origins of Municipal Reform in the Progressive Era." *Journal of Urban History* 23.2 (January 1997): 192–220.

———. *Reinventing "The People": The Progressive Movement, the Class Problem, and the Origins of Modern Liberalism.* Urbana: University of Illinois Press, 2006.

Strong, Anna Louise. *I Change Worlds.* Seattle: Seal Press, 1935.

———. "The Strike in Seattle." *Survey* 41.23 (March 1919): 821–23.

"Symposium on Julie Greene: Pure and Simple Politics." *Labor History* 40.2 (May 1999): 189–206.

Taylor, Quintard. *The Forging of a Black Community: Seattle's Central District from 1870 Through the Civil Rights Era.* Seattle: University of Washington Press, 1994.

Tentler, Leslie Woodcock. *Wage-Earning Women: Industrial Work and Family Life in the United States, 1900–1930.* New York: Oxford University Press, 1979.

Tilly, Louise A., and Patricia Gurin, eds. *Women, Politics, and Change.* New York: Russell Sage Foundation, 1990.

Van Wienen, Mark W. "A Rose by Any Other Name: Charlotte Perkins Stetson (Gilman) and the Case for American Reform Socialism." *American Quarterly* 55.4 (December 2003): 603–34.

Voss, Kim. *The Making of American Exceptionalism: The Knights of Labor and Class Formation in the Nineteenth Century.* Ithaca, NY: Cornell University Press, 1993.

Watkins, Marilyn. *Rural Democracy: Family Farmers and Politics in Western Washington, 1890–1925.* Ithaca, NY: Cornell University Press, 1995.

Webster, Janice Reiff. "Domestication and Americanization: Scandinavian Women in Seattle, 1888–1900." *Journal of Urban History* 4.3 (May 1978): 275–90.

Weinstein, James. "Organized Business and the City Commission and Manager Movements." *Journal of Southern History* 28 (1962): 166–82.

Welter, Barbara. "The Cult of True Womanhood, 1820–1860." *American Quarterly* 18 (June 1966): 151–74.

Wheeler, Marjorie Spruill. *One Woman, One Vote: Rediscovering the Woman Suffrage Movement.* Troutsdale, OR: NewSage Press, 1995.

White, Richard. *"It's Your Misfortune and None of My Own": A New History of the American West.* Norman: University of Oklahoma Press, 1991.

Wiebe, Robert. *Businessmen and Reform: A Study of the Progressive Movement.* Cambridge: Harvard University Press, 1962.

Wilentz, Sean. "Against Exceptionalism: Class Consciousness and the American Labor Movement." *International Labor and Working-Class History* 26 (Fall 1984): 1–24.

Woodruff, Clinton Rogers, ed. *City Government by Commission.* New York: D. Appleton, 1911.

Worster, Donald. "Beyond the Agrarian Myth." In *Trails: Toward a New Western History,* edited by Patricia N. Limerick, Clyde A. Milner II, and Charles E. Rankin, 3–25. Lawrence: University Press of Kansas, 1991.

———. "New West, True West: Interpreting the Region's History." *Western Historical Quarterly* 18.2 (April 1987): 141–56.

Wrobel, David M. *Promised Lands: Promotion, Memory, and the Creation of the American West.* Lawrence: University Press of Kansas, 2002.

Wrobel, David M., and Michael C. Steiner. *Many Wests: Place, Culture, and Regional Identity.* Lawrence: University Press of Kansas, 1997.

Wunder, John R. "What's Old About the New Western History? Race and Gender, Part I." *Pacific Northwest Quarterly* 85.2 (April 1994): 50–58.

———. "What's Old About the New Western History? Part II: Environment and Economy." *Pacific Northwest Quarterly* 88.2 (Spring 1998): 84–96.

Index

Made in the USA
Coppell, TX
18 May 2021

THE GAME

A Carolina Connections Novel - Book 4

SYLVIE STEWART

Rolling Hearts Press

COPYRIGHT

First Print Edition: 2017
Copyright © 2018 by Sylvie Stewart
Edited by Heather Mann

ISBN: 978-0-9989260-8-7

ALSO BY SYLVIE STEWART

for the dreamers

PATIENCE IS A VIRTUE

GAVIN

I knew it was over before my shoulder even kissed the ground—before the crunch of metal and the burn of gravel registered in my brain and flesh. I heard nothing but the crack and pop of my bones, these sounds somehow isolated among what must have been an awful cacophony of scraping metal, squealing tires, and voices raised in alarm. It was over before it even began, and I had no one to blame but myself.

Hours later, when I awoke in the hospital, the well-meaning doctor informed me I was lucky to be alive. I begged to differ but kept my mouth shut, forcing both the physical pain and the self-loathing down as deeply as I could. My mother's tear-stained face, slack with relief, was no balm. Nor was the barrage of questions posed to the doctor by my father as he paced around the hospital room. Nobody had to tell me, but they did anyway.

In a steady, matter-of-fact tone, the doctor described the extensive surgery I'd undergo to repair the damage to my right arm and

shoulder. Pins would be inserted and the healing process would begin. It would be long and arduous, not to mention painful, but I'd regain almost complete use of my arm with any luck.

They could cut the damn thing off for all I cared, because I had just thrown away the only thing I'd ever wanted or cared about—the thing I'd busted my ass the last ten years to achieve.

And all because I'd told myself nothing bad could ever happen on my birthday. There'd been a hot girl, cold beer, and a cool-as-shit motorcycle. One ride couldn't hurt. I was fucking Gavin Monroe, star pitcher, golden boy, and ripe to make my mark on the world, and hopefully that hot girl too. Instead, the only mark I left was on an isolated stretch of North Carolina country highway. That, and a deep scar on my future that could never be healed.

If I couldn't be a somebody, that meant I'd be a nobody. And I couldn't live with that. I was well and truly fucked. And not in the good way.

But life has a way of surprising us.

- Four and a half years later -

"Hey, Junior! Where do you think you're going?" Mark yelled across the lot.

I let the douchey nickname roll off my back, something I'd gotten pretty good at over the last couple years. It wasn't my fault that I had boyish charm and youthful good looks. But, as is always the case with guys, you've got to pay your dues and put up with some hazing if you're ever going to earn the respect of those above you. Mark, while definitely holding a position of authority as my

foreman, was also a friend, so I considered it my right and duty to put him in his place as well. Flipping him off seemed the most appropriate response in the moment.

"You wish!" was his reply, but I kept walking toward my Jeep, leaving the partially-constructed shell of the newest apartment building behind. I pulled off my hard hat and ran my other hand through my sweaty mass of hair, loosening the strands from the damp, tangled helmet they'd formed.

Mark knew good and well where I was going, he just couldn't resist giving me shit on the days I cut out before everyone else on the job site. But that was the whole point of working part-time. I admit, there may have been a time or two when I'd rubbed it in a few guys' faces that I'd be taking off after lunch while they slaved away under the hot Carolina sun. But, like I said, it's a guy thing.

I couldn't resist shouting back at him, "I'll tell Fiona you said hi!" That earned me a look that might make a lesser man shit his pants. Mark was built like a linebacker and was more than a little protective of his girlfriend. He made it too damn easy to rile him.

"You'll be doing it without teeth!" he growled. See, like I said —too easy.

I hopped in my Jeep and tore out of the lot, not bothering to secure my seatbelt until I was on the main road. The New Pornographers blared from my speakers, testing their limits, and possibly those of the passengers in the car to my left. I turned down the volume a smidge, probably prolonging the lifespan of my eardrums in the process. What can I say? I was in a good mood.

The workweek at my construction job was over and I'd be spending this afternoon and the remainder of the weekend on my second job—the one I was beginning to discover I was meant to do. I'd been working for the Baseball Academy for about a year and a half now, and despite my initial reservations, I was loving it.

I got to spend my time playing ball and coaching elite players, some of whom had a real shot at what I once saw as my future.

Fate and poor judgement had gotten in the way of my dreams, but I could still be a part of it all by helping to coach these high-level players. I'm not saying it didn't still sting when I thought of what could have been, but it was getting easier as time went on. And I was learning a ton on the job. It's one thing to be a player and another to be a coach. I was starting to see a future I'd never allowed myself to envision before.

Before the Academy hired me, I'd been a bit of an embarrassment. Even I can admit it. I'd been crashing in my parents' basement since dropping out of college halfway through, and most nights were spent feeling sorry for myself and getting drunk with my best friend, Brett. How I managed to keep that shit up for over two years is beyond me. But I finally pulled my head out of my ass with the help of Brett and my sister, Laney.

She was way better at adulting than me. She'd had to be. Laney got knocked up her freshman year of college and still managed to finish her associate's degree, get a decent-paying job, and raise her son. I'm not ashamed to admit Rocco probably rivals Brett as my best friend, even though he's only six. We've got an awesome relationship—one Laney claims is so strong because of our similar levels of maturity. Whatever. He's a cool kid. I like to think I had something to do with that.

I was even teaching Rocco how to play ball, although at this point our goal was getting him to focus long enough to avoid getting hit in the head. One step at a time. Laney is...how can I put this? Hell, there's no good way—she's fucking hopeless when it comes to sports. Or anything requiring basic coordination. I can't even be in the car when she's driving. It was becoming clear that Rocco's future as an athlete rested solely on

my coaching abilities and anything his stepdad, Nate, could impart.

I pulled my Jeep into the staff lot of the Academy and spotted Gerry, one of the senior coaches, coming out the side door. As usual, his rotund belly preceded the rest of him through the doorway. I raised my hand in greeting as I parked and got out.

"Just the guy I wanted to see!" Gerry greeted me with his gravelly voice.

I grabbed my bag out of the back and threw him a chin lift. "Oh yeah?"

"Buzz and I need you to check out a pitcher this weekend. Sophomore at North—name's Miller. Two o'clock. Home game."

I wracked my brain trying to come up with a face, but the name didn't ring any bells. I prided myself on keeping track of the local high school talent. It was our bread and butter. I shot Gerry a questioning look and he nodded.

"Don't worry. You haven't been slacking. He's new in town." Gerry handed me a sticky note with just two words written on it. *Jay Miller.* Far be it from him to consider entering the digital age and shoot me a text or e-mail.

"And they let him on the team mid-season? Must be good." I raised an eyebrow.

"You tell me. I'm running out but I'll catch you later," he said, brushing past me. "And have a talk with Jameson—kid's getting too big for his britches!"

I groaned inwardly. Brad Jameson was an asshole, plain and simple. Spoiled kid with too much money and not enough talent. We'd tried several times over the last couple years to let him down gently and prepare him for a future that did not involve baseball—unless coaching little league counted. But the kid refused to listen, and his parents kept sending the payments to continue his training.

Things were going to come to a head at some point and I, for one, was not looking forward to it.

If anyone could smooth it over in the end, though, it was Gerry. He's exactly what you'd picture when you think of an old-school baseball coach—shaggy graying hair, ever-present cap, toothpick permanently clenched between his teeth, a gruff exterior, and not a man to waste words. He knew his shit inside and out, and I was lucky to have him as a mentor.

I waved him off and headed toward the staff locker room. I needed to shower the grime and sweat from the job site off before I changed into my uniform and started training. Just as I passed by the open door of the players' locker room, an object flew in front of my face, missing me by inches as it sailed by and landed unceremoniously on the floor to my right. A jock strap. You have got to be shitting me.

One glance into the room told me what I already knew. I stepped inside and crossed my arms over my chest.

"Maybe once they drop you'll be able to get some poor chick to suck you off." Brad Jameson stood with his back to me, guffawing at his own lame-ass joke and facing one of the younger guys whose jock strap Brad had obviously just tossed into the hallway. This was a quintessential Brad move. Who in God's name touches another guy's nut bucket? You just don't do that—it's an unwritten rule—unwritten because anyone with a dick knows that's the last place you want your hand. Except Brad, for some inexplicable reason. It's like the kid was trying to take douchebag to a whole new level. He was succeeding spectacularly.

Chris, the younger player, stood with a towel wrapped around his skinny waist, his face a deep crimson, further highlighting his unfortunate case of acne. He stiffened as he caught sight of me, but

I shook my head in a silent cue to leave my presence a secret for the moment.

"Doubtful," came another comment from someone hidden behind a row of lockers. Ah, Brad's lackey, Dell. The kid couldn't come up with an original thought to save his life. A couple players to my right occupied themselves by tying their cleats and pretending not to hear the exchange.

"True…he'd have to get it up first. Have you ever even had a boner, *Christian*?" Brad taunted and bent closer as the kid squirmed.

What an asshole.

"Well, ladies," I finally made my presence known. "Glad to see you've got extra time on your hands to gossip."

Brad stood straight and whirled around, clearly surprised at being caught. He quickly schooled his features, however, and assumed his usual "my shit don't stink" countenance, crossing his arms over his bare chest and shrugging.

I looked at my watch. "Fifteen minutes till batting practice. Should give you girls plenty of time to do shuttle runs. You've got sixty seconds to get dressed and get your asses out there." I knew if I didn't include Chris, it would just make things worse for him, so I made sure to address everyone in the room. I understood why kids didn't stand up for one another—it didn't mean I had to like it, but I understood it. The teenage hierarchy is a complex and fragile structure, and one you don't mess with lightly. I had to trust that the Chrises of the world would win out in the end, and it was my job to offer encouragement and a listening ear when the spotlight was off. It looked like I'd be having more than one conversation off the field tonight.

"Yo!" I hollered as I walked in the front door to my townhouse. "Are we going to Jake's tonight or—" I stopped dead in my tracks and quickly spun back around to face the door. The briefest glance at the couch had revealed more than I'm sure the girl straddling Brett's lap would prefer.

"Shit!" Brett and I said simultaneously. I heard some rustling and whispering behind me.

"Hey, sorry guys. But you do know you have a room upstairs, right, asshole?" I said into the door.

Brett just grunted at me which made me grin. I had to say, the girl was pretty hot from what I'd seen.

"Oh, God, this is so embarrassing," I heard a female whisper just before the girl brushed past me and opened the door. Her shirt was still half off, but at least her bra was back on.

"I'll call you later, Ginger!" Brett yelled behind her. Something told me she may not be answering her phone for a few days.

I finally turned back to the room just as a *Men's Health* magazine whizzed by my face. What was it with people throwing things at me today?

"I wasn't expecting you home so soon," Brett said, giving his chin a good scratch. He was growing a beard—or attempting to—and had recently gotten gauges in his ears as well. It seemed the chicks were digging this new look. I had to say, before, he looked about eighteen instead of twenty-four, so it was time for a change.

"That's pretty obvious," I responded, smile firmly in place. "So, I guess you're free to go to Jake's then?" He threw a shoe at me this time, but I caught it, no problem.

"Why are you home so early? I thought you had training." Brett got up and walked to the kitchen. I trailed behind. We'd moved into this townhouse in High Point last year, and while it wasn't anything to write home about, we'd been pleased with the

place so far. Living with your best friend always leads to some great times, and it was definitely a step toward overdue adulthood for me. I'd gone from my parents' house to my sister's before finally paying rent on my own place with Brett. Yeah, definitely overdue.

"I wrapped things up early so I could have a chat with that Jameson kid, but the little prick skipped out on me." I was still pissed off.

Brett handed me a beer from the fridge and we both popped ours open. I tossed my cap over my shoulder and straight into the open trash can. Brett's landed somewhere in a vicinity of the sink. I shook my head as if ashamed and, as usual, he completely ignored me.

"Somebody needs to hand that kid his ass," Brett said, shaking his head. He'd been my sounding board regarding the little shit on many occasions.

I laughed mirthlessly. "I wish to hell I could be the one to do it, but I kind of like being employed. I would suggest you do it, but, well…" I let that sit out there. Brett was damn scrawny and I loved giving him shit about it. But he was good at dealing back in kind.

"And you wouldn't want to mess up that pretty-boy face of yours anyway," he threw back at me. "Tell me, exactly how long did you spend getting ready this morning, princess?"

I punched him in the arm and he pretended it didn't hurt.

I told Brett about Brad's disturbing locker-room behavior, and he was appropriately appalled. I may not have caught up with Brad after training, but I had been able to pull Chris aside. I'd tried to share some tips on how to maybe fit in a little better without becoming an asshole himself. Truthfully, sometimes all it took was one new impression and a bully's attention could be diverted. I'd been half tempted to communicate the age-old prison strategy of

beating someone to shit on your first day to keep people from messing with you, but even I knew that would be unwise.

"Hey, I'm going to check out some new talent tomorrow for Gerry and Buzz. You wanna come?" Brett and I had always shared a love of baseball—it was one of the main reasons we'd become friends in the first place. He revered the game almost as much as I did. He also had a damn good eye, even if he was kind of a shit player, so I often used his help.

"Got nothing better to do now that you've scared Ginger off." He set down his beer and pointed at my face. "You're gonna pay for that if she doesn't take my call, asswipe."

"Noted." My mouth tugged. It was good seeing Brett feeling more confident around girls these days. "But, just in case, let's head out in a bit and check out the talent at Jake's. Never hurts to have a back-up." I raised an eyebrow.

He sighed in resignation. "Whatever."

I headed upstairs, drink in hand, to take yet another shower before our night out. I had a good feeling.

The good feeling from the night before had not panned out as I hoped. I'd had a decent time shooting the shit with Brett and a couple other guys, but I wasn't feeling any of the girls at the bar. I decided to attribute my positive premonitions to the player I'd be scouting today instead.

I found a parking spot up close by the field at North High School. It was a good day to play ball. The sky was clear and the temperature was ideal, sitting in the low seventies. I grabbed my notebook and headed for the fence to check out pregame warmup. Brett planned to meet me at the field later since I liked to show up

early. I adjusted my cap and looked over the sea of uniforms for an unfamiliar number.

There he was. Number 52.

The kid was tall for his age, probably just under six feet, and he had a mess of dirty blond hair sticking out from under his blue cap. He was lanky as shit, but held himself confidently. His glove raised and lowered naturally as he and his teammate tossed the ball back and forth. It was impossible to see what kind of talent he may or may not have from just watching him play catch, but that was why I was prepared to stand against this fence for the rest of the afternoon.

I knew the starting pitcher for North, a senior named Wes Hartfield. He wasn't too shabby. North's record was 4-2 so far this season, and Wes had a lot to do with that. We'd worked with one of the coaches to try and set up some extra training sessions with Wes, but it was a no-go. His parents were set on him joining the family business out of high school and didn't want to shell out the money for a future they didn't see for their kid. It was a shame, but Wes didn't seem willing to fight them on it, so we'd let it lie.

His impending graduation opened up the spot for a starting pitcher on the team next season, and I could think of a couple guys who'd be gunning for it. I'd have to see for myself if this new kid could give them a run for their money.

The coach called the players in for a chat and I signaled one of the assistant coaches, a guy named Kirk. He jogged over, pulling his cap off and wiping his brow with his shirtsleeve.

We shook hands over the fence.

"Good to see you, Monroe," he greeted me.

I gave him a chin lift. "You too, man. Just wanted to give you a heads up that I'm here for Gerry and Buzz today. We're checking out the new kid."

His mouth lifted on one side in a knowing grin. "Damn, you move fast. The kid just got here last week."

"That means we're already a week behind," I threw back at him with my own grin.

That got a small chuckle out of Kirk. He settled his cap back on his head and looked to the side. "Well, patience will have to be your virtue today because he'll be riding the bench until probably the eighth. Wes has earned his time, and we got Anders and Bates fighting for relief pitcher already." He didn't look pleased.

"What's the story?" I asked.

Kirk didn't look at me or answer for several moments so I waited. Finally, he spoke. "You ask me, we could win the whole goddamn thing if we put Miller in starting today. But you know how this works—nothing's that simple."

I nodded. You can't escape politics, even in America's favorite pastime. "Well, Kirk, it's like you said—patience."

He nodded back and we both heard his name being called from across the field.

"Catch you later, Monroe. Make sure you stick around." He pointed at me as he turned and jogged toward the team.

Nothing was going to make me move from my spot today—not after that conversation.

Chapter Two

HELLO, MONDAY

EMERSON

"Do you want some dinner? I can whip something up." I lurked in the doorway to the bedroom, feeling slightly out of place. Which was odd considering this was my own house.

My brother looked up from his book, his dirty blond hair hanging over one eye. My hand itched for a pair of scissors so I could trim the messy mop right then. "Sorry, what?"

Instead, I felt my lips tip up. I remembered getting caught up in reading to the point where outside noises vanished. It was one of the things we had in common. "Dinner," I prompted.

"Oh." He self-consciously combed the errant hairs back with one hand while his blue eyes dropped back down. "I'll just fix myself a sandwich or something. You don't need to worry about me."

I took a few steps into the room. "Jay, I'm happy to make you something. I'm making myself a salad—I can easily put a meal together for you while I'm at it." He'd been refusing all my offers

of help or any type of real engagement since he'd moved in the week before. It was beginning to truly concern me.

He attempted a half smile and just shook his head.

I didn't want to push, but this was getting ridiculous. He was my brother, for God's sake. Well, technically my half-brother, but I loved him with my whole heart. Which was why it was so hard to see him this way—so unsure of his place, and obviously not wanting to make even the smallest ripple in my normally structured and orderly life. He'd always been a kid who was so comfortable in his own skin, it was unnerving to see him rattled.

"Okay," I finally conceded. "You know where everything is…" I trailed off, then switched tack. "You know, reading from paper as opposed to a screen increases your degree of comprehension and mental recall. Just thought you'd want to know you're making good choices." I shrugged.

He looked up again, and this time his grin was genuine. My inane knack for trivia always used to entertain him. I was pleased to see it could still make a dent.

"I'll file that away," he responded, his tone warmer this time.

"You do that." I turned to leave the room. But one glance back when I reached the doorway revealed his shoulders slumping in a defeated sigh.

"Crackers," I muttered under my breath. This wasn't how it was supposed to be. This wasn't the scenario I'd envisioned a month ago when I'd spoken with our mother and we'd agreed it would be best for Jay to move in with me.

"We'll be fine, Mom," I'd said for the fourth time. "You and Aldo have been wanting to do this forever. Lord knows he'll relish the chance to drive that ridiculous camper in any direction you point."

I heard a sigh and a small hum on the other end of the line.

"This is going to be our second act, Emmy. The craft-fair circuit are my people, you know what I mean?" I wanted to confess that I didn't know what she meant at all. An itinerant life on the road with uncertainty and strangers around every bend was my version of a fresh hell, but I supposed she was right. This spontaneous and somewhat flighty behavior was in no way surprising coming from the woman who called herself my "life vessel."

"I just didn't understand how strongly he felt about this," she continued. "We've moved a few times before and he's never said a word." I bit my tongue to hold back a sardonic laugh. "A few" was putting it lightly. My mother and stepfather led a practically nomadic lifestyle, always dragging Jay with them wherever the wind led. It wasn't surprising to me in the least that Jay finally wanted to put down roots somewhere. I suppressed the urge to ask why they couldn't wait another couple years until Jay could at least graduate high school. Any answer I'd receive would be less than satisfying, and more than likely just downright confusing.

Our mother's wanderlust was in her blood, no doubt, but I certainly had not inherited it. All evidence pointed to Jay's not sharing the gene either. Thank God she'd found Aldo to share her erratic tendencies with. He adored her for them, which made me adore him, as incongruous as it sounds.

"Mom, he's almost sixteen. He's thinking about his future— he's thinking about college. I'm not trying to be mean, but you can't expect him to pick up stakes and get a GED, for goodness sake. He wants to be a normal kid."

She gave a long-suffering sigh. "I wasn't suggesting he get a GED, Emmy. We could home school him on the road. Aldo is a whiz in chemistry."

I practically choked. I didn't really think colleges appreciated Aldo's form of chemistry, if you get my drift. And, God love her,

but the only thing an education from Naomi Miller would entail was how to harness the mystical powers of crystals and perhaps give a halfway decent tarot card reading. Science, in her world, mostly came in the fictional variety, and I was guessing she would dedicate much of her tutoring to the history of such useful subjects as witchcraft and the healing virtues of essential oils.

Not helpful to a sophomore boy who just wanted to make friends and play baseball.

"I have plenty of room, and I can have the paperwork drawn up without a problem. Are you absolutely sure this is what all of you want?"

"I want what he wants, and if that's to settle down in one place until he graduates, then I'm happy to let him," she reassured before sighing quietly. "So why do I feel like a terrible mother?" she asked.

That softened my heart. The last thing she was was a terrible mother. Unconventional, yes. Terrible, no. The love in her heart had no bounds and she gave it freely. In all the years growing up with her, never had I doubted either her love or her pride in me.

She just wasn't a traditional mother-type. I'd never had my permission slips signed on time or worn trendy fashions. My lunches were an odd combination of whatever she found in the pantry, sometimes to the great envy of lunch-table-mates when they'd spied chocolate bars and raisins in my brown paper sacks instead of turkey sandwiches and apple slices.

And nothing fazed her, or Aldo for that matter. A snide comment from another parent rolled right off her back. A request from the principal to please ensure my prompt arrival at school in the mornings was met with a beautiful smile and an offer to check his chakras.

No—Naomi was in no sense traditional. She was more of a free-spirited, sometimes-forgets-to-put-shoes-on, earth-mother.

And I'd always accepted that. I had not, however, emulated it. From an early age, I'd known what I wanted, and I was determined to work toward my goals. So, around third grade, I began to set my own alarm clock, pack my own lunches, and forge my mother's signature on permission slips. I was going to succeed, and the world would be mine to conquer.

But I could do all that and still love my mother.

"Mom, I love you. Jay loves you. You're a good mother. You drive us nuts sometimes, but there's no one better."

I could hear the tears in her voice. "I love you too, my sweet girl."

"Now, when are you bringing him down?"

And that was how I had inherited my very own "charge" as they used to say. I was the official temporary guardian of my fifteen-year-old brother and I was determined he'd feel at home in my—our—house. It was just going to take a bit more work than I'd anticipated.

And having unexpected hiccups in my life was something I didn't handle all that well.

"Fudgesicles!"

I clutched my pinkie toe which had just made solid contact with the leg of my bed. My phone clattered to the hardwood and I could hear the faint sound of Ari's voice on the other end of the line.

Blowing my hair out of my eyes, I retrieved the phone and sat

on the bed. I cradled my poor toe in my hand. Hello, Monday, it's awesome to see you too.

I brought the phone back to my ear as Ari yelled, "What the hell?! Did you just throw your phone at the wall?"

"I dropped it. My bed tried to kill me."

"That's a new one," Ari replied. "You okay?"

"I'm sure my toe will grow back, don't worry. Sorry, go ahead with what you were saying." I tested my toe by placing my foot gingerly on the floor and standing. Okay, not too bad, but my shoe choice for the day would have to be amended. Crap. I could have really used my heels today to face off with Craig.

Ari's voice kicked up on the other end of the line. "So, what part did I lose you at?"

"I heard the part about Elliot being a d-i-c-k to your mom in the backyard." I disliked Elliot. Intensely.

She sighed. "You know you're allowed to say the word, right? You're an adult. Dick! Say it with me now."

I echoed her sigh. This was one of our constant back-and-forths. Ari was what I would classify as an Olympic-level cusser. I, on the other hand, couldn't even imagine a curse crossing my lips. Sure, I mentally cussed sometimes, but never aloud. My father's voice always lurked in the back of my mind, telling me that well-bred women didn't curse.

"Yes, Ari. Go on." She knew I'd never cave so she gave up immediately. I limped my way to the bathroom to finish getting ready for work.

"Needless to say, Mamá didn't take that shit. She told him he could cook his own dinner if he didn't like what was on his plate. I don't know, Em, he's so sweet when it's just the two of us. I don't understand why he has to be such an ass sometimes." She sounded defeated.

This wasn't the first time we'd hashed out this dilemma. I'd seen Ari's boyfriend treat her all right, but I wouldn't ever classify his behavior as *sweet*. Elliot's first priority is Elliot. He's the kind of guy who would walk into a parking meter because he was too busy admiring his own reflection in a store window. And his idea of a thoughtful birthday present was a pair of tickets to see *his* favorite band. Sweet? I don't think so.

Ari's voice dropped and she continued, "And you know the sex is smoking." She practically purred. I set down my hairbrush and closed my eyes to keep my breakfast from reappearing. I did not need to hear about Elliot's magical penis again. Unless it held the cure for cancer, I was of the opinion that the world could do without it.

But being a good friend meant more listening and less lecturing. "Yes, Ari, I'm aware that Elliot…satisfies you." I was hoping my acknowledgement of his bedroom skills would propel the conversation forward—to other topics.

"Anyway, he left and I got another lecture from Mamá on my terrible taste in men."

Did I mention I love Ari's mom?

"I hate to say it, Ari, but did you really expect things to go well? You have met your mother before, right?"

"Shut it, bitch," she laughed. "I know, but there is this part of me that's compelled to try anyway. One of these days, she'll break."

I had to smile at her optimism—and guts. "Where was your dad during all of this?" I couldn't imagine Mr. Amante standing by while someone insulted his wife's cooking, no matter how subtly.

"Papá had to work late. Turns out that was a good thing in the end. I guess Elliot and I will just lay low for a while. I don't want to scare him off."

I had to bite my tongue. Hard. Ariana is beautiful, intelligent, talented, funny, and all-around wonderful. She deserved so much better than a jerk like Elliot. Why couldn't she see that?

I made a noncommittal noise, then looked at my watch. Darn it! I was going to be late if I didn't get moving. And I could not be late today, of all days.

I thought briefly about checking in with Jay, but I knew he'd already be gone on the bus and wouldn't answer his phone. I'd have to catch him in the evening.

"I'm sorry, but I have to run."

"Oh, shit!" Ari responded. "I totally got sidetracked and forgot today is the day!" She squealed a bit and it made me grin. "You're going to do awesome! Kick Craig's ass, woman!"

"Yes, ma'am." I mock saluted even though she couldn't see me. "I'll call you later."

I set the phone on the bathroom counter and caught my own eyes in the mirror. "You can do this, Emerson. You were born for this." My resolve in place, I swiped on my favorite red lipstick and prepared for the day ahead.

I crossed my legs and ordered myself to stay still as I sat in a chair outside Thomas Wheeler's office. Fidgeting would only indicate nervousness and weakness, so it was essential I maintain a calm and collected demeanor. My colleague and nemesis, Craig Pendleton, occupied the chair to my left as we both waited for our meeting with one of the managing partners at the law offices of Jefferson, Wheeler, and Schenk.

Craig and I were both fourth-year associates, and it was no secret that one of us would eventually be weeded out before a part-

nership was offered to the final one standing. And I fully intended to be the victor when a partnership was on the table. I'd busted my butt to be an indispensable asset to the firm, always making myself available, and billing more than the required hours, while also carving out time for pro bono cases. And I would continue to do so, no matter what.

I chanced a sideways glance at Craig and noticed his eyes were firmly planted on my crossed legs. I felt the urge to pull my skirt down, even though it sat at a perfectly modest length. Blech. I turned my head fully toward him, forcing his eyes up to mine. He didn't even have the decency to blush. A cunning grin crossed his unsettlingly pouty lips, and it suddenly occurred to me that he bore an uncanny resemblance to that creepy actor, Cillian Murphy. I repressed a shudder. Once I got the partnership, maybe Craig could move to L.A. and be a movie villain. The thought made me snicker inwardly.

"Ms. Scott, Mr. Pendleton, come on in." The door to Thomas Wheeler's office had opened and he beckoned us both inside. Mr. Wheeler was my favorite of the managing partners. He was also the only one who addressed me as "Ms. Scott" instead of "Emerson," which would not have bothered me except Craig was referred to as "Mr. Pendleton" by all three managing partners.

Mr. Wheeler crossed to the other side of his large mahogany desk and sank into his plush leather chair. He was a tall man and kept himself in decent shape through healthy eating and an even healthier appetite for golf and racquetball. His square jaw and neatly trimmed salt-and-pepper hair made a strong impression, along with his confident bearing.

He folded his hands on the desk in front of him as Craig and I settled in. "So, I know you're both aware we had to let Mr. Anderson go last week." Travis Anderson had been another of the

fourth-year associates in the corporate law department. Despite his sharp intelligence and work ethic, his work had slowly declined over the past year since he and his wife welcomed twins into their family. Travis was a great guy, but there was no slacking off at Jefferson, Wheeler, and Schenk, no matter how important the reason. It hadn't been a huge surprise when he'd been dismissed. I'd seen associates drop like flies in the past four years. But that wasn't going to be me.

Craig cleared his throat, and I knew some brown-nosing comment was soon to follow. "Well, sir, some people just don't have their priorities in order." I barely resisted making a gagging sound.

Mr. Wheeler merely gave Craig a blank look.

Ha! Insensitive jerk. Take that!

Our boss continued, "At any rate, this leaves us with more work and fewer associates to cover it. I've already reassigned a few projects, but I'll need you each to take on some of the work-load." This was the moment of truth. Travis had been working on several cases, but only one truly mattered: the AgPower agricultural startup. Whoever took that one would be working closely with Mr. Wheeler, an opportunity that was worth its weight in gold.

A project that had started as advising on a simple agricultural startup had now grown into a colossal business opportunity, thanks to a push the client's company had garnered from some big players in the industry. The company was developing a new crop that had the potential to create a biofuel alternative. Handled correctly, this could mean big things for the firm and the lawyers involved. The entire firm had been buzzing about it for weeks, and Travis had become increasingly overwhelmed by the project's scope.

I could feel Craig holding his breath along with me as Mr.

Wheeler pushed two stacks of folders across his desk, one to each of us. My breath whooshed out as I made out the word "AgPower" on the label of my top folder. *Yes!* All those extra hours and volunteering to take on undesirable cases and clients had paid off. I felt like jumping across the desk and hugging Mr. Wheeler. Of course, I would never actually do something so inappropriate. Even thinking it was uncharacteristic of me.

I was so caught up in my thoughts that I didn't notice Craig's reaction at first. He extended his hand across the desk to Mr. Wheeler. "I appreciate the opportunity, sir." It was then that I glanced at Craig's folders. No freaking way! The label on one of his was identical to mine. We were both on the AgPower start-up. I was going to have to work with the dreaded Craig.

I managed to paste on a smile and extend my hand as well. "Thank you, sir. We'll get right on it."

"I know you will. Get up to speed on AgPower for the afternoon meeting. We'll see you in the east conference room at 4:00."

That was our dismissal, so Craig and I crossed to the door. He exited before me and didn't bother holding the door. This was going to be a pleasant few months.

"I can't believe they gave it to both of you!" Ari's indignant expression made me want to hug her. She'd stopped by on her way home from her karaoke hosting gig she did a few nights a week. This was in addition to her full-time job as a receptionist at a realty office and her freelance web design business.

I shrugged because what else could I do. "I know, but I'll just have to put my head down and work my butt off. I just wish it were

Travis instead of Craig." I scrunched up my nose as I thought about Craig's smug face yet again.

"That guy is such a two-faced twat." She shoved a handful of popcorn in her mouth and offered me the bowl.

"Watch your mouth!" I whisper-yelled and took a glance at the hall behind me.

"Excuse the hell out of me," she mumbled over her mouthful of popcorn. "I hate to break it to you, Em, but you should hear the things teenagers say these days. It would burn your delicate ears clean off."

I put a hand up, not wanting to acknowledge the fact that I'd probably need a professional translator to understand half the words that came out of any teenager's mouth. "Please don't remind me. He's already about a foot taller than me. I don't need another indication of how grown up he is. That kid is a statistical anomaly —what is Aldo? Five-foot-seven, maybe?" I asked.

Ari shrugged and offered me the popcorn again. I took a handful and played with a piece between my fingers. "All he does is stay in his room—that is, when he's here at all. He's so focused on not being a bother that I hardly get a chance to see him."

She grabbed my hand. "Hey, just give him time to settle in and he'll come out of his shell."

I gave her a sad smile. "Yeah, I guess. But I'm going to be up to my ears on this case and keeping an eye on Craig. It's not like I'll be here a lot. I feel bad."

"Look. You're both making the best out of a difficult situation. You focus on work and the two-faced twat, and Jay will take care of himself."

I swatted at her for cussing again. "I know he's perfectly capable of taking care of himself, but that doesn't mean he should have to. He's only fifteen, for crying out loud."

"With the soul of a fifty-year-old." She gave me a knowing look. And she was not wrong.

I'd tried talking to him earlier in the evening, but he'd gently brushed me off again, citing homework that needed his attention. I'd have to be persistent if I wanted him to feel at home, and not like I was merely tolerating his presence.

"Didn't you say he has a game this coming weekend? We'll go and cheer him on—embarrass the shit out of him. That right there is how a brother knows he's loved." Ari winked at me. She would know. She comes from a family of four kids, and all they ever seem to do is bicker and throw insults. It had been that way since we were kids living next door to one another.

The thought of going to Jay's game made me smile. My kid brother's passion had always been baseball. From the moment he'd shoved his tiny hand into his first glove at the age of three, it had become an obsession. No matter how many times our mom and Aldo had moved him to different cities and different schools, the one thing that remained constant was baseball. There was always a home for Jay on any school or league's team.

In fact, it was one of the main reasons he'd asked to live with me until he finished out high school. There were no teams on the craft fair circuit—or the home-school program run by one self-proclaimed psychic and her pot-smoking partner. And I was more than happy to have him.

"It's a date," I told Ari, although we both knew I wouldn't embarrass Jay. She'd do that all on her own.

Ari yawned, which was contagious.

I tried to stifle mine. "I still have these files and e-mails to look over before the morning, and I'm sure you have some dirty text messages to send."

She pretended to be offended but it didn't last more than a

second. "Well, far be it from me to get in the way of you crushing Craig like the insignificant little pest he is." She bent down and began fastening the buckle of her shoe.

The mental image was pleasing, I had to admit. "Besides that, I've got to work extra hard to make an impression with Wheeler. If it were up to Jefferson and Schenk, I wouldn't be anywhere near a case this important. Those two are old-school boys' club all the way." It was a reality in my profession—one I'd been fully aware of before I decided to pursue a law degree. It was also the reason I'd taken golf lessons during all my school breaks and tried to schedule rounds with other lawyers whenever possible. Truthfully, I hated golf, but it was all part of the bigger picture. Show you're a team player and they might forget you don't have a penis.

Not to say that was the reality across all law firms, but it certainly was in mine—and in the majority of established firms like ours. Deals were still made in locker rooms and on golf courses, as archaic as that may be. But I had to believe a killer work ethic could win out in the end.

"Neanderthal mentality." Ari shook her head. "It might be fun in the bedroom, but that's where it needs to stay." She arched her eyebrows and her piercing winked at me.

I wrinkled my nose at her in return which made her laugh. "TMI, Ari." Not that I could ever stop her from sharing. The girl had always been an open book. Sometimes I found myself wishing I could be more like Ari, but I couldn't ever release my white-knuckle grip on my control in that way. I had an innate need to be taken seriously.

She abandoned her shoe. "Oh, come on! You can't tell me you wouldn't like a little bit of alpha male in your life. And maybe a spanking or two?" Now she was just baiting me with her waggling brows and ridiculous grin.

"Shut up!" I covered my ears and she threw a handful of popcorn at me. Nobody knew me better than Ari, which was why it was so easy for her to tease me. "You go ahead and get your paddle, just leave me out of it."

She cackled. "I may just have to give Elliot a call."

Oh, eww.

"Or you could just crash here," I suggested. She lived twenty minutes away and I hated the thought of her driving home after working two shifts today.

"You sound like Mamá." She fake scowled at me. "And you're just jealous because it's been...wait, how long *has* it been since you got laid?"

I huffed at her. "I don't know. When did David and I break up?" Truthfully, I didn't understand what the big deal was with sex. It was sometimes pleasant, other times awkward, and a few times, downright gross.

"Girl, that was over six months ago. Your vibrator must be working overtime." Again with the baiting.

I covered my face with a throw pillow. "Will you please shut up!" I knew my face was crimson.

She forcefully pulled the pillow off my face. "I'm just messing with you. You work too hard and you need to cut loose. Go on a date. Something!"

"I'll cut loose when I'm dead. Right now, I have a gazillion e-mails to go through and a brother to figure out." And I didn't want to talk about vibrators. Or dates. "And, besides, I can't be in a relationship while this case is in progress. I need to stay completely focused—no distractions." I pointed at her.

"Well, you'll still have to put up with me—and Jay—but I get it," she responded, finishing with the buckles of her strappy heels. She rose from the couch and adjusted her tank top over her ample

chest. I let myself be a little jealous of her endowments for a moment before pushing the thought aside. Ari is half Italian and half Puerto Rican—she got the Puerto Rican curves and the attitude of both cultures. Combine that with her dyed burgundy hair and her piercings and tattoos, and you had one unforgettable woman.

I looked down at my modest, baby-pink silk pajamas covering my slim but unremarkable build. The only thing noteworthy about me was probably my natural auburn locks, but there was nothing wrong with that. Some people were made to stand out and others were made to be the cogs in the machine. And I was a darn good cog. And, further, when it came to my career, I was bound for greatness. I just had to be persistent and play the game.

Chapter Three

THE JOYRIDE AND THE GIANT PISTACHIO

G AVIN

"He did what?!" I covered my eyes with one hand and leaned back against the refrigerator, phone still glued to my ear.

"You heard me!" Gerry growled from the other end.

Shit.

"Buzz is about to shit a brick. You wanna tell me exactly what you said to that kid to make him do something this stupid?"

"What makes you think it was something I said?!" I tried to defend myself but it was really no use with Gerry.

"Maybe the fact that he said *you told him to do it!*"

"No I didn't!" And that was no lie. I would never tell a four-teen-year-old kid to take a car for a joyride—especially in a car that belonged to someone else. A very expensive car that belonged to someone else.

It seemed Chris had taken my advice to the extreme in an attempt to prove himself to some of the older players. He'd

accepted a dare to lift the keys to Brad Jameson's neighbor's BMW Z4 and take it for a spin. The similarity to my own youthful indiscretion wasn't lost on me. Thankfully, though, no one had been hurt this time. But that didn't mean no one was in trouble. Chris Hardacre was in deep shit. And it seemed Jameson and his buddies had clammed up regarding their part in the whole fiasco.

I thought back to my conversation with Chris from the other night. To my best recollection, I'd told him to stay cool and not let the other guys see that they intimidated him. We'd talked about fitting in, but this definitely wasn't what I had meant.

Shit.

"All right, Gerry, calm down. I'm gonna call Chris's parents and find out exactly what's going on. Surely the neighbor will drop the charges when he understands the circumstances."

"You'd better hope to hell he does! You call me back the minute you get any info. I don't want this kid's ass swinging in the wind, you hear me?!"

"Loud and clear. I got this."

I so totally did not have this. Shit.

The first thing I did after hanging up with the Hardacres was to call my fairy godmother. Oh, you didn't mishear. I have a real-life fairy godmother. She's about five feet tall, has the mouth of a sailor, and I don't ever cross her if I can help it—but she's the real deal. Fiona Pierce makes things happen. And if there were ever a time when I needed something good to happen, it was now.

"What's up, Gav?" she answered breathlessly. I heard loud male cursing in the background, followed by female laughter.

"Is that Mark? Are you torturing him?" Fiona is Mark's boyfriend—yes, my boss, Mark—and the two love to go at it.

Wait. Sorry. Okay, yeah, that too.

"I'm over at Bailey's and we're watching Jake and Mark try to put together the crib for the baby. It's hilarious. For two guys who work with their hands all day, they are remarkably bad at this." She snickered.

Jake is Mark's brother, and he and his wife, Bailey, were expecting a kid in a couple months. It was going to be like watching a science experiment gone wrong—or maybe a car crash. Bailey is probably the last person on earth I'd label as maternal. I'd call Jake maternal before I'd call Bailey that, and that dude could kick my ass. Nevertheless, the train had left the station and we were just waiting for the big day.

I heard Mark's voice in the background. "Who the hell are you talking to, Shortcake?"

She didn't even bother covering the phone. "It's Gavin. Do you want me to ask him to come over and help?"

Bailey's voice chimed in, "How many burly dudes does it take to put a crib together? There's got to be a joke in there somewhere."

"Shut it, Irish!" That had to be Jake. "We're just getting our bearings."

This caused another round of female laughter.

"It seems they don't want your help, Gavin. Oh, sorry. You called me. Why was that again?"

I fought a groan. I might have found this a lot funnier if I didn't have the weight of Chris's situation on my mind. I explained the dilemma to Fiona, including the fact that the Hardacres didn't have much money for a lawyer. It was enough that they were springing for training, but the cost of an expensive (read: good) attorney

would break them. Fiona had a lot of connections, due to both her family's social status and her personality and general inability to stay out of everyone's business. In fact, she'd been the one to get me an interview at the Baseball Academy in the first place.

Like I said, she's a freaking fairy godmother.

"I'm on it!" she said, and hung up.

I paced the kitchen, wracking my brain for any ideas of how to make this go away. I could call Brad's parents and ask them to intervene, but I was guessing they would be too preoccupied with protecting Brad to want to help. But a fourteen-year-old kid was facing possible felony charges just for being stupid, something I was well versed in. I had to do something.

Twenty minutes later, my phone rang, but this time it was Jake. "Yo, Junior!" he greeted.

"Hey, man. Did you finish the crib?"

He mumbled something I couldn't make out.

"Huh?"

"I said Bailey took over."

I couldn't help it. Despite the shitstorm brewing on my end, that was fucking hilarious. I burst out laughing.

"Yeah, yeah. Laugh it up. The instructions were in Japanese, for Christ's sake! Now, shut up or I won't help you."

That did the trick and I zipped my trap.

"Fiona's fancy lawyer is in Fiji or something, but I called another lawyer here in town. We kind of worked with her before, and she agreed to hear your kid out. Got a pen?"

I quickly grabbed a pen and paper and jotted down the name and number.

Emerson Scott. What the hell kind of name is that for a woman? I immediately pictured a pointy-nosed college professor. Or maybe some older woman who dressed like a dude. It didn't

matter, though. I had a lead and that was all I cared about. Chris's future couldn't be trusted to an overworked court-appointed attorney.

After passing the information on to the Hardacres, I was unsure what to do with myself. I ended up calling Gerry to get him up to speed and then went upstairs to my computer. I had work to do, and since there was nothing else I could do for Chris tonight, I got down to it.

The next afternoon, I found myself back at North High School, leaning against the fence as I'd done the past weekend. Kirk hadn't been blowing smoke up my ass. This Miller kid had the touch. I'd only seen him pitch one inning, but his raw talent was stunning. And since I hadn't been able to catch him after the game, Gerry and I had decided I should become a fixture at team practice and weekday games. In other words, I was to develop stalking tendencies.

Still preoccupied by my numerous phone conversations the previous night, I rubbed my bloodshot eyes and waited for the team to take the field. Sleep had been elusive, even though I'd ended the night somewhat confident that Chris would have a good lawyer. Ms. Scott was meeting with the Hardacres today and I was anxious to hear how it went. Guilt gnawed at my gut over the part I'd played in this debacle.

It wasn't long before the players and coaches started trickling onto the field. I could pinpoint the moment Kirk caught sight of me because his chin sank into his chest and his head shook with his laughter. He gave me a sign that he'd come talk to me soon, so I watched the kids warm up.

About twenty minutes later, it was all I could do to keep myself from jumping the fence and hugging the shit out of the Miller kid. He'd been throwing pitches to the backup catcher, and each one was better than the one before it. And this was just practice! His fastball was tight as shit and his curve dropped like a freaking bomb when it hit the strike zone. I had to have this kid at the Academy.

By the time Kirk made his way over to me, I was practically salivating like a dog with a juicy ribeye. And that's when Kirk dealt the crushing blow.

"Sorry to say, Monroe, but it's not gonna happen. Kid's got no money. Coach even talked to him, but he was adamant. Don't know anything about his home life since he's new, but he seems like a straight shooter."

"Shit," I replied. The Academy did payment plans, of course, and we had different levels of training, but there was no scholarship system in place.

Kirk's lips quirked to the side. "I'll tell you what I can do. I can't give out his personal info to you, but I can give his parents a shout and ask them to call you to chat. That's the best I can give you, though."

I nodded distractedly, my eyes drawn again to the kid as he threw a perfect slider. Damn.

After practice, I drove over to the Academy to update Gerry since he refused to keep his damn phone turned on. But before I could make my way to his office, I caught sight of Chris coming out of the locker room, arms full of gear. Shit. Well, I guess I should have expected this.

"Chris!" I called out. He turned and as soon as he saw me, his lower lip started to tremble a bit. I looked away to give him a chance to gather himself.

"My parents are waiting in the parking lot," was all he said. His shoulders were slumped and he had dark circles under his eyes.

"Man, I'm so sorry about all this." I shook my head. "I never meant to—"

He cut me off. "I know. I'm sorry. I shouldn't have said anything. I was just really panicked, you know."

I nodded and stepped closer. "Yeah. I bet."

"Anyway, thanks for hooking us up with that lawyer. She's gonna take my case p...pora bono?"

I grinned. "Pro bono."

"Yeah," he replied, hitching his gear back up in his arms. "Anyway, she's pretty sure she can make it go away with just a fine and probably community service since I didn't mean to really steal the car."

I allowed myself a small grin. "You just had to pick a Benz, didn't you?"

The side of his mouth lifted in return. "Go big or go home, right?"

I let out a chuckle, then gestured to the gear. "This your decision or your parents'?"

"Well, I can't say I'll be disappointed not to hang out with Brad and Dell anymore, but it was my parents' choice. They said the money for the fines and court fees has to come from somewhere, and it's part of my punishment. But I may be able to come back next year." He shrugged.

"I hope you do." I cuffed the side of his head. "You let me know if you need anything, okay?"

He shifted uncomfortably. "Actually, um, do you think you might be able to come to court? You know, just to have a friend there?"

I smiled. "You bet. Just leave a message with the details and I'll be there."

He lifted his chin at me and turned toward the door. "Thanks, Coach."

Damn.

The following morning, I was still thinking about Chris as I put on my hard hat and made my way around the back of the apartment building our crew was working on. The rest of the crew was already there, along with Mark and some outside contractors. I was about to go over and give Mark shit about the crib when my phone rang. Unknown number.

"Hello?"

"Hello there."

It was a woman's voice—one I didn't recognize. When she didn't continue, I pulled the phone from my ear, thinking we were disconnected. We weren't.

"Hi," I said warily. "Who am I speaking with?"

"It's Naomi. Jupiter's mother." Her voice was light and airy.

This in no way cleared up my confusion.

"Jupiter?" This had to be a joke.

"Yes. They told me to call you. They said you'd be expecting my call," she said, as if a little put out. I had to wonder who "they" were, and I was beginning to fear it was "the voices."

"I'm sorry, ma'am—"

She cut me off. "Naomi."

I paused. Okay. "I'm sorry, Naomi, but I think you have the wrong number."

"I don't think so. I'm sure I wrote it down correctly. You're Gavin. That's a lovely name."

"Thank you?" Who in the hell was this lady?

"You're very welcome, Gavin."

"Why is it you're calling again?" I tried my nicest voice but I had to get to work and didn't really have time for the crazy train today.

"I told you. It's about Jupiter. They said you wanted to coach him in baseball."

Oh, this was a call about training. That made me feel a bit better, but I didn't know who in the hell Jupiter was. "Um, Jupiter?"

"Right," she responded, and then something seemed to click for her because she laughed. "Oh, I'm sorry. You probably know him as Jay. Jay Miller."

Holy crap! This was the call I'd been waiting for. "Yes! Jay—wow. He's an extraordinary player, ma'a—Naomi. You must be very proud."

"Thank you, Gavin. And, yes, we are very proud."

I put the oddness of the kid's name aside and continued with my best sales pitch, careful to tell her all about our payment plans and the reputation of our center. I included all the stats on former students and their college scholarships, as well as the handful who had made it to the majors. She made appropriately impressed sounds and I was feeling optimistic.

"That seems like a wonderful opportunity," she responded when I was done. She sounded oddly proud of me. For some reason I felt compelled to thank her, but I refrained.

"So, what do you say we sign Jay up?" I held my breath.

"Well, I think if he'd like to do it, you should definitely sign him up."

YES!

"Great! When can you bring him in to register?"

She paused. "Oh, me? That will be a bit of a problem, I'm afraid."

I frowned. Maybe she was an invalid? "Or we can do it online. I can even come to your house if that would make it easier…"

She laughed. "I'm afraid that would be quite a haul, Gavin, and not really worth your time."

Why did I feel ten steps behind in this entire conversation? If Jay went to North, that meant he lived in the district. "I wouldn't mind at all," I insisted. "Where do you live?"

"Right now?" she asked, strangely. Then I heard muffled sounds and a male voice before she came back to the line. "We're in New Mexico. Beautiful country! Have you been?"

What the hell?

"Um, no." I was gripping the back of my neck by this point, desperate to get the kid on board, but feeling at a total loss talking to this woman.

"Oh, you really should, Gavin. Do you have a lady friend?"

I had to stifle an exasperated laugh that tried to work its way up my throat. I had a sudden urge to look around for evidence this was a practical joke. "No one at the moment. Naomi, I'm a bit confused. When will you be back in town?"

"Well, that's a shame, what with your lovely name and your nice voice. You could take your girl on a cross-country trip sometime if you had one."

I had zero knowledge how to respond. I opened my mouth, but nothing came out.

"I haven't lived in North Carolina in ages myself, but I've visited Emmy and it's still quite beautiful there too, so I suppose you're okay where you are. At any rate, Jay is with Emmy now, so

I'll have her stop by to register him. I'm sure she'll be happy to pay for it."

"Emmy?" This was getting weirder by the second.

"I'll call her tonight. Oh, I have to run! We just pulled up to the world's largest pistachio!" She laughed. "You really should see this, Gavin! Bye for now."

And then she hung up, leaving me wondering if that conversation had actually happened or if maybe I was still in bed, asleep.

Chapter Four

SUGAR

*E*MERSON

"Is there something you forgot to tell me?"

Jay stopped in his tracks. He'd just stepped in the front door, his clothes covered in dust. His equipment bag was slung over one shoulder, his backpack over the other.

I'd just gotten off the phone with our mom. She'd explained that Jay needed to register for extra training at a local center—an expensive local center. As soon as she told me, I knew it was something Jay had deliberately kept quiet. Mom and Aldo didn't have the money for extra luxuries like private training, not that Jay would have asked them either. But, he certainly would never have asked me. My heart ached again at the thought.

"I don't think so," Jay replied warily.

I cocked my head and he turned to close the door. I waited until I had his attention again. "Are you sure you didn't forget to mention—oh, I don't know—that your coaches think you're

fantastic and they recommended training at the Baseball Academy?" I raised my eyebrows at him.

His face colored. "Oh, that."

"Yes, that." I couldn't help but grin. I didn't bother to ask why he hadn't told me. I already knew. "They're open late, so we're going tomorrow when I get home. We're getting you registered." I pointed at him.

"Em, no," he said. "You don't know how expensive that stuff is. I'm fine without it."

"Well, you'll be even more fine *with* it, then."

"I'm not even a starter—I'm hardly playing much. It's not worth it."

"You're the only one who seems to think so. I'm not going to take a no this time, Jay. Even if I have to drag you there." I pulled myself up to my full height, which, even at five-eight, was no match.

He gave me a look that said he knew he could take me. Oh well. "Mom and Dad can't afford it, and I'm not taking money from you. You're already housing and feeding me." He tried to walk past me but I stopped him with a hand on his arm.

"So? I want to do this for you. And, besides, I like having you around here. It's too quiet with just me in this place."

"Well, that's your fault for buying a gigantic house." He raised his eyebrows at me.

"I like my gigantic house—it's not that big." Was it?

"If you say so. I'm gonna go do some laundry—my clothes stink. You want me to throw some of your stuff in?"

I ignored his attempt at distraction. "When I get home tomorrow, we're going, so you'd better not bail on me."

He mumbled in response and headed down the hallway, but I was pretty certain I didn't hear the word no.

"Ms. Scott, may I have a word?" Mr. Wheeler's voice came from behind me. I turned abruptly.

"Certainly." I pinned my most accommodating smile in place. Drat. It was already 7:00 p.m. and I had been on my way out the door to get Jay.

He motioned for me to precede him back into my office.

When the door had closed behind him, he spoke again. "I've just gotten off the phone with Dietrich, and we're going to have to move the founder's agreement and non-disclosure paperwork deadline up by a week."

My heart sank. Dietrich was one of the chief clients in the AgPower start-up. That deadline was only two weeks away as it was, which meant we only had one week to get things sewn up. Fudge—that was going to be a stretch.

I refused to let my distress show on my face. "That shouldn't be a problem, Mr. Wheeler. I'll confer with Craig now and we'll get it taken care of." My nerves were frayed. How in holy hell were we going to pull this off?

"Excellent." He nodded. "I'm meeting Melanie for dinner, so I need to be off. I'll leave you to it." He walked out and I sank into my desk chair again, knowing I'd have to call Jay and cancel.

When I got home three hours later, I knocked on his bedroom door. There was no answer, and I debated whether or not I should open the door. He was fifteen, after all. I decided to take my chances.

I turned the knob and poked my head around the opening I'd created. "Hi," I said, scrunching my nose at him as I prepared my apology.

He was on his bed, his homework spread out in front of him in

a messy array of papers and books. A pair of wireless headphones covered his damp hair, and his head swung up as he spied me in his peripheral vision. Seemingly caught by surprise, he didn't have time to school his features to affect indifference, and the wide smile I remembered so well overtook his face. Darn, I missed that smile. I altered my expression to match his, just as his turned stiff.

"Hey," I ventured.

"Hey." He removed his headphones and kept my gaze.

"I'm so sorry about tonight." I felt my eyebrows rise. "Can we go tomorrow after your game?"

"Nah, don't worry about it. I already told them I'm not doing it. It's totally fine." He maintained his artificial happy expression.

I didn't really have a leg to stand on since I'd harped about this so much the previous night and then I'd been the one to bail. So I just narrowed my eyes playfully and said, "We'll see."

I was determined to make this happen with or without him. Surely, I could find time to slip out tomorrow and run over to the center. My plan in place, I kept the pretense that the issue was dropped.

"So, what's with this overachieving stuff?" I gestured to his books. "You're supposed to be texting girls and sneaking out the window, not doing your homework at ten o'clock on a Friday night," I teased.

"Oh, I did that earlier," he tossed back at me, not missing a beat. "I'm just getting this done so I can spend the rest of the weekend selling drugs and bullying kids on Facebook."

"Ha ha," I responded and then asked if he'd eaten yet. He assured me he had grabbed some pizza with one of his teammates.

"You're not going to give me some random fact about the poor nutritional quality of pizza, are you?" he teased.

I narrowed my eyes. "No…not unless you want me to."

He put his hands up to ward me off. "Don't ruin pizza for me. I'm a growing boy—I need all the calories I can get."

"Yeah, about that. If you could do me a favor and stop getting taller, that would be awesome. You're making me feel like a shrimp." The kid had grown at least three inches since the last time I'd seen him on a trip to Virginia six months before. If I didn't know how in love our mom was with Aldo, I would have questioned her faithfulness. But apparently short guys did it for her.

So, how she'd married my own father was a complete mystery. He stood over six feet, but his height was the most trivial of traits that kept me perplexed at how he and my mother had ever had a relationship—much less a marriage, even as short-lived as it had been.

"I'll do my best," Jay responded and then donned his head-phones again. I took that as my cue and went to my room to get ready for bed.

The brief thought of my father reminded me that I owed him a visit. He'd been dropping hints over e-mails and phone calls for the past month, but I hadn't been able to bring myself to accept any of his invitations. I always made sure to have an excuse at the ready. It wasn't that I didn't want to see him. Heck, he was half the reason I'd joined a law practice here in Greensboro as opposed to one of the other cities I'd been considering.

It was Candy I couldn't stomach. Okay, her name is really Mandy, but Ari and I always refer to her as Candy instead. It really suits her much better, I swear to you. She speaks in a sugary sweet voice and never fails to address me as if I'm eight years old.

"Emerson, how *arrrre* you, sweetheart?"—enunciating and dragging out the word "are" as if I were a dog or perhaps just very slow. I'm always tempted to respond in kind. "Candy, I'd be *soooo*

much *better* if you'd choke on your own stupidity and *die*." But I hold myself in check. Mostly.

All right, fine. I'm not very nice to her. Usually, I just ignore her, but she's only a year older than me, so it's not easy. She is also wife number four, so this ain't my first rodeo. But I have to give her credit—she's stuck the longest of them all, including my mom. My father and Mandy have been married for almost four years. Four very tedious years.

I'm sure my dad knows on some level that I don't care for her, but he chooses to pretend otherwise. Perhaps I should rephrase that. He has decided that his marrying Mandy trumps any feelings I have about the situation. Which, in a way, I understand and have accepted. It doesn't mean I have to like her, though.

Ari loves to give Mandy a hard time whenever possible. She's a loyal friend, that one. Ari will bring up topics she knows Mandy is clueless about and then ask her opinion. Sometimes she'll outright make things up just to see Candy the Trophy Wife squirm.

One of the worst (or best, I should say) occurred a couple months back when I'd been cornered into Sunday dinner with my father and his child bride. I dragged Ari along as my date. As soon as my dad had excused himself to take a phone call, Ari pounced.

"It's terrible about the coup in Sweden, isn't it?" Ari shook her head solemnly and tsked her general sadness over the nonexistent crisis. "All those poor Swedes trampled in the ensuing riots."

Mandy's eyes widened and then she shook her head in shared sympathy. "Yes, I know exactly what you mean. The poor Swedes. Robert and I donated to the Red Cross fund providing aid to the victims," she informed us. I'd had to pinch my leg to keep from laughing out loud.

Let's just say my dad hadn't married her for her intelligence.

I sighed and pulled out my phone to e-mail him. I truly did

want to see him. I just wished we could sometimes do it without the trophy wife in tow.

Not that I could afford to dwell on it. I had the AgPower account, a court hearing for my new pro bono case to prep for, Jay's game to attend, and an escape to the Baseball Academy to maneuver. I'd need a good night's sleep because I wasn't about to drop the ball on any of my responsibilities. No way.

"What's the matter, ump?! You need Lasik?! That was a ball!" Ari shouted.

I opted for the slightly less antagonistic, "That's okay, number twelve—you've got this!"

Ari gave me a sidelong glance. "That was bullshit."

"And insulting the umpire is going to make him change the call?"

One side of her mouth lifted. "Well, no. But it made me feel better."

I let out a small laugh and looked around the stands. It was a decent crowd, probably due to the perfect weather. Like Ari and me, the fans lining the metal bleachers around us were dressed in blue and white, while the opposite stands boasted an unfortunate combination of burgundy and orange, creating a sea of...ugly. I took a sip from my water bottle and then sighed. "I hope they put Jay in soon. I haven't seen him play in ages."

"They've got to put somebody in. Their pitcher is having a craptastic day so far." Ari checked her phone and took a sip of her soda.

I adjusted my position so my butt wouldn't fall asleep on the hard bleachers and simply nodded my head in agreement. It was

only the bottom of the third, but North's "star" pitcher had yet to impress. Our team was at bat at the moment, but not producing anything to write home about there either. Something had to give or a huge checkmark was going in the L column for the day.

"Come on, North!" I shouted again, as if my voice alone could propel them to victory. Jay had explained there was a pecking order and, as the new kid, he was at the end of the line. But if his pitching was half as good as I remembered, he could wipe the floor with this other team—one hand tied behind his back and a pirate's eyepatch in place.

Ari yawned. I knew she hadn't finished with her gig last night until sometime after midnight, after which I suspected she joined Elliot for activities I'd prefer to bleach from my mind. "So, do you think Jay will let you sign him up for that extra training thing after all? I can kind of see his point if the coach isn't even letting him play…" Ari trailed off.

I nodded. "I know, but the kid deserves something special, right? And I can manage the payments, so it's one thing I can do for him. Does that sound as pathetic to you as it does to me?" I cringed. "I'm totally trying to make up for not being around enough, aren't I?"

Ari let out a small laugh. "Maybe. But I think it's sweet." She lifted her phone to show me a text. "Ponch is going to try to make it before the end of the game."

My heart lifted a little at that. Ari's older brother used to make my heart palpitate on the regular when I was a teen, but I'd learned over time that he was only good for one thing when it came to hearts—breaking them. Enough girls had been for a ride on his Amante Express (which could appropriately refer to either his manhood or his panty-melting motorcycle with equal accuracy) that he'd earned the nickname Ponch from the cheesy eighties

show *CHiPS*. You'd think the name would make him an easy target for mockery, but he had the uncanny ability to make anything downright cool. Hardly anyone except his own parents called him Nick anymore.

And, let's be real, if you're okay with your boyfriend going by a name that celebrates his promiscuity, you need to take a good look within, ladies. That's how I'd been able to let my girlhood crush go and form a platonic relationship with my best friend's brother over time. Although it didn't stop him from flirting shamelessly with me—and just about anyone lacking a Y chromosome, so I didn't ever take it seriously.

I had to imagine Jay would be thrilled to see Ponch at his game. If he ever got to play, that was. Jay had only been a little kid when we'd lived next door to the Amante family, but Ponch had always treated him like he thought Jay was the coolest thing around. They'd played catch, and Ponch would take him on rides on the back of his motorcycle when he stopped by to visit his parents. It had always scared the pants off me, but Mom and Aldo never batted an eyelash. My mom embraced any new experience as an adventure to enrich the spirit. She'd clearly never seen *Scenes from the ER* episodes featuring such adventurous motorcycling enthusiasts. But, Jay had always returned unscathed, and had a friend for life in Ponch.

The inning turned over with North still losing 4-0, although they'd managed to get a player on second. I crossed my fingers as Jay's team took the field, but, once again, he remained in the dugout.

Sugar!

Chapter Five

WELCOME TO MILLER TOWN

GAVIN

"Come on Davidson," I murmured quietly, willing North's coach to put Miller in. His team was losing 4-2 at the top of the seventh and if they didn't make a switch soon, it was all over. The opposing team, Burlington West, wasn't exactly a top-ranked team, but they did have a few key players with talent. The Academy had done a full-team training day with Burlington West when I'd first started my job a while back, and I remembered a couple of the kids. I was happy to see the improvement in some of their techniques.

But my eye was supposed to remain fully focused on Jay Miller, and I'd been honing my stalking tendencies all week. Despite the surreal conversation with Naomi Miller, we had yet to hear from the elusive Emmy. But I was determined to pin her down today, assuming she was in attendance. When I wasn't watching the field, I was scanning the bleachers in search of Jay Miller's...

whatever. Was she a stepmom? An aunt? Not that it did me any good since I had zero clue what she looked like.

"Miller, you're up!" I heard the magic words hit my ears at the same time as a tremendously loud feminine howl pealed from North's home stands. My eyes immediately darted in its direction, as did the gaze of just about everyone in attendance. A petite woman with dark red hair and a bright blue tank top was jumping up and down, her ample breasts bobbing in tandem as she shouted, "Go, Jay!! Show 'em what you got, Miller!!" A few snickers rippled through the crowd along with a couple lighthearted shouts of agreement. I noticed several male gazes lingering on the still-bouncing breasts which I concluded must belong to none other than Emmy whoever-the-hell. I also noticed her seatmate with her head in her hands as her back shook in laughter while she attempted to sink into the bleachers at her friend's enthusiastic outburst.

Torn between watching Jay Miller take the mound and pinning this woman down about the contract, I chose to watch the kid, whose face, I noted, had turned a bit red. "Well, kid," I murmured, "looks like you've got a fan."

Over the next two innings, I watched in amazement as North soundly turned the game on its head. Jay shut out Burlington West on his first turn on the mound, and the second had been almost as good, resulting in only one runner on base and no runs scored. North managed to carry the momentum from Jay's swift dismissal of Burlington's batters, and they scored three runs, making the score 5-4 moving into the top of the ninth.

Jay dispensed with the first batter and walked the second. Burlington's third batter caught a piece of Jay's fastball but popped it up and it was picked off by one of North's senior players. It was all down to the last out, and I watched intently to see how Jay

handled himself under the pressure. I could see him drawing in deep breaths as he kneaded the ball, keeping an eye on the runner on first as he shifted off base looking for his chance to steal second. Miller nodded at the catcher's signal and then delivered a killer changeup that painted the outside corners of the plate. The batter swung about an hour early and the ump called the strike. I looked back to Jay and saw his face not cracking even the smallest of smiles. He was a cool customer, all the way. Even when another screech sounded from the bleachers. "That's right, batter! You're in Miller town now! Don't get comfortable!" I couldn't help but snicker a bit to myself.

The next pitch was a monster fastball that flew straight through the heart of the strike zone. The batter went for it and missed by a mile. I held my breath as Jay wound up again and gave the player on first the opening he'd been looking for. He stole second as Jay delivered a pitch that went a bit wide and resulted in a ball. Both sets of bleachers erupted in encouraging cheers for their teams as the ball came back to the mound and Jay prepared what I could feel would be the final pitch of the game. Another set of deep breaths and a few shake offs to the catcher, and Jay released another fastball with the most heat I'd seen yet. The batter was more prepared this time and swung only a fraction of a second too late. The ball hit the catcher's mitt with a resounding smack, and North's fans exploded in cheers as Jay's teammates swarmed him.

All eyes were on the pitcher's mound, but mine swung straight back to the bleachers, even more intent on my goal after witnessing the crushing blow Jay had just delivered. This kid was mine. All I had to do was turn on the charm and hope like hell this Emmy woman would go for it.

Weaving through the crowd like a salmon swimming upstream, I lost sight of her until I heard the familiar, loud shout somewhere

to my left. "That's right, boys! Nice ass-whooping!" I turned and caught a glimpse of the more subdued of the two women dragging Emmy away from the milling crowd. Emmy was laughing uproariously at something the other woman must have said, and let herself be led to the fence line. I quickly adjusted my path and followed.

"Oh, come on. I'm sure he loved it," Emmy was insisting, her red lips tipped up in a mischievous smile. She wore a tank top that revealed a couple tattoos on her collarbone and arm, and I noticed more than a few piercings. I couldn't fathom who this woman was to Jay Miller.

The other woman had her back to me, and I could see she was laughing along, even though she'd obviously just been scolding her friend. This woman had red hair as well, but it was pulled up into a ponytail and the color was more natural and subdued. Auburn is what Laney would probably call it. She also wore a more modest short-sleeved sweater and tailored jeans that showcased a pert little ass.

Wait. Stop right there, Gavin. Focus, please.

I cleared my throat as I approached. "Excuse me."

That got the attention of Emmy, and she shifted her dark eyes to me. This was followed by a cock of her head and a blatant perusal of my entire body from my scuffed boots to my cap-covered hair. *Jesus.* I had a sudden urge to confirm my fly was closed. One side of her mouth tipped up, almost as though she'd read my thoughts. She most certainly picked up on my discomfort —thus the smile, I was sure. I opened my mouth to speak again when her friend turned to face me.

Strands of her auburn hair had escaped the confines of the ponytail and fell around her face, a few trailing near her mouth as a breeze picked them up. A mouth that was a perfect shade of pink with a full bottom lip parted as if forming a question. A

smattering of light freckles adorned her small nose, and warm golden-brown eyes narrowed slightly as she looked at me inquiringly.

I had completely forgotten what I'd been about to say.

I *knew* this woman. Well, technically, I didn't actually *know* her, but I'd seen her before. Both in real life, and a few times in my shower, I'm not ashamed to admit.

A few months back, at Bailey and Jake's baby shower, this woman had approached the couple and they'd chatted for a few minutes. She'd immediately captured my attention, but I'd been waylaid by Fiona trying to make me eat melted chocolate out of a diaper. Even I have standards. By the time I'd gotten over to Bailey and Jake, the woman had retreated with her phone to her ear and I hadn't seen her again. Neither Bailey nor Jake would tell me who she was, claiming that she was both too old for me and way out of my league.

Ha! Bastards.

And now, here she was, almost as if she'd appeared out of thin air. It couldn't be mere coincidence that had put her in my path once again.

"H-Hi," I stammered like an idiot, suddenly glad no one had accompanied me to today's game.

She was still looking at me questioningly. Had she spoken and I'd missed it? That was entirely possible.

"Hey, handsome. You need something?" Emmy asked in a not unfriendly tone. My eyes remained glued to her friend as I tried to recall what my purpose had been.

Shit. The contract. Jay Miller.

I shook myself out of my stupor and forced my eyes back to Emmy. She had a shit-eating grin on her face. Busted.

"Um, is your name, by any chance, Emmy?"

The two women exchanged a glance before she asked, "Emmy?" in a half-amused, half-suspicious tone.

"Well, yeah. I heard you cheering for Jay Miller and I assumed..." I trailed off as both women remained silent. "I'm sorry, do either of you know Naomi Miller?"

"Oh," both women said in drawn-out unison, as if that explained everything. Thank God.

The woman with the dark red hair gestured to her friend, "That's *Emmy*," putting emphasis on the name. I was definitely not in on whatever joke this was. Clearly, everyone who associated with Naomi Miller excelled at confounding innocent guys.

The auburn-haired woman narrowed her eyes at her friend before facing me again. Her cheeks had reddened a bit, setting off the freckles. "And you are?" Her voice was soft and almost musical, even with its slightly suspicious tone.

"Gavin Monroe. I'm from the Baseball Academy." I extended my hand as her face transformed from questioning to joyful. Damn, that was a good look on this woman. Her eyes widened and warmed, causing an odd tightening sensation in my chest.

"Oh, Mr. Monroe, I'm so happy to meet you!" Emmy, the *real* Emmy, took my hand and shook it firmly. Her skin was warm and smooth and I didn't want to release her hand. I also didn't want to look like a creeper, so I let go reluctantly. "I was going to come by right after the game to get Jay registered. What a happy coincidence." She smiled up at me and the tightening turned into a thick knot in my chest cavity.

"Just Gavin is good," I murmured as I heard her friend snicker and try to cover it with a cough. Fucking brilliant, Monroe. Emmy seemed completely oblivious to my pathetic imitation of a lapdog, thank fuck.

Desperate to keep it that way, I fumbled in my back pocket for

the folded pack of documents I'd been carrying around. "I brought the forms with me on the off chance you might be here. But they need to be signed by a parent or legal guardian…" I mentally crossed my fingers, but she waved me off.

"I'm his legal guardian. His sister, in fact."

Ah, okay, this was making more sense now. She seemed way too young to be a stepmom or an aunt or something. If I had to guess, I'd say she looked about thirty, but the conservative clothes may have had something to do with that.

At this point, her friend interjected. "You've got a live one with Jay. He's amazing!" As if she had to convince me. She began to root around in her bag.

I gave her a grin. "Why do you think I've been carrying these contracts around?"

She returned my smile and unearthed a pen, passing it to Emmy, who glanced around looking for a hard surface to write on. Without a second thought, I turned around and offered her my back. "Feel free." I glanced over my shoulder just in time to see both women's eyes snap up from my ass.

Dammit. I was going to get a hard-on in front of half the high school and their parents.

Emmy approached and I felt her tentatively place the papers against my t-shirt, taking care not to actually touch me with her hand. The awkwardness of that writing position quickly became apparent, and I felt the pressure of her writing hand rest on my back while the fingers of her other hand held the papers steady.

My mind couldn't help but jump to images of her hands on me in another much more intimate, much more satisfying situation. I held in a small groan and thought about baseball, as all guys learn to do around the awkward age of thirteen.

"What do we do about the payments?" Emmy asked. "Are you hiding a credit card machine in your other pocket?"

"Or are you just happy to see her?" I heard her friend whisper a bit too loudly. That was followed by a grunt and an "Ow!" shortly after.

"No," I hurried, anxious to move on. "It's fine. I'll hand these over to admin and they'll be sending you an e-mail with payment information. You can do it online. In fact, we could have done the whole thing online, but Naomi was a bit…vague on your details."

"You have no idea," she responded in understanding. I felt the pen running across the muscles of my mid-back as her fingers continued to work their way down the papers. She finally finished with a flourish of what I assumed to be her signature, and I had to hold in a grunt as she pressed a bit too hard at the end. Clearly, she'd forgotten her desk was of the human variety, something I was all too acutely aware of.

"There," she said, lifting the forms off me. I turned around and was greeted with the brilliant smile once more.

Before I could even contemplate my next move, a tall, broad guy with dark hair and eyes walked up behind both women and put his arms around their shoulders, pulling them into him. "Hey, how's my favorite girl?" His head leaned toward Emmy. Her friend elbowed him in the gut and he pretended to be offended. "What? You know I like her better."

She rolled her eyes at him, but he'd already turned back to Emmy. I decided immediately that I hated him.

He raised his chin toward me. "Who's this?"

I stood up a little straighter, suddenly aware that this guy was a couple inches taller and instinctively feeling the need to make up the difference somehow. I held out my hand and forced a smile. "Gavin Monroe." Keep your friends close and all that.

He didn't remove his hands from the women's shoulders so I lamely dropped my hand back to my side. This caused Emmy to elbow him in the gut as well. "Born in a barn, were you?" she asked him and then spun out from under his arm. She gestured to him and said, "This is Ponch. And while we're at it, this is Ariana, his sister. Neither one is fit for public interaction." The siblings looked at each other and simply shrugged. Ponch then extended his hand.

"Sorry, man. Just messing with you. Ponch Amante. Nice to meet you." I hesitated, sure he was going to pull his hand back, but when he didn't, I took it and we shook in greeting. If his grip was a bit too firm, I ignored it. The warning had been clear from the beginning. No need to drive it home.

We stood awkwardly for a moment and then Emmy thrust the papers toward me. "Here, Gavin. We're going to wait outside the locker room for Jay. Would you like to join us?"

I noticed Ari's eyes widen a bit as Ponch's narrowed. It was almost comical, but I couldn't afford to take the time to hesitate. I nodded. "Sounds good. Ladies." I gestured for them to precede me toward the building.

Once Emmy was in front of me, I used the opportunity to quickly glance at the forms she'd filled out, homing in on the only line of info I needed: her phone number. Committing it to memory, I shoved the forms into my back pocket once again and followed the trio.

"You missed a great game, dickwad," Ari threw over her shoulder to Ponch.

"Pardon me for trying to make a living. Some of us have to be adults, you know." He shot me a sideways look, as if suggesting I was somehow guilty of not being an adult. I was dying to ask if he and Emmy were dating, but could think of no way to do it that

wouldn't have me looking like a desperate moron. I'd have to find out another way.

Despite the looks I was getting from this overprotective Neanderthal, I smiled to myself as we walked toward the school. Tucked safely in my memory was the phone number of one auburn-haired beauty, and I had every intention of using it.

Chapter Six

FEELING THE BUZZ

$\mathcal{E}$MERSON

　　I had no idea why I'd invited Gavin Monroe to join us to wait for Jay except that I'd been embarrassed by the blatant He-Man routine Ponch had displayed. Why were guys such idiots? It wasn't as if Ponch had any claim on me, and even more to the point, it wasn't as if I had any interest whatsoever in this Gavin guy. Even if he was sort of cute and had a decent backend. Okay, fine. He was hot and had an awesome ass. The mere thought had my skin turning crimson. I couldn't believe he'd caught us staring at his butt. How humiliating. And even more-so considering he was probably all of about twenty. Talk about inappropriate. Nevertheless, I felt the need to compensate for Ponch's idiotic behavior and so I'd asked Gavin to join us.

　　In step at my side, I could see Ari giving me sideways glances and practically choking in her attempts to both keep her mouth shut and stop herself from laughing outright.

　　"Don't even think about it," I warned quietly, which caused her

to snort. This would just descend into disaster if I didn't step in. But before I could, Ari gathered herself and glanced behind us.

"So, Gavin, will you be training Jay yourself? How does this work?"

I took the opportunity to look at him—it was good manners to look at someone when they were speaking, after all. *What?* He was tall, probably right around six feet or a touch taller, with naturally highlighted brown hair that sprang out in various directions from beneath his well-worn, green baseball cap. The bill shadowed his eyes, but even so, I could see the deep brown shade surrounded by an even darker ring of almost black. He had such a boyish quality to his expression, eyes a bit wide as if always responding to a question and not exactly sure of his answer. It was quite adorable, honestly.

If boyish described his face, however, it did nothing to describe the rest of him. Long, lean muscle covered his build, and the sexiest wrists—yes, wrists—extended from perfectly proportioned biceps and forearms as he forced his hands into his pockets while listening to Ari. There was clearly something wrong with me if I was now ogling guys' wrists.

His tongue swept over his bottom lip just before he spoke, and my belly dipped in awareness. Yep—definitely something wrong with me. "I'm just one of the coaching staff, but I'll be working closely with Jay since pitching is my specialty. His head trainer will be Buzz Hader, but I'll oversee a lot of day-to-day aspects."

At that, I noticed Ponch completely halt his gait. He looked as if he'd been shot with a tranquilizer dart, and I involuntarily stopped in my tracks as well, causing Gavin to barrel into me.

"Crap, I'm so sorry," he said, steadying me with his hands on the skin of my upper arms, just below the sleeves of my flimsy summer sweater. I felt my skin turn hot and I drew a quick intake

of air. I tried to force away the memory of the feel of his t-shirt-covered back under my hands when I'd been filling out the forms minutes earlier. I failed miserably and had the sudden urge to lean back into his solid form. What was I doing?! He was a child, for God's sake!

"Buzz Hader?" came Ponch's voice. I'd almost forgotten he'd been the reason I'd halted in the first place. "*The* Buzz Hader?" A glance back at Ponch showed him looking dumbstruck, his mouth practically hanging open.

"Who the hell is Buzz Hader?" asked Ari, who'd backtracked once she realized we'd all stopped.

Both Ponch and Gavin swiveled their eyes to Ari with what could only be described as horrified expressions. "*Who the hell is Buzz Hader?*" they mimicked simultaneously. I held in a snicker, relieved when Gavin's grip released my arms and I could breathe normally again. I knew I'd heard the name before, but I couldn't recall who this Buzz guy was either. Not that I would bring that up.

Ponch was shaking his head and muttering under his breath while Gavin illuminated us. "Former All-Star first baseman for the Kings?"

Ari just pursed her lips and shrugged. "If you say so."

"If I..." Gavin trailed off as if he couldn't quite believe what he'd just witnessed.

Ponch put a reassuring hand on his shoulder. "Tell me you have a sister, man."

Gavin tore his eyes from Ari and finally registered what Ponch had said. "Unfortunately," he responded, and they both gazed at the ground, seemingly lost in some kind of shared grief over the possession of sisters who didn't share the baseball gene.

It was time to get this show on the road. The sooner we saw Jay, the sooner I could be rid of these pesky, tingly sensations this

man-child kept evoking in me. "Well, I happen to be a sister too, so let's go find my little brother and tell him the good news."

As planned, this brought everyone out of their thoughts and we all moved forward, eager to find Jay and tell him that he'd be coached by a former Major League player and a hot young stud by the name of Gavin Monroe.

Well, perhaps I'd keep the latter to myself.

"I still can't believe it," Jay said again as we pulled off Horse Pen Creek Road onto the main street of my neighborhood.

"*I* still can't believe what an awesome game you pitched," I responded, grinning his way.

He gave me a playful scowl. "Buzz Hader. I mean, that's just… that's just crazy."

Ever since we'd broken the news to Jay outside the locker room, he'd had a half-awed, half-ecstatic smile plastered to his face. He'd been so bowled over by the idea of one of his idols coaching him that he hadn't even protested at my proceeding with the registration without consulting him. Ponch, of course, had been the one to butt in and break the big news to Jay. The two had high-fived and back slapped until I'd finally had to cut in and introduce Jay to Gavin, who took the whole thing very good-naturedly. He'd clearly been a star-struck young player once upon a time as well.

I'd been glad, however, when we'd all parted ways and I could escape the strangely unnerving presence of one of Jay's soon-to-be coaches. I was actually a little embarrassed for myself.

"Seriously, though, Jay. I don't get why you're not the starting pitcher. You're clearly the best pitcher on the team."

I could see him shaking his head in my peripheral vision. "Nah.

I just had a lucky day. And I'm only a sophomore, anyway. These other guys have earned their place, Em. It's just how the game is played."

"I guess," I conceded. "But if I were the coach, I'd start you. So would Ari, if you couldn't guess by her reaction today."

"She's never been very subtle, has she?"

I pressed the button for the garage door and pulled into the driveway. "Got any plans tonight? I wish I could take you out, but I've got work to do." I was doing my best to get the final draft of the AgPower founder's agreement together, but Craig hadn't been answering my e-mails this morning. I should have anticipated that, but it was frustrating regardless. He knew I couldn't move on without the data he was gathering. And then there was the pro bono case I'd taken on. I was due in court on Monday afternoon and had hardly glanced at the case, even though I was fairly confi-dent it would be cut and dried. I'd only taken it on because I felt like I owed the couple who'd asked for the favor.

"That's okay," my brother said, "I'll probably just pass out in front of the TV."

"You know, you can invite a friend over if you want."

"Nah, I'm good." He shrugged.

I knew he'd say that. Oh well. Baby steps.

Three hours later, I still hadn't heard back from Craig, so I moved on to the pro bono case. Technically, I was supposed to get these approved before accepting them, but I knew I could slide by with one on my own now and then. It wasn't like it took away from my billable hours, and the client's family was paying the court costs. I looked over the file to familiarize myself with the facts.

Christian Hardacre, age fourteen, was being charged with grand theft and driving without a license. There wasn't much I could do about the second part, but the first part was a joke.

Christian—Chris—had taken a neighbor's car for a joyride to impress some older kids. Dumb, but not a danger to society in my opinion. And besides, from what the kid's parents had said, he'd been given some not-so-wise advice from a family friend—an adult family friend—who had prompted the idea in the first place. Not that Chris shouldn't have been smart enough to ignore the advice, but this "friend" sounded like a first-class imbecile to me.

Thankfully, the neighbor—the victim of the theft—would be in court and I was confident we'd be able to dispense with the grand theft charges and get the kid off with fines and community service. It was clear to me that the neighbor didn't have the whole story, and I was only too happy to enlighten him. Chris was just an awkward young kid with crappy judgement and even crappier friends.

I poured myself a glass of Sauvignon Blanc and was just about to settle back into my task when my phone rang with an unknown local number. Worried it might have to do with one of my cases, I took a chance and answered.

"Hello?"

"Oh, hi," said a vaguely familiar male voice on the other end. "Emmy?"

My pulse automatically kicked up a notch, which startled me to the point where I completely forgot to correct the caller about my actual name. Instead, I lamely answered, "Yes?" As if I didn't know exactly who it was on the other end of the line. I face-palmed and waited.

"It's Gavin Monroe," he said. And when I failed to respond, still caught up in my own stupidity, he added, "from today."

I had to get it together. "Yes. Hi. How are you?"

"I'm great. How are you?"

I was obviously missing something here. I set the wine glass on the counter and took a breath.

"Great," I responded. "Um, did I forget to sign something?" Then it hit me. "Oh! The payment. I completely forgot. You're probably waiting on me to log in and pay. So sorry!"

He chuckled. "No. No, it's not that."

"Oh," I let out a breath.

"I was actually calling because I wanted to ask if you were free for dinner next weekend."

Huh? "Is this some kind of parent orientation or something?"

"Uh, not exactly." He seemed to hesitate before continuing, "It's more of a date kind of thing."

"Oh. Seriously?" I couldn't help myself. It just slipped out, and I was mortified by my poor manners.

"Well, based on your reaction, I'm not sure any more." He gave a self-deprecating laugh. "I'm guessing I caught you by surprise."

"You could say that. It's just…" It's just that you're jailbait?

"You don't eat? Are you part cyborg? Shit, I always end up going for the half-humans."

That got a smile out of me. I picked up the wine glass again and took a sip, settling my back into the counter as I answered. "No, I eat. And I'm human, for the record."

"Okay, then. Great! How does Friday sound?" Wow, he wasn't shy, was he? But I had to shut this thing down.

"Gavin, I'm really flattered, but I don't think that would be a good idea."

"Oh. Sorry. I didn't really get the vibe that you and Ponch were an item."

"Ponch? Um, no. Just, no." I didn't even try to explain, as that would have taken all night.

"Good to know. So why not then? I'm human, you're human... what more could you ask for?" I could hear his grin in his voice.

I blurted out, "How old are you?" Again with the impeccable manners.

"Didn't anyone ever tell you it's not polite to ask someone's age?" There was that audible grin again.

"Not when it could be considered a felony to go on a date with the person."

"Ouch."

I made my way over to the couch and settled in. "Well?"

"How about if we just say I'm old enough, and I won't ask you how old you are," he responded.

"You don't have to. I'm twenty-nine. And I'm guessing that's about two presidential terms older than you."

"Oh, please. I can't help it if I don't have wrinkles. What can I say? I take sunscreen seriously."

I pulled a throw pillow into my lap. "So, you're what? You're actually sixty with the skin of a twenty-year-old?"

"I'm taking the secret to my grave. Now, what do you say? Italian? Greek? Steakhouse? You choose."

This guy...this *boy*, I reminded myself.

"You're very sweet, and I can tell you're fun, but I'm not in a place where I can date right now. Even if you weren't thirty years older than me," I added to soften the rejection.

"Ah, I see. Still getting over your crush on Buzz Hader. Why do I always come in second to that guy?"

"Sadly, no. Although I hear he's quite a catch. I'm actually completely swamped with work, and any free time I have I'm trying to spend with Jay. I'm sure you understand."

He didn't confirm he understood anything. Instead, he switched topics entirely. "That reminds me. I've been meaning to ask. Is his name really Jupiter?"

"As shocking as it sounds, yes. But then, you've spoken to our mother so there is that."

"True. So how did you end up with a normal name? Or is Emmy short for Emulsion or something?"

Again, I didn't correct him. What was wrong with me? Apart from my mom, nobody called me Emmy. Nobody. So why did I like the sound of it coming from this random guy?

"No. My dad named me. It's a family name." That, and I secretly think he wanted a boy. I didn't add that part. Instead, I tucked my feet under my butt and took another sip of wine.

"And he lost when it came time to name Jay?"

"No. Different fathers. Jay's my half-brother."

"Ah, I see. Half-brother but full human? Just asking because with the way he pitches I wouldn't be surprised if he was part machine."

I felt my lips curve into a smile. "I'll tell him you said so. Honestly, I don't know where he gets his athletic ability. His dad's not exactly the sporting type."

"That's easy. The baseball gods," Gavin explained matter-of-factly.

"You don't say? What makes you so sure?"

"Because they gave me the gift too."

I couldn't hold in my burst of laughter at that. "Oh, yeah? Aren't we a little full of ourselves? If you're so awesome, why aren't you in the big leagues?"

"Who says I wasn't? There aren't many sixty-year-olds still in the game."

There aren't many sixty-year-olds with an ass like that either, I

wanted to say. It was then I realized I was actually caressing the throw pillow on my lap. Oh, lord. I flung the pillow to the floor and face-palmed again as he continued.

"So, have you changed your mind yet about the date?"

I had to shut this thing down. "No. Unfortunately, I have to stick to the game plan. But thank you for asking. It's been fun talking to you."

"Just imagine how much more fun it would be eating with me."

I shook my head at his persistence. "I'll have to just leave that to my imagination."

"You do that." Yikes. Why did that conjure images that had very little to do with dinner? Emerson, you idiot—stop right there!

An awkward silence followed. The first of our conversation.

"Okay, then. Um, I guess I'll be seeing you around," he finally said.

"I guess so." I didn't want to hang up.

"Sweet dreams, Emmy."

I heard the line disconnect. Sweet dreams, indeed. I picked the throw pillow back up and buried my face in it.

Chapter Seven

THE BEST EVER

*E*MERSON

"Jay, sweetheart, how *arrrre* you?"

My molars threatened to turn to dust as I ground them together in an attempt to mind my manners. In a move that was admittedly riddled in cowardice, I had coaxed my brother to join me for dreaded Sunday brunch with my dad and Mandy the next day. Although, watching Jay eye the opulent buffet at my dad's club, I was feeling less guilty by the minute.

Jay flicked his eyes to Mandy and answered, "Good, thanks," before his attention was drawn back to the large bed of iced shrimp beckoning him from six feet away. I debated advising her to never come between a teenage boy and food lest she find herself missing a hand, but then figured she could learn for herself. My dad had excused himself to take a phone call, so it was just the awkward trio left at the table, waiting for him to return before we approached the buffet. Manners, you know.

I crossed my legs in my seat and decided to suck it up, if for no

other reason than to pass the time. That, and to distract myself from thoughts that kept wandering back to my phone conversation with a certain charming guy from the previous night. "What have you been up to lately, Mandy?"

She fussed with her napkin and glanced over to me. "Oh, you know. Volunteer work, running the house. Oh, and I'm in a book club now," she said excitedly. She brushed a lock of platinum blond hair behind her shoulder.

Hmm. That was surprising. I wasn't aware she could read. *Okay, Emerson, that was below the belt.* "Sounds…interesting." But, honestly, what did she do with herself all day? Her life sounded so freaking boring.

"It is! This month, we're reading a book about two women in Afghanistan. I'm only a couple chapters in, but it's really good so far."

I thought about asking her the title, but I was fairly certain I knew the book. It had had me in tears when I read it several years earlier. I wondered if she was prepared. I wondered if her shellacked face could produce tears.

"Sorry about that, ladies, Jay," said my father as he returned to his seat, picking up his napkin and arranging it in his lap. He sighed as he took us in. "Well, isn't this wonderful? Sunday brunch with my two favorite girls and an up-and-coming baseball star." He winked at Jay.

I had to hand it to my father. He'd always been very accepting of Jay. But, then again, the kid was so easygoing, it would be nearly impossible to dislike him.

Ever since I could remember, I'd spent weekends and summers at my dad's posh house near Lake Brandt. He'd always encouraged me to invite my friends, often to the dismay of whoever his wife happened to be at the time. Considering that Ari

THE GAME • 71

was usually one of the invited friends, who could really blame them, though.

And when my mom finally remarried and had Jay, the invitation had been open to him as well. There had been times when I'd been relieved to bring Jay with me so I could watch over him and be assured he was fed actual food and received the occasional bath. Naomi and Aldo were of the school of thought that the more you're exposed to germs, the higher your tolerance would be. Predictably, I vehemently disagreed. So, having my toddler brother join me now and then at my father's was a nice treat, as well as a relief to me and my worrying mind.

But, then I'd gone off to college, and our mom took the rest of the family to one of what would turn out to be many new destinations—or "adventures for the soul" as she would say. I was acutely aware that she'd only stayed in Greensboro all that time for my sake. She knew my desire for consistency, even if she didn't understand it. And she felt the importance of keeping me near my father so he and I could have a close relationship. I was grateful she'd done that for me, even when her heart clearly wanted to kick off the dust of North Carolina and hit the road.

"Well, it's been too long," I replied to my dad. "My fault—sorry I've been so busy." I left out the end of that sentence, which would have been something along the lines of *avoiding your annoying child bride*.

"Taking the world of corporate law by storm! How can a father complain too much?" He smiled in my direction and I returned it, my chest involuntarily swelling at the notion that I'd made him proud.

"I was just telling Emerson about my book club," Mandy chimed in. Her desperation to bring focus back to herself was so transparent I found myself suddenly feeling a bit sorry for her.

My father took a sip of his coffee. "Oh, of course. That's lovely, darling." I almost cringed at his dismissive tone. See. This is what happens when you get involved with someone out of your age bracket.

Had she asked me before taking up with my dad, I'd have told Mandy the only way to impress him was to play the game his way. You could either be the trophy wife or the partner, but you had to choose. She'd made her bed, and now had to lay in it, tiara firmly in place. No use trying to change her role now. But, of course, I kept my mouth shut and gave her a half-hearted smile which I couldn't decide was genuine or not.

I took in the little tableaux we made. I'm sure to any onlooker, we appeared to be a single father—or perhaps even a widower—taking his three children out for brunch. Not that my dad looked particularly old. No, he kept himself up very well. His hair maintained its youthful light-brown shade, and it was always neatly trimmed. No stray neck hairs for Robert Scott. And he stayed in shape by pursuing the same sports I did, sometimes inviting me for a round of golf or a tennis match at his club. The managing partner at his own firm of tax attorneys, my father affected an impressive image. One that remained composed in the most difficult of situations. Cool as a cucumber, my dad was, and that was the image I had strode for my entire life.

Mandy, I noticed, was fiddling with her cloth napkin again. I could practically hear her brain working to conjure something to add to the conversation. I decided to take pity on her and gestured to the buffet. I knew Ari would have rolled her eyes at me had she been forced to attend this little scene. "Shall we?"

Mandy shot me a brief look of relief, and I felt another unexpected pang of sympathy. Hmm. That was odd. But I didn't give it much thought as I was distracted by my little brother practically

whimpering in relief as he rose from his seat and power walked to the stack of sparkling white plates at the front of the extravagant buffet.

"Well that was exhausting," I said as I shut my car door, enclosing Jay and me in the silence of my Volvo S90.

"Food coma?" Jay asked, buckling his seatbelt and settling in.

"Diabetic coma from Candy is more like it."

"I don't know why you let her bug you so much. She's harmless." Oh, my dear, sweet brother.

"I guess. She just rubs me the wrong way. Don't mind me—I'm being petty." I pulled out of the spot and maneuvered my way out of the parking lot.

I knew I was overly critical of Mandy, but she's done very little to endear herself to me over the years. From the very beginning, she'd made sure I knew she was at the top of my father's list. Trophy wife outranked daughter, in her opinion, and she'd done her best to ensure his focus was firmly on her whenever we got together. I tried not to let it bother me, and I vowed to just wait her out. Women never lasted long with him, so why should she be any different? I had to hand it to her—she'd certainly surprised me by hanging in this long. If today's interaction was any indication, however, I was thinking her days were numbered. And she knew it.

In true Mandy style, she'd compensated by pointing out the calorie count in my salad dressing ("It's so *great* that you don't worry about gaining weight, *sweetheart*. I wish *I* could be that relaxed.") and asking if I needed her help finding a new hairdresser ("I'm *soooo* jealous that you don't have to spend time getting ready in the morning, *Emerson*. But change is always good."). Like

I'd ever let someone work my hair into an overdone rat's nest like the one resting on her scalp.

Oh well, it was over now, and I wouldn't have to endure another one of these outings for several weeks, thank God.

I looked over at Jay, envious of his ability to set people's comments aside and just go about his business. He really was a great kid.

"So, do you have a ride lined up to the Academy this week or do you need me to arrange something?" He was going to his first training after school on Tuesday and the bus wasn't an option.

His eyes lit. "I got it covered. Coach is going to take me over to get me settled in." His voice was practically vibrating with excitement, and I thought again of Gavin Monroe and how he'd worked so hard to get Jay this chance.

No. No thoughts of too-young guys with sexy backsides. I wasn't going down that road. I was going to go home, prepare for my pro bono case, and curse Craig's name a few more times. And maybe Mandy's too, just for good measure.

"Sounds great, but just let me know if you need a lift home," I told Jay as I pulled onto the main street, leaving the club behind and driving us home.

Too Young for You: Change your mind yet?

My phone vibrated on the coffee table with an unexpected text from a certain young coach. After our conversation the night before, I'd created a contact name to help me remember the bigger picture. *Too Young for You.* Gavin Monroe was off limits. End of story.

I'd just ignore this text and continue focusing on my laptop.

But my phone had other ideas. It vibrated again, reminding me I had a new text I hadn't officially opened. I took off my reading glasses and closed my eyes, waiting for the third and final reminder I knew was coming. Finally, the phone vibrated again and then stilled.

There. I'd done it. I'd successfully conquered the temptation. He'd realize I was serious about not going out with him, and he'd leave me alone.

The damn phone suddenly rattled again, causing me to jump in my seat, as if Gavin had just appeared by my side on the couch. Before I could think better of it, I replaced my glasses and leaned over my laptop to peek at the new text notification.

Too Young for You: *Because I have an awesome date planned out, if I do say so myself...*

Darn it. Now I was curious. I chewed on my bottom lip as I debated what to do next, but the phone vibrated again with another new text.

Too Young for You: *Unless you don't like awesome dates.*

I smiled. Okay, it was time for a break anyway. I set the laptop on the couch beside me and picked up my phone.

Emerson: *I have nothing against awesome dates, per se. I do have other reasons, however, as I've already explained.*

There. That should do it. But, of course, the three little dots appeared, telling me he was typing his response.

Too Young for You: *We can work around those reasons. I'm a very hard worker.*

Why did that sound vaguely dirty? My pulse sped up a tad, and I ordered it to calm down.

Emerson: *I'm sure you are, but I still have to say no.*

Too Young for You: *So, you're saying I'm going to have to go on the best date ever by myself? Harsh.*

I laughed, despite myself, and typed my response.

Emerson: Oh, it's the best date ever now, is it?

Too Young for You: I guess you'll never know...

Emerson: I'll have to live with the disappointment of never having experienced the best ever.

Too Young for You: Wow. I'm flattered. I didn't know word had gotten around.

Momentarily confused, I read over my last text and realized what I had implied. I could feel my face burning as my thumbs moved frantically over my phone.

Emerson: Shut up. I meant "best DATE ever" and you know it.

It was time to stop this and get back to reality before I embarrassed myself further. Or worse, accepted a date.

Emerson: Jay is excited for Tuesday.

Too Young for You: Hell, I'm excited to train him. He's phenomenal.

Sisterly pride swelled in my chest.

Emerson: Yeah, pretty much.

Too Young for You: I know I'm completely jumping the gun, but I feel like he's really got a shot.

Emerson: A shot?

Too Young for You: At the Majors. It's a long ways down the line, I know, but I've got a gut feeling.

Wow. I had no idea.

Emerson: Seriously?

Too Young for You: I don't joke about baseball.

Emerson: Something tells me that's about the only thing you don't joke about.

Too Young for You: Well, there is one other thing.

Don't ask, Emerson.

Emerson: Do tell.

Dammit!

Too Young for You: *I think you're amazing and I want one date.*

My belly started swimming with warmth and I bit my lip.

Too Young for You: *If you don't want to see me again after that, I'll leave you alone. Hand to God.*

Honestly, what could it hurt? One little date and we'd realize we have nothing in common and go our separate ways. In fact, it was probably a good idea.

Emerson: *Coffee*

Too Young for You: *What?*

Emerson: *I'll get coffee with you. No "best date ever" business.*

Too Young for You: *That's putting a lot of pressure on a cup of beans, but I'm up to the challenge. Coffee it is. How about tomorrow?*

Best to get it over and done with, and then I could stop thinking about him and my stupid, inappropriate attraction to him. I switched to my schedule to see when I'd be free before texting him back.

Emerson: *I'm swamped the next couple days, but I could do Wednesday.*

Too Young for You: *It's a date.*

Emerson: *It's coffee.*

Too Young for You: *We'll see.*

Why did I get the feeling he knew something I didn't?

Chapter Eight

CALL THE POLICE!

*G*AVIN

Not even the mind-numbing sound of multiple nail guns simultaneously firing into drywall could dampen my good mood Monday morning. I'd somehow convinced Emmy to give me a shot. Well, it was just coffee—for now. But I'd do my best to win her over and get her to go out on a real date with me. I was dying to get to know her better, or at all, really. Right now, I only knew that she was beautiful, funny, and a great sister. I didn't even know what she did for a living and I was kicking myself for not asking more questions this weekend. But there was time.

"Yo, Junior, get that dopey-ass grin off your face and come give Trey a hand next door. You can think about giving yourself a hand job later." Mark swung past me and smacked me on my hardhat with a clipboard.

"Hey! I'll have you know my hands were behind my head the whole time—right where they should be. I didn't have to lift a finger!" I threw back at him.

"That's not what I heard. Word is you've been striking out big-time lately!" he yelled as he strode out the door, giving me zero chance to defend myself. The three other guys wielding nail guns all guffawed.

"Laugh it up, assholes! That shit is far from the truth and you know it," I grumbled as I made my way out the back and to the apartment next door. So what if Mark's comments hit a little too close to home? I'd been busy. What can I say? Between the two jobs and my online classes, I didn't have much free time to pursue extracurricular activities.

All that would change on Wednesday, though. I could feel it. I'd make the fucking time.

I spent the rest of the morning and early afternoon assisting with pipefitting before taking off to go home and grab a shower. I'd gotten word that Chris's court appearance was this afternoon, and I was determined to show up and support him. Granted, his parents weren't completely thrilled with me at the moment—but they were reasonable enough to realize I hadn't actually encouraged their son to steal a goddamn car. I hoped they wouldn't mind me showing up.

I also hoped the neighbor would see reason and drop the theft charges. In the end, most of it was resting on the shoulders of Chris's lawyer, Ms. Scott. I sure as hell hoped Jake had steered me in the right direction with that one. There wasn't a whole lot I could do at this point, though, except show up and be there for Chris.

I'd never been to court—I know, I'm as surprised as you—so I wasn't too sure what to expect. By the time I found the correct room, I was already twenty minutes late and I was sweating like a whore in church. The room was a smaller version of what I'd seen on TV, with a judge's bench at the front, two tables for prosecution

and defense, and a viewing area filled with chairs. There was no jury box, and the chairs were folding chairs, but otherwise it was like TV.

The seats were about half full, and it was easy to spot Chris and his parents sitting in one of the front rows. I took a seat a few rows back, not sure if I'd missed anything. Before I could ponder it too long, though, the judge called Chris's name and he rose from his seat. It was only then that I noticed the woman who had been sitting on his other side. She rose with him and led him to one of the tables at the front. I could only see her back, but the hairs on my neck stood at attention and my heart rate involuntarily kicked up. I knew that auburn hair pulled up into a tight bun, and I knew that pert ass, even in a business suit.

What in the hell was Emmy doing here? And with Chris? Just then, Chris glanced behind him and caught sight of me, his face lighting up despite the visible beads of sweat on his forehead. He looked even younger than usual, dressed up in an ill-fitting grey suit and blue tie. I forced myself to give him an encouraging smile and a chin lift, despite my state of utter confusion.

In the next moment, Emmy turned to see who had caught Chris's attention and her eyes widened almost comically at the sight of me. Completely at a loss, I acted like a colossal moron and gave her a thumbs-up. A fucking thumbs-up. Way to go, asshole.

Her expression turned from one of surprise to one of *"Call the police!"* and I was desperately tempted to just flee the scene and pretend I'd never been there. But I couldn't do that to Chris.

Jesus Christ. She probably thought I was stalking her and preparing to dry her skin in my basement before turning it into a cozy winter hat and scarf set. Chris leaned over and whispered something to her, after which she turned and pinned me with a death glare that shrank my balls. WTF?

It seemed I had just blown any chance I might have ever had with her, and I didn't even know how it had happened.

I managed to make it through the proceedings without either running for the hills or approaching the bench and asking the judge for an opportunity on the stand to explain myself. The fact that there was no actual stand was only a small deterrent. By the time it was all said and done, Chris received probation, fines, and community service as we'd all hoped. He hugged Emmy, and she graced him with one of her beautiful smiles that I was pretty certain would never be pointed in my direction again. Then he hugged his parents while I stood at the back of the room trying to decide my next move.

Emmy continued to chat with the older Hardacres as Chris filtered his way through an incoming group of people and found me.

"Hey, Coach. Thanks so much for coming."

I put a fist to his arm. "No problem. I'm glad to see it all worked out."

Chris glanced back to the judge's bench and then to me again. "Yeah, well, it's not ideal but I'll take it." He gave me a self-deprecating grin. "That's what I get for being a jackass, I guess."

I shrugged. "Don't beat yourself up too much. We've all done stupid things. Even me, if you can believe it." I gave him a mock surprised face and he laughed.

The next case was getting ready to start, and I saw Emmy and Chris's parents making their way toward us. Shit. This was awkward.

I raised a hand and gave a little wave—you know, because I

hadn't made a big enough ass out of myself already. The Hardacres were smiling, surely out of relief that their kid wasn't going to juvie. Apparently, I'd been forgiven for my role in this shit show.

Emmy, on the other hand, looked downright disgusted. What in the hell had I done to her?!

"Hey, Gavin." Mr. Hardacre put out a hand and I had to tear my gaze away from Emmy's scathing look, leaving myself vulnerable in the event she chose to attack or something. At this point, anything was possible.

I took his hand and we shook. "I'm so glad this is all over with," I said.

"No kidding," replied Mrs. Hardacre. "And we definitely owe you for arranging Ms. Scott's help." She squeezed Emmy's arm and some of the pieces started coming together in my brain.

Seeing Emmy for the first time at Jake and Bailey's shower and then being referred by them to an attorney named Emerson Scott. I never even thought to look at her last name on the Academy forms because, in my head, she was Emmy Miller. Stupid! She'd said she and Jay had different dads. It still didn't explain why she seemed to suddenly hate me, but I was sure she would be only too happy to explain.

"Wait," Emmy—Emerson—said in a surprised tone. "What does *he* have to do with our introduction? I was referred by Jake and Mark Beckett."

The Hardacres looked at each other and then back at Emmy. Emerson. Ms. Scott. Whoever the fuck! "We don't know any Becketts. Gavin called us with your information." They all turned their gazes to me.

I scratched the back of my neck and tried to explain. "They're friends of mine. Mark is actually my boss." I looked back at

Emmy, still feeling confused. "I thought it was Jake and Bailey who knew you. How do you know Mark?"

She took a breath and let it out like she was losing patience and just wanted to get the hell out of there. "Long story. Anyway, all's well that ends well, right?" She pasted a smile on her face and shook hands with all three Hardacres. "I'll be in touch tomorrow to follow up," she said

And without another word or glance in my direction, she left the courtroom and left me feeling more bewildered than ever.

I had to stay and make small talk with Chris and his family or I'd look like an asshole. By the time I made it out into the main corridor, Emmy was long gone. Just like our coffee date, I surmised.

"So, tell me exactly how you know Emerson Scott?"

"Shit," said Mark as I barreled my way through the door he'd just opened. "Well, come on in and make yourself at home."

"What do you mean, 'shit'?" I turned back to face him as he closed the door behind us. He eyed me, hands on hips with his ridiculous Popeye muscles practically tearing the arms off his t-shirt. Jesus, just buy a bigger shirt, man.

"I think the better question is how *you* know Emerson Scott," he responded.

It was one of my rare nights off, and although I had homework to do, I hadn't been able to focus. I needed answers. Without thinking too much about it, I'd hopped in my car and driven to Mark's place. Well, actually Fiona's place, but she and Mark were attached at the hip—or probably more accurately, the crotch—so it

hadn't been hard to find him. Fiona has a slick condo in a high-rise downtown and, if I were Mark, I'd ditch the rental house he lives in and move in here. This place is sweet. Floor to ceiling windows on a high floor, a granite and stainless-steel kitchen, and girl furniture. Fancy shit.

"I just saw her in court today. You know, helping out my dumbass player who decided he was Mario Andretti."

"Dammit. I knew that was a bad idea," came another male voice from the direction of the kitchen.

I turned around and found Jake and Bailey both leaning against the kitchen counter with drinks in their hands. "Where the hell did you two come from?"

"Uh, free dinner at Fiona's? Have you met me?" asked Bailey, pointing unnecessarily to her protruding belly that looked like it was about to explode. Her blond hair was in a messy ponytail and she looked like she was wearing Jake's clothes.

Well, that explained things, I supposed. Fiona runs a catering business with Mark and Jake's mom and she cooks the absolute best food. I was suddenly a bit put out that I hadn't been invited.

Fiona poked her head around the corner, surprising the shit out of me while simultaneously reading my mind. "You're always at games or training sessions on weeknights. How was I supposed to know you had the night off?"

I made a face at her before remembering my mission and getting back to it. "And you knew *what* was a bad idea?" I asked Jake accusingly.

"Putting that woman anywhere in the vicinity of you and your adolescent libido." He came closer and dropped onto the couch, beckoning for Bailey to sit next to him. She did so with some difficulty, looking a bit more like an elderly person balancing a giant pumpkin on her lap.

I put my hands on my hips. "I take offense to that. My libido is a very mature twenty-four. A shitload better than your ancient ass, I'm guessing."

He put his arm around his wife. "Whatever you say, Junior. I haven't gotten any complaints."

Bailey pretended to contemplate that for a moment before confirming, "That's true," and patting his knee.

Yuck. "Okay, let's drop it. I've met Emerson, we've been introduced, so it's too late anyway. I want to know how you all know her."

Bailey looked back at me and sighed. "Fine. It's not like she'd ever go for you anyway. We were just trying to save you the embarrassment of panting after her like a puppy. Don't think we didn't all see you at that shower with your tongue hanging out."

"Ohhh! I remember her. I liked her." Fiona emerged from the kitchen, suddenly way too interested in the topic.

Bailey nodded at her with a wicked grin before explaining to me, "Remember my douchebag ex—the one who tried to sue Mark? She was his attorney."

Huh? "Wait. I thought Fiona's guy was your attorney."

Mark barked from behind me. "Not *my* attorney, idiot. The douchebag ex's attorney."

I gave each of them an incredulous look. "What the fuck? You recommended someone to me who not only tried to sue you, but lost?! What the hell kind of friends are you?"

Mark and Jake both shrugged and this made them all laugh uproariously. Jesus Christ.

Finally, Fiona seemed to conjure up some basic human decency. "Oh no. Did your kid lose the case?"

That shut all of them up. Bastards.

I shuffled my feet a bit and said, "No," which made them laugh

even harder. I had to shout to be heard. "But that's beside the point!"

Fiona just patted my arm. "Come eat some leftovers. They're still warm." She led me toward the kitchen.

I scowled at her. "You can't placate me with food, you know."

She just nodded and patted my arm again. "It's stuffed pork chops with baked apples and a Dijon butter sauce."

"Oh." I replied and let her lead me to it.

After Fiona fed me, I took my ass home and did some work. I may have dropped out of college when I lost my baseball scholarship— okay, I can't blame the scholarship; it was me feeling sorry for myself—but I'd been able to keep the two years of credits I'd built up. And once I'd stopped acting like a spoiled brat, I realized I was halfway to a Sports Science degree. That was nothing to sneeze at. And nothing to throw away.

It had actually been Gerry who'd encouraged me to step up and finish my degree. Being an assistant coach at the Academy was fun and full of valuable experience, but it didn't pay all that well. Construction paid better, but I couldn't do that full time, and it wasn't where I saw myself in the long run. A degree in Sports Science, combined with the coaching experience I was getting, could lead to a solid future in coaching—hopefully at the college level, eventually.

I'd enrolled in online classes in January and I was hoping to complete my degree in another couple years. Brett was the only one who knew about it at this point, since he's my best friend and it was kind of hard to hide what I was doing on my laptop all that

time. Naturally, he'd assumed a porn addiction in the beginning, but he finally figured that even I didn't have the attention span for that much fucking. I wasn't sure why I didn't want anyone else to know. Maybe I felt like everybody was still waiting for me to fail or revert back to my sorry old ways. Maybe I was afraid of that myself. I didn't want to expose myself to that kind of pressure.

I shot my professor an e-mail with my latest assignment and closed the laptop for the night. Immediately, my mind went back to the scene in court earlier in the day. Should I try texting her?

Before I could talk myself out of it, I grabbed my phone and sent a message.

Gavin: *Hi.*

Brilliant, Gavin. You're a regular Shakespeare.

Crickets.

I figured a beer was in order since I'd kicked ass on my assignment—and I needed a distraction from the blank screen of my phone. One beer and two episodes of *Archer* later—*What? It may be a cartoon, but it's for adults*—and my phone finally sounded with a text notification.

Emmy: *Hello, Gavin. What can I do for you?*

What could she do for me? What was this? I felt like I was in the principal's office or something. Hmm, wait. I think I had a naughty fantasy about that once…nope. Lost it.

I got up to get another beer while I thought about my response. Leaning against the counter, I typed it in.

Gavin: *I think we had a miscommunication of some kind. How about if we work it out on Wednesday over our coffee?*

Emmy: *I don't think that's a good idea. I'm sorry, I'm going to have to cancel.*

WTF?

Gavin: I think I at least deserve an explanation, don't you?

Emmy: It's just for the best. Let's leave it at that. Good luck, and I'm sure I'll see you at some of Jay's games.

Huh. Well, there wasn't much I could say to that, now was there?

Chapter Nine

NOPE

MERSON

Ugh.

I put my phone back on my bedside table. There. I'd let him down gently and it was done. I breathed a sigh of relief, not realizing until right then exactly how keyed up I'd been about the impending coffee date. Coffee *non*-date.

I should have trusted my instincts from the beginning. I had absolutely no business forming any kind of friendship—much less a remotely romantic one—with a guy who still acted like a teenager.

When I'd turned around in court and caught sight of Gavin in the back of the galley, I'd felt my blood run hot. Then cold. My brain could not compute any plausible scenario that would place him in the courtroom. Thoughts flew directly to him being there to see me. But how could he have known I'd be there? I hadn't even told him I was a lawyer. That's when my thoughts raced right to

psycho town and I considered the possibility that he was a crazy stalker. That would be just my luck.

But when I realized that Chris obviously knew him, and Chris explained exactly *how* he knew him, understanding dawned. I really shouldn't have been all that surprised to find out that Gavin Monroe was just as damned immature as I'd feared. He had been the family "friend" who'd told Chris to go along with the other teenagers' antics and do what he needed to fit in. What kind of advice was that? Damn idiot kids. Gavin included.

This was exactly why I always trusted my gut and kept the big picture in mind. I didn't have the time or the freedom to let undesirable or unsuitable people into my life.

Sighing, I sank down into my pillow and pulled my blanket up to my chin. I felt the soft fibers brush against my neck and immediately felt a bit better. It was my go-to comfort. Yes, I realized the irony of my disdain for childish behavior while simultaneously clinging to what essentially amounted to a toddler's blankie. But it was soft. What can I say?

However, even my blanket couldn't entirely calm the storm in my head. My thoughts drifted back to last fall's debacle that had started this whole thing. I'd known that damn pro bono would eventually come back to haunt me. And I'd been right.

Last year I'd taken on a different pro bono case at the request of Bradford Schenk, one of the managing partners. It was a personal injury case in which his daughter's friend had been assaulted and had some property damaged in the process. The client was an artist named Anton Germaine, and he seemed both sincere and distraught when I first met with him. He explained that he'd broken up with a woman, and that woman's friend hadn't taken kindly to it. In fact, the friend had responded by threatening Anton and then punching him as well as ruining an expensive

painting Anton had been in the process of selling to a client for a large sum of money.

Mr. Schenk's daughter, Amber, explained that Mr. Germaine was a popular local artist who had a successful exhibit at a local gallery in progress at the time of the assault. Not only had he been punched and had his property ruined, but he also feared for his safety and was unable to continue with his current work due to the constant stress.

While I hadn't really bought the whole idea of not being able to work, I wasn't exactly the creative type, so what did I know? Well, I'll tell you what I did know. Bradford Schenk had asked me to represent this guy, so that's what I was going to do. I informed the party we were intending to sue—whose name was Mark Beckett— and scheduled a settlement meeting, hoping to avoid court.

Little had I known, Anton Germaine turned out not only to be a crappy artist, but he was a crappy liar too. In the end, his story fell apart faster than a house of cards. As far as I could discern, yes, he'd been punched, but he'd also deserved it. In fact, I would have liked to deliver my own punch when all was said and done. He'd manufactured the bit about the destruction of property as well as the inability to work. And then he'd proceeded to assault the ex-girlfriend right in front of me. Bailey Murphy—no, Beckett now since marrying her friend's brother—was certainly better off without the ass of an artist.

But I'd felt bad about my part in it, so when the Beckett clan asked for help last week, I hadn't hesitated long. And, besides, the client was a fourteen-year-old kid who'd taken some awful advice from a family friend—one I now knew to be Gavin Monroe. I thanked my lucky stars that my little brother was self-possessed enough not to fall for lame life lessons from an overgrown child.

I rolled over and punched my pillow, giving a huge huff.

Maybe I should steer clear of pro bono cases for a while. Yeah, that's what I should do. I took a deep breath, let it out, and finally fell asleep with my blanket cushioning my cheek.

"I still can't believe the coincidence," Ari said as we waited in line at Starbucks the next morning. She was wearing slim black pants and a flowy red blouse that brought out the burgundy in her hair. Her nose and eyebrow piercings were missing, a requirement of her receptionist job at the conservative realty office where she'd be heading after coffee.

I'd called her this morning for emergency girl time so I could get the oddness and frustration of this whole situation off my chest and refocus.

"I know. And I can't believe he'd actually talked me into coffee with him."

She tilted her head and gave me the raised eyebrows. "Seriously?"

"What?" I had no idea what she was driving at.

"Let's see." She put up a hand and started counting off on her fingers. "He's cute. He's got that ass. You haven't gotten laid in a decade." I scowled at her at that one and tried to shush her, but she continued, undeterred. "He blatantly pursued you, which is hot. And, oh yeah, that ass!" she finished, shoving her open palm in my face.

I smacked it aside. "Whatever. I just thank God I realized my mistake before I actually went out with him. I think I need a vacation."

"Damn straight. I've been telling you that for two years. But let's not kid ourselves. You're never taking a vacation. You've got

the AgPower thing and all your other cases on top of that. You're going to die at your desk and we'll just cover you in a shroud and seal the room up."

"Shut up. I am not. But, you're right, I can't take vacation anytime in the foreseeable future. Must stick to the plan: crush Craig, get partnership, kick butt, and retire to Aruba at fifty." I ticked off my list on my own fingers.

"You'd better get a tiki hut for two, because I'm joining you, girl."

I gave her a side hug as we approached the counter to place our order. "I wouldn't have it any other way."

Once we were settled at our table with our drinks, I asked Ari about her family. I needed to focus on something else.

"They're good. I still haven't dared to bring Elliot back around, but Mamá said *you'd* better get your ass to dinner one of these days."

I set my cup down and sighed. "I know. I haven't seen your parents in months. Tell her I promise I'll come soon."

Ari took a small sip of her coffee and played with her necklace with her other hand. Her tone turned to one that's usually accompanied by some form of oversharing on her part. "And Ponch has been asking about you too. I told him you were dating the baseball coach and he about blew a gasket. Granted, I didn't know at the time that you actually *were* dating Gavin, but that makes it even funnier. I think Ponch's flirting is turning into a real-life lustfest."

I shooed her off. "No it isn't. He's like that with everyone with boobs."

"I don't know…" she trailed off, still playing with the beads around her neck.

"And I wasn't dating Gavin. We were engaging in some mildly

flirty texting and were considering drinking some coffee in the same room. That's a far cry from dating."

"Uh huh. Keep telling yourself that."

I threw my napkin at her and she laughed, finally dropping the damn necklace and leaning forward on the table.

"I hate to stir things up. Okay, I love to stir things up, I admit." She gave me a wicked grin before continuing. "But, I don't really see what Gavin did that was all that bad."

I looked at her incredulously. "He told a fourteen-year-old boy to steal a car!"

"No, he didn't. That's ridiculous." This time it was her shooing me. "He gave some advice that was grossly misinterpreted and ended in a shitty situation. Which he called in favors to remedy, I might add. He didn't just ditch the kid." She sat back in her chair, having just closed her argument with what she considered to be a slam dunk. Why wasn't she the lawyer?

I supposed that was true. I played with the cardboard sleeve of my coffee cup and thought for a moment before responding. "Be that as it may, he's still way too young to consider. And, I might add, I hardly have time to see you; where would I ever find the time to date anyone?"

"All work and no play…just sayin'." She shrugged and pointed at me. "And don't forget that ass."

I searched around for another napkin to throw at her but had to settle for a dirty look instead.

Damn you, Ari, I thought to myself later that afternoon as I tried for the third time to focus on the boring paperwork in front of me. I was reviewing documents on an acquisition one of our clients was

finalizing, but my brain seemed to be stuck on Ari's words from that morning.

I admit, maybe I'd been a bit rude in my texts to Gavin the previous night. I pulled my phone out so I could review the exchange.

Nope: *Hi.*

I'd changed his contact name from *Too Young for You* to *Nope* as soon as his text came through the night before. I hadn't even intended to acknowledge his message, but after an hour it had seemed rude not to.

Emerson: *Hello, Gavin. What can I do for you?*

Nope: *I think we had a miscommunication of some kind. How about if we work it out on Wednesday over our coffee?*

Emerson: *I don't think that's a good idea. I'm sorry, I'm going to have to cancel.*

Nope: *I think I at least deserve an explanation, don't you?*

Emerson: *It's just for the best. Let's leave it at that. Good luck, and I'm sure I'll see you at some of Jay's games.*

Hmm. That had been a bit abrupt, hadn't it? I brought up the phone's keyboard and considered what I might text back to appropriately apologize for my rudeness, while also communicating that nothing was going to happen between us. I began to type.

Emerson: *I'm sorry I*

That was as far as I got when Craig burst into my office—without knocking—and proceeded to rant at me about a detail I'd missed in the non-disclosure draft. By the time I settled him down and explained that it hadn't been an oversight but an intentional omission of information, it was over an hour later. He finally left me in peace and I removed my reading glasses, closed my eyes, and squeezed the bridge of my nose to stave off the headache that usually came in the wake of any Craig encounter.

"You look beat," said a voice from the doorway. A very familiar voice.

My eyes snapped open and Gavin Monroe stood in my doorway, looking all adorable and sexy in athletic shorts and a grey t-shirt, the familiar green baseball cap covering his head. He held a cup of coffee in one hand and his face sported a sheepish grin.

"Wh-what are you doing here?"

"I got your text," he said, casual as can be.

"My…" I looked around on my desk until I unearthed my phone and dismissed the lock screen. Sure enough, there was a text from me to Gavin, and two in return. I had sent the damn unfinished text by accident. I chose to blame Craig.

Emerson: *I'm sorry I*

Nope: *You're sorry you what? Cancelled our coffee date?*

Nope: *You're forgiven, by the way. I'll even stop by your office and bring you a cup on my way to training.*

My eyes found him again and I was speechless. How had I gotten myself into this?

Seemingly needing no invitation, he sauntered into my office and set the coffee in front of me. "I didn't know how you liked it, so I took a wild guess and got you a skim vanilla latte. That's what Mark's girlfriend likes, so I chanced it."

I looked down at the coffee and back to him. I recalled the girlfriend. Fiona, I think. "Yes. I mean, that's perfect. Thank you."

Again, needing no invitation, he took a seat across from my desk and took a good look around. "This is nice. You must be pretty important."

I took a moment to look around myself and take in the surroundings from a newcomer's perspective. It was a nice office with a small sofa and table in the corner and two matching chairs in front of a maple desk. Coordinating bookshelves lined one

wall and I even had a small window with a view of the courtyard.

My eyes came back to him. "I don't know about that. I'm just a fourth-year associate. You should see the partners' offices." I stayed seated because I had no clue what to do in this situation. I hadn't wanted him to come here. "So," I began awkwardly, "I guess you have training to go to. What time does that start?"

Incredibly subtle, Emerson. Geez.

He looked at his watch. "Not for another forty-five minutes. I made sure I had plenty of time."

For what? I wanted to ask but kept my mouth shut.

"So, I was thinking—if it works with your schedule, of course —we could meet up at the Starbucks around the corner when you're done with work tomorrow. Unless, that is, you've changed your mind and want to do dinner. I don't know that I could put together that 'best date ever' in the short timeframe, but I can arrange something."

When I didn't respond, he continued, gesturing to the coffee in front of me, "I mean, technically, we've done coffee so it's only proper to move on to dinner as a second date."

"Date?" was all I managed before another visitor chose the worst possible moment to fill my office doorway.

Mr. Wheeler stood in the threshold, head bent to his phone. "Ms. Scott, is it possible to move our..." he began before glancing up and seeing I already had company. He straightened.

"Oh, I'm terribly sorry. I didn't realize you had a client."

"Oh, he's not a client," I burst out before my brain could catch up and tell me to shut my mouth.

Mr. Wheeler took the entire situation in stride and stepped forward, hand out to Gavin, who stood and shook my boss's hand.

"Gavin Monroe. Pleased to meet you."

"Thomas Wheeler. The pleasure is mine," my boss returned formally and then, just as he released Gavin's hand, his eyes widened a bit and snapped back to Gavin's face. "You're Gavin Monroe." His tone was suddenly enthusiastic and he gave a small laugh. "Well, of course you are. You just introduced yourself. I followed your career since you were in high school. My daughter went to State and I never missed a game."

Gavin seemed to be completely unaffected by this jovial outburst from my boss that had me mentally passing out in shock. My freaking boss was fan-girling all over my non-date. Who the hell was this guy?

"I appreciate it," replied Gavin. "Fans are what make the whole thing possible."

"Well, you definitely had one in me, I'll tell you that. I'm really sorry things didn't work out for you."

Gavin gave a self-deprecating smile and shrugged. "We can't all live the dream. I've moved on."

Mr. Wheeler nodded appreciatively and then turned to me. "Why didn't you tell me you were dating a local legend?"

Oh, God! "No, we're—" I began, but Gavin cut me off.

"It's new. She probably didn't want to broadcast her personal life around the office."

"True. Always the consummate professional, Ms. Scott." He nodded again and I had no earthly clue how to respond. Refuting Gavin's comment would only trigger more discussion on the topic and would make me appear indecisive or flighty. That, I could not have.

"Well, now that the cat is out of the bag, we may as well take advantage of this situation," Mr. Wheeler commented, his gaze shifting between me and Gavin.

No, no, no!

"As Ms. Scott knows, we have our Bar Association softball tournament coming up and we always encourage significant others to participate." He looked at Gavin with raised eyebrows and I wished for the largest piano possible to drop on my head. Or Gavin's. I couldn't decide.

Chapter Ten

PLAY BALL

*G*AVIN

I was feeling pretty proud of myself for how I'd maneuvered that situation. Thomas Wheeler left the office a few minutes after I agreed to be on their firm's softball team, and I'm sure I wore a shit-eating grin. One glance at Emmy, though, told me I'd better gird my loins because shit was about to rain down on my parade. Eh, maybe I mixed a few too many idioms, but I was starting to panic.

Emmy stood from behind her desk, revealing another conservative suit—this one some kind of grey tweed with a white blouse underneath. She was buttoned up into the perfect package and all I wanted to do was unbutton every little bit of her. It had been all I could do not to bite my hand when I'd seen her at her desk wearing those glasses. Talk about sexy librarian fantasies—I'd be booking some alone time this evening for sure.

Her mood did not match mine, however, as she grabbed me by the sleeve of my t-shirt and practically marched me out of her

office and down the hall toward the elevators. I thought briefly about asking her to bring those glasses with her, but wisely kept my mouth shut.

She was seething, and I'm sure I was supposed to understand why, but once again, I was at a loss when it came to this woman. Although, I did consider the possibility that maybe I shouldn't have told her colleague we were dating. I'll admit, I got a little ahead of myself.

The elevator opened and she pulled me inside. Was it wrong that I was getting a little turned on by her forceful behavior? *Down boy*, I told myself. The doors closed and she turned to me, opening her mouth and pointing her index finger in my face. I waited, but nothing came out. She closed it, then opened it again and drew in a deep breath. Still nothing. Her eyes were piercing me with anger or frustration, or maybe a bit of both. When she closed her mouth without speaking this time, I decided she'd had her turn. Now it was mine.

I stepped into her, leaned down, and covered her mouth with mine. She was stiff as a board, but I didn't let that deter me. I put one hand to the small of her back and the other to the back of her neck, drawing her into me. The kiss began gently as I took her bottom lip between mine, then switched to the top, grazing it lightly with my teeth in the process. Her lips were soft and perfect, as I'd known they'd be. I pulled back a fraction of an inch and felt her warm breath on my mouth as she exhaled. When she didn't slap me or pull back, I angled my head and deepened the kiss, gently sweeping my tongue across her bottom lip, begging for entrance.

Her lips parted in invitation and I didn't hesitate to slide my tongue against hers for a better taste. She smelled amazing—like citrus and vanilla—and she tasted even better. A combination of

coffee and mint and something else that I assumed was just Emmy. She let out a little moan and I adjusted our position, allowing my hand to travel up her back so I could press her breasts into my chest as my mouth continued its assault.

Finally, I felt her arms wrap around and grasp two fistfuls of my t-shirt at the back. The anger had all but dissipated, replaced by desire and/or the need to rip my shirt off my back. Not that I was complaining. This spurred me on, and I let my hand travel back down until it reached her ass. I pulled her in even further so she could feel the effect she was having on me.

Just then, the elevator dinged and we both jumped back, having completely forgotten where we were.

She muttered something that sounded like "sugar" before she frantically smoothed her hair and clothes just as the elevator doors parted. Two women in suits very similar to Emmy's stepped in, both of them nodding to us before continuing their conversation. Emmy extended them a strained smile and then, when the women's backs were turned to us, hissed quietly at me, "I can't *believe* you just did that."

I leaned in and heard her breath hitch, as if she thought I was moving in to kiss her again. "Did what?"

"Any of it," she whispered tersely.

The elevator doors opened to the lobby and she stalked out after the women. I raced to catch up to her, impressed at how fast she could walk in those heels. Speaking of those heels, Jesus—they made her legs look a mile long and added an extra sway to her ass as she practically sprinted out of the building ahead of me. I was acutely aware that my athletic shorts did very little to hide my condition, and I wished for some kind of folder or bag to place in front of me while I walked. Oh well. It couldn't be helped. At least not around this woman, that was for damn sure.

By the time she exited the building and was halfway down the sidewalk, I'd had enough of the chasing. I caught up to her and put a hand on her shoulder. "Emmy, wait."

She whirled on me. "Emerson. My name is Emerson. Not Emmy. Emerson." She brushed a hair out of her eyes and stood stiffly.

I pulled my head back. "Really? You don't like Emmy?"

"That's what my mother calls me. Nobody else." She looked to the side, obviously still perturbed.

"Well, you could have corrected me."

"I know." She shook her head and then brought her gaze back to me. "Anyway, that's not the point. The point is, you act *way* too familiar with me. You just told my boss we were dating and you invited yourself to join my firm's softball team, for God's sake! Not to mention that incredibly inappropriate kiss in the elevator!" She huffed, and I wouldn't have been surprised if she'd stomped her foot. I thought the whole display was kind of hot. This whole riled-up sexy librarian thing was a turn on. Big time.

I couldn't help the grin that formed on my face. "I didn't hear you complaining at the time."

She glared at me but it bounced right off.

Her hands extended in exasperation. "Now I'll have to manufacture a believable break-up that doesn't result in my boss being ticked at me for messing with the darn roster he's no doubt salivating over at this very moment." She gestured heatedly back to the building.

I raised my hand as if asking permission to speak. Yes, like a five-year-old. Hey, if she got to be the librarian, I'd volunteer to be the student. That got me another glare, so I dug in. "Or, I could just play on the team. Sounds easier."

She sighed. "You don't understand, Gavin. I can't let word get

around that I'm dating someone so much younger than me. It would seriously mess with my reputation at the firm. I'd be fodder for the office gossip chain. Don't you understand? I'm on the partner track and I have to watch my every move."

"Your boss didn't seem to think it was a big deal."

"That's because he had stars in his eyes. How was I supposed to know you're some kind of local hero?" I scowled at that but she continued, "He was envisioning holding up the championship trophy, not thinking about my career. And, believe me, the other two managing partners wouldn't miss a chance to knock me down a peg, and don't even get me started on the other associates. It's dog-eat-dog in there. You wouldn't understand." She sounded defeated, but I couldn't help but feel a bit offended.

"Oh, I couldn't possibly understand? What, because I'm just some dumb jock who works construction and plays ball?"

"That's not what I meant. You're just...young." Her voice had lost some of its fire by this point.

"Emmy. Sorry. Emerson, I'm twenty-four, not twelve. I work hard and I'm carving out a career for myself. I don't deserve the insinuations you're making. You don't even know me." I wasn't going to let anyone dismiss me that easily, much less this woman I was apparently in complete lust with.

"I know enough." The critical look was making a return.

"What's that supposed to mean?"

She raised her eyebrows. "I know you encouraged a fourteen-year-old kid to do whatever it took to fit in with the 'cool kids.' I can't think of anything as immature and shortsighted as that."

Fuck. The pieces were finally coming together here. "Is that what this is about? Jesus. I gave the kid a few pointers to help him avoid getting bullied. I didn't tell him to steal a goddamned car!"

"Keep your voice down," she hissed.

"And, by all rights, I should be pissed at you!" I threw at her. Yeah, she didn't hold the patent on annoyance.

"Me?!" She couldn't have looked more shocked.

"Yes! You sued my friend, who also happens to be my boss, and almost ruined his life!"

She sucked in a breath of shock. "I did not! That was much more complicated than you're making it out to be."

I tilted my head at her and leaned in. "Hmm, kind of like my situation with Chris?"

That shut her up.

"Where's your big lawyer talk now?" I taunted.

She actually growled at that point. Damn, her eyes were on fire. Flecks of gold glinted throughout the brown of her irises. It made me wonder how they'd look when she was aroused.

Seemingly all out of arguments, she asked, "So, what now?"

I put my hands on my hips. "I don't know. You tell me. Apparently, I'm your dirty little secret whether you like it or not. Your boss is not going to want me off that team and you know it."

Her shoulders slumped. "I know."

I just stood and stared back at the building. I guess I sort of had screwed this up for her, but I didn't understand the big deal. I'm only five years younger than her. I brought my gaze back to Emmy, unhappy that I'd caused this defeated look. "You know, guys date younger women all the time. What's the big deal if it's the other way around?"

She waved me off. "It's a complete double standard, I know, but that doesn't make it any less real. They'll skewer me for it."

"Even if we kick ass at the tournament?" I asked, giving her a wicked grin.

That brought out a small smile in response. "Well, it couldn't hurt to win, I suppose," she admitted.

"You know what I think? I think you worry too much."

She rolled her eyes. "You've been talking to Ari, haven't you?"

"No, but if we can join forces to loosen you up, I just might call her."

She sighed and paused. "Look, Gavin, I'm sorry I blew up at you. I just really need everyone at the firm to take me seriously. I can't afford to slip."

I was beginning to understand that it wasn't just her co-workers she needed to take her seriously. It was everyone. And I was certainly ready to take her seriously. Probably just not in the way she meant.

"It's okay. I can see you're under a lot of stress. I have ways of relieving that, you know." I waggled my eyebrows in an exaggerated move to keep her smiling. Her face was brilliant when she did.

"I'm sure you do." She shoved my arm and then seemed to remember herself. "Don't you have training to get to? I believe my brother is waiting with bated breath."

I looked at my watch and saw that she was right. I'd used up my free time and I'd be late if I didn't leave now.

"I suppose I'll have to save all my stress-relieving skills for our second date."

"Gavin." She left it at the one word, but it spoke volumes.

I wasn't letting go that easily. "What? If everybody already thinks we're dating, what's the harm?"

She pursed her lips, bringing my attention directly to them while my mind replayed that killer kiss in the elevator.

I leaned in close. "And don't try to tell me you didn't enjoy that kiss."

Her face flamed, and she immediately spun on her heel to head back to the office.

I just laughed, causing her to pick up the pace, providing me with another awesome view of her ass in that prim little skirt.

I spent the drive over to the Academy both reliving the hot elevator kiss and planning where to take Emmy to dinner the next night. She hadn't technically said yes, but she hadn't said no either. And I thought I'd made a good argument in my favor. She was clearly shy when it came to the physical, but I could work with that. I couldn't wait to get my mouth on her again.

It was time to change my thought pattern when I pulled into the Academy parking lot and spotted Jay and Coach Davidson talking to Buzz on one of the practice fields. It brought to mind my first interview with Buzz and Gerry, and I recalled being a little star-struck myself. Since then, I'd gotten to know the former Major League first baseman, and the awe had worn off. He was a decent guy, but to be honest, I preferred Gerry's company and mentorship.

Guessing that the guys wouldn't appreciate me sporting even the slightest wood, I went directly inside and changed into my coaching uniform of an Academy polo shirt and khaki pants before joining the trio on the field.

"Coach," I greeted Davidson as we shook hands. I turned to Jay and extended a hand to him as well, while still addressing Davidson. "Looks like you've won the lottery with this one."

That brought out polite chuckles from both men as Jay tried to wave me off. "Nah, I've got a lot to learn. I was just telling Mr. Hader how glad I am for the opportunity to learn from y'all." Damn, this kid was polite. And humble. I'm sure I was a conceited asshole at his age.

"Well, no time like the present, if everybody's ready."

"I've got to be running. Nice to see you, Buzz, Monroe." Davidson nodded at both of us. "Good luck, kid. See you at tomorrow's game," he said to Jay and then excused himself.

Buzz patted Jay on the shoulder. Hader had lost some of his stature with age, but he was still a relatively fit guy. His omnipresent sunglasses covered his eyes and an Academy baseball cap topped his head. "I'll leave you to it for now. Coach Monroe will be doing some evaluations today, as we discussed. I'll catch up with you again on Thursday." Buzz nodded to both of us and headed back to the main building, leaving Jay and me to play ball. Damn, my life was good.

Chapter Eleven
WOW

EMERSON

I put my head down and worked like an obsessed woman for the rest of the afternoon and early evening, not daring to slow down or I'd have to think about that damn kiss. That damn kiss that had lit my entire body on fire and had me thinking very, very naughty thoughts I had no business thinking. *Nope. Too Young for You.* But I'd never had a kiss like that—one that I could feel in every pore and cell. Sadly, even the most memorable sex I'd had couldn't compare to that one simple kiss. How pathetic was that?

I pulled my glasses off and squeezed the bridge of my nose. This wasn't working. My belly dipped as my mind went back to the elevator. I was pretty sure those weren't butterflies in there—they seemed more like spider monkeys, screaming and swinging around, laughing at me and my stupid predicament.

I'd concluded that there was no easy way to bow out of this softball team situation, so I'd have to make it work somehow. The trick would be finding a way to keep my reputation as a serious,

professional sharp-shooter in the process. I was at a loss as to how to accomplish that. Gavin had been right, the age difference shouldn't matter in the grand scheme of things, but that didn't change anything. It was an old-school boys' club and I'd entered the clubhouse with my eyes wide open, agreeing to play their game by their rules. If I chose to break them, it was at my own peril.

But, besides the image part, I still felt silly even considering going out with Gavin. Okay, so he was five years younger, not nine as I'd feared, but a lot happens between the ages of twenty-four and twenty-nine. Careers form, goals alter, responsibilities increase. He hadn't experienced much of that yet, as far as I could tell. We were in different stages of our lives, making this a terrible idea.

All I had to do was look at my father and all his failed relationships with younger women to drive that truth home. I'd vowed never to make the relationship mistakes he had. And then there was the need to focus on work and Jay. I couldn't forget that.

No. Dating Gavin Monroe for real, as opposed to fake-dating him for the tournament's sake, was a terrible idea all around. So, why did the spider monkeys keep telling me otherwise. Darn hormonal beasts.

I closed my laptop and packed up to go home. It was after seven and I clearly wasn't in the headspace to be productive anymore tonight. What I needed was Netflix and a bowl of ice cream.

Unfortunately, if I'd thought time at home would distract me from the unwanted younger-man temptation, I'd been dead wrong. As soon as I walked in the door, Jay regaled me with a thirty-minute monologue on how utterly amazing his afternoon at the Baseball Academy had been—meeting the famous Buzz Hader, touring the facility, and, let's not forget, hanging out with Coach

Monroe, who was apparently the coolest guy on earth. I smiled and nodded and told Jay how happy I was that things had gone so well. He couldn't wipe the sweet lopsided grin off his face. Eventually, he couldn't come up with one more unforgettable detail to share, and off he went to his room to finish his homework.

It wasn't until Jay left that I realized this was the first time since he'd moved in that he'd acted like the old Jay I knew. Happy, carefree, content with life and his place in it. And, dammit, it looked like I had one *Nope/Too Young for You* to thank for it.

I was halfway through my second episode of *The Crown*, knowing I should put the remote down and go through more paper-work, when my phone rang. My pulse jumped as if my body were on constant alert for any form of contact from Gavin. I wasn't going to answer and was about to let it go to voicemail when I glanced at my phone and saw that it wasn't Gavin at all. It was Ponch. A stab of disappointment I didn't want to examine too closely cut through me. Of course, I wasn't going to share that with Ponch—even though his ego could take it.

"Hey there," I said into the phone.

"Hey, beautiful, how's it going?"

I wondered briefly if he even knew who he was calling or if he always used terms of endearment in place of names in the event he misdialed. "I'm good. How's the world of motorcycle gear?" Ponch owned an independent gear shop for all things involving motorcycles. I'd been by a couple times, but the vibe there could be more than a little intimidating.

"Same as ever. Business could always be better, but I've got no real complaints," he answered. "So, what are you up to this weekend?"

That caught me by surprise. I mean, it wasn't as if Ponch never called me, but it was usually regarding something related to Ari or

the rest of the family. Maybe his mom had tasked him with getting me over to her house.

"Um, I'm not really sure. Ari and I had talked about dinner Friday since she's not working…" I trailed off. "Why? Is your mom having the family over this weekend?"

"No, nothing like that."

Now I was really confused. "Oh," was all I could think to say.

"I want us to go out to dinner."

Um, okay. This couldn't be what it sounded like. "You're more than welcome to come on Friday. The more the merrier." I'm sure my tone was way too cheerful.

"Sorry," he practically barked into the phone. "Forget I said anything. Have fun with Ari and I'll talk to you later."

Then he hung up.

I stared at the phone for a good minute trying to figure out what the heck had just happened. Had Ponch Amante just asked me out? What sort of alternate universe was this where I had not one hot guy, but two wanting to take me out? I looked down at myself, checking to see if maybe my boobs had grown recently, but nope. They were still a modest B-cup.

I must have misinterpreted, and I decided to pretend the call had never happened, just as Ponch requested. I also took it as a sign that I needed to get back to work, so I dove into some paperwork and soon forgot about the strange call.

A text came through when I was getting ready for bed. I froze and bit my lip, not sure which name on the screen would rattle me more. Five seconds of kidding myself that I wouldn't read it and the phone was in my hand. I swallowed hard and felt my belly flip over. For the third time this week, I'd changed the contact name.

Be Careful: *Are we still on for dinner tomorrow night?*

I harrumphed. Presumptuous much?

Be Careful: *I thought I'd take you to Gia since I know you like that place.*

How did he know that? Maybe he *had* been talking to Ari.

Emerson: *How do you know that?*

Be Careful: *It's where I first saw you.*

What? How was that possible? We'd met at Jay's game.

Emerson: *We met at Jay's game??*

Be Careful: *Correct. But I first saw you at Gia—at Jake and Bailey Beckett's shower.*

He'd been there? I'd been at Gia a few months back and noticed the Becketts having a party. I'd quietly approached the couple to give them my card and let them know that I could help if that dreadful Anton Germaine ever reared his ugly, lying head again. I didn't realize Gavin had been there, but I guess it made sense.

Emerson: *How in the world do you remember that?*

Be Careful: *Trust me. You're hard to forget.*

I felt my body flame at the compliment and the spider monkeys piped up again. I didn't know how to respond. Nobody had ever delivered such a flattering personal compliment to me before. I was used to professional compliments, but never personal ones. I think my last boyfriend's best compliment had been, "Excellent parking job." God, I was pathetic.

Emerson: *Oh. Thank you.*

Be Careful: *Don't thank me. It's true. Now, how about Gia? It will have to be around 8:00 since I have to work, but I figured you keep late hours anyway.*

I bit my lip and looked around my bedroom as if the answer was held somewhere under a pillow or behind a drape. Part of me really wanted to go and the other part was ready to smack the back of my hand with a ruler for even considering it. But one

date wouldn't hurt, would it? Heck, it was like Gavin said—the firm would all think we were dating anyway. Why not take advantage? Before the ruler could come down on me, I typed my response.

Emerson: *Okay. I'll meet you there at 8:00.*

I hit send and immediately let out a squeal, something incredibly uncharacteristic of me. I had a sudden urge to call Ari, but I held back, letting the idea of my upcoming date settle in my brain and belly for a moment. My phone vibrated again.

Be Careful: *Can't wait.*

As much as I feared it and wished it weren't true, I couldn't either. What in God's name had happened to my earlier resolve? Oh yeah, Gavin Monroe had happened.

"Wow," Gavin breathed out.

Yet another first. I'd never been wowed before and I felt my face begin to heat. Darn it. I'd been here five seconds and my grip on my well-controlled world was already slipping. I willed my skin not to betray me as Gavin took me in from head to toe in the lobby of Gia the next night. I'd struggled for ages over what to wear and finally caved and called Ari.

After she finished I-told-you-so-ing, her first words were, "For Christ's sake, tell me you're not standing in your closet looking at a suit." At that, I put the hanger holding my red Elie Tahari suit back on the rail.

"No," I said, convincing no one.

"This is a date with a hot young guy. You need to dress flirty—as in, plunging neckline or a short skirt."

I wasn't sure if I even owned a skirt that didn't at least skim the

tops of my knees. And plunging neckline? Who did she think she was talking to?

She seemed to realize this because she continued with, "Never mind. Go all the way to the back-right corner of your closet." I loved my closet. It was a huge walk-in with a built-in shoe rack that could hold twenty pairs of shoes. And don't think I didn't fill that entire sucker up. I glanced to the back-right corner, realizing at once what Ari was up to.

"Ari, those are your clothes." She liked to keep a few things at my house for when we had a bit too much wine or she wanted to escape whatever boyfriend was bugging her at the moment. "In what universe do you think I could wear anything of yours?"

I could practically hear her shrug over the phone. "So, the top might be a bit loose in the rack area—so what. There should be a green sleeveless top with sequins embroidered into the front. Grab it." I did as I was told but immediately put it right back.

"Are you kidding me?!" I screeched. The top did indeed have sequins embroidered on the front—what there was of it. I swear the neckline formed a vee that would likely reveal my belly button, not to mention anything I had up top.

"I'm deadly serious. He'll swallow his tongue, and it will look gorgeous with your hair."

"That won't matter because I'll be arrested for indecent exposure before I even make it into the restaurant!"

"Okay, drama queen, calm the hell down."

"I couldn't even wear a bra with that thing!" I continued my protest.

"And?"

"And I'm a twenty-nine-year-old professional woman. I'm legally required to wear a bra. I'd probably wear one to bed if I found one comfortable enough."

She snickered at that. "Can I make a counter-argument, counsel?" She didn't wait for me to answer. "You just proved my point. You're twenty-nine and your tits are still perky. That's not going to be the case forever. Take advantage and let the girls go free."

I couldn't believe I was even considering this. Although, I supposed I could pin the top so it didn't reveal too much. "Whatever. So, Kelly Osborne, exactly what am I going to magically pair with this slutty top?"

"You definitely can't pull off any of my skirts with that tiny ass, so I say just go with your darkest skinny jeans and some killer heels."

"Really? Jeans to dinner? My father would be appalled."

"You're going to Gia, not the White House. You'll look fab. Oh, and wear your hair down."

Shoot. I knew she'd say that.

"Are you sure I can't just wear what I wore to work?"

"Do I need to come over there and kick your ass? I would, but then I'd be late for work. I'm opening with Adele tonight."

Ari has the most beautiful singing voice. Personally, I thought she could have gone somewhere with it, but she never wanted to leave North Carolina to pursue it. I'd have to carve some time out to watch her at work one of these evenings. "I need to come to one of your gigs soon. It's been too long. Where are you setting up shop tonight?" She brings karaoke night to an array of local bars and the line-up is always changing.

"Pinky's. Should be fun. Anyway, are we all set on the outfit, or do I have to get fired in order to dress your ass in something sexy?"

"No, master, I'll do as I'm told."

"Oooh, I bet Mr. Baseball would love it if you said that to him."

My jaw dropped. "Ari! Sometimes I don't understand how we ever became friends."

"It's because my dirty mind didn't develop until it was too late to ditch me."

True. I pulled the green top back out and held it up for another inspection.

"Okay, girl," Ari said. "I gotta run. Have fun and call me later with all the details. Length, girth, you know, the usual."

I hung up on her, but not before I heard her cackling laugh.

And now I was here in the lobby of Gia, having just been wowed by an incredibly hot guy. Gavin was wearing jeans, I was relieved to see, and he'd paired them with a navy checked button-down with the sleeves rolled up to reveal those sexy wrists and forearms I'd noticed on our first meeting. The monkeys seemed to like his wrists as well, if the activity in my belly was anything to go by.

"Hi, Gavin." I managed a smile which he returned before leaning in and kissing my cheek. He smelled entirely yummy and I had the sudden ridiculous urge to bury my face in his neck and settle in. What was wrong with me? Instead, I quickly glanced down to make sure Ari's top hadn't shifted where I'd pinned it. I hadn't dared to let it dip any lower than just above my bra's front closure, despite Ari's urgings regarding my "girls" and their need to live a life of freedom.

"You look beautiful," Gavin said as he pulled back.

"Thanks. You don't look too bad yourself." Understatement of the year. He looked good enough to eat.

"They have our table ready." He gestured to the hostess who stood next to the podium, two menus in her hand.

I stepped forward and felt the heat of his hand on the small of my back. It cut directly through the flimsy shirt and sent a deli-

cious tingle up my spine. I was beginning to understand that I was in deep, deep trouble where this guy was concerned. For the third time in the last ten minutes, I second-guessed my decision to come. Nevertheless, I smiled and thanked the hostess as I took my seat across from Gavin. We were seated at a cozy corner table, offering a degree of privacy that only added to my discomfort.

"Are you okay?" Gavin asked as he unfolded his napkin and placed it on his lap. Concern clouded his features and I immediately felt ashamed. I'd agreed to this date, after all. I needed to woman up. One cleansing breath later, I summoned my best smile and answered, "Yes. Sorry. I was just having a moment."

Before Gavin could respond, our waiter arrived and requested our drink orders. It gave me the extra time I needed to clear my head and get back in the moment. I didn't hear Gavin's order, but I ordered a Sauvignon Blanc which I knew would go down way too fast. I couldn't be bothered to care.

"So, any exciting new pro bono cases? Perhaps a bank robber suing for injuries suffered during the get-away?"

"Ha, ha. Very funny."

He grinned and shrugged.

"Thankfully, it's back to basics for me. I don't actually appear before the court very often. Most of my work is a little more behind the scenes."

"Corporate law, right?"

"Yes. Mostly contracts, acquisitions…a lot of paperwork and nit-picking." I offered a self-deprecating smile and placed my own napkin in my lap.

He gave me a speculative look. "Is it safe to assume you were a straight-A student since preschool?"

"Based on your question, is it safe to assume you weren't?"

"Touché. I was a little more concerned with playing ball than doing homework."

The waiter brought our drinks, Gavin receiving a tall glass of amber liquid that was clearly a beer. We told him we needed a few minutes.

"Speaking of playing ball, I obviously missed something. Why did my boss know you? Are you famous?" I leaned in, genuinely curious.

He laughed and took a sip of his beer. "Absolutely not. I played in high school and got a scholarship to State, but things didn't pan out."

I straightened again. "Well, you must have been one heck of a player, based on how flustered you made Thomas Wheeler. That man wouldn't sweat under the Spanish Inquisition."

He waved me off. "It's a guy thing. I'd bet my last dollar he used to play and probably has a kid or two who played in school. They like to see local players climb up the chain."

"But, surely, plenty of high school kids get athletic scholarships."

He began to look uncomfortable. "We should probably figure out our order before the waiter comes back." He opened his menu and I humored him by doing the same. Not that I was done with my line of questioning. The lawyer in me wouldn't allow that.

We settled on an assortment of small plates to share and were ready with our decisions when the waiter reappeared. I took a sip of my wine and gave Gavin an expectant look.

"What?"

"You were less than subtle with your attempt at distraction."

He playfully narrowed his eyes at me. "I'm beginning to see why you got straight As."

"Hmm," was my response. "You got a scholarship. Please continue."

He took in my expression and resigned himself. "Okay. So, the thing is, scouts were interested before I went to State."

"Scouts? What kind of scouts?" I was confused. Of course, college scouts would be after him if he ended up with a scholarship.

"Major League scouts."

I almost dropped my wine glass. "Are you kidding?"

He brushed non-existent crumbs off the tablecloth and gave me a wry smile. "Remember, I don't joke about baseball."

"Right," I answered distractedly. "So, what happened?"

"Long story short, my parents begged me to go to college—my mom is a college professor—and I went along with it, figuring I'd just improve in college and get drafted afterwards. The scouts were all still around and the plan was working. But I screwed everything up, so now I'm a coach and I work construction." He lifted his glass and took another sip while his eyes took in the restaurant.

I didn't know how to respond. I had tons of questions, but he was uncomfortable and I didn't know how hard to push. I settled on the ever-brilliant, "Wow."

Chapter Twelve

THE PERFECT KISS AND THE CLOROX SHOWER

GAVIN

I felt my face tug at Emmy's single-word response. "Yeah, that's one word for it." I really didn't want to get into the nitty gritty of my past, so I turned the tables on her before she could ask any more questions. "So, enough about me. What made you decide to be a lawyer?" I took another sip of my beer while she brought her wine glass to her lips, blatantly stalling for time.

"Oh, you know, the usual. My dad is a lawyer so I was kind of born into it."

I nodded. "Based on what I know so far, it's pretty clear you don't take after your mom. Makes sense that you take after your dad."

She blew out a laugh, bringing that dazzling smile to her lips. I wanted to lean over the table and kiss her, other patrons be damned. I'd wanted to kiss her since the moment she'd walked into the restaurant in those heels and skin-tight jeans. I'd been practi-

cally speechless at the sight of her with her hair loose around her face and her eyes wide with what seemed to be a case of nerves. I'd been a bit gratified to note I hadn't been the only one feeling anxious.

"Yeah, Naomi and I couldn't possibly be more different," she confirmed.

I reminded myself not to act like a feral animal and instead demonstrate that I could be very adult and civil, despite her misgivings about our age difference. I mean, what did she think? That just because I was twenty-four I didn't know how to behave like an adult? I pushed the thought aside. "What does she do for a living?" I asked.

Emmy laughed again, causing my dick to twitch. "I think 'for a living' is pushing it, but she and her husband, Aldo, are currently touring the country on the craft-fair circuit."

I cocked my head to one side at that. "I have absolutely no idea what that even means."

She leaned forward, and her low-cut top shifted to reveal the top swell of one creamy white breast. God was clearly testing me. "It means they drive around in a camper and set up shop at craft fairs around the country. My mom sells crystals and does tarot card readings. Aldo, meanwhile, acts as her pack mule and engages in some activities I choose to remain ignorant of, given my position with the Bar Association. I'll let your imagination take over on that one."

Oh, my imagination was already in fourth gear and considering switching to fifth, but I reigned myself in. "I think I get the idea." I grinned at her and she grimaced good-naturedly. Truthfully, the idea of someone close to Emmy being involved in marijuana trade was so ironic it was funny.

She shook her head, as if dismissing the entire topic. "He

makes my mom happy, and he's a great dad, so I try not to think about it."

The waiter arrived with our food, setting out an array of carefully crafted plates before us. It all looked amazing. I'd been happy to see that Emmy hadn't tried to stick with salad and was, instead, willing to be adventurous in her choices. We had everything from some kind of grain-based salad to barbequed quail. I gestured for her to start first.

"So, Aldo is Jay's dad, right?"

She nodded while coating a chip with olive spread.

"How long have he and your mom been together?"

She gave that some thought, and I took the opportunity to fill my plate with an assortment of portions. "I think he started coming around when I was about eleven. But my parents split up when I was still a baby."

"Oh," was all I could say to that. I came from a family where the biggest issue we'd had was Laney and I fighting over the remote. I couldn't relate to her childhood. Maybe it explained some of her need to be so cautious.

"I got to spend a lot of time with my dad, but I mostly lived with my mom. Then Aldo came along, they got married, and Jay arrived." Her smile kicked up at that. She was obviously crazy about her brother.

"Did your dad ever remarry?"

Her smile turned stiff. Uh-oh. "Yes. Several times, in fact." She took a sip of her wine.

Time to reroute the conversation.

"Here, try the quail." I pushed the plate toward her. "It's delicious."

She smiled gratefully, seemingly aware I'd let her off the hook, and took the plate from me.

We continued to chat over dinner, conversation easily flowing right on into dessert and a second glass of wine and beer. My instincts about her had been spot-on and my attraction grew as the evening progressed. I didn't know what I wanted more—for her to keep talking to me in that lyrical voice, or for her to let me walk her out to her car and kiss the ever-loving daylights out of her.

The choice was taken from me when a yawn broke her face, causing her to give out a cute little squeak and cover her mouth in embarrassment. "I'm so sorry!"

I couldn't help but smile. "It's fine. Looks like I kept you out past your bedtime." I looked at my watch and noticed it was already ten-thirty. The time had flown by, and I was hoping she'd had as much fun as I had. I signaled the waiter for the bill and quickly paid it, ignoring Emmy's attempt to split it. What kind of man did she think I was? Oh, that's right. She thought I was a kid, not a man at all. I suddenly felt a bit deflated. I guess I'd just have to work harder to prove myself to her because, after tonight, I wasn't about to let her just walk away.

She stood and I neglected to tell her that her top had shifted again, this time dipping low enough that I caught a glimpse of black lace and more skin. I made myself look away, not wanting to be a perv. Instead, I led her to the door, my hand on her back. She pointed to her car and I followed her, even when she tried to turn around and say goodbye outside the door to the restaurant.

I finally let her turn once we reached the driver's side of her Volvo. Really? A Volvo? She was much too young and sexy for this car. She belonged in a sports car. Sleek, fast, and elegant.

"Well," she began. "Thanks so much for dinner. I had a lovely time."

"Me too," I responded, letting my hand lift to her face to tuck a

strand of hair behind her ear. The breeze blew it right back into her face and I smiled.

She returned it, and I took that as my cue to lean forward for a goodnight kiss. It started sweet and gentle, our lips barely grazing each other's, but ratcheted up as soon as the tip of her tongue slid along my lip. I hadn't expected her to be the one to deepen the kiss, but didn't hesitate to join right in. I held her hip with one hand as the other snaked behind her back. Her hands cradled either side of my neck and I could feel my pulse point beat into the palm of her hand as our mouths melded together in a wet slide. She tasted like wine and chocolate from our dessert, but I still detected that hint of sweetness that seemed to just be her.

I groaned into her mouth and adjusted my position so I could pull her further into me. She pulled back for a breath and her eyes were wild with lust, her cheeks pink and hot and her mouth swollen from our kiss. Her gaze flicked from my lips to my eyes and back again, her expression turning to one of almost bewilderment.

"You're a really good kisser," she said on a quick exhale.

I grinned. "Right back at you."

She stepped back and out of my arms. I wanted nothing more than to pull her back in and then take her home with me where we could make excellent use of my big bed. But she was skittish, this I knew. So I took in a breath and continued smiling at her.

"I should go." She smoothed her hair back with one hand.

"Okay." I didn't argue. "But I have two questions before you do."

She looked hesitant but asked anyway, "What are they?"

"One, when does this tournament start?"

She relaxed. "Next weekend, I think. I'll have to let you know."

I held up my hand with two fingers raised. "And, two, when are you free for our next date?"

The doubt was back, as I knew it would be. I tried not to get discouraged and told myself to remember the kiss we'd just shared. The fuck-hot kiss where she'd all but unraveled in my arms.

"Oh." She tried to back up another step but ran into the door of her car. "I think I'll have to let you know about that too." She turned to open her door and only glanced back over her shoulder once to thank me again for dinner.

This was turning out to be more difficult than I'd anticipated. But I was up for the challenge. Hopefully.

"Where is he? Where is that little fart factory?"

I used my key on my sister's front door without bothering to knock first. It may not have been my home anymore, but she's my sister, so it's my job to annoy her any chance I can get. This time, however, it completely backfired. I'd have to take a Clorox shower to recover from the sight that greeted me when I strode into the kitchen on a search for my nephew, Rocco.

The kid was not in the kitchen. Laney and her husband, Nate, however, were. My sister was up on the island and Nate was...well, I don't want to ever think about what Nate was doing again. Let's just say, I was never eating any food made in that kitchen until the end of time. Which sucked, because Fiona often cooks at my sister's house.

I retreated to the back deck and sat on a lounger, rocking back and forth until Nate came out and handed me a beer. He sat in another lounger next to me and scratched the back of his neck. We both stared at the treehouse in silence for a few minutes until he

reached over and opened my beer for me. I mean, really, it was the least he could do.

I stopped rocking and took a huge gulp of the cold liquid.

I could see out of the corner of my eye that Nate was about to speak and I threw a hand out to the side to stop him. "Nope." The asshole had the nerve to grin. If he weren't one of my bosses I'd punch him in the throat. He eventually got up and patted my shoulder a couple times on his way back into the house. I stayed where I was and drank my beer.

"Oh, for God's sake. Get over yourself," came my sister's voice from behind me. She pulled the lounger Nate had just left closer to mine and stretched out on it. She was dressed in a t-shirt and jeans, I was relieved to see.

I scowled at her. "You owe me therapy bills for the next thirty years, I hope you know that."

She punched my arm. "How do you think *I* feel? That'll teach you to walk into other people's homes at least."

"Consider the lesson learned."

She laughed. I had to admit it was good to see her so happy and carefree. "Rest assured, Gav, Rocco will be home soon and you can distract yourself with talk of poop and lizards."

Thank God for small favors. I'd come over to see my nephew in a desperate attempt to distract myself from the unreturned texts to Emmy that were mocking me on my phone. As ever, Laney sensed the disturbance in the Force.

"Hey, what's the matter?" Her face had taken on that big sister look.

"Nothing." I attempted a scoff but it was half-hearted at best.

"Jesus. It's a girl, isn't it?" She sat up in her seat, way, *way* too eager for my liking.

I narrowed my eyes at her in answer and finished the last drag of my beer, causing her to smile like a fucking Cheshire cat.

"Gavin has a girlfriend, Gavin has a girlfriend," she chanted like the incredibly mature mother she is. That earned her another scowl and a lip curl to sweeten the pot. All she did was laugh until she was finally able to speak again. "I'm sorry," she said, sounding the farthest thing from it. "This is just too good. Come on. Tell me all about it." She settled back into a reclining position.

The thought was really not very enticing, but I was pretty much at the end of my rope. I'd been seeking distraction from Rocco and, I'm a bit ashamed to admit, perhaps some advice, but my sister was here and offering. Desperate times and all that.

"Fine. There's this woman I'm interested in." I stopped and retraced my steps. "No, that's not it. I'm not just interested. She's incredible and probably way out of my league but I don't give a shit. There's something between us, and I feel like she's not even willing to give it a chance."

Laney looked a little offended on my behalf, which I greatly appreciated. Not to the point where I'd forgive her for the scene in the kitchen, but still. "How many times have you been out?"

"That's just it. We've really only been on one official date, but it was amazing. *She* was amazing. And I know she likes me...she just doesn't seem willing to let herself admit it."

"Well, that's just bizarre." Laney gave me a speculative look. "You don't think she's in another relationship, do you?"

I shook my head vehemently. "No. Absolutely not. She's just... cautious." My chin sank to my chest. "She's a little bit older than me."

Laney sat upright in her chair again, the metal squeaking against the wood of the deck. "Oh my God! It's that lawyer from the baby shower, isn't it?!"

"Jesus Christ. Do you women do nothing but gossip?!"

She looked offended. An expression I was more than familiar with. "Please. We kick ass and take names. We only gossip in our spare time." She settled back and put her feet up. "Besides, we uncover some great information through girl talk. In fact, all you'd have to do to figure out your lawyer is put her in a room with Fiona for about twenty minutes."

Hmm. That idea had some merit, I had to admit. Fiona could draw blood from a stone in the right context. I studied Laney as I considered this.

"Invite her out in a group setting—less pressure. If you want her to be your girlfriend, she's going to have to survive hanging out with us anyway. You may as well let her know what she'd be getting herself into." She opened a bottle of water and took a sip.

Again, she had a point. It also occurred to me that, apart from Brett, pretty much everyone I hung out with was older than me. Perhaps that would weigh in my favor if Emmy had reservations about my age.

"You may be onto something here," I told my sister. "I think I'll text her and see if she and her friend can meet up with us this weekend. Are you guys free tomorrow night?"

She shrugged and brushed her long dark hair behind her shoulder. "I can try to get a sitter, but even if I can't, one of us can go out. Let me check with Fiona." She pulled her phone from her back pocket.

I used the opportunity to send a text of my own to Emmy.

Gavin: *Hi. I know you're busy with work, but I'm going out with my sister and some friends tomorrow night. Do you and Ariana want to meet up with us?*

There. That sounded casual enough. And she could surely take a Saturday night off work. I'd been telling myself she wasn't

responding to my attempts at communication because she was swamped with work. I wasn't ready to concede that she just didn't want to see me again.

My phone signaled with a return text almost immediately.

Emmy: Sounds great. Ari has to work, though. Would you guys be up for karaoke?

I was more than surprised by the quick response, and it triggered some very mixed feelings. Karaoke? Jesus.

Gavin: Sure. Just name the place.

Beggars can't be choosers, I supposed.

Emmy: Ari's hosting karaoke downtown at Tate's tomorrow night. I'll be there around 8:30 to help her set up. See you there?

Gavin: Absolutely. See you tomorrow.

I had just scored myself a pseudo date. Excellent.

"Well, Laney, I hope you're up for karaoke because I just signed you on."

This caused her to laugh in a manner that sounded a bit too evil for my taste. "Wait till I tell Fiona." She typed frantically into her phone and laughed some more at whatever Fiona's response was. "This is going to be phenomenal."

I wasn't so sure anymore.

Chapter Thirteen

EVEN TRAITORS SING KARAOKE

*E*MERSON

"Okay, I'm done. Where are we going?" I asked Ari and Jay as I walked back into my living room. I'd forced myself to put my work down for the next few hours and enjoy dinner with my brother and best friend.

Jay was giving Ari a look I couldn't discern and Ari appeared...kind of smug. Not necessarily unusual, unfortunately.

"What's going on?" I was almost afraid to ask.

"That's what I want to know," Jay responded, still eyeing Ari.

"Nothing's going on," she sniffed. "I'm starving. Let's go to Rio Grande—I'm dying for some ACP and a margarita." She stood from the couch and grabbed her purse from the coffee table. She also picked up my phone from its spot on the table and handed it to me.

"Thanks," I said, still a bit wary.

"You might want to take a little peek at your phone, sis. I caught Ari red-handed."

She gasped in indignation and pretended to swat him. "Traitor!"

"At least now you know where my loyalties lie," he said in return, causing me to smile before I flipped through my phone to see what kind of trouble Ari had been causing. Nothing jumped out at me immediately.

"Come on, you two. Let's go," Ari pulled me by the arm in the direction of the garage. "I was just fooling around. No harm done," she stated.

Figuring she'd probably changed my ringtone to something embarrassing, I lowered the volume all the way and shoved the phone in my purse on our way out the door.

One margarita and a full belly later, I sat back in the booth at our favorite Mexican joint and sighed. "I'm going to regret that last basket of chips later, but I'm in heaven right now."

Jay continued to devour more chips and salsa and Ari signaled the waiter for another drink. I shook my head when he gestured to me. I was driving, and it was looking like Ari might be sleeping over.

"Hey," she said, turning to me in the booth. "Do you think you could help me set up karaoke tomorrow night? I'm working at Tate's and I can never seem to get a close enough parking spot. An extra set of hands would be awesome."

I'd helped Ari a few times in the past when she was first starting out and didn't have her routine down pat, but it had been quite a while. Guilt swelled when I thought about how long it had been since I'd seen her do her thing. I had to get better about balancing my career with my personal life or I was in danger of alienating everybody I loved.

I smiled and bumped her with my shoulder. "I'd love to. Just don't expect me to get up on stage with you."

THE GAME • 133

She scoffed playfully. "That'll be the day."

"I refuse to apologize for not voluntarily humiliating myself in public."

"She's doing you a favor, Ari. I've heard her singing in the shower and it's not safe," Jay volunteered. I gestured across the table imploring her to listen to the voice of wisdom.

"And I keep telling you that you don't have to sing well to have fun at karaoke night. You've seen how awful some of those people are, but they're having fun and keeping me in my job."

"Still not happening." I took a sip of my water as the waiter set down Ari's margarita. She smiled up at him in thanks and I swore he blushed. That made me laugh a little.

"What?" she asked.

I lifted my chin toward the retreating waiter. "The waiter. I think he's got a crush."

Her gaze flew to him. "Seriously? He's so young, he could be my child. Jay's probably older than him."

"Okay. This is my cue to take a break." Jay rose from his seat and brushed his hands on his jeans. "I'll be back." He walked away, presumably to visit the restroom.

"I wasn't suggesting you date him. I was just pointing out that he seemed to like you. Geez." Although, at this point, I'd take anyone over Elliot.

"Well, as soon as you accept another date from Mr. Baseball, I'll consider dating the twelve-year-old waiter." Damn. There was that smug look again.

I'd been shamelessly avoiding Gavin's texts for the last couple days. I mean, wasn't it dating protocol to wait a few days before texting after the first date? I was just helping him follow the rules.

Okay, that was a load of crap. The truth was, I'd enjoyed dinner with Gavin way more than I'd anticipated. Too much. And

then that kiss. Ack! It was…there were no words. I felt goose-bumps rise over my skin at the memory. This was not good. In fact, I feared if I engaged in texting with him, I'd agree to just about anything he suggested.

"Well then, it's a good thing I don't want you to date the waiter." I gave Ari my own smug smile as I reigned my wayward thoughts in.

She pursed her lips into a pout worthy of a two-year-old. "Come on! You said yourself the date was perfect. I believe I even recall a sigh that went along with the story. He's a hot young guy who's into you. You don't have to marry him. Just go out with him and have some fun. And, for God's sake, get yourself laid, will you —you're probably growing cobwebs down there."

I felt my lip curl in disgust. "Ew. Please, don't concern yourself with my…down there. I still haven't decided exactly what to do about Gavin. I haven't even returned his texts, for goodness sake." I face-palmed. "God, I'm a mess. This is yet another reason I shouldn't date."

"Didn't anyone ever tell you it's rude to ignore text messages? You're always so goddamned polite, I'm shocked." She took a healthy sip of her drink and smacked her lips.

"I know. I know."

Jay chose that moment to return. "Is it safe now?"

"Yes. Unfortunately," said Ari, sending me a little glare before looking back at Jay. "Don't you think it's time Emerson got a boyfriend?"

My brother narrowed his eyes at her. "You said it was safe!"

I elbowed her. "Leave him alone. Jay, tell Ari about your games this week. It's time for a change of subject."

When we got home, Ari and Jay decided to watch *Game of*

Thrones while I ducked back into my bedroom to check emails and see if there was anything I needed to address before the morning. Craig had, predictably, sent out a group e-mail about some changes he'd made to improve the founder's agreement draft. Changes *he'd* made, despite the fact that we'd both worked on the adjustments. I ground my molars together and tried to remind myself that karma was a b-i-t-c-h.

I was getting ready to rejoin the bloodthirsty duo in my living room when I heard my phone rattle on the bedside table next to me. I realized I had never turned the volume back up and prayed I hadn't missed anything important.

But when I picked up my phone, all I saw was a single-line text from *Ignore Until Next Week*.

Ignore Until Next Week: *Can't wait for tomorrow. Sweet dreams.*

Huh? What did that mean? I swiped to open the text exchange and felt all the blood drain from my face.

"Ari!!!"

"Oh, please. You've used up all your righteous indignation points for the day. Let. It. Go. I even have the song if you want it set to music."

I glared at Ari over the speaker we were scooting into place in a corner of Tate's small stage the next night. The monkeys were back in my belly and I was filled with a crazy cocktail of emotions. The fact that Ari didn't seem to be bothered by my ranting over her little texting stunt didn't help either.

I was just going to have to pull up my big-girl panties and be

the mature adult I am. It wasn't as if I didn't want to see Gavin. I'd had a great time with him on our date, and he was funny and sweet and smart. But I had to consider his feelings in all of this. He obviously liked me, which was really flattering in itself, but what if he started to *like* me?

"Stop it." Ari was looking at me critically. "You're thinking too hard."

"Get out of my head." How did she do that? Of course I was thinking too hard. It's what I do.

"He's a twenty-four-year-old guy. He thinks you're hot and wants to do you. It's not rocket science and you're not going to break his poor little baby heart because you have a job and responsibilities." She adjusted the mic stand. "Have a drink, do some flirting, and get yourself some. End of story. I'll even buy your first drink." She smiled a bit too sweetly.

"There is a special place in hell for people like you, Ari."

She stuck her tongue out at me in response.

Tate's was a bit of a dive, but the staff was friendly and the crowd enthusiastic. Ari used her natural charm to draw the patrons in and make them comfortable. She had her sign-up sheet half-filled by the time she started her first number. I made myself comfortable at the large high-top table we'd claimed up front and took a sip of my gin and tonic just as the first familiar strains of "Mrs. Robinson" by Simon and Garfunkle rang from the speakers. Ari winked at me and began singing while I planned her slow and painful death.

Thankfully, Ari's little ode to cougars everywhere had ended and a trio of thirty-something women were belting out Rihanna by the time I felt a warm hand on my shoulder. I looked up to find Gavin, looking as hot as ever in a faded band t-shirt and well-worn jeans, his hair catching some of the colored lights from Ari's

set-up. I couldn't stop the smile that formed on my lips, and he took it as invitation to bend down and plant a brief kiss on my mouth.

"Hey, Emmy," was all he said, but his eyes delivered a message something along the lines of *"Can we get the hell out of here so I can ravish you?"* I swallowed hard and let him get away with calling me Emmy, as usual. Heck, he could have called me Carl in that moment and I would have brushed it off.

"Long time, no see," said a bright female voice from behind me.

I shook off the Gavin haze and swung my head around to find a face I remembered. Thankfully, I found my voice and it sounded normal. "Oh, hi. Fiona, right?" The very petite blond woman had been at the settlement meeting for that horrible pro bono case from last year. She'd been there to support her boyfriend, Mark, whom my jerk of a client was trying to sue. This all felt a bit bizarre.

She smiled. "That's right. Nice to see you again, Emerson."

I wrinkled my nose a bit. "These circumstances are a bit better than our last meeting."

She laughed amiably and pulled Mark Beckett up to her side. He seemed to be completely unbothered by the situation and shook my hand warmly. Gavin then introduced me to his sister, Laney, and her husband, Nate. I hoped I could keep all the names straight. I spotted another person I recognized at the bar placing an order. It was Mark's brother, Jake, who had been the one to call me about the Chris Hardacre case.

Everyone quickly took seats and it didn't escape my notice that Gavin was the first to claim a spot—the one right next to me. Ari waved to us from her place at the side of the stage where she was prepping the music for the next "performer," and I used the opportunity to send her one last glare.

"Laney!" Fiona shouted across the table to Gavin's sister. "Are we doing Taylor Swift or Britney Spears?"

"You can get your freak on all you want. I'm not getting anywhere near that stage until I've had at least two drinks. And I'm only doing back-up." Laney pointed at her friend.

Fiona pouted in return.

"I think Ari's already got about twenty people on her list. You may want to sign up now so you don't miss out," I offered.

Fiona turned to me. "You want to do lead vocals with me?"

I shook my head vehemently. "You do not want to hear me sing. But wait until you hear Ari. She's amazing."

Ari called out the next name on the list and an overweight guy with flaming red hair and a full pint of beer mounted the stage. Everyone clapped encouragingly. "I want to dedicate this one to my girl, Tina! I love you, baby!" The music started and he began to sing the most awkward, off-key rendition of Seal's "Kiss from a Rose" ever. I had to bite my lips to keep from bursting out laughing at the poor guy. I glanced over to Gavin and he looked like he'd been hit over the head with a two-by-four.

"Just breathe," I leaned over and told him. "It will be over soon." He looked at me, eyes wide, clearly wondering if this was my idea of a perfect Saturday night—and, if so, how he could gently extract himself from the situation. The notion that he might want out of the evening after all the fretting I'd done actually caused the laughter to release. Ari was right. I needed to get over myself. I leaned into his arm and let myself laugh, which seemed to loosen him up a bit.

His hot breath blew against my ear as he said, "If you think I'm getting up there, you are freaking nuts." I giggled like a teenager as the poor guy on stage finally wrapped up his number and the audience applauded weakly. This was turning out to be fun.

"Jesus," Jake said, handing out a round of drinks as he took a seat across from us. "What the hell was that?"

All the women seemed to be laughing and the guys looked like they'd just been inappropriately frisked by the TSA.

"Welcome to karaoke night!" Laney patted him on the shoulder.

"It's almost your turn, Jake. We signed you up when you were getting our drinks. You and Mark are doing a duet," Fiona said with a genuinely sweet-looking smile.

Jake narrowed his eyes at her. "I knew I should have brought Bailey for protection."

"Where is she tonight?" I asked.

"She volunteered to babysit our son," Laney responded for him. "She's about a hundred months pregnant so she wasn't up for the bar scene."

I nodded in understanding as Ari took the mic up on stage. Her low-cut dress hugged her every curve and she put a hand to her hip. "Well, thank you, Ken, for that...heartfelt tribute. Tina is one lucky woman." She couldn't hold her sly smile in. "I have some special guests in the house tonight." Ari gestured down to our table and I cringed. What the hell was she doing now? "My lovely assistant, Emerson, and her new *friends*." She accentuated the last word just enough to give it some ambiguous extra meaning and continued, ignoring my exasperated head shake. "I'll be getting them up here later if it's the last thing I do. But, for now, let's welcome Sharon and TJ to the stage!" She handed mics to a couple as they climbed onstage and then she came over to our table.

"Hi, guys. I'm so glad you could all make it." She put a hand to her chest. "I'm Ari, the best friend. Hi, Gavin." She winked, causing Laney and Fiona to look at Gavin and grin. Introductions were made and, as usual, Ari chatted effortlessly with everyone

until it was time for her to get back to work. Everyone at the table talked and drank and seemed to be having fun.

But the entire time, all I could think about was the feeling of Gavin's knee pressing against mine and the feeling in my gut telling me to just go for it.

Chapter Fourteen

LEAVE YOUR DIGNITY AT THE DOOR AND COME ON IN

GAVIN

It would take a blind man to ignore all the meaningful looks coming my way from Laney, Fiona, and now Ari. Lord, it was like they'd never seen two humans of the opposite sex interact before. I was waiting for an Animal Planet style voiceover to start any minute. If I were ever going to make any progress, I had to get Emmy out of here.

"Wanna come with me to the bar? I'll buy you another drink." I leaned over so she could hear me above the screeching coming from the drunk college chicks on stage. She nodded and I stood, helping her by pulling her stool out in the cramped space. The bar had filled up in the time we'd been there. I gestured for her to go ahead and then made sure I delivered purposeful "back off" signals to the meddling twosome at our table before following Emmy to the bar.

My vantage point gave me a clear view of her outfit, if only from behind. She was back to conservative—a pale blue blouse

and black pants that hugged her ass, her hair up in a styled ponytail —but it had the effect of being a complete turn-on by making me use my imagination. And I was doing a damn good job of it if I did say so myself.

"So, have we convinced you to become a regular at karaoke night?" Emmy asked playfully once we found a spot to stand at the bar.

"At this point, I'm considering taking on a third job just so I can pay Ari to quit this gig. How does she stand it?"

Emmy laughed. "She actually enjoys it, if you can believe it. I don't come very often, and now I'm remembering why. I'm pretty sure you have to be drunk to really get the full effect."

"Well then, let me buy you that drink, by all means." I lifted an eyebrow at her.

"How do you do that?" she asked, raising her hand to my face and running her finger over my eyebrow. My dick twitched just from the light contact. Damn.

"Do what?"

A slow smile broke over her face. "Raise just one eyebrow."

I narrowed my eyes at her and felt my lips tug.

She let her finger linger on my skin and proceeded to contort her face in a way that resembled a stroke victim attempting a wink. Both her eyebrows rose and fell as she strained in concentration to isolate each one.

"Please, don't hurt yourself," I pleaded.

She dropped her hand from my face and laughed at herself. "See. Can't do it."

I nodded, but all I saw was how fucking adorable she was.

I couldn't help it so I leaned in for another quick kiss. The one I'd given her when we first arrived hadn't been nearly enough and I was dying to kiss her properly. I pulled back, though, conscious

that we were in a public place, and saw that her eyes were still closed. Then her lids slowly fluttered open and in that instant I was pretty sure I was a goner.

The bartender chose that moment to ask for our order and I requested another round of drinks for the table. I wouldn't mind a bit if Emmy wanted to get her drink on and let me drive her home since I was on a two-beer limit. I knew that was wishful thinking, though—she'd certainly have made other arrangements already, as careful as she always tried to be. But I'd seen glimpses of what hid under her carefully-controlled exterior, and I was going to get her to loosen up eventually or die trying.

"Hey," Emmy said, "I wanted to apologize for not responding to your texts after our date. That was rude." She looked at me earnestly.

I shrugged. "I figured you were busy with work. You agreed to meet up tonight—that's all that matters."

She opened her mouth to respond and then seemed to think better of it. She just smiled at me again instead, and my chest got tight.

"Christ, you have a beautiful smile, Emerson Scott."

She blushed and the freckles on her cheeks became more prominent.

"You also have the tendency to blush more than any girl I've ever met, I think."

Her hands went to her cheeks and then she smacked my arm. "Talk about rude!" But she was still smiling.

The bartender set some drinks down in front of us, and Emmy took a sip of hers. "Your friends seem nice. Not that we can talk very easily with all the noise in here, but they're obviously a lot of fun."

I let my gaze flip back to the table where Fiona seemed to be

making out with the back of her own hand. Christ on a cracker. What was she drinking tonight? I turned back to Emmy. "They're certainly not boring, I'll give them that."

"Yeah, I did notice a bit of overzealous enthusiasm regarding our...friendship. But, then, you've met Ari so it's really just par for the course."

Ha. Friendship, my ass. I let it go for the time being.

I shook my head. "Now that you mention it, I'm kind of wondering why the women were invited in the first place."

"I figured you needed back-up in case I stood you up or something." She played with the straw in her drink and gave me a sly look.

"No way. You'd never do that. I'm too irresistible."

She rolled her eyes, making her seem really young. It was cute as hell and I was happy to see her back to the same place of comfort we'd found at dinner.

We continued to chat and I had all but forgotten about our friends until Mark wandered over and interrupted. "Yo, Junior, are you fermenting the liquor yourself? What's taking so long?" He gave Emmy a grin and me a scowl.

"Just chatting with a pretty girl, so thanks for butting your giant head in."

"The kid thinks he's charming. Don't fall for it, Emerson," Mark told her in a conspiratorial tone, one of his big arms brushing against her and making my hackles rise.

I wanted to tell him to shut the fuck up, but I couldn't see a way to do that and maintain the nice vibe we'd had going. I knew he was just fooling around and wasn't aware of Emmy's reservations regarding my age. I'd just have to suck it up.

Luckily, a distraction presented itself before Emmy could respond. Fiona was up on stage, mic in hand, singing her ever-

loving face off to Def Leppard's "Pour Some Sugar on Me." Mark spun around just in time to see her shimmy down and run her hand all the way down her body to the hem of her short dress. I heard a growl and a mutter of something that sounded like, "I don't fucking think so, Shortcake" before he took off for the stage.

Emmy clapped a hand over her mouth to hold in the laughter as Mark stepped directly from the bar floor onto the stage, skipping the steps entirely. Fiona had turned around and was shaking her ass at the crowd by that point, and she let out a loud squeak into the mic as she spun around right into Mark's chest. He grabbed the mic from her and handed it to Ari who'd scuttled her ass on stage, then hiked Fiona up over his shoulder in a fireman's hold. One of his big hands covered the bottom of her dress, hiding anything interesting, and he stomped right off the stage and directly to the back exit of the bar, Fiona smacking his ass and yelling at him the whole way. Hoots and cheers rung out throughout the bar and my sister and Jake looked like they were going to piss themselves they were laughing so hard. Nate pulled Laney to him and laughed into her hair as the back door of the bar slammed shut behind the departing couple, and Ari spoke into the mic.

"Well, it ain't a party till someone gets their ass spanked!"

Emmy shook her head next to me, and I just took a long pull on my beer, feeling like the night was turning out to be pretty freaking awesome after all.

"Time to mix it up a bit before our next performer gets on stage. Hope you all enjoy!" said Ari before pushing a couple buttons and beginning to sing "Titanium," effectively blowing the whole crowd away.

"Holy shit," I heard myself say.

"I know," was Emmy's response.

146 · SYLVIE STEWART

I looked down at her and her eyes were glued to her friend, pride clearly glowing in her features.

When Ari finished the last notes, just about everyone in the bar stood and clapped, and she did a playful curtsey before calling the next singer up. I, for one, would never want to follow that act in a million years, even if I had lost my mind and agreed to participate in what was debatably one of the worst inventions of the last couple centuries.

We eventually made our way back to the table with everyone's drinks, and Ari joined us on her break. Mark and Fiona had re-entered the bar, both looking freshly fucked if you asked me. Further proof being the very smug look on Mark's face and the conspicuous red lipstick on his ear—not that I was going to say anything. Brett had also shown up and pulled a stool to our table. Unlike some people I could mention, he played it entirely cool with Emerson, and I bought him a beer in appreciation. As far as I could tell, Brett, Emmy, and I were by far the most mature people at the whole damn table. Mark was an overgrown animal, and the other two guys in their thirties were having a debate with Ari over which superhero movie franchise was the best. Yup, my plan to impress Emmy with my oh-so-mature friends had gone completely tits up.

Not that she seemed to notice at all. Her gorgeous smile lit her face almost the entire evening, and it was aimed at me more often than not. I even kept my hand on her knee, her arm, or her back throughout the night and she hadn't slapped me or made a move to shake me off. I was considering the night a smashing success until *it* happened.

Fiona and Laney had just finished a cringe-worthy rendition of "Hold On" by Wilson Philips, with Ari and Emmy cheering them on the whole time. Ari retrieved the microphone to introduce the

next participant. "Let's welcome Nick to the stage. Nick, come on up!" A smattering of applause sounded and a tall guy with dark hair strode from the back of the bar and onto the stage, wobbling just a bit on the steps. It looked like we would be treated to another drunken guy who'd lost a bet. Except the look on Ari's face went from smiling to surprised—even wary—once she caught sight of the guy's face. She handed him the mic hesitantly and then slowly backed away to start his song.

When he turned around, I recognized him immediately. It was Ponch, Ari's brother. What the fuck? I wondered momentarily why he hadn't just joined us at the table since he'd obviously been at the bar for a while based on his state of shit-faced-ness. Before I could think further about it, the music started and he warbled the first few lines of some eighties song I vaguely recognized. I looked at Emmy but she was talking to Laney and hadn't noticed Ponch. That was, until he got to the chorus of what I finally recognized as REO Speedwagon's "Can't Fight this Feeling" and yelled into the mic, "Emerson! I mean it, baby!" before continuing the god-awful singing about a friendship that's grown into something more.

Fuck. Me.

Our entire table silenced at once and all eyes swung to the stage. Except mine. My attention was on Emmy. I needed to see her reaction to what was essentially a declaration of love from someone she'd known her entire life. Her jaw just about hit the table and her face went crimson in no time flat. Out of the corner of my eye, I saw Ari dash to her brother and a wrestling match over the microphone ensued. I didn't see how it ended—I just heard the music cut off and Ari's voice sounding over the speakers.

"Sorry about that folks! It seems my brother misplaced his dignity somewhere between the bar and the stage." Undercurrents

of anger threaded through her voice and I was suddenly a huge fan of Ari Amante.

Her brother, not so much.

The next day was Sunday and all I had on my schedule was some studying. The previous night's activities had ended shortly after Ponch's performance. Emmy and Ari had conferred by the stage for several minutes before Emmy returned to me and very apologetically explained that she was going with Ari to take Ponch's drunk ass home. Well, she didn't put it quite like that, but she wasn't going home with me so that was the only important part. I had no idea what was going on, but she promised to text me in the morning. By mid-morning, there was still no word from her, and I wasn't about to repeat the cycle of unreturned texts from the last time we'd been out.

Given my state of mind, I decided it was a good day for the batting cages. I had a little aggression to let out and some thinking I didn't really want to do, and I knew the perfect person to take with me for distraction.

"That's right," I said. "Keep that right elbow up. Here it comes."

Rocco swung with all the might of a scrawny six-year-old and missed by a mile, his helmet shifting to cover half his face in the process.

"Good try, buddy. Remember not to close your eyes this time."

He nodded and readjusted the helmet over his mop of dark hair. The next pitch came in low and he caught a piece of it, the ball popping up and hitting the top of the cage before thudding to the ground. "Did you see that?!" he yelled excitedly.

"Absolutely. You're gonna be hitting them out of the park in no time." I paused the machine and pulled his helmet off. "You need a bigger head."

"You need a smaller helmet," he responded.

I grinned at him. "You want a drink? I think they've got lemonade in the machine."

He gave me big eyes and a smile, which I took as a yes, and we walked over to the side of the main building, under an overhang where a couple vending machines stood. The Academy was dead quiet, as I'd known it would be. People would filter in as the day wore on, but Sunday morning was always quiet. While other folks went to breakfast and church, I much preferred taking in the silence while throwing pitches into a training screen or hitting the batting cages. Laney joked that it was my heathens' church, and I couldn't really argue with that.

Rocco and I settled with our butts on the concrete and our backs to the brick wall, sipping our drinks and looking out over the practice fields.

"I'll tell you, Rocco, enjoy being a kid while you can. Don't be in any hurry to grow up, you hear me?"

"Yeah, okay." He licked the side of his bottle where a drop had escaped. "But I want to drive a semi-truck and I can't do that until I'm an adult. Shouldn't I at least want to grow up enough to get a license or something?"

I shrugged and looked down at him. "Well, sure. I see your point, and driving is fun. Just make sure you have a back-up plan in case the semi-driving gig doesn't pan out." It would be good if at least somebody learned from my mistakes.

"Oh, I already have one." He nodded and took another sip of his lemonade. "I'm gonna be a rocket scientist or an astronaut. I

haven't decided yet. The truck driving is just for my free time." He threw a hand out to the side as if this was all old hat to him.

I gave him an appraising look. "Good choice. I hear girls go crazy for astronauts. I don't know why I didn't think of that." I mean, really, astronauts were bad-ass.

But Rocco curled his lip. "I hope not. Girls like to hug all over you, and they always leave glitter everywhere. Maybe rocket scientist is the better way to go then."

I couldn't help but smile. "I don't think you'll mind the hugging. That is, if you do decide to get older."

His head shook vigorously. "Nope. My mom can hug me—and Aunt Fiona cuz she smells good—oh, and Grandma and Gigi, but I'm pretty sure that's enough." Then a thought seemed to occur to him and he looked up at me with speculation and a bit of that lip curl again. "Wait. Do you like it when girls hug on you?"

I knocked him in the arm with my now-empty plastic bottle. "I hate to break it to you, but yeah, I kinda do."

"But what about all the glitter?" He narrowed his eyes at me.

"Well, the girls I like don't tend to leave a trail of glitter. Unless it's a special occasion like a bachelor party or…never mind." I stopped, suddenly remembering who I was talking to. "Actually, there's a very non-glittery girl I like who I wish would hug on me. But I'm worried she might be hugging somebody else."

He shrugged, completely unconcerned. "So. Why can't she just hug both of you? Doesn't sound too complicated to me."

I tapped him on the arm again. "See, this is why you should stay a kid. And I'll explain the trouble with hug sharing another day—maybe when you get that long-hauler license. Just trust me when I say I want her to save all her hugs for me."

"If her hugs are so great, that sounds a little selfish of you, but

whatever." He took another sip of lemonade before continuing, "If it makes you feel any better, I promise I won't let her hug me."

I put a hand on his head. "Thanks, man. I appreciate it."

"No problem." He stood, clearly finished with the conversation. "Are we gonna hit some more balls or what?"

"Definitely." I got to my feet as well. "Let's go, Neil Armstrong."

Maybe Rocco was right and it was selfish to hope Emmy would give her childhood friend the brush off and pick me, but I couldn't bring myself to feel too bad about it. It was up to her at this point, so I needed to keep my focus on teaching my nephew how to connect with a pitch and leave all thoughts of "hugging" for later.

Chapter Fifteen

OH, BARRY MANILOW, SAY IT AIN'T SO

EMERSON

"Okay, I think I got the whole story now," Ari said with a sigh as she walked into her guestroom with two cups of coffee. I scrambled from the covers, desperate for the caffeine. Sleep had not been my friend, and I'm sure it didn't help that my blanket was lying uselessly on my own bed at home. Yes, I said it.

We'd had a heck of a time sorting Ponch out after his unbelievably embarrassing display the night before. I mean, really, what had he been thinking?! Jake and Nate had helped maneuver Ponch into the backseat of Ari's Honda CR-V while she wrapped up her gig. I wasn't ready to be alone with the drunken, asinine troubadour so I stayed in the bar and said my goodbyes to the group. The night had been going so well, I found myself not only freaked out by Ponch's stunt but sharply disappointed I wouldn't have more time with Gavin. I felt we were on the precipice of some kind of development in our acquaintance, and the interruption by my childhood friend left me feeling cheated somehow. I apologized

profusely and told Gavin I'd get in touch in the morning. There was no way Ari could handle her brother on her own, and I wanted to nip this mess in the bud before Ponch went any further with his misguided declarations.

We drove to Ari's so she could keep an eye on him overnight. I remained silent the entire twenty-minute drive while Ponch alternately apologized, sang, and doled out compliments. Each outburst was followed by Ari shouting some form of *shut your effing face before I shut it for you!* She got quite creative by the time we pulled into her driveway, at one point detailing how she was going to remove his testicles and reunite them with his body in a very different location.

To his credit, Ponch refrained from any attempts at groping me as we half-carried him inside and dumped him on the couch, and he finally stopped singing when we both threatened to call his mother. Let's just say, drunk or sober, Ari got the musical genes in the family. At least the evening had proven something.

I retreated to Ari's room to borrow a t-shirt and shorts, and by the time I returned, Ponch was passed out cold. I was prepared to testify that it was the alcohol and not Ari's fist that had gotten him there. I told Ari about the strange phone call I'd gotten from Ponch earlier in the week, and she shared again about some odd comments he'd made when he heard I might be dating Gavin.

The whole thing made no sense. We'd all known each other for almost thirty years and, while I'm sure he'd been aware of my passing teenage crush, I was also confident he knew those feelings had faded long ago. And, besides, he was not the settling-down, love-declaring, karaoke-confessing type. At all. I'd always figured he'd end up being the lecherous old man making passes outside the plastic surgery center and fancying himself his generation's Hugh Hefner.

Neither Ari nor I could make sense of the night's strange turn of events, so we decided to drink wine and watch HGTV, leaving the great mystery to hopefully explain itself in the morning. Vicariously shopping for mansions and heckling the buyers and realtors was always a good distraction. Once the couple on the show had chosen the absolute worst house, I called Jay to let him know I wouldn't be home and to make sure he was all right. Then Ari and I put a bucket by the side of the couch in case Ponch's night sought revenge, and we went to bed.

I yawned and took my first sip of the caffeinated nectar of the gods. "So where is Romeo?" I asked Ari. "I hope he has a headache."

Ari sat cross-legged on the bed and grinned like a proper wicked sister. "Oh yeah. He's hurting bigtime. And he's currently in my shower hiding from you and attempting to wash the shame off."

I snickered and motioned for her to tell me what she'd learned.

She set her cup down on the bedside table and folded her hands together in her lap. "Wait for it." She cocked her head, making sure she had my full attention. "My brother, king of the ho-bags, champion of one-night-stands, financier of condom factories the world over, breaker of bimbo's hearts everywhere...Got. Dumped."

I gasped. Literally. My inhale was so sharp and sudden I forgot I had a mouth full of coffee and ended up sputtering and coughing for the next minute.

Ponch got dumped? This did not compute.

After a few well-placed back thumps and another coughing fit, I finally regained the ability to speak. "But...but that would mean he'd been in a relationship."

Ari extended her hands. "I know! Believe me, I'm as surprised as you." She settled in to share the dirt. "Her name is Holly, and

from what Ponch said, she was apparently immune to his normal sleazy pick-up lines. She totally made him work for it, and he figured she was just playing hard to get. So, he jumped through her hoops. Problem is, he started getting into her." Ari's expression turned a bit peevish. "How he kept this from me I have no idea."

I shook my head since I was as baffled as she was.

"Anyway, this Holly woman finally agreed to date him, but then she somehow found out about all the notches in his bedpost—oh, who are we kidding? They'd never fit on one measly bedpost." Ari shook her head and snickered.

I pushed the story along. "So she dumped him. Is it wrong that it makes me like her a little?" I grimaced.

"Are you kidding? I'm considering dumping *you* as my bestie and recruiting her. I mean, it's about damn time he had a wake-up call, the big slut. Frankly, I'm surprised he's never contracted some nasty disease that made his balls fall off."

"Eww. Thanks for that visual."

She gave her head a little bow, ignoring my sarcasm, and grabbed her coffee. "How this all translated into him sniffing around you and announcing in front of an entire bar that you're the 'candle in his window' I have no idea." At this point she couldn't hold herself together anymore. I was afraid the coffee was going to come out her nose, she was laughing so hard. Between deep gasps for breath she half-laughed/half-sang the lyrics that would probably make me cringe for the rest of my life.

"He's ruined REO Speedwagon for me," I curled my lip.

"Ha! He's made them my all-time favorite band. Oh God, I can't wait to tell Tony and Gabe," she said, referring to her other brothers.

Oh God, they would eviscerate Ponch. I grinned but quickly

sobered. "Great. Now things are going to be awkward and uncomfortable between Ponch and me."

She shook her head, still recovering. "No. Not happening. I told him he could wallow in his own humiliation for the time it takes him to shower, but then he's clearing the air and we're going back to normal."

I hoped it would be that simple.

"Sooo." Ponch's voice came from behind me where I sat at the kitchen table checking my email on my phone. He crossed over and pulled a chair out, turning it around so he could straddle it. Even hungover and groveling, he still maintained some of his swagger. Although his handsome face was a bit green, I wasn't too displeased to notice. Crap, this was uncomfortable.

I pulled my lips into a thin line and raised my eyebrows. "So."

Then he put his head in his hands and sighed. "I am so fuckin' sorry, Emerson. I don't even know how to explain except to say I'm a complete asshole." He drew his hands down over his face and looked at me. "I just...I met this girl. Well, I'm sure Ari told you." I nodded and he continued. "I got this taste of something good, something special I never even knew I could have. And then it was gone."

His face held an expression I'd never seen on him before. He looked wistful and heartbroken. Part of me wanted to hug him, but I was still holding onto a little anger and frustration so I let him continue.

"The only way I could think of to stay sane was to go out and find it again. So, I guess I thought of you."

I opened my mouth to respond, but there was absolutely nothing I could say to that. Even the concept was nuts.

He gestured up and down. "I mean, you're hot in an understated kind of way, and we're friends. I figured you'd never dump me because you're so nice and, I don't know, conscientious I guess?"

He was asking me? The workings of his brain of late were as foreign to me as Swahili. I blinked slowly, making him bark out a small laugh at his own expense.

"I know I sound like a crazy person, but that day at the ball field—when I saw you look at that baseball guy—I thought, hey, maybe Emerson isn't just interested in nerds and boring dudes. No offense." His gaze flashed to mine again, suddenly realizing his words might be less than tactful.

The whole thing was so odd, I just waved him off and let him get on with it. His lips quirked up briefly and he ran a hand through his hair.

"So, anyway, I started acting all stupid towards you. And then last night, I was on my way to join you guys at the table and I saw you smile at that guy." He caught my eye and held it while he shook his head. "I've never seen you smile like that."

I swallowed, not wanting to acknowledge that he may just be right. I couldn't think about that now, so I just sat there speechless.

"Well, I think you know the rest. I saw my plan going up in smoke and I had a few too many—and, well, yeah." He let that sit out there for a moment and I knew we were both replaying the scene from the bar like the colossal train wreck it was. "I'm so sorry, Emerson. It was unfair of me to put you in that position, and it was stupid of me to think that I could just replace one girl with another and not miss a beat—like people are interchangeable and feelings just transfer like that." He snapped his fingers and then

gave a mirthless laugh. "I know It's not that simple, and I probably deserve to feel like shit after the way I've always been with women, you know?" He scrubbed his hair with both hands, leaving it sticking up in all directions. He looked a bit lost, and this time, I got up and went to his side of the table to hug him.

"All this hearts and feelings stuff is harder than it looks, isn't it?" I gave him a last squeeze and pulled back.

"No shit. I feel like I'm about fourteen. I should probably be asking Jay for advice."

I smiled. "Well, he is wiser than the lot of us put together, after all." I patted the top of Ponch's head and went back to my seat where I studied him as I sipped my coffee. Finally, I said, "You know you need to resolve this whole Holly thing, right?"

He dropped his head back and groaned. "I know. I heard she started dating this other guy, though. Probably some douchebag," he said and then caught my disapproving look. "Okay, fine, whoever he is, he's probably a damn sight better than me."

"That's more like it, Barry Manilow," Ari commented as she sauntered into the kitchen. "Nice to see you getting a little perspective, bro." She set down her cup and leaned her back against the counter with her arms crossed. "Everything sorted here?"

Ponch raised his eyebrows at me. I felt my lips tug. "Yeah. Everything's good."

And it was. Except for that niggling feeling at the base of my neck that told me if Ponch—the least emotionally aware person in the universe—could sense the chemistry and connection between Gavin and me, I was in deep, deep trouble. The question was, did I want to be?

Emerson: *Hi*

    Maybe: *Hey – you okay?*

    Emerson: *Yes. Finally got home.*

Shoot. I realized how that sounded too late. I bit my thumb. Should I clarify? Darn it. No response.

    Emerson: *FYI – whatever demon was possessing Ponch last night has been exorcised. Thought you might want to know.*

There, that was better.

    Maybe: *So he's done singing eighties love ballads to you?*

    Emerson: *Most definitely. And he's also got a doozy of a hangover as punishment.*

    Maybe: *I would say I feel bad, but he kind of cramped my style on our date.*

    Emerson: *Oh, it was a date, was it?*

    Maybe: *Uh, yeah. You're a smart woman—definitely smart enough to see through that whole casual group hangout bullshit.*

    Emerson: *Are you saying you tricked me into a second date?*

    Maybe: *Third date.*

    Emerson: *How do you figure?*

I was pretty sure dinner and then karaoke were the only two dates.

    Maybe: *Coffee in your office, dinner at Gia, karaoke nightmare —that's three.*

    Emerson: *You're counting coffee in my office as a date? You spent more time talking to my boss than with me!*

    Maybe: *Ah, but it ended with a kiss. Definitely qualifies as a date.*

    Emerson: *Hmm.*

    Maybe: *So, I was thinking we should get together to prepare for your tournament.*

    Emerson: *Prepare?*

Maybe: I need to see your moves. Maybe I can give you some pointers.

Emerson: As tempting as that sounds, I spent too much time goofing off this weekend and I have tons of work to catch up on for the next few days.

Maybe: Will you be at any of Jay's games this week? He's got one tomorrow night and one on Thursday.

He knew my brother's schedule better than I did.

Emerson: I can try to make Thursday, but there's no way I can make it tomorrow.

Maybe: Okay, then I'll make sure I'm at Thursday's game. And you let me know if any time clears up for our own training in the meantime.

I was starting to think I might make the time if it wasn't readily available. That should have sent huge red flags up in my head, but my heart and other parts were too busy waving giant green ones.

Emerson: Okay, sounds good.

Maybe: Talk later, Emmy.

The fact that I, once again, did not correct him on my name signified that his contact info would soon be changing from *Maybe* to a big fat *Yes*.

Jay walked by the couch on his way to the kitchen. I'd been worried leaving him alone the night before, but he would have laughed if I told him.

"Hey, I'm going to try to make your game on Thursday night. What time is it?"

He looked surprised that I knew he even had a game, but then his lips quirked up so I could tell the idea pleased him.

"I gotta check, but they're usually around 6:30."

"Okay, I'll do my best to be there."

"Don't worry if you can't make it. There will be other games."

I could have predicted he'd say that.

"Hey, did Mom tell you they're coming through town in a few weeks?"

"No." I was a bit taken aback. They'd only been gone for a month.

"I think they're secretly worried about me or something, but they're doing a fair in Asheville."

"I'll have to call her and get the details. I'm sure you miss them." I watched him closely to gauge his response. He seemed happy lately, but I had to keep an eye on him.

He shrugged. "Well, yeah, but you're not half bad." I caught the sly smile and it set my mind at ease.

I crooked my finger. "Come here. I need to show you something."

"Ha! I'm not falling for that." He escaped to the kitchen before I could exact my sisterly revenge.

Chapter Sixteen

SLUGGER

*G*AVIN

I went a little stir-crazy the rest of the day, despite receiving Emmy's text that things with Ponch were settled. Because that didn't exactly mean things were settled with *me*. Far from it. Thankfully, I'd at least see her Saturday since that was the first game of the Bar Association softball tournament. Emmy had explained at Tate's that each participating firm was required to fill their roster with at least one-third female players, and immediate family members and significant others were allowed on the teams as long as they were of age. She also explained that if I thought this was some light-hearted exercise in bonding and camaraderie between lawyers, I was dead wrong. They took this shit seriously.

I'd meant what I said about getting together to prepare, and it only had a little to do with me wanting to get my hands on her again. Okay, scratch that. But when she'd told me she was on the team, it gave me pause. I'm sure that made me an asshole, but

there did not appear to be a whole lot of muscle on that girl—there didn't appear to be a whole lot of anything except some cute-as-hell freckles, a head full of auburn hair, and a large expanse of pale skin I'd like to place my mouth on for a good long while.

I figured if I could give her a few tips she might impress her boss and earn some brownie points and shit. It was obvious her work was her top priority, and I respected that. Not that I wasn't hoping she could carve out some time to see if we had something between us, but I was impressed by how hard she worked to reach her goals.

Brett invited me to meet up with him and a couple guys for wings, but I figured I could take a page from Emmy's book and buckle down and finish a project for one of my classes. That didn't stop me from taking a few breaks to send her some casual yet charming texts. If this was all we had time for, I was going to take full advantage and work every angle I could.

"Hey there. I was just thinking about you," I said as I answered the phone with my free hand.

It was Wednesday and I hadn't laid eyes on Emmy since the weekend.

"Oh. Hi," Emmy responded, almost sounding surprised to hear my voice, even though she was the one to call me.

She didn't expand on that, so I continued, "Let me guess. You're stuck under a pile of client files and you need me to come and rescue you from suffocation and certain death."

I could hear the smile in her voice. "No, although that probably will be my cause of death one day, so stay alert."

"Consider me on notice." I adjusted my Academy cap and stacked up another couple orange cones.

I could hear her take a deep breath before quickly saying, "Actually, I was calling because I'm finishing up early tonight and wanted to see if your offer for softball practice was still open."

That had me stopping in my tracks. Was Emerson Scott actually asking me out? I'd most definitely been the pursuer since day one, and I was cool with that, but it felt fan-fucking-tastic to have the tables turned like this. It meant I was getting to her. I felt a grin overtake my face. "Absolutely. But I have training until 7:00. Do you think you can come over to the Academy then?"

"Sure. Um, how will I find you?"

"Don't worry. I'll find you."

"Okay then. I guess I'll see you in a couple hours."

We hung up and I found myself humming a little tune and maybe even strutting a bit on my way back to the building.

"I don't even want to know," muttered Gerry when I passed him at the side door.

"No, you do not, my man."

"Jesus Christ." He continued on his way.

I returned the cones I'd been carrying to their designated bin and made my way to the indoor training area where Jay was warming up with a pitching screen.

"There he is! You ready for your game tomorrow?"

He didn't flinch or seem to notice me at all. The ball flew from his hand with careful control. Only when it smacked the screen and rolled to the side did he acknowledge me.

"Ready as I can be, I guess, but we'll see if I play."

That thought pissed me right off, despite my chipper mood, but I didn't let it show. I hadn't seen his game on Monday but when I looked up the stats I saw that he'd stayed on the bench all night. It

was like Davidson was *trying* to throw the season away. They lost by two runs.

"All you can do is be ready with your game face on and hope for the best." I couldn't let on about my frustration. That wasn't my job, and I couldn't afford to alienate coaching staff at any of the local schools if I wanted to keep it.

"I hear you, Coach." Jay nodded.

We proceeded to work through some drills, and were joined by a couple other pitchers I was working with. By the end, they were all exhausted but the adrenaline was running high, just as it should be. I sent them to the showers while I cleaned up. I checked my watch and noted that I only had about five minutes until Emmy would be here.

I grabbed a couple clean batting helmets and a bat that would suit her and headed out to the parking lot. I waved at a few players as they walked to their cars or those of their parents until I caught sight of a particular white Volvo I recognized. I couldn't have stopped the smile forming on my face if I wanted to.

She parked and got out as I walked toward her car. Her hair was secured in a high ponytail, her eyes hidden by big sunglasses. My gaze travelled down her figure which was covered in a fitted t-shirt and dark jeans, her feet encased in flimsy canvas sneakers. She reached back in and bent over to grab something, and I stopped all motion at the sight of her ass popping up in the air like that. Fuck. I wasn't generally very picky about types of women, but I was starting to think slim, conservative and perky was my new favorite.

"Em? What are you doing here?" a voice sounded from behind me and I swung my head to find Jay looking between Emmy's car and me. I'd been completely busted staring at his sister's ass. Shit.

Emmy, meanwhile, smacked her head on the doorframe of her

car as her brother's voice alerted her to his presence. She turned and pulled herself upright, rubbing the back of her head where she'd hit it.

"Hey!" she said a bit too loudly, obviously surprised by the sight of her brother and discomfited by the unexpected situation.

Personally, I was curious how she was going to handle this. She looked from me to Jay while Jay's eyes continued to pass between his sister and me. Yeah, this was a tad awkward.

"I thought you had practice tonight," she offered.

Jay's eyes suddenly narrowed at me and he answered her without giving her his eyes. "I had it earlier, and Coach Davidson thought I might benefit from a training session since we have a game tomorrow."

I brought my hand to the back of my neck and gave it a scratch, trying to keep my face blank.

"Oh, um. Do you need a ride home?" Emmy asked lamely.

He finally looked at her again. "I'm catching a ride with one of the guys. He lives out that way. You still didn't tell me what you're doing here, sis."

She shifted uncomfortably. "Gavin's going to give me some tips for the tournament. It starts this weekend."

Jay's eyebrows hit his hairline. "Tips?" The kid was too damn perceptive.

"Sure. It's always good to put your best foot forward, right?" she said with a fake-ass laugh. She was awful at subterfuge. Entire nations would crumble if she were ever to change careers and become a spy.

"Uh huh," was all Jay said. Then he looked back to me and his voice turned hard. "I guess I'll let you get on with it." There was clear warning in his voice.

Jesus, this woman was surrounded by guys who seemed to feel

the need to protect her from me. What had I ever done? I was just a dude minding my own business and trying to get a date.

"Okay," said Emmy with an awkward smile. "See you at home in a bit."

"Yeah. See you." A player named Mason joined us and the two kids walked to Mason's car. Right before he got in, Jay said, "You know, Em, if you needed some pointers, your brother's no slouch." He narrowed his eyes at me again and got in, closing the door behind him. What had happened to "Yes, Coach" and "Thanks, Coach"? Shit. I hoped this wouldn't blow up in my face.

Emmy watched them go and then face-palmed. "Did that just happen?"

I walked closer and grabbed her free hand. "I'm afraid it did." I pulled her toward me. "Now, come on."

She lifted her head and looked at me. "Should I go home and talk to him?"

I shook my head. "Give him a bit to get his head around it and talk to him later tonight."

Her mouth twisted to the side in thought. "I guess."

I pulled on her hand again and began walking toward the spot where I'd left the equipment. "Let's hit the cages. I'll teach you how to swing."

She followed but I heard a huff. "What makes you think I don't know how to swing?"

I looked her up and down, inventorying as I went, and confirming my earlier observations about her build. "No offense, Emmy, but a strong wind could knock you over. We're going to go for technique so you can make the most of what strength you have."

She narrowed her eyes at me and I ignored it, leading her to the same batting cage Rocco and I had used a few days earlier. I set the

pitch for the slowest setting and put a helmet over her hair. I placed one on my own head as well, then positioned her at the plate while I stood behind her. She let me. Never in my life had I done batting instruction from this position, but I pretended it was old hat. I just hoped my dick didn't decide to play. Not that I had any control over him when Emmy was around.

"Okay, let's see your grip first." I reached around and held the bat in front of her. I thought I heard her sigh, but I couldn't be sure. She took the bat in both hands and gripped it with her knuckles lined up. "Good," I said. "Now, plant your feet a little wider than shoulder-width apart and flex at the knees." I unnecessarily skimmed my hands down her legs to place them exactly as I wanted. I was about to move on to her arm position when she turned her head and cut in.

"You do know I've been watching my brother play ball for over ten years, right?"

I nodded. "Of course, but watching and playing are two very different things. Trust me."

She bit her lip which sent my cock on an upward journey, and then she turned back around and followed my instructions on weight distribution and arm position. I talked her through a couple practice swings and stepped back out of the cage, not wanting to get hit if things when awry.

"You ready?"

"Sure thing, Coach," she responded with a bit of sass before I flipped the switch and a slow pitch came arcing toward the plate, aiming right for the strike zone. She kept her stance just as I'd shown her and I waited for her to try and swing.

Just as the ball approached the plate, she shifted her weight and brought the bat around in a precise swing. The ball connected solidly with the sweet spot and rocketed forward in a line drive that

hit the net with a force I had no doubt would have sent the hit over two hundred feet. I flipped the switch, not taking my eyes off the ball where it sat in the dirt. I only moved my gaze when I caught Emmy spinning my way out of the corner of my eye. One look showed her weight resting on one leg, hand on her hip, bat propping up her other hand.

"Any more pointers, Slugger?"

Fuck. Me.

I was pretty sure I'd just found the perfect woman.

An hour and countless swings later, I'd collected all the balls—as well as my ego. Emmy and I had thrown a ball back and forth a few times, and she confirmed her proficiency didn't stop at batting. We were settled on a bench outside the cages, Emmy having proved beyond a shadow of a doubt that she and Jay were related.

"How was I supposed to know you were a tennis and golf superstar?" I asked as I took off my cap and ran a hand through my hair.

"Not quite." She laughed. "I'm not bad, but I'm no pro. And I always enjoyed taking Jay to the batting cages when we'd visit each other. It was kind of our thing."

"So, what made you agree to my lame invitation to prep you for the game then?"

She looked up at me. "Besides the opportunity to see you eat crow?" I scowled at her and she grinned and then shrugged. "I don't know."

"You don't know?" I raised an eyebrow, which caught her gaze.

"Yeah."

"I think *I* know."

She looked at me speculatively. "Okay then. You tell me."

"You wanted to see me." I leaned in toward her.

She narrowed her eyes but didn't contradict me.

"I'm glad you called," I told her, and she gave me one of her bright smiles that made my chest do strange things. I wanted to kiss her but it would cover that smile—and I was enjoying the hell out of that smile. After a beat I continued quietly, "Date number four. You know what that means, right?" I reached out and ran my thumb along her jaw.

She stilled and her breath halted. Her expression changed to one of trepidation and her cheeks flamed at my insinuation. I should have felt bad but I couldn't bring myself to—not after the blow to my ego she'd just dealt in the cage.

"Listen, Gavin, I'm sorry if I sent out the wrong signals..."

I cut her off, "Ice cream."

Her gaze shot to mine and her eyebrows peaked. "Ice cream?"

"Yeah. What did you think I was going to say?" I leaned back again and played innocent.

Her lips pursed. "Tequila. I thought you were going to say Tequila. You know, the classic fourth-date tequila. Can't stand the stuff. Just thought you should know."

"I'll file it away." I grabbed her hand and pulled her up off the bench. Then we got ice cream, and when I kissed her at her car, this time she tasted of strawberries and Emmy.

Chapter Seventeen

REASONS YOU SHOULD DATE ME

*E*MERSON

"Okay, lay it on me. I'm ready." I stood in the entry to the kitchen as Jay constructed what could quite possibly qualify as the world's largest sandwich. He didn't look up.

"What exactly do you think I'm gonna say?"

I coughed out a laugh that held little humor. "Uh, let's see." I began counting off on my fingers. "He's my coach, Emerson. He's too young for you, Emerson. You don't have anything in common, Emerson. You hardly have time for me but you're making time for him, Emerson. He's basically a large child, Emerson. He's not a lawyer or an investment banker, Emerson." I dropped my hands and moved to the island. "Do I need to continue?"

He finally glanced over at me before going back to his culinary construction project. When he was done, he picked up the plate and set it on the island between us. Then he lifted half of the monstrosity and somehow managed to fit his mouth around it, taking a huge bite—all while eyeing me.

I watched him chew, and I have to say, it was pretty damn gross. The kid may be mature for his age, but he's still a teenager —a fact that made it nearly impossible for him to use good manners when it came to food.

The giant bite meant that he was unable to speak for about a minute, giving me ample time to squirm under his gaze. What did that look even mean?

He finally swallowed and wiped his mouth with the back of his hand—yuck. I refrained from retrieving the napkin holder and, instead, gestured impatiently for him to speak.

"Is that what *you* think?" He finally spoke.

My head jerked back. "No," I said quickly—too quickly. "I mean, I was just throwing things out there. You're allowed to have an opinion on this, Jay."

He nodded. "I do have an opinion."

I gestured a bit desperately this time. "Well?"

He reached for the sandwich again and I pulled the plate toward me. I couldn't handle another bite from him. He scowled at me and then gave in. "I think you should do what you want. I mean, I wish you'd told me, but the only issue I have is with him, not you."

My brow creased. "What does that mean?"

He reached for the plate again and I pulled it off the island and held it behind my back.

"I'm a growing kid. I need food, Emerson!"

I sighed and relinquished the plate, giving him a hard look in the process. He answered before taking another bite. "It means I'll use his head for batting practice if he hurts you."

I narrowed my eyes in disapproval, but felt my heart melt a little at the same time. "Take it down a notch, Babe Ruth.

Nobody's going to get hurt. Things are very casual between Gavin and me, and they're going to stay that way."

He raised his eyebrows and finished chewing. I was going to have to start looking away before I lost my ice cream. "And why's that?" he mumbled.

"Why will things stay casual?" When he nodded, I just said, "You know."

He shrugged. "I know what you rambled off a couple minutes ago. Gotta be honest, Em. Some of that sounded like your dad talking and the rest sounded like a bunch of B.S."

I frowned at him for his language and probably for the rest of it too. I knew he was right. But he was young—he didn't know how the world worked outside baseball and high school. He didn't know that some of the things I'd said, even though I felt ashamed for saying them or even entertaining the thoughts, were facts of my life the way it was—the way I'd carefully built it.

But I chose to just respond with, "I know." Then I left him to finish his sandwich while I changed my clothes and got to keep my ice cream down.

I'd lied when I told Gavin I finished work early tonight. He completely nailed me when he'd said I just wanted to see him. The truth was I had been having a hell of a time concentrating on my work all week. I suspected this had something to do with the influx of texts he'd been sending every day. They were a perfect combination of sweet, flirty, and funny, and I was afraid each one was causing me to get a dopey look on my face when I read it. Thank God I was usually alone when they came through.

But one of my particular favorites had arrived yesterday while I was supposed to be concentrating on my colleague's ramblings in a meeting.

Maybe: *I'm making a list of reasons you should date me. It's a work in progress, but here's what I have so far…*

1) I know all the best places for take-out.

2) I'm tall enough to reach lightbulbs.

3) People will always refer to you as the pretty one.

4) I'll let you touch my butt.

I'd almost laughed out loud before remembering where I was. I was pretty sure that was the text that caused me to pack up my laptop and call the guy. But playtime was over and it was time to make up for the hours I'd spent hanging out with my new coach. I settled in on the couch and got to work.

The next morning, Craig and I were summoned by Mr. Wheeler's executive assistant who informed us we were expected for a last-minute round of golf with our boss and a potential client. Like me, Craig was no idiot—he kept his game sharp and his clubs in the trunk of his car at all times. You never knew when opportunity would strike. We both made short work of collecting our belongings and getting our butts to the club in a hurry. I changed in the women's locker room, having brought my emergency change of clothes from my trunk as well. Suited up in a very respectable golf skirt and shirt with my matching visor in place, I joined Mr. Wheeler and the soon-to-be client, Mr. Weston, by the golf carts. I was secretly—and pettily—pleased to see I'd beaten Craig to the punch. But he approached moments later and we got on with the round.

I played decently and so did Craig, but Mr. Weston, who insisted we call him Brent, soundly defeated both of us and even

edged out our boss. Although it did cross my mind to wonder if Mr. Wheeler hadn't sliced his last drive on purpose.

As we were discussing some details of Brent's legal needs, I heard my voice being called. When I turned around, I was pleasantly surprised to see my father striding toward us with a smile.

"Dad," I greeted, mirroring his happy expression.

He gave me a short hug and then pulled back, turning to my companions. "Thomas," he held his hand out. "A pleasure to see you."

The two men had known each other casually for years, but introductions were made for Craig and Brent, and pleasantries were exchanged.

"I hope my daughter is doing her old man proud," my dad said, placing a hand on my shoulder. I had a momentary flash of nervousness for some inexplicable reason, as if I were still a child needing approval.

"Absolutely," assured my boss with a polite laugh. "She's a credit to the firm."

I felt my cheeks begin to warm and willed them to stop. I also noticed Craig shifting a bit impatiently on his feet, probably ticked off he wasn't the center of attention—not that I wanted to be. But it was always nice to hear you're doing a good job, no matter the situation.

"Well, she's always been determined and hard-working, that's for sure. A chip off the old block," my father felt the need to share, not caring in the least that he was laying it on way too thick.

Still, Mr. Wheeler was gracious as ever, and talk soon turned to business, to my great relief. It was only as we were all parting ways that Mr. Wheeler made mention of the upcoming tournament, which my dad's firm always participated in. "You'll want to watch

out, Robert. Your daughter is bringing along her secret weapon to the field this year."

I felt my head go light. My father, understandably, looked perplexed. How in God's name was I going to get out of this one?

"I bet you wish you'd hired her yourself now that she's dating a ringer," Mr. Wheeler taunted good-naturedly.

I grappled for something to say, but could do nothing but plaster a false smile on my face. Thankfully, my father was sharp as a tack. It wouldn't do that his daughter's boss knew more about her dating life than he did. My dad's mouth assumed an identical smile to mine and he just said, "Indeed," before departing.

I sighed with relief, but knew there would be a summons to the Scott house in my very near future. I wondered who I could drag along with me this time.

"Oh, Ms. Scott," Mr. Wheeler stopped me on my way out the conference room door late that afternoon after a meeting on AgPower. "It seems one of the patent applications hasn't been filed yet. I'm not sure how they neglected to tell us about it, but we need to get that sorted immediately."

I nodded. "Absolutely. I'm surprised they let that go this long with how much attention they're attracting."

He buttoned his suit jacket. "My thoughts exactly. It's a minor one, but still. Check your inbox."

"A bit cavalier of them. Thankfully they have us to keep things from getting out of hand," Craig weighed in as he and another associate gathered their things from the conference table.

"That's what we get paid for, Mr. Pendleton," Mr. Wheeler picked up his bag and sauntered from the room. I followed,

breaking off to the right toward my office once more. It looked like I'd be missing Jay's game after all. I hated that.

Craig appeared in my doorway twenty minutes later, his brief-case in hand. He leaned on the doorframe wearing an indiscernible expression. I sat back in my chair. "Anything I can help you with, Craig?" I fiddled with my pen while he seemed to consider this.

"I was just thinking, maybe we should bury the hatchet, you and I."

I studied him, trying to determine if this was one of his games.

"Look. I know you don't like me." He straightened. "And maybe I've given you cause. But this account is too important for us to let personal feelings get in the way. How about it?"

This was genuinely surprising coming from Craig. I would have assumed he'd never in a million years admit to any form of poor conduct on his part. Blame was always shifted when Craig had a say. What was he up to? Or was I being paranoid for assuming the worst? I decided to proceed with caution.

"I think that sounds like an excellent way to move forward," I finally responded.

His mouth formed a very modest, professional smile, creepy lips and all. Then he nodded and wrapped on the doorframe with his knuckles before bidding me goodnight. If we were calling a truce, I was going to have to stop picturing him as Cillian Murphy.

I filed the conversation away to dissect later, and called one of the paralegals to join me in my office to finish gathering what we could for the patent application.

My phone vibrated on my desk a few minutes later and I excused myself, knowing it was probably Gavin. As usual, I couldn't bring myself to ignore it. I briefly acknowledged to myself the new name I'd assigned him proved I was getting soft, and then read his text.

Slugger: Are you here? I haven't seen you yet?

Darn it. I'd forgotten to tell Jay and Gavin I wouldn't be at the game.

Emerson: No. I got stuck at work. If you talk to Jay tell him I'm so sorry!

Slugger: He'll understand. He may not even be playing tonight.

Well that stunk. Jay blew those other pitchers away—the coach had to be crazy not to play him. I felt my mouth go tight.

Emerson: I may be having a talk with that coach!

Slugger: Simmer down, Ace. Not going to help. Although, I admit the idea of you all hot and bothered is a good one.

I felt my cheeks flush. How did he do that to me so easily?

Slugger: Are you blushing?

I gasped. How did he know that? I snuck a peek around to make sure he wasn't actually lurking somewhere in the hall. He wasn't, of course.

Emerson: Shut up.

Slugger: Wish I could see your face.

Emerson: Get back to the game, jerk.

Slugger: Later, Emmy.

Even with the blush that still stained my cheeks, I was smiling when I got back to work.

"Did you win?" I shouted when I heard the front door open and close. There was no immediate response, so I ducked out of the kitchen to check the entryway.

"Only because they put the star pitcher in for the last three innings." It wasn't Jay who explained. It was Gavin. Gavin

Monroe was standing next to my brother in my entryway. And I was wearing my silk pink pajamas with my hair tied up in a messy knot and my face completely free of make-up. And, of course, I was barefoot.

It took me a moment to form words.

Jay chimed in, "I figured he should see what you look like in your natural habitat. You know, so he'd understand what he was getting into."

I was going to kill my brother. My hand went to my hair and I knew—I just knew—my face was the color of a freaking boiled lobster. They both just grinned at me, making me want to kill Gavin too. Naturally, he looked perfect in his cargo pants, casual red t-shirt and that damn green cap that he must have been born wearing.

"Congratulations," was all I managed.

Neither male seemed fazed in the least, and Jay raised a huge brown takeout bag while they both walked past me and toward the kitchen. "Thanks. Want some Chinese?"

That was an unfair question. Of course I wanted Chinese. I turned and glared at their backs as I followed them to the kitchen, running my hands over my pajamas to make sure everything was covered and there were no wardrobe malfunctions. It was too late to do anything about my outfit, but the least I could do was reassure myself I wasn't going to flash anyone. But, as if they knew exactly how flustered I was with Gavin's sudden appearance in my home, my nipples decided to poke at my pajama top as if to say, "*Hi, Gavin. In case you weren't aware, we think you're hot.*"

I stared at them, cursing to myself, and just managed to cover them with crossed arms as Gavin pivoted at my island to look at me. "We didn't know what you liked so we got an assortment. All the kid knew was that you're a fan of veggies." He mock-scowled

at Jay and my brother just shrugged his shoulders, completely unconcerned with anything apart from filling his face with food as soon as humanly possible.

I approached the island and attempted to mentally calculate how I was going to fix a plate of food while keeping my arms crossed to hide my traitorous nipples. Why hadn't I worn a bra?! Oh, right. Because I hadn't expected my ridiculously inappropriate crush to materialize in my house with take-out.

At least Jay had had the manners to pull out three plates before he piled his high and retreated to the living room. I heard the TV turn on to what was, undoubtedly, a baseball game.

"So, good surprise or bad surprise?" Gavin asked with a cocky grin on his face. I wanted to roll my eyes but managed not to.

"Well, at least you brought dinner," I responded with a little glare. "But just a hint about women for next time…we like a little advance notice."

He scooped some rice on a plate and topped it with what looked like beef and broccoli. "Ah, but then I wouldn't have gotten to see your pink pajamas." He raised that darn eyebrow at me.

This time I did roll my eyes.

"You want me to fix you a plate?" He gestured with the spoon.

I was still worried about my predicament and didn't want to uncross my arms. "That's okay. I'll get mine in a minute. Go ahead and finish yours." I gestured with my chin, knowing exactly how awkward I must look.

Gavin noticed. Terrific. He cocked his head and took in my position. "Are you cold?"

Oh God.

I bit my lip and said nothing. This was too embarrassing, so I ordered my boobs to behave and then uncrossed my arms, attempting casual and probably missing by a mile. "No."

His eyes went straight to my breasts and then back up to my eyes before a sly grin formed on his lips.

"Don't you dare say a word." I walked closer to the island to grab a plate, but Gavin just continued to look at me, his eyes getting a little smoky. Oh my. That was a good look on him.

He abandoned his plate and slowly came around the island, not stopping until he was very much in my personal space. His hand went to the side of my neck and I could smell the grass and dust on him from the game. He kept my eyes until he was too close, and then he was kissing me.

This kiss had none of the gentle hesitation or request for permission that his previous kisses held. His mouth demanded my acquiescence, and his tongue insistently probed my mouth to duel with mine in a wet collision laced heavily with heat and want. He turned us and I felt the edge of the island counter press into my spine while Gavin's hands roamed my body. I returned the kiss with everything in me. I didn't care what I was wearing, or how my hair looked. I didn't care that Gavin was twenty-four and posed potential career suicide. And I most certainly didn't care that I was starving and loved Chinese food. The only thing that mattered was Gavin's mouth on mine, his hands stroking over my body, and the need for him to be everywhere at once.

Overwhelmed by this desire that was so foreign to me, I'm ashamed to admit I practically molested the poor guy. My hands went straight for his ass, taking inventory for a good long while before traveling up his back and shoulders, my fingers taking in his lean muscle and the warmth of his body. Reading my overt behavior as invitation, Gavin's own hands moved down to my butt and he grasped it in both hands, pressing me in closer to him. I felt his hardness against my belly and the spider monkeys screamed their damn heads off.

The next thing I knew, he lifted me by my thighs, and my butt was on the island with my thighs straddling his hips. This new position placed us in perfect alignment so I could feel his arousal against my center. He was not shy, that was for certain. Of their own accord, my legs circled him and my ankles crossed behind his back as his tongue ran down my neck. I heard myself moan into the hair that was peeking out from beneath his favorite cap.

He murmured unintelligible words against my skin and I pressed him in closer with my heels. My entire body felt so tightly wound I feared what would happen to it next. I didn't understand the sensations this guy—this man—was evoking in me. I was not in control of my own faculties. I was completely at his mercy and would have gone anywhere, done anything he asked in that moment.

A shout from the other room pierced into my consciousness without warning. I jumped and felt Gavin do the same. "Come on! That was a strike!" Jay shouted. Gavin and I were both breathing heavily, still wrapped in each other's limbs. I could feel a slight burn from his five o'clock shadow on my chin and neck, and my pulse thrummed in my ears. I brought a hand to my mouth to feel my kiss-swollen lips as I unhooked my legs and Gavin took a step back. He took his cap off and scrubbed a hand through his hair before putting it back on and helping me off the island. We were completely silent. I knew my silence was the result of complete and utter awe as well as a good dose of embarrassment at the brazen behavior I'd exhibited just feet away from my teenaged brother.

It took a moment for me to meet Gavin's eyes, but when I did, all I saw was heat. This man wanted me. It was written clearly on his face, and I was guessing mine was a mirror image.

Criminy!

Chapter Eighteen

MIND OFFICIALLY BLOWN

GAVIN

Holy mother of hard-ons.

She'd had me fooled with her blushes and her coyness and all those conservative outfits, but Emerson Scott was sex on legs. I'd nearly lost my damn mind and dry humped her in the kitchen while her brother ate fucking Chinese fifteen feet away! My mind was officially blown.

I was still catching my breath and staring at her, wishing with everything in me that Jay wasn't home. The image of her spread out for me on that damn island and the thoughts of everything I would do to her were going to keep me up all night. A fully naked and aroused Emmy on that expanse of granite—Christ.

There was nothing to be done about it, though. Jay's heckling had alerted us to his presence, thank God, and we had to put the fun stuff on hold. But with the look Emmy was giving me, it wasn't going to be easy.

"Um, I guess we should eat?" She attempted, still catching her breath.

I couldn't speak yet, so I just nodded and willed my cock to calm the fuck down. I was going to have a permanent impression of my zipper on the underside of the damn thing if I hung out with this woman much longer. We finished gathering our food and joined Jay in front of the TV to watch the end of the game. Well, *they* watched the game—*I* watched Emmy, more certain than ever that we had something between us that couldn't be ignored.

When the game was over and the leftovers put away, Jay headed to his room and Emmy walked me to the door.

"So, what's the plan for the tournament this weekend?"

She shifted a little nervously on her feet. "Oh, right. Um, it's at Gibson Park off Wendover. We're supposed to be there at 11:00. I'll bring your uniform shirt for you."

"How about if I pick you up?"

"Oh," She shrugged. "I guess that would be okay."

"Don't get too enthusiastic on me," I teased at her tone, making her crack a little smile and shake out of whatever had been distracting her.

"Sorry. That would be nice. But isn't it completely out of your way?"

It was, but I didn't care. "I want to pick you up. 10:30 okay?"

She ducked her head a bit and it was fucking cute.

"Okay."

Then I kissed her again, careful not to get carried away this time. But I was scheduling some alone time with her as soon as humanly possible. Somewhere with some privacy and a nice horizontal surface, preferably.

Exhibiting a colossal error in judgment, I mentioned the tournament in passing to Nate. Nate, Bailey, and their dad, Riordan, owned Built by Murphy, the family business that employed me part time.

I'd been working at a remodel job the day after Chinese and Emmy's sweet mouth, when Nate showed up to check in with one of the independent contractors. He pulled me aside on his way out —I assumed, to talk to me about a work-related topic. Not so much.

I walked to his truck with him and he leaned back against the driver's door. He pulled off his hardhat and scratched the back of his dark hair, looking a bit tense. I started to feel worried for him until he broke the quiet with a comment I immediately wished to unhear.

"I've been thinking about asking Laney to have a baby."

The hardhat in my hand dropped and landed with a crack on the pavement. I ran both of my gloved hands over my face and around to the back of my neck, holding them there. "Why the hell do you have to talk to me about this? I don't want to hear about you and my sister. Do you not remember the horrific scene from last weekend?" I shook my head at him like he was an idiot, and I was seconds from bolting.

He put his hands on his hips and faced me. "I figured you'd have some insight." He shrugged. "You know, you did live with Laney and Rocco since the beginning and I figured you'd, I don't know, maybe have an idea of how the whole thing might go over."

I dropped my hands and shook my head again. Poor, misguided man. Didn't he know that my sister's favorite pastime was proving me wrong? "Dude, I am clueless. You've got to talk to someone else—and might I suggest you at least buy the poor soul a beer or

two first? I mean, would you want Jake talking to you about knocking up Bailey?"

"Yeah, thanks, Junior, but I'm living in the middle of that horror show right now."

I threw my hands out. "See, so you need to have some pity on me! I have no idea if she wants a baby. You think she talks to me about that stuff? Ask Fiona if you need an outside opinion."

He looked at me as if I were a complete moron. "And have Laney find out I talked to someone else first?"

"You're talking to *me* right now!" I pointed out, more than a little annoyed that I was, yet again, being forced to participate in shit that would put me in therapy.

"Yeah, but you'd do anything to avoid this topic with your sister. She'll never find out."

I looked to the sky. "All I want to do is hang out, do my job, and play some ball. Is that too much to ask?"

"Fine. Forget I said anything." He shook his head.

"As if I could. One of these days I'm going to waltz into your house, screw a woman on your kitchen table, and then ask your advice on a bunch of personal shit. How does that sound?"

"Depends on who the woman is, I guess." He shrugged.

"You are not right in the head, man."

His mouth tugged. "I'm messing with you. I'll drop the baby topic since you've been so helpful. But, hey, did you ever hear back from Emerson after she bolted last weekend?"

I couldn't help the grin that formed on my face. "Of course I did. What do you think this is, amateur hour?" I motioned to myself.

"And she's not bothered that you're a teenager?" He raised a brow.

"Your wife is only two years older than me and you're in your

thirties—you do realize that, don't you?" What was with these so-called friends of mine?

"Yeah, but she's more mature than me so it evens out." Based on this current conversation, he was not wrong.

"I guess. I'll admit the age thing has come up a time or two, but I'm compensating in other ways." I nodded.

"Compensating sounds like you've got a problem of another variety, my friend." Smug bastard.

"Yeah, right. Shut the fuck up. I was actually talking about a little strategy I've got working right now. I'm playing on her law firm's softball team and getting in good with her boss. How's that for genius?" I nodded and mimed a basketball shot hitting nothing but net.

He considered me. "Not bad, Junior. Not bad at all."

"First game in the tournament is tomorrow and I plan on impressing the shit out of her—maybe earning myself a little post-game celebration."

He threw his chin out at me. "Does Laney know you're playing ball? I know she'd love to see you—Rocco too."

Shit. I hadn't thought this through.

"It's no big deal, man. It's just softball with a bunch of out-of-shape lawyers." I fought the urge to back away slowly.

"Still, I know they'll want to come. When and where?"

Damn. There was no getting out of this, was there? I told him the info but made him promise to just keep it to the three of them. The last thing I needed was the whole peanut gallery showing up and making a scene. I suspected that would do little to advance my cause with Emmy.

He climbed into his truck and I decided to throw him a bone before he closed the door. "Hey, man." He turned to me. "If you

want to have a baby, just ask. You never know—she may be waiting for you to bring it up."

He nodded. "Thanks, Junior."

As he was pulling away, it occurred to me that another little Rocco running around wouldn't be a bad thing. Not at all.

"All right. Ms. Scott, you're in left field. And, of course, Mr. Monroe, you're pitching," Thomas Wheeler said with a beaming smile. He shook my hand and gave my shoulder a pat. This dude was stoked.

Emmy and I were wearing identical red t-shirts with the firm's logo, and matching caps shielded our eyes from the late morning sun. Thomas Wheeler and the rest of the firm's team were all dressed similarly while the opposing team sported black gear. The age range varied on both benches, with the black team having one player who appeared alarmingly elderly and looking like she could possibly benefit from an oxygen tank.

"Let's do this thing," I said, returning his smile and grabbing the softball glove I'd unearthed from my closet the night before. I was always up for playing ball. He moved on to greet some other arrivals and I turned to Emmy who looked like my idea of the perfect woman in her cap and t-shirt, slim jeans and a glove. I was beginning to think she might have been hand-made for me. I tugged on the bill of her cap and she turned to me. "Wanna warm up?"

One side of her mouth lifted. "Let's see what you've got today, Slugger."

"I'll go easy on you. Wouldn't want to embarrass you in front of your boss and all."

"Gee, thanks," she returned. I grabbed a ball from the equipment bag and we tossed it back and forth for a bit while Thomas and a couple older men—whom I assumed were Emmy's other bosses—organized the team.

I noticed Emmy eyeing another two teams on the next field over, and when I asked, she explained they were also part of the tournament. Eventually a couple umps arrived and the game was finally set to begin. I'd completely forgotten about Nate and Laney so I was momentarily surprised to hear a shout of my name from the bleachers. Emmy and I turned simultaneously and I vowed in that moment that I would methodically pull my brother-in-law's fingernails off one at a time and be quite happy doing it.

Taking up a good chunk of the available seating was not only my sister and her guys but pretty much everyone I knew. Fiona and Mark were present, of course—Mark saluting me and Fiona clapping excitedly over nothing in particular. Jake and Bailey sat a row in front of them, Bailey scarfing down food from a takeout fast food joint and paying little attention to anything but protecting her fries from Jake's hands. Then there was Riordan Murphy and his wife, Erin; as well as Trey and Court from work; Brett and that girl Ginger; Mark and Jake's mom, Kelly; and even Fiona's freaking boss, Jax.

"Fuck me," I muttered under my breath, but Emmy just waved cheerfully and got several waves back.

"You've got quite a fan club there, Slugger."

"You have no idea." I was staring daggers at Nate who caught my glare and pointed meaningfully at Laney who then pointed at Fiona. That made perfect fucking sense.

"Oh, look!" Emmy said. "There's Ari—and she brought Jay!" She waved at them as they found seats near Fiona and Laney.

Well, it looked like the whole gang was here. All we needed

was Ponch showing up and singing the National Anthem and we'd be all set. I sent up a little plea for my crew to behave themselves, knowing already that even the thought was futile.

And I was proven correct as I tossed the first strike across the plate. Pitching softball was a different animal than baseball, but I was confident in my abilities with pretty much any sport that involved a glove and a ball. The player in black from Anderson and Mellik, our opposing team, swung too late and the ump made the call. His voice was immediately drowned out by Bailey yelling, "Steeee-rike" at the top of her lungs followed shortly by a chorus of female voices shouting various forms of "Woot!" and "Woohoo!" I turned to left field after the catcher tossed me the ball, prepared to offer some kind of non-verbal apology, but Emmy was all smiles. Go figure.

Play proceeded in the same manner for the remaining top of the first inning, the guys also contributing some incredibly helpful words of encouragement, each prominently featuring "Junior" as part of the comment. I almost pitched a perfect inning, but that damn elderly lady who looked like she'd fall over any minute caught a piece of the ball and even made it to first base.

When our team prepped for batting at the bottom of the inning, I checked in with Emmy. "I'm so sorry about all that." I hooked a thumb to the bleachers. "I have no control over them."

She just smiled. "Don't worry about it. Believe me, this is way more fun than last year." She glanced meaningfully to the uber-conservative crowd lining the bench. She grabbed a bat and donned a helmet. "Wish me luck," she said as she turned for home plate as the first batter for the red team.

"You don't need it, Ace!" I yelled after her, a grin plastered to my face for sure. I turned back to the bench and the grin faltered. Thomas Wheeler was talking to the woman next to him, but three

other men's gazes were directed toward me, and none of them looked the least amused. I could identify two of them as the other managing partners, Jefferson and Schenk. But I had no idea who the third was. All I could tell was that he did not approve of me, Emmy, our friends, and probably the concept of fun in general. Shit. Maybe Emmy had been right all along and me getting involved was a stupendous mistake.

"Oh my God!" Laney wrapped her arms around me, seemingly unbothered by my sweaty state. "It's been way too long since I've seen you play. You looked great out there!"

I felt my mouth tug a little. "It's just a softball game, sis. Nothing to get all hormonal and weepy about."

She released me and smacked my arm just as Rocco attacked me in a hug from behind. I swung him up and over my shoulder. "What did you think, dude?"

"Awesome," he responded. "But they need a snack bar."

"I'll see what I can do for next time." I put him back on his feet and he ran off.

We'd cleaned the floor with the opposing team, another player even taking over at the mound when it started to get embarrassing. Emmy seemed pleased and I saw her talking to all the managing partners at one point or another, so I assumed all was okay. She wasn't at all touchy-feely with me, and I took the hint and kept my hands to myself for the most part, trying to maintain a little distance and decorum—unlike my idiot friends and family who continued to cheer as if it were game seven of the World Series. I gestured several times for them to shut the hell up when I noticed other attendees giving them sideways glances, but it did little to

help. I did, however, notice Ari maintaining a lower profile than usual, and I guessed it was because she knew the state of affairs with Emmy's job situation. That made me feel doubly guilty, but Emmy didn't say a word.

"Hey, Junior!" I heard Bailey call to me and I suppressed the urge to cover her mouth. She waddled over—there was really no other way to describe it. "Do you guys want to come over to our place later? Everybody's going to watch basketball while I lie in a recliner incubating Dexter here." She patted her belly. She insisted on calling the kid Dexter because he or she kept poking at Bailey's organs and she swore she was giving birth to a serial killer.

I looked over to Emmy who was talking to Jay. She must have sensed my gaze because she turned almost immediately and met my eyes. "Possibly, but don't count on it," I told Bailey, never tearing my eyes from Emmy's.

I heard Bailey make a gagging sound. "Gross. Did you at least get a note from your mom giving you permission to bang a grown-up?"

That brought my eyes straight back to her. "Did you get permission from Sea World to take the day off?"

She gave a fake gasp of indignation before yelling, "Jake! Junior just called me fat! Come kick his ass for me. I don't want to go into labor doing it myself!"

I decided that was my sign to leave.

Chapter Nineteen

DEAR EX-BOYFRIENDS: PLEASE TAKE A NOTE

EMERSON

I honestly didn't know what to make of the game as a whole. All three partners were pleased we'd defeated Anderson and Mellik since they'd trounced us in the semi-finals the year before, but I was getting a vaguely disapproving vibe from Mr. Schenk, and Mr. Jefferson said very little to Gavin or me the entire time. Mr. Wheeler, on the other hand gushed effusively over Gavin after he pitched what was essentially a professional-level game. Anika, a second-year associate, took over for Gavin when the black team still hadn't scored by the seventh inning. But, even then, he impressed by scoring runs and giving encouragement to other players. His love of all things baseball shone through, even though this was just some lawyers playing softball at a county park. Just watching him sent a warmth spreading through me that I knew I should be wary of, yet couldn't help but just enjoy.

His crazy friends and family, I admit, may not have made the best impression on my bosses, but there was nothing I could do

about that, and they seemed to make the game more fun for most of the participants, me included. I decided early on just to let it go and enjoy the game, keeping my fingers crossed that any of my fears would go unwarranted. I felt I was being very zen about it. My mother would be proud.

And speaking of parents, I'd nearly had a heart attack when I saw the teams assembling on the next field. I thought for sure my father's team would be one of them, but, thankfully, I'd been wrong. I'd managed to successfully dodge his calls the last couple days, still unsure what to say about my "secret weapon." Although it was only a matter of time before word filtered his way and I'd have to do some explaining.

"I don't even know what to say," Ari surprised me out of my thoughts with an arm around my shoulder and wide eyes. "Your Mr. Baseball is fucking hot. If you don't do something about this, I'm dumping Elliot and going after him myself."

A twinge of envy ran through me, unbidden. Gavin wasn't mine. I didn't even want him to be mine. I didn't have room for him to be mine. And Ari was all kinds of sexy—what guy in his right mind wouldn't want her? And, hey, if I could get rid of Elliot in the process, well...

Ari snapped her fingers in front of my eyes to regain my attention. "Joking! But not about you doing something. Get on that, woman—take that Mustang for a test drive and call me later with the report." She kissed my cheek, ignoring my grunt of annoyance, and turned toward the parking lot. "Oh, and good game!" she yelled behind her.

I waved and shook my head. "Thanks, Ari!"

Then I turned again and caught sight of Gavin hoisting a dark-haired little boy over his shoulder and I swear I felt my ovaries

sigh. I was thinking Ari was going to have to find a different substitute for Elliot after all.

"You want to pick up some food on the way home?" Gavin asked once we were on the road.

"Absolutely. I'm starving," Jay moaned from the back seat. Ari had picked him up earlier but we were dropping him off at one of his friends' houses and then they were going to the Greensboro Grasshopper's season opener in the evening.

I turned around in my seat. "You know, Mom didn't warn me about your feeding schedule. I swear you're like a hummingbird."

"Hummingbird?" Gavin asked.

"Wait for it," Jay responded for me. "Her head is filled with useless trivia."

"I think you meant *interesting* trivia," I said.

"By all means, keep telling yourself that," Jay said on a grin.

I narrowed my eyes at him before explaining to Gavin, "A hummingbird eats twice its weight in nectar every day. By ratio, of course, that makes it the hungriest animal on earth, besides insects and my brother."

Gavin looked suitably impressed and I gave Jay a smug smile. "See. Interesting. I have plenty more if you need proof."

Gavin cleared his throat. "So, that's a yes on stopping for food, right?"

Jay returned my smug smile.

"Oh, yeah. Sorry," I muttered.

I called in an order to Hops and we picked up some burgers to go. Despite having worked my butt off at the game, I could still only eat

half of mine and silently passed the remaining half back to my brother when I was finished. By the time we dropped him off, he'd probably consumed enough calories to fuel a small nation for a week.

"So, who was the guy who kept staring at you during the game?" Gavin asked. When I looked at him blankly, he expounded, "Um, probably about your age, brown hair, my height?"

I mentally ran through the roster and realized he must have been talking about Craig. "I think you mean Craig Pendleton, but I doubt he was staring at me."

"Oh, he was. Believe me. He was just subtle about it."

"Seriously?" I mean, Craig was always looking at women in what I considered a creepy and inappropriate way, but I assumed he reigned it in when the managing partners were around. And, besides, he and I were supposed to be on a truce.

"I'm pretty certain he was imagining what color underwear you're wearing."

I smacked Gavin's arm.

"Hey! Hands off the driver. Well, only if your intent is violent, I mean." I ignored his comment and he continued, "Anyway, I was just asking because he was giving me a *back the hell off* signal and I didn't know if there was something I was missing."

I felt my brow wrinkle. "That's really odd. You must have misconstrued the look. He and I are sort of rivals. I would call him my nemesis, but we've decided to call a truce while we're working on this huge account together. Eventually, one of us will probably be offered a partnership with the firm, though, and the other…" I trailed off.

"Ah," was all Gavin said as he took a left turn.

"What does that mean?"

He considered that for a moment. "I think you'd have to be a guy to understand."

I wanted to roll my eyes at that. "I highly doubt that. Try me."

He looked over at me appraisingly, then finally spoke. "He's totally into you, but he doesn't want to be. The fact that you're rivals just makes the idea of having you hotter. This truce means you'll spend more time together, which could result in: a) your appeal diminishes when your claws aren't out, and he can get over you; or b) now that your guard is down, he'll try to charm you and get in your pants. Then there's: c) you'll see he's not so bad after all and give him a real shot; or d) he's pulling one over on you, trying to appeal to your honorable side by calling a truce, but he's really after both getting you under him and swiping the partnership up in the process."

I just stared at him.

Gavin's eyes remained on the road until he felt my gaze and did a double take. "What?"

"You got all that from one look?"

He shrugged. "Well, it was more than one, but yeah. Like I said, it's a guy thing."

I sat back in my seat and considered that for a moment. "That's either the most brilliant assessment of a situation I've ever heard or you are certifiably nuts."

He flashed me a grin. "You asked."

I let myself revel in that grin for a minute before I responded, "Actually, I think you're reading way too much into this. He probably had something in his eye."

"Seriously?" Gavin actually sounded kind of annoyed.

"What?"

"You don't know how hot you are, do you?"

Aaand, cue embarrassing blush.

I felt his eyes on me even though I was staring straight ahead. "You're just proving my point, you know."

"Shut up and drive," I muttered, making him laugh.

By the time we pulled in my driveway, my face had returned to a shade that wouldn't halt traffic. Gavin didn't ask if he was coming in, and I refused to think about it too hard. Everyone we knew had seen us together and assumed we were an item. Not to mention, I was sixteen kinds of attracted to him and I knew he liked me. What could it hurt if I just spent a little more time with the guy?

I unlocked the door and he followed me in, carrying our takeout trash directly to the kitchen. I trailed him, and just the sight of Gavin near my kitchen island brought back all kinds of feelings...hot feelings. Tingly feelings. Feelings I wouldn't mind experiencing again if I were being honest.

"What I wouldn't give to know the thoughts running through your head right now."

I started, not realizing he'd been looking at me. Oh, lord. I probably looked like some kind of dog in heat. He was leaning against the counter by the refrigerator, blatantly checking me out and looking so flipping gorgeous and casual with his hands in the pockets of his jeans. Before I could think, I said the first thing that popped in my head. "Sandwiches."

It was his turn to jerk his head back in surprise. The smirk dropped from his face—smug hot guy, assuming he knew what I was thinking about. Take that!

"Yeah." I brought a hand to my hip as if to add some credence to my claim. "I was thinking of making sandwiches."

"You were?"

"Yes." Defensive much, Emerson?

"And this is because you didn't get enough to eat in the car?"

He hooked a thumb toward the door we'd just walked through. "You know, about ten minutes ago."

God. How in the world did I make a good attorney when I was so incredibly abysmal at thinking on my feet? It had to be Gavin. He rattled the hell out of me.

"I thought lawyers were supposed to be better liars than that," Gavin said, practically echoing my own thoughts as he stepped closer, grin back in place, eyes practically sparkling with mirth. Fudge. How was I supposed to fight that? I could almost hear Ari's voice in my head yelling, "You don't! You jump him instead!"

I obviously wasn't going to jump him, but I was thinking the fight was over, and Mr. Baseball had just won.

He didn't stop his advance, and I stood my ground, refusing to chicken out. I was a twenty-nine-year-old woman who had every right to engage in whatever the heck I felt like with another consenting adult. I didn't need to feel worried or ashamed or anything but the heat in my belly and the thrum of my pulse in my neck. And if the kisses we'd shared were any indication, I was going to enjoy the ever-loving hell out of whatever Gavin and I did together.

When his hand reached out to wrap around the side of my neck, I willed my nerves and those damn monkeys to settle and let any doubt or trepidation drain away so I could, for once in my life, just live in the moment and take a chance. Gavin's eyes burned into mine, and then I lost sight of them as his mouth crashed down on mine and I was lost in the feel of his lips on mine and his tongue against my own.

How had I never realized how awesome kissing was? This was amazing. I could feel it down to my toes as they curled inside my sneakers and electricity zinged along my spine, landing with a zap in the center of my womb. Gavin's kisses reached every part of my

body and had me moving against him involuntarily—instinctually. There was nothing mechanical about this joining of mouths and bodies as there had always been in my past experiences. I had assumed there was something wrong with me or that other people overexaggerated when speaking of their sexual adventures. It turned out all I'd needed all along was somebody who knew what they were doing. Either that, or whatever chemistry Gavin and I were sparking. It was ironic this was all coming from a guy I'd figured to be too young to take seriously. If this situation proved anything, it was that Gavin Monroe was *seriously good* at making out.

I hardly realized we were moving until I felt the wall at my back and Gavin's hand move to my thigh, hitching it up along his waist. I took the hint in no time and matched the position with my other leg, at which point his hands grabbed my butt and didn't let go.

"God, I love your ass." He squeezed and murmured the words into my neck. I locked my ankles behind his back as he pressed in.

"Thank you. I love your wrists," I said in response, my hormonal high rendering me a blathering idiot.

I felt his smile against my neck and silently thanked him for not calling me on my ridiculous statement. Instead, I leaned my head back on a groan and gave him better access.

At the sound, he abruptly turned us and began walking with me wrapped around him like a pretzel. I didn't care where he was taking me at that point. It could have been outside to the lawn for all I cared. I just needed him to keep doing what he was doing so I could keep feeling the delicious tingles all over and through my body. This sex stuff was awesome, and we hadn't even removed our clothes! I had the fleeting urge to write a letter to my past sexual partners telling them to sign up for Gavin Monroe's "How

to Do It Right" class because they'd all clearly been doing it very wrong.

It turned out Gavin was not taking me outside, but instead to my bedroom, some internal homing beacon having led him directly there without my assistance. Not that I would have been much help at this point anyway. His hardness was pressing into the perfect spot between my legs and I was shifting restlessly against him, needing more. More of what, I couldn't decide, but I just knew I needed it. I moaned his name, not even recognizing my own voice as it bubbled up my throat in a breathy plea.

"Jesus." I heard him say just as he lowered me to the bed, remaining firmly on top of me in the process. Which was a good thing, because if he had tried to remove himself, I probably would have tackled him to the ground to maintain contact. What in God's name was coming over me?

I threaded my fingers through his hair as he continued to kiss and nip down my neck until his mouth hit the barrier of my t-shirt's crew neck.

"Off," he said, sparing no time for complete sentences. Who needed grammar when there was amazing sex to be had? I mean, I was assuming it would be amazing—I was pretty much assuming Gavin was good at *everything* at this point.

He lifted off me for the split second it took for him to pull my shirt over my head, and then his mouth was everywhere. I didn't have time to worry about the sweat from the game that had surely dried on my skin, or the size of my breasts, or the freckles that dotted my chest. There was just his lips on me and the smell of grass and sweat from his hair that acted as some kind of aphrodisiac for me as I breathed it in and tried to memorize it.

My bra somehow disappeared without me realizing it—undoubtedly due to Gavin's magic hands. But I didn't care because

my nipple was in his mouth, and his teeth and tongue were doing unbelievable things to it—things that revealed a theretofore unknown nerve channel that ran directly from my nipple to my vagina. It disregarded the presence of all my internal organs and drove straight lines through me, connecting all my erogenous zones and making my body light on fire.

"Oh, God," I moaned, my fingers tripping over the muscles of his back and shoulders as he shifted over me and switched to my other breast. In a move that was completely unlike me, I pulled on his shirt until his bare skin was revealed to my fingertips. Then I impatiently tugged it over his head, sighing disappointedly when the motion caused his lips to lift from my breast. Luckily, he seemed just as eager as I was to get his mouth back to business.

I felt one of his hands slide between our bodies and easily undo the button of my jeans before sliding the zipper down. I hadn't fully allowed myself to contemplate the gravity of the entire encounter until that moment. I must have tensed involuntarily because his hand stilled.

I was about to have sex with Gavin Monroe. I didn't have sex with men unless we were in a committed relationship. How had I let it get to this point? What had happened to the numerous dates ending in chaste kisses? The gradual transition to light petting and then to a bit heavier, eventually leading to the bedroom after a few months had passed? Months. Not days.

This wasn't me!

A tiny voice in my head—one that had clearly been talking to my boobs—offered up a conflicting viewpoint. *But it could be you*, the voice said.

Indeed.

While my mind had been racing, Gavin had brought his head up. His eyes were heavy with desire, but there was also concern in

his expression. I bit my lip, knowing this was the moment of decision. If I did this, did that make me a slut? If I didn't, did that make
me a tease? I didn't want to be either one—I just wanted to be
Emerson. Oh, God, why didn't life have an instruction manual? I
mean, really, it would make things so much easier.

Chapter Twenty

DON'T DISS THE WOOBIE

GAVIN

Emmy's brain was running a mile a minute, that was clear from just looking at her. I saw those flushed cheeks and hooded eyes, but indecision was written all over her face.

"Emmy, we don't have to do this. Just say the word and this is as far as we'll go." I gestured down with my chin. "I'm very happy to concentrate my attention on areas we've already covered, believe me." I went for a light tone so she'd stop worrying. But her bottom lip was still clutched between her teeth, and her brow was creased.

She finally let her gaze fall to the side, her arms still wound around my back, her firm tits pressed against my chest. I had never coerced an unwilling woman and I never would. I was about to change positions so I could button her jeans back up, when her eyes came back to me.

"No." She motioned to the bed and then to me. "It's just that I've never done this."

Holy fuck. I felt the blood drain from my face. She was a virgin? How was that even possible in this day and age?

Her urgent tone cut into my panic. "No! That's not what I meant. Of course I've done...*it*."

I wasn't convinced if she couldn't even say the word, so I eyed her warily as she continued.

"I've just always been in a long-term relationship with the guy. I hardly even know you." She gestured wildly with her hand, almost catching me in the face.

I felt a bit put out by that statement. "I wouldn't say that. I've even stopped counting the number of dates we've been on."

She narrowed her eyes at me. "Showing up randomly at my house and kissing me in my kitchen isn't a date, Gavin."

"Sure it is." I gave a shrug and then rolled off her so I was laying on my side, my head propped up in my hand. This gave me a perfect view of her naked breasts. I resisted the urge to reach out for a touch. When my eyes came back to her face, I noted her gaze was on my chest and travelling downward by the second. I grinned and the movement brought her eyes back to my face. She shook her head, as if trying to gather her thoughts again.

Her protest continued. "And neither is playing softball with my bosses and my arch-rival."

"Now, wait a minute." I pulled my chin back in shock. "I got to first, second, *and* third base. I could have hit a home run, I just didn't want to be greedy. That, my friend, is a date."

She shoved my chest, but the crease in her brow loosened and her lips tipped up. I fell on my back, pretending she'd knocked me over. "So violent," I teased.

"I'm trying to be serious here."

"Then stop beating me up. It's a total turn-on, just so you know." I propped myself back up.

She growled. I grinned, letting my eyes wander.

"I'm obviously attracted to you," she admitted and then suddenly seemed to remember she was topless. She quickly—and tragically—pulled a blanket over her gorgeous tits.

I sighed as she continued, "I just don't think I see this relationship going anywhere, and I've never thrown caution to the wind and just gone on primal instinct. I'm more of a...planner."

I had to admit, that stung. I mean, she'd told me she didn't have time for a relationship, what with her work obligations and the new responsibility of being Jay's guardian. But I still thought I could make her change her mind. And *I* was busy too. It wasn't like I was asking her to marry me or anything. At least I was open to possibilities, though. She'd already made up her mind that this wasn't going anywhere.

I was mentally forming my response when I did a double take at the blanket she'd used to unfairly hide her goods from me. It was green and fuzzy and—no, my eyes hadn't deceived me—had small pink pigs sewn all over it. I opened my mouth, completely forgetting what I'd been about to say.

"Um, are those...pigs?"

Emmy's eyes flashed down to her body as she registered my words, and her face, already flushed from our activities, flamed an even darker shade. She flung the blanket off and onto the floor as if it were on fire. Then, realizing she'd exposed herself again, she frantically looked around for something else before futilely pulling at the covers I was laying on. The motions only served to jostle the very items she was attempting to hide, and I decided to take over.

I rolled onto her again and brought her arms over her head, holding them in place with my hands. "Emmy?" I asked slowly and deliberately. "Do you have a pig blanket?"

She sealed her lips together and shook her head vehemently.

Her wild auburn locks had come loose from the ponytail and were spread all around her. She looked like every fantasy I'd ever had.

I nodded. "See now, I think you're lying. I have a very clear memory of a pig blanket."

She strained her arms, trying to break free. I didn't let her.

"If you don't feel like we know each other very well, here's a great opportunity to remedy that," I suggested. "Tell me about the pig blanket, Emerson. I can't express to you exactly how eager I am to hear this."

She scowled at me, keeping her lips sealed.

"Oh, and feel free to blush all you want. You know how much that turns me on." I grinned. Yeah, I was a bit of an ass. But this was priceless. This woman had vehemently stressed how important it was to maintain the image of a serious adult, all the while cuddling up with a special pig blankie at night. It meant she had a chink in her armor. It meant she had a tender spot and wasn't so rigid. It meant I had a chance.

"Fine!" she finally huffed. "I have a woobie!"

That made me throw my head back and laugh.

"Shut up and let me go!"

I looked down at her, still laughing. "Not until you say, 'My name is Emerson Scott and I have a fuzzy pig woobie.'"

She shot daggers at me, her mouth pinched. Finally, the words escaped. "My name is Emerson Scott and I happily confess to the murder of Gavin Monroe by suffocation with a fuzzy pig woobie."

I had tears in my eyes from laughter at this point, but I swear I felt myself fall half-way in love with this woman as I watched her face and heard those words fall from her lips.

What can I say? I'm easy.

Needless to say, we didn't have sex. And I was completely fine with that. My cock? Not so much. But the evening ended up being

one of the best I could remember. We talked, we made out, we cooled down, we had a late dinner, and we made out some more. Then we both fell asleep in our jeans, covered with the pig blanket —which I had to admit was damn comfy.

And I found out the origin of the Emmy's childhood blanket. It was the only gift she could ever remember receiving from her dad that was purely frivolous and entirely girly. I was sure that revealed a lot more than she wanted me to know, but I held onto the knowledge just the same.

"Sugar!"

That single, strange word was the thing that woke me. Not Emmy shaking my shoulder like she was attempting to revive a dead person. I lifted my hand to stop her before she dislocated something. So violent, that one.

"Watch the shoulder. Do you want to break it again?" She'd discovered my scars from the motorcycle accident during her thorough exploration of my skin last night. I gave her the short version of the story, playing it down so things didn't get too heavy. "What's wrong?" I asked on a yawn.

"We fell asleep!" She said in an urgent whisper.

I kept my eyes closed and tried to roll over. "I sometimes do that in bed. It's perfectly normal. I promise."

The shaking resumed. I opened my eyes and turned to look at her. She sat next to me in bed, a white tank top covering her, but doing a very poor job of hiding her nipples. This shirt was now my favorite.

I motioned for her to come closer. "C'mere. I have something to show you."

"Stop it," she hissed. "We have to get you out of here before Jay wakes up."

That's what this vicious wake-up call was all about?

"Seriously?"

She just nodded and gestured for me to get my ass moving.

"Emmy, the kid's fifteen. He won't be up until noon at the earliest. And, speaking of fifteen, I'm pretty sure he already assumes we're having sex—which, I might note, we aren't."

She gasped. "That is totally untrue. Fifteen-year-olds don't think like that." She frowned. "Do they?"

I nodded. "I'm around them a lot. Trust me."

She shook her head. "That doesn't matter. I'm his sister and his guardian. I'm supposed to be setting a good example, and having you—a man I've been seeing for a nanosecond; a man who's his coach, no less—spend the night in my bed is not the bar I want to set!"

I let the unintended dig slide because I knew she wasn't going to like what came out of my mouth next. "I hate to break it to you, Emmy, but that ship sailed the minute his friend dropped him off last night. Correct me if I'm wrong, but my Jeep in your driveway is a pretty big tip off."

She sunk her face into her hands. "Criminy."

"I thought you didn't cuss."

That earned me a scowl.

I sat up and pulled her into me. "He'll survive. I highly doubt he'll go out and get a girl pregnant. Not today, at least." She tried to shove me away at that last comment, but I laughed and held her firmly. "You know, Emmy, if my ego weren't healthy, I might be offended that you keep trying to get away from me."

She mumbled her response into my chest. "If you weren't such an a-s-s, I wouldn't have to."

That made me pull back. "Did you just spell the word 'ass'?" I really couldn't hold my smile back, even if I'd wanted to.

"Yes." Her look dared me to comment further.

"Just checking," I responded before kissing her soundly.

"So, this isn't awkward or anything," Jay said as he spooned more cereal into his mouth. Emmy and I had migrated to the kitchen after a healthy morning make-out session, only to find Jay preparing his breakfast.

"I already told you. We didn't *do* anything!" Emmy said in exasperation, the statement causing Jay to turn a mild shade of green.

I interjected, "For Christ's sake, you're just making it worse. Quit while you're ahead, woman!" At least she'd stopped pacing like she'd done the first five minutes we'd been in the kitchen.

Jay took a moment and then resumed eating.

I pulled Emmy to a position behind Jay so he couldn't see us, and then I wrapped her in my arms. "Breathe," I whispered in her ear. I felt her sigh against my chest.

It was time to change the subject.

"How are you feeling about your game today?" I asked Jay as I released his sister.

He swallowed his bite before responding. "Good. I think Coach will put me in a bit earlier today. Wes was having some shoulder pain at Friday's practice so he might take it easy."

I pulled out a chair and sat across from him. Emmy set a cup of coffee down in front of me and I smiled at her before responding. "That's great news. I mean, obviously not the part about Wes's

shoulder, but I'm happy you're looking at more time on the mound."

He nodded before turning to Emmy. "Hey, I forgot to tell you Mom called me last night. They're coming the Friday after next and staying until Monday."

She stilled and looked back at him. "As in, less than two weeks from now?"

"Yeah," Jay returned with a smile. Then he got up from the table and took his bowl to the sink. "Good news, huh?" he asked before walking toward the hall.

"Yeah," Emmy responded distractedly, staring at a spot on the wall. I had no idea what that meant, but I was guessing things got complicated when Naomi was around.

"Oh," Jay's voice carried from down the hall. "And she said to tell Gavin hello."

Emmy didn't appreciate the snicker that comment elicited from me.

Despite the less-than-ideal encounter with Jay, Emmy loosened up and we had breakfast together, exchanging casual conversation and touches as if we'd been doing this for ages. For a woman who didn't see this going anywhere, she sure seemed comfortable with me inserting myself into her life. I took that as a good sign.

Then I took off, after a lingering kiss at the door, so Emmy and I could both get some work done before meeting up for Jay's game in the afternoon. I bought her a drink and some popcorn, which we promptly spilled when Jay completed a double play at the top of the fifth, catching a fly ball and throwing an opposing player out as he attempted a return to second base. Jay pitched an amazing few innings and I loved the look of pride on Emmy's face as she watched her brother lead his team to a win. It was also great seeing

her relax, even though I caught her checking e-mails on her phone a couple times.

We finally parted ways in the school parking lot, but not before I got in some last words. "Don't even think of telling me that wasn't a date."

To which she smiled her dazzling smile that hit me squarely in the chest and left me in high spirits the whole rest of the day. She was getting to me, and I could only hope I was doing the same to her.

Chapter Twenty-One

COCKTAIL THERAPY

$\mathcal{E}$MERSON

I sighed and leaned back into my desk chair. It was no use trying to lie to myself. I missed Gavin Monroe. It had only been thirty-six hours since I'd laid eyes on the guy and I freaking *missed* him. How pathetic was that?

It was Tuesday morning and I was supposed to be reviewing contracts for a merger, but there I was mooning over a man instead. This was so entirely unlike me. It was as if an alien form of me named Emmy had taken over my body and filled it with fluff and hormones. I'd practically fallen all over myself when he'd called the night before and asked me out to dinner for tonight.

Even the slightest recollection of Saturday afternoon and evening brought goosebumps to my skin. Gavin had known exactly how to touch and caress me to elicit the most delicious feelings I'd ever experienced. Had I known those feelings were possible, I'd have probably been a lot more tolerant of a couple of Ari's ex-boyfriends. It was obvious some men wielded magical powers, and

I should consider the possibility that she'd found a few along the line. Who was I to begrudge a girl some of that same blissful heat Gavin had triggered in me? And then there was the amazing feel of his skin under my fingers—the contrast of warm, smooth skin over taut, lean muscle was divine. I practically squirmed in my chair at the mere thought.

"Am I interrupting something?" a voice came from the doorway.

I tried to quickly school my features even as I felt my face flame. Traitorous fair skin! "No," I said a bit too loudly to Craig's inquiring expression. "Just thinking about what to order for lunch." *Seriously, Emerson? Is that the best you can do?*

"Okay," he replied simply, and I mentally thanked him for letting the blatant lie slide. Maybe Craig *was* serious about this truce. I waved him into the room and he seated himself in a chair across from me. He was dressed in his usual dark suit, and there wasn't a hair on his head that was out of place. Craig was the picture of composure while I was a flustered wreck.

I put my palms flat on my desk to keep them from betraying me. "What's up?" *What's up?* I had to get my act together. This was not how I spoke to colleagues at work.

Luckily, Craig let that slide as well. "I was just reviewing the completed patent applications you and Melissa prepared, and I noticed a slight discrepancy. Here, take a look." He passed a small stack of papers over and leaned in to point to a section he'd marked.

Sure enough, the date had been transposed. I looked up to him, my mind reaching back to the night last week when the paralegal and I had filled out the paperwork. I'd been a bit tired, but it was so unlike me not to catch something like that. Mistakes happened, I supposed—they just usually didn't happen to me. I sighed and

nodded, seeing my date with Gavin slipping through my fingers. "I'm so relieved you caught that. It could have caused a mess down the line."

He smiled in a decidedly non-creepy fashion. "Happy to help. It could happen to anyone."

"You're kind to say so." I returned his smile. Who was this guy and what had he done with my nemesis?

"I see you're busy, so I won't take up any more of your time." He gestured to the papers littering my desk.

I nodded. "The Jackson-Pancote merger."

"Ah. I dodged a bullet on that one," he returned good-naturedly.

I thought back to Gavin's assessment of Craig's behavior at the game and I just couldn't reconcile it with the man standing in my office. Gavin had to have been mistaken.

I handed the patent paperwork back to Craig. "I'll get this changed immediately and re-file. Thanks again."

He nodded, then said, "I have it up on my computer right now. I can easily take care of it so you can get back to the thrilling world of mergers." He raised his eyebrows, causing a genuine smile to cross my face.

A few weeks ago, I wouldn't have trusted Craig to pump my gas. Now I only hesitated for a moment before responding, "You know, that would be terrific. Thank you, Craig." I felt my pulse jump, realizing that Craig had just unknowingly saved my date with Gavin. I couldn't wait to tell Gavin how wrong he'd been—how wrong *I'd* been—about the man.

The rest of the week flew by, probably because I got to spend every night either hanging out with Gavin or talking on the phone with him until all hours. It was just like they say—time flies when you're having fun, and I'd never had so much fun in all my life. I'd

never laughed as hard, felt as light, or felt as *much*, period. I was starting to see possibility where it hadn't been before. And I was trying hard not to think about it too much—quite the feat for a woman who overanalyzed just about every decision she ever made.

The only fly in the ointment was my father. I was still avoiding him like a complete coward, but I didn't know what to say—especially considering my new revelations about all things Gavin Monroe. It was all too complicated and I couldn't deal with my dad quite yet. So, I was amassing an impressive collection of e-mails and voicemails, feeling rotten about it and knowing I'd have to face him soon.

Meanwhile, Jay was positively thriving. His grades were excellent, he was getting more playing time, and both he and Gavin raved about the extra training sessions. Coach Davidson was even starting Jay at a game next week. That prospect, along with the upcoming visit from Mom and Aldo, had Jay talking non-stop and back to the carefree teenager I knew and loved.

Even work was sailing along smoothly. Despite the time I was spending with Gavin, I was able to keep up with all my cases and accounts. I still had some work to do on the weekend in preparation for a meeting with the AgPower team on Monday, but that was par for the course. And there were two games in the tournament this weekend, so hopefully we'd win those and make it to the championship. Nothing would please the managing partners more than that, and if Gavin and I could help make that happen, all the better.

"I have to say, I love seeing you like this," Ari said as she sipped her cranberry and vodka and assessed me from her spot across the table. Gavin was out with the guys, giving me some overdue girl time.

I usually saw Ari several times a week, mostly due to her

boundless energy and willingness to accommodate my work sched-ule. I was undeserving of such a wonderful friend, but we'd been inseparable since childhood, so I supposed it wasn't so surprising that we continued to do whatever it took to maintain our close bond.

I'd always gone to all her school plays and performances, and I'd held her hand when she'd gotten her first piercing—and her first tattoo. I'd also stood by her side as her mother read her the riot act and prayed to whatever patron saint whose duty it was to look after unruly teenagers who liked to dye their hair and pierce their noses. And I'd been there to hold that dyed hair back when some awful boy broke her heart and she'd drunken herself into oblivion to drown the pain.

We were each other's touchstones. Ari understood how impor-tant my professional pursuits were to me, and she supported me wholeheartedly in my aspirations. She wouldn't let a busy work schedule on either of our ends cause our friendship to suffer. So, there she was, sitting across from me after a full day of work and with an evening of karaoke hosting ahead of her—just so we could catch up and lay eyes on one another. But this time, the reason for our almost week-long separation had been a guy. Sure, there had been times when Ari first started seeing someone and she'd been swept up in the guy, losing touch with me for a week here or there. But it had never been the other way around. This was a first, and Ari was apparently the number one fan of Team Gavin.

"I don't know what you're talking about." I shooed her away, taking a sip of my own drink to cover my lie.

"Nice try, chica. You're in *lurve* with Mr. Baseball," she cooed, making me practically choke on my Pinot Grigio.

"You've got to be kidding me," I managed to say. "I've known the guy for a few weeks!"

She chewed on her straw and gave me an innocent look. "Sometimes that's all the time it takes. So, tell me. What kind of bat is he swinging?"

"Okay, no more liquor for you." I tried to pull her glass away but she snatched it up.

"Oh, please. This is my first one. I thought the homerun king would have loosened you up by now. I haven't talked to you in days—you owe me some juicy details."

I had to admit part of me was tempted, given my newly-discovered sex drive and Gavin's apparent ability to find and push every single one of my buttons. But I didn't even know how to begin to talk about this kind of thing. "Relax," I said. "We haven't...you know."

Her mouth fell open and her eyes narrowed. "You can't be serious! What's the point of spending all your time with that tight, young ass if you're not gettin' you some?"

It was my turn to drop my jaw. "Oh my God. He's not a piece of meat, Ari!"

"Well, you clearly don't know the first thing about meat if his is still in his pants. I'd have been all over that by now."

"I'm aware." I took another sip of wine, wanting to change the subject to anything else before she started suggesting sexual positions and asking my thoughts on butt stuff. "What would Elliot say about you lusting after another man? Shame, shame, shame." I shook my head at her.

"Eh," was all she said in return.

This perked me right up. Was it possible there was a break-up on the horizon? Don't get me wrong—I'd never want my best friend to suffer heartbreak, but I was pretty sure this relationship with Elliot the Egomaniac wasn't the real deal. "Do you care to expand on that?"

Ari eyed me. "Are you a therapist now?"

"That depends. Do you want me to be?" I answered cheekily.

"That depends too. Do you have anything useful to share?" she shot back.

"Probably not." I let myself smile, dropping the act. "But you can still tell me."

"Ugh. It's probably going to sound stupid, but he hurt my feelings and he refuses to apologize."

That was entirely unsurprising, and I felt a pang of guilt that I hadn't been there for her immediately after Elliot acted like, well, Elliot. "What did he do?" I braced.

"Like I said, it's probably stupid," she prefaced before continuing, "So, his birthday is coming up in a couple weeks and I asked him what he wanted. I had some ideas and needed to see if I was on the right track. Anyway, after we settled that, I said, 'Don't you want to know what I want for my birthday?' I mean, I know it's still a few weeks out, but you know how much I like presents."

I did. Ari got ridiculously excited about gifts, no matter the occasion. "Of course. What did he say?" I wasn't sure I wanted to hear the answer.

Her lip curled. "He said, 'Oh, I already know what I'm getting you. A six-month membership to my gym.'"

Good God. It was worse than I thought.

"Oh, Ari," I said, reaching over to grab her hand. "He's an idiot." I couldn't help it. He had to be an utter moron not to see the stunningly gorgeous woman he was lucky enough to be dating. She shouldn't have to change a single thing for him.

She sighed. "I know. But he's my idiot."

"So, what happened then?"

"I tried to stay calm and explain how that was the worst present

in the history of the universe. He got totally offended and called me selfish."

I was ready to hunt Elliot down and ensure he would never participate in the propagation of the human species. I'd be doing all of us a favor, really.

"So, not only did he basically call me fat, but he called me selfish on top of that. We both refuse to apologize, so we're not speaking right now."

"I'm proud of you for standing your ground. Not that you ever have a problem doing that," I grinned. "But I'm proud none-theless." I received a small smile in return. "I'm sorry he treated you that way, sweetie."

She scrunched her nose up a bit. "Yeah, me too. But I'm not letting it ruin my night. Fuck men!" She lifted her glass in a toast to no one in particular.

I darted my eyes around us, hoping nobody heard her proclamation.

"Oh, but when it comes to Mr. Baseball," Ari said with a grin, "I mean that in the literal sense. You should definitely fuck that man." She nodded and I thunked my forehead on the table.

Chapter Twenty-Two

SCRABBLE WITH JENNIFER BEALS

*G*AVIN

"Come on, Ace! You got this!" I cupped my hands around my mouth and shouted as Emmy took a couple practice swings outside the batter's box. Despite the fact that the game was almost over and we were winning, I knew Emmy wasn't satisfied with her level of play thus far. She'd missed a catch earlier, which had resulted in the orange team scoring a run, and she was anxious to redeem herself. If her bosses considered a dropped ball an indicator of her level of commitment to the firm, I'd suggest a new profession. But I was fairly certain Emmy's need to prove herself had very little to do with her firm and more to do with her personality in general. Nevertheless, I wanted to see her do well—especially if it brought out that smile that went straight to my cock every time.

Today's game was considerably more subdued than the last one, owing to my bat-shit-crazy crew's absence. In fact, even Ari and Jay had skipped this one, promising to make an appearance at

Sunday's game instead—assuming we'd win today and advance to the next round. This was a foregone conclusion in my mind, of course.

The orange team's pitcher adjusted his cap and gripped the ball, all while keeping an eye on Emmy as she stepped up to the plate. He got into position, shifted forward and swung his pitching arm around, releasing a fastball with a snap of his wrist. Emmy's swing would have brought Jay to his feet had he been there. It was perfection. The ball connected with her bat right in the sweet spot and went sailing directly over the centerfielder's head, causing him to chase after it. Our bench went nuts, shouting and cheering for Emmy and the other player on base to run like hell. By the time the ball made it back to the infield, we'd scored one run and Emmy was safely on third, that smile firmly in place. I wanted to run up and kiss the living hell out of her. Instead I settled for a loud, "That's how you do it, Ace!" and my own smile. It was safe to say Emmy's reputation with the firm—and herself—was once again in good standing.

The game wrapped up shortly after, and the players milled around exchanging handshakes and discussing strategies for tomorrow's semi-final game. Thomas Wheeler checked in with me to ensure I'd be there, but the remaining managing partners still gave me a wide berth. It was odd, to say the least, and I didn't want to admit that Emmy may have had a point all those weeks ago when she'd told me her reputation could be tarnished simply by her choosing to date the likes of me. It was hard to believe people could be so shallow, yet I knew it was one of life's unfortunate truths.

I'd also been keeping an eye on this Craig guy throughout the afternoon. Emmy had told me he'd turned a corner and was actually being helpful and perfectly professional with her, but I still

THE GAME • 223

didn't trust the guy one bit. If he was even entertaining the thought of backstabbing my woman, let alone hitting on her, I'd set him straight in no time, probably with my fists. Yeah, Emmy was my woman, no doubt in my mind at this point. And I was her man. Well, at least that was the plan. And there was no room for dickwad Craig anywhere in the mix. He'd been more careful in eyeing her today, but there was still something off about him. And he made no attempt to hide his feelings for me, sending daggers my way whenever possible. That was one guy I'd be glad never to see again once this tournament was over.

"You ready?" Emmy asked, sidling up beside me, looking cute as fuck in her uniform. I was hoping for a repeat of last weekend's events since the only times I'd seen her this week had been in public. And I'd be lying if I said I wasn't hoping for things to progress to the next level this time. I was very open to any and all naked activities.

I nodded and we waved to a few more people as we headed to my Jeep and got in. Admittedly, it wasn't the nicest vehicle, but I didn't have any payments to make on it, so that was good enough for me. And Emmy didn't appear to mind. In fact, she seemed to enjoy the warm spring air as it swept over her sun-kissed and freckled cheeks. The honk of a horn alerted me to the fact I was sitting still at a freaking green light, and I quickly stepped on the gas. I was going to have to keep my focus on the road and off her if we were going to make it to her place in one piece.

I'd gone out with Brett and a couple guys from my construction job the night before, and they'd mocked me pretty severely about Emmy. I tried to play it cool, of course, but I did a pretty shitty job of it, provoking them to make cougar jokes all evening. They were just a bunch of jealous assholes, though, and none of them were taking a hot, funny, sweet woman back to her place

tonight. All they had were their right hands and maybe some half-way decent porn if they were lucky. Although Brett may have scored another date with Ginger, so I couldn't be sure in his case. He was still a jealous asshole, though, on principle.

"What do you want to do about dinner?" Emmy asked.

That brought a smile to my face. I loved that we'd progressed to the point where it was just assumed we'd be hanging out for the evening. It hadn't taken nearly as long as I'd expected and I gave myself a mental pat on the back for a job well done. "Why don't we grill out? It'll be hot as hell before we know it—may as well enjoy the awesome weather while we've got it."

She nodded and smiled. "I've got chicken and we can throw together some sides."

"Works for me." I turned the wheel, taking the on ramp to the highway. "Is Jay going to be eating with us?" I asked, knowing that the kid's presence would dictate both the tone of the evening and the probability of Emmy and I both having to fight for our fair share of food.

"No. Ponch is taking him to a concert in Raleigh tonight. Some band I've never heard of but is apparently 'epic.'" She made air quotes, not that I couldn't have guessed that word hadn't originated from her. "I'm the very uncool big sister," she said with a self-deprecating laugh.

"Crap. I don't usually hang out with uncool people."

She gave me the stink eye. "Well, I appreciate you making an exception for me."

"You're gonna owe me. I only take payment in naked form, though, just to warn you."

Of course, she blushed.

"Nice try. 'Sagittal' is not a word."

"Are you officially challenging me? You know what that means if you're wrong, don't you?" I asked.

Emmy eyed me and I maintained my best poker face.

The gods had intervened and I'd somehow convinced her to play strip Scrabble with me. Either she was super confident in her Scrabble abilities or she was suddenly down with getting naked in front of me. I suspected it was the former and she figured she'd get an easy look at my naked ass. I didn't care. Either way, I was in.

The rules are simple. Each player takes a turn. The one whose word scores the least points has to remove an article of clothing. Play continues until the game is over. If a player challenges a word and loses, they have to remove two articles. If they challenge and win, they can put an article back on.

The whole thing started when I made a joke over dinner about strip poker and learned that she'd never played. That was down-right un-American, in my opinion. She insisted she sucked at poker, so I suggested Scrabble.

I was down to boxer briefs and one sock. Emmy, who had showered and changed when we got to her house, was left wearing a collared shirt and jeans. In my defense, though, she'd claimed her hair tie and jewelry as articles of clothing, something I thought was bullshit, but I allowed because she smiled at me and distracted me with ice cream. I know, I'm a total sucker.

But things were about to get interesting. She only had four pieces of clothing left before she was bare-assed, and she was about to challenge me.

"Hmm." She continued to examine my expression before doing an inventory of her remaining clothing. "Nope. It's not a word," she declared with confidence. "I'm officially challenging."

That was when I let myself grin, causing her smug smile to

falter. Not taking my eyes from her, I pulled my phone from my discarded jeans and handed it over to her. "Look it up, Ace."

She snatched my phone and frantically typed, her eyes glued to the screen. I pinpointed the exact moment she found it. It was the same moment she pulled her bottom lip between her teeth and bit down. My cock took notice and twitched in my boxer briefs, catching her attention. Her eyes were suddenly not so interested in my phone—instead, they were pretty intent on my junk. Good thing I wasn't shy.

She released her lip from her teeth and the tip of her pink tongue darted out to lick the bitten spot. Fuck. There was no helping it now—my cock had a mind of his own. I saw her eyes widen a bit and I did my damn best not to smile. She was just this fantastic combination of sophisticated and innocent. It was such a fucking turn-on.

I finally cleared my throat and her eyes snapped up to mine, still wide. "I think you owe me some clothes."

That caused her head to jerk down, as if she'd forgotten what we'd been doing. Then she went for a pathetically transparent stall tactic. "Where in the heck did you get the word 'sagittal' anyway?"

I decided to humor her, for the moment. "I study sports science so I know tons of terms about the human body."

Her eyebrows popped up. "You do? How did I not know that?"

I shrugged. "Brett's the only person who knows, and now you."

She gave me a look like she thought I was insane.

She wasn't going to let me leave it at that, so I kept talking. "You remember when I told you about that accident I was in? Well, I'd been studying sports science—mostly because it was what my coaches had all studied and partly because I have a knack for that kind of thing." Emmy just nodded and watched me. "Anyway, once I started coaching at the Academy, I realized if I finished my

degree I could have a shot at a real career in coaching." I shrugged again. "So that's what I'm doing."

She cocked her head to the side. "But how do you have time to do that when you work two jobs?"

I grinned, thinking that was hilarious coming from a workaholic like her. "It's mostly online so I do it at night and on the weekends. I work it in whenever I need to."

"Wow," she said. "I'm impressed. And a little scared now over what other obscure terms you're going to put on the board."

I put my hand out in a beckoning gesture. "Speaking of...off with your clothes."

She pushed my hand aside. "Wait. One more question."

I sighed, letting her know my patience was reaching its limit. There was naked skin to be seen!

"Why are Brett and I the only ones who know about your classes?"

Shit. That was way too hard to explain. And it probably wouldn't reflect well on me. I still hadn't told her about the two-plus years I'd spent as a pathetic cry baby.

I put a finger up. "That is a story for another time."

She scowled.

"Enough stalling, you little cheater."

She sighed in resignation. Her brow creased in indecision and I knew I was smirking. After a moment, she stood and unbuttoned her jeans, then slid the zipper down and lowered the denim, all while keeping her eyes averted from mine. But her shirt was long, and when she straightened I realized it covered all the good stuff. I couldn't even tell what color her panties were! Then I remembered she had to remove two articles of clothing. Ha!

That was when she finally met my eyes again. I was ready for the big reveal, assuming she'd remove her shirt next. But she

reached behind her back with both hands, and I was momentarily confused. Until I realized what she was doing.

Damn you, Jennifer Beals! Damn you for teaching women how to remove their bras without taking their shirts off!

When Emmy finally pulled the white lace bra from one of the sleeves of her shirt, she extended her hand out over the coffee table and dropped it right on my rock-hard cock as it tested the fabric of my boxer briefs. Then she sat back down with that damn smug look. "My turn."

I narrowed my eyes and resisted adjusting myself. "This isn't over by a long shot."

She responded by placing her tiles on the board and spelling "quest" over a double word score space.

Dammit. I looked at my tiles and the best I could do was still about ten points shy. I played my tiles and lost my sock.

The next turn, I beat her by putting an s at the end of "quest," and she lost her panties. While I now knew they were white lace to match her bra—*holy fuck*, by the way—I still couldn't see a single part of her with that damn shirt in the way. My dick was clamoring for us to finish this game immediately and I couldn't have agreed with him more.

But Emmy was taking forever to put her next word down. It took me a minute to realize she was nervous. One of us would be completely naked in a couple minutes and it occurred to me that she might not want that. We'd been laughing and joking, and I knew she was turned on, but naked led to all sorts of things. Things she might not be ready for.

"Hey," I said quietly. "We can stop now if you want." I couldn't quite believe the words coming out of my mouth. That right there is what I call maturity. I hoped she took note of it if she was still somehow caught up with the age difference.

"No," she said. "I just...I just need a second. Believe it or not, I'm kind of nervous about...you know."

You know could encompass a hell of a lot of different things, but I got the gist of it. "We can do whatever you want, Emmy. No pressure here," I reassured.

"I know. I'm just...more of a lights-off kind of girl."

Well, that wasn't happening, that was for damn sure. She was fucking gorgeous and I was going to see and touch every single inch of her, even if tonight wasn't the night.

"Hey, if you don't want to look at me, feel free to keep your eyes shut. I promise I won't be offended." One side of her mouth twitched. "But I'm sure as hell looking at every bit of you—when you're ready. You're too stunning to keep the lights off, Emmy."

She looked up at me, and her eyes turned soft and warm. The anxiety in her features drained away and she just looked at me for what seemed like minutes. I looked back, drinking her in.

Finally, she opened her mouth and spoke. "Gavin, will you kiss me?"

Chapter Twenty-Three

CUTTING LOOSE WITH JUNIOR

EMERSON

The words were out of my mouth and nothing could have stopped them. I needed him to kiss me, to touch me. I'd been staring at his face, so open and without a touch of pretense. Gavin had zero ulterior motives or agendas. He didn't play games. He was kind and funny and sweet. And he was so easy to be with. I felt cherished when I was around him, and I realized in those minutes that Gavin had become precious to me.

I wasn't in love with him, although being with him made me realize I'd never actually been in love before. My past relationships had been more like arrangements based on convenience and mutual interest more than a sharing of hearts. With Gavin, everything was so different. I felt closer to him in a matter of weeks than I had to any of my past boyfriends—few though they were—after months. No, I wasn't in love with Gavin Monroe, but I knew in the very center of me that it would be so easy to fall.

If he was surprised or amused by my request, he didn't show it. He just stood and skirted around the coffee table before dropping to his knees so he was level with me. Without saying a word, he took my face in both hands and held my eyes for a moment. Then he leaned in and placed the sweetest of kisses on my parted lips. Just the simple touch of lips to mine sent my stomach clenching as electricity raced down to my womb.

I lifted my hands to his biceps and up to his shoulders, feeling the uneven skin on one of his arms where scar tissue resided. I had the sudden urge to place kisses along the scars, as if I could erase his past pain. But the feeling of his mouth on mine, his tongue sweeping along my lower lip, had my mind losing focus and my head angling to offer better access. I loved his mouth. It seemed to know mine in a way that made me want to permanently fuse our lips and tongues together. Sure, it might make everyday activities a bit difficult, but it would be worth it to keep these sensations he was provoking in me.

Gavin's hands slid from my face down my back to press me into him. I was acutely aware that I was naked save for this thin shirt. All he would have to do was lift the flimsy fabric and I'd be completely bared to him—a notion that had intimidated me earlier but was sounding like the best idea in the history of the world now. I moaned into his mouth as his hands continued down to my butt, his fingers brushing the bare skin right below my behind. Goosebumps overtook my skin and I pulled back from the kiss, feeling a mix of pure need and uncharacteristic boldness. I released Gavin and reached down to grasp the bottom of my shirt, pulling it up and over my head until I knelt there completely naked and practically panting. It was a strangely liberating feeling and I had a crazy urge to laugh out loud. That was, until I saw the fire in Gavin's eyes.

His gaze blazed a trail over my body, taking in every inch of bared skin. I could see the rise and fall of his chest as he took in my breasts with their tightened nipples and continued down to the juncture of my thighs. If he'd hollered and beaten his chest at that moment, I wouldn't have been surprised. His expression was tense and carnal and I thought his jaw might crack when he forced out the words, "Fuck. Emmy." For some reason, his dirty mouth turned me way the heck on.

And then he was on me, taking me down to the carpet beside the coffee table. His lips were everywhere at once, covering as much skin as they could and leaving little kisses, nips, and licks in their wake. His hardness pressed against my bare thighs through the cotton of his boxer briefs and I just wanted them off. I craved the feeling of all of his skin against all of mine.

"Gavin," I said, almost as a plea, as I slid a hand under his waistband. He seemed to understand my intent because he lifted and quickly shucked his boxer briefs, exposing himself entirely.

Now, as we've established, I'm not one to share details about… you know. But the next time Ari asked, I just might have to set things straight regarding "Junior" being a horrid nickname for Gavin Monroe.

Before I could register much, he was on top of me again, and my legs circled his back of their own accord. I had my head thrown back, and he was kissing my neck. Again, I couldn't believe that I'd missed out on this for all those years. Why had I wasted my time on men who engaged in sexual activity like they were following an instruction manual?

Gavin groaned into my neck, "God, Emmy. You're so soft, so sweet." I swooned and dug my fingernails into his back, causing him to rumble and bite my earlobe. His hot breath sent a shiver down my spine and I felt him press against my center. His hips

moved against me and all I wanted was to feel him inside me. But, even in my hazy lustful state, I knew we were missing a step.

"Condom," I managed to say before kissing the skin of his shoulder.

"Shit," he responded, and then rose up again. He turned on his knees and fumbled for his jeans. It gave me my first view of his bare ass, and *oh my*. I kind of wanted to bite it. What was happening to me? I was turning into a horny sex fiend.

Before I could follow through on my ridiculous notion, Gavin was back, condom in hand. He dropped it on the coffee table and sank down to kiss my breasts and tease my nipples while one of his hands caressed down my belly and over my thigh. He used it to part my legs and all I could do was grasp onto his hair, knowing where he was headed.

I felt the gentle stroke of his finger parting me, and then he was circling my clitoris. My back arched up and he simultaneously bit my nipple. I yelped in surprise, pulling his hair and feeling his growl against my breast. He continued his ministrations, making me squirm and moan and probably say all sorts of unintelligible things. When he slid a finger inside me, I thought I was going to climax right then. But I needed him inside me. The need was urgent. It was primal.

I began to push him away, but before he could misconstrue my intent, I muttered, "Gavin, I need you. Now."

He brought his eyes up to mine and they were liquid with lust and want. I knew mine were the same. He snatched up the condom packet, quickly opening it and rolling it on himself. I watched in a mix of fascination and impatience. And then he was on top of me again. My thighs parted of their own accord and he was pushing inside me. I moaned and let my hands slide down to his butt, urging him forward. I didn't want gentleness or hesitation. I

wanted him to take me. It was ridiculously animalistic, my desires in this moment, but I didn't care. It felt too good and right.

"Jesus, you're so tight," Gavin said on a groan. I wanted to tell him it was just because he was so…gifted. But it had been a long time for me, so he was probably right anyway. The delicious friction dissolved all rational thought, though, and I gave myself up to meeting the movements of his hips with my own.

It. Was. Amazing.

Just as I'd known it would be the first time he kissed me in that damn elevator.

Our bodies joined over and over, and when he began to thrust harder, I made noises I'm sure I'd never made in my life. Then Gavin paused, drawing in deep breaths, sweat beading on his brow. He surprised me by quickly rolling us over so I was on top of him, our bodies never separating. I gave him a questioning look.

"I don't want you to get rug burn," he said.

The thought hadn't even occurred to me, I had been so wrapped up in the sensations of our bodies lighting each other on fire. "What about you?" I asked, still breathless.

He grinned. "Totally worth it for the view I'm getting right now."

I looked down, realizing that I was straddling his hips, my hands propped on his chest and my breasts bared. Any other day, any other moment, I would have been shy or embarrassed, but I wasn't with Gavin. The only thing I felt was beautiful as his eyes drank me in and his hips pressed up into me. I bit my lip, this position seating him differently inside me.

"God, I could look at you all day," Gavin said, thrusting again, this time more forcefully.

I moaned and began my own movements on top of him. Soon we were both panting again, and words were unnecessary. I

could feel sweat dripping between my breasts and down my stomach. Strands of hair were stuck to my face and I didn't care about anything but the feel of this man inside me. Our movements picked up speed until I felt my climax begin to form at the very bottom of my belly. It rushed down to where we were joined and then ran up my spine, causing me to arch and cry out. I couldn't hold my rhythm through the overwhelming sensations, but Gavin continued to thrust into me, taking over for the both of us until I heard him grunt and curse, his own orgasm ripping through him.

I finally collapsed in a heap on his chest, feeling our sweat mingling and wanting nothing but to stay exactly where I was until the end of time. Or at least until work on Monday.

I felt Gavin's hand stroke the back of my head, but I had no energy to reciprocate. "Are you okay?" he asked.

An exhausted laugh bubbled from me and sounded against his bare chest.

"I'll take that as a yes," he chuckled lightly and the vibration caused my head to shake. Gavin ran both hands down my back and squeezed my butt. "Have I told you how much I love your ass?"

"Right back at you," I mumbled into his chest.

"I know."

That cocky statement gave me the burst of energy I needed to raise my head a fraction and meet his eyes. "I see someone has a healthy ego." I tried to scowl at him.

He grinned. "Don't think I didn't catch you and Ari both checking my ass out the first time we met."

Oops.

I just huffed and settled my cheek back onto his chest.

He chuckled again, giving my butt one more squeeze before reaching between us. "Sorry, but I have to take care of this," he

said. I reluctantly rolled off him and watched him walk naked to the bathroom. I sighed.

When he was out of sight, I looked around, taking in the Scrabble board and our discarded glasses from the drinks we'd shared. Then I looked down at myself. I had streaks of pink on my skin from the abrasion of his stubble, and a few darker marks on my thighs that I knew were the result of our exertions. I vaguely wondered if my face showed any evidence. I sighed again, reveling in the foreign feeling of being well and truly sexed up. Gavin's touch was still on my skin, even though he wasn't even in the room.

It occurred to me that maybe I should regret getting caught up in the moment. It certainly wasn't anything I'd ever done before. But I couldn't bring myself to feel anything other than giddiness, satiation, and a good measure of exhaustion.

Gavin returned, still gloriously naked, his lean muscular frame making me feel not quite as tired as I'd been a moment before. "What time is Jay coming home?" he asked.

Oh God! I'd been so wrapped up in the awesome sex I hadn't been paying any attention to the time. I snatched my shirt up before grabbing my phone and checking the time. My pulse slowed a fraction. It was only ten-thirty. "I don't think he'll be back for another couple hours," I said.

"Good," Gavin said before bending down and pulling me up by my hands. He walked backwards to the hall, dragging me with him.

"Wait!" I protested.

"No. We can clean up the game later." He practically pouted.

"Fine, but I'm not leaving our underwear out here for Jay and Ponch to see."

He glanced back at the floor, taking in my discarded bra and underwear as well as the rest of our clothes. "Point taken."

He quickly swiped up all our clothes in one hand and then pulled me down the hall to my bedroom.

I followed willingly, a huge smile on my face. It looked like Emerson Scott had finally cut loose.

Chapter Twenty-Four

ME AND TOM CRUISE

*G*AVIN

I sang along to Japandroids all the way home, like fucking Jerry Maguire, ignoring any strange looks I received and just feeling sheer contentment from my night with Emmy.

Last night would go down as possibly the best night of my life. The vision of her gorgeous body straddling me with her flushed face and heavy-lidded eyes would be burned on my brain for an eternity. The fact that she took unabashed pleasure in each new sensation and seemed almost surprised as her body responded did things for my ego, I must admit. And, as much as I despised the mere thought of her with any other man, I had to wonder what kinds of idiots she'd been dating.

I may have been the younger one in this relationship—yes, relationship—but I was clearly the more experienced. Emerson Scott was an undiscovered treasure and I couldn't wait to help her explore all the incredible things we could do together.

After our second round last night—in her bed this time—I was in desperate need of a shower. I couldn't coax Emmy to join me, something I'd have to work on for next time. Instead, she washed our clothes since we'd have to wear our uniforms again for the semi-final game, and I had nothing else to wear anyway. We heard Jay wander in eventually, and Emmy went out to talk to him. I stayed in the bedroom, figuring Jay wanted to see my naked ass about as much as I wanted him to. Ponch's voice was also audible, giving me double the reason to stay put. Eventually, Emmy came back to bed and we fell asleep, her back to me and my arm around her, my hand staking claim to her right breast, just as it should be.

When I got home, Brett was nowhere to be found so I assumed he'd gotten an invitation to crash at Ginger's the night before. I grabbed a soda and got down to work, trying to complete an assignment that was due by midnight. The game wasn't until three o'clock so I had some time.

I heard the front door open and slam shut about an hour later, then the sounds of cursing filtered up the stairs and I decided to investigate. I found Brett with his head in the refrigerator, muttering something unintelligible.

"Hey, man," I said, startling him and causing him to smack his head on the bottom of the freezer.

"Shit," he said, turning around with a hand on his head.

"Sorry. I figured you saw my Jeep." I wanted to laugh but he looked like he'd been through the ringer.

"Must have missed it," he grumbled, pulling a beer out of the fridge and closing the door.

I looked at my watch purposefully. "Um, a bit early, isn't it?" My brows raised in question.

He unscrewed the cap and tossed it toward the trash can, missing as usual. "Not after the night I had."

I leaned back against the counter and watched him down half the beer. "What the hell happened? I thought you'd be with Ginger."

He laughed mirthlessly. "Yeah, Ginger," he responded, his voice dripping with scorn. He wiped his mouth with the back of his hand and I refrained from telling him about the drops he'd spilled in his sort-of-beard.

This did not sound good. "What happened?" I asked again.

Brett took another swig. "She dragged me out to Limelight with some of her friends last night. I drove, of course, so I was dead-ass sober."

I cringed at that. A sober Brett at a dance club was tantamount to a nun at a strip club.

"Turns out, some of her other friends—guy friends—were meeting us there. She got wasted and I caught her on the dance floor with some asshole's tongue down her throat. I tried to get out of there, but she followed me outside saying it was no big deal. That she and this guy are just fuck buddies."

"Ouch."

"Yeah. I tried to walk away, but she started crying and shit. You know I can't handle that."

I nodded. Girl tears are Brett's kryptonite. "You drove her home, didn't you?" I had to ask.

"Of course I did. Have you met me?!"

I suppressed my chuckle as best I could.

"But that isn't even the worst of it."

I was beginning to think I might need my own beer if there was more to this train wreck.

"She puked in my fucking car!"

Oh, shit.

"And then I had to help her up to her apartment and hold her

goddamned hair back while the demons escaped. Her roommate wasn't home and I didn't want to leave her in case she choked or something, so I fell asleep on her fucking hallway floor."

"Jesus, man. That sucks." There really wasn't much else to say. "So, where have you been all morning?"

He drained the rest of his beer and slammed the bottle down on the counter. "Some asshole parked me in, so I had to wait for him to move his car. Then I went and paid a fortune to get the damn car detailed. I had to drive with the windows down and my hand over my mouth." He looked at me. "I'm fucking done with women. At least the young ones. Does Emmy have any friends?" he asked.

I laughed. "Well, you've met Ari, but I don't think she'd make your life any easier."

He shook his head. "She's hot, but no way, man. I don't need that kind of crazy in my life." I had to agree.

"Maybe you should go it alone for a while," I suggested.

He scratched his beard. "Yeah, you're probably right." Then he threw his chin out. "How about you? Any luck with Emmy last night?"

I couldn't help the shit-eating grin that overtook my face.

Brett nodded and smiled back. "Well done, my friend. I like her."

"I do too," was all I said in return, but I was thinking my feelings ran deeper than like. How much deeper, I wasn't sure yet, but I was looking forward to finding out.

And there was no reason I couldn't keep my eye out for a nice girl for Brett along the way. He could use some nice in his life. Damn, if I wasn't feeling like one cheerful son of a bitch.

"Go! Go! Go!" I kept yelling as Emmy rounded second base. I was standing by third and waving her forward, confident she could make it. Her foot hit the base seconds before the third baseman in blue caught the ball. The ump made the safe call and I grinned widely. "Way to go, Ace!" She smiled that gorgeous smile at me and bent to catch her breath, her hands resting on her knees. We were only up by one and Emmy's hard-hit grounder that landed her on third base was exactly what we needed.

"Go, red!" I heard Ari yell from the stands. I glanced over and almost laughed at the look on Brett's face as Ari stood on the seat and cheered. He shook his head and then dropped it in his hand. I'd talked him into coming to the game, figuring it might bring him out of his foul mood, but I was afraid Ari was just a little too far toward crazy to help cheer him up. Luckily, he and Jay had been talking most of the game, so at least he was distracted.

I made my way toward the backstop and watched our next batter step up to the plate. It was that damn Craig guy. He swung at a drop pitch and missed before catching a piece of a fastball and taking off for first. Everyone on our bench and in the stands yelled out as Emmy took off for home, running like a bat out of hell and crossing the plate. She turned my way and hardly paused before running and launching herself at me, her legs circling my waist and her arms snaking around my neck as I caught her.

"Damn, woman!" I smiled at her and she dipped her head to plant a hard kiss on my mouth. I squeezed her one last time and she hopped down. It surprised the hell out of me that she'd been so publicly affectionate, but I wasn't going to complain. I looked over to see that Craig was safely on first and we were now up by two runs. There was a championship in our near future. The blue team still had one more turn at bat, but I was confident we could keep our lead.

"Way to go, Emerson!" I heard Jay cheering for his sister. She waved at him and went to take her place on the bench. I stayed where I was and enjoyed the view from behind.

A tiny paralegal named Tracy was up next and I reminded her to keep her elbow up and assume a good stance. She couldn't bat for shit, but her height made her strike zone narrower than an apple peel so she got walked almost every damn time. This time was no different and she sashayed her way to first, making everybody laugh, while Craig advanced to second. Unfortunately, our next batter struck out, turning the inning over. I grabbed my glove and walked out to the mound.

When I turned back around, I noticed more people had shown up, and most of them were watching us from behind the team benches. Some wore gray shirts while the rest wore yellow. Thomas Wheeler and the other managing partners greeted a few of the newcomers and I remembered that the other semi-final game was being played right after ours. Whoever won that game would go up against us at the championship next weekend. That was, if I did my job right.

I didn't think much of it as I threw a few warm-up pitches to our catcher, a funny guy named Pete. But when I happened to turn and see Emmy in her position at left field, it was impossible not to notice she'd lost most of the color in her face. She just stood there, staring in the direction of the opposing bench. I glanced that way and saw one of the new arrivals—an older man dressed in a gray team shirt—beckoning with his hand for her to come over. When I looked back at Emmy, I could see she was mouthing something to him, but I couldn't make it out. Who the hell was that guy? By the look on Emmy's face, he wasn't just some random weirdo, that was for sure. I wanted to send her a questioning look, but she wasn't facing my way and the bottom of the ninth was about to

start. I needed to focus on the win and then I could find out what the hell was going on.

"Well done, Mr. Monroe!" Thomas Wheeler clapped me on the shoulder and shook my hand. "We certainly couldn't have done it without you."

I returned his shake and his smile. "Thank you, but you've got to stop calling me Mr. Monroe. I keep looking for my dad when you say that."

He chuckled but didn't call me Gavin. Instead, he moved on to shake more hands. A few other teammates came up for high fives or handshakes, and Brett wandered over as well. I hadn't seen Emmy since the end of the game and I was looking forward to a celebratory kiss at the very least. "Hey, man, have you seen Emmy?"

He shook his head. "No, sorry. I was talking to Jay. That kid is something."

I nodded. "No kidding. Now you see why I can't shut up about him." I craned my neck, looking around for my girl.

"Anyway, good game. I'm taking off so I'll catch you later," Brett said.

"Thanks for coming," I returned as I gathered up our gear. "I'll probably be back late, if at all."

He grinned and shook his head, offering a wave before heading for the parking lot.

Where in the hell had Emmy gone? Then I remembered that guy. Shit. I filtered my way through the milling crowd and finally spotted her as I dropped our gear in the backseat of my Jeep. She was standing in the parking lot next to a silver BMW, talking

intensely with the older guy in the gray shirt. I started to head their way and then paused. They seemed to be arguing. He had his hands on his hips and Emmy's arms were crossed over her chest. He leaned down to say something and she threw her arms out to her sides before turning from him and stalking back toward the field. She swiped a hand under one eye and then the other. I felt my blood begin to boil. Whoever this asshole was, he'd just made her cry. I was still a good forty feet away and she hadn't seen me yet. My gaze shifted past her and to the man I was considering throat punching. But he wasn't watching Emmy's retreating back. His eyes were shooting daggers at me. I didn't even know this guy. What could I possibly have done to piss him off so badly? I returned the glare out of principle and after several seconds, he just shook his head and turned to his car.

My eyes found Emmy again just as she spotted me. Her steps faltered a bit and then she resumed her pace, attempting and failing to school her features. As she neared, I could see the tears sparkling in her eyes and the flush on her cheeks. I closed the distance between us and wrapped her up in my arms. "Hey," I said.

"Hey," she answered weakly, her voice muffled by the fabric of my shirt.

We were having a talk on the way home, no doubt about it.

Chapter Twenty-Five

EXPECTATIONS AND FUNDAMENTAL TRUTHS

*E*MERSON

I gripped the back of Gavin's shirt as he held me to him. I had no idea how he knew I needed his arms around me, but I was so grateful he did. Tears pricked my eyes and threatened to fall again, but I did my best to hold them back. Gavin placed his lips on my hair and gave my head a small kiss, making me sigh into his chest.

"Let's get out of here," he said into my hair.

I didn't trust my voice to respond, so I just nodded and let him hold me for one more minute before he led me by the hand to his Jeep. I climbed in and fastened my seatbelt while he did the same, and then we were pulling out of the parking lot. I didn't even have my glove or hat and had no idea if Gavin had grabbed any of the gear we'd brought, but I didn't care. I just needed the breeze across my skin and the calming presence of the man next to me. Everything would be all right, I told myself. It had to be.

For a twenty-nine-year-old woman, I suppose it was unusual

that I'd never had an argument with my father. Never. I'd always been his shining star. From the moment I'd chosen tennis lessons over ballet at age six, his approving smile had become an addiction —one I began chasing and, apparently, never stopped. When I came in third place at the middle school science fair, I got a pat on the back, but when I came back the next year with a horizontal-axis windmill and a study on its energy output, I took home the blue ribbon and one of my dad's beaming smiles.

I'd always been somewhat aware that, had I been a boy, things would have been simpler growing up with my dad. But with all the loving reassurance and encouragement to "just be myself" that came with my mother's parenting, it never seemed like a burden. I took it as more of a challenge to be met—one that came with its own rewards. My mother's love and acceptance was given so freely, I had no expectations to live up to. There was no bar set, no push to achieve. But my father's blood ran through my veins and I needed the challenge of setting goals and working to achieve them.

Each time my father boasted to a friend or colleague about my accomplishments, it added another point to the tally I kept inside. When I followed in his footsteps and applied to law school, I thought he would burst with pride. And I reveled in it, soaking up the praise and adding the points to my ledger.

The fact that so many of my life choices were made to garner his approval or to please him should have struck me as trouble-some, but I'd honestly never given it much thought. I had two families, and they were so different, I'd needed to develop one personality—one life plan—and stick with it or I'd go nuts. I just happened to develop one that aligned more closely with my dad's expectations. It should have sent huge, blue-whale-size red flags up, but it didn't.

Until today.

Until I found myself on the receiving end of a look I'd never in my life gotten from my dad.

Disapproval.

Disdain.

It caught me by complete surprise and stung me like a venomous wasp.

I'd known I couldn't avoid my father forever, and my confrontation with him probably would have been much less dramatic and hurtful if I'd just womaned up and responded to his first phone call after our encounter at the golf course. How I'd thought we'd be gone before his team showed up today, I had no idea. I must have been in a post-hot-sex stupor that turned me temporarily stupid.

There I'd been in the outfield when I caught sight of my dad standing behind the blue team's bench aiming a stern look my way. It was no use to pretend I hadn't seen him, so I gave a weak wave. In response, he beckoned me over. I was not in the habit of disobeying my father, but the inning was about to start and there was no way either of us would tolerate any kind of public scene anyway. I mouthed that I'd talk to him later and did my best to finish out the game while wracking my brain for a good explanation.

But, really, what was the big deal? So I hadn't told him I was dating a guy—so what? But I knew why I hadn't told him. I'd known all along. There would be questions, there would be expectations, and the answers would not please him, no matter how I tried to spin it.

My dad is, in a word, a snob. I knew it and I accepted it, just as I accepted that my mom is a slightly batty hippie. I didn't have to approve or emulate if I didn't want to, but I had to accept it. They're my parents. But having a snob for a father

makes things a bit difficult when you bring other people into the mix. I may not mind adjusting my behavior and choices to meet his approval, but I could hardly expect other people to do the same.

Luckily, I'd never had to. Sure, Ari is a bit wild and my dad wouldn't ever want to claim her as his own, but he'd known her since she'd been a toddler so she was kind of grandfathered in. And my past boyfriends who'd lasted long enough to be introduced to my dad had all been stuffy lawyers or accountants—just the types he associated with on a daily basis.

I knew he envisioned a future where I achieved a partnership at a prestigious law firm, then got married and had perhaps one or two children while my husband worked at his own high-profile job (or if not high-profile, at least high-earning) and our nanny cared for the kids while we joined my dad for rounds of golf at *our* club and spent holidays skiing and sending charitable donations to all the right philanthropic entities.

I knew it because it was the same future I'd always envisioned for myself.

"I'm going to give you the benefit of the doubt and presume you've been too wrapped up in work to return my calls and e-mails," my dad opened as we stood by his car after my game. We were far from the crowd, so we had plenty of privacy for our talk.

"I'm sorry," I said. "That was rude of me. And I'm sorry you had to find out from Thomas Wheeler that I'm dating someone. That put you in an awkward position and I apologize." I was hoping that would do it and he wouldn't dig deeper. I also hoped that triple-fudge brownies would suddenly become a health-food staple, but neither had a snowball's chance in hell of ever happening.

He suddenly looked as if he'd smelled something foul. "Yes,

dating." His eyes locked on mine. "I saw your little display, Emerson. I have to say, I don't understand what's come over you."

I felt my brow crease. "Display?"

His hands went to his hips and his mouth tightened. "I may be getting older, but my eyesight is still quite sharp. Really, Emerson, you jumped on that...*boy* as if you were some kind of rodeo queen, not a damn officer of the court. I can only imagine what the partners thought."

That sent my cheeks flaming. I'd never heard him use that tone with me. I thought back to my race toward home plate and the natural way my feet had taken me straight to Gavin. I'd felt such joy in that moment, and now it was overshadowed by shame. He was right, of course. It had been wildly inappropriate. How had I not realized it at the time?

"I'm...I'm sorry. Of course, you're right. I can't think what came over me."

My father sighed, some of the disdain draining from his expression. "Well, at least this whole tournament business will be over soon. I understand you wanting to go the extra mile to impress Thomas, but associating with some second-rate local athlete just to secure Wheeler's precious trophy is going too far, in my opinion. Impress him with your hard work and intelligence. I'd hate for you to gain the wrong reputation."

"Oh," was all I could say for the moment. He was under the impression that I was fake-dating Gavin for the sake of the tournament. A notion that shouldn't surprise me given that it had been my original plan. And he also clearly disapproved of Gavin, something that in no way surprised me.

I finally cleared my throat and spoke, "His name is Gavin Monroe. He's actually a terrific guy."

My father's brows shot up. "You think I don't know who he is?

The minute I left the club that day, I was on the phone finding out exactly who my daughter was supposedly *dating*." He said the last word so caustically I almost winced. This conversation was not going well. At all. "Do you know he doesn't even have a full-time job?"

I inhaled sharply. "Yes, he does! He works more than full time. He could give me a run for my money with how many hours he works!"

My father looked shocked at my outburst. "Why are you championing this young man? Don't tell me you've become attached." He scoffed as if the notion were preposterous.

I felt my face flame again.

"You've got to be kidding me!" He raised his voice in anger. Then he coughed out a humorless laugh. "Oh, I'm sure your mother just loves this. Her 'baby' hitching herself to a falling star, rubbing shoulders with the underachievers of the world so she can help lift them up."

I was appalled. "That's not fair!" I couldn't decide who it was more insulting to—Gavin, my mom, or me.

"Who ever said life was fair?!" He thundered at me.

I felt the urge to retreat but I stood my ground. "You don't know anything about Gavin. He's smart and kind and hardworking. And he's good to me."

He leaned down over me. "Don't be naïve, Emerson. I'm sure he's a swell good-ole-boy. But he's nowhere close to your league! You need to keep your eye on your future. This boy may be Thomas's best friend on the softball field, but he'll never sit at a dinner table with the man. Which means, if you keep associating with this Gavin character, neither will you."

I hated his words. I hated that he felt this way, and even more, I hated that he was probably not wrong.

He straightened and brought his voice down a notch. "Did you know that your baseball player dropped out of college and spent over two years living practically as a bum?" My head snapped up at that, catching his eyes. My dad continued. "I see he didn't share that little bit of information with you. He sponged off his family and friends, spending all that time drinking and doing God knows what, not working a single day for over two years. Does this sound like someone you should be affiliating yourself with?"

I was speechless. I knew Gavin had dropped out of school because of his accident and scholarship, but I didn't know the rest. I shook my head, trying to gather my thoughts. I couldn't just take my dad's word for it. Surely, Gavin could clear the air. I looked at my dad, his face now calm, assuming he'd convinced me to see reason. But I was getting angry now. Even if all those things he said were true, that wasn't the Gavin I knew. He'd changed. He'd grown up.

I crossed my arms over my chest. "If you knew him, you'd see that you're wrong."

"Facts don't lie, Emerson. We're lawyers. It's a fundamental truth."

I threw my arms out to the sides, feeling tears of frustration and sadness forming in my eyes and willing them back. I couldn't let him see me cry, see me weak.

"Maybe in court, but not in life. I think we need to table this conversation until we've both had a chance to calm down. I'll speak with you later, Dad." And I turned and walked away, a few tears spilling from my eyes. I wiped them away quickly and plodded back toward the field, not realizing Gavin stood waiting for me.

"So, are you going to tell me who that guy was?"

Gavin had given me the first half of the drive to sit in silence,

but my reprieve was apparently over. We sat at a red light on Wendover Avenue and he turned to look at me. I swallowed.

"It was my father," I said quietly.

"Your father?" He couldn't have sounded more surprised if he tried.

I just nodded in response.

"But you guys were obviously fighting. I thought it was his wife you didn't get along with."

I sighed. "Well, today it was him, I guess."

"What were you fighting about?" Gavin asked, sounding more serious.

There was no way I was going to tell him my dad thought he wasn't good enough for me and that I was making a fool of myself and committing career suicide by dating him. That's not exactly something a guy wants to hear, I was guessing. So, I went with the ever-lame, "It's complicated."

I saw Gavin's grip tighten on the steering wheel, but he didn't respond. We continued driving for another few minutes before I broke the silence. "So, did you get that assignment for your class finished?"

"Yeah," he said. "How about you? Ready for your AgPower meeting in the morning?"

I groaned. "Not quite. I've got more to do tonight."

"I guess that means I should just drop you off, then?" Gavin asked, sounding half resigned and half hopeful.

"Yeah. Probably." But I wanted Gavin to come over, if for no other reason than to remind me how right I was about him and how wrong my dad was.

I half-hated myself for what I knew I was going to ask next. I hadn't brought up his class out of idle curiosity. "So, I've been meaning to ask, what did you do after your accident? I mean, after

you left college. Because you said you've only been working your current jobs for a couple years..." I kept my eyes forward, but I saw his head turn to look at me.

"Um, what made you think of that?" He sounded wary—as he had every right to. God, I was bad at this.

"It's just that you never talk about it." Way to go, Emerson. Turn it back on him, just like a good little lawyer. Ugh.

He sighed. "That's because I don't like to think about it."

I felt that like an arrow to the heart. What was I doing?

"I'm sorry." I finally looked at him, but his eyes were now on the road. "You don't have to talk about it."

We were both silent for the remainder of the drive back to my place. Gavin pulled the Jeep into my driveway and put it in park, leaving the engine running.

"I don't like to think about it or talk about it because I'm embarrassed about the kind of guy I was," he said quietly.

"Gavin," I interrupted. "Please. You don't have to tell me this. It was wrong of me to question you like that."

"No," he responded, taking his hat off and running a hand through his hair. "You deserve to know who you're dating."

"I'm dating a hot baseball coach." I tried a smile but it didn't hit its mark.

He laughed without much conviction. "If you say so, but you're also dating the exact guy your dad just described to you."

Chapter Twenty-Six

MILEY CYRUS RUINS EVERYTHING

GAVIN

I'm no idiot, despite what Emmy's dad might think. He was probably right about a lot of the things he thought about me, but that wasn't one of them. As soon as Emmy told me the guy from the game was her dad, the pieces started falling into place. Then, when she'd brought up my classes, I knew exactly where this was going—and exactly where it had come from.

But, really, how could I blame him? If I had a smart, driven, successful daughter like her, I'd want better for her than a guy like me. She could have any guy she wanted, and I was fucking thrilled that she was dating me. But I'd never be able to buy her a BMW or some McMansion in a fancy-ass neighborhood. I wouldn't be hanging some Ivy League diploma on my wall, and I'd probably never have a job that didn't have me coming home covered in sweat and dirt. And I'd never see the need for more than three utensils at the table. I mean, why the hell do you need a different

fork for your salad, your main course, and your dessert? That's just a whole hell of a lot of wasted dish detergent if you ask me.

And, though I'd been keeping quiet about the years when I'd been an asshole freeloader, she had a right to know who she was getting into bed with. So I told her. I told her all about the accident and the aftermath. About how I'd caused the whole damn thing in the first place with my arrogance and disregard for common sense. And about how I'd fallen into a well of self-pity and whining worthy of any four-year-old kid who didn't get his way. How I'd taken advantage of my parents' kindness and sympathy. And how I'd sponged off everyone and drank beer like it was my new career. She just let me talk as we sat in her driveway, the engine of my Jeep still running.

Only when I finished did she speak. "Gavin, anybody else would do the same. I know if my dream had been taken from me, I'd wallow in regret and what-ifs. Who wouldn't?" She reached her hand out and grabbed my arm.

I raised an eyebrow at her. "I think once you pass the two-month mark, you're all out of your allotted wallowing time. I milked this thing for over two *years*, Emmy. And that's two years I'll never get back." I'd never said it aloud like that, and I felt a fresh wave of guilt and regret wash over me. But I shook it off as best I could. I didn't do that shit anymore.

She gave me a sad smile. "Well, either way, you can't go back and change it. You have to move on. And that's what you've done."

"I'm trying to," I responded. "This probably wasn't what you expected when you signed on to that first date with me, was it?" I tried to lighten the mood. It worked.

She scoffed. "I was tricked into that!"

"I am pretty sly, I have to say."

"Yeah, and about as subtle as a wrecking ball." She pursed her lips.

"Well, now you've done it. I'm going to have the image of you naked and swinging on a wrecking ball stuck in my head all damn night. You'd better kiss me quick and get out if you hope to get any work done tonight."

She scurried out of the car without kissing me, her cheeks pink and her voice muttering something about Miley Cyrus ruining everything.

I laughed and watched her go, suddenly feeling a bit lighter after sharing that part of my past with her. I just hoped it wouldn't come back to bite me in the ass.

"Yo, Junior!" Mark yelled as he crossed the lot in my direction. I felt the sweat drip down my spine as I straightened. So much for mild springtime weather. It was a scorcher and it was only mid-April.

"What's up, man? You need me at a site with air conditioning? Shoot. Well, all right. I guess I can do it."

"Always the smartass," he said, shaking his head and curling his lip. He came to a stop in front of me.

"I like to think of it as providing comic relief," I told him.

He ignored me. "Fiona's cooking a pot roast. You're supposed to bring Emerson over."

My stomach immediately growled at the thought. Fiona's pot roast was a religion of its own. There was no way I was missing it. "Your place or hers?" I asked.

"*Our* place," he said with a shit-eating grin.

"Please tell me she didn't sell the condo."

"Do I look stupid to you?" He scowled at me.

"You sure you want me to answer that?"

"Get your ass back to work." He hit me in the arm and I almost fell over.

"Ow!" I cried to his departing back.

"You deserved it. Quit your crying." He didn't even have the decency to look at me while he talked.

"Just for that, I'm taking an extra serving!"

"Go ahead and try. Seven o'clock!"

I rubbed my arm and pulled out my phone to text Emmy. I knew she had a busy day with her meeting but I was hoping she'd get off in time for pot roast. I opened our text thread.

Gavin: Fiona is cooking tonight at 7:00. I promise you don't want to miss it.

I waited for a minute but there was no reply. Not all that surprising. I'd have to check back later. I scrolled up so I could read our text exchange from the night before. I felt my face tug.

Gavin: I was just listening to Miley Cyrus so I had to check in. Are you decent?

Emmy: Ha, ha. There is no way you listen to Miley Cyrus.

Gavin: That's pretty presumptuous. How do you know? I might have her whole damn collection.

Emmy: That's about as likely as me having Run-DMC's whole collection.

Emmy: You still there.

Gavin: Sorry. I can't type and laugh at the same time. Run-DMC? Really? How old are you?

Emmy: Old enough to know that this line of questioning is going to get you in trouble if you don't watch it.

Gavin: Shutting up now. You done with work?

Emmy: I wish.

Gavin: *I'll let you get back to it.*

Emmy: *Okay. Thanks for the distraction. Talk to you tomorrow?*

Gavin: *Anytime. Sweet dreams, Emmy.*

I quickly looked around, sure I had a stupid smile on my face and not wanting to catch any heat for it. Then I got my ass back to work.

When quitting time rolled around and I still hadn't heard back from Emmy, I was in a conundrum of sorts. I wanted the pot roast, but I also wanted to see Emmy. I was experiencing one of man's age-old dilemmas. Our three essential needs of food, sleep, and sex sometimes conflicted and we had to make a choice. My very male brain chose sex. So I went home and took a shower. Then I made a last-ditch effort to call her, and when there was still no answer I decided on a whim to just head over to her office. It wasn't too far from Fiona's place anyway, so maybe I'd get to kill two birds with one stone after all.

I parked and made my way up to her floor, looking down at my t-shirt and jeans and realizing too late that I probably should have dressed a bit nicer. I remembered where her office was, so I bypassed the front desk and walked down a couple hallways until I reached her door. It was closed and the lights were off.

I assumed I must have just missed her and reached for my phone to check for a text. It was odd, not only that she finished with work so early, but that she hadn't returned my text or call. I was pressing the button to turn on my phone when that Craig guy stepped out from another office. He did a double take, and when he recognized me, his lips curved into a self-satisfied smile. I knew right then that something was very wrong.

"Looking for your girlfriend?" He asked.

I didn't respond. I just held his eyes.

He sighed, as if I were playing some game he was tired of. "I'd check the unemployment office. She was let go about a half hour ago. You just missed her."

He brushed by me and walked casually down the hall in the direction I'd come from. I was speechless.

Let go? How was that possible?

That slimy fucking son of a bitch. He was behind this, that was one thing I knew for damn sure. The other thing I knew? He was going to get his ass handed to him one way or another. You don't mess with my girlfriend and get away with it.

I turned and went after him, catching up with him at the elevators. "What the hell happened?" I demanded as he pressed the down button and kept his eyes on the closed doors.

"I'm not really sure," he said, feigning innocence. "But our firm doesn't tolerate slackers." That was when he turned and let his eyes deliberately take in my clothes.

If I weren't so pissed I probably would have rolled my eyes at him. I backed away toward the stairs and pointed at him. "This isn't over, asswipe."

He assumed a bored expression and I took off down the stairs, anxious to track Emmy down and find out what the hell was going on. I didn't see her car anywhere, so I hopped in my Jeep and tore out of there, hitting her contact on my phone. My call went directly to voicemail so I knew she'd turned her phone off. I pointed my Jeep in the direction of her house, but I knew before I even rang the bell that nobody was home. Dammit! I could find Jay's number if I went over to the Academy, but he was at practice so he wouldn't have his phone on him. And I didn't have Ari's number or address so I was shit out of luck. I wracked my brain for the name of Ponch's shop, but drew a complete blank. The only thing I could remember was that it sounded slightly dirty. I did a quick

Google search and found it. Stroke. That was it. Jesus, that guy. I hit call and waited while it rang once, twice, three times.

"Stroke, whaddya want?" blurted a female voice over the line.

"Yeah, hi. Is Ponch around?"

"That depends on who's askin'."

I did not have time for this shit.

"Tell him it's Gavin Monroe, and Emerson's in trouble."

"Hold on." There was a bang on the other end as if the phone had just been dropped. Then I heard muffled voices and the tail end of Ponch's statement to whoever the hell had answered the phone. "...or I'm not letting you answer the goddamn phone anymore!" Then his voice spoke into the phone clearly. "Gavin. What the hell is going on? Is Emerson all right?"

I took a moment to consider how to answer that. Then I just laid it out. "I'm probably going to get my ass kicked for telling you this, but she got fired today. I can't find her—she's not home and her phone is turned off. I figured she might be with Ari but I don't have her number or address."

"Shit. How the hell did that happen?"

"I don't have a fucking clue. That's why I need to call Ari. Can I have the number, man?" If he gave me a hard time, I was going to reach through the phone and nut-punch him.

"Yeah." He rattled off the number and I wrote it down on the back of a fast food receipt.

"I'd appreciate it if you didn't let on that you know about the job."

"No problem. I'll call Ari later. Good luck, kid."

I grunted irritably.

He coughed out a short laugh. "You're way too easy to mess with. Later." And he hung up.

I quickly dialed Ari's number. It rang a few times and went to

voicemail. "Ari, it's Gavin. I'm looking for Emerson. I know what happened at work. Please call me when you get this."

About a minute later, I got a text.

Ari: I'm hiding in the bathroom. She doesn't want me talking to anyone.

Gavin: So she's with you? Is she okay?

Ari: She was here when I got home. She's acting really weird.

Gavin: What do you mean?

Ari: She's not crying. She's sending out resumés and pacing. She won't tell me what happened—just that she got fired and she keeps saying "stupid!" over and over. How did you find out?

Gavin: I went to her office and ran into that Craig asshole.

Ari: I knew that two-faced twat had something to do with this. That guy is a fuckwad!

Gavin: No arguments here. Can I come over?

Ari: Shit. I don't think she's ready to see anybody yet. I'll work on her and try to get her to call you.

Gavin: Okay. Thanks.

Ari: We'll get this figured out. Don't worry.

Ari: I've gotta get back. TTYL

I lowered the phone and looked up and down Emmy's street, not sure what I was expecting to see. Ari's news had not sounded good and it kind of hit me in the gut that Emmy didn't want to see me. I had no idea what to do with myself, so I did the only thing I could think of. I went to the batting cages.

Chapter Twenty-Seven

JERKS ARE THE WORST

EMERSON

"Sampson and Dornet! They like me! Oh, but I beat Dornet at our last round of golf. Probably not great, but there's nothing I can do about it now," I muttered to no one in particular. I looked up the e-mail address and started composing another personalized cover letter.

Six down and…about three hundred to go.

"What was that?" Ari asked, coming back into the room.

"Nothing. I just thought of another one."

"That's good," Ari answered and came closer until she was standing with her hand on the back of the dining chair I was using as my desk chair. Her kitchen table had become my makeshift office. "Anything I can do to help? Want me to Google 'corporate law in Greensboro'?"

I nodded. "Better make it the whole Triad area. Thanks." I continued to type.

I could feel Ari behind me, just standing there. I knew she was going to speak before she opened her mouth.

"So, are you ready to talk about it yet?" She sounded like she was addressing a crazy person holding a gun.

"Nope." My fingers flew over the keyboard. I wasn't stopping until I'd exhausted every possibility.

"Okay. I'm gonna make some dinner. Do you want some?"

"No, but thanks," I responded distractedly. "Do you think including a recommendation from your law professor is tacky when you've been out of school for four years?"

"Ummm…" was all she said, and I finally turned to her. She looked stricken that she didn't have an answer for me. Shoot. I wasn't being a very good friend right now.

"It's okay, Ari. I really appreciate you helping me out."

She got the sappy eyes and started to come in for a hug. I put a hand out to stop her. "I can't hug right now. If I do, I'll start crying. And I can't cry right now. I can't cry until I get a new job."

That made her look even more sad.

"I'm sorry. I just…"

She gave me a half-hearted smile. "It's okay. We'll figure it out. Go back to your letter and I'll get that Google search for you. And I'll make enough dinner so you can have yours later."

"Thanks, Ari. You're the best." I attempted a smile.

"Damn straight," she said, trying to lighten the mood. Then she went off to the kitchen, leaving me to it.

Luckily, I'm an organizational freak, so my resumé was already up to date. How I was going to get a new job without a reference from my old job, though, I had no idea. And the fact that—apart from some internships I'd done—Jefferson, Wheeler, and Schenk was the *only* professional job I'd had was a huge problem.

Crap! If only I hadn't gotten in that argument with my dad, I

could ask for his advice. Of course, I could always grovel and admit he'd been right all along. Because he had been. I was so stupid! There I'd been, trying to hold the moral high ground as he spouted prejudicial judgments, all the while forgetting that I worked for people who thought just like him! I was so angry with myself, I could hardly breathe when I let myself think about it.

So stop thinking about it, Emerson! Get back to work. Find a job so you can pay your mortgage and your car payment and take care of your brother!

Right. Back to work. I'd worry about references later.

Oh! Travis. I wondered where he was working now. Maybe they had an opening. I shot off a quick text message to him, ignoring the unanswered texts from Gavin. I most definitely couldn't think about Gavin right now.

I researched, typed, and sent e-mails, only stopping for coffee and a quick bite Ari forced on me before finally giving in to exhaustion at two in the morning. Ari had tried to stay up with me but fell asleep on the couch around midnight. I covered her with a blanket and staggered my way to her guest room where I put on the t-shirt she'd left for me and climbed into bed.

Despite my fatigue, sleep didn't come. Instead, memories of the worst day in my professional life bombarded me.

My first clue should have been the moment my new "ally" refused to meet my gaze. Our team was meeting in the east conference room ahead of the official AgPower meeting. Their executives weren't due for another hour, and we were taking the opportunity to get all our ducks in a row so the meeting would run as smoothly as possible. Because of the importance of the case to our entire firm, Mr. Schenk and Mr. Jefferson were slated to make an appearance.

Everything was in line. I knew this because I'd spent the

previous night checking and rechecking each piece. The articles of incorporation, the IP assignment agreement, the bylaws, the founder's agreement, the NDAs, the employment contracts... everything. I even checked over items that were not part of our firm's scope of the project. The main goal was to help the client succeed, and we did whatever that took. The only thing I didn't have in my hands was the patent re-file, but I'd spoken with Craig the night before and he e-mailed me the confirmation receipt he'd gotten from the patent office.

I had my laptop and files out in front of me, as did the other associates in the room, Craig included. We were just waiting on the managing partners. A second-year associate named Shelly was asking me a question about a merger when Mr. Wheeler stalked in the room and sat without a word. This was unusual. He wore a grim expression and his eyes were on the conference table.

A feeling of dread crept over me. I looked over to Craig and his eyes remained fixed on his laptop. That was when I knew.

Mr. Wheeler cleared his throat and then his eyes came directly to me.

"Thirty minutes ago, I got a call from Dietrich. One of their patents wasn't filed and a rival company filed on Friday. EnerGro."

"That's not possible," I said, trying to ignore what I already knew. "Which one?"

He set a folder on the table and slid it across the surface until it was stopped by my hand. My fingers shook as I opened the folder and saw the specs for the very patent Craig had found the mistake on and re-filed for me.

I quickly brought up my e-mail and tried to open the forwarded confirmation, but it was gone. Disappeared as if it had never been there in the first place. I looked at Craig again, but he was typing furiously into his laptop.

That slimy, two-faced, conniving jerk. Why had I trusted him? He was never interested in the good of the firm—he was only interested in the good of Craig Pendleton. I randomly thought that he and Elliot should get together, but realized I must be losing my mind.

Think, Emerson!

Melissa, the paralegal, had sent the original filing. All I had to do was get her to e-mail me that one. But it had the wrong date! Shoot. But it was better than nothing.

"Ms. Scott," Mr. Wheeler interrupted my train of thought, his voice stern. "How did this happen?"

"I'm sorry, Mr. Wheeler. I'm trying to get a confirmation e-mail right now. One moment, please."

I finished my e-mail to Melissa and prayed she was at her desk. I pulled out my phone to call her just as her e-mail response came through. *"I'm currently out of the office until April 24th. I'll respond to e-mails upon my return. If you need immediate assistance, please contact Isaac Garcia at igarcia@jwslaw.com."*

My stomach dropped and I lifted my eyes slowly to Craig. Only then did he meet my eyes, and his expression could only be described with one word: victory.

I swallowed hard and turned to Mr. Wheeler, just as the other two managing partners entered the room. All I had was a draft of the patent application. I had no record it had ever been filed. I was essentially screwed. "I'm so sorry, sir, I don't know what happened. I believe Melissa Yates has a record of the patent application but she's out of the office. However, there was a date discrepancy and we had to re-file." There was no way I was throwing Melissa under the bus, and any attempt to blame Craig would be met with his denial. I had no record of our interaction over the patent. It would make me look desperate and even more

unprofessional than I already appeared. I swallowed hard and forced the words out. "I'm afraid I failed to do so."

And, in the end, that was the truth. It was *my* responsibility. I'd let Craig pull one over on me because my focus hadn't been where it should be. And I'd allowed him to do me the "favor" of re-filing because I hadn't wanted to miss my dinner date with Gavin. Stupid! Why hadn't I followed my instincts?

I knew exactly why. I let sexual attraction and a nice smile divert my attention from what was truly important. I'd worked my butt off for this partnership for the last four years and it was slipping away because I suddenly discovered that sex could be great. I could hear my father's voice in my head and I wanted to scream.

Mr. Jefferson and Mr. Schenk sent me disgusted looks while Mr. Wheeler simply turned to the rest of the table and said, "Damage control. What can we do?"

Of course, Craig was ridiculously prepared. "I was just looking up EnerGro, and we'll have to gather as much data as possible from AgPower to prove they have the rights to the patent over the new company. Hopefully the new guys are just throwing spitballs trying to see if they can get one to stick. I'm sending you the data I've already gathered." His fingers sailed over the keyboard of his laptop, and all I could do was stare blankly.

"Excellent," was Mr. Wheeler's response.

"Emerson," Mr. Schenk addressed me. "I think you can go now."

I looked to Mr. Wheeler in a last-ditch effort to salvage things. He just nodded absently and read the new message from Craig on his laptop. I quietly gathered my things, carefully avoiding all eyes in the room and made my way to the hallway and back to my office.

It was no surprise when Mr. Schenk knocked on my door thirty

minutes later, accompanied by a security guard, and gave me my walking papers.

I woke up the next morning feeling like I'd been run over by a bus. My body begged for coffee and I prayed I'd have enough time to grab some before I had to get to work. And then I remembered. Ugh. My limbs felt heavy as I forced myself out of bed and on a hunt for caffeine. Ari was in the kitchen, coffee cup in hand and her phone to her ear.

She spotted me and gave me a weak smile. "I gotta run, but I'll talk to you later," she said to the person on the other end. Then she tucked her phone in the back pocket of her pants and filled a second coffee mug from the pot on the counter. She approached me where I sat slumped on the couch and passed the cup over.

"Thanks."

"So," she said as she sat next to me. "I know you weren't ready last night, but you need to tell me what happened. I'm worried about you."

I ran a hand over my hair and found it in a tangled mess. "You're going to be late for work." My pathetic stall tactic failed.

She shooed me away. "Pshhht. I've got time, and besides, Amara owes me one. She can answer a few calls."

"I have to check and see if any of my e-mails got responses." I tried again.

"After you talk to me. And if you don't open your mouth and spill it, I'm calling Mamá to get her ass over here. You choose."

I gave her a betrayed look. Her mom would be all over me and I wouldn't be released until I'd shared every secret I ever had and

accepted a job with one of about twenty people she'd call and demand hire me. It wouldn't even matter what field the job was in.

But Ari just stared at me and sipped her coffee, her expression making it clear she was not letting up.

I finally sighed. "Fine. It was Craig."

Ari stood abruptly, her coffee sloshing over the side and spilling on her shoe. She didn't even notice. "I knew it! That mother fucker. I'm going to junk punch him so hard he'll be eating his balls for breakfast! Then I'll drag him over to your boss's office and make him confess."

I put a hand out to calm her. "There's nothing you can do. He was way too sneaky. Ari, I should have seen it coming. I let myself get distracted."

She cut me off. "Oh no you don't. Don't make this about Gavin. You deserve a life outside of work."

"We can debate that later, but the truth is I brought Gavin right into my work by agreeing to the whole tournament thing. I flaunted him in front of all my colleagues and lost sight of what was expected of me."

She shook her head. "Just because he's not some lawyer or senator or something? That's crazy! Other people had their spouses and partners there, and you can't tell me they were all members of all the right clubs and associations. Why should they expect different from you?"

"Because they do! They did. I forgot what game I was playing."

"I'm sorry, but that's a load of double-standard bullshit." She finally sat back down and set her coffee on the side table.

"Yes. And I agreed to it the moment I signed on at their firm."

"That's got to be illegal."

I looked at her earnestly—my fierce friend who would take on

the world for me. "They didn't fire me for dating a twenty-four-year-old construction worker. They fired me for not filing a patent application, Ari. They are well within their rights. I failed to do the job I was hired for and they let me go."

"Emerson, never in your life would you fail to do something you were hired for."

"But I did. Craig laid out the breadcrumbs, but I followed the trail."

I explained to her about me getting the initial application wrong and Craig offering to submit the new one. How he tricked me into thinking he'd actually done it, and how he'd timed the bomb to explode when Melissa wasn't there to back me up. Not that it would have done much good since I was the one to screw up the date in the first place. I still didn't know how EnerGro had gotten the specs to file the patent, but I wouldn't put it past Craig to screw over a client as long as it ended with him looking like the hero.

"Shit," Ari said when I finished.

"Yup. That about sums it up."

"So what do we do now?" she asked. I managed a small smile at her use of "we." I appreciated it more than I could express.

"I find a new job and start over. I buckle down and work twice as hard to prove myself, and I don't lose sight of what's important again."

She looked at me disapprovingly. "You're dumping Gavin, aren't you?"

"I don't have any other choice, Ari. I knew it was a bad idea from the start and I let it happen anyway."

"But he makes you happy. I've never seen you that happy."

"Happy doesn't pay my mortgage and secure my future."

"Oh, Em."

"I'll be fine, Ari. Go ahead to work. I'm going to go home and continue the job hunt."

"You're more than welcome to stay here. You know that."

"I do, and thanks. But I need to be home for Jay. I don't like leaving him—overnight especially. Yet another thing I need to reprioritize. My brother deserves better than I've been giving him."

"Emerson Scott, you stop right now. You're an amazing sister."

I smiled and hugged her. "There's always room for improvement."

Chapter Twenty-Eight

ADULTING WITH A HACKER AND THE POPE

*G*AVIN

"Thanks, Ari." I hung up the phone after her abrupt goodbye. Emmy must have woken up. I still hadn't heard back from Emmy, and Ari hadn't sounded too encouraging. Emmy had apparently spent about ten hours on her computer sending out resumés and reaching out to her contacts in the world of corporate law. She hadn't shared any details with Ari about what had happened, but we were both confident Craig was at the center of it.

I sighed and donned my hard hat and gloves before going to find Trey and getting started with my day. I could tell it was going to be a long one.

When I finally finished up for the day, I headed over to the Academy, hoping that Jay would show up as scheduled. Not that I could really ask him about Emmy and her job. I figured she wouldn't tell him so as not to worry him. But just being around Jay would hopefully ease the feeling in my gut that she was drifting away from me with every second that passed.

I got my wish. After showering and changing into my uniform, I found Jay and a couple other players throwing pitches at screens in the indoor facility. They were all buzzing with energy since the regular season was winding down and playoffs were on the horizon. Jay's mood matched those of the other players so I assumed I'd been right and Emmy hadn't told him a thing. We got down to work and I tried to push my growing sense of dread aside.

Given the fact that Emmy had been avoiding me for the last day, I was more than a little surprised when my phone rang and her name popped up as I was walking to my car after training.

"Emmy, Christ. I'm so glad you called. How are you doing?" I didn't even let her say hello.

"Hi, Gavin." She sounded defeated.

"Hey," I answered gently.

"So, I got fired," she said with a laugh that held absolutely no humor.

"I know, Ace. I stopped by your office and ran into that Craig asshole. What happened?"

She sighed. "It's a really long story, but let's just say that one of your theories about Craig was right on target."

I brought my fist down on the roll bar of my Jeep. "Dammit. I wish I'd been wrong."

She inhaled deeply. "Well, I can't blame it all on him. I screwed up, Gavin." Her voice cracked and I wanted to pull her into my arms and make it all better somehow.

"Are you at home? Let me come over."

"No." I heard a small sniffle. "I can't. I can't do this anymore, Gavin. We can't see each other anymore."

"What? Why?" Was she blaming me for her getting fired? Well, maybe I was to blame after all. I'd bulldozed my way into

her life. I'd told her boss we were dating. I'd joined that damn team. Shit.

"I need to focus on finding a new job and taking care of Jay. Whatever job I get is going to take even more time than my last one. I'll be starting at the beginning and I'll need to dedicate all my spare time to catching up. I didn't work this hard over the past four years to just give up now."

I couldn't respond. It was as if I'd been struck by a lightning bolt. The similarity between our two situations was uncanny. I'd worked for years for a dream, and when it had been taken—whether from my own poor decisions or fate—I'd taken the coward's way out. I'd wallowed and cursed the world. I'd let it beat me.

Emmy wasn't doing that. She'd never do that. Her dream had just been ripped out from under her, and instead of giving up, she was fighting. She wasn't going to play the victim and feel sorry for herself. She was getting back on that horse and pushing forward, even though she knew the new road would be even harder than the old one.

I knew right then that I was in love with this woman. And I also knew I had to let her go. At least for now. But I was going to set some wrongs right whether she wanted me in her life or not.

Damn, this adulting thing was no joke.

The first thing I did was to call Ari. I'd learned a lot about Emmy in our time together, but I had a few questions I needed answered, and Ari had those answers. Luckily, she was only too happy to oblige. She may have even broken the girl code when she gave me the details of Emmy's firing, but she assured me she'd always colored outside the lines. That wasn't hard to believe.

The next thing I did was to call—you guessed it—my fairy godmother.

"Hey, Gav. We missed you at dinner last night. Did everything turn out okay?"

I'd called Fiona the night before to tell her something unsettling had come up at Emmy's work and we'd have to bail on dinner.

"No, I'm afraid it didn't," I responded. "So, tell me, who do you know who's got some hacking skills and puts the greater good above, say, the law?" It was a long shot, but this was Fiona we were talking about.

"Oooooh. This sounds juicy. I may have just the guy."

"So, we're not talking about the greatest firewall here, so don't be too impressed," Ollie said, pushing his glasses up his nose before getting back to the fastest typing I'd ever seen in my life.

It was the next day, and we were at the office of Fiona's day job at Precision Lawns and Landscaping. Jax, her boss, sat at his desk talking on his phone and eyeing us. Fiona and I leaned over Ollie's desk, watching as he hacked his way into the system of Jefferson, Wheeler and Schenk. Ollie did the accounts for Jax, but in his spare time he was some kind of computer wizard and comic book freak, among other things. The guy was scrawny and wore black hipster glasses that almost perfectly matched the color of his hair.

"Okay," said Ollie. "Do we know the last name of this Melissa?"

I scratched the back of my neck. "No, but she's a paralegal. There can't be too many with the same name, right?"

"Just a sec." Ollie continued to type. I heard the creak of a

chair and Fiona and I both turned around in time to see Jax emerging from his office.

"I got it," Fiona whispered and sashayed towards Jax to cut him off. We were guessing he wouldn't exactly approve of our activities. "Jax, can I have a word?" I heard her ask in her sweetest voice.

"Melissa Yates. Got her," Ollie said quietly. "Let me get into her e-mail. You said we're looking for anything to do with the patent office, right?"

"Right," I said, trying to keep an eye on both Fiona and Ollie's computer screen.

Jax crossed his arms and grinned at Fiona. Shit. "Darlin', you seem to be under the impression I was born yesterday. Now, you and your high heels need to step aside." Jax came striding over to where we sat.

"Jax," I managed to whisper to Ollie. He snapped his laptop closed and we both sat there, our guilt painfully obvious. We'd make the absolute shittiest actors.

"You boys wanna tell me what you're up to?"

I considered that. "Not exactly." I decided to go for partial honesty.

Fiona caught up with Jax. "Oh, come on. It's for the betterment of humanity," she pleaded.

We all looked at her. She shrugged. "Well, it sort of is. It's for Gavin's girlfriend." She proceeded to give the short version of events.

Jax scrubbed at his wild blond hair with both hands and let out a breath before looking at each of us in turn. "I trust this isn't gonna come back and bite me in the ass?"

Ollie looked almost offended. "Please. Who do you think you're dealing with?"

"Well, carry on if you must," Jax said, and Fiona hugged him.

Just then, the door to the building swung open and Ari rushed in. "I'm here! I'm here! Sorry I'm late," she panted. Her chest was heaving, and I'm no perv, but even the pope would have noticed. Turns out neither Ollie nor Jax were feeling very papal either. Fiona made a disapproving noise at us and beckoned Ari forward for a hug. Ari hugged her back and then said, "I tried as hard as I could, but I couldn't get Emerson's computer. It's attached to her like a barnacle. I even tried to get Jay to help, but he asked too many questions."

"That's okay. We can get by without it. I can always reach it remotely if we need to," Ollie said, as if he were discussing an alternate beverage choice instead of illegally hacking into various computers.

His laptop was open again and he continued to search the paralegal's account as Fiona got Ari up to speed. He shook his head. "I'm not seeing anything."

"That's impossible," Ari protested. "Emerson said she and Melissa drafted it together and then Melissa filed it with the patent office. She would have gotten a confirmation e-mail at the very least. Isn't there some record of websites she's accessed?"

Ollie continued to type and then suddenly sat up. "This is interesting."

"What?" we all asked at once. Even Jax had come back to investigate.

"It looks like I'm not the first person to be in here uninvited."

Ari and I looked at each other. "Craig," we both said.

"Well, whoever it was, he was messy as shit. And I believe I just found what we've been looking for," Ollie announced, leaning back in his chair and leaving us all a good view.

"Holy shit," was all I could think to say.

I rang the doorbell and heard what sounded like about a hundred windchimes going off at once. I stepped back involuntarily. Jesus, this place was practically a mansion.

The ornate front door opened and a woman about Emmy's age with perfectly-styled blond hair and an overly made-up face greeted me with a smile. "Hello."

"Hi," I said. "You must be Mandy."

She cocked her head to the side but still gave me a friendly look. "Yes. Do I know you?"

I shook my head. "No. No. I'm a friend of Emerson. Gavin Monroe." I held out my hand and she accepted it with a limp shake.

"Well, it's lovely to meet you, Gavin. Please, come in." She paused then. "You do know Emerson doesn't live here, right?"

I smiled. "Yes. Of course. I was actually hoping to speak with her father."

"Oh!" She suddenly looked way too interested, her polished nails coming to rest over her mouth. I realized my mistake a moment too late.

"No! God. It's nothing like that." We both released a laugh.

"Sorry," she said. "I shouldn't have assumed. It's just that we don't meet too many of Emerson's friends. I figured you must be… special." She looked me over. I'd chosen to dress a little more formally than usual. And, by that, I mean my shirt had buttons.

I didn't have a good response, so I gave a noncommittal noise.

"Anyway, please come in. I'll go see if I can tear Robert away from his computer."

"Like father like daughter," I said.

She gave a stiff smile at that and left me in the entryway while

she went to retrieve her husband. Annoyance gnawed at my gut over Richard Scott's blatant hypocrisy.

I turned in a circle, taking in the place. Hand-rubbed hardwood floors extended throughout the first floor, and an enormous stonework fireplace stood as the focal point of the great room beyond the entry. Two wide hallways forked off on either side and a high ceiling opened the space, making it feel enormous. I didn't even want to think about how much this place must be worth. Or the fact that this was the world Emmy came from.

"So, you couldn't settle for ruining my daughter's career. You had to sully my doorstep as well." I turned to see the same man from the game, except this time he was wearing suit pants and a white dress shirt rolled up at the sleeves.

Wow. What a complete asshole.

I decided to ignore his comment. I hadn't come here to live up to the stereotype he'd obviously pegged me with. And, since a handshake was unlikely, given his opening line, I got on with it.

"Hello, Mr. Scott. I'm guessing I don't need to introduce myself." He gave a little scoff but I soldiered on. "I'm not here to plead my case, so don't worry. I just want to talk to you about Emerson."

His eyebrows rose almost to his hairline. "And you think you know things about my daughter that I don't? You've been in her life for all of a few weeks."

I took a second to remind myself to stay calm. "I understand. I just wanted you to know it was a colleague who got her fired, not anything Emerson did or didn't do. She doesn't even know the full extent of it yet, but even if she did, I knew she wouldn't tell you. She's not one to pass blame."

"I should hope not."

"But, I assure you, this was not her fault." I refrained from

adding it wasn't my fault either. I just didn't get this guy. Aren't parents supposed to be unconditionally loving and supportive? From everything I'd suspected and Ari had confirmed, this guy's love did not come cheap.

"Why are you telling me this?" He tried to look bored but his jaw was tight.

"Because, like I said, I knew she wouldn't. And she's working her tail off trying to get a new job, trying to salvage her career. I figured it was worth appealing to you to help her. Even if it's just emotional support."

"Oh, I'm sure you're taking care of the emotional support in your own special way." He practically sneered at me. This guy took dickhead to a whole new level.

"Actually, you'll be happy to know that we broke up so she can focus on her professional life and her brother."

He huffed. "She wouldn't have to worry about Jay if her mother hadn't shirked her own responsibilities. I'm happy to hear Emerson isn't letting herself follow Naomi's path to mediocrity anymore." Then something seemed to occur to him. "If you broke up, why are you here, pleading her case?"

I didn't understand this man one bit. "Just because we broke up doesn't mean I don't care for her. That's not how relationships work."

He sniffed. "If that's all, I need to get back to work. I'm sure you can see yourself out." He turned to go.

I couldn't stop the next words from coming out. "Emmy shouldn't have to earn your love. She's your daughter."

He stopped and turned momentarily. "It's not my love *Emerson* has to earn. It's my respect." He resumed his steps down the hall.

Jesus. This guy.

"If that's how you feel, maybe it should go both ways."

I didn't look to see if he even heard me. I just walked out the door and closed it behind me.

Then I made a mental note to call my parents.

With help, I'd done everything I could to ease things for Emmy. Now I just had to wait and hope it was enough.

Chapter Twenty-Nine

SOMETIMES BROWNIES ARE THE BEST MEDICINE

*E*MERSON

Day three with no job and I was going nutballs.

And the worst part of it was, now that I was down to applying for the dregs of potential job opportunities I had more time to think. Of course, my thoughts liked to wander to all things Gavin. I was so conflicted. I knew I'd made the right choice to end things, but I also knew he wasn't to blame for the situation I was currently in. And I missed him.

The oven timer beeped, and I went to retrieve the pan of brownies. No matter how many times I'd tried to make brownies from scratch—okay, the two times I'd tried—they always tasted better from the boxed mix. This was one area where I wasn't ever going to be an overachiever.

"Oh, wow," came Jay's voice from the entry to the kitchen. "I'm sorry if this is totally insensitive, but I hope you never get another job."

I narrowed my eyes at him. I'd finally had to tell Jay about my

job, but I glossed it over by saying I had numerous offers on the way. I couldn't remember ever lying to my brother, with the exception of the existence of Santa and maybe sasquatches, but I didn't want him to worry. Knowing him, he'd be on the next bus to Mom and Aldo if he thought I was at all struggling.

Which I wasn't, technically. Like any responsible adult with a good-paying job, I set aside money each month for savings and retirement. And I had an investment portfolio. Suffice it to say, we weren't going to starve anytime soon, but I needed a job. Not just for income, but for my sanity.

"Well, give it a minute or you'll burn a hole in your esophagus." I looked around at the counter and saw the crock pot bubbling away with chicken tortilla soup, as well as the stack of cookies I'd baked earlier, the soda bread that had turned out a bit dry, and the chocolate chip banana bread I was planning on giving to Ari. Hmm, perhaps I'd gone a little overboard.

But offers were not flooding in and I needed a distraction. It turns out it's next to impossible to get a job with a reputable firm when you've been fired from another one. I needed somebody with clout to recommend me, and my one letter from Travis wasn't going to cut it. His firm wasn't hiring, but he'd kindly written me a reference and wished me luck. I tried not to think too much about the step down he'd had to take when he switched firms after getting the ax like me.

Jay hovered over the brownie pan, inhaling the scent. "Please try not to drool on those," I said with very little hope.

"No promises," he responded.

I took another look around. "Do you have any hungry friends you could invite over? I need my counter space back."

He gave me a sharp look of betrayal. "No way. These are

mine." One arm reached toward the cookie plate to bring it closer for protection. "Well, you can have a few, I guess."

"Gee, thanks." But I wasn't hungry. I just needed something to keep my hands busy so they didn't dial Gavin's number. I had yet to hear from him, but that was what I'd wanted, right?

As if my thoughts had triggered it, my phone rang from its spot on the counter. I froze. Jay leaned over for a look. "It's your dad," he said.

I groaned. I hadn't called my dad yet, but I had no doubt he knew all about my current predicament. He had too many friends in the law community not to know all the comings and goings. I didn't think I could stomach it if this was an "I told you so" phone call, but the last time I'd avoided him hadn't turned out so well. I sighed and went to grab the phone before it went to voicemail.

"Hi, Dad." I tried to sound chipper, God knows why.

"Emerson. How are you holding up?"

Huh, maybe this wouldn't be so awful. I walked into the living room and toward the hallway, leaving Jay to stand sentry over the baked goods.

"Well, obviously things could be better, but I'm doing my best to find a new position."

"Yes, well. That's actually why I'm calling. I had an interesting conversation with Larry Henderson, and he said he would be open to an interview."

I stopped in my tracks at my bedroom door. Larry Henderson? I'd already gotten a "Thanks, but no thanks" reply from his firm. "Really?"

This was the dad I loved—the one who supported me in my pursuits and didn't throw judgments in my face.

"Yes, but it would be with the understanding that you're ready to re-focus."

Oh.

That burned a little, but I swallowed it down. "Of course."

"It wouldn't be just your reputation on the line; it would be mine. I can't tolerate any more of this careless behavior or galivanting around with local nobodies. If you want a boyfriend, I have plenty of suitable suggestions for you. Ones that won't cause you to lose your head and your job."

I had definitely spoken too soon. My dad was tossing the judgments around like confetti. I bit my tongue hard and my blood began to simmer. Yes, I'd been careless, but this was going too far. Who was he to condemn me so harshly, just because I carried half of his DNA?! This was humiliating.

But I couldn't afford to stand on my soapbox, could I? Not if I wanted a job. Not if I wanted Jay to stay with me.

I was beginning to feel like a child again, and that wouldn't do. I still had some of my pride. "That sounds a little ruthless, to be honest. I am an extremely hard worker as you know, and I made one mistake. It's hardly grounds to condemn me. Having said that, I appreciate your offer of help and I'll do my best not to disappoint." There. I'd said enough but not too much.

"I suppose I'll have to accept that. It's true that you've always taken after me more than your mother, thank God. I suppose I was afraid you were beginning to lean in the other direction. I'm pleased to hear I was mistaken."

He just had to go there, didn't he?

I leaned against my doorframe. "Dad, can I ask you a question?"

"Certainly."

"If you abhor everything about Mom, why did you marry her?" I wasn't used to being so bold with my father. Neither was he, apparently.

He tsked in my ear, but finally answered. "Because it was the right thing to do, of course. You know that." I did know that. My mom had been pregnant with me when they got married.

"Maybe that was the wrong question. Why were you with her in the first place? I mean, you must have found some of her qualities redeeming."

He paused for a few moments and then I heard a sigh before he answered. "Because I was young and didn't understand how the world works."

It was next to impossible to imagine my dad ever being open-minded enough to mesh with my mom, much less convince her to be with him. But he must have been at some point, I realized, or she wouldn't have given him the time of day.

The other thing I was beginning to realize was that perhaps there was more of my mom in me than I'd ever acknowledged.

"So, should I have Henderson's assistant call you?" Back to business.

"Please," I answered. I was not in a position to pass up help of any kind. "Thank you."

"And I'll invite a suitable young man over next time you come for dinner."

I didn't want to get into an argument so I just said goodbye and hung up. I knew my dad's version of suitable, and it was the polar opposite of Gavin Monroe. Unfortunately.

A brownie was suddenly sounding better and better. I headed back to the kitchen and found Jay at the table, brownie pan in front of him and a fork in his hand.

I snatched it from his fingers.

"Hey!" he protested.

"You could at least eat like a human," I told him, coming back

to the table with a knife and a couple plates. "And just for that, I'm texting Ari to come over for dessert."

"Let me look at you!" my mom said as she held Jay's hands and took him in from head to toe. He rolled his eyes but let her look her fill. "You're more handsome than ever."

"Hi, Aldo," I said as I hugged my step-father and we both grinned over my mom.

Yes, as if the universe had some grand plan I had no hope of understanding, my mom and Aldo arrived on my doorstep the next afternoon. I hadn't yet told them about my job, but I had managed to get that interview with Larry Henderson set up for the following Tuesday. I wished it were already over so I'd have a better idea of the outcome one way or the other.

"And Emmy!" My mom turned to me with her bright smile and began to approach, no doubt to give me the same treatment as Jay. But her smile fell, along with her arms. "You look terrible."

"Wow. Don't shower me with so many compliments, Mom. I'll get a big head."

"Naomi," said Aldo, but she ignored him.

"What's wrong? Haven't you been sleeping? You're working too hard! I knew it! You need some down time, sweetie."

The irony of that caused a slightly maniacal laugh to escape from my throat. Everyone fell silent. Crap. I was losing it. Mom and Aldo both eyed me with suspicion and concern.

Jay struggled for something to say, finally settling on, "So, Asheville. I love that town."

They both turned to him. His hands were in his pockets and he was rocking on his heels. This was not going well.

"Somebody better tell me what the hell is going on here," our mom said, her mouth forming a straight line and her eyes pinning us.

I put a hand out. "It's fine. I lost my job." My mom and Aldo both inhaled sharply. I sighed and steeled myself to continue. "*But*, I'm getting a new one, so we don't need to talk about it. Or worry about it. Okay? Okay." I answered for everyone, essentially closing the subject.

Nothing could have held my mom back from hugging me after that, so I took it and even squeezed her back. "My poor baby! What happened?"

Oh, no. I wasn't getting into this with her.

Aldo, bless his heart, took pity on me. "So, do you have anything to drink around here?" He clapped his hands together and I extracted myself from my mom's tight embrace. I wasn't going to cry.

"Of course! Let's go to the kitchen."

My mom gave me a look that promised this conversation wasn't over, then followed us to the kitchen where the blessed alcohol lived.

We ate leftover chicken tortilla soup for dinner, along with some bread I'd baked and a frozen burrito for the human garbage disposal I called Jay. Mom and Aldo told us about some of their adventures thus far, entertaining us with stories of new friends they'd made and some mishaps they'd had along their craft-fair journey. They were both practically glowing. Our mother had always been beautiful, with her long strawberry-blond hair and her golden-brown eyes. Her skin was radiant and she had somehow managed to stave off many of the typical symptoms of aging. Aldo was his typical laid-back self, and he was the picture of contentment sitting in my kitchen basking in the presence of family.

"Oh, and Emmy, I got into juicing," my mother said, nodding as if this were something I must make a note of immediately.

"Okay," I said, not sure what response she was looking for.

"It's terrific for your body. It cleanses you and makes you feel completely revived. We're going to get you juicing before we leave." She patted my hand. I looked to Aldo for help, but he just shook his head.

"Actually," I said, "I already juice, so I'm all set." Total lie. I just couldn't handle anything revolting right now.

"Drinking wine is not juicing," Jay mumbled.

I gave him a death glare.

"Although technically, I suppose it's grape juice, so…" he tried to redeem himself. Too late.

"No more brownies for you," I told him sternly.

He responded with a ridiculous pout. "Hey, that's just mean,"

"I brought brownies," Aldo volunteered.

"No!" my mom and I yelled in unison.

Three hours later, I'd put Mom and Aldo's things into Jay's room and made up the pull-out couch for Jay in the office I never actually used. He'd gone off with Aldo to watch some zombie show, and my mom and I sat curled up on the couch with pillows and glasses of wine.

"It's so good to have us all in one house again, isn't it?" She sighed, making me genuinely smile for probably the first time all week.

"It is. Definitely."

"So, since you don't want to talk about you, tell me, how has Jupiter really been? He sounds great on the phone, but

we all know how good he is at sweeping things under the rug."

I thought about it before answering, "I think he's happy. At first, I was worried. He tip-toed around the place as if his mere presence was a bother, but he's definitely loosened up. And you should see him play ball!" I pretended to swoon. "He's gotten so good, and he's having the time of his life out there."

"So this training with Gavin has turned out to be a blessing—in more ways than one." She wiggled her eyebrows.

Well, I'd walked right into that one.

"Jay loves it. He says he's learning techniques he's never even heard of before. It seems pretty remarkable, and his head trainer is a former major leaguer." I took a sip of my wine, hoping that would end the subject.

"And what about you? A little bird told me you're seeing Gavin for some extracurricular activities of your own."

I gasped. "Mom!"

"What? We're both adults."

"I am not talking to you about this." I shook my head.

"Emmy, it's perfectly natural. Women have needs just as—"

I threw a hand out to cut her off. "Please. No more."

She sniffed. "Fine."

Truthfully, I didn't even know what I would say. Last night, Gavin had started texting me again—just a few short one-liners over the last twenty-four hours, but they had the effect I'm sure he intended. Doubt was creeping in and trying to overtake my resolve. Regardless, the last thing I needed was to tell my mom about Gavin and me. That would propel her into an unavoidable line of questioning I'd never be able to work my way out of.

"I had hoped you'd be more open to talking to me about these things the older you got. But you're allowed to be whoever you

are, even if that means we'll never have a conversation about orgasms."

I chugged the rest of my wine. "Need another?" I asked, standing up and gripping my glass.

"No. I'm all right," she answered, completely oblivious to the fact that I was quickly losing my mind.

I returned with a refill and sat back down, pulling a pillow over my lap. It wouldn't kill me to open up a little, I supposed. Just not about Gavin. And certainly not about sex. Good God.

"So, I've been doing a lot of thinking this week—you know, since I've had some free time." I sent her a self-deprecating smile. "We've never really talked about how you and Dad got together. I mean, I know you got married because you were pregnant and he was…Dad. But I don't get how you ever got along in the first place."

She bobbed her head back and forth as if weighing what she wanted to say. "Truthfully, it's kind of hard to remember, it's been so long. And time warps your memories anyway. But he was a different man in a lot of ways back then. Not so concerned with appearances."

I couldn't help the scoff that came from me. She smiled in understanding.

"I suppose I was a novelty." She shrugged. "And you know me. I catch a glimpse of someone's free spirit trying to get out and I grab on and pull. It turned out his wasn't going to budge, no matter what I did. And by the time I realized it, we were already married with our precious Emmy on the way." She smiled.

"So, he wasn't always so rigid? So unforgiving?" I asked quietly.

She looked at me with concern then. I'd said too much.

I sighed. "Sorry. He and I got into a fight."

She looked shocked.

"I know. The first one ever, and it was a doozy, let me tell you." I tried to laugh it off but she wasn't buying it. "I disappointed him."

"How is that even possible?" She set her wine glass on the coffee table and looked at me with bewilderment.

"Believe me, it's definitely possible."

"Emmy." she shook her head, her brow creased. "Please don't let yourself internalize his criticism. He has his own set of rules and standards and it's not your job to meet them. You only need to worry about your own standards, which I know are already sky high."

"But I didn't."

"You didn't what?" She looked puzzled again.

"I didn't meet my own standards. I made a mistake." I picked at a loose thread on the pillow in my lap.

"Well, heaven forbid you be human." She put a hand to her chest in an overly dramatic fashion. I rolled my eyes, as she'd intended me to. "Everyone makes mistakes. Even your father. You need to forgive yourself and move on. Just don't let other people decide what constitutes a failure on your behalf. One person's idea of a shortcoming can be another's greatest gift."

In that moment, I wished more than anything that I were more like my mom. But maybe I was, and I needed to accept the real me who was more complex than I'd realized—just like she'd always told me.

Chapter Thirty

TEAM GAVIN

G AVIN

"I think you broke him," Laney said.

"No way, little man. This is nothing," I told Rocco in a barely intelligible voice as I kept my head tilted back and a wad of tissues pressed to my nose.

"Sorry, Uncle Gavin."

"Nothing to be sorry about. I was the one who wasn't paying attention to the ball." I pulled the tissues away to see if the bleeding had stopped and gave Rocco a smile so he'd know I was okay. "What are you feeding this kid, Laney? His muscles are getting huge!"

That comment had the desired effect as I saw a smile creep over Rocco's face.

"Just the usual—other small children plus some chicken nuggets now and then." She pulled Rocco to her and covered his head in kisses. "You want a bag of frozen peas?" she asked me.

"No. I'm good."

I'd come over on my break between the job site and training on Thursday evening to catch up with the kid and to distract myself from thoughts of Emmy. Turns out that plan sucked and only ended up with a baseball to my face. The kid was getting better, that was for sure, if the throbbing pain in my nose was anything to go by. I may have earned myself a couple black eyes with this one. Nothing I hadn't dealt with a dozen times before, though.

"Hey, buddy," Laney said as she released Rocco. "Why don't you give your uncle a few minutes to recover and go feed Pickles?"

Pickles was his gecko he'd conned his Aunt Bailey into buying him last year. I had to hand it to him, the kid was good. Or Bailey was a sucker. Both were likely equally true. Rocco headed to his room to feed the beast.

"Round two starts in ten minutes, dude!" I yelled after him.

Laney just shook her head at me. "You're a glutton for punishment."

"What? I need to redeem myself."

"Well, if you can refrain from breaking *his* nose, I'd be grateful," she added, putting a fresh box of tissues on her kitchen table.

I scowled at her and then winced at the pain that caused. "Please. He didn't break my nose. I'm made of steel." I swiped my nose with the tissues again and took a seat at the table.

"Soooo," she began as she took a seat as well. That should have been my sign to get up and leave. "What is going on with Emerson? Fiona filled me in and it sounds like high drama."

"Yeah, that asshole she worked with screwed her right out of her job—and a future partnership."

"And right out of a boyfriend too, it sounds like," Laney said, sounding bummed.

"So, you heard that, huh?"

"You're not going to take it lying down, though, are you?" She picked at a rough spot on the surface of the tabletop.

That put my hackles up a bit. I may have let Emmy go for the time being, but I had no intention of bowing out entirely. She just had to figure her work shit out and then I was getting back in there. We'd figure out a way for her to be comfortable with balancing a job and a relationship.

"You think I'm just going to give up?" I was feeling defensive.

"No way! You're not that guy anymore." Her gaze shot to mine and she looked almost offended.

Oh. Well, that was much better. It seems she'd let go of my past transgressions a little more than I'd assumed. Maybe it was my own paranoia that made me assume everybody was just waiting for me to fail again.

I looked at her and noted her fierce expression. She had my back. That felt pretty fucking great. "Thanks for the vote of confidence," I told her with complete sincerity.

"So, what's the plan?" Crap, I'd walked right into that one, hadn't I? She looked way too interested for my liking.

"Well, the details of her asshole colleague's illegal behavior have been anonymously sent to her boss—her former boss—but it doesn't directly implicate him, unfortunately. I think it should be enough to get her job back, though, if she wants it."

"Thank God for that," Laney said.

"Yeah, but I'm kind of pissed at her now."

She reared her head back. "What the hell kind of support is that?"

"No, I mean, she let them fire her for a mistake she didn't even make in the first place. This Craig guy orchestrated the whole thing. Emmy just *thought* she made a mistake and let them get away with firing her."

"I'm sure it's more complicated than that," my sister said, propping her chin up on her hand, her elbow resting on the table.

"Yeah, I guess. I mean, I'm blown away by her single-mindedness in terms of fighting for a new job, but now I feel like she should have fought harder for her old job."

"Well, I'm sure it's a different view from the outside looking in," Laney offered.

I sighed and swiped at my nose again. "Yeah. Maybe I'm just projecting. Either way, I want her to get the redemption she deserves. She's worked hard for everything she's got."

"That kind of makes you guys a great couple, doesn't it?" My sister raised her eyebrows and grinned.

My chest tightened a bit at that. Eighteen months ago, Laney never would have even inadvertently hinted that I'd worked hard for anything. She'd had a front-row seat to my two-year pity party. It meant more than I could say that she was now my champion.

To hell with it. I may as well go all in.

"So, I'm taking online classes to finish my Sports Science degree."

Laney gasped. "Shut. Up! You're kidding me?!"

"Would I lie to you?" I couldn't help the upward curve of my lips.

"Absolutely." She didn't even hesitate.

"Well, I'm not lying about this."

She got up and hugged me while I stayed seated. I pretended to reluctantly tolerate her hug while she rolled her eyes at my reaction. Pretty much par for the course.

"I am so freaking proud of you," she said.

"Don't go busting an ovary over it."

She smacked the side of my head.

"Ow! Broken face here!"

"Whatever."

She sat back down and just smiled at me. For God's sake.

"Soooo," I threw her own opener back at her. "What's going on with you?"

She stuck her tongue out at me and then looked down at the table. Uh oh. I had no idea what that meant.

"Um, Nate and I are trying to have a baby."

A spectacularly stupid smile overtook my face. I couldn't help it. "No fucking way!"

"Yes fucking way." She looked up and her face was the picture of happiness. I loved that for her.

"Well, let's just hope this new one has better aim."

She threw her head back and laughed.

I hadn't spoken to Emmy in two days, and it sucked. Our phone call from Tuesday had ended with her having the impression I wasn't going to fight her on our break-up. It was time to begin re-inserting myself into her life. I just needed to remind her why she needed me, even if it was just for inserting a little levity into her stressful situation.

Gavin: *So, did you know that over 10,000 trees are planted each year by forgetful squirrels?*

I knew she probably wouldn't answer, but at least she'd think of me. And hopefully smile. I was surprised to hear the notification as a text came in. I was momentarily disappointed at the name until I read the message.

Ari: *Nice one. First smile I've seen all week ;-)*

I supposed it wasn't surprising that Ari was with Emmy. Those two were a package deal.

Ari: Oh, and btw - you're listed as "Don't Cave" on her phone. I'm thinking she'll last maybe a week.

Don't Cave? Well, it could be worse.

Gavin: Thanks, Ari. How's she doing?

Ari: I think she's sent her resumé to every law firm in the state, and now she's slowly going insane waiting.

Gavin: Has Wheeler called yet?

I would have expected him to make contact with her by now. He had the evidence in his hands, so what was he waiting for?

Ari: No! I don't get it. Maybe he's having a hard time convincing the asshole partners.

That sounded like a distinct possibility. Damn.

I wanted to ask if Emmy had talked about me, but last I checked, I hadn't grown a vagina.

Ari: Anyway, her mom's coming to visit tomorrow so hopefully it will take her mind off things.

Gavin: I'll be at Jay's playoff game on Sunday. I'm assuming you guys are going?

Ari: Yeah. How are you holding up? You're not going to start writing shitty poetry, are you?

Gavin: Who's side are you on?

Ari: No comment.

Ari: Hey, on another note, what do you know about Fiona's boss?

Gavin: Jax? Great guy. Why?

I would venture to guess many a woman has asked about Jax over time. He definitely had the whole southern charm thing down pat.

Gavin: I thought you had a boyfriend.

Ari: Maybe. Anyway, Ollie said Jax wants me to design a new

website for his business. I'm sure Ollie could do it blindfolded, but Jax asked for me for some reason.

I could guess that reason in two words: cup size.

Gavin: *He's solid. Just watch out if you don't want to be charmed out of your...well, you can guess.*

Ari: *That's to be determined. I kind of hate Elliot right now. Anyway, Emerson is getting suspicious. Gotta run. See you Sunday!*

Gavin: *Later.*

Shit. If Jax had Ari in his sights, he was in for a surprise. I was pretty sure she had a tattoo that said, "Hard to Handle," and if not, she certainly should.

Chapter Thirty-One

THERE'S NEVER A PRIEST AROUND WHEN YOU NEED ONE

*E*MERSON

Since I'd used most of the groceries in my house over the course of my cooking and baking marathon, Saturday morning called for a trip to the grocery store to restock.

I also wanted to keep busy because I knew the championship softball game was today and neither Gavin nor I would be playing. My former colleagues, however, would be taking on my father's team. I almost had to laugh at that, as the universe once again proved it had a God-awful sense of humor.

Mom and Aldo had stayed behind with Jay, no doubt making up for lost time by smothering him. Which left me wandering the aisles of Harris Teeter with a shopping list that ran the gamut from chia seeds to pizza rolls. I was in the produce section choosing some Honeycrisp apples when I caught sight of Mandy out of the corner of my eye. I froze, as if a lack of motion would somehow make me invisible to her. Before I could decide what to do next,

she spotted me, doing a double take before looking for her own escape route.

This was ridiculous. I sighed and accepted the inevitable, steering my cart around the banana display and approaching her.

"Hi, Mandy. How are you?" My eyes travelled to her cart, which held a half-gallon of ice cream, a tube of pre-made cookie dough, and a bottle of Moscato. She had clearly exchanged carts with a pre-menstrual college student who'd just had a fight with her boyfriend. Mandy didn't "do" sugar. Or carbs. Or anything that tasted good. My eyes shot to her face and found her wearing a broken expression. Her make-up was half gone and she had smudges of mascara under her red and swollen eyes.

Well, shoot.

My dad had finally reached his marriage threshold and asked for a divorce.

I didn't have it in me to be smug about it, but I was also leery to put my guard down. Mandy tended to strike when wounded. I finally settled on, "Are you okay?"

She sniffed and then pulled a tissue out of her Gucci purse. She wiped her nose and sighed in defeat. "No." Then a tear ran down her cheek and she swiped it away with the tissue. "I'm most definitely not okay."

I looked around hoping for one of her girlfriends or perhaps a priest to appear. But it was just me. I cleared my throat. "You know," I began and then paused, searching for the right words. "It's not you. It's him. This is what he does." Although, really, when you marry someone who's already divorced two carbon copies of you, can you really be that surprised? At any rate, she was obviously hurting, so I put on my compassion hat and squeezed her arm with a sad smile.

But then I noticed her looking at me with a baffled expression.

"What does that mean?" She wiped her nose again.

"My father," I prompted.

"What about Robert?" she asked, beginning to sound impatient. Huh?

It occurred to me I might have been way off base. "Wait. Why are you crying and buying junk food?" I gestured to her cart.

Her cheeks colored at the mention of the food. She sniffled again. "I'm supposed to go to my book club and I can't."

Good lord. "What?" That was all I had. I should have guessed this would be about something ridiculous.

"I just finished reading the book I told you about and I can't stop crying. It was so sad. I mean, I just...I've never read anything so sad in my whole life." Tears sprang anew and spilled over her cheeks. "They killed that woman and then..." She couldn't continue.

I opened my mouth but nothing came out.

Finally, she continued in a high-pitched voice as sobs threatened. "I can't go to my book club like this. Emerson, I didn't know things were like that. I mean, I know the book isn't real, but they said it was based on things that really happen. *Every day*. How is that possible?"

Oh my. It looked like the rose-colored glasses had been callously ripped from Barbie's eyes.

"It's just so...sad." Another sniff.

I nodded and patted her arm. "Yes, it's very sad. The world is a very unfair place for most of humanity."

Her eyes widened and I quickly amended my statement. "For *some* of humanity."

She grabbed another tissue. "Well, I knew that already, I guess. I just never thought about other people in such a personal way, you know?"

This did not surprise me in any way. "Yeah. Hey, maybe you should join a different book club. There are lots of really uplifting books out there," I suggested.

She blew out a breath. "The whole point was to read things that would broaden my horizons. You know, give me more things to talk to Robert about."

Oh. I held in my wince at that one.

"It's probably a lost cause anyway." Mandy sighed and looked into her cart.

"What do you mean?" I was pretty sure I knew but I felt compelled to ask, regardless.

She rolled her puffy eyes. "Please. Like you don't know. You practically gave me the break-up pity line a few minutes ago."

"Oh."

"He hasn't said anything yet, but I know it's coming. I'm sure you're thrilled." Here came the claws.

"I wouldn't go that far." *What? I couldn't feign that much disappointment.*

"Well, I'll never be Saint Emerson, that's for sure. I really don't know why he didn't just marry someone like you in the first place."

The eternal mystery. Who knew why my dad only went for women with half his years and half his brains?

"Believe me, I'm not in great standing with him right now, either," I told her.

"Maybe for the next five minutes, but you'll be back on that pedestal soon enough. It's not fair, you know. You get three parents and a brother who worship you, you get this fancy career and all this respect, and on top of that, you get a hot guy who's freaking in love with you."

That set my head back and my eyebrows arching.

She practically curled her lip. "I met him when he came to the house. Geez. I don't understand how you got a guy like that to fall for you when you're so...plain."

I ignored the dig, too distracted by what she'd just said. "Who in the world are you talking about?"

"Like you don't know. That Gavin guy" she practically spat.

"Wait. Gavin came to my dad's house?" I was ignoring the part about the l-word for now. One shock at a time was all I could handle.

"Yes, he came to *our* house. Poor perfect Emerson was in a bind and her hot boyfriend came to defend her honor."

Holy. Cow.

Gavin had gone to my dad on my behalf? The sweet, lovely, *stupid* guy. I really could have saved him the trouble. My dad would never listen to anyone. But Gavin had tried. He knew my dad practically hated him, certainly viewed him with utter contempt, yet he'd still gone and tried.

A huge knot formed in my chest and I thought I might cry. There we were, two pathetic messes hanging out by the bananas at Harris Teeter on a Saturday morning.

There wasn't really anything else I could say to Mandy. She was in attack mode so nothing would penetrate at this point. "Well, I hope things get better for you, Mandy. I'll see you later." I turned my cart and began to steer toward the deli counter, all thoughts turning to Gavin and what he'd done for me.

Her voice sounded after me, having lost all its fire. "What's it like to matter to so many people? How do you...make that happen?"

I stopped in my tracks.

Darn it.

I turned my head as she spoke again. "I've always just been

somebody's plus one." She shrugged. "I think it would feel a whole lot better if somebody saw me as the best part of their day. You know, instead of just something pretty to hang onto."

What could I say to that?

Was I the best part of anyone's day?

Something in my chest told me I might have been the best part of Gavin's day. And he may have been the best part of mine. Yeah.

I looked up at Mandy, her make-up a huge mess and her mouth turned down in a frown. And, darn it, she was still pretty. "You do matter. And if somebody makes you feel like you don't, they don't deserve your time."

She half-smiled and rolled her eyes. "Thanks, *mom*." Then she turned and steered away, probably to pick up a bag of Twizzlers. I knew that's what I would do.

It didn't occur to me until I was at the checkout that, despite her waspish tone, Mandy hadn't used an ounce of her Candy when speaking with me. That was a first. And it was probably also the first time I'd seen her as just Mandy, a woman who happened to be married to my dad. Maybe he wasn't the only one wearing judgy pants in the family.

I sat in my car in the parking lot of Harris Teeter, staring down at my phone. As if his ears were burning, a new text had come in from Gavin and, as usual, it brought a smile to my face. I shook my head and laughed out loud in the silent space of my car.

Don't Cave: *Did you know that 43% of statistics are made up? I'm 85% sure that's true.*

I scrolled up to read the one from last night.

Don't Cave: *Did you know that on his deathbed, the founder of*

Rolls Royce actually said, "I wish I'd spent more time at the office"?

I wanted to text him back, but I wasn't ready. I could feel myself on the precipice of…something. I just didn't know exactly what yet. But another change in his contact name was a distinct possibility. For someone who'd been so sure of everything a few weeks before, I was quite the mess.

I sighed and put my phone down, then headed home before all the frozen foods in my trunk melted. Aldo was brewing a batch of iced tea and my mom was on the back deck with Jay, both of them laughing. She reached a hand over and pushed his hair out of his eyes and he tolerated it. When I looked back at Aldo, I noticed his attention had been diverted the same way mine had. Sensing my gaze, his eyes moved to me next. He smiled and took a deep breath, letting it out slowly with a nod.

"It's been harder on her than she thought."

I gave him a questioning look.

"Being away from Jay," he explained.

"Ah." Not entirely surprising.

"We've decided to stay on the circuit through the summer and then we're going to settle here till he graduates."

"Really?" I asked, feeling both happy and somewhat disappointed at the same time. I loved having Jay live with me. But I could still hang out with him if they moved to town again. And it would be good to have my mom and Aldo close by. I hugged Aldo, feeling my heart swell.

"Plenty of time for road trips down the line. It's more important to be with your kids when you have the chance." He winked at me and I grinned back.

Then we took the iced tea and glasses out to the porch and sat down as a family to enjoy the spring day.

Ari and Ponch came over later in the afternoon to catch up with Mom and Aldo, and Ari brought their mom with her. The two older women shared a bottle of wine on the deck, erupting into cackles every now and then, sending Ari and me shaking our heads at each other. Ponch announced he was going to teach Jay to ride a motorcycle, something Aldo thought was a grand idea, and I had to remind all of them that Jay wouldn't even be sixteen for another couple weeks. Sheesh. I was then deemed the dasher of dreams.

I told Ari about my run-in with Mandy at the grocery store, making sure we were well out of my mom's earshot. For once, Ari didn't laugh, and neither did I. It was a minor miracle when it came to our history with my dad's wives.

Just before dinner, the doorbell rang and I went to answer it, having no clue who it might be, but hearing a tiny voice in my head chanting, "Please be Gavin. Please be Gavin." Never before had I hoped for someone to disregard my wishes and barrel right through my defenses. The monkeys started up in my belly again as I turned the knob and swung the door open.

But it wasn't Gavin.

It was Thomas Wheeler of all people. And he was dressed in his team uniform, complete with red cap and dusty jeans.

"Mr. Wheeler," I said in surprise.

"Ms. Scott. Sorry for dropping by unannounced like this, but I...it's been a strange week," he finished, running his thumb along his chin and looking a bit harried. That was new.

"Come in." I opened the door wider for him to enter. No matter what had happened with the firm, he'd always been fair to me, even if his partners hadn't necessarily been so.

Laughter came from the kitchen behind me and Mr. Wheeler motioned to my front porch. "Do you mind if we talk out here? The subject is a bit sensitive."

"Not a problem," I replied, more curious than ever. I stepped out and closed the door behind me, signaling for him to take a seat on one of my Adirondack chairs. I settled in the other one and waited to hear what he'd come to say.

He cleared his throat. "I suppose you've heard by now that your father's firm took home the trophy."

I shook my head. "No, I hadn't. I'm sorry you lost."

His mouth twitched on one side. "Our own fault, really." He breathed in deeply and let it out. "Anyway, I came by because I owe you an apology," he said, shocking the daylights out of me. He continued, "The day you were let go, my focus was on the client and I failed to fight for you. I considered it my responsibility to do both, and I didn't."

"Mr. Wheeler, please. The client comes first. And I made a mistake that…well, I don't even know the outcome, and you're not allowed to tell me, are you?"

He gave a chagrinned quirk of his lips and shook his head. "I'll tell you what I can, and the first thing you need to know is that you didn't make a mistake." I started to protest but he put a hand out to cut me off. "And even if you had, one typo doesn't ruin a company, especially one that neglected to file their own damn patents in the first place."

I let out a small laugh at that, and he continued. "It's our job to find and fix oversights, but one lawyer, even one as dedicated and talented as you, doesn't have the power to bring down an entire company." He gave me a half smile in return. "I hate to break it to you." It meant the world to me that he still thought I was a good lawyer, even if I didn't work for him any longer.

"But, what do you mean I didn't make a mistake? I did. Even if it began as only a typo, the bottom line is that you asked me to file the patent and it wasn't filed."

He tilted his head to the side, considering me. Then he just looked confused before his expression morphed again into amusement. "You have no idea what happened, do you?"

Then it was my turn to be perplexed. I opened my mouth to ask a question and then realized I had no clue which one to ask.

"Did you know that we had to get a new IT company in this week to shore up our firewall and security?"

I didn't bother to answer because how in the world would I know that, and for that matter, why was he talking to me about firewalls? Had he gotten hit in the head by a softball?

"Earlier this week, I received some anonymous information that was most interesting, both in its content and its implication that our network wasn't nearly as secure as we'd thought. Hackers," he explained. "More than one. Let's just say the first had a vested interest in seeing you bungle the AgPower account, and the second had a very different interest in you—one that, I gather, was to see you reinstated at the firm."

My jaw dropped. He was being fairly vague, but I was getting the picture. I mean, I'd known Craig had done some kind of IT tricks to make his fake e-mail disappear, but it sounded like it went deeper than that—a lot deeper.

"Unfortunately, in both cases, we were unable to pinpoint the hacker in question, but I have a few very specific guesses."

I shook my head. There was no way he thought I was a hacker, was there? I knew how to use about four programs, and one of them was Solitaire.

"Not you, Ms. Scott. Don't worry." That sent my blood pressure back toward normal. His face got serious then. "Now, I don't have the power to reinstate you. I'm sure you won't be surprised to discover the decision to let you go was two to one, and I doubt that will change in your favor. And you're right that, technically speak-

ing, it was your task to file the patent and it wasn't filed—no matter who was actually at fault. The illegal means by which the absolving evidence was revealed makes it particularly sticky, as I'm sure you can imagine."

I nodded. He was right. If I tried to sue to get my job back, I'd just end up broke and jobless, no matter how unfair that was. And the alternative was almost worse—if I won, I'd still have to work for Jefferson and Schenk, except this time they'd absolutely despise me. That sounded fun. "Of course. Well, I appreciate you sharing what you could. It does shed some light on things." I stood, assuming we were done. But I had one more question, one he probably wasn't even at liberty to answer. "Can I ask how AgPower is doing? Does EnerGro have the patent?"

His lips twitched again. "Now, would I let that happen?" I chuckled and he stood. "I will, of course, be happy to act as a reference on your behalf. Any firm would be lucky to have you. I'll also keep my ears open for a good opportunity." He put his hand out.

I shook it. "Thank you very much, sir."

"You're most welcome. Take care, Ms. Scott."

"You too, Mr. Wheeler."

He stepped off the front porch and I had to shield my eyes from the sun in its low position in the sky. Halfway down my walk, he turned. "Tell Mr. Monroe thanks for bringing some new blood to the tournament." He smiled and shook his head. "Damn. We almost had it."

I smiled back and waited until his car had pulled away before opening my front door and shouting. "Ari Amante! What have you done now?!"

Chapter Thirty-Two

PEANUTS AND CRACKER JACK

GAVIN

It was the perfect day for a ball game. The air was still and the humidity low, with the temperature hovering in the high seventies. On days like this, I missed the game more than ever. But I had a player who was the starting pitcher in the first playoff game of the season, and he had fire in his eyes and probably a lightning bolt somewhere in his arm. I was happy with that. I was happy for him.

I was also nervous as shit—both about the game and about seeing Emmy for the first time in a week. I'd received a cryptic message from Ari last night that just said, "SHE KNOWS!" I wasn't quite sure what to make of it, but I gathered I'd find out soon enough.

I arrived early and took my spot by the fence waiting for players to arrive and coaches to take them to the locker rooms for speeches and game prep. I took a deep breath, inhaling the sharp scent of grass and dirt and taking in the relative silence.

"Hey, Slugger, what happened to your eye?" a very familiar voice came from beside me.

I turned and there she was. My heart fell to my stomach and I drank in the sight of Emmy standing there in a red sundress and a flimsy, white short-sleeved sweater. Her fiery hair was up in that neat ponytail and her eyes were soft and aimed right at me. I wanted to go kiss her, but I hadn't grown stupid over the past week. Desperate, maybe, but not stupid.

"Car jacking. You should see the other guy. Name was Rocco or something." I felt my mouth tug and her lips curved up in response. Damn, she was fucking perfect. "Hi, Emmy."

"You should be more careful. I hear six-year-olds can be vicious." She continued to look at me with that smile, and then her eyes fell to her sandals. "I heard about what you did for me. Thomas Wheeler stopped by yesterday." She looked back up and pursed her lips. "And the rest I got out of Ari. You guys are sneaky, I'll give you that."

"We're thinking of starting our own super-hero alliance. Fiona wants costumes. You're welcome to join." I raised an eyebrow.

She laughed out loud at that. "You're also wonderful—all of you. I can't believe you all did that for me."

I shrugged. "Did it work?"

She stayed where she was standing, so I did too, even though I wanted to pull her close and finish this conversation with my hands on her ass. Or somewhere in that vicinity.

She rocked her head side to side. "Kind of. I didn't get my job back, but Mr. Wheeler is going to give me a reference. My dad also got me an interview at another firm on Tuesday, so that's good." She paused. "Speaking of my dad, I heard about that too."

I wrinkled my nose and adjusted my hat. "Yeah, I don't know

314 • SYLVIE STEWART

that I'll be invited to dinner anytime soon, but I'm glad he was able to help you. You didn't deserve what happened to you."

She opened her mouth, looking like she wanted to refute me or make an important point, but then she closed it again and bit her lip instead. Which, of course, made my cock wake up. This woman was the one with super powers—all she had to do was look at me and I was practically ready to go.

"So," I continued when she stayed silent, "do you think you—"

I didn't get to finish my question because another female voice interrupted. "I finally get to put a face with the name and the voice! Give me a hug, sweet boy!" A woman who could only be Naomi Miller pulled me in for a short hug and then held me at arm's length to look me over. She bore some resemblance to her daughter, but her hair was longer and crazier and she dressed like she was waiting for the second coming of Jerry Garcia.

Naomi raised her eyebrows and gave Emmy a sidelong glance. "I knew it the minute I heard his voice on the phone. I can tell these things, you know."

What these things were, I had no idea, but based on the good-natured head shake the comment earned from Emmy, I gathered this wasn't unusual. It was just Naomi.

"Come sit with us, Gavin. We got here early so we could get the best seats." Since they were all high school bleacher seats, that didn't mean much, but I nodded and let her lead me by the arm to the stands as she peppered me with questions about everything from my black eye to my astrological sign. I figured we could chat for a bit and then I'd get back to my conversation with Emmy, but to my disappointment, Emmy bypassed the open seat next to me and sat herself next to her stepdad who she then introduced me to.

Maybe I'd read our interaction at the fence all wrong, but it had felt like it was leading to something—maybe not taking us to

exactly where we'd left off last week, but somewhere in the same neighborhood. If Naomi noticed the change in my mood, she didn't mention it. She just kept chattering until the teams took the field to warm up.

Ari showed up a few minutes before the first pitch and sat on Emmy's other side, essentially boxing her in. I tried to get Ari's attention but all she did was smile and say hi. What was going on here? Emmy did look at me a couple times, but she almost seemed on the verge of laughter when she did. I guess she was finding it amusing that I'd been trapped in her mother's web.

My personal shit would have to wait, though, because the game was about to start and one Jay Miller was taking the mound. All of us stood at once and shouted our loudest. Ari's voice, of course, carried the farthest, and Naomi looked like she might cry. Jay managed to ignore us all, just as he should. He threw a couple more practice pitches and then the ump called the start of the game. Naomi grabbed my hand and it made me laugh.

East Forsyth's first batter stepped up to the plate. I knew this kid and he was usually good for a hard-hit grounder or a line drive. Jay nodded to the catcher and delivered a fastball the batter passed on. Pitch two was the same, but the batter swung and barely missed, causing Naomi to crunch a few of my knuckles together. Aldo nudged her to let go of me, and I finally got my hand back just as Jay wound up and threw a beautiful slider that the batter had no chance of connecting with. The out was called and our row went batshit crazy. Damn, this was going to be one great game.

But, by the bottom of the fourth, I was feeling a bit put out— and not about the game. I asked Emmy if she wanted to come with me to get some popcorn and she brought Ari along. Then, when we returned to the seats and I tried to switch places with Ari, Naomi protested and insisted I resume my former seat. There were a

couple times when I could have sworn I saw the three women exchanging grins that felt like they were somehow at my expense. If I thought Aldo would help a brother out, I was sorely mistaken; his attention was completely centered on every play of the game.

And it wasn't hard to see why. His son was pitching a phenomenal game. When the sixth inning turned over and it was clear a relief pitcher would be taking over for the seventh, every ass on North's bleachers was up and out of its seat as the crowd celebrated Jay's performance. He hadn't let a single run in.

By the top of the seventh, when the relief pitcher took over, I excused myself, saying I was headed to the restroom. Instead, I took a spot at the fence. Looking over at North's dugout, I could see the white of Jay's teeth as he smiled and fist-bumped his teammates as they headed for the field. For a split second, I allowed myself to feel what could have been, and then I pushed it aside and only felt joy for this remarkable kid and the future that lay ahead of him.

I cheered North's team as the relief pitcher made a valiant effort but let one run in. They were still up by five, so I was feeling confident going into the seventh inning stretch. I realized I'd been gone a while and Naomi might send a search party out for me, so I turned to head back to the stands. North's mascot spoke over the loudspeaker, priming the crowd for "Take Me Out to the Ball Game." Most of the crowd stood, preparing to sing along as I made my way back to our row. When I approached, Naomi and Ari were giving me a look I'd only ever seen on two other people: Laney and Fiona. That could not be good. Just as I craned my neck looking for Emmy, I heard a new voice over the loudspeaker.

"Um, hi. Thanks for letting me take over, and I apologize ahead of time." I knew that voice. It took me a moment to track her down, but there was Emmy, standing by home plate with a micro-

phone in her hand. What the hell was she doing? I looked to Naomi and Ari—and, hell, even Aldo—for some explanation but at her next words, my eyes shot straight back to Emmy before I could get any explanation. "This one's for Gavin!" She thrust an awkward fist up in the air and I felt my mouth stretch in a big-ass grin as she began to sing—*terribly*—the first words of the iconic song. It was God-awful and fucking awesome all at the same time. But I'll give her one thing, when that woman commits to something, she doesn't half-ass it. She sang and swayed and beckoned for the crowd to join in. And we did. Even through tears of laughter, we did. I'd never be able to hear that song again without the image of Emmy in her red sundress butchering it just for me.

And that's when I knew beyond a shadow of a doubt that everything would be all right.

"Celebratory dinner at Hops!" yelled Ari.

The first game of the playoffs was over and North had made it to the next round.

"Jay might want to hang out with the team, so don't give him a hard time if he begs off," said Aldo. From what I'd seen today, Jay had the ideal dad for a player—someone to talk baseball with and play catch, but also someone who understood when you needed to roll with the team dynamic. He reminded me a little of my dad, but with the added flavor of slightly illegal substances.

"Ari, call your folks to join us," Naomi suggested, and Ari pulled out her phone to increase the crowd to a number that didn't have a hope of getting a table. Not that I had a vested interest. Emmy and I were abandoning the party to have a little get-together of our own even if we had to ninja fight our way out of there.

After the worst rendition of "Take Me Out to the Ball Game" in the history of the world, Emmy had politely handed the microphone back to the mascot who, though I can't confirm it because of his costume, I strongly suspect had just peed himself with laughter. Then she'd very gracefully made her way off the field and up the bleachers directly to me and planted a hard kiss on my smiling lips. She was literally shaking and I pulled her onto my lap and took the cap from my head to place it on hers. That earned me a brilliant smile as she took deep breaths to calm herself. I couldn't even imagine what it had taken for her to go so far outside of herself to get on that field and belt the hell out of that song. I was awestruck. She had just set the bar for our entire relationship going forward. I'd never be able to impress her with anything less than a public striptease or maybe the donation of a kidney. Not that I was concerned because Emerson Scott was not only absolutely certifiable, but she was mine.

"I think Gavin and I will catch up with you guys later," Emmy said, clearly on the same page as me.

Naomi hugged us both. "Have fun, kids."

"Yeah, have *fun*!" Ari echoed, leaving no doubt as to the kind of fun she was suggesting.

Emmy blushed, of course, and I grabbed her hand to pull her toward the parking lot.

I turned and yelled back, "Hey, Naomi! Ask Ari about Jax!"

I caught a glimpse of Ari's death glare just as Naomi's face lit up and she clasped her hands together, readying herself for the inquisition. Gavin, one; Ari, well, probably more than one.

"What was that about?" Emmy asked.

"Probably nothing, but it was fun anyway." We continued toward my Jeep.

"I'm going to have to dig into this one later." She gave me a sidelong glance.

"Definitely later. Right now, I'm taking you to my place and you're going to tell me how Emerson Scott got the brilliant idea of serenading a couple hundred people."

She put her free hand over her face. "Was it really that many?"

"Afraid so." I shook my head and grinned. "But you definitely killed it."

"Yeah, something tells me you're using that word in its literal sense."

I laughed and pulled her hand so she had no choice but to stumble into me. She gave a little yelp and I lowered my head, not able to wait any longer for another taste of her. She kissed me back and sighed into my mouth. Damn, I'd missed this.

She parted her lips and I took the invitation to slide my tongue inside to meet hers. I felt her arms circle my neck and I wrapped mine around her waist, closing any remaining space between us and fitting her body against mine. I angled to get a better taste and felt my cock clamoring to join in.

Then I remembered where we were and groaned—in disappointment this time. I tore my mouth from hers and she pulled in a deep breath, looking a bit dazed. "Let's get the hell out of here," I practically growled. She just nodded her head and we ran the rest of the way to my Jeep.

Chapter Thirty-Three

SANDWICHES

*E*MERSON

I laughed out loud as we sped down the highway, the wind whipping my hair around and the sound of my laugh getting lost in the breeze. Gavin looked over and gave me an inquisitive glance accompanied by an adoring smile. It was too loud to talk, but I shouted nonetheless.

"I can't believe I did that!"

He coughed out a quick laugh, then signaled to take the off-ramp, driving us toward his place in High Point. I'd never been there and was curious to see where he lived.

Last night, when Ari told me what they'd all done for me I'd been completely floored and not a little overwhelmed. As I listened to her explain about Fiona and this Ollie guy and how she and Gavin had been communicating with each other all week to ensure my personal life and my career didn't fall apart, I felt like crying—in a good way.

Mandy's words from the grocery store echoed in my head and I

thought about how incredibly lucky I was to have so many people championing me—caring for me. My mom, Aldo, Jay, Ari, Ari's whole darn family, my dad—in his own way, even Thomas Wheeler and Gavin's friends who hardly knew me! And then there was Gavin. I mattered to a lot of people, and that was a gift I didn't ever want to squander.

If I couldn't find a way to balance my career aspirations with my personal life, there was a problem with my priorities. I didn't want to end up like my father, where partnerships only belonged in his professional life, not his personal one. Truthfully, it made me feel a bit sorry for my dad, something I'd never in my life felt toward him.

My mother and Mrs. Amante butted their way into the conversation, of course, and Ari was more than happy to share the details of my saga. I had to endure a bit of admonishing from my mom for not telling her everything in the first place, but I didn't mind it much—not with the new revelations seating themselves in my heart and mind. Then all three women tasked themselves with hatching a plan—a plan to reclaim my life and reclaim my boyfriend. And not necessarily in that order.

We all decided the situation called for a big gesture. And nothing gets bigger for me than standing in front of a crowd of people and making a complete idiot of myself. Gavin had let me have my freak out when I lost my job and he'd supported my need for space. Then he'd gone and worked behind the scenes as my biggest ally, even taking on my dad and spearheading an illegal hacking endeavor. All for me. He needed to know that his actions, his kindness, meant the world to me. So I had to go big or go home. And I was Emerson Scott. I wasn't about to go home.

The seventh-inning stretch had been my mom's idea. Ari's suggestion was luring Gavin to karaoke and singing some incred-

ibly cheesy love song, but plenty of people do that. I needed something a bit more terrifying and significant, and if the smile on
Gavin's face was anything to go by, I'd hit the mark perfectly. The
surprising part was, even though I was trembling with fear the
entire time I held that microphone, it was also freeing in a sense. If
I could survive that, I could survive just about anything.

We pulled into a complex of townhouses, and Gavin steered to
a parking spot a few buildings down the road. The outside was tidy
and the place relatively new.

"So, ready to get the grand tour?"

I was kind of thinking I just wanted him to show me the
bedroom first, and that thought alone shocked me.

"Wait, why are you blushing?" Gavin asked, turning fully in
his seat to face me as he removed his seatbelt.

"No reason," I managed while I busied myself getting out.

Gavin met me on the walkway and stopped me with a hand on
my arm. "Are you thinking of sandwiches again?" His grin was
wicked.

"Shut up and show me your place."

He chuckled as I preceded him up the walkway to his front
door. He caught up with me and unlocked the door, pushing it open
so I could go in ahead of him. "Just to be clear, I *really* like
sandwiches."

I scowled, making him laugh again.

He showed me the main floor, which was comprised of a
kitchen, dining room, and living room, all surprisingly neat considering he hadn't been expecting company. I don't know why I was
surprised, though. Gavin had a history of disproving all my preconceived notions about guys, and especially guys his age. If I'd
learned anything over the last couple months, it was that judging
people only made your life narrower. When I met him, I'd been

under the impression that I knew way more about life than he did, but all evidence suggested that Gavin Monroe could teach me a thing or two. Or ten.

"So, are you going to tell me how you ended up at home plate singing your heart out to all your fans?" He pulled me to him and our bodies met front to front, fitting together perfectly.

"Um, let's just say I needed a change in perspective and I have some really pushy broads in my life."

"I like the pushy broads in your life. But I like you the most."

"What a coincidence. I'm pretty fond of you as well." I felt my lips curve up as his head descended so his mouth could claim mine. It was exactly what I wanted—what I needed. His mouth on mine, his body on mine, our separation over the last week obliterated.

He seemed to be feeling the same, because he claimed my mouth with his own just as his hands took possession of my butt, pulling me in to feel his arousal. He was hard and I relished the feel of the evidence against my stomach. I couldn't believe I'd ever thought I could do without this—without him—in my life. And it was about so much more than the physical. The electricity he brought to my body just reaffirmed everything else I knew about the two of us and the way we belonged together.

I answered the claim of his hands with a claiming of my own. I grasped his biceps and then slid my hands up until they threaded through his hair. I felt the sudden and unfamiliar urge to tug on the handfuls of hair I held—so I did. He responded with a growl and I smiled against his mouth. What had I been doing my whole adult life? Sex and lust and love—yes, I said it—was supposed to be liberating and fun. How had I not known that before?

Not that I had a lot of time to think about it, because Gavin suddenly hiked me up so I had no choice but to encircle his waist

with my legs while he strode toward the stairs. God, I'd never wanted anything so badly in my life as I wanted this man. My mouth took over and burned a path from his neck to his ear where my teeth nipped at the lobe, drawing a curse from Gavin.

Before I knew what was happening, I felt a mattress at my back and a hard, male body descending over my front, covering me from head to toe. He kissed my neck and I threw my head back to give him better access as my back arched under the caress of his hand on my breast.

"We need to get this sweater off. Now," he murmured into the skin of my throat before running his tongue over my pulse point. That sent a shock to the lowest part of my belly, and I was up on my elbows in no time, working to discard my sweater. Gavin lowered the straps of my sundress and then the bodice, exposing my naked breasts to him. Yes, Ari had finally convinced me to let the girls go free, and I was beyond grateful for it at this moment. Gavin took one of my nipples in his mouth while his hand played with the other. All I could do was wrap my legs around him and run my fingers through his hair while he worshipped my breasts— there was no other word for it.

When he switched his mouth to my other breast, he let his hand travel down to my thigh, where my dress had ridden up. His fingers traced a path to the edge of my panties before slipping under the silky fabric. I moaned in anticipation and he lifted his head from my chest to look into my face. I wasn't sure what he was looking for, but he must have found it because he got up on his knees, pulled my dress up to my waist and slid my panties completely off—all before I even knew what was happening.

But I didn't have any time to be embarrassed or protest—not that any woman in her right mind ever would in this situation. He lowered his mouth to the juncture of my thighs and proceeded to

use his fingers and tongue in a combination of caresses and strokes that had me panting and moaning and probably speaking in tongues. My climax washed over me, but his attentions continued until the last shudder ran through my body.

He wiped his mouth on the sheet but I was too shocked and boneless to be embarrassed. Then he came back up over me, still completely dressed, mind you, and smiled. "Did you just say, 'Heavens to Mergatroyd'?" He looked like he was about to laugh.

"Quite possibly," I panted in response, not even caring that he was laughing at me.

"Just checking." He pressed a hard kiss to my mouth and then went back up on his knees, removing his shirt in the process and then going to the button of his jeans.

Finally!

I drank in the sight of his bare upper body, lean and muscled with only the scars on his right arm and shoulder breaking the smooth expanse of skin and smattering of hair. My hands stroked his stomach of their own volition and I was pleased to feel his muscles clench in response. A new boldness overtook me and I pushed his hands out of the way so I could lower his zipper and yank his jeans down—then his boxer briefs until he was completely exposed to me.

He quickly shucked the garment the rest of the way and I dispensed with my dress. Then we were on each other, fully naked, our skin soaking up the sensations each of us provoked in the other. I was considering never wearing clothes again, this felt so right. We explored and caressed with hands and mouths, our fingers and tongues tracing paths over one another's skin until I thought I might pass out from the adrenaline rush and the clenching of my belly and sex.

As if reading my mind, Gavin lifted himself up and opened the

drawer of his bedside table. He removed a condom and quickly tore the packet open before rolling it down his length. Then he settled on top of me and took my face between his hands.

"I missed you," he said, and it made my nose sting a bit as my eyes got wet.

"I missed you too. I'm sorry."

"Nothing to be sorry about, Emmy. I'm just happy to have you back."

"I'm happy to be back," I said quietly as I encircled his waist with my legs and silently urged him to get down to business.

Which he did—spectacularly.

When we were both spent and satisfied, we snuggled together in a sweaty heap, exchanging small kisses now and then while we silently basked in each other's company and closeness.

Finally, Gavin sighed. "Well that didn't suck."

I laughed out loud.

He pulled me even closer and placed a kiss on my head. "The only thing that could have made this better is if we had your woobie."

I smacked his chest and he laughed at his own joke. Then he rolled me over and covered me with his body once more, essentially obliterating any protests on my part. As he came in for a kiss, he still had that smile I loved plastered on his face. I couldn't help but smile back, and then his lips were on mine and our bodies awoke. It looked like our time-out was over and we were ready to resume play.

EPILOGUE

MERSON
One Month Later

"There they are!" Ari pointed to a blue tent in the middle of a long row. My mom and Aldo were under the tent chatting with some potential customers. Ari and Jay headed that way and Gavin pulled me along by the hand.

The School for Visual Arts in Winston-Salem was hosting an art fair this weekend, complete with demonstrations and vendors of all kinds. Of course, Mom and Aldo had jumped at the chance to do a big event so close to home.

The place was busy with crowds of people checking out all the different booths and the wares up for purchase. Fiona had already bought a pair of earrings, a leather belt, and a bag of kettle corn, and we'd only been here ten minutes. The entire gang had come along, just to add to the chaos of the event. I had gotten to know Gavin's friends a lot better over the past few weeks, and they had accepted both Ari and me with open arms. It felt great to expand

my personal life to include more friends and experience more of what life had to offer. I was so grateful that I'd finally let myself embrace it.

And, speaking of change, a lot of unexpected changes had occurred over the last month—and not just in my life. Mandy uncovered some long-forgotten bravery and good sense and left my dad. He'd been a bit blindsided, although I can't think why. And I was hoping the experience would cause him to rethink some of his established behaviors and ways of thinking. I was done killing myself trying to please him or condone his choices by remaining silent. We still talked, and when we did, I expressed my opinions as the context called for. This made things a bit tense between us these days, but I was hopeful we could carve out a comfortable middle ground in the future.

One thing that had left my dad particularly annoyed with me had been my choice to turn down the job with Larry Henderson. The interview had gone well, but throughout it, I'd had the uncomfortable feeling that I'd be jumping from the frying pan into the fire. There was no Thomas Wheeler at this firm, and it was fairly clear from the start that I'd only be getting an offer because of my father's relationship with Mr. Henderson—not because I was a good lawyer. As fate would have it, though, a call came in from Mr. Wheeler the day after the interview. It turned out Brent Weston had decided against hiring a corporate law firm, realizing that it made better business sense to hire internal counsel. Ironically, my golf game had come in handy after all. When Mr. Wheeler mentioned my name to Brent as a potential candidate, he'd jumped on the chance to snatch me up. Five minutes into the interview for the position of General Counsel for Weston Enterprises, I knew it was the job for me. The pay was great, the hours were predictable, and my co-workers weren't out to get me fired.

Which brings me to the last bit of news—a true confirmation that karma is indeed a b-i-t-c-h. One of the new IT workers at Jefferson, Wheeler and Schenk decided to dig a little deeper into the AgPower debacle and found evidence that Craig Pendleton had leaked the patent specs to EnerGro. Craig was not only immediately fired, but he was being disbarred and was up on potential criminal charges. I felt bad about it for about a half a day and then got over it. I had other things in my life that deserved my thoughts and attention.

One of whom was physically pulling me toward a booth where we were all sure to receive a tarot card reading whether we wanted one or not. Gavin dismissed my reluctance and told me to suck it up. I promised him some pretty good things if we could just avoid my mom a few minutes longer, but he just laughed and said he'd get those *things* anyway. Which was true.

Over the last month or so, I'd been discovering that I was a bit of a sex maniac. It must have been all those years of underwhelming sex I'd endured. But I knew better—it was all Gavin. Well, that, and the fact that, in Ari's words, we were in *lurve*.

Following a humiliating sequence of events that required Gavin's landlord to replace the glass shower door, all bets were off and the l-word was spoken. The simple fact alone that he'd spared me any blame and claimed he'd just lost his balance while showering before work probably earned him more than just love—by all rights, I should have paid him in cash or…you know. But he was more than happy with my declaration of emotions and he returned them on the spot.

I'd heard people say, "when you know, you know" and I'd always dismissed it in favor of a well thought out plan. Turned out I was wrong again. Because I knew. And, luckily, so did Gavin. I'd never been happier to be wrong.

GAVIN

Emmy pretended she didn't want to see her mom just yet, but I knew better. She missed her mom and was looking forward to Naomi and Aldo moving back to Greensboro. She was going to miss having Jay live with her, but I was confident I could offer enough distraction to compensate.

The high school baseball season was wrapping up, and North had a spot in the state semi-final in the coming week. Jay was pitching better than ever and my gut was telling me he had a real shot at a huge career in the game. Helping him achieve his goals felt like a remarkable gift.

Ari was hugging Naomi as we approached the tent, and then it was our turn to receive hugs and comments about how "cute" Emmy and I were. I was just glad Mark, Jake, and Nate were out of earshot, having been waylaid by their significant others to look at art shit. Despite her advanced state of pregnancy, Bailey had been the first one to jump on the idea of coming to the fair with us. As an artist herself, she ate up this kind of event. As for the guys, Jake wasn't leaving Bailey's side this close to her due date; Mark didn't trust Fiona not to come home with an entire apartment's worth of crap; and Nate just liked to walk behind my sister and stare at her ass, something that made me slightly nauseous. I just came to the fair because I'd take any opportunity to hang out with my girlfriend.

I had yet to meet the infamous Elliot, but he'd passed on the grounds that he didn't "do cheesy shit like that." The guy sounded like a complete douchebag, but Ari had yet to eject him from the picture. She was starting on Jax's website soon, though, so I was

mentally rubbing my hands together in anticipation of that shit show.

The rest of the gang eventually caught up, and Laney and Fiona eagerly forked over some cash for tarot card readings. Jake and Bailey were talking to Aldo about Bailey's paintings, and the other guys chatted with Ari and Jay.

I felt Emmy lean into my side and I put my arm around her to pull her in closer.

"Did you know..." she began, but I interrupted.

"Wait, are you going to give me useless trivia?"

She narrowed her eyes at me. "*Interesting* trivia."

My lips tugged up and she continued.

"Did you know that tarot cards were originally called triumph cards?"

"I did not know that." I shook my head and held my grin. There were way too many things I liked about this woman.

"Did you also know they had that name due to the triumphant feeling the card reader had whenever she tricked somebody out of their hard-earned money?" She smiled her gorgeous smile and I was half tempted to take her up on her earlier offer.

"I'm going to have to call bullshit on that one."

"Okay, that part was completely made up," she confessed and I bent to kiss her.

"Hey, they're having karaoke later," Ari interrupted our kiss, showing us the event schedule.

"Hey, Ari," I said. "Did you know that karaoke is Japanese for 'drunk'?"

She cocked her head. "It is?"

Emmy laughed into my chest and then I got a punch in the arm from Ari.

"Liar," said Ari, going back to the schedule. "Naomi said we

have to check out the glass-blowing demonstration. Apparently, it's amazing."

"That does sound cool," Emmy agreed.

I was up for whatever, so when the card readings were over, we wandered over to the school building and followed the directions to the glass-blowing studio. Jay had opted to stay behind with his parents. I suspected glass-blowing sounded about as interesting to a sixteen-year-old kid as shopping for socks. The room was fairly packed with spectators. It also felt akin to standing directly next to the sun.

"Jesus, it's hot as balls in here," said Jake. "Are you sure it's safe for you to be in here, Irish?"

When I didn't hear a response from Bailey, I glanced over and noticed all five women were paying absolutely no attention to any of us guys. Well, that's not quite accurate. They were paying plenty of attention to one guy, and that guy just happened to be the one standing in a wife-beater t-shirt turning some long metal stick in what looked like a giant oven, flames flying every which way. I took another look around the room and realized that, apart from Mark, Jake, Nate, and me, the place was filled entirely with chicks. And all of them had their eyes aimed in one direction.

Jesus Christ.

Awareness of the situation hit the other guys as a muttering of curses sounded down the line of us. Okay, so the glass-blowing dude probably had that whole muscle-bound, sweaty, worker-of-the-earth thing about him, but I didn't really get what the big deal was. He was just some guy.

He brought the end of the stick to his mouth and blew, making me understand it was a hollow tube.

"Good God, Shortcake. Avert your eyes, would you?" Mark growled at Fiona.

She responded by passing her shopping bags to him, never taking her eyes off the glass-blowing dude for a second. "Here, hold these, will you?" She didn't bother checking his hold on them before she released them from her hands.

That resulted in a snarl.

"Sweet mother of hotness," Ari muttered to Emmy, her eyes similarly glued to one spot. "Do you hear that?"

"Hear what?" Emmy responded, sounding a bit too distracted for my taste.

"That's the sound of a hundred ovaries simultaneously exploding."

All the women in our group laughed at that.

Then the stupid guy took a second to glance at his audience and the fucker had the nerve to wink.

"We're done here!" shouted Nate, pulling on Laney's arm to get her moving.

"Five more minutes!" Fiona protested, but Mark picked her up by the waist.

"Five more hours!" Ari responded, beginning to laugh her ass off.

I looked to Emmy and she was laughing too, now watching my cavemen friends dragging their women about.

"Um, I'm ready to go," Bailey's voice came out sounding odd. She hadn't even insulted any of the guys, which was totally out of character.

"Holy shit!" Jake's voice was panicked.

That's when we all looked at Bailey and saw a small puddle forming around her feet.

"Oh my God!" Fiona and Laney shouted simultaneously.

"Let go, you beast!" Fiona smacked Mark's arm and he released her so she could join Laney by Bailey's side.

Bailey smiled tremulously. "Forget spicy food and long walks —why don't the books tell you about half-naked glass blowers to induce labor?"

The women snickered, but us guys were too out of our element to do anything but stand there and panic.

"Okay, let's get you out of here," Emmy finally spoke up as the only voice of reason and assurance.

This seemed to snap Laney out of her surprise, and, as the only mother in the group, she began asking Bailey questions and leading her to the exit.

Four hours later, Emmy and I were eating ice cream on her couch and waiting for word from the hospital. Most of the group had accompanied Jake and Bailey, but Ari, Jay, Emmy, and I hadn't wanted to overwhelm the couple with too many people at once. And besides, Laney said these things could take hours, something I had no interest in thinking about any further.

Emmy set her empty bowl on the coffee table and stood up. She stopped in front of me and bent down, placing a lingering kiss on my lips. It tasted like chocolate and Emmy.

"I'm going to see if Jay wants some ice cream. Be right back." I watched her walk toward the hall, enjoying the view immensely.

My phone rang and I quickly swiped it from my pocket. "Hey."

"It's a girl!" Laney shouted in my ear, causing me to instinctively pull it away a few inches until it was safe again. "She's perfect. I can't believe how beautiful she is, Gavin. You have to come see her."

"How's Bailey doing?"

"Exhausted but happy," she answered and then laughed. "Jake is the one I'd worry about, though. He looks like he just came home from war."

I chuckled at that.

Laney sighed. "I can't wait to have a baby too."

"Then I suggest you don't let Nate talk to Jake right now," I advised with another laugh.

"Yeah, good point," she responded. "Is Emerson there? I want to tell her all the girl details. I don't trust you to remember them."

That was a valid point. "Yeah, just a sec." I covered the microphone and yelled for Emmy. She didn't respond so I quickly opened my text app.

Gavin: *Baby was born. Laney wants to talk girl shit.*

I pressed send and then heard the sound of a text notification coming from the couch cushions. I fished Emmy's phone out and saw my message on the screen. And that's when I noticed my contact info had been changed.

I was now "Gavin" with a big-ass heart emoji right next to it.

My lips curved in the smile of a man who knew exactly what he had and wasn't ever going to take it for granted. I put my own phone back to my ear and asked Laney to hang on a minute. Then I went and fetched my girl.

~THE END ~

Brett is up to bat in the next Carolina Connections book, **The Way You Are**. *Read on for an excerpt!*

Stay up to date on Sylvie's upcoming books and projects by subscribing to her newsletter! http://bit.ly/NewsSylvie

ABOUT THE AUTHOR

USA Today bestselling author Sylvie Stewart is addicted to Romantic Comedy and Contemporary Romance, and she's not looking for a cure. She hails from the great state of North Carolina, so it's no surprise that most of her books are set in the Tar Heel state. She's a wife to a hilarious dude and mommy to ten-year-old twin boys who tend to take after their father in every way. Sylvie often wonders if they're actually hers, but then she remembers being a human incubator for a gazillion months. Ah, good times.

Sylvie began publishing when her kids started elementary school, and she loves sharing her stories with readers and hopefully making them laugh and swoon a bit along the way. If she's not in her comfy green writing chair, she's probably camping or kayaking with her family or having a glass of wine while binge-watching Hulu. Or she's been kidnapped—so what are you doing just sitting there?!!

**Winner of the 2017 National Indie Excellence Award for Romantic Comedy

**Winner of the 2017 Readers' Favorite Silver Medal for Romantic Comedy

Thank you so much for reading *The Game* – I hope you enjoyed it.

If you did, a **review** on your favorite book site is always appreciated!

Use these links to grab special **bonus** content!
http://bit.ly/BonusTheGame & http://bit.ly/ColorCC

Want to stay updated on new releases, promotions and giveaways?
Subscribe to my newsletter! http://bit.ly/NewsSylvie

Want to hang out with me and my other readers?
Join my reader group on Facebook: **Sylvie's Spot - for the Sexy, Sassy, and Smartassy!** http://facebook.com/groups/SylviesSpot

XOXO,
Sylvie

Keep up to date and keep in touch!
www.sylviestewartauthor.com
sylvie@sylviestewartauthor.com

f facebook.com/SylvieStewartAuthor

🐦 twitter.com/sylvie_stewart_

📷 instagram.com/sylvie.stewart.romance

ACKNOWLEDGMENTS

As always, I need to send a big thanks to my friend and editor, Heather Mann, and to my hubby and kids for enduring the "worst summer ever"—in part due to me holing myself up in the office like a vampire, but also due to the unfortunate tumble down the stairs that rearranged my husband's leg. Good times. Next summer will be EPIC, dudes!

I also want to send a shout out to Diane for inspiring the epilogue, and to Gwen, just because I can't thank Heather and Diane and not include Gwen—they're a package deal and always will be!

Next up are my fellow indie authors...I am proud to be a member of a community that's so nurturing and generous. To my pals at IAS and to the Super Squad, thanks for your support and friendship. You guys rock it hard!

And, lastly, none of this would be possible without my read-ers!! Thank you so much for buying and reading my stories, and

for your messages, feedback, and rants about the jerks in my books. You make all the hard work worth it!

ALSO BY SYLVIE STEWART

The Carolina Connection Series:

The Fix (*Carolina Connections, Book 1*)

The Spark (*Carolina Connections* Book 2)

The Lucky One (*Carolina Connections* Book 3)

The Way You Are (*Carolina Connections* Book 5)

The Runaround (*Carolina Connections* Book 6)

The Nerd Next Door (*Carolina Kisses, Book 1*)

Then Again

Happy New You

Game Changer

About That

Full-On Clinger

Between a Rock and a Royal (*Kings of Carolina, Book 1*)

Blue Bloods and Backroads (*Kings of Carolina*, Book 2)

THE WAY YOU ARE:

"They say nice guys always finish last. I say the only place that should apply is in the bedroom—it's just good manners, after all."

– Brett MacKinnon, *nice guy and frequent resident of the friend zone*

Liv:

There are really only three things I need in life: sex, baseball, and winning. My hot boyfriend and season tickets take care of the first two, while I always do my best to cover the last. So developing an unexpected crush on a new friend is more than a little inconvenient. I don't have anything but friendship to offer Brett, but with the way he looks at me, he has me wishing I did.

Brett:

I've been put in the friend zone so often, they've got a sandwich named after me. You'd think I'd be used to it by now. But when it comes to the delectable Liv, I'm determined to ditch the friend zone and show her I'm boyfriend material. Too bad the position's already been filled by a ball-playing caveman who could flatten me with his pinky.

What will it take to show Liv that nice guys can be more than just friends, and that love is the one game truly worth winning?

Order your copy of *The Way You Are today!*

THE FIX:

My life is a friggin' fairytale—just not the kind any single girl would ever want to star in.

Laney:

Like any good heroine, I have challenges to face. Getting my son to wear pants is one; dealing with my snooze-fest of a job is another. Then there's the Beast, my freeloading brother who's worn a permanent dent in the couch at my new place. And no fairytale would be complete without a smoking hot prince, of course. Too bad he's a complete ass.

My instincts scream at me to steer clear of Nate Murphy. Because, if life has taught me anything, there is no such thing as happily ever after.

Nate:

I may not be a superhero, but I do my best to come to the rescue when I'm needed. And, hey, I just moved halfway across the country after a single phone call from my mom. But being back home and taking on the responsibilities involved makes me a bit cranky at times. Unfortunately, the one time I completely lose my cool is in front of the hottest girl I've ever met. I've got my work cut out for me if I'm going to fix this. But I *will* fix this.

I'll be anything Laney Monroe needs me to be … a superhero, a prince, or just a guy she might take a chance on.

Order your copy of *The Fix* today!

BETWEEN A ROCK AND A ROYAL:

Two foreign princes, one local girl in a serious jam, and a '65 Mustang headed for Georgia. What could go wrong?

LEO: My brother likes to think he's the clever one, and I usually let him. He's the crown prince, after all. But he's cocked things up royally this

time, pardon the pun. It will take some quick thinking and a heavy dose of luck, but I'll pull us out of it. Even if it means putting my trust in a stranger... a tempting stranger who carries a wrench and an attitude.

RUBY: I knew before I even agreed that this would be a bad idea. But given my circumstances, I had little choice but to take these rich country-club rejects up on their offer. A ride in exchange for the money my uncle and I owe. How bad could it be? I'm sure I'll survive and hopefully fix my problems in the process, but my heart might not be so lucky.

Order your copy of ***Between a Rock and a Royal*** today!

THEN AGAIN:

It's been two years since the divorce papers slapped Jenna in the face, and it's high time to dive back in.

Step one: find a romance-novel-worthy man for a hot summer fling.

How hard could it be?

But disastrously bad flirting, a failed honky-tonk hookup, and a mix-up with one of Sunview's finest have Jenna seriously doubting if this is all worth it. Maybe she's better off leaving the world of love and sex to others—or maybe she's just looking in the wrong place …

Order your copy of ***Then Again*** today!

EXCERPT FROM THE WAY YOU ARE

Carolina Connections, Book 5

BRETT:

It was then I realized I was wearing a t-shirt, boxer briefs, and nothing else. Fuck. Me. I snatched the beer bottle up in a panic and turned to the sink. "Uh, yeah. So, I hope it's okay that your dog just drank a beer."

"Bo!" She scolded the dog but didn't sound like she meant it. "You pledging a fraternity now?" I heard her pat him. "Go on. You cleaned it up enough."

The dog smacked his jaws one more time and his nails clicked on the tile floor as he retreated to the living room.

I glanced over my shoulder. "Sorry I woke you up."

"You didn't. I was having trouble sleeping." She sidled up to the counter next to the sink where I stood with my crotch pressed against the cabinet. "You know, unfamiliar bed," she explained, leaning forward and propping her cheek on a hand. "What about you?" I swear I caught a smirk threatening.

"Uh, same. Couldn't sleep." This was ridiculous. "You want a

beer? I've got a couple more in the fridge, unless you want to finish the one your dog started."

"No, thanks." She pushed back off the counter and I turned around without thinking. Her eyes shot right to my junk and I winced inwardly. My only hope was that it was too dark for her to see much of anything.

But it was no hope. She pulled her lips between her teeth to suppress her smile... or laugh... or whatever the hell she was thinking.

I threw my hands out, launching the paper towel roll over the counter and into the next room. "I'm a guy! What do you want me to say?" I brought one hand back in a gesture up and down her small frame. "A girl walks around in her underwear and the cock gets a mind of his own."

Her mouth flew open and she looked down at her skimpy clothes. "I'm not in my underwear!"

"May as well be," I shot back. I had nothing to lose at this point. I might as well have been standing there stark raving naked with my dick bobbing in the air.

"You're the one in your underwear!" Again, she drew attention back to my straining cock before having the decency to look back up at my face.

"I guarantee the material I'm wearing could make six of what you're wearing!"

"These are pajamas." She pulled at the material of her top, making it stretch tighter over her tits.

"You're not helping!" I shouted, which just brought her attention to my dick yet again. At this rate, it was likely to make an appearance over the waistband of my boxer briefs.

She crossed her arms. "Are you sure about that?" She raised a brow and I couldn't take it anymore. I stalked past her. It wasn't

that I couldn't find humor in the situation—or, more likely, wouldn't be able to a few weeks from now. It was that I didn't want to be a joke to her, and I was afraid that's what I might be.

"I'm sorry." She grabbed my arm as I passed, and the feel of her fingers flexing on my skin stilled me. "Sometimes I can't help myself. I mean, you're standing here in your underwear with a sizeable hard-on. It's not like I can just ignore it."

"I'd actually prefer if you did." Then I paused and backtracked a few seconds. She said sizeable. *Nice.*

The Way You Are by Sylvie Stewart is now available in e-book and paperback.

EXCERPT FROM THE FIX

Carolina Connections, Book 1

Chapter 14: *Scarlett O'Hara Had and Excellent Point*

LANEY

I ran my tongue around the shell of his ear and sucked his earlobe. Apparently that was the last straw. Nate physically picked me up and headed to my bedroom with his hands on my ass, and I had no choice but to hang on for dear life. This was shocking and a bit embarrassing on many levels, the least of which being the chronically untidy state of my bedroom.

Let me explain.

In all these romance novels, the buff guys are constantly picking the girls up and throwing them on the bed or having vertical make-out sessions—all while not straining a single muscle. I am not that girl. I have tits and I have ass, and I'm not saying that in some cute little "oh, look at her perky booty" kind of way. I have double Ds and a very proportionate ass to match. That very often puts me into the plus-size department and then on to a tailor

to fit the smaller parts of me. Everyone loves to talk about boobs and booty like they are thrilled the old bombshell figure is back in style, but I can tell you two things: (1) a rack like this wreaks havoc on your back, and (2) tailors are not inexpensive.

So Nate carrying me to my bedroom, an event which should have been a romantic milestone complete with "Up Where We Belong" playing in the background, was instead an episode that filled me with self-doubt and imagined trips to the emergency room. A hernia, at the very least, was a distinct possibility in this little scenario—how romantic can you get?

Amazingly, though, we made it without injury and he deposited me gently on the bed. He honestly didn't look any worse for wear, and his lustful look implied I'd better kick my insecurities to the curb. Shit was about to get real. *Yowza!*

"You're wearing too many clothes," he growled while gazing at me from his elevated viewpoint at the side of the bed. "Lose the pants and the blouse. I'll take care of the rest."

Holy shit. It seemed someone was putting on his alpha pants.

The Fix by Sylvie Stewart is now available in e-book and paperback.